CHARLES KINGSLEY

HYPATIA

ANDROMEDA
AND
OTHER POEMS

Elibron Classics
www.elibron.com

Elibron Classics series.

© 2006 Adamant Media Corporation.

ISBN 0-543-90324-9 (paperback)
ISBN 0-543-90323-0 (hardcover)

Dedication

PREFACE

A PICTURE of life in the fifth century must needs contain much which will be painful to any reader, and which the young and innocent will do well to leave altogether unread. It has to represent a very hideous, though a very great, age; one of those critical and cardinal eras in the history of the human race, in which virtues and vices manifest themselves side by side — even, at times, in the same person — with the most startling openness and power. One who writes of such an era labours under a troublesome disadvantage. He dare not tell how evil people were; he will not be believed if he tells how good they were. In the present case that disadvantage is doubled; for while the sins of the Church, however heinous, were still such as admit of being expressed in words, the sins of the heathen world, against which she fought, were utterly indescribable; and the Christian apologist is thus compelled, for the sake of decency, to state the Church's case far more weakly than the facts deserve.

Not, be it ever remembered, that the slightest suspicion of immorality attaches either to the heroine of this book, or to the leading philosophers of her school, for several centuries. Howsoever base and profligate their disciples, or the Manichees, may have been, the great Neo-Platonists were, as Manes himself was, persons of the most rigid and ascetic virtue.

For a time had arrived, in which no teacher who did not put forth the most lofty pretensions to righteousness could expect a hearing. That Divine Word, who is "The Light who lighteth every man which cometh into the world," had awakened in the heart of mankind a moral craving never before felt in any strength, except by a few isolated philosophers or prophets. The Spirit had been poured out on all flesh; and from one end of the Empire to the other, from the slave in the mill to the emperor on his throne, all hearts were either hungering and thirsting after righteousness, or learning to do homage to those who did so. And He who excited the craving, was also furnishing that which would satisfy it; and was teaching mankind, by a long and painful education, to distinguish the truth from its innumerable counterfeits, and to find, for the first time in the world's life, a good news not merely for the select few, but for all mankind without respect of rank or race.

For somewhat more than four hundred years, the Roman Empire and the Christian Church, born into the world almost at the same moment, had been developing themselves side by side as two great rival powers, in deadly struggle for the possession of the human race. The weapons of the Empire had been not merely an overwhelming physical force, and a ruthless lust of aggressive conquest: but, even more powerful still, an unequalled genius for organization, and an uniform system of external law and order. This was generally a real boon to conquered nations, because it substituted a fixed and regular spoliation for the fortuitous and arbitrary miseries of savage warfare: but it arrayed, meanwhile, on the side of the Empire the wealthier citizens of every province, by allowing them their share in the plunder of the labouring masse below them. These, in the country districts, were utterly enslaved; while in the cities, nominal freedom was of little use to masses kept from starvation by the alms of the government, and drugged into brutish good-humour by a vast system of public spectacles, in which the realms of nature and of art were ransacked to glut the wonder, lust, and ferocity of a degraded populace.

Against this vast organization the Church had been fighting for now four hundred years, armed only with its own mighty and all-embracing message, and with the manifestation of a spirit of purity and virtue, of love and self-sacrifice, which had proved itself mightier to melt and weld together the hearts of men, than all the force and terror, all the mechanical organization, all the sensual baits with which the Empire had been contending against that Gospel in which it had recognized instinctively and at first sight, its internecine foe.

And now the Church had conquered. The weak things of this world had confounded the strong. In spite of the devilish cruelties of persecutors; in spite of the contaminating atmosphere of sin which surrounded her; in spite of having to form herself, not out of a race of pure and separate creatures, but by a most literal "new birth" out of those very fallen masses who insulted and persecuted her; in spite of having to endure within herself continual outbursts of the evil passions in which her members had once indulged without check; in spite of a thousand counterfeits which sprung up around her and within her, claiming to be parts of her, and alluring men to themselves by that very exclusiveness and party arrogance which disproved their claim; in spite of all, she had conquered. The very emperors had arrayed themselves on her side. Julian's last attempt to restore paganism by imperial influence had only proved that the old faith had lost all hold upon the hearts of the masses; at his death the great tidewave of new opinion rolled on unchecked, and the rulers of earth were fain to swim with the stream; to accept, in words at least, the Church's laws as theirs; to acknowledge a King of kings to whom even they owed homage and obedience; and to call their own slaves their "poorer brethren," and often, too, their "spiritual superiors."

But if the emperors had become Christian, the Empire had not. Here and there an abuse was lopped off; or an edict was passed for the visitation of prisons and for the welfare of prisoners; or a Theodosius was recalled to justice and humanity for a while by the stern rebukes of an Ambrose. But the Empire was still the same: still a great tyranny, enslaving the masses, crushing national life, fattening itself and its officials on a system of world-wide robbery; and while it was paramount, there could be no hope for the human race. Nay, there were even those among the Christians who saw, like Dante afterwards, in the "fatal gift of Constantine," and the truce between the Church and the Empire, fresh and more deadly danger. Was not the Empire trying to extend over the Church itself that upas shadow with which it had withered up every other form of human existence; to make her, too, its stipendiary slave-official, to be pampered when obedient, and scourged whenever she dare assert a free will of her own, a law beyond that of her tyrants; to throw on her, by a refined hypocrisy, the care and support of the masses on whose lifeblood it was feeding? So thought many then, and, as I believe, not unwisely.

But if the social condition of the civilized world was anomalous at the beginning of the fifth century, its spiritual state was still more so. The universal fusion of races, languages, and customs, which had gone on for four centuries under the Roman rule, had produced a corresponding fusion of creeds, an universal fermentation of human thought and faith. All honest belief in the old local superstitions of paganism had been long dying out before the more palpable and material idolatry of Emperor-worship; and the gods of the nations, unable to deliver those who had trusted in them, became one by one the vassals of the "Divus Cæsar," neglected by the philosophic rich, and only worshipped by the lower classes, where the old rites still pandered to their grosser appetites, or subserved the wealth and importance of some particular locality.

In the meanwhile, the minds of men, cut adrift from their ancient moorings, wandered wildly over pathless seas of speculative doubt, and especially in the more metaphysical and contemplative East, attempted to solve for themselves the questions of man's relation to the unseen, by those thousand schisms, heresies, and theosophies (it is a disgrace to the word philosophy to call them by it), on the records of which the student now gazes bewildered, unable alike to count or to explain their fantasies.

Yet even these, like every outburst of free human thought, had their use and their fruit. They brought before the minds of churchmen a thousand new questions which must be solved, unless the Church was to relinquish for ever her claims as the great teacher and satisfier of the human soul. To study these bubbles, as they formed and burst on every wave of human life; to feel, too often by sad experience, as Augustine felt, the charm of their allurements; to divide the truths at which they aimed from the falsehood which they offered as its substitute; to exhibit the Catholic Church as possessing, in the great facts which she proclaimed, full satisfaction, even for the most subtle metaphysical cravings of a diseased age; — that was the work of the time; and men were sent to do it, and aided in their labour by the very causes which had produced the intellectual revolution. The general intermixture of ideas, creeds, and races, even the mere physical facilities for intercourse between different parts of the Empire, helped to give the great Christian fathers of the fourth and fifth centuries a breadth of observation, a depth of thought, a large-hearted and large-minded patience and tolerance, such as, we may say boldly, the Church has since beheld but rarely, and the world never; at least, if we are to judge those great men by what they had, and not by what they had not, and to believe, as we are bound, that had they lived now, and not then, they would have towered as far above the heads of this generation as they did above the heads of their own. And thus an age, which, to the shallow insight of a sneerer like Gibbon, seems only a rotting and sinless chaos of sensuality and anarchy, fanaticism and hypocrisy, produced a Clement and an Athanase, a Chrysostom and an Augustine; absorbed into the sphere of Christianity all which was most valuable in the philosophies of Greece and Egypt, and in the social organization of Rome, as an heir-loom for nations yet unborn; and laid in foreign lands, by unconscious agents, the foundations of all European thought and ethics.

But the health of a Church depends, not merely on the creed which it professes, not even on the wisdom and holiness of a few great ecclesiastics, but on the faith and virtue of its individual members. The *mens sana* must have a *corpus sanum* to inhabit. And even for the Western Church, the lofty future which was in store for it would have been impossible, without some infusion of new and healthier blood into the veins of a world drained and tainted by the influence of Rome.

And the new blood, at the era of this story, was at hand. The great tide of those Gothic nations, of which the Norwegian and the German are the purest remaining types, though every nation of Europe, from Gibraltar to St. Petersburg, owes to them the most precious elements of strength, was sweeping onward, wave over wave, in a steady south-western current, across the whole Roman territory, and only stopping and recoiling when it reached the shores of the Mediterranean. Those wild tribes were bringing with t-hem into the magic circle of the Western Church's influence the very materials which she required for the building up of a future Christendom, and which she could find as little in the Western Empire, as in the Eastern; comparative purity of morals; sacred respect for woman, for family life, law, equal justice, individual freedom, and, above all, for honesty in word and deed; bodies untainted by hereditary effeminacy, hearts earnest though genial, and blest with a strange willingness to learn, even from those whom they despised; a brain equal to that of the Roman in practical power, and not too far behind that of the Eastern in imaginative and speculative acuteness.

And their strength was felt at once. Their vanguard, confined with difficulty for three centuries beyond the Eastern Alps, at the expense of sanguinary wars, had been adopted, wherever it was practicable, into the service of the Empire; and the heart's core of the Roman legions was composed of Gothic officers and soldiers. But now the main body had arrived. Tribe after tribe was crowding down to the Alps, and trampling upon each other on the frontiers of the Empire. The Huns, singly their inferiors, pressed them from behind with the irresistible weight of numbers; Italy, with her rich cities and fertile lowlands, beckoned them on to plunder; as auxiliaries, they had learned their own strength and Roman weakness; a *casus belli* was soon found. How iniquitous was the conduct of the sons of Theodosius, in refusing the usual bounty, by which the Goths were bribed not to attack the empire I — The whole pent-up deluge burst over the plains of Italy, and the Western Empire became from that day forth a dying idiot, while the new invaders divided Europe among themselves. The fifteen years before the time of this tale had decided the fate of Greece; the last four that of Rome itself. The countless treasures which five centuries of rapine had accumulated round the Capitol had become the prey of men clothed in sheep-skins and horse-hide; and the sister of an emperor had found her beauty, virtue, and pride of race, worthily matched by those of the hard-handed Northern hero who led her away from Italy as his captive and his bride, to found new kingdoms in South France and Spain, and to drive the newly-arrived Vandals across the Straits of Gibraltar into the then blooming coast-land of Northern Africa. Everywhere the mangled limbs of the Old World were seething in the Medea's caldron, to come forth whole, and young, and strong. The Longbeards, noblest of their race, had found a temporary resting-place upon the Austrian frontier, after long southward wanderings from the Swedish mountains, soon to be dispossessed again by the advancing Huns, and, crossing the Alps, to give their names for ever to the plains of Lombardy. A few more tumultuous years, and the Franks would find themselves lords of the Lower Rhineland; and before the hairs of Hypatia's scholars had grown grey, the mythic Hengst and Horsa would have landed on the shores of Kent, and an English nation have begun its world-wide life.

But some great Providence forbade to our race, triumphant in every other quarter, a footing beyond the Mediterranean, or even in Constantinople, which to this day preserves in Europe the faith and manners of Asia. The Eastern World seemed barred, by some stern doom, from the only influence which could have regenerated it. Every attempt of the Gothic races to establish themselves beyond the sea, whether in the form of an organized kingdom, as the Vandals attempted in Africa; or of a mere band of brigands, as did the Goths in Asia Minor, under Gainas; or of a praetorian guard, as did the Varangens of the middle age; or as religious invaders, as did the Crusaders, ended only in the corruption and disappearance of the colonists. That extraordinary reform in morals, which, according to Salvian and his contemporaries, the Vandal conquerors worked in North Africa, availed them nothing; they lost more than they gave. Climate, bad example, and the luxury of power degraded them in one century into a race of helpless and debauched slaveholders, doomed to utter extermination before the semi-Gothic armies of Belisarius; and with them vanished the last chance that the Gothic races would exercise on the Eastern World the same stem yet wholesome discipline under which the Western had been restored to life.

The Egyptian and Syrian Churches, therefore, were destined to labour not for themselves, but for us. The signs of disease and decrepitude were already but too manifest in them. That very peculiar turn of the Græco-Eastern mind, which made them the great thinkers of the then world, had the effect of drawing them away from practice to speculation; and the races of Egypt and Syria were effeminate, over-civilized, exhausted by centuries during which no infusion of fresh blood had come to renew the stock. Morbid, self-conscious, physically indolent, incapable then, as now, of personal or political freedom, they afforded material out of which fanatics might easily be made, but not citizens of the kingdom of God. The very ideas of family and national life — those two divine roots of the Church, severed from which she is certain to wither away into that most godless and most cruel of spectres, a religious world — had perished in the East from the evil influence of the universal practice of slaveholding, as well as from the degradation of that Jewish nation which had been for ages the great witness for those ideas; and all classes, like their forefather Adam — like, indeed "the old Adam" in every man and in every age — were shifting the blame of sin from their own consciences to human relationships and duties — and therein, to the God who had appointed them; and saying as of old, *"The woman whom thou gavest to be with me, she gave me of the tree, and I did eat."* The passionate Eastern character, like all weak ones, found total abstinence easier than temperance, religious thought more pleasant than godly action; and a monastic world grew up all over the East, of such vastness that in Egypt it was said to rival in numbers the lay population, producing, with an enormous decrease in the actual amount of moral evil, an equally great enervation and decrease of the population. Such a people could offer no resistance to the steadily-increasing tyranny of the Eastern Empire. In vain did such men as Chrysostom and Basil oppose their personal influence to the hideous intrigues and villanies of the Byzantine court; the ever-downward career of Eastern Christianity went on unchecked for two more miserable centuries, side by side with the upward development of the Western Church; and, while the successors of the great Saint Gregory were converting and civilizing a new-born Europe, the Churches of the East were vanishing before Mohammedan invaders, strong by living trust in that living God, whom the Christians, while they hated and persecuted each other for arguments about Him, were denying and blaspheming in every action of their lives.

But at the period whereof this story treats, the Græco-Eastern mind was still in the middle of its great work. That wonderful metaphysic subtlety, which, in phrases and definitions too often unmeaning to our grosser intellect, saw the symbols of the most important spiritual realities, and felt that on the distinction between *homoousios* and *homoiousios* might hang the solution of the whole problem of humanity, was set to battle in Alexandria, the ancient stronghold of Greek philosophy, with the effete remains of the very scientific thought to which it owed its extraordinary culture. Monastic isolation from family and national duties especially fitted the fathers of that period for the task, by giving them leisure, if nothing else, to face questions with a lifelong earnestness impossible to the more social and practical Northern mind. Our duty is, instead of sneering at them as pedantic dreamers, to thank Heaven that men were found, just at the time when they were wanted, to do for us what we could never have done for ourselves; to leave to us, as a precious heirloom, bought most truly with the lifeblood of their race, a metaphysic at once Christian and scientific, every attempt to improve on which has hitherto been found a failure; and to battle victoriously with that strange brood of theoretic monsters begotten by effete Greek philosophy upon Egyptian symbolism, Chaldee astrology, Parsee dualism, Brahminic spiritualism — graceful and gorgeous phantoms, whereof somewhat more will be said in the coming chapters.

I have, in my sketch of Hypatia and her fate, closely followed authentic history, especially Socrates' account of the closing scene, as given in Book vii. § 15, of his "Ecclesiastical History." I am inclined, however, for various historical reasons, to date her death two years earlier than he does. The tradition that she was the wife of Isidore, the philosopher, I reject, with Gibbon, as a palpable anachronism of at least fifty years (Isidore's master, Proclus, not having been born till the year before Hypatia's death), contradicted, moreover, by the very author of it, Photius, who says distinctly, after comparing Hypatia and Isidore, that Isidore married a certain "Domna." No hint, moreover, of her having been married, appears in any contemporary authors; and the name of Isidore nowhere occurs among those of the many mutual "lends to whom Synesius sends messages in his letters to Hypatia, in which, if anywhere, we should find mention of a husband, had one existed. To Synesius's most charming letters, as well as to those of Isidore, the good Abbot of Pelusium, I beg leave to refer those readers who wish for further information about the private life of the fifth century.

I cannot hope that these pages will be altogether free from anachronisms and errors. I can only say that I have laboured honestly and industriously to discover the truth, even in its minutest details, and to sketch the age, its manners and its literature, as I found them — altogether artificial, slipshod, effete, resembling far more the times of Louis Quinze than those of Sophocles and Plato. And so I send forth this little sketch, ready to give my hearty thanks to any reviewer who, by exposing my mistakes, shall teach me and the public somewhat more about the last struggle between the Young Church and the Old World.

HYPATIA

or
NEW FOES WITH AN OLD FACE

CHAPTER I
THE LAURA

IN the four hundred and thirteenth year of the Christian Era, some three hundred miles above Alexandria, the young monk Philammon was sitting on the edge of a low range of inland cliffs, crested with drifting sand. Behind him the desert sand-waste stretched, lifeless, interminable, reflecting its lurid glare on the horizon of the cloudless vault of blue. At his feet the sand dripped and trickled, in yellow rivulets, from crack to crack and ledge to ledge, or whirled past him in tiny jets of yellow smoke, before the fitful summer airs. Here and there, upon the face of the cliffs which walled in the opposite side of the narrow glen below, were cavernous tombs, huge old quarries, with obelisks and half-cut pillars, standing as the workmen had left them centuries before; the sand was slipping down and piling up around them; their heads were frosted with the arid snow; everywhere was silence, desolation — the grave of a dead nation, in a dying land. And there he sat musing above it all, full of life and youth and health and beauty — a young Apollo of the desert. His only clothing was a ragged sheep-skin, bound with a leathern girdle. His long black locks, unshorn from childhood, waved and glistened in the sun; a rich dark down on cheek and chin showed the spring of healthful manhood; his hard hands and sinewy sunburnt limbs told of labour and endurance; his flashing eyes and beetling brow, of daring, fancy, passion, thought, which had no sphere of action in such a place. What did his glorious young humanity alone among the tombs?

So perhaps he, too, thought, as he passed his hand across his brow, as if to sweep away some gathering dream, and sighing, rose and wandered along the cliffs, peering down-ward at every point and cranny, in search of fuel for the monastery from whence he came.

Simple as was the material which he sought, consisting chiefly of the low arid desert shrubs, with now and then a fragment of wood from some deserted quarry or ruin, it was becoming scarcer and scarcer round Abbot Pambo's Laura at Scetis, and long before Philammon had collected his daily quantity, he had strayed further from his home than he had ever been before.

Suddenly, at a turn of the glen, he came upon a sight new to him.... a temple carved in the sandstone cliff; and in front, a smooth platform, strewn with beams and mouldering tools, and here and there a skull bleaching among the sand, perhaps of some workman slaughtered at his labour in one of the thousand wars of old. The abbot, his spiritual father — indeed, the only father whom he knew, for his earliest recollections were of the Laura and the old man's cell — had strictly forbidden him to enter, even to approach any of those relics of ancient idolatry: but a broad terrace-road led down to the platform from the table land above; the plentiful supply of fuel was too tempting to be passed by.... He would go down, gather a few sticks, and then return, to tell the abbot of the treasure which he had found, and consult him as to the propriety of revisiting it.

So down he went, hardly daring to raise his eyes to the alluring iniquities of the painted imagery which, gaudy in crimson and blue, still blazed out upon the desolate solitude, uninjured by that rainless air. But he was young, and youth is curious; and the devil, at least in the fifth century, busy with young brains. Now Philammon believed most utterly in the devil, and night and day devoutly prayed to be delivered from him; so he crossed himself, and ejaculated, honestly enough, "Lord, turn away mine eyes, lest they behold vanity!".... and looked nevertheless.....

And who could have helped looking at those four colossal kings, who sat there grim and motionless, their huge hands laid upon their knees in everlasting self-assured repose, seeming to bear up the mountain of their stately heads? A sense of awe, weakness, all but fear, came over him. He dare not stoop to take up the wood at his feet, their great stern eyes watched him so steadily.

Round their knees and round their thrones were mystic characters engraven, symbol after symbol, line below line — the ancient wisdom of the Egyptians, wherein Moses the man of God was learned of old — why should not he know it too? What awful secrets might not be hidden there about the great world, past, present, and future, of which he knew only so small a speck? Those kings who sat there, they had known it all; their sharp lips seem parting, ready to speak to him..... Oh, that they would speak for once!.... and yet that grim sneering smile, that seemed to look down on him from the heights of their power and wisdom, with calm contempt.... him, the poor youth, picking up the leaving and rags of their past majesty.... He dare look at them no more.

So he looked past them, into the temple halls; into a lustrous abyss of cool green shade, deepening on and inward, pillar after pillar, vista after vista, into deepest night. And dimly through the gloom he could descry, on every wall and column, gorgeous arabesques, long lines of pictured story; triumphs and labours; rows of captives in foreign and fantastic dresses, leading strange animals, bearing the tributes of unknown lands; rows of ladies at feasts, their heads crowned with garlands, the fragrant lotus-flower in every hand, while slaves brought wine and perfumes, and children sat upon their knees, and husbands by their side; and dancing girls, in transparent robes and golden girdles, tossed their tawny limbs wildly among the throng.... What was the meaning of it all? Why had it all been? Why had it gone on thus, the great world, century after century, millennium after millennium, eating and drinking, and marrying and giving in marriage, and knowing nothing better.... how could they know anything better? Their forefathers had lost the light ages and ages before they were born..... And Christ had not come for ages and ages after they were dead.... How could they know?.... And yet they were all in hell.... every one of them. Every one of these ladies who sat there, with her bushy locks, and garlands, and jewelled collars, and lotus-flowers, and gauzy dress, displaying all her slender limbs — who, perhaps, when she was alive, smiled so sweetly, and went so gaily, and had children, and friends, and never once thought of what was going to happen to her — what must happen to her..... She was in hell.... Burning for ever, and ever, and ever, there below his feet. He stared down on the rocky floors. If he could but see through them.... and the eye of faith could see through them.... he should behold her writhing and twisting among the flickering flame, scorched, glowing.... in everlasting agony, such as the thought of enduring for a moment made him shudder. He had burnt his hands once, when a palm-leaf hut caught fire..... He recollected what that was like..... She was enduring ten thousand times more than that, for ever..... He should hear her shrieking in vain for a drop of water to cool her tongue..... He had never heard a human being shriek but once.... a boy bathing on the opposite Nile bank, whom a crocodile had dragged down.... and that scream, faint and distant as it came across the mighty tide, had rung intolerable in his ears for days.... and to think of all which echoed through those vaults of fire — for ever! Was the thought bearable? — was it possible? Millions upon millions burning for ever for Adam's fall..... Could God be just in that?....

It was the temptation of a fiend! He had entered the un-hallowed precincts, where devils still lingered about their ancient shrines; he had let his eyes devour the abominations of the hea-then, and given place to the devil. He would flee home to confess it all to his father. He would punish him as he deserved, pray for him, forgive him. And yet could he tell him all? Could he, dare he confess to him the whole truth — the insatiable craving to know the mysteries of learning — to see the great roaring world of men, which had been growing up in him slowly, month after month, till now it had assumed this fearful shape? He could stay no longer in the desert. This world which sent all souls to hell — was it as bad as monks declared it was? It must be, else how could such be the fruit of it? But it was too awful a thought to be taken on trust. No; he must go and see.

Filled with such fearful questionings, half-inarticulate and vague, like the thoughts of a child, the untutored youth went wandering on, till he reached the edge of the cliff below which lay his home.

It lay pleasantly enough, that lonely Laura, or lane of rude Cyclopean cells, under the perpetual shadow of the southern wall of crags, amid its grove of ancient date-trees. A branching cavern in the cliff supplied the purposes of a chapel, a storehouse, and a hospital; while on the sunny slope across the glen lay the com-mon gardens of the brotherhood, green with millet, maize, and beans, among which a tiny streamlet, husbanded and guided with the most thrifty care, wandered down from the cliff foot, and spread perpetual verdure over the little plot which voluntary and fraternal labour had painfully redeemed from the inroads of the all-devouring sand. For that garden, like everything else in the Laura, except each brother's seven feet of stone sleeping-hut, was the common property, and therefore the common care and joy, of all. For the common good, as well as for his own, each man had toiled up the glen with his palm-leaf basket of black mud from the river Nile, over whose broad sheet of silver the glen's mouth yawned abrupt. For the common good, each man had swept the ledges clear of sand, and sown in the scanty artificial soil, the harvest of which all were to share alike. To buy clothes, books, and chapel-furniture for the common necessities, education, and worship, each man sat, day after day, week after week, his mind full of high and heavenly thoughts, weaving the leaves of their little palmcopse into baskets, which an aged monk exchanged for goods with the more prosperous and frequented monasteries of the opposite bank. Thither Philammon rowed the old man over, week by week, in a light canoe of papyrus, and fished, as he sat waiting for him, for the common meal. A simple, happy, gentle life was that of the Laura, all portioned out by rules and methods, which were held hardly less sacred than those of the Scriptures, on which they were supposed (and not so wrongly either) to have been framed. Each man had food and raiment, shelter on earth, friends and counsellors, living trust in the continual care of Almighty God; and, blazing before his eyes, by day and night, the hope of everlasting glory beyond all poets' dreams..... And what more would man have had in those days? Thither they had fled out of cities, compared with which Paris is earnest and Gomorrha chaste, — out of a rotten, infernal, dying world of tyrants and slaves, hypocrites and wantons, — to ponder undisturbed on duty and on judgment, on death and eternity, heaven and hell; to find a common creed, a common interest, a common hope, common duties, pleasures, and sorrows..... True, they had many of them fled from the post where God had placed them, when they fled from man into the Thebaid waste..... What sort of post and what sort of an age they were, from which those old monks fled, we shall see, perhaps, before this tale is told out.

"Thou art late, son," said the abbot, steadfastly working away at his palm-basket, as Philammon approached.

"Fuel is scarce, and I was forced to go far."

"A monk should not answer till he is questioned. I did not ask the reason. Where didst thou find that wood?"

"Before the temple, far up the glen."

"The temple! What didst thou see there?"

No answer. Pambo looked up with his keen black eye.

"Thou hast entered it, and lusted after its abominations."

"I — I did not enter; but I looked —— "

"And what didst thou see? Women?"

Philammon was silent.

"Have I not bidden you never to look on the face of women? Are they not the first-fruits of the devil, the authors of all evil, the subtlest of all Satan's snares? Are they not accursed for ever, for the deceit of their first mother, by whom sin entered into the world? A woman first opened the gates of hell; and, until this day, they are the portresses thereof. Unhappy boy! what hast thou done?"

"They were but painted on the walls."

"Ah!" said the abbot, as if suddenly relieved from a heavy burden. "But how knewest thou them to be women, when thou hast never yet, unless thou liest — which I believe not of thee — seen the face of a daughter of Eve?"

"Perhaps — perhaps," said Philammon, as if suddenly relieved by a new suggestion — "perhaps they were only devils. They must have been, I think, for they were so very beautiful."

"Ah! how knowest thou that devils are beautiful?"

"I was launching the boat, a week ago, with Father Aufugus; and on the bank,.... not very near,.... there were two creatures.... with long hair, and striped all over the lower half of their bodies with black, and red and yellow.... and they were gathering flowers on the shore. Father Aufugus turned away; but I.... I could not help thinking them the most beautiful things that I had ever seen.... so I asked him why he turned away; and he said that those were the same sort of devils which tempted the blessed St. Anthony. Then I recollected having heard it read aloud, how Satan tempted Anthony in the shape of a beautiful woman..... And so.... and so.... those figures on the wall were very like.... and I thought they might be...."

And the poor boy, who considered that he was making confession of a deadly and shameful sin, blushed scarlet, and stammered, and at last stopped.

"And thou thoughtest them beautiful? Oh utter corruption of the flesh! — oh subtilty of Satan! The Lord forgive thee, as I do, my poor child: henceforth thou goest not beyond the garden walls."

"Not beyond the walls! Impossible! I cannot! If thou wert not my father, I would say, I will not! — I must have liberty! — I must see for myself — I must judge for myself, what this world is of which you all talk so bitterly. I long for no pomps and vanities. I will promise you this moment, if you will, never to re-enter a heathen temple — to hide my face in the dust whenever I approach a woman. But I must — I must see the world; I must see the great mother-church in Alexandria, and the patriarch, and his clergy. If they can serve God in the city, why not I? I could do more for God there than here..... Not that I despise this work — not that I am ungrateful to you — oh, never, never that! — but I pant for the battle. Let me go! I am not discontented with you, but with myself. I know that obedience is noble; but danger is nobler still. If you have seen the world, why should not I? If you have fled from it because you found it too evil to live in, why should not I, and return to you here of my own will, never to leave you?.... And yet Cyril and his clergy have not fled from it....."

Desperately and breathlessly did Philammon drive this speech out of his inmost heart; and then waited, expecting the good abbot to strike him on the spot. If he had, the Young man would have submitted patiently; so would any man, however venerable, in that monastery. Why not? Duly, after long companionship, thought, and prayer, they had elected Pambo for their abbot — abba — father — the wisest, eldest-hearted and headed of them — if he was that, it was time that he should be obeyed. And obeyed he was, with a loyal, reasonable love, and yet with an implicit, soldier-like obedience, which many a king and conqueror might envy. Were they cowards and slaves? The Roman legionaries should be good judges on that point. They used to say that no armed barbarian, Goth or Vandal, Moor or Spaniard, was so terrible as the unarmed monk of the Thebaid.

Twice the old man lifted his staff to strike; twice he laid it down again; and then, slowly rising, left Philammon kneeling there, and moved away deliberately, and with eyes fixed on the ground, to the house of the brother Aufugus.

Every one in the Laura honoured Aufugus. There was a mystery about him which heightened the charm of his surpassing sanctity, his childlike sweetness and humility. It was whispered — when the monks seldom and cautiously did whisper together in their lonely walks — that he had been once a great man; that he had come from a great city — perhaps from Rome itself. And the simple monks were proud to think that they had among them a man who had seen Rome. At least, Abbot Pambo respected him. He was never beaten; never even reproved — perhaps he never required it; but still it was the meed of all; and was not the abbot a little partial? Yet, certainly, when Theophilus sent up a messenger from Alexandria, rousing every Laura with the news of the sack of Rome by Alaric, did not Pambo take him first to the cell of Aufugus, and sit with him there three whole hours in secret consultation, before he told the awful story to the rest of the brotherhood? And did not Aufugus himself give letters to the messenger, written with his own hand, containing, as was said, deep secrets of worldly policy, known only to himself? So, when the little lane of holy men, each peering stealthily over his plaiting-work from the doorway of his sandstone cell, saw the abbot, after his unwonted passion, leave the culprit kneeling, and take his way toward the sage's dwelling, they judged that something strange and delicate had befallen the common weal, and each wished without envy, that he were as wise as the man whose counsel was to solve the difficulty.

For an hour or more the abbot remained there, talking earnestly and low; and then a solemn sound as of the two old men praying with sobs and tears; and every brother bowed his head, and whispered a hope that He whom they served might guide them for the good of the Laura, and of his Church, and of the great heathen world beyond; and still Philammon knelt motionless, awaiting his sentence; his heart filled — who can tell how? "The heart knoweth its own bitterness, and a stranger intermeddleth not with its joy." So thought he as he knelt; and so think I, too, knowing that in the pettiest character there are unfathomable depths, which the poet, all-seeing though he may pretend to be, can never analyze, but must only dimly guess at, and still more dimly sketch them by the actions which they beget.

At last Pambo returned, deliberate, still, and slow, as he had gone, and seating himself within his cell, spoke —

"And the youngest said, Father, give me the portion of goods that falleth to my share..... And he took his journey into a far country, and there wasted his substance with riotous living. Thou shalt go, my son. But first come after me, and speak with Aufugus."

Philammon, like every one else, loved Aufugus; and when the abbot retired and left the two alone together, he felt no dread or shame about unburdening his whole heart to him. Long and passionately he spoke, in answer to the gentle questions of the old man, who, without the rigidity or pedantic solemnity of the monk, interrupted the youth, and let himself be interrupted in return, gracefully, genially, almost playfully. And yet there was a melancholy about his tone as he answered to the youth's appeal —

"Tertullian, Origen, Clement, Cyprian — all these moved in the world; all these, and many more beside, whose names we honour, whose prayers we invoke, were learned in the wisdom of the heathen, and fought and laboured, unspotted, in the world; and why not I? Cyril the Patriarch himself, was he not called from the caves of Nitria to sit on the throne of Alexandria?"

Slowly the old man lifted his hand, and putting back the thick locks of the kneeling youth, gazed, with soft pitying eyes, long and earnestly into his face.

"And thou wouldst see the world, poor fool? And thou Wouldst see the world?"

"I would convert the world!"

"Thou must know it first. And shall I tell thee what that world is like, which seems to thee so easy to convert? Here I sit, the poor unknown old monk, until I die, fasting and praying, if perhaps God will have mercy on my soul: but little thou knowest how I have seen it. Little thou knowest, or thou wouldst be well content to rest here till the end. I was Arsenius..... Ah! vain old man that I am! Thou hast never heard that name, at which once queens would whisper and grow pale. Vanitas vanitatum! omnia vanitas! And yet he, at whose frown half the world trembles, has trembled himself at mine. I was the tutor of Arcadius."

"The Emperor of Byzantium?"

"Even so, my son, even so. There I saw the world which thou wouldst see. And what saw I? Even what thou wilt see. Eunuchs the tyrants of their own sovereigns. Bishops kissing the feet of parricides and harlots. Saints tearing saints in pieces for a word, while sinners cheer them on to the unnatural fight. Liars thanked for lying, hypocrites taking pride in their hypocrisy. The many sold and butchered for the malice, the caprice, the vanity of the few. The plunderers of the poor plundered in their turn by worse devourers than themselves. Every attempt at reform the parent of worse scandals; every mercy begetting fresh cruelties; every persecutor silenced, only to enable others to persecute him in their turn: every devil who is exorcised, returning with seven others worse than himself; falsehood and selfishness, spite and lust, confusion seven times confounded, Satan casting out Satan everywhere — from the emperor who wantons on his throne, to the slave who blasphemes beneath his fetters."

" If Satan cast out Satan, his kingdom shall not stand. "

"In the world to come. But in this world it shall stand and conquer, even worse and worse, until the end. These are the last days spoken of by the prophets, the beginning of woes such as never have been on the earth before — 'On earth distress of nations with perplexity, men's hearts failing them for fear, and for the dread of those things which are coming on the earth.' I have seen it long. Year after year I have watched them coming nearer and ever nearer in their course, like the whirling sandstorms of the desert, which sweep past the caravan, and past again, and yet overwhelm it after all — that black flood of the northern barbarians. I foretold it; I prayed against it; but, like Cassandra's of old, my prophecy and my prayers were alike unheard. My pupil spurned my warnings. The lusts of youth, the intrigues of courtiers, were stronger than the warning voice of God; then I ceased to hope; I ceased to pray for the glorious city, for I knew that her sentence was gone forth; I saw her in the spirit, even as Saint John saw her in the Revelations; her, and her sins, and her ruin. And I fled secretly at night, and buried myself here in the desert, to await the end of the world. Night and day I pray the Lord to accomplish his elect, and to hasten his kingdom. Morning by morning I look up trembling, and yet in hope, for the sign of the Son of Man in heaven, when the sun shall be turned into darkness, and the moon into blood, and the stars shall fall from heaven, and the skies pass away like a scroll, and the fountains of the nether fire burst up around our feet, and the end of all shall come. And thou wouldst go into the world from which I fled?"

24

"If the harvest be at hand, the Lord needs labourers. If the times be awful, I should be doing awful things in them. Send me, and let that day find me, where I long to be, in the forefront of the battle of the Lord."

"The Lord's voice be obeyed! Thou shalt go. Here are letters to Cyril the patriarch. He will love thee for my sake: and for thine own sake, too, I trust. Thou goest of our free will as well as thine own. The abbot and I have watched thee long, knowing that the Lord had need of such as thee elsewhere. We did but prove thee, to see by thy readiness to obey, whether thou wert fit to rule. Go, and God be with thee. Covet no man's gold or silver. Neither eat flesh nor drink wine, but live as thou hast lived — a Nazarite of the Lord. Fear not the face of man; but look not on the face of woman. In an evil hour came they '"to the world, the mothers of all mischiefs which I have seen under the sun. Come; the abbot waits for us at the gate."

With tears of surprise, joy, sorrow, almost of dread, Philammon hung back.

"Nay — come. Why shouldst thou break thy brethren's hearts and ours by many leave-takings? Bring from the store-house a week's provision of dried dates and millet. The papyrus boat lies at the ferry; thou shalt descend in it. The Lord will re-place it for us when we need it. Speak with no man on the river except the monks of God. When thou hast gone five days' jour-ney downward, ask for the mouth of the canal of Alexandria. Once in the city, any monk will guide thee to the archbishop. Send us news of thy welfare by some holy mouth. Come."

Silently they paced together down the glen to the lonely beach of the great stream. Pambo was there already, his white hair glittering in the rising moon, as with slow and feeble arms he launched the light canoe. Philammon flung himself at the old men's feet, and besought, with many tears, their forgiveness and their blessing.

"We have nothing to forgive. Follow thou thine inward call. If it be of the flesh, it will avenge itself; if it be of the Spirit, who are we that we should fight against God? Farewell."

A few minutes more, and the youth and his canoe were lessening down the rapid stream in the golden summer twilight.

Again a minute, and the swift southern night had fallen, and all was dark but the cold glare of the moon on the river, and on the rock-faces, and on the two old men, as they knelt upon the beach, and with their heads upon' each other's shoulders, like two children, sobbed and prayed together for the lost darling of their age.

CHAPTER II
THE DYING WORLD

IN the upper story of a house in the Museum-street of Alexandria, built and fitted up on the old Athenian model, was a small room. It had been chosen by its occupant, not merely on account of its quiet; for though it was tolerably out of hearing of the female slaves who worked, and chattered, and quarrelled under the cloisters of the women's court on the south side, yet it was exposed to the rattle of carriages and the voices of passengers in the fashionable street below, and to strange bursts of roaring, squealing, and trumpeting from the Menagerie, a short way off, oil] the opposite side of the street. The attraction of the situation lay, perhaps, in the view which it commanded over the wall of the Museum gardens, of flower-beds, shrubberies, fountains, statues, walks, and alcoves, which had echoed for nearly seven hundred years to the wisdom of the Alexandrian sages and poets. School after school, they had all walked, and taught, and sung there, beneath the spreading planes and chestnuts, figs and palm-trees. The place seemed fragrant with all the riches of Greek thought and song, since the days when Ptolemy Philadelphus walked there with Euclid and Theocritus, Callimachus and Lycophron.

On the left of the garden stretched the lofty eastern front of the Museum itself, with its picture-galleries, halls of statuary, dining-halls and lecture-rooms; one huge wing containing that famous library, founded by the father of Philadelphus, which held in the time of Seneca, even after the destruction of a great part of it in Cæsar's siege, four hundred thousand manuscripts. There it towered up, the wonder of the world, its white roof bright against the rainless blue; and beyond it, among the ridges and pediments of noble buildings, a broad glimpse of the bright blue sea.

The room was fitted up in the purest Greek style, not without an affectation of archaism, in the severe forms and subdued half-tints of the frescoes which ornamented the walls with scenes from the old myths of Athene. Yet the general effect, even under the blazing sun which poured in through the mosquito nets of the court-yard windows, was one of exquisite coolness, and cleanliness, and repose. The room had neither carpet nor fireplace; and the only moveables in it were a sofa-bed, a table, and an arm-chair, all of such delicate and graceful forms, as may be seen on ancient vases of a far earlier period than that whereof we write. But, most probably, had any of us entered that room that morning, we should not have been able to spare a look either for the furniture, or the general effect, or the Museum gardens, or the sparkling Mediterranean beyond; but we should have agreed that the room was quite rich enough for human eyes, for the sake of one treasure which 't possessed, and, beside which, nothing was worth a moment's glance. For in the light arm-chair, reading a manuscript which lay on the table, sat a woman, of some five-and-twenty years, evidently the tutelary goddess of that little shrine, dressed in perfect keeping with the archaism of the chamber, in a simple old snow-white Ionic robe, falling to the feet and reaching to the throat, and of that peculiarly severe and graceful fashion in which the upper part of the dress falls downward again from the neck to the waist in a sort of cape, entirely hiding the outline of the bust, while it leaves the arms and the point of the shoulders bare. Her dress was entirely without ornament, except the two narrow purple stripes down the front, which marked her rank as a Roman citizen, the gold-embroidered shoes upon her feet, and the gold net, which looped back, from her forehead to her neck, hair the colour and gloss of which were hardly distinguishable from that of the metal itself, such as Athene herself might have envied for tint, and mass, and ripple. Her features, arms, and hands were of the severest and grandest type of old Greek beauty, at once showing everywhere the high development of the bones, and covering them with that firm, round, ripe, outline, and waxy morbidezza of skin, which the old Greeks owed to their continual use not only of the bath and muscular exercise, but also of daily unguents. There might have seemed to us too much sadness in that clear grey eye; too much self-conscious restraint in those sharp curved lips; too much affectation in the studied severity of her posture as she read, copied, as it seemed, from some old vase or bas-relief. But the glorious grace and beauty of every line of face and figure would have excused, even hidden those defects, and we should have only recognized the marked resemblance to the ideal portraits of Athene which adorned every panel of the walls.

She has lifted her eyes off her manuscript; she is looking out with kindling countenance over the gardens of the Museum; her ripe curling Greek lips, such as we never see now, even among our own wives and sisters, open. She is talking to herself. Listen!

"Yes. The statues there are broken. The libraries are plundered. The alcoves are silent. The oracles are dumb. And yet — who says that the old faith of heroes and sages is dead? The beautiful can never die. If the gods have deserted their oracles, they have not deserted the souls who aspire to them. If they have ceased to guide nations, they have not ceased to speak to their own elect. If they have cast off the vulgar herd, they have not cast off Hypatia.

* * * * * *

" Ay. To believe in the old creeds, while every one else is dropping away from them..... To believe in spite of disappointments..... To hope against hope..... To show oneself superior to the herd, by seeing boundless depths of living glory in myths which have become dark and dead to them..... To struggle to the last against the new and vulgar superstitions of a rotting age, for the faith of my forefathers, for the old gods, the old heroes, the old sages who gauged the mysteries of heaven and earth — and perhaps to conquer — at least to have my reward! To be welcomed into the celestial ranks of the heroic — to rise to the immortal gods, to the ineffable powers, onward, upward ever, through ages and through eternities, till I find my home at last, and vanish in the glory of the Nameless and the Absolute One!...."

And her whole face flashed out into wild glory, and then sank again suddenly into a shudder of something like fear and disgust, as she saw, watching her from under the wall of the gardens opposite, a crooked, withered Jewish crone, dressed out in the most gorgeous and fantastic style of barbaric finery.

"Why does that old hag haunt me? I see her everywhere — till the last month at least — and here she is again! I will ask the prefect to find out who she is, and get rid of her, before she fascinates me with that evil eye. Thank the gods, there she moves away! Foolish! — foolish of me, a philosopher. I, to believe, against the authority of Porphyry himself, too, in evil eyes and magic! But there is my father, pacing up and down in the library."

As she spoke, the old man entered from the next room. He was a Greek also, but of a more common, and, perhaps, lower type; dark and fiery, thin and graceful; his delicate figure and cheeks, wasted by meditation, harmonized well with the staid and simple philosophic cloak which he wore as a sign of his profession. He paced impatiently up and down the chamber, while his keen, glittering eyes and restless gestures betokened intense inward thought.....

.....“I have it..... No; again it escapes — it contradicts itself. Miserable man that I am! If there is faith in Pythagoras, the symbol should be an expanding series of the powers of three; and yet that accursed binary factor will introduce itself. Did not you work the sum out once, Hypatia?”

“Sit down, my dear father, and eat. You have tasted no food yet this day.”

“What do I care for food! The inexpressible must be expressed. The work must be done, if it cost me the squaring of the circle. How can he, whose sphere lies above the stars, stoop every moment to earth?”

“Ay,” she answered, half bitterly, “and would that we could live without food, and imitate perfectly the immortal gods. But while we are in this prison-house of matter, we must wear our chain; even wear it gracefully, if we have the good taste; and make the base necessities of this body of shame symbolic of the divine food of the reason. There is fruit, with lentils and rice, waiting for you in the next room; and bread, unless you despise it too much.”

“The food of slaves!” he answered. “Well, I will eat, and be ashamed of eating. Stay, did I tell you? Six new pupils in the mathematical school this morning. It grows! It spreads! We shall conquer yet!”

She sighed. “How do you know that they have not come to you, as Critias and Alcibiades did to Socrates, to learn a merely political and mundane virtue? Strange! that men should be content to grovel, and be men, when they might rise to the rank of gods! Ah, my father I that is my bitterest grief; to see those who have been pretending in the morning lecture-room to worship every word of mine as an oracle, lounging in the afternoon round

Pelagia's litter; and then at night — for I know that they do it — the dice, and the wine, and worse. That Pallas herself should be conquered every day by Venus Pandemos! That Pelagia should have more power than I! Not that such a creature as that disturbs me: no created thing, I hope, can move my equanimity; but if I could stoop to hate — I should hate her — hate her."

And her voice took a tone which made it somewhat uncertain whether, in spite of all the lofty impassibility which she felt bound to possess, she did not hate Pelagia with a most human and mundane hatred.

But at that moment the conversation was cut short by the hasty entrance of a slave-girl, who, with fluttering voice, announced —

"His excellency, madam, the prefect! His chariot has been at the gate for these five minutes, and he is now coming upstairs."

"Foolish child!" answered Hypatia, with some affectation of indifference. "And why should that disturb me? Let him enter."

The door opened, and in came, preceded by the scent of half-a-dozen different perfumes, a florid, delicate-featured man, gorgeously dressed out in senatorial costume, his fingers and neck covered with jewels.

"The representative of the Cæsars honours himself by offering at the shrine of Athene Polias, and rejoices to see in her priestess as lovely a likeness as ever of the goddess whom she serves..... Don't betray me, but I really cannot help talking sheer paganism whenever I find myself within the influence of your eyes."

"Truth is mighty," said Hypatia, as she rose to greet him with a smile and a reverence.

"Ah, so they say — Your excellent father has vanished. He is really too modest — honest, though — about his incapacity for state secrets. After all, you know it was your Minervaship which I came to consult. How has this turbulent Alexandrian rascaldom been behaving itself in my absence?"

"The herd has been eating, and drinking, and marrying, as usual, I believe," answered Hypatia, in a languid tone.

"And multiplying, I don't doubt. Well, there will be less loss to the empire if I have to crucify a dozen or two, as I positively will, the next riot. It is really a great comfort to a states-man that the masses are so well aware that they deserve hanging, and therefore so careful to prevent any danger of public justice depopulating the province. But how go on the schools?"

Hypatia shook her head sadly.

"Ah, boys will be boys..... I plead guilty myself. Video meliora proboque, deteriora sequor. You must not be hard on us..... Whether we obey you or not in private life, we do in public; and if we enthrone you queen of Alexandria, you must allow your courtiers and bodyguards a few court-licences. Now don't sigh, or I shall be inconsolable. At all events, your worst rival has betaken herself to the wilderness, and gone to look for the city of the gods above the cataracts."

"Whom do you mean?" asked Hypatia, in a tone most un-philosophically eager.

"Pelagia, of course. I met that prettiest and naughtiest of humanities halfway between here and Thebes, transformed into a perfect Andromache of chaste affection."

"And to whom, pray?"

"To a certain Gothic giant. What men those barbarians do breed! I was afraid of being crushed under the elephant's foot at every step I took with him!"

"What!" asked Hypatia, "did your excellency condescend to converse with such savages?"

"To tell you the truth, he had some forty stout countrymen *of* his with him, who might have been troublesome to a per-plexed prefect; not to mention that it is always as well to keep on good terms with these Goths. Really, after the sack of Rome, and Athens cleaned out like a beehive by wasps, things begin to look serious. And as for the great brute himself, he has rank enough in his way, — boasts of his descent from some cannibal god or other, — really hardly deigned to speak to a paltry Roman gov-ernor, till his faithful and adoring bride interceded for me. Still, the fellow understood good living, and we celebrated our new treaty of friendship with noble libations — but I must not talk about that to you. However, I got rid of them; quoted all the geo-graphical lies I had ever heard, and a great many more; quick-ened their appetite for their fool's errand notably, and started them off again. So now the star of Venus is set, and that of Pallas in the ascendant. Wherefore tell me — what am I to do with

Saint Firebrand?"

"Cyril?"

"Cyril."

"Justice."

"Ah, Fairest Wisdom, don't mention that horrid word out of the lecture-room. In theory it is all very well; but in poor imperfect earthly practice, a governor must be content with doing very much what comes to hand. In abstract justice, now, I ought to nail up Cyril, deacons district visitors, and all, in a row, on the sand-hills outside. That is simple enough; but, like a great many simple and excellent things, impossible."

"You fear the people?"

"Well, my dear lady, and has not the villanous demagogue got the whole mob on his side? Am I to have the Constantinople riots re-enacted here? I really cannot face it; I have not nerve for it; perhaps I am too lazy. Be it so."

Hypatia sighed. "Ah, that your excellency but saw the great duel, which depends on you alone! Do not fancy that the battle is merely between Paganism and Christianity ———— "

"Why, if it were, you know, I, as a Christian, under a Christian and sainted emperor, not to mention his august sister ———— "

"We understand," interrupted she, with an impatient wave of her beautiful hand. "Not even between them; not even between philosophy and barbarianism. The struggle is simply one between the aristocracy and the mob, — between wealth, refinement, art, learning, all that makes a nation great, and the savage herd of child-breeders below, the many ignoble, who were meant to labour for the noble few. Shall the Roman empire command or obey her own slaves? is the question which you and Cyril have to battle out; and the fight must be internecine."

"I should not wonder if it became so, really," answered the prefect, with a shrug of his shoulders. "I expect every time I ride, to have my brains knocked out by some mad monk."

"Why not? In an age when, as has been well and often said, emperors and consulars crawl to the tombs of a tent-maker and a fisherman, and kiss the mouldy bones of the vilest slaves? Why not, among a people whose God is the crucified son of a carpenter? Why should learning, authority, antiquity, birth, rank, the system of empire which has been growing up, fed by the accumulated wisdom of ages, — why, I say, should any of these things protect your life a moment from the fury of any beggar who believes that the Son of God died for him as much as for you, and that he is your equal, if not your superior, in the sight of his low-born and illiterate deity?" [1]

"My most eloquent philosopher, this may be — and perhaps is — all very true. I quite agree that there are very great practical inconveniences of this kind in the new — I mean, the catholic faith; but the world is full of inconveniences. The wise man does not quarrel with his creed for being disagreeable, any more than he docs with his finger for aching: he cannot help it, and must make the best of a bad matter. Only tell me how to keep the peace."

"And let philosophy be destroyed?"

"That it never will be, as long as Hypatia lives to illuminate the earth; and, as far as I am concerned, I promise you a clear stage and — a great deal of favour; as is proved by my visiting you publicly at this moment, before I have given audience to one of the four hundred bores, great and small, who are waiting in the tribunal to torment me. Do help me and advise me. What am I to do?"

"I have told you."

"Ah, yes, as to general principles. But out of the lecture-room I prefer a practical expedient: for instance, Cyril writes to me here — plague on him I he would not let me even have a week's hunting in peace — that there is *a* plot on the part of the Jews to murder all the Christians. Here is the precious document — do look at it, in pity. For aught I know or care, the plot may be an exactly opposite one, and the Christians Intend to murder all the Jews. But I must take some notice of the letter."

"I do not see that, your excellency."

"Why, if anything did happen, after all, conceive the missives which would be sent flying off to Constantinople against me!"

"Let them go. If you are secure in the consciousness of innocence, what matter?"

---

[1] These are the arguments and the language which were commonly employed by Porphyry, Julian, and the other opponents of Christianity.

"Consciousness of innocence! I shall lose my prefecture!"

"Your danger would be just as great if you took notice of it. Whatever happened, you would be accused of favouring the Jews."

"And really there might be some truth in the accusation. How the finances of the provinces would go on without their kind assistance, I dare not think. If those Christians would but lend me their money, instead of building alms-houses and hospitals with it, they might burn the Jews' quarter to-morrow for aught I care. But now...."

"But now, you must absolutely take no notice of this letter. The very tone of it forbids you, for your own honour, and the honour of the empire. Are you to treat with a man who talks of the masses at Alexandria as 'the flock whom the King of kings has committed to his rule and care?' Does your excellency, or this proud bishop, govern Alexandria?"

"Really, my dear lady, I have given up inquiring."

"But he has not. He comes to you as a person possessing an absolute authority over two-thirds of the population, which he does not scruple to hint to you is derived from a higher source than your own. The consequence is clear. If it be from a higher source than yours, of course it ought to control yours; and you will confess that it ought to control it — you will acknowledge the root and ground of every extravagant claim which he makes, if you deign to reply."

"But I must say something, or I shall be pelted in the streets. You philosophers, however raised above your own bodies you may be, must really not forget that we poor worldlings have bones to be broken."

"Then tell him, and by word of mouth merely, that as the information which he sends you comes from his private knowledge, and concerns not him as bishop, but you as magistrate, you can only take it into consideration when he addresses you as a private person, laying a regular information at your tribunal."

"Charming! queen of diplomatists as well as philosophers! I go to obey you. Ah! why were you not Pulcheria? No, for then Alexandria had been dark, and Orestes missed the supreme happiness of kissing a hand which Pallas, when she made you, must have borrowed from the workshop of Aphrodite."

"Recollect that you are a Christian," answered Hypatia,

half smiling.

So the prefect departed; and passing through the outer hall, which was already crowded with Hypatia's aristocratic pupils and visitors, bowed his way out past them, and regained his chariot, chuckling over the rebuff which he intended to administer to Cyril, and comforting himself with the only text of Scripture of the inspiration of which he was thoroughly convinced — "Sufficient for the day is the evil thereof."

At the door was a crowd of chariots, slaves with their masters' parasols, and the rabble of on-looking boys and market-folk, as usual in Alexandria then, as in all great cities since, who were staring at the prefect, and having their heads rapped by his guards, and wondering what sort of glorious personage Hypatia might be, and what sort of glorious house she must live in, to be fit company for the great governor of Alexandria. Not that there was not many a sulky and lowering face among the mob, for the great majority of them were Christians, and very seditious and turbulent politicians, as Alexandrians, "men of Macedonia," were bound to be; and there was many a grumble among them, all but audible, at the prefect's going in state to the heathen woman's house — heathen sorceress, some pious old women called her — before he heard any poor soul's petition in the tribunal, or even said his prayers in church.

Just as he was stepping into his curricle, a tall young man, as gorgeously bedizened as himself, lounged down the steps after him, and beckoned lazily to the black boy who carried his parasol.

"Ah, Raphael Aben-Ezra! my excellent friend, what propitious deity — ahem! martyr — brings you to Alexandria just as I want you! Get up by my side, and let us have a chat on our way to the tribunal."

The man addressed came slowly forward with an ostentatiously low salutation, which could not hide, and indeed was not intended to hide, the contemptuous and lazy expression of his face; and asked, in a drawling tone —

"And for what kind purpose does the representative of the Cæsars bestow such an honour on the humblest of his, &c. &c. — your penetration will supply the rest."

"Don't be frightened; I am not going to borrow money of you," answered Orestes, laughingly, as the Jew got into the curricle.

"I am glad to hear it. Really one usurer in a family is enough. My father made the gold, and if I spend it, I consider that I do all that is required of a philosopher."

"A charming team of white Nisæans, is not this? And only one grey hoof among all the four."

"Yes.... horses are a bore, I begin to find, like every thing else. Always falling sick, or running away, or breaking one's peace of mind in some way or other. Besides, I have been pestered out of my life there in Cyrene, by commissions for dogs and horses and bows from that old episcopal Nimrod, Synesius."

"What, is the worthy man as lively as ever?"

"Lively? He nearly drove me into a nervous fever in three days. Up at four in the morning, always in the most disgustingly good health and spirits, farming, coursing, shooting, riding over hedge and ditch after rascally black robbers; preaching, intriguing, borrowing money; baptizing and excommunicating; bullying that bully, Andronicus; comforting old women, and giving pretty girls dowries; scribbling one half-hour on philosophy, and the next on farriery; sitting up all night writing hymns and drinking strong liquors; off again on horseback at four the next morning; and talking by the hour all the while about philosophic abstraction from the mundane tempest. Heaven defend me from all two-legged whirlwinds! By the by, there was a fair daughter of my nation came back to Alexandria in the same ship with me, with a cargo that may suit your highness."

"There are a great many fair daughters of your nation who might suit me, without any cargo at all."

"Ah, they have had good practice, the little fools, ever since the days of Jeroboam the son of Nebat. But I mean old Miriam — you know. She has been lending Synesius money to fight the black fellows with; and really it was high time. They had burnt every homestead for miles through the province. But the daring old girl must do a little business for herself; so she went off, in the teeth of the barbarians, right away to the Atlas, bought all their lady prisoners, and some of their own sons and daughters, too, of them, for beads and old iron; and has come back with as pretty a cargo of Lybian beauties as a prefect of good taste could wish to have the first choice of. You may thank me for that privilege."

"After, of course, you had suited yourself, my cunning Raphael?"

"Not I. Women are bores, as Solomon found out long ago. Did I never tell you? I began, as he did, with the most select harem in Alexandria. But they quarrelled so, that one day I went out, and sold them all but one, who was a Jewess — so there were objections on the part of the Rabbis. Then I tried one, as Solomon did; but my 'garden shut up,' and my 'sealed fountain' wanted me to be always in love with her, so I went to the lawyers, allowed her a comfortable maintenance, and now I am as free as a monk, and shall be happy to give your excellency the benefit of any good taste or experience which I may possess."

"Thanks, worthy Jew. We are not yet as exalted as yourself, and will send for the old Erictho this very afternoon. Now listen a moment to base, earthly, and political business. Cyril has written to me, to say that you Jews have plotted to murder all the Christians."

"Well — why not? I most heartily wish it were true, and think, on the whole, that it very probably is so."

"By the immortal — saints, man! you are not serious?"

"The four archangels forbid! It is no concern of mine. All I say is, that my people are great fools, like the rest of the world; and have, for aught I know or care, some such intention. They won't succeed, of course; and that is all you have to care for. But if you think it worth the trouble — which I do not — I shall have to go to the synagogue on business in a week or so, and then I would ask some of the Rabbis."

"Laziest of men! — and I must answer Cyril this very day."

"An additional reason for asking no questions of our people. Now you can honestly say that you know nothing about the matter."

"Well, after all, ignorance is a stronghold for poor statesmen. So you need not hurry yourself.'

"I assure your excellency I will not."

"Ten days hence, or so, you know."

"Exactly, after it is all over."

"And can't be helped. What a comfort it is, now and then, that Can't be helped!"

"It is the root and marrow of all philosophy. Your practical man, poor wretch, will try to help this and that, and torment his soul with ways and means, and preventives and forestallings: your philosopher quietly says — It can't be helped. If it ought to be, it will be: if it is, it ought to be. We did not make the world, and we are not responsible for it. — There is the sum and substance of all true wisdom, and the epitome of all that has been said and) written thereon, from Philo the Jew to Hypatia the Gentile. By the way, here's Cyril coming down the steps of the Cæsareum. A very handsome fellow, after all, though he is looking as sulky as a bear."

"With his cubs at his heels. What a scoundrelly visage that tall fellow — deacon, or reader, or whatever he is by his dress — has!"

"There they are — whispering together. Heaven give them pleasant thoughts and pleasanter faces!"

"Amen!" quoth Orestes, with a sneer: and he would have said Amen in good earnest, had he been able to take the liberty — which we shall — and listen to Cyril's answer to Peter, the tall reader.

"From Hypatia's, you say? Why, he only returned to the city this morning."

"I saw his four-in-hand standing at her door, as I came down the Museum-street hither, half-an-hour ago."

"And twenty carriages besides, I don't doubt?"

"The street was blocked up with them. There! Look round the corner now. — Chariots, litters, slaves, and fops. — When shall we see such a concourse as that where it ought to be?"

Cyril made no answer; and Peter went on — "Where it ought to be, my father — in front of your door at the Serapeium?"

"The world, the flesh, and the devil know their own, Peter: and as long as they have their own to go to, we cannot expect them to come to us."

"But what if their own were taken out of the way!"

"They might come to us for want of better amusement.... devil and all. Well — if I could get a fair hold of the two first, I would take the third into the bargain, and see what could be done with him. But never, while these lecture-rooms last — these Egyptian chambers of imagery — these theatres of Satan, where the devil transforms himself into an angel of light, and apes

Christian virtue, and bedizens his ministers like ministers of righteousness, as long as that lecture-room stands, and the great and powerful flock to it, to learn excuses for their own tyrannies and atheisms, so long will the kingdom of God be trampled underfoot in Alexandria; so long will the princes of this world, with their gladiators, and parasites, and moneylenders, be masters here, and not the bishops and priests of the living God."

It was now Peter's turn to be silent; and as the two, with their little knot of district-visitors behind them, walk moodily along the great esplanade which overlooked the harbour, and then vanish suddenly up some dingy alley into the crowded misery of the sailors' quarter, we will leave them to go about their errand of mercy, and, like fashionable people, keep to the grand parade, and listen again to our two fashionable friends in the carved and gilded curricle with four white blood-horses.

"A fine sparkling breeze outside the Pharos, Raphael — fair for the wheat-ships too."

"Are they gone yet?"

"Yes — why? I sent the first fleet off three days ago; and the rest are clearing outwards to-day."

"Oh — ah — so! — Then you have not heard from Heraclian?"

"Heraclian? What the — blessed saints has the Count of Africa to do with my wheat-ships?"

"Oh, nothing. It's no business of mine. Only he is going to rebel..... But here we are at your door."

"To what?" asked Orestes, in a horrified tone.

"To rebel, and attack Rome."

"Good gods — God I mean! A fresh bore! Come in, and tell a poor miserable slave of a governor — speak low, for heaven's sake! — I hope these rascally grooms haven't overheard you."

"Easy to throw them into the canal, if they have," quoth Raphael, as he walked coolly through hall and corridor after the perturbed governor.

Poor Orestes never stopped till he reached a little chamber of the inner court, beckoned the Jew in after him, locked the door, threw himself into an arm-chair, put his hands on his knees, and sat, bending forward, staring into Raphael's face with a ludicrous terror and perplexity.

"Tell me all about it. Tell me this instant!"

"I have told you all I know," quoth Raphael, quietly! seating himself on a sofa, and playing with a jewelled dagger. "I thought, of course, that you were in the secret, or I should have said nothing. It's no business of mine, you know."

Orestes, like most weak and luxurious men, Romans especially, had a wild-beast vein in him — and it burst forth.

"Hell and the furies! You insolent provincial slave — you will carry these liberties of yours too far! Do you know who I am, you accursed Jew? Tell me the whole truth, or, by the head of the emperor, I'll twist it out of you with red-hot pincers!"

Raphael's countenance assumed a dogged expression, which showed that the old Jewish blood still beat true, under all its affected shell of Neo-Platonist nonchalance; and there was a quiet unpleasant earnest in his smile, as he answered —

"Then, my dear governor, you will be the first man on earth who ever yet forced a Jew to say or do what he did not choose."

"We'll see!" yelled Orestes. "Here, slaves!" And he clapped his hands loudly.

"Calm yourself, your excellency," quoth Raphael, rising. "The door is locked; the mosquito net is across the window; and this dagger is poisoned. If anything happens to me, you will offend all the Jew money-lenders, and die in about three days in a great deal of pain, having missed our assignation with old Miriam, lost your pleasantest companion, and left your own finances and those of the prefecture in a considerable state of embarrassment. How much better to sit down, hear all I have to say philosophically, like a true pupil of Hypatia, and not expect a man to tell you what he really does not know."

Orestes, after looking vainly round the room for a place to escape, had quietly subsided into his chair again; and by the time that the slaves knocked at the door, he had so far recovered his philosophy as to ask, not for the torturers, but for a page and wine.

"Oh, you Jews!" quoth he, trying to laugh off matters. "The same incarnate fiends that Titus found you!"

"The very same, my dear prefect. Now for this matter, which is really important — at least to Gentiles. Heraclian will certainly rebel. Synesius let out as much to me. He has fitted out an armament for Ostia, stopped his own wheat-ships, and is going to write to you to stop yours, and to starve out the Eternal City, Goths, senate, emperor, and all. Whether you will comply with his reasonable little request depends of course on yourself."

"And that, again, very much on his plans."

"Of course. You cannot be expected to — we will euphemize — unless it be made worth your while."

Orestes sat buried in deep thought.

"Of course not," said he at last, half unconsciously. And then, in sudden dread of having committed himself, he looked up fiercely at the Jew.

"And how do I know that this is not some infernal trap of yours? Tell me how you found out all this, or by Hercules (he had quite forgotten his Christianity by this time) — by Hercules and the Twelve Gods, I'll —— "

"Don't use expressions unworthy of a philosopher. My source of information was very simple and very good. He has been negotiating a loan from the Rabbis at Carthage. They were either frightened, or loyal, or both, and hung back. He knew — as all wise governors know when they allow themselves time — that it is no use to bully a Jew; and applied to me. I never lend money — it is unphilosophical: but I introduced him to old Miriam, who dare do business with the devil himself; and by that move, whether he has the money or not, I cannot tell: but this I can tell, that we have his secret — and so have you now; and if you want more information, the old woman, who enjoys an intrigue as much as she does Falernian, will get it you."

"Well, you are a true friend, after all."

"Of course I am. Now, is not this method of getting at the truth much easier and pleasanter than setting a couple of dirty negroes to pinch and pull me, and so making it a point of honour with me to tell you nothing but lies? Here comes Ganymede with the wine, just in time to calm your nerves, and fill you with the spirit of divination..... To the goddess of good counsels, my lord? What wine this is!"

"True Syrian — fire and honey; fourteen years old next vintage, my Raphael. Out, Hypocorisma! See that he is not listening. The impudent rascal! I was humbugged into giving two thousand gold pieces for him two years ago, he was so pretty — they said he was only just rising thirteen — and he has been the plague of my life ever since and is beginning to want the barber already. Now what is the count dreaming of?"

"His wages for killing Stilicho."

"What, is it not enough to be Count of Africa?"

"I suppose he sets off against that his services during the last three years."

"Well, he saved Africa."

"And thereby Egypt also. And you, too, as well as the emperor, may be considered as owing him somewhat."

"My good friend, my debts are far too numerous for me to think of paying any of them. But what wages does he want?"

"The purple."

Orestes started, and then fell into thought. Raphael sat watching him a while.

"Now, most noble lord, may I depart? I have said all I have to say; and unless I get home to luncheon at once, I shall hardly have time to find old Miriam for you, and get through our little affair with her before sunset."

"Stay. What force has he?"

"Forty thousand already, they say. And those Donatist ruffians are with him to a man, if he can but scrape together wherewith to change their bludgeons into good steel."

"Well, go..... So. A hundred thousand might do it," said he, meditating, as Raphael bowed himself out. "He won't get them. I don't know, though; the man has the head of a Julius. Well — that fool Attains talked of joining Egypt to the Western Empire..... Not such a bad thought either. Anything is better than being governed by an idiot child and three canting nuns. I expect to be excommunicated every day for some offence against Pulcheria's prudery..... Heraclian emperor at Rome.... and I lord and master on this side the sea.... the Donatists pitted again fairly against the orthodox, to cut each other's throats in peace.... no more of Cyril's spying and tale-bearing to Constantinople..... Not such a bad dish of fare..... But then — it would take so much trouble!"

With which words, Orestes went into his third warm bath for that day.

CHAPTER III
THE GOTHS

FOR two days the young monk held on, paddling and floating rapidly down the Nile-stream, leaving city after city to right and left with longing eyes, and looking back to one villa after another, till the reaches of the banks hid them from his sight, with many a yearning to know what sort of places those gay buildings and gardens would look like on a nearer view, and what sort of life the thousands led who crowded the busy quays, and walked and drove, in an endless stream, along the great high roads which ran along either bank. He carefully avoided every boat that passed him, from the gilded barge of the wealthy land-lord or merchant, to the tiny raft buoyed up with empty jars, which was floating down to be sold at some market in the Delta. Here and there he met and hailed a crew of monks, drawing their nets in a quiet bay, or passing along the great watery highway from monastery to monastery: but all the news he received from them was, that the canal of Alexandria was still several days' journey below him. It seemed endless, that monotonous vista of the two high clay banks, with their sluices and water-wheels, their knots of palms and date-trees; endless seemed that weari-some succession of bars of sand and banks of mud, every one like the one before it, every one dotted with the same line of logs and stones strewn along the water's edge, which turned out, as he approached them, to be basking crocodiles and sleeping peli-cans. His eye, wearied with the continual confinement and want of distance, longed for the boundless expanse of the desert, for the jagged outlines of those far-off hills, which he had watched from boyhood rising mysteriously at morn out of the eastern sky, and melting-mysteriously into it again at even, beyond which dwelt a whole world of wonders, elephants and dragons, satyrs and anthropophagi, — ay, and the phœnix itself. Tired and mel-ancholy, his mind returned inward to prey on itself, and the last words of Arsenius rose again and again to his thoughts. "Was his call of the spirit or of the flesh?" How should he test that prob-lem? He wished to see the world.... that might be carnal. True; but, he wished to convert the world.... was not that spiritual?

Was he not going on a noble errand?.... thirsting for toil, for saintship, for martyrdom itself, if it would but come and cut the Gordian knot of all temptations, and save him — for he dimly felt that it would save him — a whole sea of trouble in getting safe and triumphant out of that world into which he had not yet entered.... and his heart shrunk back from the untried homeless wilderness before him. But no! the die was cast, and he must down and onward, whether in obedience to the spirit or the flesh. Oh, for one hour of the quiet of that dear Laura and the old familiar faces!

At last, a sudden turn of the bank brought him in sight of a gaudily-painted barge, on board of which armed men, in uncouth and foreign dresses, were chasing with barbaric shouts some large object in the water. In the bows stood a man of gigantic stature, brandishing a harpoon in his right hand, and in his left holding the line of a second, the head of which was fixed in the huge purple sides of a hippopotamus, who foamed and wallowed a few yards down the stream. An old grizzled warrior at the stem, with a rudder in either hand, kept the boat's head continually towards the monster, in spite of its sudden and frantic wheelings; and when it dashed madly across the stream, some twenty oars flashed through the water in pursuit. All was activity and excitement; and it was no wonder if Philammon's curiosity had tempted him to drift down almost abreast of the barge, ere he descried, peeping from under a decorated awning in the after-part, some dozen pair of languishing black eyes, turned alternately to the game and to himself. The serpents! — chattering and smiling, with pretty little shrieks and shaking of glossy curls and gold necklaces, and fluttering of muslin dresses, within a dozen yards of him! Blushing scarlet, he knew not why, he seized his paddle, and tried to back out of the snare.... but somehow, his very efforts to escape those sparkling eyes diverted his attention from everything else: the hippopotamus had caught sight of him, and furious with pain, rushed straight at the unoffending canoe; the harpoon line became entangled round his body, and in a moment he and his frail bark were overturned, and the monster, with his huge white tusks gaping wide, close on him as he struggled in the stream.

Luckily Philammon, contrary to the wont of monks, was a bather, and swam like a water-fowl: fear he had never known:

death from childhood had been to him, as to the other inmates of the Laura, a contemplation too perpetual to have any paralysing terror in it, even then, when life seemed just about to open on him anew. But the monk was a man, and a young one, and had no intention of dying tamely or unavenged. In an instant he had freed himself from the line; drawn the short knife which was his only weapon; and diving suddenly, avoided the monster's rush, and attacked him from behind with stabs, which, though not deep, still dyed the waters with gore at every stroke. The barbarians shouted with delight. The hippopotamus turned furiously against his new assailant, crushing, alas I the empty canoe to fragments with a single snap of his enormous jaws; but the turn was fatal to him; the barge was close upon him, and as he presented his broad side to the blow, the sinewy arm of the giant drove a harpoon through his heart, and with one convulsive shudder the huge blue mass turned over on its side and floated dead.

Poor Philammon! He alone was silent, amid the yells of triumph; sorrowfully he swam round and round his little paper wreck.... it would not have floated a mouse. Wistfully he eyed the distant banks, half minded to strike out for them, and escape,.... and thought of the crocodiles,.... and paddled round again,.... and thought of the basilisk eyes;.... he might escape the crocodiles, but who could escape women?.... and he struck out valiantly for shore.... when he was brought to a sudden stop by finding the stem of the barge close on him, a noose thrown over him by some friendly barbarian, and himself hauled on board, amid the laughter, praise, astonishment, and grumbling of the good-natured crew, who had expected him, as a matter of course, to avail himself at once of their help, and could not conceive the cause of his reluctance.

Philammon gazed with wonder on his strange hosts, their pale complexions, globular heads and faces, high cheekbones, tall and sturdy figures; their red beards, and yellow hair knotted fantastically above the head; their awkward dresses, half Roman or Egyptian, and half of foreign fur, soiled and stained in many a storm and fight, but tastelessly bedizened with classic jewels, brooches and Roman coins, strung like necklaces. Only the steersman, who had come forward to wonder at the hippopotamus, and to help in dragging the unwieldy brute on board, seemed to keep genuine and unornamented the costume of his race, the white linen leggings, strapped with thongs of deerskin, the quilted leather cuirass, the bear's-fur cloak, the only ornaments of which were the fangs and claws of the beast itself, and a fringe of grizzled tufts, which looked but too like human hair. The language which they spoke was utterly unintelligible to Philammon, though it need not be so to us.

"A well-grown lad and a brave one, Wulf the son of Ovida," said the giant to the old hero of the bearskin cloak; "and understands wearing skins, in this furnace-mouth of a climate, rather better than you do."

"I keep to the dress of my forefathers, Amalric the Amal. What did to sack Rome in, may do to find Asgard in."

The giant, who was decked out with helmet, cuirass, and senatorial boots, in a sort of mongrel mixture of the Roman military and civil dress, his neck wreathed with a dozen gold chains, and every finger sparkling with jewels, turned away with an impatient sneer.

"Asgard — Asgard? If you are in such a hurry to get to Asgard up this ditch in the sand, you had better ask the fellow how far it is thither."

Wulf took him quietly at his word, and addressed a question to the young monk, which he could only answer by a shake of the head.

"Ask him in Greek, man."

"Greek is a slave's tongue. Make a slave talk to him in it, not me."

"Here — some of you girls! Pelagia! you understand this fellow's talk. Ask him how far it is to Asgard."

"You must ask me more civilly, my rough hero," replied a soft voice from underneath the awning. "Beauty must be sued, and not commanded."

"Come, then, my olive-tree, my gazelle, my lotus-flower, my — what was the last nonsense you taught me? — and ask this wild man of the sands how far it is from these accursed endless rabbit-burrows to Asgard."

The awning was raised, and lying luxuriously on a soft mattress, fanned with peacock's feathers, and glittering-with rubies and topazes, appeared such a vision as Philammon had never seen before.

A woman of some two-and-twenty summers, formed in the most voluptuous mould of Grecian beauty, whose complexion showed every violet vein through its veil of luscious brown. Her little bare feet, as they dimpled the cushions, were more perfect than Aphrodite's, softer than a swan's bosom. Every swell of her bust and arms showed through the thin gauze robe, while her lower limbs were wrapped in a shawl of orange silk, embroidered with wreaths of shells and roses. Her dark hair lay carefully spread out upon the pillow, in a thousand ringlets entwined with gold and Jewels; her languishing eyes blazed like diamonds from a cavern, under eyelids darkened and deepened with black antimony; her lips pouted of themselves, by habit or by nature, into a perpetual kiss; slowly she raised one little lazy hand; slowly the ripe lips opened; and in most pure and melodious Attic, she lisped her huge lover's question to the monk, and repeated it before the boy could shake off the spell, and answer....

"Asgard? What is Asgard?"

The beauty looked at the giant for further instructions.

"The City of the immortal Gods," interposed the old warrior, hastily and sternly, to the lady.

"The city of God is in heaven," said Philammon to the interpreter, turning his head away from those gleaming, luscious searching glances.

His answer was received with a general laugh by all except the leader, who shrugged his shoulders.

"It may as well be up in the skies as up the Nile. We shall be just as likely, I believe, to reach it by flying, as by rowing up this big ditch. Ask him where the river comes from, Pelagia."

Pelagia obeyed.... and thereon followed a confusion worse confounded, composed of all the impossible wonders of that mythic fairy-land with which Philammon had gorged himself from boyhood in his walks with the old monks, and of the equally trustworthy traditions which the Goths had picked up at Alexandria. There was nothing which that river did not do. It rose in the Caucasus. Where was the Caucasus? He did not know. In Paradise — in Indian ^Ethiopia — in ^Ethiopian India. Where were they? He did not know. Nobody knew. It ran for a hundred and fifty days' journey through deserts where nothing but flying serpents and satyrs lived, and the very lions' manes were burnt off by the heat.....

"Good sporting there, at all events, among these dragons," quoth Smid the son of Troll, armourer to the party.

"As good as Thor's when he caught Snake Midgard with the bullock's head," said Wulf.

It turned to the East for a hundred days' journey more, all round Arabia and India, among forests full of elephants and dog-headed women.

"Better and better, Smid!" growled Wulf, approvingly.

"Fresh beef cheap there, Prince Wulf, eh?" quoth Smid; "I must look over the arrow-heads."

— To the mountains of the Hyperboreans, where there was eternal night, and the air was full of feathers..... That is, one-third of it came from thence, and another third came from the Southern ocean, over the Moon mountains, where no one had ever been, and the remaining third from the country where the phœnix lived, and nobody knew where that was. And then there were the cataracts, and the inundations — and — and — and above the cataracts, nothing but sand-hills and ruins, as full of devils as they could hold.... and as for Asgard, no one had ever heard of it.... till every face grew longer and longer, as Pelagia went on interpreting and misinterpreting; and at last the giant smote his hand upon his knee, and swore a great oath that Asgard might rot till the twilight of the gods before he went a step farther up the Nile.

"Curse the monk!" growled Wulf. "How should such a poor beast know anything about the matter?"

"Why should not he know as well as that ape of a Roman governor?" asked Smid.

"Oh, the monks know everything," said Pelagia. "They go hundreds and thousands of miles up the river, and cross the deserts among fiends and monsters, where any one else would be eaten up, or go mad at once."

"Ah, the dear holy men! It's all by the sign of the blessed cross!" exclaimed all the girls together, devoutly crossing themselves, while two or three of the most enthusiastic were half-minded to go forward and kneel to Philammon for his blessing; but hesitated, their Gothic lovers being heathenishly stupid and prudish on such points.

"Why should he not know as well as the prefect? Well said, Smid! I believe that prefect's quill-driver was humbugging us when he said Asgard was only ten days' sail up."

"Why?" asked Wulf.

"I never give any reasons. What's the use of being an Amal, and a son of Odin, if one has always to be giving reasons like a rascally Roman lawyer? I say the governor looked like a liar; and I say this monk looks like an honest fellow; and I choose to believe him, and there's an end of it."

"Don't look so cross at me, Prince Wulf; I'm sure it's not my fault; I could only say what the monk told me," whispered poor Pelagia.

"Who looks cross at you, my queen?" roared the Amal. "Let me have him out here, and by Thor's hammer, I'll ——— "

"Who spoke to you, you stupid darling?" answered Pelagia, who lived in hourly fear of thunderstorms. "Who is going to be cross with any one, except I with you, for mishearing and misunderstanding, and meddling, as you are always doing? I shall do as I threatened, and run away with prince Wulf, if you are not good. Don't you see that the whole crew are expecting you to make them an oration?"

Whereupon the Amal rose.

"See you here, Wulf, the son of Ovida, and warriors all! If we want wealth, we shan't find it among the sand-hills. If we want women, we shall find nothing prettier than these among dragons and devils. Don't look angry, Wulf. You have no mind to marry one of those dog-headed girls the monk talked of, have you? Well, then, we have money and women; and if we want sport, it's better sport killing men than killing beasts; so we had better go where we shall find most of that game, which we certainly shall not up this road. As for fame and all that, though I've had enough, there's plenty to be got anywhere along the shores of that Mediterranean. Let's burn and plunder Alexandria: forty of us Goths might kill down all those donkey-riders in two days, and hang up that lying prefect who sent us here on this fool's errand. Don't answer, Wulf. I knew he was humbugging us all along, but you were so open-mouthed to all he said, that I was bound to let my elders choose for me. Let's go back; send over for any of the tribes; send to Spain for those Vandals — they have had enough of Adolph by now, curse him! — I'll warrant them; get together an army, and take Constantinople. I'll be Augustus, and Pelagia, Augusta; you and Smid here, the two

Cæsars; and we'll make the monk the chief of the eunuchs, eh? — anything you like for a quiet life; but up this accursed kennel of hot water I go no farther. Ask your girls, my heroes, and I'll ask mine. Women are all prophetesses, every one of them."

"When they are not harlots," growled Wulf to himself.

"I will go to the world's end with you, my king!" sighed Pelagia; "but Alexandria is certainly pleasanter than this."

Old Wulf sprang up fiercely enough.

"Hear me, Almaric the Amal, son of Odin, and heroes all! When my fathers swore to be Odin's men, and gave up the kingdom to the holy Amals, the sons of the Æsir, what was the bond between your fathers and mine? Was it not that we should move and move, southward and southward ever, till we came back to Asgard, the city where Odin dwells for ever, and gave into his hands the kingdom of all the earth? And did we not keep our oath? Have we not held to the Amals? Did we not leave Adolf, because we would not follow a Balth, while there was an Amal to lead us? Have we not been true men to you, son of the Æsir?"

" No man ever saw Wulf, the son of Ovida, fail friend or foe."

"Then why does his friend fail him? Why does his friend fail himself? If the bison-bull lie down and wallow, what will the herd do for a leader? If the king-wolf lose the scent, how will the pack hold it? If the Yngling forgets the song of Asgard, who will sing it to the heroes?"

"Sing it yourself, if you choose. Pelagia sings quite well enough for me."

In an instant the cunning beauty caught at the hint, and poured forth a soft, low, sleepy song: —

> " Loose the sail, rest the oar, float away down,
> Fleeting and gliding by tower and town;
> Life is so short at best! snatch, while thou can'st, thy rest,
> Sleeping by me! "

"Can you answer that, Wulf?" shouted a dozen voices.

"Hear the song of Asgard, warriors of the Goths! Did not Alaric the king love it well! Did I not sing it before him in the palace of the Cæsars, till he swore, for all the Christian that he was, to go southward in search of the holy city? And when he went to Valhalla, and the ships were wrecked off Sicily, and Adolf the Balth turned back like a lazy hound, and married the daughter of the Romans, whom Odin hates, and went northward again to Gaul, did not I sing you all the song of Asgard in Messina there, till you swore to follow the Amal through fire and water, until we found the hall of Odin, and received the mead-cup from his own hand? Hear it again, warriors of the Goths!"

Not that song!" roared the Amal, stopping his ears with both his hands. "Will you drive us blood-mad again, just as we are settling down into our sober senses, and finding out what our lives were given us for?"

"Hear the song of Asgard I On to Asgard, wolves of the Goths!" shouted another; and a babel of voices arose.

"Haven't we been fighting and marching these seven years?"

"Haven't we drank blood enough to satisfy Odin ten times over? If he wants us, let him come himself and lead us!"

"Let us get our winds again before we start afresh."

"Wulf the Prince is like his name, and never tires; he has a winter-wolf's legs under him; that is no reason why we should have."

"Haven't you heard what the monk says? — we can never get over those cataracts."

"We'll stop his old-wives' tales for him, and then settle for ourselves," said Smid; and springing from the thwart where he had been sitting, he caught up a bill with one hand, and seized Philammon's throat with the other.... in a moment more, it would have been all over with him....

For the first time in his life Philammon felt a hostile gripe upon him, and a new sensation rushed through every nerve, as he grappled with the warrior, clutched with his left hand the uplifted wrist, and with his right the girdle, and commenced without any definite aim, a fierce struggle, which, strange to say, as it went on, grew absolutely pleasant.

The women shrieked to their lovers to part the combatants, but in vain.

"Not for worlds! A very fair match and a very fair fight! Take your long legs back, Itho, or they will be over you! That's right, my Smid, don't use the knife! They will be overboard in a moment! By all the Valkyrs, they are down! and Smid undermost!"

There was no doubt of it; and in another moment Philammon would have wrenched the bill out of his opponent's hand, when, to the utter astonishment of the onlookers, he suddenly loosed his hold, shook himself free by one powerful wrench, and quietly retreated to his seat, conscience-stricken at the fearful thirst for blood which had suddenly boiled up within him as he felt his enemy under him.

The on-lookers were struck dumb with astonishment; they had taken for granted that he would, as a matter of course, have used his right of splitting his vanquished opponent's skull — an event which they would of course have deeply deplored, but with which, as men of honour, they could not on any account interfere, but merely console themselves for the loss of their comrade by flaying his conqueror alive, "carving him into the blood-eagle," or any other delicate ceremony which might serve as a vent for their sorrow and a comfort to the soul of the deceased.

Smid rose, with a bill in his hand, and looked round him — perhaps to see what was expected of him. He half lifted his weapon to strike..... Philammon, seated, looked him calmly in the face..... The old warrior's eye caught the bank, which was now receding rapidly past them; and when he saw that they were really floating downwards again, without an effort to stem the stream, he put away his bill, and sat himself down deliberately in his place, astonishing the on-lookers quite as much as Philammon had done.

"Five minutes' good fighting, and no one killed! This is a shame!" quoth another. "Blood we must see, and it had better be yours, master monk, than your betters'," — and therewith he rushed on poor Philammon.

He spoke the heart of the crew; the sleeping wolf in them had been awakened by the struggle, and blood they would have; and not frantically, like Celts or Egyptians, but with the cool, humorous cruelty of the Teuton, they rose altogether, and turning Philammon over on his back, deliberated by what death he should die.

Philammon quietly submitted — if submission have anything to do with that state of mind in which sheer astonishment and novelty have broken up all the custom of man's nature, till the strangest deeds and sufferings are taken as matters of course.

His sudden escape from the Laura, the new world of thought and action into which he had been plunged, the new companions with whom he had fallen in, had driven him utterly from his moorings, and now anything and everything might happen to him. He who had promised never to look upon woman found himself, by circumstances over which he had no control, amid a boatful of the most objectionable species of that most objectionable genus — and the utterly worst having happened, everything else which happened must be better than the worst. For the rest, he had gone forth to see the world — and this was one of the ways of it. So he made up his mind to see it, and be filled with the fruit of his own devices.

And he would have been certainly filled with the same in five minutes more, in some shape too ugly to be mentioned: but, as even sinful women have hearts in them, Pelagia shrieked out —

"Almaric! Almaric! do not let them! I cannot bear it!"

"The warriors are free men, my darling, and know what is proper. And what can the life of such a brute be to you?"

Before he could stop her, Pelagia had sprung from her cushions, and thrown herself into the midst of the laughing ring of wild beasts.

"Spare him! Spare him for my sake!" shrieked she.

"Oh, my pretty lady! you mustn't interrupt warriors' sport!"

In an instant she had torn off her shawl, and thrown it over Philammon; and as she stood, with all the outlines of her beautiful limbs revealed through the thin robe of spangled gauze, —

" Let the man who dares, touch him beneath that shawl! — though it be a saffron one!"

The Goths drew back. For Pelagia herself they had as little respect as the rest of the world had. But for a moment she was not the Messalina of Alexandria, but a woman; and true to the old woman-worshipping instinct, they looked one and all at her flashing eyes, full of noble pity and indignation, as well as of mere woman's terror — and drew back, and whispered together.

Whether the good spirit or the evil one would conquer, seemed for a moment doubtful, when Pelagia felt a heavy hand on her shoulder, and turning, saw Wulf the son of Ovida.

"Go back, pretty woman! Men, I claim the boy. Smid, give

him to me. He is your man. You could have killed him if you had chosen, and did not; and no one else shall."

"Give him us, Prince Wulf! We have not seen blood for many a day!"

"You might have seen rivers of it, if you had had the hearts to go onward. The boy is mine, and a brave boy. He has upset a warrior fairly this day, and spared him; and we will make a warrior of him in return."

And he lifted up the prostrate monk.

"You are my man now. Do you like fighting?"

Philammon, not understanding the language in which he was addressed, could only shake his head — though if he had known what its import was, he could hardly in honesty have said, No.

"He shakes his head! He does not like it! He is craven! Let us have him!"

"I had killed kings when you were shooting frogs," cried Smid." Listen to me, my sons! A coward grips sharply at first, and loosens his hand after a while, because his blood is soon hot and soon cold. A brave man's gripe grows the firmer the longer he holds, because the spirit of Odin comes upon him. I watched the boy's hands on my throat; and he will make a man; and I will make him one. However, we may as well make him useful at once; so give him an oar."

"Well," answered his new protector, "he can as well row us as be rowed by us; and if we are to go back to a cow's death and the pool of Hela, the quicker we go the better."

And as the men settled themselves again to their oars, one was put into Philammon's hand, which he managed with such strength and skill, that his late tormentors, who, in spite of an occasional inclination to robbery and murder, were thoroughly goodnatured, honest fellows, clapped him on the back, and praised him as heartily as they had just now heartily intended to torture him to death, and then went forward, as many of them as were not rowing, to examine the strange beast which they had just slaughtered, pawing him over from tusks to tail, putting their heads into his mouth, trying their knives on his hide, comparing him to all beasts, like and unlike, which they had ever seen, and laughing and shoving each other about with the fun and childish wonder of a party of schoolboys; till Smid, who was the wit of the party, settled the comparative anatomy of the subject for them —

"Valhalla! I've found out what he's most like! — One of those big blue plums, which gave us all the stomach-ache when we were encamped in the orchards above Ravenna!"

CHAPTER IV
MIRIAM

ONE morning in the same week, Hypatia's favourite maid entered her chamber with a somewhat terrified face.

"The old Jewess, madam — the hag who has been watching so often lately under the wall opposite. She frightened us all out of our senses last evening by peeping in. We all said she had the evil eye, if any one ever had —— "

"Well, what of her?"

"She is below, madam, and will speak with you. Not that I care for her; I have my amulet on. I hope you have?"

"Silly girl! Those who have been initiated as I have in the mysteries of the gods, can defy spirits and command them. Do you suppose that the favourite of Pallas Athene will condescend to charms and magic? Send her up."

The girl retreated, with a look half of awe, half of doubt at the lofty pretensions of her mistress, and returned with old Miriam, keeping, however, prudently behind her, in order to test as little as possible the power of her own amulet by avoiding the basilisk eye which had terrified her.

Miriam came in, and advancing to the proud beauty, who remained seated, made an obeisance down to the very floor, without, however, taking her eyes for an instant off Hypatia's face.

Her countenance was haggard and bony, with broad sharp-cut lips, stamped with a strangely mingled expression of strength and sensuality. But the feature about her which instantly fixed Hypatia's attention, and from which she could not in spite of herself withdraw it, was the dry, glittering, coal-black eye which glared out from underneath the grey fringe of her swarthy brows, between black locks covered with gold coins. Hypatia could look at nothing but those eyes; and she reddened, and grew all but unphilosophically angry, as she saw that the old woman intended her to look at them, and feel the strange power which she evidently wished them to exercise.

After a moment's silence, Miriam drew a letter from her bosom, and with a second low obeisance presented it.

"From whom is this?"

"Perhaps the letter itself will tell the beautiful lady, the fortunate lady, the discerning lady," answered she, in a fawning, wheedling tone. "How should a poor old Jewess know great folks' secrets?"

"Great folks?" ———

Hypatia looked at the seal which fixed a silk cord round the letter. It was Orestes'; and so was the handwriting..... Strange, that he should have chosen such a messenger! What message could it be which required such secrecy?

She clapped her hands for the maid. "Let this woman wait in the ante-room." Miriam glided out backwards, bowing as she went. As Hypatia looked up over the letter to see whether she was alone, she caught a last glance of that eye still fixed upon her, and an expression in Miriam's face which made her, she knew not why, shudder and turn chill.

"Foolish that I am! What can that witch be to me? But now for the letter."

"To the most noble and most beautiful, the mistress of philosophy, beloved of Athene, her pupil and slave sends greeting."....

"My slave! and no name mentioned!"

"There are those who consider that the favourite hen of Honorius, which bears the name of the Imperial City, would thrive better under a new feeder; and the Count of Africa has been despatched by himself and by the immortal gods to superintend for the present the poultry-yard of the Cæsars — at least during the absence of Adolph and Placidia. There are those also who consider that in his absence the Numidian lion might be prevailed on to become the yoke-fellow of the Egyptian crocodile; and a farm which, ploughed by such a pair, should extend from the upper cataract to the pillars of Hercules, might have charms even for a philosopher. But while the ploughman is without a nymph, Arcadia is imperfect. What were Dionusos; without his Ariadne, Ares without Aphrodite, Zeus without! Here? Even Artemis has her Endymion; Athene alone remains unwedded; but only because Hephæstus was tow rough a wooer. Such is not he who now offers to the representative of Athene the opportunity of sharing that! which may be with the help of her wisdom, which without; her is impossible. Φωναντα

60

συνέτοισιν. Shall Eros, invincible for ages, be balked at last of the noblest game against; which he ever drew his bow?"....

If Hypatia's colour had faded a moment before under the withering glance of the old Jewess, it rose again swiftly! enough, as she read line after line of this strange epistle; till at last, crushing it together in her hand, she rose and hurried into the adjoining library, where Theon sat over his books.

"Father, do you know anything of this? Look what Orestes has dared to send me by the hands of some base' Jewish witch!" — And she spread the letter before him, and stood impatient, her whole figure dilated with pride; and anger, as the old man read it slowly and carefully, and then looked up, apparently not ill pleased with the contents.

"What, father?" asked she, half reproachfully." Do not you, too, feel the insult which has been put upon your daughter?"

"My dear child," with a puzzled look, "do you not see that he offers you —— "

"I know what he offers me, father. The Empire of Africa..... I am to descend from the mountain heights of science, from the contemplation of the unchangeable and I the ineffable glories, into the foul fields and farm-yards of earthly practical life, and become a drudge among political chicanery, and the petty ambitions, and sins, and falsehoods of the earthly herd..... And the price which he offers me — me, the stainless — me, the virgin — me, the; untamed, — is — his hand! Pallas Athene! dost thou not blush with thy child?"

"But, my child — my child, — an empire ——— "

"Would the empire of the world restore my lost self-respect — my just pride? Would it save my cheek from blushes every time I recollected that I bore the hateful and degrading name of wife? — The property, the puppet of a man — submitting to his pleasure — bearing his children — wearing myself out with all the nauseous cares of wife-hood — no longer able to glory in myself, pure and self-sustained, but forced by day and night to recollect that my very beauty is no longer the sacrament of Athene's love for me, but the plaything of a man; — and such a man as that! Luxurious, frivolous, heartless — courting my society, as he has done for years, only to pick up and turn to his own base earthly uses the scraps which fall from the festal table of the gods! I have encouraged him too much — vain fool that I have been! No, I wrong myself! It was only — I thought — I thought that by his being seen at our doors, the cause of the immortal gods would gain honour and strength in the eyes of the multitude..... I have tried to feed the altars of heaven with earthly fuel..... And this is my just reward! I will write to him this moment; — return by the fitting messenger which he has sent, insult for insult!"

"In the name of Heaven, my daughter! — for your father's sake! — for my sake! Hypatia! — my pride, my joy, my only hope! — have pity on my grey hairs!"

And the poor old man flung himself at her feet, and clasped her knees imploringly.

Tenderly she lifted him up, and wound her long arms round him, and laid his head on her white shoulder, and her tears fell fast upon his grey hair; but her lip was firm and determined.

"Think of my pride — my glory in your glory; think of me..... Not for myself! You know I never cared for myself!" sobbed out the old man. "But to die seeing you empress!"

"Unless I died first in childbed, father, as many a woman dies who is weak enough to become a slave, and submit to tortures only fit for slaves."

"But — but — " said the old man, racking his bewildered brains for some argument far enough removed from nature and common sense to have an effect on the beautiful fanatic — "but the cause of the gods! What you might do for it!.... Remember Julian!"

Hypatia's arms dropped suddenly. Yes; it was true! The thought flashed across her mind with mingled delight and terror..... Visions of her childhood rose swift and thick — temples — sacrifices — priesthoods — colleges — museums! What might she not do? What might she not make Africa? Give her ten years of power, and the hated name of Christian might be forgotten, and Athene Polias; colossal in ivory and gold, watching in calm triumph over the harbours of a heathen Alexandria..... But the price!

And she hid her face in her hands, and bursting into bitter tears, walked slowly away into her own chamber, her whole body convulsed with the internal struggle.

The old man looked after her, anxiously and perplexed, and then followed, hesitating. She was sitting at the table, her face buried in her hands. He did not dare to disturb her. In addition to all the affection, the wisdom, the glorious beauty, on which his whole heart fed day by day, he believed her to be the possessor of those supernatural powers and favours, to which she so boldly laid claim. And he stood watching her in the doorway, praying in his heart to all gods and demons, principalities and powers, from Athene down to his daughter's guardian spirit, to move a determination which he was too weak to gainsay, and yet too rational to approve.

At last the struggle was over, and she looked up, clear, calm, and glorious again.

"It shall be. For the sake of the immortal gods — for the sake of art, and science, and learning, and philosophy..... It shall be. If the gods demand a victim, here am I. If a second time in the history of the ages the Grecian fleet cannot sail forth, conquering and civilizing, without the sacrifice of a virgin, I give my throat to the knife. Father, call me no more Hypatia: call me Iphigenia!"

"And me Agamemnon?" asked the old man, attempting a faint jest through his tears of joy. "I dare say you think me a very cruel father; but —— "

"Spare me, father — I have spared you."

And she began to write her answer.

"I have accepted his offer — conditionally, that is. And on whether he have courage or not to fulfil that condition, depends —— Do not ask me what it is. While Cyril is leader of the Christian mob, it may be safer for you, my father, that you should be able to deny all knowledge of my answer. Be content. I have said this — that if he will do as I would have him do, I will do as you would have me do."

"Have you not been too rash? Have you not demanded of him something which, for the sake of public opinion, he dare not grant openly, and yet which he may allow you to do for yourself when once —— "

"I have. If I am to be a victim, the sacrificing priest shall at least be a man, and not a coward and a time-server. If he believes this Christian faith, let him defend it against me; for either it or I shall perish. If he does not — as he does not — let him give up living in a lie, and taking on his lips blasphemies against the immortals, from which his heart and reason revolt!"

And she clapped her hands again for the maid-servant, gave her the letter silently, shut the doors of her chamber, and tried to resume her Commentary on Plotinus. Alas! what were all the wire-drawn dreams of metaphysics to her in that real and human struggle of the heart? What availed it to define the process by which individual souls emanated from the universal one, while her own soul had, singly and on its own responsibility, to decide so terrible an act of will? or to write fine words with pen and ink about the immutability of the supreme Reason, while her own reason was left there to struggle for its life amid a roaring shoreless waste of doubts and darkness? Oh, how grand, and clear, and logical it had all looked half-an-hour ago! And how irrefragably she had been deducing from it all, syllogism after syllogism, the non-existence of evil! — how it was but a lower form of good, one of the countless products of the one great all-pervading mind which could not err or change, only so strange and recondite in its form as to excite antipathy in all minds but that of the philosopher, who learnt to see the stem which connected the apparently bitter fruit with the perfect root from whence it sprung. Could she see the stem there? — the connexion between the pure and supreme Reason, and the hideous caresses of the debauched and cowardly Orestes? Was not that evil, pure, unadulterate with any vein of good, past, present, or future?....

True; — she might keep her spirit pure amid it all; she might sacrifice the base body, and ennoble the soul by the self-sacrifice.... And yet, would not that increase the horror, the agony, the evil of it — to her, at least, most real evil, not to be explained away — and yet the gods required it? Were they just, merciful in that? Was it like them, to torture her, their last unshaken votary? Did they require it? Was it not required of them by some higher power, of whom they were only the emanations, the tools, the puppets? — and required of that higher power by some still higher one — some nameless, absolute destiny of which Orestes and she, and all heaven and earth, were but the victims, dragged along in an inevitable vortex, helpless, hopeless, toward that for which each was meant? — And she was meant for this! The thought was unbearable; it turned her giddy. No! she would not! She would rebel! Like Prometheus, she would dare destiny, and brave its worst! And she sprang up to recall the letter..... Miriam was gone; and she threw herself on the floor, and wept bitterly.

And her peace of mind would certainly not have been improved, could she have seen old Miriam hurry home with her letter to a dingy house in the Jews' quarter, where it was unsealed, read, and sealed up again with such marvellous skill, that no eye could have detected the change; and finally, still less would she have been comforted could she have heard the conversation which was going on in a summer-room of Orestes' palace, between that illustrious statesman and Raphael Aben-Ezra, who were lying on two divans opposite each other, whiling away, by a throw or two of dice, the anxious moments which delayed her answer.

"Trays again! The devil is in you, Raphael!"

"I always thought he was," answered Raphael, sweeping up the gold pieces.....

"When will that old witch be back?"

"When she has read through your letter, and Hypatia's answer."

"Read them?"

"Of course. You don't fancy she is going to be fool enough to carry a message without knowing what it is? Don't be angry; she won't tell. She would give one of those two grave lights there, which she calls her eyes, to see the thing prosper."

"Why?"

"Your excellency will know when the letter comes. Here she is; I hear steps in the cloister. Now, one bet before they enter. I give you two to one she asks you to turn pagan."

"What in? Negro-boys?"

"Anything you like."

"Taken. Come in, slaves!"

And Hypocorisma entered, pouting.

"That Jewish fury is outside with a letter, and has the impudence to say she won't let me bring it in!"

"Bring her in then. Quick!"

"I wonder what I am here for, if people have secrets that I am not to know," grumbled the spoilt youth.

"Do you want a blue ribbon round those white sides of yours, you monkey?" answered Orestes. "Because, if you do, the hippopotamus hide hangs ready outside."

"Let us make him kneel down here for a couple of hours, and use him as a dice-board," said Raphael, "as you used to do to the girls in Armenia."

"Ah, you recollect that? — and how the barbarian papas used to grumble, till I had to crucify one or two, eh? That was something like life! I love those out-of-the-way stations, where nobody asks questions: but here one might as well live among the monks in Nitria. Here comes Canidia! Ah, the answer? Hand it here, my queen of go-betweens!"

Orestes read it, — and his countenance fell.

"I have won?"

"Out of the room, slaves! and no listening!"

"I have won, then?"

Orestes tossed the letter across to him, and Raphael read

—

"The immortal gods accept no divided worship; and he who would command the counsels of their prophetess must remember that they will vouchsafe to her no illumination till their lost honours be restored. If he who aspires to be the lord of Africa dare trample on the hateful cross, and restore the Cæsareum to those for whose worship it was built — if he dare proclaim aloud with his lips, and in his deeds, that contempt for novel and barbarous superstitions, which his taste and reason have already taught him, then he would prove himself one with whom it were a glory to labour, to dare, to die in a great cause. But till then —
_____ "

And so the letter ended.

"What am I to do?"

"Take her at her word."

"Good heavens! I shall be excommunicated! And — and — what is to become of my soul?"

"What will become of it in any case, my most excellent lord?" answered Raphael, blandly.

"You mean — I know what you cursed Jews think will happen to every one but yourselves. But what would the world say? I an apostate! And in the face of Cyril and the populace! I daren't, I tell you!"

"No one asked your excellency to apostatize."

"Why, what? What did you say just now?"

"I asked you to promise. It will not be the first time that

promises before marriage have not exactly coincided with performance afterwards.

"I daren't — that is, I won't promise. I believe, now, this is some trap of your Jewish intrigue, just to make me commit myself against those Christians, whom you hate."

"I assure you, I despise all mankind far too profoundly to hate them. How disinterested my advice was when I proposed this match to you, you never will know; Indeed, it would be boastful in me to tell you. But really you must make a little sacrifice to win this foolish girl. With all the depth and daring of her intellect to help you, you might be a match for Romans, Byzantines, and Goths at once. And as for beauty — why, there is one dimple inside that wrist, just at the setting on of the sweet little hand, worth all the other flesh and blood in Alexandria."

"By Jove! you admire her so much, I suspect you must be in love with her yourself. Why don't you marry her? I'll make you my prime minister, and then we shall have the use of her wits without the trouble of her fancies. By the twelve Gods! If you marry her and help me, I'll make you what you like!"

Raphael rose, and bowed to the earth,

"Your serene high-mightiness overwhelms me. But I assure you, that never having as yet cared for any one's interest but my own, I could not be expected, at my time of life, to devote myself to that of another, even though it were to yours."

"Candid I"

"Exactly so; and moreover, whosoever I may marry, will be practically, as well as theoretically, my private and peculiar property..... You comprehend?"

"Candid again."

"Exactly so; and waiving the third argument, that she probably might not choose to marry me, I beg to remark that it would not be proper to allow the world to say, that I, the subject, had a wiser and fairer wife than you, the ruler; especially a wife who had already refused that ruler's complimentary offer."

"By Jove! and she has refused me in good earnest! I'll make her repent it! I was a fool to ask her at all I What's the use of having guards, if one can't compel what one wants? If fair means can't do it, foul shall! I'll send for her this moment!"

"Most illustrious majesty — it will not succeed. You do not know that woman's determination. Scourges and red-hot pincers will not shake her, alive; and dead, she will be of no use whatsoever to you, while she will be of great use to Cyril."

"How?"

"He will be most happy to make the whole story a handle against you, give out that she died a virgin-martyr, in defence of the most holy catholic and apostolic faith, get miracles worked at her tomb, and pull your palace about your ears on the strength thereof."

"Cyril will hear of it anyhow: that's another dilemma into which you have brought me, you intriguing rascal! Why this girl will be boasting all over Alexandria that I have offered her marriage, and that she has done herself the honour to refuse me!"

"She will be much too wise to do anything of the kind; she has sense enough to know that if she did so, you would inform a Christian populace what conditions she offered you, and, with all her contempt for the burden of the flesh, she has no mind to be lightened of that pretty load by being torn in pieces by Christian monks: a very probable ending for her in any case, as she herself, in her melancholy moods, confesses!"

"What will you have me to do, then?"

"Simply nothing. Let the prophetic spirit go out of her, as it will, in a day or two, and then — I know nothing of human nature, if she does not bate a little of her own price. Depend on it, for all her ineffabilities, and impassibilities, and all the rest of the seventh-heaven moonshine at which we play here in Alexandria, a throne is far too pretty a bait for even Hypatia the Pythoness to refuse. Leave well alone is a good rule, but leave ill alone is a better. So now another bet before we part, and this time three to one. Do nothing either way, and she sends to you of her own accord before a month is out. In Caucasian mules? Done? Be it so."

"Well, you are the most charming counsellor for a poor perplexed devil of a prefect! If I had but a private fortune like you, I could just take the money, and let the work do itself."

"Which is the true method of successful government. Your slave bids you farewell. Do not forget our bet. You dine with me to-morrow?"

And Raphael bowed himself out.

As he left the prefect's door, he saw Miriam on the opposite side of the street, evidently watching for him. As soon as she saw him, she held on her own side, without appearing to notice him, till he turned a corner, and then crossing, caught him eagerly by the arm.

"Does the fool dare?"

"Who dare what?"

"You know what I mean. Do you suppose old Miriam carries letters without taking care to know what is inside them? Will he apostatize? Tell me. I am secret as the grave!"

"The fool has found an old worm-eaten rag of conscience somewhere in the corner of his heart, and dare not."

"Curse the coward! And such a plot as I had laid! I would have swept every Christian dog out of Africa within the year. What is the man afraid of?"

"Hell-fire."

"Why, he will go there in any case, the accursed Gentile!"

"So I hinted to him, as delicately as I could; but, like the rest of the world, he had a sort of partiality for getting thither by his own road."

"Coward! And whom shall I get now? Oh, if that Pelagia had as much cunning in her whole body as Hypatia has in her little finger, I'd seat her and her Goth upon the throne of the Cæsars. But ——— "

" But she has five senses, and just enough wit to use them, eh?"

"Don't laugh at her for that, the darling! I do delight in her, after all. It warms even my old blood to see how thoroughly she knows her business, and how she enjoys it, like a true daughter of Eve."

"She has been your most successful pupil, certainly, mother. You may well be proud of her."

The old hag chuckled to herself a while; and then suddenly turning to Raphael —

"See here! I have a present for you;" and she pulled out a magnificent ring.

"Why, mother, you are always giving me presents. It was but a month ago you sent me this poisoned dagger."

"Why not, eh? — why not? Why should not Jew give to Jew? Take the old woman's ring!"

"What a glorious opal!"

"Ah, that is an opal, indeed! And the unspeakable name upon it; just like Solomon's own. Take it, I say! Whosoever wears that never need fear fire, steel, poison, or woman's eye."

"Your own included, eh?"

"Take it, I say!" and Miriam caught his hand, and forced the ring on his finger. "There! Now you're safe. And now call me mother again. I like it. I don't know why, but I like it. And — Raphael Aben-Ezra — don't laugh at me, and call me witch and hag, as you often do. I don't care about it from any one else; I'm accustomed to it. But when you do it, I always long to stab you. That's why I gave you the dagger. I used to wear it; and I was afraid I might be tempted to use it some day, when the thought came across me how handsome you'd look, and how quiet, when you were dead, and your soul up there so happy in Abraham's bosom, watching all the Gentiles frying and roasting for ever down below. Don't laugh at me, I say; and don't thwart me I I may make you the emperor's prime minister, some day. I can if I choose."

"Heaven forbid I" said Raphael, laughing.

"Don't laugh. I cast your nativity last night, and I know you have no cause to laugh. A great danger hangs over you, and a deep temptation. And if you weather this storm, you may be chamberlain, prime minister, emperor, if you will. And you shall be — by the four archangels, you shall!"

And the old woman vanished down a by-lane, leaving Raphael utterly bewildered.

"Moses and the prophets! Does the old lady intend to marry me? What can there be in this very lazy and selfish per- sonage who bears my name, to excite so romantic an affection? Well, Raphael Aben-Ezra, thou hast one more friend in the world beside Bran the mastiff; and therefore one more trouble — see- ing that friends always expect a due return of affection and good offices, and what not. I wonder whether the old lady has been getting into a scrape kidnapping, and wants my patronage to help her out of it..... Three-quarters of a mile of roasting sun between me and home!.... I must hire a gig, or a litter, or something, off the next stand.... with a driver who has been eating onions.... and of course there is not a stand for the next half-mile. Oh, divine æther! as Prometheus has it, and ye swift-winged breezes (I wish there were any here), when will it all be over? Three-and-thirty years have I endured already of this Babel of knaves and fools; and with this abominable good health of mine, which won't even help me with gout or indigestion, I am likely to have three-and-thirty years more of it..... I know nothing, and I care for nothing, and I expect nothing; and I actually can't take the trouble to prick a hole in myself, and let the very small amount of wits out, to see something really worth seeing, and try its strength at something really worth doing — if, after all, the other side the grave does not turn out to be just as stupid as this one..... When will it be all over, and I in Abraham's bosom — or any one else's, provided it be not a woman's?"

CHAPTER V
A DAY IN ALEXANDRIA

IN the meanwhile Philammon, with his hosts, the Goths, had been slipping down the stream. Passing, one after another, world-old cities now dwindled to decaying towns, and numberless canal-mouths, now fast falling into ruin with the fields to which they ensured fertility, under the pressure of Roman extortion and misrule, they had entered one evening the mouth of the great canal of Alexandria, slid easily all night across the star-bespangled shadows of Lake Mareotis, and found themselves when the next morning dawned, among the countless masts and noisy quays of the greatest seaport in the world. The motley crowd of foreigners, the hubbub of all dialects from the Crimea to Cadiz, the vast piles of merchandise, and heaps of wheat, lying unsheltered in that rainless air, the huge bulk of the corn-ships lading for Rome, whose tall sides rose story over story, like floating palaces, above the buildings of some inner dock — these sights, and a hundred more, made the young monk think that the world did not look at first sight a thing to be despised. In front of heaps of fruit, fresh from the market-boats, black groups of glossy negro slaves were basking and laughing on the quay, looking anxiously and coquettishly round in hopes of a purchaser; they evidently did not think the change from desert toil to city luxuries a change for the worse. Philammon turned away his eyes from beholding vanity; but only to meet fresh vanity wheresoever they fell. He felt crushed by the multitude of new objects, stunned by the din around; and scarcely recollected himself enough to seize the first opportunity of escaping from his dangerous companions.

"Holloa!" roared Smid the armourer, as he scrambled on to the steps of the slip; '' you are not going to run away without bidding us good-by?"

"Stop with me, boy!" said old Wulf. "I saved you; and you are my man."

Philammon turned and hesitated.

"I am a monk, and God's man."

"You can be that anywhere. I will make you a warrior."

"The weapons of my warfare are not of flesh and blood, but prayer and fasting," answered poor Philammon, who felt already that he should have ten times more need of the said weapons in Alexandria than ever he had had in the desert..... "Let me go! I am not made for your life! I thank you, bless you! I will pray for you, sir! but let me go!"

"Curse the craven hound!" roared half-a-dozen voices. "Why did you not let us have our will with him, Prince Wulf? You might have expected such gratitude from a monk."

"He owes me my share of the sport," quoth Smid. "And here it is!" And a hatchet, thrown with practised aim, whistled right for Philammon's head — he had just time to swerve, and the weapon struck and snapped against the granite wall behind.

"Well saved!" said Wulf, coolly, while the sailors and market-women above yelled murder, and the custom-house officers, and other constables and catchpolls of the harbour, rushed to the place — and retired again quietly at the thunder of the Amal from the boat's stern —

"Never mind my good fellows! we're only Goths; and on a visit to the prefect, too."

"Only Goths, my donkey-riding friends!" echoed Smid, and at that ominous name the whole posse comitatus tried to look unconcerned, and found suddenly that their presence was absolutely required in an opposite direction.

"Let him go," said Wulf, as he stalked up the steps. "Let the boy go. I never set my heart on any man yet," he growled to himself in an under voice, "but what he disappointed me — and I must not expect more from this fellow. Come, men, ashore, and get drunk!"

Philammon, of course, now that he had leave to go, longed to stay — at all events, he must go back and thank his hosts. He turned unwillingly to do so, as hastily as he could, and found Pelagia and her gigantic lover just entering a palanquin. With downcast eyes he approached the beautiful basilisk, and stammered out some commonplace; and she, full of smiles, turned to him at once.

"Tell us more about yourself before we part. You speak such beautiful Greek — true Athenian. It is quite delightful to hear one's own accent again. Were you ever at Athens?"

"When I was a child; I recollect — that is, I think —— "

"What?" asked Pelagia, eagerly.

"A great house in Athens — and a great battle there — and coming to Egypt in a ship."

"Heavens!" said Pelagia, and paused..... "How strange! Girls, who said he was like me?"

"I'm sure we meant no harm, if we did say it in a joke," pouted one of the attendants.

"Like me! — you must come and see us. I have something to say to you..... You must!"

Philammon misinterpreted the intense interest of her tone, and if he did not shrink back, gave some involuntary gesture of reluctance. Pelagia laughed aloud.

"Don't be vain enough to suspect, foolish boy, but come! Do you think that I have nothing to talk about but nonsense? Come and see me. It may be better for you. I live in — —," and she named a fashionable street, which Philammon, though he inwardly vowed not to accept the invitation, somehow could not help remembering.

"Do leave the wild man, and come," growled the Amal from within the palanquin. "You are not going to turn nun, I hope?"

"Not while the first man I ever met in the world stays in it," answered Pelagia, as she skipped into the palanquin, taking care to show the most lovely white heel and ankle, and, like the Parthian, send a random arrow as she retreated. But the dart was lost on Philammon, who had been already hustled away by the bevy of laughing attendants, amid baskets, dressing-cases, and bird-cages, and was fain to make his escape into the Babel round, and inquire his way to the patriarch's house.

"Patriarch's house?" answered the man whom he first addressed, a little lean, swarthy fellow, with merry black eyes, who, with a basket of fruit at his feet, was sunning himself on a baulk of timber, meditatively chewing the papyrus-cane, and examining the strangers with a look of absurd sagacity. "I know it; without a doubt I know it; all Alexandria has good reason to know it. Are you a monk?"

"Yes."

"Then ask your way of the monks; you won't go far without finding one."

"But I do not even know the right direction: what is your

grudge against monks, my good man?"

"Look here, my youth; you seem too ingenuous for a monk. Don't flatter yourself that it will last. If you can wear the sheepskin, and haunt the churches here for a month, without learning to lie, and slander, and clap, and hoot, and perhaps play your part in a sedition-and-murder satyric drama — why, you are a better man than I take you for. I, sir, am a Greek, and a philosopher; though the whirlpool of matter may have, and indeed has, involved my ethereal spark in the body of a porter. Therefore, youth," continued the little man, starting up upon his baulk like an excited monkey, and stretching-out one oratorio paw, "I bear a treble hatred to the monkish tribe. First, as a man and a husband;.... for as for the smiles of beauty, or otherwise, — such as I have, I have; and the monks, if they had their wicked will, would leave neither men nor women in the world. Sir, they would exterminate the human race in a single generation, by a voluntary suicide! Secondly, as a porter; for if all men turned monks, nobody would be idle, and the profession of portering would be annihilated. Thirdly, sir, as a philosopher; for as the false coin is odious to the true, so is the irrational and animal asceticism of the monk, to the logical and methodic self-restraint of one who, like your humblest of philosophers, aspires to a life according to the pure reason."

"And pray," asked Philammon, half-laughing, "who has been your tutor in philosophy?"

"The fountain of classic wisdom, Hypatia herself. As the ancient sage — the name is unimportant to a monk — pumped water nightly that he might study by day, so I, the guardian of cloaks and parasols at the sacred doors of her lecture-room, imbibe celestial knowledge. From my youth I felt in me a soul above the matter-entangled herd. She revealed to me the glorious fact, that I am a spark of Divinity itself. A fallen star, I am, sir!" continued he, pensively, stroking his lean stomach — "a fallen star! — fallen, if the dignity of philosophy will allow of the simile, among the hogs of the lower world — indeed, even into the hog-bucket itself. Well, after all, I will show you the way to the Archbishop's. There is a philosophic pleasure in opening one's treasures to the modest young. Perhaps you will assist me by carrying this basket of fruit?" And the little man jumped up, put his basket on Philammon's headland trotted off up a neighbouring street.

Philammon followed, half contemptuous, half wondering at what this philosophy might be, which could feed the self-conceit of anything so abject as his ragged little apish guide; but the novel roar and whirl of the street, the perpetual stream of busy faces, the line of curricles, palanquins, laden asses, camels, elephants, which met and passed him, and squeezed him up steps and into doorways, as they threaded their way through the great Moon-gate into the ample street beyond, drove everything from his mind but wondering curiosity, and a vague, helpless dread of that great living wilderness, more terrible than any dead wilderness of sand which he had left behind. Already he longed for the repose, the silence of the Laura — for faces which knew him and smiled upon him; but it was too late to turn back now. His guide held on for more than a mile up the great main street, crossed in the centre of the city, at right angles, by one equally magnificent, at each end of which, miles away, appeared, dim and distant over the heads of the living stream of passengers, the yellow sand-hills of the desert; while at the end of the vista in front of them gleamed the blue harbour, through a network of countless masts.

At last they reached the quay at the opposite end of the street; and there burst on Philammon's astonished eyes a vast semicircle of blue sea, ringed with palaces and towers..... He stopped involuntarily; and his little guide stopped also, and looked askance at the young monk, to watch the effect which that grand panorama should produce on him.

"There! ——— Behold our works! Us Greeks! — us be-nighted heathens! Look at it and feel yourself what you are, a very small, conceited, ignorant young person, who fancies that your new religion gives you a right to despise every one else. Did Christians make all this? Did Christians build that Pharos there on the left horn — wonder of the world? Did Christians raise that mile-long mole which runs towards the land, with its two drawbridges, connecting the two ports? Did Christians build this esplanade, or this gate of the Sun above our heads? Or that Cжsareum on our right here? Look at those obelisks before it!" And he pointed upwards to those two world-famous ones, one of which still lies on its ancient site, as Cleopatra's needle. "Look up! look up, I say, and feel small — very small indeed! Did Christians raise them, or engrave them from base to point with the wisdom of the ancients? Did Christians build that Museum next to it, or design its statues and its frescoes — now, alas! re-echoing no more to the hummings of the Attic bee? Did they pile up out of the waves that palace beyond it, or that Exchange? or fill that Temple of Neptune with breathing brass and blushing marble? Did they build that Timonium on the point, where Antony, worsted at Actium, forgot his shame in Cleopatra's arms? Did they quarry out that island of Antirrhodus into a nest of docks, or cover those waters with the sails of every nation under heaven? Speak! Thou son of bats and moles — thou six feet of sand — thou mummy out of the cliff caverns! Can monks do works like these?"

"Other men have laboured, and we have entered into their labours," answered Philammon, trying to seem as unconcerned as he could. He was, indeed, too utterly astonished to be angry at anything. The overwhelming vastness, multiplicity, and magnificence of the whole scene; the range of buildings, such as mother earth never, perhaps, carried on her lap before or since, the extraordinary variety of form — the pure Doric and Ionic of the earlier Ptolemies, the barbaric and confused gorgeousness of the later Roman, and here and there an imitation of the grand elephantine style of old Egypt, its gaudy colours relieving, while they deepened, the effect of its massive and simple outlines; the eternal repose of that great belt of stone contrasting with the restless ripple of the glittering harbour, and the busy sails which crowded out into the sea beyond, like white doves taking their flight into boundless space; — all dazzled, overpowered, saddened him..... This was the world..... Was it not beautiful?.... Must not the men who made all this have been — if not great.... yet.... he knew not what? Surely they had great souls and noble thoughts in them! Surely there was something godlike in being able to create such things! Not for themselves alone, too; but for a nation — for generations yet unborn..... And there was the sea.... and beyond it, nations of men innumerable..... His imagination was dizzy with thinking of them..... Were they all doomed — lost?.... Had God no love for them?

At last, recovering himself, he recollected his errand, and again asked his way to the archbishop's house.

"This way, O youthful nonentity!" answered the little man, leading the way round the great front of the Cæsareum, at the foot of the obelisks.

Philammon's eye fell on some new masonry in the pediment, ornamented with Christian symbols.

"How? Is this a church?"

"It is the Cæsareum. It has become temporarily a church. The immortal gods have, for the time being, condescended to waive their rights; but it is the Cæsareum, nevertheless. This way; down this street to the right. There," said he, pointing to a doorway in the side of the Museum, "is the last haunt of the Muses — the lecture' room of Hypatia, the school of my unworthiness..... And here," stopping at the door of a splendid house on the opposite side of the street, "is the residence of that blest favourite of Athene — Neith, as the barbarians of Egypt would denominate the goddess — we men of Macedonia retain the time-honoured Grecian nomenclature..... You may put down your basket." And he knocked at the door, and delivering the fruit to a black porter, made a polite obeisance to Philammon, and seemed on the point of taking his departure.

"But where is the archbishop's house?"

"Close to the Serapeium. You cannot miss the place: four hundred columns of marble, now ruined by Christian persecutors, stand on an eminence —— "

"But how far off?"

"About three miles; near the gate of the Moon."

"Why, was not that the gate by which we entered the city on the other side?"

"Exactly so; you will know your way back, having already traversed it."

Philammon checked a decidedly carnal inclination to seize the little fellow by the throat, and knock his head against the wall, and contented himself by saying —

"Then do you actually mean to say, you heathen villain, that you have taken me six or seven miles out of my road?"

"Good words, young man. If you do me harm, I call for help; we are close to the Jews' quarter, and there are some thousands there who will swarm out like wasps on the chance of beating a monk to death. Yet that which I have done, I have done with a good purpose. First, politically, or according to practical wisdom — in order that you, not I, might carry the basket. Next, philosophically, or according to the intuitions of the pure reason

— in order that you might, by beholding the magnificence of that great civilization which your fellows wish to destroy, learn that you are an ass, and a tortoise, and a nonentity, and so beholding yourself to be nothing, may be moved to become something."

And he moved off.

Philammon seized him by the collar of his ragged tunic, and held him in a grip from which the little man, though he twisted like an eel, could not escape.

"Peaceably, if you will; if not, by main force. You shall go back with me, and show me every step of the way. It is a just penalty."

"The philosopher conquers circumstances by submitting to them. I go peaceably. Indeed, the base necessities of the hog-bucket side of existence compel me of themselves. back to the Moon-gate, for another early fruit job."

So they went back together.

Now why Philammon's thoughts should have been running on the next new specimen of womankind to whom he had been introduced, though only in name, let psychologists tell, but certainly, after he had walked some half-mile in silence, he suddenly woke up, as out of many meditations, and asked —

"But who is this Hypatia, of whom you talk so much?"

"Who is Hypatia, rustic? The queen of Alexandria! In wit, Athene; Hera in majesty; in beauty, Aphrodite!"

"And who are they?" asked Philammon.

The porter stopped, surveyed him slowly from foot to head with an expression of boundless pity and contempt, and was in the act of walking off in the ecstasy of his disdain, when he was brought-to suddenly by Philammon's strong arm.

"Ah! — I recollect. There is a compact..... Who is Athene? The goddess, giver of wisdom. Hera, spouse of Zeus, queen of the Celestials. Aphrodite, mother of love..... You are not expected to understand."

Philammon did understand, however, so much as this, that Hypatia was a very unique and wonderful person in the mind of his little guide; and therefore asked the only further question by which he could as yet test any Alexandrian phenomenon —

"And is she a friend of the patriarch?"

The porter opened his eyes very wide, put his middle finger in a careful and complicated fashion between his fore and third finger, and extending it playfully towards Philammon, performed therewith certain mysterious signals, the effect whereof being totally lost on him, the little man stopped, took another look at Philammon's stately figure, and answered —

"Of the human race in general, my young friend. The philosopher must rise above the individual, to the contemplation of the universal..... Aha! — Here is something worth seeing, and the gates are open." And he stopped at the portal of a vast building.

"Is this the patriarch's house?"

"The patriarch's tastes are more plebeian. He lives, they say, in two dirty little rooms — knowing what is fit for him. The patriarch's house? Its antipodes, my young friend — that is, if such beings have a cosmic existence, on which point Hypatia has her doubts. This is the temple of art and beauty; the Delphic tripod of poetic inspiration; the solace of the earth-worn drudge; in a word, the theatre; which your patriarch, if he could, would convert to-morrow into a ——— but the philosopher must not revile. Ah! I see the prefect's apparitors at the gate. He is making the polity, as we call it here; the dispositions; settling, in short, the bill of fare for the day, in compliance with the public palate. A facetious pantomime dances here on this day every week — admired by some, the Jews especially. To the more classic taste, many of his movements — his recoil, especially — are wanting in the true antique severity — might be called, perhaps, on the whole, indecent. Still the weary pilgrim must be amused. Let us step in and hear."

But before Philammon could refuse, an uproar arose within, a rush outward of the mob, and inward of the prefect's apparitors.

"It is false!" shouted many voices. "A Jewish calumny! The man is innocent!"

"There's no more sedition in him than there is in me," roared a fat butcher, who looked as ready to fell a man as an ox. "He was always the first and the last to clap the holy patriarch at sermon."

"Dear tender soul," whimpered a woman; "and I said to him only this morning, why don't you flog my boys, Master Hierax? how can you expect them to learn if they are not flogged? And he said, he never could abide the sight of a rod, it made his back tingle so."

"Which was plainly a prophecy!"

"And proves him innocent; for how could he prophesy if he was not one of the holy ones?"

"Monks, to the rescue! Hierax, a Christian, is taken and tortured in the theatre!" thundered a wild hermit, his beard and hair streaming about his chest and shoulders.

"Nitria! Nitria! For God and the mother of God, monks of Nitria! Down with the Jewish slanderers! Down with heathen tyrants!" — And the mob, reinforced as if by magic by hundreds from without, swept down the huge vaulted passage, carrying Philammon and the porter with them.

"My friends," quoth the little man, trying to look philosophically calm, though he was fairly off his legs, and hanging between heaven and earth on the elbows of the bystanders; "whence this tumult?"

"The Jews got up a cry that Hierax wanted to raise a riot. Curse them and their sabbath, they're always rioting on Saturdays about this dancer of theirs, instead of working like honest Christians!"

"And rioting on Sunday instead. Ahem! sectarian differences, which the philosopher" ———

The rest of the sentence disappeared with the speaker, as a sudden opening of the mob let him drop, and buried him under innumerable legs.

Philammon, furious at the notion of persecution, maddened by the cries around him, found himself bursting fiercely through the crowd, till he reached the front ranks, where tall gates of open ironwork barred all further progress, but left a full view of the tragedy which was enacting within, where the poor innocent wretch, suspended from a gibbet, writhed and shrieked at every stroke of the hide whips of his tormentors.

In vain Philammon and the monks around him knocked and beat at the gates; they were only answered by laughter and taunts from the apparitors within, curses on the turbulent mob of Alexandria, with its patriarch, clergy, saints, and churches, and promises to each and all outside, that their turn would come next; while the piteous screams grew fainter and more faint, and at last, with a convulsive shudder, motion and suffering ceased for ever in the poor mangled body.

"They have killed him! Martyred him! Back to the arch-bishop! To the Patriarch's house: he will avenge us!" And as the horrible news, and the watchword which followed it, passed outwards through the crowd, they wheeled round as one man, and poured through street after street towards Cyril's house; while Philammon, beside himself with horror, rage, and pity, hurried onward with them.

A tumultuous hour, or more, was passed in the street, before he could gain entrance; and then he was swept, along with the mob in which he had been fast wedged, through a dark low passage, and landed breathless in a quadrangle of mean and new buildings, overhung by the four hundred stately columns of the ruined Serapeium. The grass was already growing on the ruined capitals and architraves..... Little did even its destroyers dream then, that the day would come when one only of that four hundred would be left, as "Pompey's Pillar," to show what the men of old could think and do.

Philammon at last escaped from the crowd, and putting the letter which he had carried in his bosom into the hands of one of the priests who was mixing with the mob, was beckoned by him into a corridor, and up a flight of stairs, and into a large, low, mean room, and there, by virtue of the world-wide freemasonry which Christianity had, for the first time on earth, established, found himself in five minutes awaiting the summons of the most powerful man south of the Mediterranean.

A curtain hung across the door of the inner chamber, through which Philammon could hear plainly the steps of some one walking up and down hurriedly and fiercely.

"They will drive me to it!" at last burst out a deep sono-rous voice. "They will drive me to it..... Their blood be on their own head! Is it not enough for them to blaspheme God and his church, to have the monopoly of all the cheating, fortune-telling, usury, sorcery, and coining of the city, but they must deliver my clergy into the hands of the tyrant?"

"It was so even in the apostles' time," suggested a softer, but far more unpleasant voice.

"Then it shall be so no longer! God has given me the power to stop them; and God do so to me, and more also, if I do not use that power. To-morrow I sweep out this Augean stable of villany, and leave not a Jew to blaspheme and cheat in Alexandria."

"I am afraid such a judgment, however righteous, might offend his excellency."

"His excellency! His tyranny! Why does Orestes truckle to these circumcised, but because they lend money to him and to his creatures? He would keep up a den of fiends in Alexandria if they would do as much for him I And then to play them off against me and mine, to bring Religion into contempt by setting the mob together by the ears, and to end with outrages like this! Seditious? Have they not cause enough? The sooner I remove one of their temptations, the better: let the other tempter beware, lest his judgment be at hand!"

"The prefect, your holiness?" asked the other voice, slily.

"Who spoke of the prefect? Whosoever is a tyrant, and a murderer, and an oppressor of the poor, and a favourer of the philosophy which despises and enslaves the poor, should not he perish, though he be seven times a prefect!"

At this juncture Philammon, thinking perhaps that he had already heard too much, notified his presence by some slight noise, at which the secretary, as he seemed to be, hastily lifted the curtain, and somewhat sharply demanded his business. The names of Pambo and Arsenius, however, seemed to pacify him at once; and the trembling youth was ushered into the presence of him who in reality, though not in name, sat on the throne of the Pharaohs.

Not, indeed, in their outward pomp; the furniture of the chamber was but a grade above that of the artisan's; the dress of the great man was coarse and simple; if personal vanity peeped out anywhere, it was in the careful arrangement of the bushy beard, and of the few curling locks which the tonsure had spared. But the height and majesty of his figure, the stern and massive beauty of his features, the flashing eye, curling lip, and project-ing brow — all marked him as one born to command. As the youth entered, Cyril stopped short in his walk, and looking him through and through, with a glance which burnt upon his cheeks like fire, and made him all but wish the kindly earth would open and hide him, took the letters, read them, and then began:

"Philammon. A Greek. You are said to have learned to obey. If so, you have also learned to rule. Your father-abbot has transferred you to my tutelage. You are now to obey me."

"And I will."

"Well said. Go to that window, then, and leap into the court."

Philammon walked to it, and opened it. The pavement was full twenty feet below; but his business was to obey, and not take measurements. There was a flower in a vase upon the sill. He quietly removed it, and in an instant more would have leapt, for life or death, when Cyril's voice thundered "Stop!"

"The lad will pass, my Peter. I shall not be afraid, now, for the secrets which he may have overheard."

Peter smiled assent, looking all the while as if he thought it a great pity that the young man had not been allowed to put talebearing out of his own power, by breaking his neck.

"You wish to see the world? Perhaps you have seen something of it to-day."

"I saw the murder ——— "

"Then you saw what you came hither to see; what the world is, and what justice and mercy it can deal out. You would not dislike to see God's reprisals to man's tyranny?.... Or to be a fellow-worker with God therein, if I judge rightly by your looks?"

"I would avenge that man."

"Ah! my poor simple schoolmaster! And his fate is the portent of portents to you now! Stay a while, till you have gone with Ezekiel into the inner chambers of the devil's temple, and you will see worse things than these — women weeping for Thammuz; bemoaning the decay of an idolatry which they themselves disbelieve — That, too, is on the list of Hercules' labours, Peter mine."

At this moment a deacon entered..... "Your holiness, the rabbis of the accursed nation are below, at your summons. We brought them in through the back gate, for fear of ——— "

"Right, right. An accident to them might have ruined us. I shall not forget you. Bring them up. Peter, take this youth, introduce him to the parabolani.... Who will be the best man for him to work under?"

"The brother Theopompus is especially sober and gentle."

Cyril shook his head laughingly.... "Go into the next room, my son.... No, Peter, put him under some fiery saint, some true Boanerges, who will talk him down, and work him to death, and show him the best and worst of everything. Cleitophon will be the man. Now then, let me see my engagements: five minutes for these Jews — Orestes did not choose to frighten them: let us see whether Cyril cannot; then an hour to look over the hospital accounts; an hour for the schools; a half-hour for the reserved cases of distress; and another half-hour for myself; and then divine service. See that the boy is there. Do bring in every one in their turn, Peter mine. So much time goes in hunting for this man and that man.... and life is too short for all that. Where are these Jews?" and Cyril plunged into the latter half of his day's work with that untiring energy, self-sacrifice and method which commanded for him, in spite of all suspicions of his violence, ambition, and intrigue, the loving awe and implicit obedience of several hundred thousand human beings.

So Philammon went out with the parabolani, a sort of organized guild of district visitors.... And in their company he saw that afternoon the dark side of that world, whereof the harbour-panorama had been the bright one. In squalid misery, filth, profligacy, ignorance, ferocity, discontent, neglected in body, house, and soul, by the civil authorities, proving their existence only in aimless and sanguinary riots, there they starved, and rotted, heap on heap, the masses of the old Greek population, close to the great food-exporting harbour of the world. Among these, fiercely perhaps, and fanatically, but still among them, and for them, laboured those district visitors, night and day. And so Philammon toiled away with them, carrying food and clothing, helping sick to the hospital, and dead to the burial; cleaning out the infected houses — for the fever was all but perennial in those quarters — and comforting the dying with the good news of forgiveness from above; till the larger number had to return for evening service. He, however, was kept by his superior, watching at a sick-bedside, and it was late at night before he got home, and was reported to Peter the Reader as having acquitted himself like "a man of God," as, indeed, without the least thought of doing anything noble or self-sacrificing, he had truly done, being a monk. And so he threw himself on a truckle bed, in one of the many cells which opened off a long corridor, and fell fast asleep in a minute.

He was just weltering about in a dreary dream-jumble of Goths dancing with district visitors, Pelagia as an angel, with peacock's wings; Hypatia with horns and cloven feet, riding three hippopotami at once round the theatre; Cyril standing at an open window, cursing frightfully, and pelting him with flower-pots; and a similar self-sown after-crop of his day's impressions; when he was awakened by the tramp of hurried feet in the street outside, and shouts, which gradually, as he became conscious, shaped themselves into cries of "Alexander's church is on fire! Help, good Christians! Fire! Help!"

Whereat he sat up in his truckle bed, tried to recollect where he was, and having with some trouble succeeded, threw on his sheepskin, and jumped up to ask the news from the deacons and monks who were hurrying along the corridor outside. "Yes, Alexander's church was on fire;" and down the stairs they poured, across the courtyard, and out into the street, Peter's tall figure serving as a standard and a rallying point.

As they rushed out through the gateway, Philammon, dazzled by the sudden transition from the darkness within to the blaze of moon and starlight which flooded the street, and walls, and shining roofs, hung back a moment. That hesitation probably saved his life; for in an instant he saw a dark figure spring out of the shadow, a long knife flashed across his eyes, and a priest next to him sunk upon the pavement with a groan, while the assassin dashed off down the street, hotly pursued by monks and parabolani.

Philammon, who ran like a desert ostrich, had soon outstripped all but Peter, when several more dark figures sprang out of doorways and corners, and joined, or seemed to join, the pursuit. Suddenly, however, after running a hundred yards, they drew up opposite the mouth of a side street; the assassin stopped also. Peter, suspecting something wrong, slackened his pace, and caught Philammon's arm.

"Do you see those fellows in the shadow?"

But, before Philammon could answer, some thirty or forty men, their daggers gleaming in the moonlight, moved out into the middle of the street, and received the fugitives into their ranks. What was the meaning of it? Here was a pleasant taste of the ways of the most Christian and civilized city of the Empire!

"Well," thought Philammon," I have come out to see the world, and I seem, at this rate, to be likely to see enough of it."

Peter turned at once, and fled as quickly as he had pursued; while Philammon, considering discretion the better part of valour, followed, and they rejoined their party breathless.

"There is an armed mob at the end of the street."

"Assassins!" "Jews!" "A conspiracy!" Up rose a Babel of doubtful voices. The foe appeared in sight, advancing stealthily, and the whole party took to flight, led once more by Peter, who seemed determined to make free use, in behalf of his own safety, of the long legs which nature had given him.

Philammon followed, sulkily and unwillingly, at a foot's pace; but he had not gone a dozen yards when a pitiable voice at his feet called to him —

"Help! mercy! Do not leave me here to be murdered! I am a Christian; indeed I am a Christian!"

Philammon stooped, and lifted from the ground a comely negro-woman, weeping, and shivering in a few tattered remnants of clothing.

"I ran out when they said the church was on fire," sobbed the poor creature, "and the Jews beat and wounded me. They tore my shawl and tunic off me before I could get away from them; and then our own people ran over me and trod me down. And now my husband will beat me, if I ever get home. Quick! up this side street, or we shall be murdered!"

The armed men, whosoever they were, were close on them. There was no time to be lost; and Philammon, assuring her that he would not desert her, hurried her up the side street which she pointed out. But the pursuers had caught sight of them, and while the mass held on up the main street, three or four turned aside and gave chase. The poor negress could only limp along, and Philammon, unarmed, looked back, and saw the bright steel points gleaming in the moonlight, and made up his mind to die as a monk should. Nevertheless, youth is hopeful. One chance for life. He thrust the negress into a dark doorway, where her colour hid her well enough, and had just time to ensconce himself behind a pillar, when the foremost pursuer reached him. He held his breath in fearful suspense. Should he be seen? He would not die without a struggle at least. No! the fellow ran on, panting. But in a minute more, another came up, saw him suddenly, and sprang aside startled. That start saved Philammon. Quick as a cat, he leapt upon him, felled him to the earth with a single blow, tore the dagger from his hand, and sprang to his feet again just in time to strike his new weapon full into the third pursuer's face. The man put his hand to his head, and recoiled against a fellow-ruffian, who was close on his heels. Philammon, flushed with victory, took advantage of the confusion, and before the worthy pair could recover, dealt them half-a-dozen blows which, luckily for them, came from an unpractised hand, or the young monk might have had more than one life to answer for. As it was, they turned and limped off, cursing in an unknown tongue; and Philammon found himself triumphant and alone, with the trembling negress and the prostrate ruffian, who, stunned by the blow and the fall, lay groaning on the pavement.

It was all over in a minute..... The negress was kneeling under the gateway, pouring out her simple thanks to Heaven for this unexpected deliverance; and Philammon was about to kneel too, when a thought struck him; and coolly despoiling the Jew of his shawl and sash, he handed them over to the poor negress, considering them fairly enough as his own by right of conquest; but, lo and behold! as she was overwhelming him with thanks, a fresh mob poured into the street from the upper end, and were close on them before they were aware..... A flush of terror and despair,.... and then a burst of joy, as, by mingled moonlight and torchlight, Philammon descried priestly robes, and in the fore-front of the battle — there being no apparent danger — Peter the Reader, who seemed to be anxious to prevent inquiry, by beginning to talk as fast as possible.

"Ah, boy! Safe? The saints be praised! We gave you up for dead! Whom have you here? A prisoner? And we have another. He ran right into our arms up the street, and the Lord delivered him into our hand. He must have passed you."

"So he did," said Philammon, dragging up his captive, "and here is his fellow-scoundrel." Whereon the two worthies were speedily tied together by the elbows; and the party marched on once more in search of Alexander's church, and the supposed conflagration.

Philammon looked round for the negress, but she had vanished. He was far too much ashamed of being known to have been alone with a woman to say anything about her. Yet he longed to see her again; an interest — even something like an affection — had already sprung up in his heart toward the poor simple creature whom he had delivered from death. Instead of thinking her ungrateful for not staying to tell what he had done for her, he was thankful to her for having saved his blushes, by disappearing so opportunely..... And he longed to tell her so — to know if she was hurt — to —— Oh, Philammon! only four days from the Laura, and a whole regiment of women acquaintances already! True, Providence having sent into the world about as many women as men, it may be difficult to keep out of their way altogether. Perhaps, too, Providence may have intended them to be of some use to that other sex, with whom it has so mixed them up. Don't argue, poor Philammon; Alexander's church is on fire! — forward!

And so they hurried on, a confused mass of monks and populace, with their hapless prisoners in the centre, who hauled, cuffed, questioned, and cursed by twenty self-elected inquisitors at once, thought fit, either from Jewish obstinacy, or sheer bewilderment, to give no account whatsoever of themselves.

As they turned the corner of a street, the folding-doors of a large gateway rolled open; a long lane of glittering figures poured across the road, dropped their spear-butts on the pavement with a single rattle, and remained motionless. The front rank of the mob recoiled; and an awe-struck whisper ran through them....."The Stationaries!"

"Who are they?" asked Philammon, in a whisper.

"The soldiers — the Roman soldiers," answered a whisperer to him.

Philammon, who was among the leaders, had recoiled too — he hardly knew why — at that stern apparition. His next instinct was to press forward as close as he dared..... And these were Roman soldiers! — the conquerors of the world! — the men whose name had thrilled him from his childhood with vague awe and admiration, dimly heard of up there in the lonely Laura..... Roman soldiers! And here he was face to face with them at last!

His curiosity received a sudden check, however, as he found his arm seized by an officer, as he took him to be, from the gold ornaments on his helmet and cuirass, who lifted his vine-stock threateningly over the young monk's head, and demanded —

"What's all this about? Why are you not quietly in your beds, you Alexandrian rascals?"

"Alexander's church is on fire," answered Philammon, thinking the shortest answer the wisest.

"So much the better."

"And the Jews are murdering the Christians."

"Fight it out, then. Turn in, men, it's only a riot."

And the steel-clad apparition suddenly flashed round, and vanished, trampling and jingling, into the dark jaws of the guardhouse-gate, while the stream, its temporary barrier removed, rushed on wilder than ever.

Philammon hurried on too with them, not without a strange feeling of disappointment. "Only a riot!" Peter was chuckling to his brothers over their cleverness in "having kept the prisoners in the middle, and stopped the rascals' mouths till they were past the guardhouse." "A fine thing to boast of," thought Philammon, "in the face of the men who make and unmake kings and Cæsars!" "Only a riot!" He, and the corps of district visitors — whom he fancied the most august body on earth — and Alexander's church, Christians murdered by Jews, persecution of the Catholic faith, and all the rest of it, was simply, then, not worth the notice of those forty men, alone and secure in the sense of power and discipline, among tens of thousands..... He hated them, those soldiers. Was it because they were indifferent to the cause of the Church?.... or because they were indifferent to the cause of which he was inclined to think himself a not unimportant member, on the strength of his late Samsonic defeat of Jewish persecutors? At least, he obeyed the little porter's advice, and "felt very small indeed."

And he felt smaller still, being-young and alive to ridicule, when, at some sudden ebb or flow, wave or wavelet of the Babel sea, which weltered up and down every street, a shrill female voice informed them from an upper window, that Alexander's church was not on fire at all; that she had gone to the top of the house, as they might have gone, if they had not been fools, &c. &c.; and that it "looked as safe and as ugly as ever;" wherewith a brickbat or two having been sent up in answer, she shut the blinds, leaving them to halt, inquire, discover gradually and piecemeal, after the method of mobs, they had been following the nature of mobs; that no one had seen the church on fire, or seen any one else who had seen the same, or even seen any light in the sky in any quarter, or knew who raised the cry; or — or —

in short, Alexander's church was two miles off; if it was on fire, it was either burnt down or saved by this time; if not, the night-air was, to say the least, chilly: and, whether it was or not, there were ambuscades of Jews — Satan only knew how strong — in every street between them and it..... Might it not be better to secure their two prisoners, and then ask for further orders from the archbishop? Wherewith, after the manner of mobs, they melted off the way they came, by twos and threes, till those of a contrary opinion began to find themselves left alone, and having a strong dislike to Jewish daggers, were fain to follow the stream.

With a panic or two, a cry of "The Jews are on us!" and a general rush in every direction (in which one or two, seeking shelter from the awful nothing in neighbouring houses, were handed over to the watch as burglars, and sent to the quarries accordingly), they reached the Serapeium, and there found, of course, a counter-mob collected to inform them that they had been taken in — that Alexander's church had never been on fire at all — that the Jews had murdered a thousand Christians at least, though three dead bodies, including the poor priest who lay in the house within, were all of the thousand who had yet been seen — and that the whole Jews' quarter was marching upon them. At which news it was considered advisable to retreat into the archbishop's house as quickly as possible, barricade the doors, and prepare for a siege — a work at which Philammon performed prodigies, tearing woodwork from the rooms, and stones from the parapets, before it struck some of the more sober-minded that it was as well to wait for some more decided demonstration of attack before incurring so heavy a carpenter's bill of repairs.

At last the heavy tramp of footsteps was heard coming-down the street, and every window was crowded in an instant with eager heads; while Peter rushed down stairs to heat the large coppers, having some experience in the defensive virtues of boiling water. The bright moon glittered on a long line of helmets and cuirasses. Thank Heaven! it was the soldiery.

"Are the Jews coming?" "Is the city quiet?" "Why did not you prevent this villany?" "A thousand citizens murdered while you have been snoring?" — and a volley of similar ejaculations, greeted the soldiers as they passed, and were answered by a cool — "To your perches, and sleep, you noisy chickens, or we'll set the coop on fire about your ears."

A yell of defiance answered this polite speech, and the soldiery, who knew perfectly well that the unarmed ecclesiastics within were not to be trifled with, and had no ambition to die by coping-stones and hot water, went quietly on their way.

All danger was now past; and the cackling rose jubilant, louder than ever, and might have continued till daylight, had not a window in the courtyard been suddenly thrown open, and the awful voice of Cyril commanded silence.

"Every man sleep where he can. I shall want you at daybreak. The superiors of the parabolani are to come up to me with the two prisoners, and the men who took them."

In a few minutes Philammon found himself, with some twenty others, in the great man's presence: he was sitting at his desk, writing, quietly, small notes on slips of paper.

"Here is the youth who helped me to pursue the murderer, and, having outrun me, was attacked by the prisoners," said Peter. "My hands are clean from blood, I thank the Lord!"

"Three set on me with daggers," said Philammon, apologetically, "and I was forced to take this one's dagger away, and beat off the two others with it."

Cyril smiled, and shook his head.

"Thou art a brave boy; but hast thou not read, 'If a man smite thee on one cheek, turn to him the other?' "

"I could not run away, as Master Peter and the rest did."

"So you run away, eh? my worthy friend?"

"Is it not written," asked Peter, in his blandest tone " 'If they persecute you in one city, flee unto another?' "

Cyril smiled again. "And why could not you run away boy?"

Philammon blushed scarlet, but he dared not lie. "There was a — a poor black woman, wounded and trodden down, and I dare not leave her, for she told me she was a Christian."

"Right, my son, right. I shall remember this. What was her name?"

"I did not hear it. — Stay, I think she said Judith."

"Ah! the wife of the porter who stands at the lecture-room door, which God confound! A devout woman, full of good works, and sorely ill-treated by her heathen husband. Peter, thou shalt go to her to-morrow with the physician, and see if she is in need of anything. Boy, thou hast done well. Cyril never forgets. Now bring up those Jews. Their Rabbis were with me two hours ago promising peace: and this is the way they have kept their promise. So be it. The wicked is snared in his own wickedness."

The Jews were brought in, but kept a stubborn silence.

"Your holiness perceives," said some one, "that they have each of them rings of green palm-bark on their right hand."

"A very dangerous sign! An evident conspiracy!" commented Peter.

"Ah? What does that mean, you rascals? Answer me, as you value your lives."

"You have no business with us: we are Jews, and none of your people," said one, sulkily.

"None of my people? You have murdered my people! None of my people? Every soul in Alexandria is mine, if the kingdom of God means anything; and you shall find it out. I shall not argue with you, my good friends, any more than I did with your Rabbis. Take these fellows away, Peter, and lock them up in the fuel-cellar, and see that they are guarded. If any man lets them go. his life shall be for the life of them."

And the two worthies were led out.

"Now, my brothers, here are your orders. You will divide these notes among yourselves, and distribute them to trusty and godly catholics in your districts. Wait one hour, till the city be quiet; and then start, and raise the church. I must have thirty thousand men by sunrise."

"What for, your holiness?" asked a dozen voices.

"Read your notes. Whosoever will fight to-morrow under the banner of the Lord, shall have free plunder of the Jews' quarter, outrage and murder only forbidden. As I have said it, God do so to me, and more also, if there be a Jew left in Alexandria by to-morrow at noon. Go."

And the staff of orderlies filed out, thanking Heaven that they had a leader so prompt and valiant, and spent the next hour over the hall fire, eating millet cakes, drinking bad beer, likening Cyril to Barak, Gideon, Samson, Jephtha, Judas Maccabeus, and all the worthies of the Old Testament, and then started on their pacific errand.

Philammon was about to follow them, when Cyril stopped him.

"Stay, my son; you are young and rash, and do not know the city. Lie down here and sleep in the anteroom. Three hours hence the sun rises, and we go forth against the enemies of the Lord."

Philammon threw himself on the floor in a corner, and slumbered like a child, till he was awakened in the grey dawn by one of the parabolani.

"Up, boy! and see what we can do. Cyril goes down greater than Barak the son of Abinoam, not with ten, but with thirty thousand men at his feet!"

"Ay, my brothers!" said Cyril, as he passed proudly out in full pontificals, with a gorgeous retinue of priests and deacons — "the Catholic Church has her organization, her unity, her common cause, her watchwords, such as the tyrants of the earth, in their weakness and their divisions, may envy and tremble at, but cannot imitate. Could Orestes raise, in three hours, thirty thousand men, who would die for him?"

"As we will for you!" shouted many voices.

" Say for the kingdom of God." And he passed out.

And so ended Philammon's first day in Alexandria.

CHAPTER VI
THE NEW DIOGENES

ABOUT five o'clock the next morning, Raphael Aben-Ezra was lying in bed, alternately yawning over a manuscript of Philo Judæus, pulling the ears of his huge British mastiff, watching the sparkle of the fountain in the court outside, wondering when that lazy boy would come to tell him that the bath was warmed, and meditating, half aloud.......

"Alas! poor me! Here I am, back again — just at the point from which I started!.... How am I to get free from that heathen Siren? Plagues on her! I shall end by falling in love with her..... I don't know that I have not got a barb of the blind boy in me already. I felt absurdly glad the other day when that fool told me he dare not accept her modest offer. Ha! ha! A delicious joke it would have been to have seen Orestes bowing down to stocks and stones, and Hypatia installed in the ruins of the Serapeium, as High Priestess of the Abomination of Desolation!.... And now.... Well: I call all heaven and earth to witness, that I have fought valiantly. I have faced naughty little Eros like a man, rod in hand. What could a poor human being do more than try to marry her to some one else, in hopes of sickening himself of the whole matter? Well, every moth has its candle, and every man his destiny. But the daring of the little fool! What huge imaginations she has! She might be another Zenobia, now, with Orestes as Odenatus, and Raphael Aben-Ezra to play the part of Longinus.... and receive Long-inus's salary of axe or poison. She don't care for me; she would sacrifice me, or a thousand of me, the cold-blooded fanatical archangel that she is, to water with our blood the foundation of some new temple of cast rags and broken dolls.... Oh, Raphael Aben-Ezra, what a fool you are!.... You know you are going off as usual to her lecture, this very morning!"

At this crisis of his confessions the page entered, and announced, not the bath, but Miriam.

The old woman, who, in virtue of her profession, had the private entry of all fashionable chambers in Alexandria, came in hurriedly; and instead of seating-herself as usual, for a gossip, remained standing, and motioned the boy out of the room.

"Well, my sweet mother? Sit; Ah? I see! You rascal, you have brought in no wine for the lady. Don't you know her little ways yet?"

"Eos has got it at the door, of course," answered the boy with a saucy air of offended virtue.

"Out with you, imp of Satan!" cried Miriam. "This is no time for wine-bibbing. Raphael Aben-Ezra, why are you lying here? Did you not receive a note last night?"

"A note? So I did: but I was too sleepy to read it. There it lies. Boy, bring it here..... What's this? A scrap out of Jeremiah? 'Arise, and flee for thy life, for evil is determined against the whole house of Israel!' — Does this come from the chief rabbi; I always took the venerable father for a sober man..... Eh, Miriam?"

"Fool! instead of laughing at the sacred words of the prophets, get up and obey them. I sent you the note."

"Why can't I obey them in bed? Here I am, reading hard at the Cabbala, or Philo — who is stupider still — and what more would you have!"

The old woman, unable to restrain her impatience, literally ran at him, gnashing her teeth, and, before he was aware, dragged him out of bed upon the floor, where he stood meekly wondering what would come next.

"Many thanks, mother, for having saved me the one daily torture of life — getting out of bed by one's own exertion."

"Raphael Aben-Ezra! are you so besotted with your philosophy and your heathenry, and your laziness, and your contempt for God and man, that you will see your nation given up for a prey, and your wealth plundered by heathen dogs? I tell you, Cyril has sworn that God shall do so to him, and more also, if there be a Jew left in Alexandria by to-morrow about this time."

"So much the better for the Jews, then, if they are half as tired of this noisy Pandemonium as I am. But how can I help it? Am I Queen Esther, to go to Ahasuerus there in the prefect's palace, and get him to hold out the golden sceptre to me?"

"Fool I if you had read that note last night, you might have gone and saved us, and your name would have been handed down for ever from generation to generation as second Mordecai."

"My dear mother, Ahasuerus would have been either fast asleep, or far too drunk to listen to me. Why did you not go yourself?"

"Do you suppose that I would not have gone if I could? Do you fancy me a sluggard like yourself? At the risk of my life I have got hither in time, if there be time to save you."

"Well: shall I dress? What can be done now?"

"Nothing! The streets are blockaded by Cyril's mob — There! do you hear the shouts and screams? They are attacking the further part of the quarter already."

"What! are they murdering them?" asked Raphael, throwing on his pelisse. "Because, if it has really come to a practical joke of that kind, I shall have the greatest pleasure in employing a counter-irritant. Here, boy! My sword and dagger! Quick!"

"No, the hypocrites! No blood is to be shed, they say, if we make no resistance, and let them pillage. Cyril and his monks are there, to prevent outrage, and so forth..... The Angel of the Lord scatter them!"

The conversation was interrupted by the rushing in of the whole household, in an agony of terror; and Raphael, at last thoroughly roused, went to a window which looked into the street. The thoroughfare was full of scolding women and screaming children; while men, old and young, looked on at the plunder of their property with true Jewish doggedness, too prudent to resist, but too manful to complain; while furniture came flying out of every window, and from door after door poured a stream of rascality, carrying off money, jewels, silks, and all the treasures which Jewish usury had accumulated during many a generation. But unmoved amid the roaring sea of plunderers and plundered, stood, scattered up and down, Cyril's spiritual police, enforcing, by a word, an obedience which the Roman soldiers could only have compelled by hard blows of the spear-butt. There was to be no outrage, and no outrage there was; and more than once some man in priestly robes hurried through the crowd, leading by the hand, tenderly enough, a lost child in search of its parents.

Raphael stood watching silently, while Miriam, who had followed him up stairs, paced the room in an ecstasy of rage, calling vainly to him to speak or act.

"Let me alone, mother," he said, at last. "It will be full ten minutes more before they pay me a visit, and in the mean time what can one do better than watch the progress of this, the little Exodus?"

"Not like that first one! Then we went forth with cymbals and songs to the Red Sea triumph! Then we borrowed, every woman of her neighbour, jewels of silver, and jewels of gold, and raiment."

"And now we pay them back again;.... it is but fair, after all. We ought to have listened to Jeremiah a thousand years ago, and never gone back again, like fools, into a country to which we were so deeply in debt."

"Accursed land!" cried Miriam. "In an evil hour our fore-fathers disobeyed the prophet; and now we reap the harvest of our sins! — Our sons have forgotten the faith of their forefathers for the philosophy of the Gentiles, and fill their chambers" (with a contemptuous look round) "with heathen imagery; and our daughters are — Look there!"

As she spoke a beautiful girl rushed shrieking out of an adjoining house, followed by some half-drunk ruffian, who was clutching at the gold chains and trinkets with which she was profusely bedecked, after the fashion of Jewish women. The rascal had just seized with one hand her streaming black tresses, and with the other a heavy collar of gold, which was wound round her throat, when a priest, stepping up, laid a quiet hand upon his shoulder. The fellow, too maddened to obey, turned, and struck back the restraining arm.... and in an instant was felled to the earth by a young monk.....

"Touchest thou the Lord's anointed, sacrilegious wretch?" cried the man of the desert, as the fellow dropped on the pavement, with his booty in his hand.

The monk tore the gold necklace from his grasp, looked at it for a moment with childish wonder, as a savage might at some incomprehensible product of civilized industry, and then, spitting on it in contempt, dashed it on the ground, and trampled it into the mud.

"Follow the golden wedge of Achan, and the silver of Iscariot, thou root of all evil!" And he rushed on, yelling," Down with the circumcision! Down with the blasphemers!" — while the poor girl vanished among the crowd.

Raphael watched him with a quaint thoughtful smile while Miriam shrieked aloud at the destruction of the precious trumpery.

"The monk is right, mother. If those Christians go on upon that method, they must beat us. It has been our ruin from the first, our fancy for loading ourselves with the thick clay."

"What will you do?" cried Miriam, clutching him by the arm.

"What will you do?"

"I am safe. I have a boat waiting for me on the canal at the garden gate, and in Alexandria I stay; no Christian hound shall make old Miriam move a foot against her will. My jewels are all buried — my girls all sold; save what you can, and come with me!"

"My sweet mother, why so peculiarly solicitous about my welfare, above that of all the sons of Judah?" '

"Because — because — No, I'll tell you that another time. But I loved your mother, and she loved me. Come!"

Raphael relapsed into silence for a few minutes, and' watched the tumult below.

"How those Christian priests keep their men in order! There is no use resisting destiny. They are the strong men of the time, after all; and the little Exodus must needs have its course. Miriam, daughter of Jonathan —— "

"I am no man's daughter! I have neither father nor mother, husband nor ——— Call me mother again!"

"Whatsoever I am to call you, there are jewels enough in that closet to buy half Alexandria. Take them. I am going."

"With me?"

"Out into the wide world, my dear lady. I am bored with riches. That young savage of a monk understood them better than we Jews do. I shall just make a virtue of necessity, and turn beggar."

"Beggar?"

"Why not? Don't argue. These scoundrels will make me one, whether I like or not; so forth I go. There will be few leave-takings. This brute of a dog is the only friend I have on earth; and I love her, because she has the true old, dogged, spiteful, cunning, obstinate Maccabee spirit in her — of which if we had a spark left in us just now, there would be no little Exodus; eh,

Bran, my beauty?''

"You can escape with me to the prefect's, and save the mass of your wealth."

"Exactly what I don't want to do. I hate that prefect as I hate a dead camel, or the vulture who eats him. And to tell the truth, I am growing a great deal too fond of that heathen woman there — — "

"What?" shrieked the old woman — "Hypatia?"

"If you choose. At all events, the easiest way to cut the knot is to expatriate. I shall beg my passage on board the first ship to Cyrene, and go and study life in Italy with Heraclian's expedition. Quick — take the jewels, and breed fresh troubles for yourself with them. I am going. My liberators are battering the outer door already."

Miriam greedily tore out of the closet diamonds and pearls, rubles and emeralds, and concealed them among her ample robes — "Go! go! Escape from her! I will hide your jewels!"

"Ay, hide them, as mother earth does all things, in that all-embracing bosom. You will have doubled them before we meet again, no doubt. Farewell, mother!"

"But not for ever, Raphael! not for ever I Promise me, in the name of the four archangels, that if you are in trouble or danger, you will write to me, at the house of Eudaimon."

"The little porter philosopher, who hangs about Hypatia's lecture-room?"

"The same, the same. He will give me your letter, and I swear to you, I will cross the mountains of Kaf to deliver you! — I will pay you all back. By Abraham, Isaac, and Jacob I swear! May my tongue cleave to the roof of my mouth, if I do not account to you for the last penny!"

"Don't commit yourself to rash promises, my dear lady. If I am bored with poverty, I can but borrow a few gold pieces of a rabbi, and turn pedler. I really do not trust you to pay me back, so I shall not be disappointed if you do not. Why should I?"

"Because — because — Oh, God! No — never mind! You shall have all back. Spirit of Elias! where is the black agate? Why is it not among these? — The broken half of the black agate talisman!"

Raphael turned pale. "How did you know that I have; a black agate?"

"How did I? How did I not?" cried she, clutching? him by the arm. "Where is it? All depends on that! Fool!" she went on, throwing him off from her at arm's length, as a sudden suspicion stung her — "you have not given it to the heathen woman?"

"By the soul of my fathers, then, you mysterious old witch, who seem to know everything, that is exactly what I have done."

Miriam clapped her hands together wildly. "Lost! lost! lost! No! I will have it, if I tear it out of her heart! I will be avenged of her — the strange woman who flatters with her words, to whom the simple go in, and know not that the dead are there, and that her guests are in the depths of hell! God do so to me, and more also, if she and her sorceries be on earth a twelve-month hence!"

"Silence, Jezebel! Heathen or none, she is as pure as the sunlight! I only gave it her because she fancied the talisman upon it."

"To enchant you with it, to your ruin!"

"Brute of a slave-dealer! you fancy every one as base as the poor wretches whom you buy and sell to shame, that you may make them as much the children of hell, if that be possible, as yourself!"

Miriam looked at him, her large black eyes widening and kindling. For an instant she felt for her poniard — and then burst into an agony of tears, hid her face in her withered hands, and rushed from the room, as a crash and shout below announced the bursting of the door.

"There she goes with my jewels. And here come my guests, with the young monk at their head. — One rising when the other sets. A worthy pair of Dioscuri! Come, Bran!.... Boys! Slaves! Where are you? Steal every one what he can lay his hands on, and run for your lives through the back gate."

The slaves had obeyed him already. He walked smiling down stairs through utter solitude, and in the front passage, met face to face the mob of monks, costermongers and dock-workers, fishwives and beggars, who were thronging up the narrow entry, and bursting into the doors right and left; and at their head, alas! the young monk who had just trampled the necklace into the mud.... no other, in fact, than Philammon.

"Welcome, my worthy guests I Enter, I beseech you, and

fulfil, in your own peculiar way, the precepts which bid you not be over anxious for the good things of this life..... For eating and drinking, my kitchen and cellar are at your service. For clothing, if any illustrious personage will do me the honour to change his holy rags with me, here are an Indian shawl-pelisse and a pair of silk trousers at his service. Perhaps you will accommodate me, my handsome young captain, choragus of this new school of the prophets?"

Philammon, who was the person addressed, tried to push by him contemptuously.

"Allow me, sir. I lead the way. This dagger is poisoned, — a scratch and you are dead. This dog is of the true British breed; if she seizes you, red-hot iron will not loose her, till she hears the bone crack. If any one will change clothes with me, all I have is at your service. If not, the first that stirs is a dead man."

There was no mistaking the quiet, high-bred determination of the speaker. Had he raged and blustered, Philammon could have met him on his own ground: but there was an easy self-possessed disdain about him, which utterly abashed the young monk, and abashed, too, the whole crowd of rascals at his heels.

"I'll change clothes with you, you Jewish dog!" roared a dirty fellow out of the mob.

"I am your eternal debtor. Let us step into this side room. Walk up stairs, my friends. Take care there, sir! — That porcelain, whole, is worth three thousand gold pieces; broken, it is not three pence. I leave it to your good sense to treat it accordingly. Now then, my friend!" And in the midst of the raging vortex of plunderers, who were snatching up everything which they could carry away, and breaking everything which they could not, he quietly divested himself of his finery, and put on the ragged cotton tunic, and battered straw hat, which the fellow handed over to him.

Philammon, who had had from the first no mind to plunder, stood watching Raphael with dumb wonder; and a shudder of regret, he knew not why, passed through him, as he saw the mob tearing down pictures, and dashing statues to the ground. Heathen they were, doubtless; but still, the Nymphs and Venuses looked too lovely to be so, brutally destroyed..... There was something almost humanly pitiful in their poor broken arms and legs, as they lay about upon the pavement..... He laughed at himself for the notion; but he could not laugh it away.

Raphael seemed to think that he ought not to laugh it away; for he pointed to the fragments, and with a quaint look at the young monk —

"Our nurses used to tell us,

' If you can't make it,
You ought not to break it.' "

"I had no nurse," said Philammon.

"Ah! — that accounts — for this and other things. Well," he went on, with the most provoking good-nature, "you are in a fair road, my handsome youth; I wish you joy of your fellow-workmen, and of your apprenticeship in the noble art of monkery. Riot and pillage, shrieking women and houseless children in your twentieth summer, are the sure path to a saintship, such as Paul of Tarsus, who, with all his eccentricities, was a gentleman, certainly never contemplated. I have heard of Phœbus Apollo under many disguises, but this is the first time I ever saw him in the wolf's hide."

"Or in the lion's," said Philammon, trying in his shame to make a fine speech.

"Like the Ass in the Fable. Farewell! Stand out of the way, friends! 'Ware teeth and poison!"

And he disappeared among the crowd, who made way respectfully enough for his dagger and his brindled companion.

CHAPTER VII
THOSE BY WHOM OFFENCES COME

PHILAMMON's heart smote him all that day, whenever he thought of his morning's work. Till then all Christians, monks above all, had been infallible in his eyes: all Jews and heathens insane and accursed. Moreover, meekness under insult, fortitude in calamity, the contempt of worldly comfort, the worship of poverty as a noble estate, were virtues which the Church Catholic boasted as her peculiar heritage: on which side had the balance of those qualities inclined that morning? The figure of Raphael, stalking out ragged and penniless into the wide world, haunted him, with its quiet self-assured smile. And there haunted him, too, another peculiarity in the man, which he had never before remarked in any one but Arsenius — that ease and grace, that courtesy and self-restraint, which made Raphael's rebukes rankle all the more keenly, because he felt that the rebuker was in some mysterious way superior to him, and saw through him, and could have won him over, or crushed him in argument, or in intrigue — or in anything, perhaps, except mere brute force. Strange — that Raphael, of all men, should in those few moments have reminded him so much of Arsenius; and that the very same qualities which gave a peculiar charm to the latter should give a peculiar unloveliness to the former, and yet be, without a doubt, the same. What was it? Was it rank which gave it? Arsenius had been a great man, he knew — the companion of kings. And Raphael seemed rich. He had heard the mob crying out against the prefect for favouring him. Was it then familiarity with the great ones of the world which produced this manner and tone? It was a real strength, whether in Arsenius or in Raphael. He felt humbled before it — envied it. If it made Arsenius a more complete and more captivating person, why should it not do the same for him? Why should not he, too, have his share of it?

Bringing with it such thoughts as these, the time ran on till noon, and the midday meal, and the afternoon's work, to which Philammon looked forward joyfully, as a refuge from his own thoughts.

He was sitting on his sheepskin upon a step, basking, like a true son of the desert, in a blaze of fiery sunshine, which made the black stonework too hot to touch with the bare hand, watching the swallows, as they threaded the columns of the Serapeium, and thinking how often he had delighted in their air-dance, as they turned and hawked up and down the dear old glen at Scetis. A crowd of citizens with causes, appeals, and petitions, were passing in and out from the patriarch's audience-room. Peter and the archdeacon were waiting-in the shade close by, for the gathering of the parabolani, and talking over the morning's work in an earnest whisper, in which the names of Hypatia and Orestes were now and then audible.

An old priest came up, and bowing reverently enough to the archdeacon, requested the help of one of the parabolani. He had a sailor's family, all fever-stricken, who must be removed to the hospital at once.

The archdeacon looked at him, answered an off-hand "Very well," and went on with his talk.

The priest, bowing lower than before, represented the immediate necessity for help.

"It is very odd," said Peter to the swallows in the Serapeium, "that some people cannot obtain influence enough in their own parishes to get the simplest good works performed without tormenting his holiness the patriarch."

The old priest mumbled some sort of excuse, and the archdeacon, without deigning-a second look at him, said — "Find him a man, brother Peter. Anybody will do. What is that boy — Philammon — doing there? Let him go with Master Hieracas."

Peter seemed not to receive the proposition favourably, and whispered something to the archdeacon....

"No. I can spare none of the rest. Importunate persons must take their chance of being well served. Come — here are our brethren; we will all go together."

"The further together the better for the boy's sake," grumbled Peter, loud enough for Philammon — perhaps for the old priest — to overhear him.

So Philammon went out with them, and as he went questioned his companions, meekly enough, as to who Raphael was.

" A friend of Hypatia!" — that name, too, haunted him;

and he began, as stealthily and indirectly as he could, to obtain information about her. There was no need for his caution; for the very mention of her name roused the whole party into a fury of execration.

"May God confound her, siren, enchantress, dealer in spells and sorceries! She is the strange woman of whom Solomon prophesied."

"It is my opinion," said another, "that she is the forerunner of Antichrist."

"Perhaps the virgin of whom it is prophesied that he will be born," suggested another.

"Not that, I'll warrant her," said Peter, with a savage sneer.

"And is Raphael Aben-Ezra her pupil in philosophy?" asked Philammon.

"Her pupil in whatsoever she can find wherewith to delude men's souls," said the old priest. "The reality of philosophy has died long ago, but the great ones find it still worth their while to worship its shadow."

"Some of them worship more than a shadow, when they haunt her house," said Peter." Do you think Orestes goes thither only for philosophy?"

"We must not judge harsh judgments," said the old priest; "Synesius of Cyrene is a holy man, and yet he loves Hypatia well."

"He a holy man? — and keeps a wife? One who had the insolence to tell the blessed Theophilus himself that he would not be made bishop unless he were allowed to remain with her; and despised the gift of the Holy Ghost in comparison of the carnal joys of wedlock, not knowing the Scriptures, which saith that those who are in the flesh cannot please God! Well said Siricius of Rome of such men — 'Can the Holy Spirit of God dwell in other than holy bodies?' No wonder that such a one as Synesius grovels at the feet of Orestes' mistress!"

"Then she is profligate?" asked Philammon.

"She must be. Has a heathen faith and grace? And without faith and grace, are not all our righteousnesses as filthy rags? What says St. Paul? — That God has given them over to a reprobate mind, full of all injustice, unclean-ness, covetousness, maliciousness, you know the catalogue — why do you ask me?"

"Alas! and is she this?"

"Alas! And why alas? How would the Gospel be glorified if heathens were holier than Christians? It ought to be so, therefore it is so. If she seems to have virtues, they, being done without the grace of Christ, are only bedizened vices, cunning shams, the devil transformed into an angel of light. And as for chastity, the flower and crown of all virtues — whosoever says that she, being yet a heathen, has that, blasphemes the Holy Spirit, whose peculiar and highest gift it is, and is anathema maranatha for ever! Amen!" And Peter devoutly crossing himself, turned angrily and contemptuously away from his young companion.

Philammon was quite shrewd enough to see that assertion was not identical with proof. But Peter's argument of "it ought to be, therefore it is," is one which saves a great deal of trouble.... and no doubt he had very good sources of information. So Philammon walked on, sad, he knew not why, at the new notion which he had formed of Hypatia, as a sort of awful sorceress-Messalina, whose den was foul with magic rites and ruined souls of men. And yet if that was all she had to teach, whence had her pupil Raphael learned that fortitude of his? If philosophy had, as they said, utterly died out, then what was Raphael?

Just then, Peter and the rest turned up a side street, and Philammon and Hieracas were left to go on their joint errand together. They paced on for some way in silence, up one street and down another, till Philammon, for want of anything better to say, asked where they were going?

"Where I choose, at all events. No, young man! If I, a priest, am to be insulted by archdeacons and readers, I won't be insulted by you."

"I assure you I meant no harm."

"Of course not; you all learn the same trick, and the young ones catch it of the old ones fast enough. Words smoother than butter, yet very swords."

"You do not mean to complain of the archdeacon and his companions?" said Philammon, who of course was boiling over with pugnacious respect for the body to which he belonged.

No answer.

"Why, sir, are they not among the most holy and devoted of men?"

"Ah — yes," said his companion, in a tone which sounded

very like "Ah — no."

"You do not think so?" asked Philammon, bluntly. "You are young, you are young. Wait a while till you have seen as much as I have. A degenerate age this, my son; not like the good old times, when men dare suffer and die for the faith. We are too prosperous nowadays; and fine ladies walk about with Magdalens embroidered on their silks, and gospels hanging round their necks. When I was young, they died for that with which they now bedizen themselves."

"But I was speaking of the parabolani."

"Ah, there are a great many among them who have not much business where they are. Don't say I said so. But many a rich man puts his name on the list of the guild just to get his exemption from taxes, and leaves the work to poor men like you. Rotten, rotten! my son, and you will find it out. The preachers, now — people used to say — I know Abbot Isidore did — that I had as good a gift for expounding as any man in Pelusium; but since I came here, eleven years since, if you will believe it, I have never been asked to preach in my own parish church."

"You surely jest!"

"True, as I am a christened man. I know why — I know why: they are afraid of Isidore's men here..... Perhaps they may have caught the holy man's trick of plain speaking — and ears are dainty in Alexandria. And there are some in those parts, too, that have never forgiven him the part he took about those three villains, Maro, Zosimus, and Martinian, and a certain letter that came of it; or another letter either, which we know of, about taking alms for the church from the gains of robbers and usurers. 'Cyril never forgets.' So he says to every one who does him a good turn..... And so he does to every one who he fancies has done him a bad one. So here am I slaving away, a subordinate priest, while such fellows as Peter the Reader look down on me as their slave. But it's always so. There never was a bishop yet, except the blessed Augustine — would to Heaven I had taken my abbot's advice and gone to him at Hippo! — who had not his flatterers and his talebearers, and generally the archdeacon at the head of them, ready to step into the bishop's place when he dies, over the heads of hard-working parish priests. But that is the way of the world. The sleekest and the oiliest, and the noisiest; the man who can bring in most money to the charities, never mind whence or how; the man who will take most of the bishop's work off his hands, and agree with him in everything he wants, and save him, by spying and eavesdropping, the trouble of using his own eyes; that is the man to succeed in Alexandria, or Constantinople, or Rome itself. Look now; there are but seven deacons to this great city, and all its priests; and they and the archdeacon are the masters of it and us. They and that Peter manage Cyril's work for him, and when Cyril makes the archdeacon a bishop, he will make Peter archdeacon..... They have their reward, they have their reward; and so has Cyril, for that matter."

"How?"

"Why, don't say I said it. But what do I care? I have nothing to lose, I 'm sure. But they do say that there are two ways of promotion in Alexandria: one by deserving it, the other by paying for it. That's all."

"Impossible!"

"Oh, of course, quite impossible. But all I know is just this, that when that fellow Martinian got back again into Pelusium, after being turned out by the late bishop for a rogue and hypocrite as he was, and got the ear of his present bishop, and was appointed his steward, and ordained priest — I'd as soon have ordained that street-dog — and plundered him and brought him to disgrace — for I don't believe this bishop is a bad man, but those who use rogues must expect to be called rogues — and ground the poor to the earth, and tyrannized over the whole city so that no man's property, or reputation, scarcely their lives, were safe; and after all, had the impudence, when he was called on for his accounts, to bring the church in as owing him money; I just know this, that he added to all his other shamelessness this, that he offered the patriarch a large sum of money to buy a bishopric of him..... And what do you think the patriarch answered?"

"Excommunicated the sacrilegious wretch, of course!"

"Sent him a letter to say that if he dared to do such a thing again he should really be forced to expose him! So the fellow taking courage, brought his money himself the next time; and all the world says that Cyril would have made him a bishop after all, if Abbot Isidore had not written to remonstrate."

"He could not have known the man's character," said poor Philammon, hunting for an excuse.

"The whole Delta was ringing with it. Isidore had written to him again and again."

"Surely, then, his wish was to prevent scandal, and preserve the unity of the church in the eyes of the heathen."

The old man laughed bitterly.

"Ah, the old story — of preventing scandals by retaining them, and fancying that sin is a less evil than a little noise; as if the worst of all scandals was not the being discovered in hushing up a. scandal. And as for unity, if you want that, you must go back to the good old times of Dioclesian and Decius."

"The persecutors?"

"Ay, boy — to the times of persecution, when Christians died like brothers, because they lived like brothers. You will see very little of that now, except in some little remote county bishopric, which no one ever bears of from year's end to year's end. But in the cities it is all one great fight for place and power. Every man is jealous of his neighbour. The priests are jealous of the deacons, and good cause they have. The county bishops are jealous of the metropolitan, and he is jealous of the North African bishops, and quite right he is. What business have they to set up for themselves, as if they were infallible? It's a schism, I say — a complete schism. They are just as bad as their own Donatists. Did not the Council of Nice settle that the Metropolitan of Alexandria should have authority over Libya and Pentapolis, according to the ancient custom?"

"Of course he ought," said Philammon, jealous for the honour of his own patriarchate.

"And the patriarchs of Rome and Constantinople are jealous of our patriarch."

"Of Cyril?"

"Of course, because he won't be at their beck and nod, and let them be lords and masters of Africa."

"But surely these things can be settled by councils?"

"Councils? Walt till you have been at one. The blessed Abbot Isidore used to say, that if he ever was a bishop — which he never will be — he is tar too honest for that, — he would never go near one of them; for he never had seen one which did not call out every evil passion in men's hearts, and leave the question more confounded with words than they found it, even if the whole matter was not settled beforehand by some chamberlain, or eunuch, or cook sent from court, as if he were an anointed vessel of the Spirit, to settle the dogmas of the Holy Catholic Church."

"Cook?"

"Why, Valens sent his chief cook to stop Basil of Cæsarea from opposing the Court doctrine..... I tell you, the great battle in these cases is to get votes from courts, or to get to court yourself. When I was young, the Council of Antioch had to make a law to keep bishops from running off to Constantinople to intrigue, under pretence of pleading the cause of orphan and widow. But what's the use of that, when every noisy and ambitious man shifts and shifts, from one see to another, till he settles himself close to Rome or Byzantium, and gets the emperor's ear, and plays into the hands of his courtiers?"

"Is it not written, 'Speak not evil of dignities?' " said Philammon, in his most sanctimonious tone.

"Well, what of that? I don't speak evil of dignities, when I complain of the men who fill them badly, do I?"

"I never heard that interpretation of the text before."

"Very likely not. That's no reason why it should not be true and orthodox. You will soon hear a good many more things, which are true enough — though whether they are orthodox or not, the court cooks must settle. Of course, I am a disappointed, irreverent old grumbler. Of course; and of course, too, young men must needs buy their own experience, instead of taking old folks' at a gift. There — use your own eyes, and judge for yourself. There you may see what sort of saints are bred by this plan of managing the Catholic Church. There comes one of them. Now! I say no more!"

As he spoke, two tall negroes came up to them, and set down before the steps of a large church which they were passing, an object new to Philammon — a sedan-chair, the poles of which were inlaid with ivory and silver, and the upper part enclosed in rose-coloured silk curtains.

"What is inside that cage?" asked he of the old priest, as the negroes stood wiping the perspiration from their foreheads, and a smart slave-girl stepped forward, with a parasol and slippers in her hand, and reverently lifted the lower edge of the curtain.

"A saint, I tell you!"

An embroidered shoe, with a large gold cross on the instep, was put forth delicately from beneath the curtain, and the kneeling maid put on the slipper over it.

"There!" whispered the old grumbler. "Not enough, you see, to use Christian men as beasts of burden — Abbot Isidore used to say — ay, and told Iron, the pleader, to his face, that he could not conceive how a man who loved Christ, and knew the grace which has made all men free, could keep a slave."

"Nor can I," said Philammon.

"But we think otherwise, you see, in Alexandria here. We can't even walk up the steps of God's temple without an additional protection to our delicate feet."

"I had thought it was written, 'Put off thy shoes from off thy feet, for the place where thou standest is holy ground.' "

"Ah! there are a good many more things written which we do not find it convenient to recollect ——— Look! There is one of the pillars of the church — the richest and most pious lady in Alexandria."

And forth stepped a figure, at which Philammon's eyes opened wider than they had done even at the sight of Pelagia. Whatever thoughts the rich and careless grace of her attire might have raised in his mind, it had certainly not given his innate Greek good taste the inclination to laugh and weep at once, which he felt at this specimen of the tasteless fashion of an artificial and decaying civilization. Her gown was stuffed out behind in a fashion which provoked from the dirty boys who lay about the steps, gambling for pistachios on their fingers, the same comments with which St. Clement had upbraided from the pulpit the Alexandrian ladies of his day. The said gown of white silk was bedizened, from waist to ankle, with certain mysterious red and green figures at least a foot long, which Philammon gradually discovered to be a representation, in the very lowest and ugliest style of fallen art, of Dives and Lazarus; while down her back hung, upon a bright blue shawl, edged with embroidered crosses, Job sitting, potsherd in hand, surrounded by his three friends — a memorial, the old priest whispered, of a pilgrimage which she had taken a year or two before, to Arabia, to see and kiss the identical dunghill on which the patriarch had sat.

Round her neck hung, by one of half-a-dozen necklaces, a manuscript of the Gospels, gilt-edged and clasped with jewels;

the lofty diadem of pearls on the head carried in front a large gold cross; while above and around it her hair, stiffened with pomatum, was frizzled out half a foot from the wilderness of plaits and curls, which must have cost some hapless slave-girl an hour's work, and perhaps j more than one scolding, that very morning.

Meekly, with simpering face and downcast eyes, and now; and then a penitent sigh and shake of the head and pressure of her hand on her jewelled bosom, the fair penitent was proceeding up the steps, when she caught sight of the! priest and the monk, and turning to them, with an obeisance of the deepest humility, entreated to be allowed to kiss the hem of their garments.

"You had far better, madam," said Philammon, bluntly enough, "kiss the hem of your own. You carry two lessons there which you do not seem to have learnt yet."

In an instant her face flashed up into pride and fury. "I asked for your blessing, and not for a sermon. I can have that when I like."

"And such as you like," grumbled the old priest, as she swept up the steps, tossing some small coin to the ragged boys, and murmuring to herself, loud enough for Philammon's hearing, that she should certainly inform the confessor, and that she would not be insulted in the streets by savage monks.

"Now she will confess her sins inside — all but those which she has been showing off to us here outside, and beat her breast, and weep like a very Magdalen; and then the worthy man will comfort her with — 'What a beautiful chain! And what a shawl! — allow me to touch it! How soft and delicate this Indian wool! Ah! if you knew the debts which I have been compelled to incur in the service of the sanctuary! ———— ' And then of course the answer will be, as, indeed, he expects it should, that if it can be of the least use in the service of the Temple, she, of course, will think it only too great an honour..... And he will keep the chain, and perhaps the shawl, too. And she will go home, believing that she has fulfilled to the very letter the command to break off her sins by almsgiving, and only sorry that the good priest happened to hit on that particular gewgaw!"

"What," asked Philammon; "dare she actually not refuse such importunity?"

"From a poor priest like me, stoutly enough; but from a

popular ecclesiastic like him.... As Jerome says, in a letter of his I once saw, ladies think twice in such cases before they offend the city newsmonger. Have you anything more to say?"

Philammon had nothing to say; and wisely held his peace, while the old grumbler ran on —

"Ah, boy, you have yet to learn city fashions I When you are a little older, instead of speaking unpleasant truths to a fine lady with a cross on her forehead, you will be ready to run to the pillars of Hercules at her beck and nod, for the sake of her disinterested help toward a fashionable pulpit, or perhaps a bishopric. The ladies settle that for us here."

"The women?"

"The women, lad. Do you suppose that they heap priests and churches with wealth for nothing? They have their reward. Do you suppose that a preacher gets into the pulpit of that church there, without looking anxiously, at the end of each peculiarly flowery sentence, to see whether her saintship there is clapping or not? She, who has such a delicate sense for orthodoxy, that she can scent out Novatianism or Origenism where no other mortal nose would suspect it? She who meets at her own house weekly all the richest and most pious women of the city, to settle our discipline for us, as the court cooks do our doctrine? She who has even, it is whispered, the ear of the Augusta Pulcheria herself, and sends monthly letters to her at Constantinople, and might give the patriarch himself some trouble, if he crossed her holy will?"

"What! will Cyril truckle to such creatures?"

"Cyril is a wise man in his generation — too wise, some say, for a child of the light. But at least, he knows there is no use fighting with those whom you cannot conquer; and while he can get money out of these great ladies for his almshouses, and orphan-houses, and lodging-houses, and hospitals, and workshops, and all the rest of it — and in that, I will say for him, there is no man on earth equal to him, but Ambrose of Milan and Basil of Cæsarea — why, I don't quarrel with him for making the best of a bad matter; and a very bad matter it is, boy, and has been ever since emperors and courtiers have given up burning and crucifying us, and taking to patronizing and bribing us instead."

Philammon walked on in silence by the old priest's side, stunned and sickened..... "And this is what I have come out to see — reeds shaken in the wind, and men clothed;! in soft raiment, fit only for kings' palaces!" For this he had left the dear old Laura, and the simple joys and friendships of childhood, and cast himself into a roaring whirlpool of labour and temptation! This was the harmonious strength and unity of that Church Catholic, in which, as he had been taught from boyhood, there was but one Lord, one Faith, one Spirit. This was the indivisible body, "without spot or wrinkle, which fitly joined together and compacted by that which every member supplied, according to the effectual and proportionate working of every part, increased the body, and enabled it to build itself up in Love!" He shuddered as the well-known words passed through his memory, and seemed to mock the base and chaotic reality around him. He felt angry with the old man for having broken his dream; he longed to believe that his complaints were only exaggerations of cynic peevishness, of selfish disappointment: and yet, had hot Arsenius warned him? Had he not foretold, word for word, what the youth would find — what he had found? Then was Saint Paul's great idea an empty and an impossible dream? No! God's word could not fail; the Church could not err. The fault could not be in her, but in her enemies; not, as the old man said, in her too great prosperity, but in her slavery. And then the words which he had heard from Cyril at their first interview rose before him as the true explanation. How could the Church work freely and healthily while she was crushed and fettered by the rulers of this world? And how could they be anything but the tyrants and antichrists they were, while they were menaced and deluded by heathen philosophy, and vain systems of human wisdom? If Orestes was the curse of the Alexandrian Church, then Hypatia was the curse of Orestes. On her head the true blame lay. She was the root of the evil. Who would extirpate it?....

Why should not he? It might be dangerous: yet, successful or unsuccessful, it must be glorious. The cause of Christianity wanted great examples. Might he not — and his young heart beat high at the thought — might he not, by some great act of daring, self-sacrifice, divine madness of faith, like David's of old, when he went out against the giant — awaken selfish and luxurious souls to a noble emulation, and recall to their minds, perhaps to their lives, the patterns of those martyrs who were the pride, the glory, the heirloom of Egypt? And as figure after figure rose before his imagination, of simple men and weak women who had conquered temptation and shame, torture and death, to live for ever on the lips of men, and take their seats among the patricians of the heavenly court, with brows glittering through all eternities with the martyr's crown, his heart beat thick and fast, and he longed only for an opportunity to dare and die.

And the longing begot the opportunity. For he had hardly rejoined his brother visitors when the absorbing thought took word again, and he began questioning them eagerly for more information about Hypatia.

On that point, indeed, he obtained nothing but fresh invective; but when his companions, after talking of the triumph which the true faith had gained that morning, went on to speak of the great overthrow of Paganism twenty years before, under the patriarch Theophilus; of Olympiodorus and his mob, who held the Serapeium for many days by force of arms against the Christians, making sallies into the city, and torturing and murdering the prisoners whom they took; of the martyrs who, among those very pillars which overhung their heads, had died in torments rather than sacrifice to Serapis; and of the final victory, and the soldier who, in presence of the trembling mob, clove the great jaw of the colossal idol, and snapped for ever the spell of heathenism, Philammon's heart burned to distinguish himself like that soldier, and to wipe out his qualms of conscience by some more unquestionable deed of Christian prowess. There were no idols now to break: but there was philosophy — "Why not carry war into the heart of the enemy's camp, and beard Satan in his very den? Why does not some man of God go boldly into the lecture-room of the sorceress, and testify against her to her face?"

"Do it yourself, if you dare," said Peter. "We have no wish to get our brains knocked out by all the profligate young gentlemen in the city."

"I will do it," said Philammon.

"That is, if his holiness allows you to make such a fool of yourself."

"Take care, sir, of your words. You revile the blessed martyrs, from St. Stephen to St. Telemachus, when you call such a deed foolishness."

"I shall most certainly inform his holiness of your insolence.''

"Do so," said Philammon, who, possessed with a new idea, wished for nothing-more. And there the matter dropped for the time.

* * * * * *

"The presumption of the young in this generation is growing insufferable," said Peter to his master that evening.

"So much the better. They put their elders on their mettle in the race of good works. But who has been presuming to-day?"

"That mad boy whom Pambo sent up from the deserts, dared to offer himself as champion of the faith against Hypatia. He actually proposed to go into her lecture-room and argue with her to her face. What think you of that for a specimen of youthful modesty, and self-distrust?"

Cyril was silent a while.

"What answer am I to have the honour of taking back? A month's relegation to Nitria on bread and water? You, I am sure, will not allow such things to go unpunished; indeed, if they do, there is an end to all authority and discipline."

Cyril was still silent; whilst Peter's brow clouded fast. At last he answered —

"The cause wants martyrs. Send the boy to me."

Peter went down with a shrug, and an expression of face which looked but too like envy, and ushered up the trembling youth, who dropped on his knees as soon as he entered.

"So you wish to go into the heathen woman's lecture-room and defy her? Have you courage for it?"

"God will give it me."

"You will be murdered by her pupils."

"I can defend myself," said Philammon, with a pardonable glance downward at his sinewy limbs. And if not: what death more glorious than martyrdom?"

Cyril smiled genially enough. "Promise me two things."

"Two thousand, if you will."

"Two are quite difficult enough to keep. Youth is rash in promises, and rasher in forgetting them. Promise me that, whatever happens, you will not strike the first blow."

"I do."

"Promise me again, that you will not argue with her."

"What then?"

"Contradict, denounce, defy. But give no reasons. If you do, you are lost. She is subtler than the serpent, skilled in all the tricks of logic, and you will become a laughingstock, and run away in shame. Promise me."

"I do."

"Then go."

"When?"

"The sooner the better. At what hour does the accursed woman lecture to-morrow, Peter?"

"We saw her going to the Museum at nine this morning."

"Then go at nine to-morrow. There is money for you."

"What is this for?" asked Philammon, fingering curiously the first coins which he ever had handled in his life.

"To pay for your entrance. To the philosopher none enters without money. Not so to the Church of God, open all day long to the beggar and the slave. If you convert her, well. And if not".... And he added to himself between his teeth, "And if not, well also — perhaps better."

"Ay!" said Peter, bitterly, as he ushered Philammon out. "Go up to Ramoth Gilead, and prosper, young fool! What evil spirit sent you here to feed the noble patriarch's only weakness?"

"What do you mean?" asked Philammon, as fiercely as he dare.

"The fancy that preachings, and protestations, and martyrdoms can drive out the Canaanites, who can only be got rid of with the sword of the Lord and of Gideon. His uncle Theophilus knew that well enough. If he had not, Olympiodorus might have been master of Alexandria, and incense burning before Serapis to this day. Ay, go, and let her convert you! Touch the accursed thing, like Achan, and see if you do not end by having it in your tent. Keep company with the daughters of Midian, and see if you do not join yourself to Baalpeor, and eat the offering's of the dead!"

And with this encouraging sentence, the two parted for the night.

CHAPTER VIII
THE EAST WIND

As Hypatia went forth the next morning, in all her glory, with a crowd of philosophers and philosophasters, students, and fine gentlemen, following her in reverend admiration across the street to her lecture-room, a ragged beggar-man, accompanied by a huge and villanous-looking dog, planted himself right before her, and extending a dirty hand, whined for an alms.

Hypatia, whose refined taste could never endure the sight, much less the contact, of anything squalid and degraded, recoiled a little, and bade the attendant slave get rid of the man, with a coin. Several of the younger gentlemen, however, considered themselves adepts in that noble art of "upsetting" then in vogue in the African universities, to which we all have reason enough to be thankful,. seeing that it drove Saint Augustine from Carthage to Rome; and they, in compliance with the usual fashion of tormenting any simple creature who came in their way by mystification and insult, commenced a series of personal witticisms, which the beggar bore stoically enough. The coin was offered him, but he blandly put aside the hand of the giver, and keeping his place on the pavement, seemed inclined to dispute Hypatia's further passage.

"What do you want? Send the wretch and his frightful dog away, gentlemen!" said the poor philosopher, in some trepidation.

"I know that dog," said one of them;" it is Aben-Ezra's. Where did you find it before it was lost, you rascal?"

"Where your mother found you when she palmed you off upon her goodman, my child — in the slave-market. Fair sibyl, have you already forgotten your humblest pupil, as these young dogs have, who are already trying to upset their master and instructor in the angelic science of bullying?"

And the beggar, lifting his broad straw hat, disclosed the features of Raphael Aben-Ezra. Hypatia recoiled with a shriek of surprise.

"Ah! you are astonished. At what, I pray?"

"To see you, sir, thus!"

"Why, then? You have been preaching to us all a long time the glory of abstraction from the allurements of sense. It augurs ill, surely, for your estimate either of your pupils, or of your own eloquence, if you are so struck with consternation because one of them has actually at last obeyed you."

"What is the meaning of this masquerade, most excellent sir?" asked Hypatia and a dozen voices beside.

"Ask Cyril. I am on my way to Italy, in the character of the New Diogenes, to look, like him, for a man. When I have found one, I shall feel great pleasure in returning to acquaint you with the amazing news. Farewell! I wished to look once more at a certain countenance, though I have turned, as you see, Cynic; and intend henceforth to attend no teacher but my dog, who will luckily charge no fees for instruction; if she did, I must go untaught, for my ancestral wealth made itself wings yesterday morning. You are aware, doubtless, of the Plebiscitum against the Jews, which was carried into effect under the auspices of a certain holy tribune of the people?"

"Infamous!"

"And dangerous, my dear lady. Success is inspiriting.... and Theon's house is quite as easily sacked as the Jew's quarter..... Beware."

"Come, come, Aben-Ezra," cried the young men; "you are far too good company for us to lose you for that rascally patriarch's fancy. We will make a subscription for you, eh? And you shall live with each of us, month and month about. We shall quite lose the trick of joking without you."

"Thank you, gentlemen. But really you have been my butts far too long for me to think of becoming yours. Madam, one word in private before I go."

Hypatia leant forward, and speaking in Syriac, whispered hurriedly, —

"Oh, stay, sir, I beseech you! You are the wisest of my pupils — perhaps my only true pupil..... My father will find some concealment for you from these wretches; and if you need money, remember, he is your debtor. We have never repaid you the gold which —— "

"Fairest Muse, that was but my entrance-fee to Parnassus. It is I who am in your debt; and I have brought my arrears, in the form of this opal ring. As for shelter near you," he went on, lowering his voice, and speaking like her, in Syriac — "Hypatia the Gentile is far too lovely for the peace of mind of Raphael the Jew." And he drew from his finger Miriam's ring, and offered it.

"Impossible!" said Hypatia, blushing scarlet; "I cannot accept it."

"I beseech you. It is the last earthly burden I have, except this snail's prison of flesh and blood. My dagger will open a crack through that when it becomes intolerable. But as I do not intend to leave my shell, if I can help it, except just when and how I choose; and as, if I take this ring with me, some of Heraclian's Circumcellions will assuredly knock my brains out for the sake of it — I must entreat."

"Never! Can you not sell the ring, and escape to Synesius? He will give you shelter."

"The hospitable hurricane! Shelter, yes; but rest, none. As soon pitch my tent in the crater of Ætna, Why, he will be trying day and night to convert me to that eclectic farrago of his, which he calls philosophic Christianity. Well, if you will not have the ring, it is soon disposed of. We Easterns know how to be magnificent, and vanish as the lords of the world ought."

And he turned to the philosophic crowd.

"Here, gentlemen of Alexandria! Does any gay youth wish to pay his debts once and for all? Behold the Rainbow of Solomon, an opal such as Alexandria never saw before, which would buy any one of you, and his Macedonian papa, and Macedonian mamma, and his Macedonian sisters, and horses, and parrots, and peacocks, twice over, In any slave-market in the world. Any gentleman who wishes to possess a jewel worth ten thousand gold pieces, will only need to pick it out of the gutter into which I throw it. Scramble for it, you young Phædrias and Pamphili! There are Laides and Thaides enough about, who will help you to spend it."

And raising the jewel on high, he was in the act of tossing it into the street, when his arm was seized from behind, and the ring snatched from his hand. He turned, fiercely enough, and saw behind him, her eyes flashing fury and contempt, old Miriam.

Bran sprung at the old woman's throat in an instant: but recoiled again before the glare of her eye. Raphael called the dog off, and turning quietly to the disappointed spectators —

"It is all right, my luckless friends. You must raise money

for yourselves, after all; which, since the departure of my nation, will be a somewhat more difficult matter than ever. The over-ruling destinies, whom, as you all know so well when you are getting tipsy, not even philosophers can resist, have restored the Rainbow of Solomon to its original possessor. Farewell, Queen of Philosophy! When I find the man, you shall hear of it. Mother, I am coming with you for a friendly word before we part, though," he went on laughing as the two walked away together, "it was a scurvy trick of you to balk one of The Nation of the exquisite pleasure of seeing those heathen dogs scrambling in the gutter for his bounty."

Hypatia went on to the Museum, utterly bewildered by this strange meeting, and its still stranger end. She took care, never-theless, to betray no sign of her deep interest till she found her-self alone in her little waiting-room adjoining the lecture-hall; and there, throwing herself into a chair, she sat and thought, till she found, to her surprise and anger, the tears trickling down her cheeks. Not that her bosom held one spark of affection for Raph-ael. If there had ever been any danger of that, the wily Jew had himself taken care to ward it off, by the sneering and frivolous tone with which he quashed every approach to deep feeling, ei-ther in himself or in others. As for his compliments to her beauty, she was far too much accustomed to such, to be either pleased or displeased by them. But she felt, as she said, that she had lost perhaps her only true pupil; and more — perhaps her only true master. For she saw clearly enough, that under that Si-lenus' mask was hidden a nature capable of — perhaps more than she dare think of. She had always felt him her superior in practical cunning; and that morning had proved to her what she had long suspected, that he was possibly also her superior in that moral earnestness and strength of will for which she looked in vain among the enervated Greeks who surrounded her. And even in those matters in which he professed himself her pupil, she had long been alternately delighted by finding that he alone, of all her school, seemed thoroughly and instinctively to comprehend her every word, and chilled by the disagreeable suspicion that he was only playing with her, and her mathematics and geometry, and metaphysic and dialectic, like a fencer practising with foils, while he reserved his real strength for some object more worthy of him. More than once some paradox or question of his had shaken her neatest systems into a thousand cracks, and opened up ugly depths of doubt, even on the most seemingly-palpable certainties; or some half-jesting allusion to those Hebrew Scriptures, the quantity and quality of his faith in which he would never confess, made her indignant at the notion that he considered himself in possession of a reserved ground of knowledge, deeper and surer than her own, in which he did not deign to allow her to share.

And yet she was irresistibly attracted to him. That deliberate and consistent luxury of his, from which she shrank, he had always boasted that he was able to put on and take off at will like a garment: and now he seemed to have proved his words; to be a worthy rival of the great stoics of old time. Could Zeno himself have asked more from frail humanity? Moreover, Raphael had been of infinite practical use to her. He worked out, unasked her mathematical problems; he looked out authorities, kept her pupils in order by his bitter tongue, and drew fresh students to her lectures by the attractions of his wit, his arguments, and last, but not least, his unrivalled cook and cellar. Above all, he acted the part of a fierce and valiant watch-dog on her behalf, against the knots of clownish and often brutal sophists, the wrecks of the old Cynic, Stoic, and Academic schools, who, with venom increasing, after the wont of parties, with their decrepitude, assailed the beautifully bespangled card-castle of Neo-Platonism, as an empty medley of all Greek philosophies with all Eastern superstitions. All such Philistines had as yet dreaded the pen and tongue of Raphael, even more than those of the chivalrous Bishop of Cyrene, though he certainly, to judge from certain of his letters, hated them as much as he could hate any human being; which was after all not very bitterly.

But the visits of Synesius were few and far between; the distance between Carthage and Alexandria, and the labour of his diocese, and, worse than all, the growing difference in purpose between him and his beautiful teacher, made his protection all but valueless. And now Aben-Ezra was gone too, and with him were gone a thousand plans and hopes. To have converted him at last to a philosophic faith in the old gods! To have made him her instrument for turning back the stream of human error!.... How often had that dream crossed her! And now, who would take his place? Athanasius? Synesius in his good-nature might dignify

him with the name of brother, but to her he was a powerless pedant, destined to die without having wrought any deliverance on
the earth, as indeed the event proved. Plutarch of Athens? He
was superannuated. Syrianus? A mere logician, twisting Aristotle to mean what she knew, and he ought to have known, Aristotle never meant. Her father? A man of triangles and conic
sections. How paltry they all looked by the side of the unfathomable Jew! — Spinners of charming cobwebs.... But would the
flies condescend to be caught in them! Builders of pretty
houses.... If people would but enter and live in them! Preachers
of superfine morality.... which their admiring pupils never
dreamt of practising. Without her, she well knew, philosophy
must die in Alexandria. And was it her wisdom — or other and
more earthly charms of hers — which enabled her to keep it
alive? Sickening thought! Oh, that she were ugly, only to test the
power of her doctrines!....

Ho! The odds were fearful enough already; she would be
glad of any help, however earthly and carnal. But was not the
work hopeless? What she wanted was men who could act while
she thought. And those were just the men whom she would find
nowhere but — she knew it too well — in the hated Christian
priesthood. And then that fearful Iphigenia sacrifice loomed in
the distance as inevitable. The only hope of philosophy was in
her despair!

* * * * * *

She dashed away the tears, and proudly entered the lecture-hall, and ascended the tribune like a goddess, amid the
shouts of her audience..... What did she care for them? Would
they do what she told them? She was half through her lecture
before she could recollect herself, and banish from her mind the
thought of Raphael. And at that point we will take the lecture up.

* * * * * *

"Truth! Where is truth but in the soul itself? Facts, objects,
are but phantoms matter-woven — ghosts of this earthly night, at
which the soul, sleeping here in the mire and clay of matter,
shudders and names its own vague tremors sense and perception.
Yet, even as our nightly dreams stir in us the suspicion of mysterious and immaterial presences, unfettered by the bonds of time
and space, so do these waking dreams which we call sight and
sound. They are divine messengers, whom Zeus, pitying his

children, even when he pent them in this prison-house of flesh, appointed to arouse in them dim recollections of that real world of souls whence they came. Awakened once to them; seeing, through the veil of sense and fact, the spiritual truth of which they are but the accidental garment, concealing the very thing which they make palpable, the philosopher may neglect the fact for the doctrine, the shell for the kernel, the body for the soul, of which it is but the symbol and the vehicle. What matter, then, to the philosopher whether these names of men, Hector or Priam, Helen or Achilles, were ever visible as phantoms of flesh and blood before the eyes of men? What matter whether they spoke or thought as he of Scios says they did? What matter, even, whether he himself ever had earthly life? The book is here — the word which men call his. Let the thoughts thereof have been at first whose they may, now they are mine. I have taken them to myself, and thought them to myself, and made them parts of my own soul. Nay, they were and ever will be parts of me; for they, even as the poet was, even as I am, are but a part of the universal soul. What matter, then, what myths grew up around those mighty thoughts of ancient seers? Let others try to reconcile the Cyclic fragments, or vindicate the Catalogue of ships. What has the philosopher lost, though the former were proved to be con-tradictory, and the latter interpolated? The thoughts are there, and ours. Let us open our hearts lovingly to receive them, from whence so ever they may have come. As in men, so in books, the soul is all with which our souls must deal; and the soul of the book is whatsoever beautiful, and true, and noble we can find in it. It matters not to us whether the poet was altogether conscious of the meanings which we can find in him. Consciously or un-consciously to him, the meanings must be there; for were they not there to be seen, how could we see them? There are those among the uninitiate vulgar — and those, too, who carry under the philosophic cloak hearts still uninitiate — who revile such interpretations as merely the sophistic and arbitrary sports of fancy. It lies with them to show what Homer meant, if our spiri-tual meaning's be absurd; to tell the world why Homer is admi-rable, if that for which we hold him up to admiration does not exist in him. Will they say that the honour which he has enjoyed for ages was inspired by that which seems to be his first and lit-eral meaning? And more, will they venture to impute that literal meaning to him? Can they suppose that the divine soul of Homer could degrade itself to write of actual and physical feastings, and nuptials, and dances, actual nightly thefts of horses, actual fidelity of dogs and swineherds, actual intermarriages between deities and men, or that it is this seeming vulgarity which has won for him from the wisest of every age the title of the father of poetry? Degrading thought! fit only for the coarse and sense-bound tribe who can appreciate nothing but what is palpable to sense and sight I As soon believe the Christian scriptures, when they tell us of a deity who has hands and feet, eyes and ears, who condescends to command the patterns of furniture and culinary utensils, and is made perfect by being born — disgusting thought I — as the son of a village maiden, and defiling himself with the wants and sorrows of the lowest slaves!"

"It is false! blasphemous! The Scriptures cannot lie!" cried a voice from the further end of the room.

It was Philammon's. He had been listening to the whole lecture, and yet not so much listening as watching, in bewilderment, the beauty of the speaker, the grace of her action, the melody of her voice, and last, but not least, the maze of her rhetoric, as it glittered before his mind's eye like a cobweb diamonded with dew. A sea of new thoughts and questions, if not of doubts, came rushing in at every sentence on his acute Greek intellect, all the more plentifully and irresistibly because his speculative faculty was as yet altogether waste and empty, undefended by any scientific culture from the inrushing flood. For the first time in his life he found himself face to face with the root-questions of all thought — "What am I, and where?" "What can I know?" And in the half-terrified struggle with them, he had all but forgotten the purpose for which he entered the lecture-hall. He felt that he must break the spell. Was she not a heathen and a false prophetess? Here was something tangible to attack; and half in indignation at the blasphemy, half in order to force himself into action, he had sprung up and spoken.

A yell arose. "Turn the monk out!" "Throw the rustic through the window!" cried a dozen young gentlemen. Several of the most valiant began to scramble over the benches up to him; and Philammon was congratulating himself on the near approach of a glorious martyrdom, when Hypatia's voice, calm and silvery, stifled the tumult in a moment.

"Let the youth listen, gentlemen. He is but a monk and a plebeian, and knows no better; he has been taught thus. Let him sit here quietly, and perhaps we may be able to teach him otherwise."

And without interrupting, even by a change of tone, the thread of her discourse, she continued —

"Listen, then, to a passage, from the sixth book of the 'Iliad,' in which last night I seemed to see glimpses of some mighty mystery. You know it well: yet I will read it to you; the very sound and pomp of that great verse may tune our souls to a fit key for the reception of lofty wisdom. For well said Abamnon the Teacher, that 'the soul consisted first of harmony and rhythm, and ere it gave itself to the body, had listened to the divine harmony. Therefore it is that when, after having come into a body, it hears such melodies as most preserve the divine footstep of harmony, it embraces such, and recollects from them that divine harmony, and is impelled to it, and finds its home in it, and shares of it as much as it can share."

And therewith fell on Philammon's ear, for the first time, the mighty thunder-roll of Homer's verse: —

So spoke the stewardess: but Hector rushed
From the house, the same way back, down stately streets,
Through the broad city, to the Scaian gates,
Whereby he must go forth toward the plain,
There running toward him came Andromache,
His ample-dowered wife, Eetion's child —
Eetion the great-hearted, he who dwelt
In Thebé under Placos, and the woods
Of Places, ruling over Kilic men.
His daughter wedded Hector brazen-helmed,
And met him then; and with her came a maid,
Who bore in arms a playful-hearted babe,
An infant still, akin to some fair star,
Only and well-loved child of Hector's house,
Whom he had named Scamandrios, but the rest
Astyanax, because his sire alone
Upheld the weal of Ilion the holy.
He smiled in silence, looking on his child:
But she stood close to him, with many tears;
And hung upon his hand, and spoke, and called him.

"My hero, thy great heart will wear thee out;
Thou pitiest not thine infant child, nor me
The hapless, soon to be thy widow;
The Greeks will slay thee, falling one and all
Upon thee: but to me were sweeter far,
Having lost thee, to die; no cheer to me
Will come thenceforth, if thou shouldst meet thy fate;
Woes only: mother have I none, nor sire.
For that my sire divine Achilles slew,
And wasted utterly the pleasant homes
Of Kilic folk in Thebé lofty-walled,
And slew Eetion with the sword; yet spared
To strip the dead: awe kept his soul from that.
Therefore he burnt him in his graven arms,
And heaped a mound above him; and around
The damsels of the Ægis-holding Zeus,
The nymphs who haunt the upland, planted elms,
And seven brothers bred with me in the halls,
All in one day went down to Hades there;
For all of them swift-foot Achilles slew
Beside the lazy kine and snow-white sheep.
And her, my mother, who of late was queen
Beneath the woods of Placos, he brought here
Among his other spoils; yet set her free
Again, receiving ransom rich and great.
But Artemis, whose bow is all her joy,
Smote her to death within her father's halls.
Hector! so thou art father to me now,
Mother, and brother, and husband fair and strong!
Oh, come now, pity me, and stay thou here
Upon the tower, nor make thy child an orphan
And me thy wife a widow; range the men
Here by the fig-tree, where the city lies
Lowest, and where the wall can well be scaled;
For here three times the best have tried the assault
Round either Ajax, and Idomeneus,
And round the Atridai both, and Tydeus' son,
Whether some cunning seer taught them craft,
Or their own spirit stirred and drove them on."
    Then spake tall Hector, with the glancing helm:

"All this I too have watched, my wife; yet much
I hold in dread the scorn of Trojan men
And Trojan women with their trailing shawls,
If, like a coward, I should skulk from war.
Beside, I have no lust to stay; I have learnt
Aye to be bold, and lead the van of fight,
To win my father, and myself, a name.
For well I know, at heart and in my thought,
The day will come when Ilios the holy
Shall lie in heaps, and Priam, and the folk
Of ashen-speared Priam, perish all.
But yet no woe to come to Trojan men,
Nor even to Hecabe, nor Priam king,
Nor to my brothers, who shall roll in dust,
Many and fair, beneath the strokes of foes,
So moves me, as doth thine, when thou shalt go
Weeping, led off by some brass-harnessed Greek,
Robbed of the daylight of thy liberty,
To weave in Argos at another's loom,
Or bear the water of Messeis home,
Or Hypereia, with unseemly toils,
While heavy doom constrains thee, and perchance
The folk may say, who see thy tears run down,
'This was the wife of Hector, best in fight
At Ilium, of horse-taming Trojan men.'
So will they say perchance; while unto thee
Now grief will come, for such a husband's loss,
Who might have warded off the day of thrall.
But may the soil be heaped above my corpse
Before I hear thy shriek and see thy shame!"
    He spoke, and stretched his arms to take the child:
But back the child upon his nurse's breast
Shrank crying, frightened at his father's looks,
Fearing the brass and crest of horse's hair
Which waved above the helmet terribly.
Then out that father dear and mother laughed,
And glorious Hector took the helmet off,
And laid it gleaming on the ground, and kissed
His darling child, and danced him in his arm;
And spoke in prayer to Zeus, and all the gods:

"Zeu, and ye other gods, oh grant that this
My child, like me, may grow the champion here
As good in strength, and rule with might in Troy.
That men may say, 'The boy is better far
Than was his sire,' when he returns from war,
Bearing a gory harness, having slain
A foeman, and his mother's heart rejoice."
Thus saying, on the hands of his dear wife
He laid the child; and she received him back
In fragrant bosom, smiling through her tears.[2]

" Such is the myth. Do you fancy that in it Homer meant
to hand down to the admiration of ages such earthly common-
places as a mother's brute affection, and the terrors of an infant?
Surely the deeper insight of the philosopher may be allowed,
without the reproach of fancifulness, to see in it the adumbration
of some deeper mystery!

"The elect soul, for instance — is not its name Astyanax,
king of the city; but the fact of its ethereal parentage, the leader
and lord of all around it, though it knows it not? A child as yet, it
lies upon the fragrant bosom of its mother Nature, the nurse and
yet the enemy of man — Andromache, as the poet well names
her, because she fights with that being, when grown to man's
estate, whom as a child she nourished. Fair is she, yet unwise;
pampering us, after the fashion of mothers, with weak indul-
gences; fearing to send us forth into the great realities of speculation, there to forget her in the pursuit of glory, she would have
us while away our prime within the harem, and play for ever
round her knees. And has not the elect soul a father, too, whom it
knows not? Hector, he who is without — unconfined, uncondi-
tioned by Nature, yet its husband? — the all-pervading, plastic
Soul, informing, organizing, whom men call Zeus the lawgiver,

---

[2] The above lines are not meant as a " translation," but as an
humble attempt to give the literal sense in some sort of metre. It would
be an act of arrogance even to aim at success where Pope and Chapman
failed. It is simply, I believe, impossible to render Homer into English
verse; because, for one reason among many, it is impossible to preserve
the pomp of sound, which invests with grandeur his most common
words. How can any skill represent the rhythm of Homeric Greek in a
language which — to take the first verse which comes to hand —
transforms "boos megaloio boeien," into " great ox's hide "?

Æther the fire, Osiris the lifegiver; whom here the poet has set forth as the defender of the mystic city, the defender of harmony, and order, and beauty throughout the universe? Apart sits his great father — Priam, the first of existences, father of many sons, the Absolute Reason; unseen, tremendous, immovable, in distant glory; yet himself amenable to that abysmal unity which Homer calls Fate, the source of all which is, yet in Itself Nothing, without predicate, unnameable.

"From It and for It the universal Soul thrills through the whole Creation, doing the behests of that Reason from which it overflowed, unwillingly, into the storm and crowd of material appearances; warring with the brute forces of gross matter, crushing all which is foul and dissonant to itself, and clasping to its bosom the beautiful, and all wherein it discovers its own reflex; impressing on it its signature, reproducing from it its own likeness, whether star, or dæmon, or soul of the elect: — and yet, as the poet hints in anthropomorphic language, haunted all the while by a sadness — weighed down amid all its labours by the sense of a fate — by the thought of that First One from whom the Soul is originally descended; from whom it, and its Father the Reason before it, parted themselves when they dared to think and act, and assert their own freewill.

"And in the meanwhile, alas! Hector, the father, fights around, while his children sleep and feed; and he is away in the wars, and they know him not — know not that they the individuals are but parts of him the universal. And yet at moments — oh! thrice blessed they whose celestial parentage has made such moments part of their appointed destiny — at moments flashes on the human child the intuition of the unutterable secret. In the spangled glory of the summer-night — in the roar of the Nile-flood, sweeping down fertility in every wave — in the awful depths of the temple-shrine — in the wild melodies of old Orphic singers, or before the images of those gods of whose perfect beauty the divine theosophists of Greece caught a fleeting shadow, and with the sudden might of artistic ecstasy smote it, as by an enchanter's wand, into an eternal sleep of snowy stone — in these there flashes on the inner eye a vision beautiful and terrible, of a force, an energy, a soul, an idea, one and yet million-fold, rushing through all created things, like the wind across a lyre, thrilling the strings into celestial harmony — one life-blood through the million veins of the universe, from one great unseen heart, whose thunderous pulses the mind hears far away, beating for ever in the abysmal solitude, beyond the heavens and the galaxies, beyond the spaces and the times, themselves but veins and runnels from its all-teeming sea.

"Happy, thrice happy! they who once have dared, even though breathless, blinded with tears of awful joy, struck down upon their knees in utter helplessness, as they feel themselves but dead leaves in the wind which sweeps the universe — happy they who have dared to gaze, if but for an instant, on the terror of that glorious pageant; who have not, like the young Astyanax, clung shrieking to the breast of mother Nature, scared by the heaven-wide flash of Hector's arms, and the glitter of his rainbow crest! Happy, thrice happy! even though their eyeballs, blasted by excess of light, wither to ashes in their sockets! — Were it not a noble end to have seen Zeus, and die like Semele, burnt up by his glory? Happy, thrice happy! though their mind reel from the divine intoxication, and the hogs of Circe call them henceforth madmen, and enthusiasts. Enthusiasts they are; for Deity is in them, and they in It. For the time, this burden of individuality vanishes, and recognizing themselves as portions of the universal Soul, they rise upward, through and beyond that Reason from whence the soul proceeds, to the fount of all — the ineffable and Supreme One — and seeing It, become by that act portions of Its essence. They speak no more, but It speaks in them, and their whole being, transmuted by that glorious sunlight into whose rays they have dared, like the eagle, to gaze without shrinking, becomes an harmonious vehicle for the words of Deity, and passive itself, utters the secrets of the immortal gods. What wonder if to the brute mass they seem as dreamers? Be it so..... Smile if you will. But ask me not to teach you things unspeakable, above all sciences, which the word-battle of dialectic, the discursive struggles of reason can never reach, but which must be seen only, and when seen confessed to be unspeakable. Hence, thou disputer of the Academy! — hence, thou sneering Cynic! — hence, thou sense-worshipping Stoic, who fanciest that the soul is to derive her knowledge from those material appearances which she herself creates!.... hence ——; and yet no; stay and sneer if you will. It is but a little time — a few days longer in this prison-house of our degradation, and each thing shall return to its own fountain; the blood-drop to the abysmal heart, and the water to the river, and the river to the shining sea; and the dewdrop which fell from heaven shall rise to heaven again, shaking off the dust-grains which weighed it down, thawed from the earth-frost which chained it here to herb and sward, upward and upward ever through stars and suns, through gods, and through the parents of the gods, purer and purer through successive lives, till it enters The Nothing, which is The All, and finds its home at last.".....

And the speaker stopped suddenly, her eyes glistening with tears, her whole figure trembling and dilating with rapture. She remained for a moment motionless, gazing earnestly at her audience, as if in hopes of exciting in them some kindred glow; and then recovering herself, added in a more tender tone, not quite unmixed with sadness —

"Go now, my pupils. Hypatia has no more for you today. Go now, and spare her at least — woman as she is after all — the shame of finding that she has given you too much, and lifted the veil of Isis before eyes which are not enough purified to behold the glory of the goddess. — Farewell!"

She ended: and Philammon, the moment that the spell of her voice was taken off him, sprung up, and hurried out through the corridor into the street.....

So beautiful! So calm and merciful to him! So enthusiastic towards all which was noble! Had not she too spoken of the unseen world, of the hope of immortality, of the conquest of the spirit over the flesh, just as a Christian might have done? Was the gulf between them so infinite? If so, why had her aspirations awakened echoes in his own heart — echoes too, just such as the prayers and lessons of the Laura used to awaken? If the fruit was so like, must not the root be like also?.... Could that be a counterfeit? That a minister of Satan in the robes of an angel of light? Light, at least, it was: purity, simplicity, courage, earnestness, tenderness, flashed out from eye, lip, gesture..... A heathen, who disbelieved?.... What was the meaning of it all?

But the finishing stroke yet remained which was to complete the utter confusion of his mind. For before he had gone fifty yards up the street, his little friend of the fruit-basket, whom he had not seen since he vanished under the feet of the mob, in the gateway of the theatre, clutched him by the arm, and burst forth, breathless with running, —

"The — gods — heap their favours — on those who — who least deserve them! Rash and insolent rustic! And this is the reward of thy madness!"

"Off with you!" said Philammon, who had no mind at the moment to renew his acquaintance with the little porter. But the guardian of parasols kept a firm hold on his sheepskin.

"Fool! Hypatia herself commands! Yes, you will see her, have speech with her! while I — I the illuminated — I the appreciating — I the obedient — I the adoring — who for these three years past have grovelled in the kennel, that the hem of her garment might touch the tip of my little finger — I — I — I — ——"

"What do you want, madman?"

"She calls for thee, insensate wretch! Theon sent me — breathless at once with running and with envy — Go! favourite of the unjust gods!"

"Who is Theon?"

"Her father, ignorant! He commands thee to be at her house — here — opposite — to-morrow at the third hour. Hear and obey! There! they are coming out of the Museum, and all the parasols will get wrong! Oh, miserable me!" And the poor little fellow rushed back again, while Philammon, at his wits' end between dread and longing, started off, and ran the whole way home to the Serapeium, regardless of carriages, elephants, and foot-passengers; and having been knocked down by a surly porter, and left a piece of his sheepskin between the teeth of a spiteful camel — neither of which insults he had time to resent — arrived at the archbishop's house, found Peter the Reader, and tremblingly begged an audience from Cyril.

CHAPTER IX
THE SNAPPING OF THE BOW

CYRIL heard Philammon's story and Hypatia's message with a quiet smile, and then dismissed the youth to an afternoon of labour in the city, commanding him to mention no word of what had happened, and to come to him that evening and receive his order, when he should have had time to think over the matter. So forth Philammon went with his companions, through lanes and alleys hideous with filth and poverty, compulsory idleness and native sin. Fearfully real and practical it all was; but he saw it all dimly, as in a dream. Before his eyes one face was shining; in his ears one silvery voice was ringing..... "He is a monk, and knows no better".... True! And how should he know better? How could he tell how much more there was to know, in that great new universe, in such a cranny whereof his life had till now been past? He had heard but one side already. What if there were two sides? Had he not a right — that is, was it not proper, fair, prudent, that he should hear both, and then judge?

Cyril had hardly, perhaps, done wisely for the youth in sending him out about the practical drudgery of benevolence, before deciding for him what was his duty with regard to Hypatia's invitation. He had not calculated on the new thoughts which were tormenting the young monk; perhaps they would have been unintelligible to him had he known of them. Cyril had been bred up under the most stern dogmatic training, in those vast monastic establishments, which had arisen amid the neighbouring saltpetre quarries of Nitria, where thousands toiled in voluntary poverty and starvation at vast bakeries, dyeries, brickfields, tailors' shops, carpenters' yards; and expended the profits of their labour, not on themselves, for they had need of nothing, but on churches, hospitals, and alms. Educated in that world of practical industrial production as well as of religious exercise, which by its proximity to the great city accustomed monks to that world which they despised; entangled from boyhood in the intrigues of his fierce and ambitious uncle Theophilus, Cyril had succeeded him in the patriarchate of Alexandria without having felt a doubt, and stood free to throw his fiery energy and clear practical intel-

lect into the cause of the Church without scruple, even, where
necessary, without pity. How could such a man sympathize with
the poor boy of twenty, suddenly dragged forth from the quiet
cavern-shadow of the Laura into the full blaze and roar of the
world's noonday? He, too, was cloister-bred. But the busy and
fanatic atmosphere of Nitria, where every nerve of soul and body
was kept on a life-long artificial strain, without rest, without
simplicity, without human affection, was utterly antipodal to the
government of the remote and needy, though no less industrious
commonwealths of Cœnobites, who dotted the lonely mountain-
glens, far up into the heart of the Nubian desert. In such a one
Philammon had received, from a venerable man, a mother's
sympathy as well as a father's care; and now he yearned for the
encouragement of a gentle voice, for the greeting of a kindly eye,
and was lonely and sick at heart..... And still Hypatia's voice
haunted his ears, like a strain of music, and would not die away.
That lofty enthusiasm, so sweet and modest in its grandeur, —
that tone of pity — in one so lovely it could not be called contempt — for the many; that delicious phantom of being an elect
spirit.... unlike the crowd..... "And am I altogether like the
crowd?" said Philammon to himself, as he staggered along under
the weight of a groaning fever-patient. "Can there be found no
fitter work for me than this, which any porter from the quay
might do as well? Am I not somewhat wasted on such toil as
this? Have I not an intellect, a taste, a reason? I could appreciate
what she said. — Why should not my faculties be educated?
Why am I only to be shut out from knowledge? There is a Christian Gnosis as well as a heathen one. What was permissible to
Clement" — he had nearly said to Origen, but checked himself
on the edge of heresy — "is surely lawful for me! Is not my very
craving for knowledge a sign that I am capable of it? Surely my
sphere is the study rather than the street!"

And then his fellow-labourers — he could not deny it to
himself — began to grow less venerable in his eyes. Let him try
as he might to forget the old priest's grumblings and detractions,
the fact was before him. The men were coarse, fierce, noisy.... so
different from her! Their talk seemed mere gossip — scandalous
too, and hard-judging, most of it; about that man's private ambition, and that woman's proud looks; and who had stayed for the
Eucharist the Sunday before, and who had gone out after the

sermon; and how the majority who did not stay could possibly dare to go, and how the minority who did not go could possibly dare to stay..... Endless suspicions, sneers, complaints.... what did they care for the eternal glories and the beatific vision? Their one test for all men and things, from the patriarch to the prefect, seemed to be — did he or it advance the cause of the Church? — which Philammon soon discovered to mean their own cause, their influence, their self-glorification. And the poor boy, as his faculty for fault-finding quickened under the influence of theirs, seemed to see under the humble stock-phrases in which they talked of their labours of love, and the future reward of their present humiliations, a deep and hardly-hidden pride, a faith in their own infallibility, a contemptuous impatience of every man, however venerable, who differed from their party on any, the slightest, matter. They spoke with sneers of Augustine's Latinizing tendencies, and with open execrations of Chrysostom, as the vilest and most impious of schismatics; and, for aught Philammon knew, they were right enough. But when they talked of wars and desolation past and impending, without a word of pity for the slain and ruined, as a just judgment of Heaven upon heretics and heathens; when they argued over the awful struggle for power which, as he gathered from their words, was even then pending between the Emperor and the Count of Africa, as if it contained but one question of interest to them — would Cyril, and they as his bodyguard, gain or lose power in Alexandria? and lastly, when at some mention of Orestes, and of Hypatia as his counsellor, they broke out into open imprecations of God's curse, and comforted themselves with the prospect of everlasting torment for both; he shuddered and asked himself involuntarily — were these the ministers of a Gospel? — were these the fruits of Christ's Spirit?.... And a whisper thrilled through the inmost depth of his soul — "Is there a Gospel? Is there a Spirit of Christ? Would not their fruits be different from these?"

Faint, and low, and distant, was that whisper, like the mutter of an earthquake miles below the soil. And yet, like the earthquake-roll, it had in that one moment jarred every belief, and hope, and memory of his being each a hair's-breadth from its place..... Only one hair's-breadth. But that was enough; his whole inward and outward world changed shape, and cracked at every joint. What if it were to fall in pieces? His brain reeled with the thought. He doubted his own identity. The very light of heaven had altered its hue. Was the firm ground on which he stood after all no solid reality, but a fragile shell which covered — what?

The nightmare vanished, and he breathed once more. What a strange dream! The sun and the exertion must have made him giddy. He would forget all about it.

Weary with labour, and still wearier with thought, he returned that evening, longing, and yet dreading, to be permitted to speak with Hypatia. He half hoped at moments that Cyril might think him too weak for it; and the next, all his pride and daring, not to say his faith and hope, spurred him on. Might he but face the terrible enchantress, and rebuke her to her face! And yet so lovely, so noble as she looked! Could he speak to her, except in tones of gentle warning, pity, counsel, entreaty? Might he not convert her — save her? Glorious thought I to win such a soul to the true cause! To be able to show, as the first fruits of his mission, the very champion of heathendom! It was worth while to have lived only to do that; and having done it, to die.

The archbishop's lodgings, when he entered them, were in a state of ferment even greater than usual. Groups of monks, priests, parabolani, and citizens rich and poor, were hanging about the courtyard, talking earnestly and angrily. A large party of monks fresh from Nitria, with ragged hair and beards, and the peculiar expression of countenance which fanatics of all creeds acquire, fierce and yet abject, self-conscious and yet ungoverned, silly and yet sly, with features coarsened and degraded by continual fasting and self-torture, prudishly shrouded from head to heel in their long ragged gowns, were gesticulating wildly and loudly, and calling on their more peaceable companions, in no measured terms, to revenge some insult offered to the Church.

"What is the matter?" asked Philammon of a quiet portly citizen, who stood looking up, with a most perplexed visage, at the windows of the patriarch's apartments.

"Don't ask me; I have nothing to do with it. Why does not his holiness come out and speak to them? Blessed Virgin, mother of God! that we were well through it all! —— "

"Coward!" bawled a monk in his ear. "These shopkeepers care for nothing but seeing their stalls safe. Rather than lose a day's custom, they would give the very churches to be plundered by the heathen!"

"We do not want them!" cried another. "We managed Dioscuros and his brother, and we can manage Orestes. What matter what answer he sends? The devil shall have his own!"

"They ought to have been back two hours ago; they are murdered by this time."

"He would not dare to touch the archdeacon!"

"He will dare anything. Cyril should never have sent them forth as lambs among wolves. What necessity was there for letting the prefect know that the Jews were gone? He would have found it out for himself fast enough, the next time he wanted to borrow money!"

"What is all this about, reverend sir?" asked Philammon of Peter the Reader, who made his appearance at that moment in the quadrangle, walking with great strides, like the soul of Agamemnon across the meads of Asphodel, and apparently beside himself with rage.

"Ah! you here? You may go to-morrow, young fool! The patriarch can't talk to you. Why should he? Some people have a great deal too much notice taken of them, in my opinion. Yes; you may go. If your head is not turned already, you may go and get it turned to-morrow. We shall see whether he who exalts himself is not abased, before all is over!" And he was striding away, when Philammon, at the risk of an explosion, stopped him.

"His holiness commanded me to see him, sir, before ——"

Peter turned on him in a fury. "Fool! will you dare to intrude your fantastical dreams on him at such a moment as this?"

"He commanded me to see him," said Philammon, with the true soldierlike discipline of a monk; "and see him I will, in spite of any man. I believe in my heart you wish to keep me from his counsels and his blessing."

Peter looked at him for a moment with a right wicked expression, and then, to the youth's astonishment, struck him full in the face, and yelled for help.

If the blow had been given by Pambo in the Laura a week before, Philammon would have borne it. But from that man, and coming unexpectedly as the finishing stroke to all his disappointment and disgust, it was intolerable; and in an instant Peter's long legs were sprawling on the pavement, while he bellowed like a bull for all the monks of Nitria.

A dozen lean brown hands were at Philammon's throat as Peter rose.

"Seize him! hold him!" half blubbered he. "The traitor! the heretic! He holds communion with heathens!"

"Down with him!" "Cast him out!" "Carry him to the archbishop!" while Philammon shook himself free, and Peter returned to the charge.

"I call all good Catholics to witness! He has beaten an ecclesiastic in the courts of the Lord's house even in the midst of thee, O Jerusalem! And he was in Hypatia's lecture-room this morning!"

A groan of pious horror rose. Philammon set his back against the wall.

"His holiness the patriarch sent me."

"He confesses, he confesses! He deluded the piety of the patriarch into letting him go, under colour of converting her; and even now he wants to intrude on the sacred presence of Cyril, burning only with carnal desire that he may meet the sorceress in her house to-morrow!''

"Scandal!" "Abomination in the holy place!" and a rush at the poor youth took place.

His blood was thoroughly up. The respectable part of the crowd, as usual in such cases, prudently retreated, and left him to the mercy of the monks, with an eye to their own reputation for orthodoxy, not to mention their personal safety; and he had to help himself as he could. He looked round for a weapon. There was none. The ring of monks were baying at him like hounds round a bear: and though he might have been a. match for any one of them singly, yet their sinewy limbs and determined faces warned him that against such odds the struggle would be desperate.

"Let me leave this court in safety! God knows whether I am an heretic; and to Him I commit my cause! The holy patriarch shall know of your iniquity. I will not trouble you; I give you leave to call me heretic, or heathen, if you will, if I cross this threshold till Cyril himself sends for me back to shame you."

And he turned, and forced his way to the gate, amid a yell of derision which brought every drop of blood in his body into his cheeks. Twice, as he went down the vaulted passage, a rush was made on him from behind, but the soberer of his persecutors checked it. Yet he could not leave them, young and hot-headed as he was, without one last word, and on the threshold he turned.

"You I who call yourselves the disciples of the Lord, and are more like the demoniacs who abode day and night in the tombs, crying and cutting themselves with stones ———"

In an instant they rushed upon him; and, luckily for him, rushed also into the arms of a party of ecclesiastics, who were hurrying inwards from the street, with faces of blank terror.

"He has refused!" shouted the foremost. "He declares war against the Church of God!"

"Oh, my friends," panted the archdeacon, "we are escaped like the bird out of the snare of the fowler. The tyrant kept us waiting two hours at his palace-gates, and then sent lictors out upon us, with rods and axes, telling us that they were the only message which he had for robbers and rioters."

"Back to the patriarch!" and the whole mob streamed in again, leaving Philammon alone in the street ——— and in the world.

Whither now?

He strode on in his wrath some hundred yards or more before he asked himself that question. And when he asked it, he found himself in no humour to answer it. He was adrift, and blown out of harbour upon a shoreless sea, in utter darkness; all heaven and earth were nothing to him. He was alone in the blindness of anger.

Gradually one fixed idea, as a light-tower, began to glimmer through the storm..... To see Hypatia, and convert her. He had the patriarch's leave for that. That must be right. That would justify him — bring him back, perhaps, in a triumph more glorious than any Cæsar's, leading captive, in the fetters of the Gospel, the Queen of Heathendom. Yes, there was that left, for which to live.

His passion cooled down gradually as he wandered on in the fading evening-light, up one street and down another, till he had utterly lost his way. What matter? He should find that lecture-room to-morrow at least. At last he found himself in a broad avenue, which he seemed to know. Was that the Sun-gate in the distance? He sauntered carelessly down it, and found himself at last on the great Esplanade, whither the little porter had taken him three days before. He was close then to the Museum, and to her house. Destiny had led him, unconsciously, towards the scene of his enterprise. It was a good omen; he would go thither at once. He might sleep upon her door-step as well as upon any other. Perhaps he might catch a glimpse of her going out or coming in, even at that late hour. It might be well to accustom himself to the sight of her. There would be the less chance of his being abashed tomorrow before these sorceress eyes. And moreover, to tell the truth, his self-dependence, and his self-will too, crushed, or rather laid to sleep, by the discipline of the Laura, had started into wild life, and gave him a mysterious pleasure, which he had not felt since he was a disobedient little boy, of doing what he chose, right or wrong, simply because he chose it. Such moments come to every free-willed creature. Happy are those who have not, like poor Philammon, been kept by a hotbed cultivation from knowing how to face them! But he had yet to learn, or rather his tutors had to learn, that the sure path toward willing obedience and manful self-restraint, lies not through slavery, but through liberty.

He was not certain which was Hypatia's house; but the door of the Museum he could not forget. So there he sat himself down under the garden-wall, soothed by the cool night, and the holy silence, and the rich perfume of the thousand foreign flowers which filled the air with enervating balm. There he sat, and watched, and watched, and watched in vain for some glimpse of his one object. Which of the houses was hers? Which was the window of her chamber? Did it look into the street? What business had his fancy with women's chambers?.... But that one open window, with the lamp burning bright inside — he could not help looking up to it — he could not help fancying — hoping. He even moved a few yards, to see better the bright interior of the room. High up as it was, he could still discern shelves of books — pictures on the walls. Was that a voice? Yes! a woman's voice — reading aloud in metre — was plainly distinguishable in the dead stillness of the night, which did not even awaken a whisper in the trees above his head. He stood, spellbound by curiosity.

Suddenly the voice ceased, and a woman's figure came forward to the window, and stood motionless, gazing upward at the spangled star-world overhead, and seeming to drink in the glory, and the silence, and the rich perfume..... Could it be she? Every pulse in his body throbbed madly..... Could it be? What was she doing? He could not distinguish the features; but the full blaze of the eastern moon showed him an upturned brow, between a golden stream of glittering tresses which hid her whole figure, except the white hands clasped upon her bosom..... Was she praying? were these her midnight sorceries?....

And still his heart throbbed and throbbed, till he almost fancied she must hear its noisy beat — and still she stood motionless, gazing upon the sky, like some exquisite chryselephantine statue, all ivory and gold. And behind her, round the bright room within, painting, books, a whole world of unknown science and beauty.... and she the priestess of it all.... inviting him to learn of her and be wise! It was a temptation! He would flee from it! — Fool that he was! — and it might not be she after all!

He made some sudden movement. She looked down, saw him, and, shutting the blind, vanished for the night. In vain, now that the temptation had departed, he sat and waited for its reappearance, half cursing himself for having broken the spell. But the chamber was dark and silent henceforth; and Philammon, wearied out, found himself soon wandering back to the Laura in quiet dreams, beneath the balmy semi-tropic night.

CHAPTER X
THE INTERVIEW

PHILAMMON was aroused from his slumbers at sunrise the next morning by the attendants who came in to sweep out the lecture-rooms, and wandered, disconsolately enough, up and down the street; longing for, and yet dreading, the three weary hours to be over which must pass before he would be admitted to Hypatia. But he had tasted no food since noon the day before: he had had but three hours' sleep the previous night, and had been working, running, and fighting for two whole days without a moment's peace of body or mind. Sick with hunger and fatigue, and aching from head to foot with his hard night's rest on the granite-flags, he felt as unable as man could well do to collect his thoughts or brace his nerves for the coming interview. How to get food he could not guess; but having two hands, he might at least earn a coin by carrying a load; so he went down to the Esplanade in search of work. Of that, alas! there was none. So he sat down upon the parapet of the quay, and watched the shoals of sardines which played in and out over the marble steps below, and wondered at the strange crabs and sea-locusts which crawled up and down the face of the masonry, a few feet below the surface, scrambling for bits of offal, and making occasional fruitless dashes at the nimble little silver arrows which played round them. And at last his whole soul, too tired to think of anything else, became absorbed in a mighty struggle between two great crabs, who held on stoutly, each by a claw, to his respective bunch of seaweed, while with the others they tugged, one at the head and the other at the tail of a dead fish. Which would conquer?.... Ay, which? And for five minutes Philammon was alone in the world with the two struggling heroes..... Might not they be emblematic? Might not the upper one typify Cyril? — the lower one Hypatia? — and the dead fish between, himself?.... But at last the dead-lock was suddenly ended — the fish parted in the middle: and the typical Hypatia and Cyril, losing hold of their respective seaweeds by the jerk, tumbled down, each with its half-fish, and vanished head over heels into the blue depths in so undignified a manner, that Philammon burst into a shout of laughter.

"What's the joke?" asked a well-known voice behind him; and a hand patted him familiarly on the back. He looked round, and saw the little porter, his head crowned with a full basket of figs, grapes, and water-melons, on which the poor youth cast a longing eye. "Well, my young friend, and why are you not at church? Look at all the saints pouring into the Cæsareum there, behind you."

Philammon answered sulkily enough something inarticulate.

"Ho, ho! Quarrelled with the successor of the Apostles already? Has my prophecy come true, and the strong meat of pious riot and plunder proved too highly spiced for your young palate. Eh?"

Poor Philammon! Angry with himself for feeling that the porter was right; shrinking from the notion of exposing the failings of his fellow-Christians; shrinking still more from making such a jackanapes his confidant: and yet yearning in his loneliness to open his heart to some one, he dropped out, hint by hint, word by word, the events of the past evening, and finished by a request to be put in the way of earning his breakfast.

"Earning your breakfast! Shall the favourite of the gods — shall the guest of Hypatia — earn his breakfast, while I have an obol to share with him? Base thought! Youth! I have wronged you. Unphilosophically I allowed, yesterday morning, envy to ruffle the ocean of my intellect. We are now friends and brothers, in hatred to the monastic tribe."

"I do not hate them, I tell you," said Philammon. "But these Nitrian savages —— "

"Are the perfect examples of monkery, and you hate them; and therefore, all greaters containing the less, you hate all less monastic monks — I have not heard logic lectures in vain. Now, up! The sea woos our dusty limbs; Nereids and Tritons charging no cruel coin, calls us to Nature's baths. At home a mighty sheatfish smokes upon the festive board; beer crowns the horn, and onions deck the dish: come then, my guest and brother!"

Philammon swallowed certain scruples about becoming the guest of a heathen, seeing that otherwise there seemed no chance of having anything else to swallow; and after a refreshing plunge in the sea, followed the hospitable little fellow to Hypatia's door, where he dropped his daily load of fruit, and then into a narrow by-street, to the ground-floor of a huge block of lodgings, with a common staircase, swarming with children, cats, and chickens; and was ushered by his host into a little room, where the savoury smell of broiling fish revived Philammon's heart.

"Judith! Judith! where lingerest thou? Marble of Pentelicus! foam-flake of the wine-dark main! lily of the Mareotic lake! You accursed black Andromeda, if you don't bring the breakfast this moment, I'll cut you in two!"

The inner door opened, and in bustled, trembling, her hands full of dishes, a tall lithe negress dressed in true negro fashion, in a snow-white cotton shift, a scarlet cotton petticoat, and a bright yellow turban of the same, making a light in that dark place which would have served as a landmark a mile off. She put the dishes down, and the porter majestically waved Philammon to a stool; while she retreated, and stood humbly waiting on her lord and master, who did not deign to introduce to his guest the black beauty which composed his whole seraglio..... But, indeed, such an act of courtesy would have been needless; for the first morsel of fish was hardly safe in poor Philammon's mouth, when the negress rushed upon him, caught him by the head, and covered him with rapturous kisses.

Up jumped the little man with a yell, brandishing a knife in one hand and a leek in the other; while Philammon, scarcely less scandalized, jumped up too, and shook himself free of the lady, who, finding it impossible to vent her feelings further on his head, instantly changed her tactics, and, wallowing on the floor, began frantically kissing his feet.

"What is this? Before my face! Up, shameless baggage, or thou diest the death!" and the porter pulled her up upon her knees.

"It is the monk! the young man I told you of, who saved me from the Jews the other night! What good angel sent him here that I might thank him?" cried the poor creature, while the tears ran down her black shining face.

"I am that good angel," said the porter, with a look of intense self-satisfaction. "Rise, daughter of Erebus; thou art pardoned, being but a female. What says the poet? —

> Woman is passion's slave, while rightful lord
> O'er her and passion, rules the nobler male.

Youth! to my arms! Truly say the philosophers, that the universe is magical in itself, and by mysterious sympathies links like to like. The prophetic instinct of thy future benefits towards me drew me to thee as by an invisible warp, hawser, or chain-cable, from the moment I beheld thee. Thou wert a kindred spirit, my brother, though thou knewest it not. Therefore I do not praise thee — no, nor thank thee in the least, though thou hast preserved for me the one palm which shadows my weary steps — the single lotus-flower (in this case black, not white) which blooms for me above the mud-stained ocean-wastes of the Hylic Borboros. That which thou hast done, thou hast done by instinct — by divine compulsion — thou couldst no more help it than thou canst help eating that fish, and art no more to be praised for it."

"Thank you," said Philammon.

"Comprehend me. Our theory in the schools for such cases is this — has been so at least for the last six months: similar particles, from one original source, exist in you and me. Similar causes produce similar effects; our attractions, antipathies, impulses, are therefore, in similar circumstances, absolutely the same; and therefore you did the other night exactly what I should have done in your case."

Philammon thought the latter part of the theory open to question, but he had by no means stopped eating when he rose, and his mouth was much too full of fish to argue.

"And therefore," continued the little man," we are to consider ourselves henceforth as one soul in two bodies. You may have the best of the corporeal part of the division.... yet it is the soul which makes the person. You may trust me, I shall not disdain my brotherhood. If any one insults you henceforth, you have but to call me; and if I be within hearing, why, by this right arm ——— "

And he attempted a pat on Philammon's head, which, as there was a head and shoulder's difference between them, might on the whole have been considered, from a theatric point of view, as a failure. Whereon the little man seized the calabash of beer, and filling therewith a cow's-horn, his thumb on the small end, raised it high in the air.

"To the Tenth Muse, and to your interview with her!"

And removing his thumb, he sent a steady jet into his open

mouth, and having drained the horn without drawing breath, licked his lips, handed it to Philammon, and flew ravenously upon the fish and onions.

Philammon, to whom the whole was supremely absurd, had no invocation to make, but one which he felt too sacred for his present temper of mind: so he attempted to imitate the little man's feat, and, of course, poured the beer into his eyes, and up his nose, and in his bosom, and finally choked himself black in the face, while his host observed, smilingly —

"Aha, rustic! unacquainted with the ancient and classical customs preserved in this centre of civilization by the descendants of Alexander's heroes? Judith! clear the table. Now to the sanctuary of the Muses!"

Philammon rose, and finished his meal by a monkish grace. A gentle and reverend "Amen" rose from the other end of the room. It was the negress. She saw him look up at her, dropped her eyes modestly, and bustled away with the remnants, while Philammon and his host started for Hypatia's lecture-room.

"Your wife is a Christian?" asked he when they were outside the door.

"Ahem —— ! The barbaric mind is prone to superstition. Yet she is, being but a woman and a negress, a good soul, and thrifty, though requiring, like all lower animals, occasional chastisement. I married her on philosophic grounds. A wife was necessary to me, for several reasons: but mindful that the philosopher should subjugate the material appetite, and rise above the swinish desires of the flesh, even when his nature requires him to satisfy them, I purposed to make pleasure as unpleasant as possible. I had the choice of several cripples — their parents, of ancient Macedonian family like myself, were by no means adverse; but I required a housekeeper, with whose duties the want of an arm or a leg might have interfered."

"Why did you not marry a scold?" asked Philammon.

"Pertinently observed: and indeed the example of Socrates rose luminous more than once before my imagination. But philosophic calm, my dear youth, and the peaceful contemplation of the ineffable? I could not relinquish those luxuries. So having, by the bounty of Hypatia and her pupils, saved a small sum, I went out, bought me a negress, and hired six rooms in the block we have just left, where I let lodgings to young students of the Divine Philosophy."

"Have you any lodgers now?"

"Ahem! Certain rooms are occupied by a lady of rank. The philosopher will, above all things, abstain from babbling. To bridle the tongue, is to ———— But there is a closet at your service; and for the hall of reception, which you have just left — are you not a kindred and fraternal spark? We can combine our meals, as our souls are already united."

Philammon thanked him heartily for the offer, though he shrank from accepting it; and in ten minutes more found himself at the door of the very house which he had been watching the night before. It was she, then, whom he had seen!.... He was handed over by a black porter to a smart slave-girl, who guided him up, through cloisters and corridors, to the large library, where five or six young men were sitting, busily engaged, under Theon's superintendence, in copying manuscripts and drawing geometric diagrams.

Philammon gazed curiously at these symbols of a science unknown to him, and wondered whether the day would ever come when he too would understand their mysteries; but his eyes fell again as he saw the youths staring at his ragged sheepskin and matted locks with undisguised contempt. He could hardly collect himself enough to obey the summons of the venerable old man, as he beckoned him silently out of the room, and led him, with the titters of the young students ringing in his ears, through the door by which he had entered, and along a gallery, till he stopped and knocked humbly at a door..... She must be within!.... Now!.... At last!.... His knees knocked together under him. His heart sank and sank into abysses! Poor wretch!.... He was half-minded once to escape and dash into the street.... but was it not his one hope, his one object?.... But why did not that old man speak? If he would have but said something.... If he would only have looked cross, contemptuous.... But with the same impressive gravity as of a man upon a business in which he had no voice, and wished it to be understood that he had none, the old man silently opened the door, and Philammon followed..... There she was! looking more glorious than ever; more than when glowing with the enthusiasm of her own eloquence; more than when transfigured last night in golden tresses and glittering moonbeams. There she sat, without moving a finger, as the two entered. She greeted her father with a smile, which made up for all her seeming want of courtesy to him, and then fixed her large grey eyes full on Philammon.

"Here is the youth, my daughter. It was your wish, you know; and I always believe that you know best ——— "

Another smile put an end to the speech, and the old man retreated humbly toward another door, with a somewhat anxious visage, and then lingering and looking back, his hand upon the latch,

"If you require any one, you know, you have only to call — we shall be all in the library."

Another smile; and the old man disappeared, leaving the two alone.

Philammon stood trembling, choking, his eyes fixed on the floor. Where were all the fine things he had conned over for the occasion? He dared not look up at that face, lest it should drive them out of his head. And yet the more he kept his eyes turned from the face, the more he was conscious of it, conscious that it was watching him; and the more all the fine words were, by that very knowledge, driven out of his head..... When would she speak? Perhaps she wished him to speak first. It was her duty to begin; for she had sent for him..... But still she kept silence, and sat scanning him intently from head to foot, herself as motionless as a statue; her hands folded together before her, over the manuscript which lay upon her knee. If there was a blush on her cheek at her own daring, his eyes swam too much to notice it.

When would the intolerable suspense end? She was, perhaps, as unwilling to speak as he. But some one must strike the first blow; and, as often happens, the weaker party, impelled by sheer fear, struck it, and broke the silence in a tone half indignant, half apologetic —

"You sent for me hither!"

"I did. It seemed to me, as I watched you during my lecture, both "before and after you were rude enough to interrupt me, that your offence was one of mere youthful ignorance. It seemed to me that your countenance bespoke a nobler nature than that which the gods are usually pleased to bestow upon monks. That I may now ascertain whether or not my surmises were correct, I ask you for what purpose are you come hither?"

Philammon hailed the question as a godsend. — Now for his message! And yet he faltered, as he answered, with a desperate effort, — "To rebuke you for your sins."

"My sins? What sins?" she asked, as she looked up with a stately, slow surprise in those large grey eyes, before which his own glance sank abashed, he knew not why. What sins? — He knew not. Did she look like a Messalina? But was she not a heathen and a sorceress? — And yet he blushed, and stammered, and hung down his head, as, shrinking at the sound of his own words, he replied —

"The foul sorceries — and profligacy worse than sorceries, in which, they say ——— " He could get no farther: for he looked up again and saw an awful quiet smile upon that face. His words had raised no blush upon the marble cheek.

"They say! The bigots and slanderers; wild beasts of the desert, and fanatic intriguers, who, in the words of Him they call their master, compass heaven and earth to make one proselyte, and when they have found him, make him twofold more the child of hell than themselves. Go — I forgive you: you are young, and know not yet the mystery of the world. Science will teach you some day that the outward frame is the sacrament of the soul's inward beauty. Such a soul I had fancied your face expressed; but I was mistaken. Foul hearts alone harbour such foul suspicions, and fancy others to be what they know they might become themselves. Go! Do I look like ———? The very tapering of these fingers, if you could read their symbolism, would give your dream the lie." And she flashed full on him, like sun-rays from a mirror, the full radiance of her glorious countenance.

Alas, poor Philammon! where were thy eloquent arguments, thy orthodox theories then? Proudly he struggled with his own man's heart of flesh, and tried to turn his eyes away; the magnet might as well struggle to escape from the spell of the north. In a moment, he knew not how, utter shame, remorse, longing for forgiveness, swept over him, and crushed him down; and he found himself on his knees before her, in abject and broken syllables entreating pardon.

"Go — I forgive you. But know before you go, that the celestial milk which fell from Here's bosom, bleaching the plant which it touched to everlasting whiteness, was not more taintless than the soul of Theon's daughter."

He looked up in her face as he knelt before her. Unerring instinct told him that her words were true. He was a monk, accustomed to believe animal sin to be the deadliest and worst of all sins — indeed, "the great offence" itself, beside which all others were comparatively venial: where there was physical purity, must not all other virtues follow in its wake? All other failings were invisible under the dazzling veil of that great loveliness: and in his self-abasement he went on —

"Oh, do not spurn me! — do not drive me away! I have neither friend, home, nor teacher. I fled last night from the men of my own faith, maddened by bitter insult and injustice — disappointed and disgusted with their ferocity, narrowness, ignorance. I dare not, I cannot, I will not return to the obscurity and the dulness of a Thebaid Laura. I have a thousand doubts to solve, a thousand questions to ask, about that great ancient world of which I know nothing — of whose mysteries, they say, you alone possess the key! I am a Christian; but I thirst for knowledge..... I do not promise to believe you — I do not promise to obey you; but let me hear! Teach me what you know, that I may compare it with what I know..... If indeed" (and he shuddered as he spoke the words) "I do know anything!"

"Have you forgotten the epithets which you used to me just now!"

"No, no! But do you forget them; they were put into my mouth. I — I did not believe them when I said them. It was agony to me; but I did it, as I thought, for your sake — to save you. Oh, say that I may come and hear you again! Only from a distance — in the very farthest corner of your lecture-room. I will be silent; you shall never see me. But your words yesterday awoke in me — no, not doubts; but still I must, I must hear more, or be as miserable and homeless inwardly as I am in my outward circumstances!" And he looked up imploringly for consent.

"Rise. This passion and that attitude are fitting neither for you nor me."

And as Philammon rose, she rose also, went into the library to her father, and in a few minutes returned with him.

"Come with me, young man," said he, laying his hand kindly enough on Philammon's shoulder..... "The rest of this matter you and I can settle;" and Philammon followed him, not daring to look back at Hypatia, while the whole room swam before his eyes.

"So, so I hear you have been saying rude things to my daughter. Well, she has forgiven you ———— "

"Has she?" asked the young monk, with an eager start.

"Ah! you may well look astonished. But I forgive you too. It is lucky for you, however, that I did not hear you, or else, old man as I am, I can't say what I might not have done. Ah! you little know, you little know what she is!" — and the old pedant's eyes kindled with loving pride. "May the gods give you some day such a daughter! — that is, if you learn to deserve it — as virtuous as she is wise, as wise as she is beautiful. Truly, they have repaid me for my labours in their service. Look, young man! little as you merit it, here is a pledge of your forgiveness, such as the richest and noblest in Alexandria are glad to purchase with many an ounce of gold — a ticket of free admission to all her lectures henceforth! Now go; you have been favoured beyond your deserts, and should learn that the philosopher can practise what the Christian only preaches, and return good for evil." And he put into Philammon's hand a slip of paper, and bid one of the secretaries show him to the outer door.

The youths looked up at him from their writing as he passed, with faces of surprise and awe, and evidently thinking no more about the absurdity of his sheepskin and his tanned complexion; and he went out with a stunned, confused feeling, as of one who, by a desperate leap, has plunged into a new world. He tried to feel content; but he dare not. All before him was anxiety, uncertainty. He had cut himself adrift; he was on the great stream. Whither would it lead him? Well — was it not the great stream? Had not all mankind, for all the ages, been floating on it? Or, was it but a desert-river, dwindling away beneath the fiery sun, destined to lose itself a few miles on, among the arid sands? Were Arsenius and the faith of his childhood right? And was the Old World coming speedily to its death-throe, and the Kingdom of God at hand? Or, was Cyril right, and the Church Catholic appointed to spread, and conquer, and destroy, and rebuild, till the kingdoms of this world had become the kingdoms of God and of His Christ? If so, what use in this old knowledge which he craved? And yet, if the day of the destruction of all things were at hand, and the times destined to become worse and not better, till the end — how could that be?....

"What news?" asked the little porter, who had been waiting for him at the door all the while. "What news, O favourite of the gods!"

"I will lodge with you, and labour with you. Ask me no more at present. I am — I am ——— "

"Those who descended into the Cave of Trophonius, and beheld the unspeakable, remained astonished for three days, my young friend — and so will you!" And they went forth together to earn their bread.

But what is Hypatia doing all this while, upon that cloudy Olympus, where she sits enshrined far above the noise and struggle of man and his work-day world?

She is sitting again, with her manuscripts open before her: but she is thinking of the young monk, not of them.

"Beautiful as Antinous!.... Rather as the young Phœbus himself, fresh glowing from the slaughter of the Python. Why should not he, too, become a slayer of Pythons, and loathsome monsters, bred from the mud of tense and matter? So bold and earnest! I can forgive him those words for the very fact of his having dared, here in my father's house, to say them to me.... And yet so tender, so open to repentance and noble shame! — That is no plebeian by birth; patrician blood surely flows in those veins; it shows out in every attitude, every tone, every motion of the hand and lip. He cannot be one of the herd. Who ever knew one of them crave after knowledge for its own sake?.... And I have longed so for one real pupil! I have longed so to find one such man, among the effeminate selfish triflers who pretend to listen to me. I thought I had found one — and the moment that I had lost him, behold, I find another; and that a fresher, purer, simpler nature than ever Raphael's was at its best. By all the laws of physiognomy — by all the symbolism of gesture and voice and complexion — by the instinct of my own heart, that young monk might be the instrument, the ready, valiant, obedient instrument, for carrying out all my dreams. If I could but train him into a Longinus, I could dare to play the part of a Zenobia, with him as counsellor..... And for my Odenatus — Orestes! Horrible!"

She covered her face with her hand a minute. "No!" she said, dashing away the tears — "That — and anything — and everything for the cause of Philosophy and the gods!"

CHAPTER XI
THE LAURA AGAIN

NOT a sound, not a moving object, broke the utter stillness of the glen of Scetis. The shadows of the crags, though paling every moment before the spreading dawn, still shrouded all the gorge in gloom. A winding line of haze slept above the course of the rivulet. The plumes of the palm-trees hung motionless, as if awaiting in resignation the breathless blaze of the approaching day. At length, among the green ridges of the monastery garden, two grey figures rose from their knees, and began, with slow and feeble strokes, to break the silence by the clatter of their hoes among the pebbles.

"These beans grow wonderfully, brother Aufugus. We shall be able to sow our second crop, by God's blessing, a week earlier than we did last year."

The person addressed returned no answer; and his companion, after watching him for some time in silence, recommenced —

"What is it, my brother? I have remarked lately a melancholy about you, which is hardly fitting: for a man of God."

A deep sigh was the only answer. The speaker laid down his hoe, and placing his hand affectionately on the shoulder of Aufugus, asked again —

"What is it, my friend? I will not claim with you my abbot's right to know the secrets of your heart: but surely that breast hides nothing which is unworthy to be spoken to me, however unworthy I may be to hear it!"

"Why should I not be sad, Pambo, my friend? Does not Solomon say that there is a time for mourning?"

"True: but a time for mirth also."

"None to the penitent, burdened with the guilt of many

"Recollect what the blessed Anthony used to say — 'Trust not in thine own righteousness, and regret not that which is past.'"

"I do neither, Pambo."

"Do not be too sure of that. Is it not because thou art still trusting in thyself, that thou dost regret the past, which shows thee that thou art not that which thou wouldst gladly pride thyself on being?"

"Pambo, my friend," said Arsenius, solemnly, "I will tell thee all. My sins are not yet past; for Honorius, my pupil, still lives, and in him lives the weakness and the misery of Rome. My sins past? If they are, why do I see rising before me, night after night, that train of accusing spectres, ghosts of men slain in battle, widows and orphans, virgins of the Lord shrieking in the grasp of barbarians, who stand by my bedside and cry, 'Hadst thou done thy duty, we had not been thus! Where is that imperial charge which God committed to thee?' ".... And the old man hid his face in his hands, and wept bitterly.

Pambo laid his hand again tenderly on the weeper's shoulder.

"Is there no pride here, my brother? Who art thou, to change the fate of nations and the hearts of emperors, which are in the hand of the King of kings? If thou wert weak, and imperfect in thy work — for unfaithful, I will warrant thee, thou wert never — He put thee there, because thou wert imperfect, that so that which has come to pass might come to pass; and thou bearest thine own burden only — and yet not thou, but He who bore it for thee."

"Why then am I tormented by these nightly visions?"

"Fear them not, friend. They are spirits of evil, and therefore lying spirits. Were they good spirits, they would speak to thee only in pity, forgiveness, encouragement. But be they ghosts or demons, they must be evil, because they are accusers, like the Evil One himself, the accuser of the saints. He is the father of lies, and his children will be like himself. What said the blessed Anthony? That a monk should not busy his brain with painting spectres, or give himself up for lost; but rather be cheerful, as one who knows that he is redeemed, and in the hands of the Lord, where the Evil One has no power to hurt him. 'For,' he used to say, 'the demons behaved to us even as they find us. If they see us cast down and faithless, they terrify us still more, that they may plunge us in despair. But if they see us full of faith, and joyful in the Lord, with our souls filled with the glory which shall be, then they shrink abashed, and flee away in confusion.' Cheer up, friend! such thoughts are of the night, the hour of Satan and of the powers of darkness; and with the dawn they flee away."

"And yet things are revealed to men upon their beds, in visions of the night."

"Be it so. Nothing, at all events, has been revealed to thee upon thy bed, except that which thou knowest already far better than Satan does, namely, that thou art a sinner. But for me, my friend, though I doubt not that such things are, it is the day, and not the night, which brings revelations."

"How then?"

"Because by day I can see to read that book which is written, like the Law given on Sinai, upon tables of stone, by the finger of God himself."

Arsenius looked up at him inquiringly. Pambo smiled.

"Thou knowest that, like many holy men of old, I am no scholar, and knew not even the Greek tongue, till thou, out of thy brotherly kindness, taughtest it to me. But hast thou never heard what Anthony said to a certain Pagan who reproached him with his ignorance of books? 'Which is first,' he asked, 'spirit, or letter? — Spirit, sayest thou? Then know, the healthy spirit needs no letters. My book is the whole creation, lying open before me, wherein I can read, whensoever I please, the word of God.' "

"Dost thou not undervalue learning, my friend?"

"I am old among monks, and have seen much of their ways; and among them my simplicity seems to have seen this — many a man wearing himself with study, and tormenting his soul as to whether he believed rightly this doctrine and that, while he knew not with Solomon that in much learning is much sorrow, and that while he was puzzling at the letter of God's message, the spirit of it was going fast and faster out of him."

"And how didst thou know that of such a man?"

"By seeing him become a more and more learned theologian, and more and more zealous for the letter of orthodoxy; and yet less and less loving-and merciful — less and less full of trust in God, and of hopeful thoughts for himself and for his brethren, till he seemed to have darkened his whole soul with disputations, which breed only strife, and to have forgotten utterly the message which is written in that book wherewith the blessed Anthony was content."

"Of what message dost thou speak?"

"Look," said the old abbot, stretching his hand toward the

Eastern desert, "and judge, like a wise man, for thyself!"

As he spoke, a long arrow of level light flashed down the gorge from crag to crag, awakening every crack and slab to vividness and life. The great crimson sun rose swiftly through the dim night-mist of the desert, and as he poured his glory down the glen, the haze rose in threads and plumes, and vanished, leaving the stream to sparkle round the rocks, like the living, twinkling eye of the whole scene. Swallows flashed by hundreds out of the cliffs, and began their air-dance for the day; the jerboa hopped stealthily homeward on his stilts from his stolen meal in the monastery garden; the brown sand-lizards underneath the stones opened one eyelid each, and having satisfied themselves that it was day, dragged their bloated bodies and whip-like tails out into the most burning patch of gravel which they could find, and nestling together as a further protection against cold, fell fast asleep again; the buzzard, who considered himself lord of the valley, awoke with a long querulous bark, and rising aloft in two or three vast rings, to stretch himself after his night's sleep, hung motionless, watching every lark which chirruped on the cliffs; while from the far-off Nile below, the awakening croak of pelicans, the clang of geese, the whistle of the godwit and curlew, came ringing up the windings of the glen; and last of all the voices of the monks rose chanting a morning hymn to some wild Eastern air; and a new day had begun in Scetis, like those which went before, and those which were to follow after, week after week, year after year, of toil and prayer as quiet as its sleep.

"What does that teach thee, Aufugus, my friend?"

Arsenius was silent.

"To me it teaches this: that God is light, and in Him is no darkness at all. That in His presence is life, and fulness of joy for evermore. That He is the giver, who delights in His own bounty; the lover, whose mercy is over all His works — and why not over thee, too, O thou of little faith? Look at those thousand birds — and without our Father not one of them shall fall to the ground: and art thou not of more value than many sparrows, thou for whom God sent His Son to die?.... Ah, my friend, we must look out and around to see what God is like. It is when we persist in turning our eyes inward, and prying curiously over our own imperfections, that we learn to make a God after our own image, and fancy that our own darkness and hardness of heart are the patterns of His light and love."

"Thou speakest rather as a philosopher than as a penitent Catholic. For me, I feel that I want to look more, and not less, inward. Deeper self-examination, completer abstraction, than I can attain even here, are what I crave for. I long — forgive me, my friend — but I long more and more, daily, for the solitary life. This earth is accursed by man's sin: the less we see of it, it seems to me, the better."

"I may speak as a philosopher, or as a heathen, for aught I know: yet it seems to me that, as they say, the half loaf is better than none; that the wise man will make the best of what he has, and throw away no lesson because the book is somewhat torn and soiled. The earth teaches me thus far already. Shall I shut my eyes to those invisible things of God which are clearly manifested by the things which are made, because some day they will be more clearly manifested than now? But as for more abstraction, are we so worldly here in Scetis?"

"Nay, my friend, each man has surely his vocation, and for each some peculiar method of life is more edifying-than another. In my case, the habits of mind which I acquired in the world will cling to me in spite of myself even here. I cannot help watching the doings of others, studying their characters, planning and plotting for them, trying to prognosticate their future fate. Not a word, not a gesture of this our little family, but turns away my mind from the one thing needful."

"And do you fancy that the anchorite in his cell has fewer distractions?"

"What can he have but the supply of the mere necessary wants of life? and them, even, he may abridge to the gathering of a few roots and herbs. Men have lived like the beasts already, that they might at the same time live like the angels — and why should not I also?"

"And thou art the wise man of the world — the student of the hearts of others — the anatomizer of thine own? Hast thou not found out that, besides a craving stomach, man carries with him a corrupt heart? Many a man I have seen who, in his haste to fly from the fiends without him, has forgotten to close the door of his heart against worse fiends who were ready to harbour within him. Many a monk, friend, changes his place, but not the anguish of his soul. I have known those who, driven to feed on their own thoughts in solitude, have desperately cast themselves from cliffs, or ripped up their own bodies, in the longing to escape from thoughts, from which one companion, one kindly voice, might have delivered them. I have known those, too, who have been so puffed up by those very penances which were meant to humble them, that they have despised all means of grace, as though they were already perfect, and refusing even the holy Eucharist, have lived in self-glorying dreams and visions suggested by the evil spirits. One such I knew, who, in the madness of his pride, refused to be counselled by any mortal man — saying that he would call no man master: and what befel him? He who used to pride himself on wandering a day's journey into the desert without food or drink, who boasted that he could sustain life for three months at a time only on wild herbs and the Blessed Bread, seized with an inward fire, fled from his cell back to the theatres, the circus, and the taverns, and ended his miserable days in desperate gluttony, holding all things to be but phantasms, denying his own existence, and that of God himself."

Arsenius shook his head.

"Be it so. But my case is different. I have yet more to confess, my friend. Day by day I am more and more haunted by the remembrance of that world from which I fled. I know that if I returned I should feel no pleasure in those pomps, which, even while I battened on them, I despised. Can I hear any more the voice of singing men and singing women; or discern any longer what I eat or what I drink? And yet — the palaces of those seven hills, their statesmen and their generals, their intrigues, their falls, and their triumphs — for they might rise and conquer yet! — for no moment are they out of my imagination, — no moment in which they are not tempting me back to them, like a moth to the candle which has already scorched him, with a dreadful spell, which I must at last obey, wretch that I am, against my own will, or break by fleeing into some outer desert, from whence return will be impossible!"

Pambo smiled.

"Again I say, this is the worldly-wise man, the searcher of hearts! And he would fain flee from the little Laura, which does turn his thoughts at times from such vain dreams, to a solitude where he will be utterly unable to escape those dreams. Well, friend! — and what if thou art troubled at times by anxieties and schemes for this brother and for that? Better to be anxious for others than only for thyself. Better to have something to love — even something to weep over — than to become in some lonely cavern thine own world, — perhaps, as more than one whom I have known, thine own God."

"Do you know what you are saying?" asked Arsenius, in a startled tone.

"I say, that by fleeing into solitude a man cuts himself off from all which makes a Christian man; from law, obedience, fellow-help, self-sacrifice — from the communion of saints itself."

"How then?"

"How canst thou hold communion with those toward whom thou canst show no love? And how canst thou show thy love but by works of love?"

"I can, at least, pray day and night for all mankind. Has that no place — or rather, has it not the mightiest place — in the communion of saints?"

"He who cannot pray for his brothers whom he does see, and whose sins and temptations he knows, will pray but dully, my friend Aufugus, for his brothers whom he does not see, or for anything else. And he who will not labour for his brothers, the same will soon cease to pray for them, or love them either. And then, what is written? 'If a man love not his brother whom he hath seen, how will he love God whom he hath not seen?' "

"Again, I say, do you know whither your argument leads?"

"I am a plain man, and know nothing about arguments. If a thing be true, let it lead where it will, for it leads where God wills."

"But at this rate, it were better for a man to take a wife, and have children, and mix himself up in all the turmoil of carnal affections, in order to have as many as possible to love, and fear for, and work for."

Pambo was silent for a while.

"I am a monk, and no logician. But this I say, that thou leavest not the Laura for the desert with my good will. I would rather, had I my wish, see thy wisdom installed somewhere nearer the metropolis — at Troë or Canopus, for example — where thou mightest be at hand to fight the Lord's battles. Why wert thou taught worldly wisdom, but to use it for the good of the Church? It is enough. Let us go."

And the two old men walked homeward across the valley, little guessing the practical answer which was ready for their argument, in Abbot Pambo's cell, in the shape of a tall and grim ecclesiastic, who was busily satisfying his hunger with dates and millet, and by no means refusing the palm-wine, the sole delicacy of the monastery, which had been brought forth only in honour of a guest.

The stately and courteous hospitality of Eastern manners, as well as the self-restraining kindliness of monastic Christianity, forbade the abbot to interrupt the stranger; and it was not till he had finished a hearty meal that Pambo asked his name and errand.

" My unworthiness is called Peter the Reader. I come from Cyril, with letters and messages to the brother Aufugus."

Pambo rose, and bowed reverentially.

"We have heard your good report, sir, as of one zealously affected in the cause of the Church Catholic. Will it please you to follow us to the cell of Aufugus?"

Peter stalked after them with a sufficiently important air to the little hut, and there taking from his bosom Cyril's epistle, handed it to Arsenius, who sat long, reading and re-reading with a clouded brow, while Pambo watched him with simple awe, not daring to interrupt by a question lucubrations which he considered of unfathomable depth.

"These are indeed the last days," said Arsenius, at length, "spoken of by the prophet, when many shall run to and fro. So Heraclian has actually sailed for Italy?"

"His armament was met on the high seas by Alexandrian merchantmen, three weeks ago."

"And Orestes hardens his heart more and more?"

"Ay, Pharaoh that he is; or rather, the heathen woman hardens it for him."

"I always feared that woman above all the schools of the heathen," said Arsenius." But the Count Heraclian, whom I always held for the wisest as well as the most righteous of men! Alas! — alas! what virtue will withstand, when ambition enters the heart!"

"Fearful, truly," said Peter, "is that same lust of power: but for him, I have never trusted him since he began to be indulgent to those Donatists."

"Too true. So does one sin beget another."

"And I consider that indulgence to sinners is the worst of all sins whatsoever."

"Not of all, surely, reverend sir?" said Pambo, humbly. But Peter, taking no notice of the interruption, went on to Arsenius —

"And now, what answer am I to bear back from your wisdom to his holiness?"

"Let me see — let me see. He might — It needs consideration — I ought to know more of the state of parties. He has, of course, communicated with the African bishops, and tried to unite them with him?"

"Two months ago. But the stiff-necked schismatics are still jealous of him, and hold aloof."

"Schismatics is too harsh a term, my friend. But has he sent to Constantinople?"

"He needs a messenger accustomed to courts. It was possible, he thought, that your experience might undertake the mission."

"Me? Who am I? Alas! alas! fresh temptation daily! Let him send by the hand of whom he will..... And yet — were I — at least in Alexandria — I might advise from day to day..... I should certainly see my way clearer..... And unforeseen chances might arise, too..... Pambo, my friend, thinkest thou that it would be sinful to obey the Holy Patriarch?"

"Aha!" said Pambo, laughing, "and thou art he who was for fleeing into the desert an hour agone! And now, when once thou smellest the battle afar off, thou art pawing in the valley, like the old war-horse. Go, and God be with thee! Thou wilt be none the worse for it. Thou art too old to fall in love, too poor to buy a bishopric, and too righteous to have one given thee."

"Art thou in earnest?"

"What did I say to thee in the garden? Go, and see our son, and send me news of him."

"Ah! shame on my worldly-mindedness! I had forgotten all this time to inquire for him. How is the youth, reverend sir?"

"Whom do you mean?"

"Philammon, our spiritual son, whom we sent down to you

three months ago," said Pambo. "Risen to honour he is, by this time, I doubt not?"

"He? He is gone!"

"Gone?"

"Ay, the wretch, with the curse of Judas on him. He had not been with us three days before he beat me openly in the patriarch's court, cast off the Christian faith, and fled away to the heathen woman, Hypatia, of whom he is enamoured."

The two old men looked at each other with blank and horror-stricken faces.

"Enamoured of Hypatia?" said Arsenius, at last.

"It is impossible!" sobbed Pambo. "The boy must have been treated harshly, unjustly I Some one has wronged him, and he was accustomed only to kindness, and could not bear it. Cruel men that you are, and unfaithful stewards. The Lord will require the child's blood at your hands!"

"Ay," said Peter, rising fiercely, "that is the world's justice! Blame me, blame the patriarch, blame any and every one but the sinner. As if a hot head and a hotter heart were not enough to explain it all! As if a young fool had never before been bewitched by a fair face?"

"Oh, my friends, my friends," cried Arsenius, "why revile each other without cause? I, I only am to blame. I advised you, Pambo! — I sent him — I ought to have known — what was I doing, old worldling that I am, to thrust the poor innocent forth into the temptations of Babylon? This comes of all my schemings and my plot-tings! And now his blood will be on my head — as if I had not sins enough to bear already, I must go and add this over and above all, to sell my own Joseph, the son of my old age, to the Midianites! Here, I will go with you — now — at once — I will not rest till I find him, clasp his knees till he pities my grey hairs. Let Heraclian and Orestes go their way for aught I care — I will find him, I say. O Absalom, my son! would to God I had died for thee, my son! my son!"

CHAPTER XII
THE BOWER OF ACRASIA

THE house which Pelagia and the Amal had hired after their return to Alexandria, was one of the most splendid in the city. They had been now living there three months or more, and in that time Pelagia's taste had supplied the little which it needed to convert it into a paradise of lazy luxury. She herself was wealthy; and her Gothic guests, overburdened with Roman spoils, the very use of which they could not understand, freely allowed her and her nymphs to throw away for them the treasures which they had won in many a fearful fight. What matter? If they had enough to eat, and more than enough to drink, how could the useless surplus of their riches be better spent than in keeping their ladies in good humour?.... And when it was all gone.... they would go somewhere or other — who cared whither? — and win more. The whole world was before them waiting to be plundered, and they would fulfil their mission, whensoever it suited them. In the meantime they were in no hurry. Egypt furnished in profusion every sort of food which could gratify palates far more nice than theirs. And as for wine — few of them went to bed sober from one week's end to another. Could the souls of warriors have more, even in the halls of Valhalla?

So thought the party who occupied the inner court of the house, one blazing afternoon in the same week in which Cyril's messenger had so rudely broken in on the repose of the Scetis.

Their repose, at least, was still untouched. The great city roared without; Orestes plotted, and Cyril counter-plotted, and the fate of a continent hung — or seemed to hang — trembling in the balance; but the turmoil of it no more troubled those lazy Titans within, than did the roll and rattle of the carriage-wheels disturb the parakeets and sunbirds which peopled, under an awning of gilded wire, the inner court of Pelagia's house. Why should they fret themselves with it all? What was every fresh riot, execution, conspiracy, bankruptcy, but a sign — that the fruit was growing ripe for the plucking? Even Heraclian's rebellion, and Orestes' suspected conspiracy, were to the younger and coarser Goths a sort of child's play, at which they could look on and laugh, and bet, from morning to night; while to the more cunning heads, such as Wulf and Smid, they were but signs of the general rottenness — new cracks in those great walls over which they intended, with a simple and boyish consciousness of power, to mount to victory when they chose.

And in the meantime, till the right opening offered, what was there better than to eat, drink, and sleep? And certainly they had chosen a charming retreat in which to fulfil that lofty mission. Columns of purple and green porphyry, among which gleamed the white limbs of delicate statues, surrounded a basin of water, fed by a perpetual jet, which sprinkled with cool spray the leaves of the oranges and mimosas, mingling its murmurs with the warblings of the tropic birds which nestled among the branches.

On one side of the fountain, under the shade of a broad-leaved palmetto, lay the Amal's mighty limbs, stretched out on cushions, his yellow hair crowned with vine-leaves, his hand grasping a golden cup, which had been won from Indian Rajahs by Parthian Chosroos, from Chosroos by Roman generals, from Roman generals by the heroes of sheepskin and horsehide; while Pelagia, by the side of the sleepy Hercules-Dionysos, lay leaning over the brink of the fountain, lazily dipping her fingers into the water, and basking, like the gnats which hovered over its surface, in the mere pleasure of existence.

On the opposite brink of the basin, tended each by a dark-eyed Hebe, who filled the wine-cups, and helped now and then to empty them, lay the especial friends and companions in arms of the Amal, Goderic the son of Ermenric, and Agilmund the son of Cniva, who both, like the Amal, boasted a descent from gods; and last, but not least, that most important and all but sacred personage, Smid the son of Troll, reverenced for cunning beyond the sons of men; for not only could he make and mend all matters, from a pontoon bridge to a gold bracelet, shoe horses and doctor them, charm all diseases out of man and beast, carve runes, interpret war-omens, foretell weather, raise the winds, and, finally, conquer in the battle of mead-horns all except Wulf the son of Ovida; but he had actually, during a sojourn among the half-civilized Mæsogoths, picked up a fair share of Latin and Greek, and a rough knowledge of reading and writing.

A few yards off lay old Wulf upon his back, his knees in the air, his hands crossed behind his head, keeping up, even in his sleep, a half-conscious comment of growls on the following intellectual conversation: —

"Noble wine this, is it not?"

"Perfect. Who bought it for us?"

"Old Miriam bought it, at some great tax-farmer's sale. The fellow was bankrupt, and Miriam said she got it for the half what it was worth."

"Serve the penny-turning rascal right. The old vixen-fox took care, I'll warrant her, to get her profit out of the bargain."

"Never mind if she did. We can afford to pay like men, if we earn like men."

"We shan't afford it long, at this rate," growled Wulf.

"Then we'll go and earn more. I am tired of doing nothing."

"People need not do nothing, unless they choose," said Goderic. "Wulf and I had coursing fit for a king, the other morning, on the sand-hills. I had had no appetite for a week before, and I have been as sharp-set as a Danube pike ever since."

"Coursing? What, with those long-legged brush-tailed brutes, like a fox upon stilts, which the prefect cozened you into buying."

"All I can say is, that we put up a herd of those — what do they call them here — deer with goat's horns?"

"Antelopes?"

"That's it — and the curs ran into them as a falcon does into a skein of ducks. Wulf and I galloped and galloped over those accursed sand-heaps till the horses stuck fast; and when they got their wind again, we found each pair of dogs with a deer down between them — and what can man want more, if he cannot get fighting? You eat them, so you need not sneer."

"Well, dogs are the only things worth having, then, that this Alexandria does produce."

"Except fair ladies!" put in one of the girls.

"Of course. I'll except the women. But the men ——— "

"The what? I have not seen a man since I came here, except a dock-worker or two — priests and fine gentlemen they are all — and you don't call them men, surely?"

"What on earth do they do, beside riding donkeys?"

"Philosophize, they say."

"What's that?"

"I'm sure I don't know; some sort of slave's quill-driving, I suppose."

"Pelagia! do you know what philosophizing is?"

"No — and I don't care."

"I do," quoth Agilmund, with a look of superior wisdom; "I saw a philosopher the other day."

"And what sort of thing was it?"

"I'll tell you. I was walking down the great street, there, going to the harbour; and I saw a crowd of boys — men they call them here — going into a large doorway. So I asked one of them what was doing, and the fellow, instead of answering me, pointed at my legs, and set all the other monkeys laughing. So I boxed his ears, and he tumbled down."

"They all do so here, if you box their ears," said the Amal, meditatively, as if he had hit upon a great inductive law.

"Ah," said Pelagia, looking up with her most winning smile, "they are not such giants as you, who make a poor little woman feel like a gazelle in the lion's paw!"

" Well — it struck me that, as I spoke in Gothic, the boy might not have understood me, being a Greek. So I walked in at the door, to save questions, and see for myself. And there a fellow held out his hand — I suppose for money. So I gave him two or three gold pieces, and a box on the ear, at which he tumbled down of course, but seemed very well satisfied. So I walked in."

"And what did you see?"

"A great hall, large enough for a thousand heroes, full of these Egyptian rascals scribbling with pencils on tablets. And at the farther end of it the most beautiful woman I ever saw — with right fair hair and blue eyes, talking, talking — I could not understand it; but the donkey-riders seemed to think it very fine; for they went on looking first at her, and then at their tablets, gaping like frogs in drought. And, certainly, she looked as fair as the sun, and talked like an Alruna-wife. Not that I knew what it was about, but one can see somehow, you know. — So I fell asleep; and when I woke, and came out, I met some one who understood me, and he told me that it was the famous maiden, the great philosopher. And that's what I know about philosophy."

"She was very much wasted, then, on such soft-handed starvelings. Why don't she marry some hero?"

"Because there are none here to marry," said Pelagia; "except some who are fast netted, I fancy, already."

"But what do they talk about, and tell people to do, these philosophers, Pelagia?"

"Oh, they don't tell any one to do anything, — at least, if they do nobody ever does it, as far as I can see; but they talk about suns and stars, and right and wrong, and ghosts and spirits, and that sort of thing; and about not enjoying oneself too much. Not that I ever saw that they were any happier than any one else."

"She must have been an Alruna-maiden," said Wulf, half to himself.

"She is a very conceited creature, and I hate her," said Pelagia.

"I believe you," said Wulf.

"What is an Alruna-maiden?" asked one of the girls.

"Something as like you as a salmon is like a horse-leech. Heroes, will you hear a saga?"

"If it is a cool one," said Agilmund; "about ice, and pine-trees, and snow-storms. I shall be roasted brown in three days more."

"Oh," said the Amal, "that we were on the Alps again for only two hours, sliding down those snow-slopes on our shields, with the sleet whistling about our ears! That was sport!"

"To those who could keep their seat," said Goderic. "Who went head over heels into a glacier-crack, and was dug out of fifty feet of snow, and had to be put inside a fresh-killed horse before he could be brought to life?"

"Not you, surely," said Pelagia. "Oh, you wonderful creature! what things you have done and suffered!"

"Well," said the Amal, with a look of stolid self-satisfaction, "I suppose I have seen a good deal in my time, eh?"

"Yes, my Hercules, you have gone through your twelve labours, and saved your poor little Hesione after them all, when she was chained to the rock, for the ugly sea-monsters to eat; and she will cherish you, and keep you out of scrapes now, for her own sake;" and Pelagia threw her arms round the great bull-neck, and drew it down to her.

"Will you hear my saga," said Wulf, impatiently.

"Of course we will," said the Amal; "anything to pass the time."

"But let it be about snow," said Agilmund.

"Not about Alruna-wives?"

"About them, too," said Goderic; "my mother was one, so I must needs stand up for them."

"She was, boy. Do you be her son. Now hear, Wolves of the Goths!"

And the old man took up his little lute, or as he would probably have called it, "fidel," and began chanting, to his own accompaniment.

Over the camp fires
Drank I with heroes,
Under the Donau bank
Warm in the snow-trench,
Sagamen heard I there,
Men of the Longbeards,
Cunning and ancient,
Honey-sweet-voiced.
Scaring the wolf-cub,
Scaring the horn-owl out,
Shaking the snow-wreaths
Down from the pine boughs,
Up to the star-roof
Rang out their song.
Singing how Winil men
Over the icefloes
Sledging from Scanland on
Came unto Scoring;
Singing of Gambara
Freya's beloved.
Mother of Ayo,
Mother of Ibor.
Singing of Wendel men,
Ambri and Assi;
How to the Winilfolk
Went they with war-words —
"Few are ye, strangers,
And many are we;

Pay us now toll and fee,
Clothyarn, and rings, and beeves;
Else at the raven's meal
Bide the sharp bill's doom."

Clutching the dwarfs' work then,
Clutching the bullock's shell,
Girding grey iron on,
Forth fared the Winils all,
Fared the Alruna's sons,
Ayo and Ibor.
Mad of heart stalked they:
Loud wept the women all,
Loud the Alruna-wife;
Sore was their need.

Out of the morning land,
Over the snowdrifts,
Beautiful Freya came,
Tripping to Scoring.
White were the moorlands.
And frozen before her;
But green were the moorlands,
And blooming behind her,
Out of her golden locks
Shaking the spring flowers,
Out of her garments
Shaking the south wind,
Around in the birches
Awaking the throstles,
And making chaste housewives all
Long for their heroes home,
Loving and love-giving,
Came she to Scoring.
Came unto Gambara,
Wisest of Valas —
"Vala, why weepest thou?
Far in the wide-blue,
High up in the Elfin-home,
Heard I thy weeping."

" Stop not my weeping,
Till one can fight seven.
Sons have I, heroes tall,
First in the sword-play;
This day at the Wendels' hands
Eagles must tear them;
While their mothers, thrall-weary,
Must grind for the Wendels."

Wept the Alruna-wife;
Kissed her fair Freya —
"Far off in the morning land
High in Valhalla,
A window stands open,
Its sill is the snow-peaks,
Its posts are the water-spouts,
Storm-rack its lintel,
Gold cloud-flakes above it,
Are piled for the roofing.
Far up to the Elfin-home,
High in the wide-blue.
Smiles out each morning thence
Odin Allfather;
From under the cloud-eaves,
Smiles out on the heroes,
Smiles out on chaste housewives all,
Smiles on the brood-mares,
Smiles on the smith's work:
And theirs is the sword-luck,
With them is the glory,
So Odin hath sworn it —
Who first in the morning,
Shall meet him and greet him."

Still the Alruna wept —
" Who then shall greet him?
Women alone are here;
Far on the moorlands
Behind the war-lindens,

In vain for the bill's doom
Watch Winil heroes all.
One against seven."

Sweetly the Queen laughed —
" Hear thou my counsel now,
Take to thee cunning,
Beloved of Freya.
Take thou thy women-folk,
Maidens and wives:
Over your ankles
Lace on the white war-hose;
Over your bosoms
Link up the hard mailnets;
Over your lips
Plait long tresses with cunning; —
So war-beasts full-bearded
King Odin shall deem you,
When oft the grey sea-beach
At sunrise ye greet him."

Night's son was driving
His golden-haired horses up;
Over the Eastern firths
High flashed their manes.
Smiled from the cloud-eaves out
Allfather Odin,
Waiting the battle-sport:
Freya stood by him.
" Who are these heroes tall —
Lusty-limbed Longbeards?
Over the swans' bath
Why cry they to me?
Bones should be crashing fast,
Wolves should be full-fed,
Where'er such, mad-hearted,
Swing hands in the sword-play."

Sweetly laughed Freya —
" A name thou hast given them —

Shames neither thee nor them,
Well can they wear it.
Give them the victory,
First have they greeted thee;
Give them the victory,
Yokefellow mine I
Maidens and wives are these —
Wives of the Winils;
Few are their heroes
And far on the war-road,
So over the swans' bath
They cry unto thee."

Royally laughed he then;
Dear was that craft to him,
Odin Allfather,
Shaking the clouds.
" Cunning are women all,
Bold and importunate!
Longbeards their name shall be,
Ravens shall thank them:
Where the women are heroes,
What must the men be like?
Theirs is the victory;
No need of me!"[3]

"There!" said Wulf, when the song was ended; "is that cool enough for you?"

"Rather too cool; eh, Pelagia?" said the Amal, laughing.

"Ay," went on the old man, bitterly enough, "such were your mothers; and such were your sisters; and such your wives must be, if you intend to last much longer on the face of the earth — women who care for something better than good eating, strong drinking, and soft lying."

"All very true, Prince Wulf," said Agilmund, "but I don't like the saga after all. It was a great deal too like what Pelagia here says those philosophers talk about — right and wrong, and

---

[3] This punning legend may be seen in Paul Warnйfrid's *Gesta Langobardorum. The* metre and language are intended as imitations of those of the earlier Eddaic poems.

that sort of thing."

"I don't doubt it."

"Now I like a really good saga, about gods and giants, and the fire kingdoms and the snow kingdoms, and the Æsir making men and women out of two sticks, and all that."

"Ay," said the Amal, "something like nothing one ever saw in one's life, all stark mad and topsy-turvy, like one's dreams when one has been drunk; something grand which you cannot understand, but which sets you thinking over it all the morning after."

"Well," said Goderic, "my mother was an Alruna-woman, so I will not be the bird to foul its own nest. But I like to hear about wild beasts and ghosts, ogres, and fire-drakes, and nicors — something that one could kill if one had a chance, as one's fathers had."

"Your fathers would never have killed nicors," said Wulf, "if they had been —— "

"Like us — I know," said the Amal. "Now tell me, prince, you are old enough to be our father; and did you ever see a nicor?"

"My brother saw one, in the Northern sea, three fathoms long, with the body of a bison-bull, and the head of a cat, and the beard of a man, and tusks an ell long lying down on its breast, watching for the fishermen; and he struck it with an arrow, so that it fled to the bottom of the sea, and never came up again."

"What is a nicor, Agilmund?" asked one of the girls.

"A sea-devil who eats sailors. There used to be plenty of them where our fathers came from, and ogres too, who came out of the fens into the hall at night, when the warriors were sleeping, to suck their blood, and steal along, and steal along, and jump upon you — so!"

Pelagia, during the saga, had remained looking into the fountain, and playing with the water-drops, in assumed indifference. Perhaps it was to hide burning blushes, and something very like two hot tears, which fell unobserved into the ripple. Now she looked up suddenly —

"And of course you have killed some of these dreadful creatures, Amalric?"

"I never had such good luck, darling. Our forefathers were in such a hurry with them, that by the time we were born, there was hardly one left."

"Ay, they were men," growled Wulf.

"As for me," went on the Amal, "the biggest thing I ever killed was a snake in the Donau fens. How long was he, prince? You had time to see, for you sat eating your dinner and looking on, while he was trying to crack my bones."

"Four fathom," answered Wulf.

"With a wild bull lying by him, which he had just killed. I spoilt his dinner, eh, Wulf?"

"Yes," said the old grumbler, mollified, "that was a right good fight."

"Why don't you make a saga about it, then, instead of about right and wrong, and such things?"

"Because I am turned philosopher. I shall go and hear that Alruna-maiden this afternoon."

"Well said. Let us go too, young men: it will pass the time, at all events."

"Oh, no! no! no! do not! you shall not!" almost shrieked Pelagia.

"Why not, then, pretty one?"

"She is a witch — she — I will never love you again if you dare to go. Your only reason is that Agilmund's report of her beauty."

"So? You are afraid of my liking her golden locks better than your black ones?"

"I? Afraid?" And she leapt up, panting with pretty rage. "Come, we will go too — at once — and brave this nun, who fancies herself too wise to speak to a woman, and too pure to love a man! Look out my jewels! Saddle my white mule! We will go royally. We will not be ashamed of Cupid's livery, my girls — saffron shawl and all! Come, and let us see whether saucy Aphrodite is not a match after all for Pallas Athene and her owl!"

And she darted out of the cloister.

The three younger men burst into a roar of laughter, while Wulf looked with grim approval.

"So you want to go and hear the philosopher, Prince?" said Smid.

"Wheresoever a holy and a wise woman speaks, a warrior need not be ashamed of listening. Did not Alaric bid us spare the nuns in Rome, comrade? And though I am no Christian as he was, I thought it no shame for Odin' man to take their blessing; nor will I to take this one's Smid, son of Troll."

CHAPTER XIII
THE BOTTOM OF THE ABYSS

"HERE am I, at last !" said Raphael Aben-Ezra to himself." Fairly and safely landed at the very bottom of the bottomless; disporting myself on the firm floor of the primeval nothing, and finding my new element, like boys when they begin to swim, not so impracticable after all. No man, angel, or demon, can this day cast it in my teeth that I am weak enough to believe or disbelieve any phenomenon or theory in or concerning heaven or earth; or even that any such heaven, earth, phenomena, or theories exist — or otherwise..... I trust that is a sufficiently exhaustive statement of my opinions?.... I am certainly not dogmatic enough to deny — or to assert either — that there are sensations.... far too numerous for comfort.... but as for proceeding any further, by induction, deduction, analysis, or synthesis, I utterly decline the office of Arachne, and will spin no more cobwebs out of my own inside — if I have any. Sensations? What are they, but parts of oneself — if one has a self! What put this child's fancy into one's head, that there is anything outside of one which produces them? You have exactly similar feelings in your dreams, and you know that there is no reality corresponding to them — No, you don't! How dare you be dogmatic enough to affirm that? Why should not your dreams be as real as your waking thoughts? Why should not your dreams be the reality, and your waking thoughts the dream? What matter which?

"What matter, indeed? Here have I been staring for years — unless that, too, is a dream, which it very probably is — at every mountebank 'ism' which ever tumbled and capered on the philosophic tight-rope; and they are every one of them dead dolls, wooden, worked with wires, which are *petitiones principii*..... Each philosopher begs the question in hand, and then marches forward, as brave as a triumph, and prides himself — on proving it all afterwards. No wonder that his theory fits the universe, when he has first clipped the universe to fit his theory. Have I not tried my hand at many a one — starting, too, no one can deny, with the very minimum of clipping,.... for I suppose one cannot begin lower than at simple 'I am I'.... unless —

which is equally demonstrable — at 'I am not I.' I recollect — or dream — that I offered that sweet dream, Hypatia, to deduce all things in Heaven and earth, from the Astronomics of Hipparchus to the number of plumes in an archangel's wing, from that one simple proposition, if she would but write me out a demonstration of it first, as some sort of που στω for the apex of my inverted pyramid. But she disdained.... people are apt to disdain what they know they cannot do.... 'It was an axiom,' it was, 'like one and one making two.'.... How cross the sweet dream was, at my telling her that I did not consider that any axiom either, and that one thing and one thing seeming to us to be two things, was no more proof that they really were two, and not three hundred and sixty-five, than a man seeming to be an honest man, proved him not to be a rogue; and at my asking her, moreover, when she appealed to universal experience, how she proved that the combined folly of all fools resulted in wisdom?

" 'I am I' an axiom, indeed! What right have I to say that I am not any one else? How do I know it? How do I know that there is any one else for me not to be? I, or rather something, feels a number of sensations, longings, thoughts, fancies — the great devil take them all — fresh ones every moment, and each at war tooth and nail with all the rest; and then on the strength of this infinite multiplicity and contradiction, of which alone I am aware, I am to be illogical enough to stand up, and say, 'I by myself I;' and swear stoutly that I am one thing, when all I am conscious of is the devil only knows how many things. Of all quaint deductions from experience, that is the quaintest! Would it not be 'more philosophical to conclude that I, who never saw or felt or heard this which I call myself, am what I have seen, heard, and felt — and no more and no less — that sensation which I call that horse, that dead man, that jackass, those forty thousand two-legged jackasses who appear to be running for their lives below there, having got hold of this same notion of their being one thing each — as I choose to fancy in my foolish habit of imputing to them the same disease of thought which I find in myself — crucify the word! — The folly of my ancestors — if I ever had any — prevents my having any better expression..... Why should I not be all I feel — that sky, those clouds — the whole universe? Hercules! what a creative genius my sensorium must be! — I'll take to writing poetry — a mock-epic, in seventy-two books, entitled, 'The Universe; or, Raphael Aben-Ezra;' and take Homer's Margites for my model. Homer's? Mine! Why must not the Margites, like everything else, have been a sensation of my own? Hypatia used to say Homer's poetry was a part of her.... only she could not prove it.... but I have proved that the Margites is a part of me.... not that I believe my own proof — scepticism forbid! Oh, would to heaven that the said whole disagreeable universe were annihilated, if it were only just to settle by fair experiment whether any of master 'I' remained when they were gone! Buzzard and dogmatist! And how do you know that that would settle it? And if it did — why need it be settled?....

"I dare say there is an answer pat for all this. I could write a pretty one myself in half an hour. But then I should not believe it.... nor the rejoinder to that.... nor the demurrer to that again.... So.... I am both sleepy and hungry.... or rather, sleepiness and hunger are me. Which is it? Heigh-ho...." and Raphael finished his meditation by a mighty yawn.

This hopeful oration was delivered in a fitting lecture-room. Between the bare walls of a doleful fire-scarred tower in the Campagna of Rome, standing upon a knoll of dry brown grass, ringed with a few grim pines, blasted and black with smoke; there sat Raphael Aben-Ezra, working out the last formula of the great world-problem — "Given Self; to find God." Through the doorless stone archway he could see a long vista of the plain below, covered with broken trees, trampled crops, smoking villas, and all the ugly scars of recent war, far onward to the quiet purple mountains and the silver sea, towards which struggled, far in the distance, long dark lines of moving specks, flowing together, breaking up, stopping short, recoiling back to surge forward by some fresh channel, while now and then a glitter of keen white sparks ran through the dense black masses.... The Count of Africa had thrown for the empire of the world — and lost.

"Brave old Sun!" said Raphael, "how merrily he flashes off the sword-blades yonder, and never cares that every tiny sparkle brings a death-shriek after it! Why should he? It is no concern of his. Astrologers are fools. His business is to shine; and on the whole, he is one of my few satisfactory sensations. How now? This is questionably pleasant!"

As he spoke, a column of troops came marching across the

field, straight towards his retreat.

"If these new sensations of mine find me here, they will infallibly produce in me a new sensation, which will render all further ones impossible.... Well? What kinder thing could they do for me?.... Ay — but how do I know that they would do it? What possible proof is there that if a two-legged phantasm pokes a hard iron-grey phantasm in among my sensations, those sensations will be my last? Is the fact of my turning pale, and lying still, and being in a day or two converted into crow's flesh, any reason why I should not feel? And how do I know that would happen? It seems to happen to certain sensations of my eyeball — or something else — who cares? which I call soldiers; but what possible analogy can there be between what seems to happen to those single sensations called soldiers, and what may or may not really happen to all my sensations put together, which I call me? Should I bear apples if a phantasm seemed to come and plant me? Then why should I die if another phantasm seemed to come and poke me in the ribs?"

"Still, I don't intend to deny it.... I am no dogmatist. Positively the phantasms are marching straight for my tower! Well, it may be safer to run away, on the chance. But as for losing feeling," continued he, rising, and cramming a few mouldy crusts into his wallet, "that, like everything else, is past proof. Why — if now, when I have some sort of excuse for fancying myself one thing in one place, I am driven mad with the number of my sensations, what will it be when I am eaten, and turned to dust, and undeniably many things in many places..... Will not the sensations be multiplied by — unbearable! I would swear at the thought, if I had anything to swear by! To be transmuted into the sensoria of forty different nasty carrion crows, besides two or three foxes, and a large black-beetle! I'll run away, just like anybody else.... if anybody existed. Come, Bran!"

* * * * * *

"Bran! where are you; unlucky inseparable sensation of mine? Picking up a dinner already off these dead soldiers? Well, the pity is that this foolish contradictory taste of mine, while it makes me hungry, forbids me to follow your example. Why am I to take lessons from my soldier-phantasms, and not from my canine one? Illogical! Bran! Bran!" and he went out and whistled in vain for the dog.

"Bran! unhappy phantom, who will not vanish by night or day, lying on my chest even in dreams; and who would not even let me vanish, and solve the problem — though I don't believe there is any — why did you drag me out of the sea there at Ostia? Why did you not let me become a whole shoal of crabs? How did you know, or I either, that they may not be very jolly fellows, and not in the least troubled with philosophic doubts?.... But perhaps there were no crabs, but only phantasms of crabs..... And, on the other hand, if the crab-phantasms give jolly sensations, why should not the crow-phantasms? So whichever way it turns out, no matter; and I may as well wait here, and seem to become crows, as I certainly shall do. — Bran!.... Why should I wait for her? What pleasure can it be to me to have the feeling of a four-legged, brindled, lop-eared, toad-mouthed thing always between what seem to be my legs? There she is! Where have you been, madam? Don't you see I am in marching order, with staff and wallet ready shouldered? Come!"

But the dog, looking up in his face as only dogs can look, ran toward the back of the ruin, and up to him again, and back again, until he followed her.

"What's this? Here is a new sensation with a vengeance! Oh, storm and cloud of material appearances, were there not enough of you already, that you must add to your number these also? Bran! Bran! Could you find no other day in the year but this, whereon to present my ears with the squeals of — one — two — three — nine blind puppies?"....

Bran answered by rushing into the hole where her new family lay tumbling and squalling, bringing out one in her mouth, and laying it at his feet.

"Needless, I assure you. I am perfectly aware of the state of the case already. What! another? Silly old thing! — do you fancy, as the fine ladies do, that burdening the world with noisy likenesses of your precious self, is a thing of which to be proud? Why, she's bringing out the whole litter!.... What was I thinking of last? Ah — the argument was self-contradictory, was it, because I could not argue without using the very terms which I repudiated. Well.... And — why should it not be contradictory? Why not? One must face that too, after all. Why should not a thing be true, and false also? What harm in a thing's being false? What necessity for it to be true? True? What is truth? Why should a thing be the worse for being illogical? Why should there be any logic at all? Did I ever see a little beast flying about with 'Logic' labelled on its back? What do I know of it, but as a sensation of my own mind — if I have any? What proof is that that I am to obey it, and not it me? If a flea bites me, I get rid of that sensation; and if logic bothers me, I 'll get rid of that too. Phantasms must be taught to vanish courteously. One's only hope of comfort lies in kicking feebly against the tyranny of one's own boring notions and sensations — every philosopher confesses that — and what god is logic, pray, that it is to be the sole exception?.... What, old lady? I give you fair warning, you must choose this day, like any nun, between the ties of family and those of duty."

Bran seized him by the skirt, and pulled him down towards the puppies; took up one of the puppies and lifted it towards him; and then repeated the action with another.

"You unconscionable old brute! You don't actually dare to expect me to carry your puppies for you?" and he turned to go.

Bran sat down on her tail, and began howling.

Farewell, old dog! you have been a pleasant dream after all..... But if you will go the way of all phantasms ".... And he walked away.

Bran ran with him, leaping and barking; then recollected her family and ran back; tried to bring them, one by one, in her mouth, and then to bring them all at once: and failing sat down and howled.

"Come, Bran! Come, old girl!"

She raced halfway up to him; then halfway back again to the puppies; then towards him again: and then suddenly gave it up, and dropping her tail, walked slowly back to the blind suppliants, with a deep reproachful growl.

"* * * * *!" said Raphael, with a mighty oath; "you are right after all! Here are nine things come into the world; phantasms or not, there it is; I can't deny it. They are something, and you are something, old dog; or at least like enough to something to do instead of it; and you are not I, and as good as I, and they too, for aught I know, and have as good a right to live as I; and by the seven planets and all the rest of it, I'll carry them!"

And he went back, tied up the puppies in his blanket, and set forth, Bran barking, squeaking, wagging, leaping, running between his legs and upsetting him, in her agonies of joy.

"Forward! Whither you will, old lady! The world is wide. You shall be my guide, tutor, queen of philosophy, for the sake of this mere common sense of yours. Forward, you new Hypatia! I promise you I will attend no lectures but yours this day!"

He toiled on, every now and then stepping across a dead body, or clambering a wall out of the road, to avoid some plunging, shrieking horse, or obscene knot of prowling camp followers, who were already stripping and plundering the slain..... At last, in front of a large villa, now a black and smoking skeleton, he leaped a wall, and found himself landed on a heap of corpses..... They were piled up against the garden fence for many yards. The struggle had been fierce there some three hours before.

"Put me out of my misery! In mercy kill me!" moaned a voice beneath his feet.

Raphael looked down; the poor wretch was slashed and mutilated beyond all hope.

"Certainly, friend, if you wish it," and he drew his dagger. The poor fellow stretched out his throat, and awaited the stroke with a ghastly smile. Raphael caught his eye; his heart failed him, and he rose.

"What do you advise, Bran?" But the dog was far ahead, leaping and barking impatiently.

"I obey," said Raphael; and he followed her, while the wounded man called piteously and upbraidingly after him.

"He will not have long to wait. Those plunderers will not be as squeamish as I..... Strange, now! From Armenian reminiscences I should have fancied myself as free from such tender weakness as any of my Canaanite-slaying ancestors..... And yet by some mere spirit of contradiction, I couldn't kill that fellow, exactly because he asked me to do it..... There is more in that than will fit into the great inverted pyramid of 'I am I.'.... Never mind, let me get the dog's lessons by heart first. What next, Bran? Ah! Could one believe the transformation? Why this is the very trim villa which I passed yesterday morning, with the garden-chairs standing among the flower-beds, just as the young ladies had left them, and the peacocks and silver pheasants running about, wondering why their pretty mistresses did not come to feed them. And here is a trampled mass of wreck and corruption for the girls to find, when they venture back from Rome, and complain how horrible war is for breaking down all their shrubs, and how cruel soldiers must be to kill and cook all their poor dear tame turtle-doves! Why not? Why should they lament over other things — which they can just as little mend — and which perhaps need no more mending? Ah! there lies a gallant fellow underneath that fruit-tree!"

Raphael walked up to a ring of dead, in the midst of which lay, half-sitting against the trunk of the tree, a tall and noble officer, in the first bloom of manhood. His casque and armour, gorgeously inlaid with gold, were hewn and battered by a hundred blows; his shield was cloven through and through; his sword broken in the stiffened hand which grasped it still. Cut off from his troop, he had made his last stand beneath the tree, knee-deep in the gay summer flowers, and there he lay, bestrewn, as if by some mockery — or pity — of mother nature, with faded roses, and golden fruit, shaken from off the boughs in that last deadly struggle. Raphael stood and watched him with a sad sneer.

"Well! — you have sold your fancied personality dear! How many dead men?.... Nine.... Eleven! Conceited fellow! Who told you that your one life was worth the eleven which you have taken?"

Bran went up to the corpse — perhaps from its sitting posture fancying it still living — smelt the cold cheek, and recoiled with a mournful whine.

"Eh? That is the right way to look at the phenomenon, is it? Well, after all, I am sorry for you.... almost like you..... All your wounds in front, as a man's should be. Poor fop! Lais and Thais will never curl those dainty ringlets for you again! What is that bas-relief upon your shield? Venus receiving Psyche into the abode of the gods!.... Ah! you have found out all about Psyche's wings by this time..... How do I know that? And yet, why am I, in spite of my common sense — if I have any — talking to you as you, and liking you, and pitying you, if you are nothing now, and probably never were anything? Bran! What right had you to pity him without giving your reasons in due form, as Hypatia would have done? Forgive me, sir, however — whether you exist or not, I cannot leave that collar round your neck for these camp-wolves to convert into strong liquor."

And as he spoke, he bent down, and detached, gently

enough, a magnificent necklace.

"Not for myself, I assure you. Like Até's golden apple, it shall go to the fairest. Here, Bran!"

And he wreathed the jewels round the neck of the mastiff, who, evidently exalted in her own eyes by the burden, leaped and barked forward again, taking, apparently as a matter of course, the road back towards Ostia, by which they had come thither from the sea. And as he followed, careless where he went, he continued talking to himself aloud after the manner of restless self-discontented men.

.... "And then man talks big about his dignity and his intellect, and his heavenly parentage, and his aspirations after the unseen and the beautiful, and the infinite — and everything else unlike himself. How can he prove it? Why, these poor black-guards lying about are very fair specimens of humanity. — And how much have they been bothered since they were born with aspirations after anything infinite, except infinite sour wine? To eat, to drink; to destroy a certain number of their species; to re-produce a certain number of the same, two-thirds of whom will die in infancy, a dead waste of pain to their mothers, and of ex-pense to their putative sires.... and then — — what says Solomon? What befals them befals beasts. As one dies, so dies the other; so that they have all one breath, and a man has no pre-eminence over a beast; for all is vanity. All go to one place; all are of the dust, and turn to dust again. Who knows that the breath of man goes upward, and that the breath of the beast goes downward to the earth? Who, indeed, my most wise ancestor? Not I, certainly. Raphael Aben-Ezra, how art thou better than a beast? What pre-eminence hast thou, not merely over this dog, but over the fleas whom thou so wantonly cursest? Man must painfully win house, clothes, fire..... A pretty proof of his wis-dom, when every flea has the wit to make my blanket, without any labour of his own, lodge him a great deal better than it lodges me! Man makes clothes, and the fleas live in them..... Which is the wiser of the two?....

"Ah, but — man is fallen..... Well — and the flea is not. So much better he than the man; for he is what he was intended to be, and so fulfils the very definition of virtue.... which no one can say of us of the red-ochre vein. And even if the old myth be true, and the man only fell, because he was set to do higher work than the flea; what does that prove — but that he could not do it?

"But his arts and his sciences?.... Apage! The very sound of those grown-children's rattles turns me sick..... One conceited ass in a generation increasing labour and sorrow, and dying after all even as the fool dies, and ten million brutes and slaves, just where their forefathers were, and where their children will be after them, to the end of the farce..... The thing that has been, it is that which shall be; and there is no new thing under the sun.....

"And as for your palaces, and cities, and temples.... look at this Campagna, and judge. Flea-bites go down after a while — and so do they. What arc they but the bumps which we human fleas make in the old earth's skin?.... Make them? We only cause them, as fleas cause flea-bites..... What are all the works of man, but a sort of cutaneous disorder in this unhealthy earth-hide, and we a race of larger fleas, running about among its fur, which we call trees? Why should not the earth be an animal? How do I know it is not? Because it is too big? Bah! What is big, and what is little? Because it has not the shape of one?.... Look into a fisherman's net, and see what forms are there! Because it does not speak?.... Perhaps it has nothing to say, being too busy. Perhaps it can talk no more sense than we..... In both cases it shows its wisdom by holding its tongue. Because it moves in one necessary direction?.... How do I know that it does? How can I tell that it is not flirting with all the seven spheres at once, at this moment? But if it does — so much the wiser of it, if that be the best direction for it. Oh, what a base satire on ourselves and our notions of the fair and fitting, to say that a thing cannot be alive and rational, just because it goes steadily on upon its own road, instead of skipping and scrambling fantastically up and down without method or order, like us and the fleas, from the cradle to the grave! Besides, if you grant, with the rest of the world, that fleas are less noble than we, because they are our parasites, then you are bound to grant that we are less noble than the earth, because we are its parasites..... Positively, it looks more probable than anything I have seen for many a day..... And, by-the-by, why should not earthquakes, and floods, and pestilences, be only just so many ways which the cunning old brute earth has of scratching herself, when the human fleas and their palace and city bites get too troublesome?"

At a turn of the road he was aroused from this profitable

meditation by a shriek, the shrillness of which told him that it was a woman's. He looked up, and saw close to him, among the smouldering ruins of a farm-house, two ruffians driving before them a young girl, with her hands tied behind her, while the poor creature was looking back piteously after something among the ruins, and struggling in vain, bound as she was, to escape from her captors, and return.

"Conduct unjustifiable in any fleas, — eh, Bran? How do I know that, though? Why should it not be a piece of excellent fortune for her, if she had but the equanimity to see it? Why — what will happen to her? She will be taken to Rome, and sold as a slave..... And in spite of a few discomforts in the transfer, and the prejudice which some persons have against standing an hour on the catasta to be handled from head to foot in the minimum of clothing, she will most probably end in being far better housed, fed, bedizened, and pampered to her heart's desire, than ninety-nine out of a hundred of her sister-fleas.... till she begins to grow old.... which she must do in any case..... And if she have not contrived to wheedle her master out of her liberty, and to make up a pretty little purse of savings, by that time — why, it is her own fault. Eh, Bran?"

But Bran by no means agreed with his view of the case; for after watching the two ruffians, with her head stuck on one side, for a minute or two, she suddenly and silently, after the manner of mastiff's, sprang upon them, and dragged one to the ground.

"Oh! that is the 'fit and beautiful,' in this case, as they say in Alexandria, is it? Well — I obey. You are at least a more practical teacher than ever Hypatia was. Heaven grant that there may be no more of them in the ruins!"

And rushing on the second plunderer, he laid him dead with a blow of his dagger, and then turned to the first, whom Bran was holding down by the throat.

"Mercy, mercy I" shrieked the wretch. "Life! only life!"

"There was a fellow half-a-mile back begging me to kill him: with which of you two am I to agree? — for you can't both be right."

"Life! Only life!"

"A carnal appetite, which man must learn to conquer," said Raphael, as he raised the poniard..... In a moment it was over, and Bran and he rose. — Where was the girl? She had rushed back to the ruins, whither Raphael followed her; while Bran ran to the puppies, which he had laid upon a stone, and commenced her maternal cares.

"What do you want, my poor girl?" asked he, in Latin. "I will not hurt you."

"My father! My father!"

He untied her bruised and swollen wrists; and without stopping to thank him, she ran to a heap of fallen stones and beams, and began digging wildly with all her little strength, breathlessly calling "Father!"

"Such is the gratitude of flea to flea! What is there, now, in the mere fact of being accustomed to call another person father, and not master, or slave, which should produce such passion as that?.... Brute habit!.... What services can the said man render, or have rendered, which make him worth — — Here is Bran!.... What do you think of that, my female philosopher?"

Bran sat down and watched too. The poor girl's tender hands were bleeding from the stones, while her golden tresses rolled down over her eyes, and entangled in her impatient fingers: but still she worked frantically. Bran seemed suddenly to comprehend the case, rushed to the rescue, and began digging too, with all her might.

Raphael rose with a shrug, and joined in the work.

* * * * * *

"Hang these brute instincts! They make one very hot. What was that?"

A feeble moan rose from under the stones. A human limb was uncovered. The girl threw herself on the place, shrieking her father's name. Raphael put her gently back, and exerting his whole strength, drew out of the ruins a stalwart elderly man, in the dress of an officer of high rank.

He still breathed. The girl lifted up his head and covered him with wild kisses. Raphael looked round for water; found a spring and a broken sherd, and bathed the wounded man's temples till he opened his eyes, and showed signs of returning life.

The girl still sat by him, fondling her recovered treasure, and bathing the grizzled face in holy tears.

"It is no business of mine," said Raphael. "Come, Bran!"

The girl sprang up, threw herself at his feet, kissed his

hands, called him her saviour, her deliverer, sent by God.

"Not in the least, my child. You must thank my teacher the dog, not me."

And she took him at his word, and threw her soft arms round Bran's neck; and Bran understood it, and wagged her tail, and licked the gentle face lovingly.

"Intolerably absurd, all this!" said Raphael. "I must be going, Bran."

"You will not leave us? You surely will not leave an old man to die here?"

"Why not? What better thing could happen to him?"

"Nothing," murmured the officer, who had not spoken before.

"Ah God t he is my father!"

"Well?"

"He is my father!"

"Well?"

"You must save him! You shall, I say!" And she seized Raphael's arm in the imperiousness of her passion.

He shrugged his shoulders: but felt, he knew not why, marvellously inclined to obey her.

"I may as well do this as anything else, having nothing else to do. Whither now, sir?"

"Whither you will. Our troops are disgraced, our eagles taken. We are your prisoners by right of war. We follow you."

"Oh my fortune! A new responsibility! Why cannot I stir, without live animals, from fleas upward, attaching themselves to me? Is it not enough to have nine blind puppies at my back, and an old brute at my heels, who will persist in saving my life, that I must be burdened over and above with a respectable elderly rebel and his daughter? Why am I not allowed by fate to care for nobody but myself? Sir, I give you both your freedom. The world is wide enough for us all. I really ask no ransom."

"You seem philosophically disposed, my friend."

"I? Heaven forbid! I have gone right through that slough, and come out sheer on the other side. For sweeping the last lingering taint of it out of me, I have to thank, not sulphur and exorcisms, but your soldiers and their morning's work. Philosophy is superfluous in a world where all are fools."

"Do you include yourself under that title?"

"Most certainly, my best sir. Don't fancy that I make any exceptions. If I can in any way prove my folly to you, I will do it."

"Then help me and my daughter to Ostia."

"A very fair instance. Well — my dog happens to be going that way; and, after all, you seem to have a sufficient share of human imbecility to be a very fit companion for me. I hope, though, you do not set up for a wise man!"

"God knows — no I Am I not of Heraclian's army?"

"True; and the young lady, here, made herself so great a fool about you, that she actually infected the very dog."

"So we three fools will forth together."

"And the greatest one, as usual, must help the rest. But I have nine puppies in my family already. How am I to carry you and them?"

"I will take them," said the girl; and Bran, after looking on at the transfer with a somewhat dubious face, seemed to satisfy herself that all was right, and put her head contentedly under the girl's hand.

"Eh? You trust her, Bran?" said Raphael, in an undertone. "I must really emancipate myself from your instructions if you require a similar simplicity in me. Stay! there wanders a mule without a rider; we may as well press him into the service."

He caught the mule, lifted the wounded man into the saddle, and the cavalcade set forth, turning out of the highroad into a by-lane, which the officer, who seemed to know the country thoroughly, assured him would lead them to Ostia by an unfrequented route.

"If we arrive there before sundown, we are saved," said he.

"And in the meantime," answered Raphael, "between the dog and this dagger, which, as I take care to inform all comers, is delicately poisoned, we may keep ourselves clear of marauders. And yet, what a meddling fool I am!" he went on to himself. "What possible interest can I have in this uncircumcised rebel? The least evil is, that if we are taken, which we most probably shall be, I shall be crucified for helping him to escape. But even if we get safe off — here is a fresh tie between me and those very brother fleas, to be rid of whom I have chosen beggary and starvation. Who knows where it may end? Pooh! The man is like other men. He is certain, before the day is over, to prove ungrateful, or attempt the mountebank-heroic, or give me some other excuse for bidding him good evening. And in the meantime, there is something quaint in the fact of finding so sober a respectability, with a young daughter too, abroad on this fool's errand, which really makes me curious to discover with what variety of flea I am to class him."

But while Aben-Ezra was talking to himself about the father, he could not help, somehow, thinking about the daughter. Again and again he found himself looking at her. She was, undeniably, most beautiful. Her features were not as regularly perfect as Hypatia's, nor her stature so commanding; but her face shone with a clear and joyful determination, and with a tender and modest thoughtful-ness, such as he had never beheld before united in one countenance; and as she stepped along, firmly and lightly, by her father's side, looping up her scattered tresses as she went, laughing at the struggles of her noisy burden, and looking up with rapture at her father's gradually brightening face, Raphael could not help stealing glance after glance, and was surprised to find them returned with a bright, honest, smiling gratitude, which met him full-eyed, as free from prudery as it was from coquetry..... "A lady she is," said he to himself; "but evidently no city one. There is nature — or something else, there, pure and unadulterated, without any of man's additions or beautifications." And as he looked, he began to feel it a pleasure, such as his weary heart had not known for many a year, simply to watch her.....

"Positively there is a foolish enjoyment after all in making other fleas smile..... Ass that I am! As if I had not drank all that ditch-water cup to the dregs years ago!"

They went on for some time in silence, till the officer, turning to him —

"And may I ask you, my quaint preserver, whom I would have thanked before but for this foolish faintness, which is now going off, what and who you are?"

"A flea, sir — a flea — nothing more."

"But a patrician flea, surely; to judge by your language and manners?"

"Not that exactly. True, I have been rich, as the saying is; I may be rich again, they tell me, when I am fool enough to choose."

"Oh if we were but rich!" sighed the girl.

"You would be very unhappy, my dear young lady. Believe a flea who has tried the experiment thoroughly."

"Ah! but we could ransom my brother! and now we can find no money till we get back to Africa."

"And none then," said the officer, in a low voice. "You forget, my poor child, that I mortgaged the whole estate to raise my legion. We must not shrink from looking at things as they are."

"Ah! and he is prisoner! he will be sold for a slave_ perhaps — ah! perhaps crucified, for he is not a Roman! Oh, he will be crucified!" and she burst into an agony of weeping..... Suddenly she dashed away her tears and looked up clear and bright once more. "No! forgive me, father! God will protect his own!"

"My dear young lady," said Raphael, "if you really dislike such a prospect for your brother, and are in want of a few dirty coins wherewith to prevent it, perhaps I may be able to find you them in Ostia."

She looked at him incredulously, as her eye glanced over his rags, and then, blushing, begged his pardon for her unspoken thoughts.

"Well — as you choose to suppose. But my dog has been so civil to you already, that perhaps she may have no objection to make you a present of that necklace of hers. I will go to the Rabbis, and we will make all right; so don't cry. I hate crying; and the puppies are quite chorus enough for the present tragedy."

"The Rabbis? Are you a Jew?" asked the officer.

"Yes, sir, a Jew. And you, I presume, a Christian: perhaps you may have scruples about receiving — your sect has generally none about taking — from one of our stubborn and unbelieving race. Don't be frightened, though, for your conscience; I assure you I am no more a Jew at heart than I am a Christian."

"God help you, then!"

"Some one, or something, has helped me a great deal too much, for three-and-thirty years of pampering. But, pardon me, that was a strange speech for a Christian."

"You must be a good Jew, sir, before you can be a good Christian."

"Possibly. I intend to be neither — nor a good Pagan either. My dear sir, let us drop the subject. It is beyond me. If I can be as good a brute animal as my dog there — it being first demonstrated that it is good to be good — I shall be very well content."

The officer looked down on him with a stately, loving sorrow. Raphael caught his eye, and felt that he was in the presence of no common man.

"I must take care what I say here, I suspect, or I shall be entangled shortly in a regular Socratic dialogue.... And now, sir, may I return your question, and ask who and what are you? I really have no intention of giving you up to any Cæsar, Antiochus, Tiglath-Pileser, or other flea-devouring flea.... They will fatten well enough without your blood. So I only ask as a student of the great nothing-in-general, which men call the universe."

"I was prefect of a leg-ion this morning. What I am now, you know as well as I."

"Just what I do not. I am in deep wonder at seeing your hilarity, when, by all flea-analogies, you ought to be either behowling your fate like Achilles on the shores of Styx, or pretending to grin and bear it, as I was taught to do when I played at Stoicism. You are not of that sect certainly, for you confessed yourself a fool just now."

"And it would be long, would it not, before you made one of them do as much? Well, be it so. A fool I am; yet, if God helps us as far as Ostia, why should I not be cheerful?"

"Why should you?"

"What better thing can happen to a fool, than that God should teach him that he is one, when he fancied himself the wisest of the wise? Listen to me, sir. Four months ago I was blessed with health, honour, lands, friends — all for which the heart of man could wish. And if, for an insane ambition, I have chosen to risk all those, against the solemn warnings of the truest friend, and the wisest saint, who treads this earth of God's — should I not rejoice to have it proved to me, even by such a lesson as this, that the friend who never deceived me before was right in this case too; and that the God who has checked and turned me for forty years of wild toll and warfare, whenever I dared to do what was right in the sight of my own eyes, has not forgotten me yet, or given up the thankless task of my education?"

"And who, pray, is this peerless friend?"

"Augustine of Hippo."

"Humph! It had been better for the world in general, if the great dialectician had exerted his powers of persuasion on Heraclian himself."

"He did so, but in vain."

"I don't doubt it. I know the sleek Count well enough to judge what effect a sermon would have upon that smooth vulpine determination of his..... An instrument in the hands of God, my dear brother..... We must obey His call, even to the death," &c., &c. And Raphael laughed bitterly.

"You know the Count?"

"As well, sir, as I care to know any man."

"I am sorry for your eyesight, then, sir," said the Prefect, severely, "if it has been able to discern no more than that in so august a character."

"My dear sir, I do not doubt his excellence — nay, his inspiration. How well he divined the perfectly fit moment for stabbing his old comrade Stilicho! But really, as two men of the world, we must be aware by this time that every man has his price."....

"Oh, hush! hush!" whispered the girl. "You cannot guess how you pain him. He worships the Count. It was not ambition, as he pretends, but merely loyalty to him, which brought him here against his will."

"My dear madam, forgive me. For your sake I am silent."....

"For her sake! A pretty speech for me! What next?" said he to himself. "Ah, Bran, Bran, this is all your fault!"

"For my sake? Oh, why not for your own sake? How sad to hear one — one like you, only sneering and speaking evil!"

"Why then? If fools are fools, and one can safely call them so, why not do it?"

"Ah — if God was merciful enough to send down his own Son to die for them, should we not be merciful enough not to judge their failings harshly?"

"My dear young lady, spare a worn-out philosopher any new anthropologic theories. We really must push on a little faster, if we intend to reach Ostia to-night."

But, for some reason or other, Raphael sneered no more

for a full half-hour.

Long, however, ere they reached Ostia, the night had fallen; and their situation began to be more than questionably safe. Now and then a wolf, slinking across the road towards his ghastly feast, glided like a lank ghost out of the darkness, and into it again, answering Bran's growl by a gleam of his white teeth. Then the voices of some marauding party rang coarse and loud through the still night, and made them hesitate and stop a while. And at last, worst of all, the measured tramp of an imperial column began to roll like distant thunder along the plain below. They were advancing upon Ostia! What if they arrived there before the routed army could rally, and defend themselves long enough to re-embark?.... What if — a thousand ugly possibilities began to crowd up.

"Suppose we found the gates of Ostia shut, and the Imperialists bivouacked outside?" said Raphael, half to himself.

"God would protect his own," answered the girl; and Raphael had no heart to rob her of her hope, though he looked upon their chances of escape as growing smaller and smaller every moment. The poor girl was weary; the mule weary also; and as they crawled along, at a pace which made it certain that the fast passing column would be at Ostia an hour before them, to join the vanguard of the pursuers, and aid them in investing the town, she had to lean again and again on Raphael's arm. Her shoes, unfitted for so rough a journey, had been long since torn off, and her tender feet were marking every step with blood. Raphael knew it by her faltering gait; and remarked, too, that neither sigh nor murmur passed her lips. But as for helping her, he could not; and began to curse the fancy which had led him to eschew even sandals as unworthy the self-dependence of a Cynic.

And so they crawled along, while Raphael and the Prefect, each guessing the terrible thoughts of the other, were thankful for the darkness which hid their despairing countenances from the young girl; she, on the other hand, chatting cheerfully, almost laughingly, to her silent father.

At last the poor child stepped on some stone more sharp than usual — and with a sudden writhe and shriek, sank to the ground. Raphael lifted her up, and she tried to proceed, but sank down again..... What was to be done?

"I expected this," said the Prefect, in a slow stately voice. "Hear me, sir! Jew, Christian, or philosopher, God seems to have bestowed on you a heart which f can trust. To your care I commit this girl — your property, like me, by right of war. Mount her upon this mule. Hasten with her — where you will — for God will be there also. And may He so deal with you, as you deal with her henceforth. An old and disgraced soldier can do no more than die."

And he made an effort to dismount; but fainting from his wounds, sank upon the neck of the mule. Raphael and his daughter caught him in their arms.

"Father! Father! Impossible! Cruel! Oh — do you think that I would have followed you hither from Africa, against your own entreaties, to desert you now?"

"My daughter, I command!''

The girl remained firm and silent.

"How long have you learned to disobey me? Lift the old disgraced man down, sir, and leave him to die in the right place — on the battle-field where his general sent him." The girl sunk down on the road in an agony of weeping. "I must help myself, I sec," said her father, dropping to the ground. "Authority vanishes before old age and humiliation. Victoria! Has your father no sins to answer for already, that you will send him before his God with your blood too upon his head?"

Still the girl sat weeping on the ground; while Raphael, utterly at his wits' end, tried hard to persuade himself that it was no concern of his.

"I am at the service of either or of both, for life or death; only be so good as to settle it quickly.... Hell! here it is settled for us, with a vengeance!"

And as he spoke, the tramp and jingle of horsemen rang along the lane, approaching rapidly.

In an Instant Victoria had sprung to her feet — weakness and pain had vanished.

"There is one chance — one chance for him! Lift him over the bank, sir! Lift him over, while I run forward and meet them. My death will delay them long enough for you to save him!"

"Death?" cried Raphael, seizing her by the arm. "If that were all —— "

"God will protect his own," answered she, calmly, laying

her finger on her lips; and then breaking from his grasp in the strength of her heroism, vanished into the night.

Her father tried to follow her, but fell on his face, groaning. Raphael lifted him, strove to drag him up the steep bank: but his knees knocked together; a faint sweat seemed to melt every limb.... There was a pause, which seemed ages long.... Nearer and nearer came the trampling.... A sudden gleam of the moon revealed Victoria standing with outspread arms, right before the horses' heads. A heavenly glory seemed to bathe her from head to foot.... or was it tears sparkling in his own eyes?.... Then the grate and jar of the horse-hoofs on the road, as they pulled up suddenly.... He turned his face away and shut his eyes....

"What are you?" thundered a voice.

"Victoria, the daughter of Majoricus the Prefect."

The voice was low, but yet so clear and calm, that every syllable rang through Aben-Ezra's tingling ears.....

A shout — a shriek — the confused murmur of many voices.... he looked up, in spite of himself — a horseman had sprung to the ground, and clasped Victoria in his arms. The human heart of flesh, asleep for many a year, leaped into mad life within his breast, and drawing his dagger, he rushed into the throng —

"Villains! Hellhounds! I will balk you! She shall die first!"

And the bright blade gleamed over Victoria's head.... He was struck down — blinded — half-stunned — but rose again with the energy of madness.... What was this? Soft arms around him.... Victoria's!

"Save him! spare him! He saved us! Sir! It is my brother! We are safe! Oh, spare the dog! It saved my father!"

"We have mistaken each other, indeed, sir!" said a gay young Tribune, in a voice trembling with joy. "Where is my father?"

"Fifty yards behind. Down, Bran! Quiet! Oh Solomon mine ancestor, why did you not prevent me making such an egregious fool of myself? Why, I shall be forced, in self-justification, to carry through the farce!"

There is no use telling what followed during the next five minutes, at the end of which time Raphael found himself astride of a goodly war-horse, by the side of the young Tribune, who carried Victoria before him. Two soldiers in the mean time were supporting the Prefect on his mule, and convincing that stubborn bearer of burdens that it was not quite so unable to trot as it had fancied, by the combined arguments of a drench of wine and two sword-points, while they heaped their general with blessings, and kissed his hands and feet.

"Your father's soldiers seem to consider themselves in debt to him: not, surely, for taking them where they could best run away?"

"Ah, poor fellows!" said the Tribune; "we have had as real a panic among us as I ever read of in Arrian or Polybius. But he has been a father rather than a general to them. It is not often that, out of a routed army, twenty gallant men will volunteer to ride back into the enemy's ranks, on the chance of an old man's breathing still."

"Then you knew where to find us?" said Victoria.

"Some of them knew. And he himself showed us this very by-road yesterday, when we took up our ground, and told us it might be of service on occasion — and so it has been."

"But they told me that you were taken prisoner. Oh, the torture I have suffered for you!"

"Silly child! Did you fancy my father's son would be taken alive? I and the first troop got away over the garden walls, and cut our way out into the plain, three hours ago."

"Did I not tell you," said Victoria, leaning toward Raphael, "that God would protect his own?"

"You did," answered he; and fell into a long and silent meditation.

CHAPTER XIV
THE ROCKS OF THE SIRENS

THESE four months had been busy and eventful enough to Hypatia and to Philammon; yet the events and the business were of so gradual and uniform a tenour, that it is as well to pass quickly over them, and show what had happened principally by its effects.

The robust and fiery desert-lad was now metamorphosed into the pale and thoughtful student, oppressed with the weight of careful thought and weary memory. But those remembrances were all recent ones. With his entrance into Hypatia's lecture-room, and into the fairy realms of Greek thought, a new life had begun for him; and the Laura, and Pambo, and Arsenius, seemed dim phantoms from some antenatal existence, which faded day by day before the inrush of new and startling knowledge.

But though the friends and scenes of his childhood had fallen back so swiftly into the far horizon, he was not lonely. His heart found a lovelier, if not a healthier home, than it had ever known before. For during those four peaceful and busy months of study there had sprung up between Hypatia and the beautiful boy one of those pure and yet passionate friendships — call them rather, with St. Augustine, by the sacred name of love — which, fair and holy as they are when they link youth to youth, or girl to girl, reach their full perfection only between man and woman. The unselfish adoration with which a maiden may bow down before some strong and holy priest, or with which an enthusiastic boy may cling to the wise and tender matron, who, amid the turmoil of the world, and the pride of beauty, and the cares of wifehood, bends down to him with counsel and encouragement — earth knows no fairer bonds than these, save wedded love itself. And that second relation, motherly rather than sisterly, had bound Philammon with a golden chain to the wondrous maid of Alexandria.

From the commencement of his attendance in her lecture-room she had suited her discourses to what she fancied were his especial spiritual needs; and many a glance of the eye towards him, on any peculiarly important sentence, set the poor boy's heart beating at that sign that the words were meant for him. But before a month was past, won by the intense attention with which he watched for every utterance of hers, she had persuaded her father to give him a place in the library as one of his pupils, among the youths who were employed there daily in transcribing, as well as in studying, the authors then in fashion.

She saw him at first but seldom — more seldom than she would have wished: but she dreaded the tongue of scandal, heathen as well as Christian, and contented herself with inquiring daily from her father about the progress of the boy. And when at times she entered for a moment the library, where he sat writing, or passed him on her way to the Museum, a look was interchanged, on her part of most gracious approval, and on his of adoring gratitude, which was enough for both. Her spell was working surely; and she was too confident in her own cause and her own powers to wish to hurry that transformation for which she so fondly hoped.

"He must begin at the beginning," thought she to herself. "Mathematics and the Parmenides are enough for him as yet. Without training in the liberal sciences he cannot gain a faith worthy of those gods to whom some day I shall present him; and I should find his Christian ignorance and fanaticism transferred, whole and rude, to the service of those gods whose shrine is unapproachable save to the spiritual man, who has passed through the successive vestibules of science and philosophy."

But soon, attracted herself, as much as wishing to attract him, she employed him in copying manuscripts for her own use. She sent back his themes and declamations, corrected with her own hand; and Philammon laid them by in his little garret at Eudæmon's house as precious badges of honour, after exhibiting them to the reverential and envious gaze of the little porter. So he toiled on, early and late, counting himself well paid for a week's intense exertion by a single smile or word of approbation, and went home to pour out his soul to his host on the one inexhaustible theme which they had in common — Hypatia and her perfections. He would have raved often enough on the same subject to his fellow-pupils, but he shrank not only from their artificial city manners, but also from their morality, for suspecting which he saw but too good cause. He longed to go out into the streets, to proclaim to the whole world the treasure which he had found, and call on all to come and share it with him. For there was no jealousy in that pure love of his. Could he have seen her lavishing on thousands far greater favours than she had conferred on him, he would have rejoiced in the thought that there were so many more blest beings upon earth, and have loved them all and every one as brothers, for having deserved her notice. Her very beauty, when his first flush of wonder was past, he ceased to mention — ceased even to think of it. Of course she must be beautiful. It was her right; the natural complement of her other graces: but it was to him only what the mother's smile is to the infant, the sunlight to the skylark, the mountain-breeze to the hunter — an inspiring element, on which he fed unconsciously. Only when he doubted for a moment some especially startling or fanciful assertion, did he become really aware of the great loveliness of her who made it; and then his heart silenced his judgment with the thought — Could any but true words come out of those perfect lips? — any but royal thoughts take shape within that queenly head?.... Poor fool! Yet was it not natural enough?

Then, gradually, as she passed the boy, poring over his book in some alcove of the Museum Gardens, she would invite him by a glance to join the knot of loungers and questioners who dangled about her and her father, and fancied themselves to be reproducing the days of the Athenian sages amid the groves of another Academus. Sometimes, even, she had beckoned him to her side as she sat in some retired arbour, attended only by her father; and there some passing observation, earnest and personal, however lofty and measured, made him aware, as it was intended to do, that she had a deeper interest in him, a livelier sympathy for him, than for the many; that he was in her eyes not merely a pupil to be instructed, but a soul whom she desired to educate. And those delicious gleams of sunlight grew more frequent and more protracted; for by each she satisfied herself more and more that she had not mistaken either his powers or his susceptibilities; and in each, whether in public or private, Philammon seemed to bear himself more worthily. For over and above the natural ease and dignity which accompanies physical beauty, and the modesty, self-restraint, and deep earnestness, which he had acquired under the discipline of the Laura, his Greek character was developing itself in all its quickness, subtlety, and versatility, until he seemed to Hypatia some young Titan, by the side of the flippant, hasty, and insincere talkers who made up her chosen circle.

But man can no more live upon Platonic love than on the more prolific species of that common ailment; and for the first month Philammon would have gone hungry to his couch full many a night, to lie awake from baser causes than philosophic meditation, had it not been for his magnanimous host, who never lost heart for a moment, either about himself, or any other human being. As for Philammon's going out with him to earn his bread, he would not hear of it. Did he suppose that he could meet any of those monkish rascals in the street, without being knocked down and carried off by main force? And besides, there was a sort of impiety in allowing so hopeful a student to neglect the "Divine Ineffable" in order to supply the base necessities of the teeth. So he should pay no rent for his lodgings — positively none; and as for eatables — why, he must himself work a little harder in order to cater for both. Had not all his neighbours their litters of children to provide for, while he, thanks to the immortals, had been far too wise to burden the earth with animals who would add to the ugliness of their father the Tartarean hue of their mother? And after all, Philammon could pay him back when he became a great sophist, and made money, as of course he would some day or other; and in the mean time, something might turn up — things were always turning up for those whom the gods favoured; and besides, he had fully ascertained that on the day on which he first met Philammon, the planets were favourable, the Mercury being in something or other, he forgot what, with Helios, which portended for Philammon, in his opinion, a similar career with that of the glorious and devout Emperor Julian.

Philammon winced somewhat at the hint; which seemed to have an ugly verisimilitude in it: but still, philosophy he must learn, and bread he must eat; so he submitted.

But one evening, a few days after he had been admitted as Theon's pupil, he found, much to his astonishment, lying on the table in his garret, an undeniable glittering gold piece. He took it down to the porter the next morning, and begged him to discover the owner of the lost coin, and return it duly. But what was his surprise, when the little man, amid endless capers and gesticulations, informed him, with an air of mystery, that it was anything but lost; that his arrears of rent had been paid for him; and that, by the bounty of the upper powers, a fresh piece of coin would be forthcoming every month! In vain Philammon demanded to know who was his benefactor. Eudæmon resolutely kept the secret, and imprecated a whole Tartarus of unnecessary curses on his wife if she allowed her female garrulity — though the poor creature seemed never to open her lips from morning till night — to betray so great a mystery.

Who was the unknown friend? There was but one person who could have done it..... And yet he dared not — the thought was too delightful — think that it was she. It must have been her father. The old man had asked him more than once about the state of his purse. True, he had always returned evasive answers; but the kind old man must have divined the truth. Ought he not — must he not — go and thank him? No; perhaps it was more courteous to say nothing. If he — she — for of course she had permitted, perhaps advised, the gift — had intended' him to thank them, would they have so carefully concealed their own generosity?.... Be it so, then. But how would he not repay them for it! How delightful to be in her debt for anything — for everything! Would that he could have the enjoyment of owing her existence itself!

So he took the coin, bought unto himself a cloak of the most philosophic fashion, and went his way, such as it was, rejoicing.

But his faith in Christianity? What had become of that?

What usually happens in such cases. It was not dead; but nevertheless it had fallen fast asleep for the time being. He did not disbelieve it; he would have been shocked to hear such a thing asserted of him: but he happened to be busy believing something else — geometry, conic sections, cosmogonies, psychologies and what not. And so it befel that he had not just then time to believe in Christianity. He recollected at times its existence; but even then he neither affirmed nor denied it. When he had solved the great questions — those which Hypatia set forth as the roots of all knowledge — how the world was made, and what was the origin of evil, and what his own personality was, and — that being settled — whether he had one, with a few other preliminary matters, then it would be time to return, with his enlarged light, to the study of Christianity; and if, of course, Christianity should be found to be at variance with that enlarged light, as Hypatia seemed to think.... Why, then — What then?.... He would not think about such disagreeable possibilities. Sufficient for the day was the evil thereof. Possibilities? It was impossible..... Philosophy could not mislead. Had not Hypatia defined it, as man's search after the unseen? And if he found the unseen by it, did it not come to just the same thing as if the unseen had revealed itself to him? And he must find it — for logic and mathematics could not err. If every step was correct, the conclusion must be correct also; so he must end, after all, in the right path — that is, of course, supposing Christianity to be the right path — and return to fight the church's battles, with the sword which he had wrested from Goliath the Philistine..... But he had not won the sword yet: and in the mean while, learning was weary work; and sufficient for the day was the good, as well as the evil, thereof.

So, enabled by his gold coin each month to devote himself entirely to study, he became very much what Peter would have coarsely termed a heathen. At first, indeed, he slipped into the Christian churches, from a habit of conscience. But habits soon grow sleepy; the fear of discovery and recapture made his attendance more and more of a labour. And keeping himself apart as much as possible from the congregation, as a lonely and secret worshipper, he soon found himself as separate from them in heart as in daily life. He felt that they, and even more than they, those flowery and bombastic pulpit rhetoricians, who were paid *for* their sermons by the clapping and cheering of the congregation, were not thinking of, longing after, the same things as himself. Besides, he never spoke to a Christian; for the negress at his lodgings seemed to avoid him — whether from modesty or terror, he could not tell; and cut off thus from the outward "communion of saints," he found himself fast parting away from the inward one. So he went no more to church; and looked the other way, he hardly knew why, whenever he passed the Cæsareum; and Cyril, and all his mighty organization, became to him another world, with which he had even less to do than with those planets over his head, whose mysterious movements, and symbolisms, and influences Hypatia's lectures on astronomy were just opening before his bewildered imagination.

Hypatia watched all this with growing self-satisfaction, and fed herself with the dream that through Philammon she might see her wildest hopes realized. After the manner of women, she crowned him, in her own imagination, with all powers and excellences which she would have wished him to possess, as well as with those which he actually manifested, till Philammon would have been as much astonished as self-glorified could he have seen the idealized caricature of himself which the sweet enthusiast had painted for her private enjoyment. They were blissful months, those, to poor Hypatia. Orestes, for some reason or other, had neglected to urge his suit, and the Iphigenia-sacrifice had retired mercifully into the background. Perhaps she should be able now to accomplish all without it. And yet — it was so long to wait! Years might pass before Philammon's education was matured, and with them golden opportunities which might never recur again.

"Ah!" she sighed at times, "that Julian had lived a generation later! That I could have brought all my hard-earned treasures to the feet of the Poet of the Sun, and cried, ' Take me! — Hero, warrior, statesman, sage, priest of the God of Light! Take thy slave! Command her — send her — to martyrdom, if thou wilt!' A petty price would that have been wherewith to buy the honour of being the meanest of thy apostles, the fellow-labourer of Iamblichus, Maximus, Libanius, and the choir of sages who upheld the throne of the last true Cæsar!"

CHAPTER XV
NEPHELOCOCCUGUIA

HYPATIA had always avoided carefully discussing with Philammon any of those points on which she differed from his former faith. She was content to let the divine light of philosophy penetrate by its own power, and educe its own conclusions. But one day, at the very time at which this history reopens, she was tempted to speak more openly to her pupil than she yet had done. Her father had introduced him, a few days before, to a new work of hers on Mathematics; and the delighted and adoring look with which the boy welcomed her, as he met her in the Museum Gardens, pardonably tempted her curiosity to inquire what miracles her own wisdom might have already worked. She stopped in her walk, and motioned her father to begin a conversation with Philammon.

"Well!" asked the old man, with an encouraging smile, "and how does our pupil like his new —— "

"You mean my conic sections, father? It is hardly fair to expect an unbiassed answer in my presence."

"Why so?" said Philammon. "Why should I not tell you, as well as all the world, the fresh and wonderful field of thought which they have opened to me, in a few short hours?"

"What then?" asked Hypatia, smiling, as if she knew what the answer would be. "In what does my commentary differ from the original text of Apollonius, on which I have so faithfully based it?"

"Oh, as much as a living body differs from a dead one. Instead of mere dry disquisitions on the properties of lines and curves, I found a mine of poetry and theology. Every dull mathematical formula seemed transfigured, as if by a miracle, into the symbol of some deep and noble principle of the unseen world."

"And do you think that he of Perga did not see as much? or that we can pretend to surpass, in depth of insight, the sages of the elder world? Be sure that they, like the poets, meant only spiritual things, even when they seem to talk only of physical ones, and concealed heaven under an earthly garb, only to hide it from the eyes of the profane; while we, in these degenerate days, must interpret and display each detail to the dull ears of men."

"Do you think, my young friend," asked Theon, "that mathematics can be valuable to the philosopher otherwise than as vehicles of spiritual truth? Are we to study numbers merely that we may be able to keep accounts; or as Pythagoras did, in order to deduce from their laws the ideas by which the universe, man, Divinity itself, consists?"

"That seems to me certainly to be the nobler purpose."

"Or conic sections, that we may know better how to construct machinery; or rather to devise from them symbols of the relations of Deity to its various emanations?"

"You use your dialectic like Socrates himself, my father," said Hypatia.

"If I do, it is only for a temporary purpose. I should be sorry to accustom Philammon to suppose that the essence of philosophy was to be found in those minute investigations of words and analyses of notions, which seem to constitute Plato's chief power in the eyes of those who, like the Christian sophist Augustine, worship his letter while they neglect his spirit; not seeing that those dialogues, which they fancy the shrine itself, are but vestibules ———— "

"Say rather, veils, father."

"Veils, indeed, which were intended to baffle the rude gaze of the carnal-minded; but still vestibules, through which the enlightened soul might be led up to the inner sanctuary, to the Hesperid gardens and golden fruit of the Timæus and the oracles..... And for myself, were but those two books left, I care not whether every other writing in the world perished to-morrow." [4]

"You must except Homer, father."

"Yes, for the herd..... But of what use would he be to them without some spiritual commentary?"

"He would tell them as little, perhaps, as the circle tells to the carpenter who draws one with his compasses."

"And what is the meaning of the circle?" asked Philammon.

"It may have infinite meanings, like every other natural

---

[4] This astounding speech is usually attributed to Proclus, Hypatia's "great" successor.

phenomenon; and deeper meanings in proportion to the exalta-tion of the soul which beholds it. But, consider, is it not, as the one perfect figure, the very symbol of the totality of the spiritual world; which, like it, is invisible, except at its circumference, where it is limited by the dead gross phenomena of sensuous matter? And even as the circle takes its origin from one centre, itself unseen, — a point, as Euclid defines it, whereof neither parts nor magnitude can be predicated, — does not the world of spirits revolve round one abysmal being, unseen and indefinable — in itself, as I have so often preached, nothing, for it is con-ceivable only by the negation of all properties, even of those of reason, virtue, force: and yet, like the centre of the circle, the cause of all other existences?"

"I see," said Philammon; for the moment, certainly, the said abysmal Deity struck him as a somewhat chill and barren notion.... but that might be caused only by the dulness of his own spiritual perceptions. At all events, if it was a logical conclusion, it must be right.

"Let that be enough for the present. Hereafter you may be — I fancy that I know you well enough to prophesy that you will be — able to recognise in the equilateral triangle inscribed within the circle, and touching it only with its angles, the three supra-sensual principles of existence, which are contained in Deity as it manifests itself in the physical universe, coinciding with its utmost limits, and yet, like it, dependent on that unseen central One which none dare name."

"Ah!" said poor Philammon, blushing scarlet at the sense of his own dulness, "I am, indeed, not worthy to have such wis-dom wasted upon my imperfect apprehension.... But, if I may dare to ask.... does not Apollonius regard the circle, like all other curves, as not depending primarily on its own centre for its exis-tence, but as generated by the section of any cone by a plane at right angles to its axis?"

"But must we not draw, or at least conceive a circle, in or-der to produce that cone? And is not the axis of that cone deter-mined by the centre of that circle?"

Philammon stood rebuked.

"Do not be ashamed; you have only, unwittingly, laid open another, and, perhaps, as deep a symbol. Can you guess what it is?"

Philammon puzzled in vain.

"Does it not show you this? That, as every conceivable right section of the cone discloses the circle, so in all which is fair and symmetric you will discover Deity, if you but analyze it in a right and symmetric direction?"

"Beautiful!" said Philammon, while the old man added,

"And does it not show us, too, how the one perfect and original philosophy may be discovered in all great writers, if we have but that scientific knowledge, which will enable us to extract it?"

"True, my father: but just now, I wish Philammon, by such thoughts as I have suggested, to rise to that higher and more spiritual insight into nature, which reveals her to us as instinct throughout — all fair and noble forms of her at least — with Deity itself; to make him feel that it is not enough to say, with the Christians, that God has made the world, if we make that very assertion an excuse for believing that his presence has been ever since withdrawn from it."

"Christians, I think, would hardly say that," said Philammon.

"Not in words. But, in fact, they regard Deity as the maker of a dead machine, which, once made, will move of itself thenceforth, and repudiate as heretics every philosophic thinker, whether Gnostic or Platonist, who, unsatisfied with so dead, barren, and sordid a conception of the glorious all, wishes to honour the Deity by acknowledging his universal presence, and to believe, honestly, the assertion of their own Scriptures, that he lives and moves, and has his being in the universe."

Philammon gently suggested that the passage in question was worded somewhat differently in the Scripture.

"True. But if the one be true, its converse will be true also. If the universe lives and moves, and has its being in Him, must He not necessarily pervade all thing's?"

"Why? — Forgive my dulness, and explain."

"Because, if He did not pervade all things, those things which He did not pervade would be as it were interstices in His being, and in so far, without Him."

"True, but still they would be within His circumference."

"Well argued. But yet they would not live in Him, but in themselves. To live in Him they must be pervaded by His life.

Do you think it possible — do you think it even reverent to affirm that there can be anything within the infinite glory of Deity which has the power of excluding from the space which it occupies that very being from which it draws its worth, and which must have originally pervaded that thing, in order to bestow on it its organization and its life? Does He retire after creating, from the spaces which he occupied during creation, reduced to the base necessity of making room for His own universe, and endure the suffering — for the analogy of all material nature tells us that it is suffering — of a foreign body, like a thorn within the flesh, subsisting within His own substance? Rather believe that His wisdom and splendour, like a subtle and piercing fire, insinuates itself eternally with resistless force through every organized atom, and that were it withdrawn but for an instant from the petal of the meanest flower, gross matter, and the dead chaos from which it was formed, would be all which would remain of its loveliness.....

"Yes" — she went on, after the method of her school, who preferred, like most decaying ones, harangues to dialectic, and synthesis to induction..... "Look at yon lotus-flower, rising like Aphrodite from the wave in which it has slept throughout the plight, and saluting, with bending swan-neck, that sun which it will follow lovingly around the sky. Is there no more there than brute matter, pipes and fibres, colour and shape, and the meaningless life-in-death which men call vegetation? Those old Egyptian priests knew better, who could see in the number and the form of those ivory petals and golden stamina, in that mysterious daily birth out of the wave, in that nightly baptism, from which it rises each morning re-born to a new life, the signs of some divine idea, some mysterious law, common to the flower itself, to the white-robed priestess who held it in the temple-rites, and to the goddess to whom they both were consecrated..... The flower of Isis!.... Ah — well. Nature has her sad symbols, as well as her fair ones. And in proportion as a misguided nation has forgotten the worship of her to whom they owed their greatness, for novel and barbaric superstitions, so has her sacred flower grown rarer and more rare, till now — fit emblem of the worship over which it used to shed its perfume — it is only to be found in gardens such as these — a curiosity to the vulgar, and, to such as me, a lingering monument of wisdom and of glory past away."

Philammon, it may be seen, was far advanced by this time; for he bore the allusions to Isis without the slightest shudder. Nay — he dared even to offer consolation to the beautiful mourner.

"The philosopher," he said, "will hardly lament the loss of a mere outward idolatry. For if, as you seem to think, there were a root of spiritual truth in the symbolism of nature, that cannot die. And thus the lotus-flower must still retain its meaning, as long as its species exists on earth."

"Idolatry!" answered she, with a smile. "My pupil must not repeat to me that worn-out Christian calumny. Into whatsoever low superstitions the pious vulgar may have fallen, it is the Christians now, and not the heathens, who are idolaters. They who ascribe miraculous power to dead men's bones, who make temples of charnel-houses, and bow before the images of the meanest of mankind, have surely no right to accuse of idolatry the Greek or the Egyptian, who embodies in a form of symbolic beauty ideas beyond the reach of words!"

"Idolatry? Do I worship the Pharos when I gaze at it, as I do for hours, with loving awe, as the token to me of the all-conquering might of Hellas? Do I worship the roll on which Homer's words are written, when I welcome with delight the celestial truths which it unfolds to me, and even prize and love the material book for the sake of the message which it brings? Do you fancy that any, but the vulgar worship the image itself, or dream that it can help or hear them? Does the lover mistake his mistress's picture for the living, speaking reality? We worship the idea of which the image is a symbol. Will you blame us because we use that symbol to represent the idea to our own affections and emotions, instead of leaving it a barren notion, a vague imagination of our own intellect?"

"Then," asked Philammon, with a faltering voice, yet unable to restrain his curiosity, "then you do reverence the heathen gods?"

Why Hypatia should have felt this question a sore one, puzzled Philammon; but she evidently did feel it as such, for she answered haughtily enough —

"If Cyril had asked me that question, I should have disdained to answer. To you I will tell, that before I can answer your question you must learn what those whom you call heathen gods are. The vulgar, or rather those who find it their interest to calumniate the vulgar for the sake of confounding philosophers with them, may fancy them mere human beings, subject like man to the sufferings of pain and love, to the limitations of personality. We, on the other hand, have been taught by the primeval philosophers of Greece, by the priests of ancient Egypt, and the sages of Babylon, to recognise in them the universal powers of nature, those children of the all-quickening spirit, which are but various emanations of the one primeval unity — say rather, various phases of that unity, as it has been variously conceived, according to the differences of climate and race, by the wise of different nations. And thus, in our eyes, he who reverences the many, worships by that very act, with the highest and fullest adoration, the one of whose perfection they are the partial antitypes; perfect each in themselves, but each the image of only one of its perfections."

"Why, then," said Philammon, much relieved by this explanation, "do you so dislike Christianity? may it not be one of the many methods ——?"

"Because," she answered, interrupting him impatiently, "because it denies itself to be one of those many methods, and stakes its existence on the denial; because it arrogates to itself the exclusive revelation of the Divine, and cannot see, in its self-conceit, that its own doctrines disprove that assumption by their similarity to those of all creeds. There is not a dogma of the Galileans which may not be found, under some form or other, in some of those very religions from which it pretends to disdain borrowing."

"Except," said Theon, "its exaltation of all which is human and low-born, illiterate and levelling."

"Except that —— but look! here comes some one whom I cannot — do not choose to meet. Turn this way — quick!"

And Hypatia, turning pale as death, drew her father with unphilosophic haste down a side-walk.

"Yes," she went on to herself, as soon as she had recovered her equanimity. "Were this Galilean superstition content to take its place humbly among the other 'religiones licitas' of the empire, one might tolerate it well enough, as an anthropomorphic adumbration of divine things fitted for the base and toiling herd; perhaps peculiarly fitted, because peculiarly flattering to them. But now —— "

"There is Miriam again," said Philammon, "right before us!"

"Miriam?" asked Hypatia, severely. "You know her, then? How is that?"

"She lodges at Eudæmon's house, as I do," answered Philammon, frankly. "Not that I ever interchanged, or wish to interchange, a word with so base a creature."

"Do not! I charge you!" said Hypatia, almost imploringly. But there was now no way of avoiding her, and perforce Hypatia and her tormentress met face to face.

"One word! one moment, beautiful lady," began the old woman, with a slavish obeisance. "Nay, do not push by so cruelly. I have — see what I have for you!" and she held out, with a mysterious air, "The Rainbow of Solomon."

"Ah! I knew you would stop a moment — not for the ring's sake, of course, nor even for the sake of one who once offered it to you. — Ah! and where is he now? Dead of love, perhaps! At least, here is his last token to the fairest one, the cruel one..... Well, perhaps she is right..... To be an empress — an empress..... Far finer than anything the poor Jew could have offered..... But still..... An empress need not be above hearing her subjects' petition"....

All this was uttered rapidly, and in a wheedling undertone, with a continual snaky writhing of her whole body, except her eye, which seemed, in the intense fixity of its glare, to act as a fulcrum for all her limbs; and from that eye, as long as it kept its mysterious hold, there was no escaping.

"What do you mean? What have I to do with this ring?" asked Hypatia, half frightened.

"He who owned it once, offers it to you now. You recollect a little black agate — a paltry thing..... If you have not thrown it away, as you most likely have, he wishes to redeem it with this opal.... a gem surely more fit for such a hand as that.''

"He gave me the agate, and I shall keep it."

"But this opal — worth, oh worth ten thousand gold pieces — in exchange for that paltry broken thing not worth one?"

"I am not a dealer, like you, and have not yet learnt to value thing's by their money price. If that agate had been worth money, I would never have accepted it."

"Take the ring, take it, my darling," whispered Theon, impatiently; "it will pay all our debts."

"Ah, that it will — pay them all," answered the old woman, who seemed to have mysteriously overheard him.

"What! — my father! Would you, too, counsel me to be so mercenary? My good woman," she went on, turning to Miriam, "I cannot expect you to understand the reason of my refusal. You and I have a different standard of worth. But, for the sake of the talisman engraven on that agate, if for no other reason, I cannot give it up."

"Ah! for the sake of the talisman! That is wise, now! That is noble! Like a philosopher! Oh, I will not say a word more. Let the beautiful prophetess keep the agate, and take the opal too; for see, there is a charm on it also! The name by which Solomon compelled the demons to do his bidding. Look! What might you not do now, if you knew how to use that! To have great glorious angels, with six wings each, bowing at your feet whensoever you called them, and saying, 'Here am I, mistress; send me.' Only look at it!"

Hypatia took the tempting bait, and examined it with more curiosity than she would have wished to confess; while the old woman went on: —

"But the wise lady knows how to use the black agate, of course? Aben-Ezra told her that, did he not?"

Hypatia blushed somewhat; she was ashamed to confess that Aben-Ezra had not revealed the secret to her, probably not believing that there was any, and that the talisman had been to her only a curious plaything, of which she liked to believe one day that it might possibly have some occult virtue, and the next day to laugh at the notion as unphilosophical and barbaric; so she answered, rather severely, that her secrets were her own property.

"Ah, then! she knows it all — the fortunate lady! And the talisman has told her whether Heraclian has lost or won Rome by this time, and whether she is to be the mother of a new dynasty of Ptolemies, or to die a virgin, which the Four Angels avert! And surely she has had the great Dæmon come to her already, when she rubbed the flat side, has she not?"

"Go, foolish woman! I am not, like you, the dupe of childish superstitions."

"Childish superstitions! Ha! ha! ha!" said the old woman, as she turned to go, with obeisances more lowly than ever. "And she has not seen the Angels yet!.... Ah well! perhaps some day, when she wants to know how to use the talisman, the beautiful lady will condescend to let the poor old Jewess show her the way."

And Miriam disappeared down an alley, and plunged into the thickest shrubberies, while the three dreamers went on their way.

Little thought Hypatia that the moment the old woman had found herself alone, she had dashed herself down on the turf, rolling and biting at the leaves like an infuriated wild beast....." I will have it yet! I will have it, if I tear out her heart with it!"

CHAPTER XVI
VENUS AND PALLAS

As Hypatia was passing across to her lecture-room that afternoon, she was stopped midway by a procession of some twenty Goths and damsels, headed by Pelagia herself, in all her glory of jewels, shawls, and snow-white mule; while by her side rode the Amal, his long legs, like those of Gang-Rolf the Norseman, all but touching the ground, as he crushed down with his weight a delicate little barb, the best substitute to be found in Alexandria for the huge black chargers of his native land.

On they came, followed by a wondering and admiring mob, straight to the door of the Museum, and stopping, began to dismount, while their slaves took charge of the mules and horses.

There was no escape for Hypatia; pride forbade her to follow her own maidenly instinct, and to recoil among the crowd behind her; and in another moment the Amal had lifted Pelagia from her mule, and the rival beauties of Alexandria stood, for the first time in their lives, face to face.

"May Athene befriend you this day, Hypatia!" said Pelagia, with her sweetest smile. "I have brought my guards to hear somewhat of your wisdom, this afternoon. I am anxious to know whether you can teach them anything more worth listening to than the foolish little songs which Aphrodite taught me, when she raised me from the sea-foam, as she rose herself, and named me Pelagia."

Hypatia drew herself up to her stateliest height, and returned no answer.

"I think my body-guard will well bear comparison with yours. At least they are princes, and the descendants of deities. So it is but fitting that they should enter before your provincials. Will you show them the way?"

No answer.

"Then I must do it myself. Come, Amal!" and she swept up the steps, followed by the Goths, who put the Alexandrians aside right and left, as if they had been children.

"Ah! treacherous wanton that you are!" cried a young man's voice out of the murmuring crowd. "After having plundered us of every coin out of which you could dupe us, here you are squandering our patrimonies on barbarians!"

"Give us back our presents, Pelagia," cried another, "and you are welcome to your herd of wild bulls!"

"And I will!" cried she, stopping suddenly; and clutching at her chains and bracelets, she was on the point of dashing them among the astonished crowd —

"There! take your gifts! Pelagia and her girls scorn to be debtors to boys, while they are worshipped by men like these!"

But the Amal, who luckily for the students, had not understood a word of this conversation, seized her arm, asking if she were mad.

"No, no!" panted she, inarticulate with passion. "Give me gold — every coin you have. These wretches are twitting me with what they gave me before — before — oh Amal, you understand me?" And she clung imploringly to his arm.

"Oh! Heroes! each of you throw his purse among these fellows! They say that we and our ladies arc living on their spoils." And he tossed his purse among the crowd.

In an instant every Goth had followed his example: more than one following it up by dashing a bracelet or necklace into the face of some hapless philosophaster.

"I have no lady, my young friends," said old Wulf, in good enough Greek, "and owe you nothing; so I shall keep my money, as you might have kept yours; and as you might, too, old Smid, if you had been as wise as I."

"Don't be stingy, Prince, for the honour of the Goths," said Smid, laughing.

"If I take in gold I pay in iron," answered Wulf, drawing half out of its sheath the huge broad blade, at the ominous brown stains of which the studentry recoiled; and the whole party swept into the empty lecture-room, and seated themselves at their ease in the front ranks.

Poor Hypatia! At first she determined not to lecture — then to send for Orestes — then to call on her students to defend the sanctity of the Museum; but pride, as well as prudence, advised her better; to retreat would be to confess herself conquered — to disgrace philosophy — to lose her hold on the minds of all waverers. No! she would go on and brave everything, insults, even violence; and with trembling limbs and a pale cheek she mounted the tribune and began.

To her surprise and delight, however, her barbarian auditors were perfectly well-behaved. Pelagia, in childish good-humour at her triumph, and perhaps, too, determined to show her contempt for her adversary by giving her every chance, enforced silence and attention, and checked the tittering of the girls, for a full half-hour. But at the end of that time the heavy breathing of the slumbering Amal, who had been twice awoke by her, resounded unchecked through the lecture-room, and deepened into a snore; for Pelagia herself was as fast asleep as he. But now another censor took upon himself the office of keeping order. Old Wulf, from the moment Hypatia had begun, had never taken his eyes off her face; and again and again the maiden's weak heart had been cheered, as she saw the smile of sturdy intelligence and honest satisfaction which twinkled over that scarred and bristly visage; while every now and then the greybeard wagged approval, until she found herself, long before the end of the oration, addressing herself straight to her new admirer.

At last it was over, and the students behind, who had sat meekly through it all, without the slightest wish to "upset" the intruders, who had so thoroughly upset them, rose hurriedly, glad enough to get safe out of so dangerous a neighbourhood. But to their astonishment, as well as to that of Hypatia, old Wulf rose also, and stumbling along to the foot of the tribune, pulled out his purse, and laid it at Hypatia's feet.

"What is this?" asked she, half terrified at the approach of a figure more rugged and barbaric than she had ever beheld before.

"My fee for what I have heard to-day. You are a right noble maiden, and may Freya send you a husband worthy of you, and make you the mother of kings!"

And Wulf retired with his party.

Open homage to her rival, before her very face! Pelagia felt quite inclined to hate old Wulf.

But at least he was the only traitor. The rest of the Goths agreed unanimously that Hypatia was a very foolish person, who was wasting her youth and beauty in talking to donkey-riders; and Pelagia remounted her mule, and the Goths their horses, for a triumphal procession homeward.

And yet her heart was sad, even in her triumph. Right and

wrong were ideas as unknown to her as they were to hundreds of thousands in her day. As far as her own consciousness was concerned, she was as destitute of a soul as the mule on which she rode. Gifted by nature with boundless frolic and good-humour, wit and cunning, her Greek taste for the physically beautiful and graceful developed by long training, until she had become, without a rival, the most perfect pantomime, dancer, and musician who catered for the luxurious tastes of the Alexandrian theatres, she had lived since her childhood only for enjoyment and vanity, and wished for nothing more. But her new affection, or rather worship, for the huge manhood of her Gothic lover had awoke in her a new object — to keep him — to live for him — to follow him to the ends of the earth, even if he tired of her, ill-used her, despised her. And slowly, day by day, Wulf's sneers had awakened in her a dread that perhaps the Amal might despise her..... Why, she could not guess: but what sort of women were those Alrunas, of whom Wulf sung, of whom even the Amal and his men spoke with reverence, as something nobler, not only than her, but even than themselves? And what was it which Wulf had recognised in Hypatia which had bowed the stern and coarse old warrior before her in that public homage?.... It was not difficult to say what..... But why should that make Hypatia or any one else attractive?.... And the poor little child of nature gazed in deep bewilderment at a crowd of new questions, as a butterfly might at the pages of the book on which it has settled, and was sad and discontented — not with herself, for was she not Pelagia the perfect? — but with these strange fancies which came into other people's heads. — Why should not every one be as happy as they could? And who knew better than she how to be happy, and to make others happy?....

"Look at that old monk standing on the pavement, Amalric Why does he stare so at me? Tell him to go away."

The person at whom she pointed, a delicate-featured old man, with a venerable white beard, seemed to hear her; for he turned with a sudden start, and then, to Pelagia's astonishment, put his hands before his face, and burst convulsively into tears.

"What does he mean by behaving in that way? Bring him here to me this moment! I will know!" cried she, petulantly catching at the new object, in order to escape from her own thoughts.

In a moment a Goth had led up the weeper, who came without demur to the side of Pelagia's mule.

"Why were you so rude as to burst out crying in my face?" asked she, petulantly.

The old man looked up sadly and tenderly, and answered In a low voice, meant only for her ear, —

"And how can I help weeping-, when I see anything as beautiful as you are destined to the flames of hell for ever?"

"The flames of hell?" said Pelagia, with a shudder. "What for?"

"Do you not know?" asked the old man, with a look of sad surprise. "Have you forgotten what you are?"

"I? I never hurt a fly!"

"Why do you look so terrified, my darling? What have you been saying to her, you old villain?" and the Amal raised his whip.

"Oh! do not strike him. Come, come to-morrow, and tell me what you mean."

"No, we will have no monks within our doors, frightening silly women. Off, sirrah! and thank the lady that you have escaped with a whole skin." And the Amal caught the bridle of Pelagia's mule, and pushed forward, leaving the old man gazing sadly after them.

But the beautiful sinner was evidently not the object which had brought the old monk of the desert into a neighbourhood so strange and ungenial to his habits; for, recovering himself in a few moments, he hurried on to the door of the Museum, and there planted himself, scanning earnestly the faces of the passers-out, and meeting, of course, with his due share of student ribaldry.

"Well, old cat, and what mouse are you on the watch for, at the hole's mouth here?"

"Just come inside, and see whether the mice will not singe your whiskers for you."....

"Here is my mouse, gentlemen," answered the old monk, with a bow and a smile, as he laid his hand on Philammon's arm, and presented to his astonished eyes the delicate features and high retreating forehead of Arsenius.

"My father!" cried the boy, in the first impulse of affectionate recognition; and then — he had expected some such meeting all along, but now that it was come at last, he turned pale as death. The students saw his emotion.

"Hands off, old Heautontimoroumenos! He belongs to our guild now! Monks have no more business with sons than with wives. Shall we hustle him for you, Philammon?"

"Take care how you show off, gentlemen: the Goths are not yet out of hearing!" answered Philammon, who was learning fast how to give a smart answer; and then, fearing the temper of the young dandies, and shrinking from the notion of any insult to one so reverend and so beloved as Arsenius, he drew the old man gently away, and walked up the street with him in silence, dreading what was coming.

"And are these your friends?"

"Heaven forbid! I have nothing in common with such animals but flesh and blood, and a seat in the lecture-room!''

"Of the heathen woman?"

Philammon, after the fashion of young men in fear, rushed desperately into the subject himself, just because he dreaded Arsenius's entering on it quietly.

"Yes, of the heathen woman. Of course you have seen Cyril before you came hither?"

"I have, and —— "

"And," went on Philammon, interrupting him, "you have been told every lie which prurience, stupidity, and revenge can invent. That I have trampled on the cross — sacrificed to all the deities in the pantheon — and probably" — (and he blushed scarlet) — "that that purest and holiest of beings — who, if she were not what people call a pagan, would be, and deserves to be, worshipped as the queen of saints — that she — and I ——" and he stopped.

"Have I said that I believed what I may have heard?"

"No — and therefore, as they are all simple and sheer falsehoods, there is no more to be said on the subject. Not that I shall not be delighted to answer any questions of yours, my dearest father —— "

"Have I asked any, my child?"

"No. So we may as well change the subject for the present," — and he began overwhelming the old man with inquiries about himself, Pambo, and each and all of the inhabitants of the Laura: to which Arsenius, to the boy's infinite relief, answered cordially and minutely, and even vouchsafed a smile at some jest of Philammon's on the contrast between the monks of Nitria and those of Scetis.

Arsenius was too wise not to see well enough what all this flippancy meant; and too wise, also, not to know that Philammon's version was probably quite as near the truth as Peter's and Cyril's; but for reasons of his own, merely replied by an affectionate look, and a compliment to Philammon's growth.

"And yet you seem thin and pale, my boy."

"Study," said Philammon, "study. One cannot burn the midnight oil without paying some penalty for it..... However, I am richly repaid already; I shall be more so hereafter."

"Let us hope so. But who are those Goths whom I passed in the streets just now?"

"Ah! my father," said Philammon, glad in his heart of any excuse to turn the conversation, and yet half uneasy and suspicious at Arsenius's evident determination to avoid the very object of his visit. "It must have been you, then, whom I saw stop and speak to Pelagia at the farther end of the street. What words could you possibly have had wherewith to honour such a creature?"

"God knows. Some secret sympathy touched my heart..... Alas! poor child! But how came you to know her?"

"All Alexandria knows the shameless abomination," interrupted a voice at their elbow — none other than that of the little porter, who had been dodging-and watching the pair the whole way, and could no longer restrain his longing to meddle. "And well it had been for many a rich young man had old Miriam never brought her over, in an evil day, from Athens hither."

"Miriam?"

"Yes, monk; a name not unknown, I am told, in palaces as well as in slave-markets."

"An evil-eyed old Jewess?"

"A Jewess she is, as her name might have informed you; and as for her eyes, I consider them, or used to do so, of course — for her injured nation have been long expelled from Alexandria by your fanatic tribe — as altogether divine and demoniac, let the base imagination of monks call them what it likes."

"But how did you know this Pelagia, my son? She is no fit company for such as you."

Philammon told, honestly enough, the story of his Nile journey, and Pelagia's invitation to him.

"You did not surely accept it?"

"Heaven forbid that Hypatia's scholar should so degrade himself!"

Arsenius shook his head sadly.

"You would not have had me go?"

"No, boy. But how long hast thou learned to call thyself Hypatia's scholar, or to call it a degradation to visit the most sinful, if thou mightest thereby bring back a lost lamb to the Good Shepherd? Nevertheless, thou art too young for such employment — and she meant to tempt thee, doubtless."

"I do not think it. She seemed struck by my talking Athenian Greek, and having come from Athens."

"And how long since she came from Athens?" said Arsenius, after a pause. "Who knows?"

"Just after it was sacked by the barbarians," said the little porter, who, beginning to suspect a mystery, was peaking and peering like an excited parrot. "The old dame brought her hither among a cargo of captive boys and girls."

"The time agrees..... Can this Miriam be found?"

"A sapient and courteous question for a monk to ask! Do you not know that Cyril has expelled all Jews four months ago?"

"True, true..... Alas!" said the old man to himself, "how little the rulers of this world guess their own power! They move a finger carelessly, and forget that that finger may crush to death hundreds whose names they never heard — and every soul of them as precious in God's sight as Cyril's own."

"What is the matter, my father?" asked Philammon. "You seem deeply moved about this woman.".....

"And she is Miriam's slave?"

"Her freedwoman this four years past," said the porter. "The good lady — for reasons doubtless excellent in themselves, though not altogether patent to the philosophic mind — thought good to turn her loose on the Alexandrian republic, to seek what she might devour."

"God help her! And you are certain that Miriam is not in Alexandria?"

The little porter turned very red, and Philammon did so likewise; but he remembered his promise, and kept it.

"You both know something of her, I can see. You cannot deceive an old statesman, sir!" — turning to the little porter with a look of authority — "poor monk though he be now. If you think fitting to tell me what you know, I promise you that neither she nor you shall be losers by your confidence in me. If not, I shall find means to discover."

Both stood silent.

" Philammon, my son! and art thou too in league against — no, not against me; against thyself, poor misguided boy?"

"Against myself?"

"Yes — I have said it. But unless you will trust me, I cannot trust you."

"I have promised."

"And I, sir statesman, or monk, or both, or neither, have sworn by the immortal gods!" said the porter, looking very big.

Arsenius paused.

"There are those who hold that an oath by an idol, being nothing, is of itself void. I do not agree with them. If thou thinkest it sin to break thine oath, to thee it is sin. And for thee, my poor child, thy promise is sacred, were it made to Iscariot himself. But hear me. Can either of you, by asking this woman, be so far absolved as to give me speech of her? Tell her — that is, if she be in Alexandria, which God grant — all that has passed between us here, and tell her, on the solemn oath of a Christian, that Arsenius, whose name she knows well, will neither injure nor betray her. Will you do this?"

"Arsenius?" said the little porter, with a look of mingled awe and pity.

The old man smiled. "Arsenius, who was once called the Father of the Emperors. Even she will trust that name."

"I will go this moment, sir; I will fly!" and off rushed the little porter.

"The little fellow forgets," said Arsenius, with a smile, "to how much he has confessed already, and how easy it were now to trace him to the old hag's lair.... Philammon, my son.... I have many tears to weep over thee — but they must wait a while. I have thee safe now," and the old man clutched his arm. "Thou wilt not leave thy poor old father? Thou wilt not desert me for the heathen woman?"

"I will stay with you, I promise you, indeed! if — if you

will not say unjust things of her."

"I will speak evil of no one, accuse no one, but myself. I will not say one harsh word to thee, my poor boy. But listen now! Thou knowest that thou earnest from Athens. Knowest thou that it was I who brought thee hither?"

"You?"

"I, my son: but when I brought thee to the Laura, it seemed right that thou, as the son of a noble gentleman, shouldest hear nothing of it. But tell me: Dost thou recollect father or mother, brother or sister; or anything of thy home in Athens?"

"No!"

"Thanks be to God. But Philammon, if thou hadst had a sister — hush! And if — I only say if —— "

"A sister!" interrupted Philammon. "Pelagia?"

"God forbid, my son! But a sister thou hadst once — some three years older than thee she seemed."

"What? did you know her?"

"I saw her but once — on one sad day. — Poor children both! I will not sadden you by telling you where and how."

"And why did you not bring her hither with me? You surely had not the heart to part us?"

"Ah, my son, what right had an old monk with a fair young girl? And, indeed, even had I had the courage, it would have been impossible. There were others, richer than I, to whose covetousness her youth and beauty seemed a precious prize. When I saw her last, she was in company with an ancient Jewess. Heaven grant that this Miriam may prove to be the one!"

"And I have a sister!" gasped Philammon, his eyes bursting with tears. "We must find her! You will help me? — Now — this moment! There is nothing else to be thought of, spoken of, done, henceforth, till she is found!"

"Ah, my son, my son! Better, better, perhaps, to leave her in the hands of God! What if she were dead? To discover that, would be to discover needless sorrow. And what if — God grant that it be not so! she had only a name to live, and were dead, worse than dead, in sinful pleasure? —— "

"We would save her, or die trying to save her! Is it not enough for me that she is my sister?"

Arsenius shook his head. He little knew the strange new light and warmth which his words had poured in upon the young heart beside him..... "A sister!" What mysterious virtue was there in that simple word, which made Philammon's brain reel and his heart throb madly? A sister! not merely a friend, an equal, a helpmate, given by God himself, for loving whom none, not even a monk, could blame him. — Not merely something delicate, weak, beautiful — for of course she must be beautiful — whom he might cherish, guide, support, deliver, die for, and find death delicious. Yes — all that, and more than that, lay in the sacred word. For those divided and partial notions had flitted across his mind too rapidly to stir such passion as moved him now; even the hint of her sin and danger had been heard heedlessly, if heard at all. It was the word itself which bore its own message, its own spell, to the heart of the fatherless and motherless foundling, as he faced for the first time the deep, everlasting, divine reality of kindred..... A sister! of his own flesh and blood — born of the same father, the same mother — his, his, for ever! How hollow and fleeting seemed all "spiritual sonships," "spiritual daughterhoods," inventions of the changing fancy, the wayward will of man! Arsenius — Pambo — ay, Hypatia herself — what were they to him now? Here was a real relationship..... A sister! What else was worth caring for upon earth?

"And she was at Athens when Pelagia was" — he cried at last — "perhaps knew her — let us go to Pelagia herself!"

"Heaven forbid!" said Arsenius. "We must wait at least till Miriam's answer comes."

"I can show you her house at least in the meanwhile; and you can go in yourself when you will. I do not ask to enter. Come! I feel certain that my finding her is in some way bound up with Pelagia. Had I not met her on the Nile, had you not met her in the street, I might never have heard that I had a sister. And if she went with Miriam, Pelagia must know her — she may be in that very house at this moment!"

Arsenius had his reasons for suspecting that Philammon was but too right. But he contented himself with yielding to the boy's excitement, and set off with him in the direction of the dancer's house.

They were within a few yards of the gate, when hurried footsteps behind them, and voices calling them by name, made them turn; and behold, evidently to the disgust of Arsenius as much as Philammon himself, Peter the Reader and a large party of monks!

Philammon's first impulse was to escape: Arsenius himself caught him by the arm, and seemed inclined to hurry on.

"No!" thought the youth, "am I not a free man, and a philosopher?" and facing round, he awaited the enemy.

"Ah, young apostate! So you have found him, reverend and ill-used sir. Praised be Heaven for this rapid success!"

"My good friend," asked Arsenius, in a trembling voice, "what brings you here?"

"Heaven forbid that I should have allowed your sanctity and age to go forth, without some guard against the insults and violence of this wretched youth and his profligate companions. We have been following you afar oil all the morning, with hearts full of filial solicitude."

"Many thanks; but indeed your kindness has been superfluous. My son here, from whom I have met with nothing but affection, and whom, indeed, I believe far more innocent than report declared him, is about to return peaceably with me. Are you not, Philammon?"

"Alas! my father," said Philammon, with an effort, "how can I find courage to say it? — but I cannot return with you."

"Cannot return?"

"I vowed that I would never again cross that threshold till ———"

"And Cyril does. He bade me, indeed he bade me, assure you that he would receive you back as a son, and forgive and forget all the past."

"Forgive and forget? That is my part — not his. Will he right me against that tyrant and his crew? Will he proclaim me openly to be an innocent and persecuted man, unjustly beaten and driven forth for obeying his own commands? Till he does that, I shall not forget that I am a free man."

"A free man?" said Peter, with an unpleasant smile; "that remains to be proved, my gay youth; and will need more evidence than that smart philosophic cloak and those well-curled locks which you have adopted since I saw you last."

"Remains to be proved?"

Arsenius made an imploring gesture to Peter to be silent.

"Nay, sir. As I foretold to you, this one way alone remains; the blame of it, if there be blame, must rest on the unhappy youth whose perversity renders it necessary."

"For God's sake, spare me!" cried the old man, dragging Peter aside, while Philammon stood astonished, divided between indignation and vague dread.

"Did I not tell you again and again that I never could bring myself to call a Christian man my slave? And him, above all, my spiritual son?"

"And, most reverend sir, whose zeal is only surpassed by your tenderness and mercy, did not the holy patriarch assure you that your scruples were groundless? Do you think that either he or I can have less horror than you have of slavery in itself? Heaven forbid! But when an immortal soul is at stake — when a lost lamb is to be brought back to the fold — surely you may employ the authority which the law gives you for the salvation of that precious charge committed to you? What could be more conclusive than his Holiness's argument this morning? 'Christians are bound to obey the laws of this world for conscience' sake, even though, in the abstract, they may disapprove of them, and deny their authority. Then, by parity of reasoning, it must be lawful for them to take the advantage which those same laws offer them, when by so doing the glory of God may be advanced.' "

Arsenius still hung back, with eyes brimming with tears; but Philammon himself put an end to the parley.

"What is the meaning of all this? Are you, too, in a conspiracy against me? Speak, Arsenius!"

"This is the meaning of it, blinded sinner!" cried Peter. "That you are by law the slave of Arsenius, lawfully bought with his money, in the city of Ravenna; and that he has the power, and, as I trust, for the sake of your salvation, the will also, to compel you to accompany him."

Philammon recoiled across the pavement, with eyes flashing defiance. A slave! The light of heaven grew black to him..... Oh, that Hypatia might never know his shame! Yet it was impossible. Too dreadful to be true.....

"You lie!" almost shrieked he. "I am the son of a noble citizen of Athens. Arsenius told me so, but this moment, with his own lips!"

"Ay, but he bought you — bought you in the public market; and he can prove it!"

"Hear me — hear me, my son!" cried the old man, springing toward him. Philammon, in his fury, mistook the gesture, and thrust him fiercely back.

"Your son? — your slave! Do not insult the name of son by applying it to me. Yes, sir; your slave in body, but not in soul! Ay, seize me — drag home the fugitive — scourge him — brand him — chain him in the mill, if you can; but even for that the free heart has a remedy. If you will not let me live as a philosopher, you shall see me die like one!"

"Seize the fellow, my brethren!" cried Peter, while Arsenius, utterly unable to restrain either party, hid his face, and wept.

"Wretches!" cried the boy; "you shall never take me alive, while I have teeth or nails left. Treat me as a brute beast, and I will defend myself as such!"

"Out of the way there, rascals! Place for the Prefect! What are you squabbling about here, you unmannerly monks?" shouted peremptory voices from behind. The crowd parted, and disclosed the apparitors of Orestes, who followed in his robes of office.

A sudden hope flashed before Philammon, and in an instant he had burst through the mob, and was clinging to the Prefect's chariot.

"I am a free-born Athenian, whom these monks wish to kidnap back into slavery! I claim your protection!"

"And you shall have it, right or wrong, my handsome fellow. By Heaven, you are much too good-looking to be made a monk of! What do you mean, you villains, by attempting to kidnap free men? Is it not enough for you to lock up every mad girl whom you can dupe, but you must —— "

"His master is here present, your Excellency, who will swear to the purchase."

"Or to anything else for the glory of God. Out of the way I And take care, you tall scoundrel, that I do not get a handle against you. You have been one of my marked men for many a month. Off!"

"His master demands the rights of the law as a Roman citizen," said Peter, pushing forward Arsenius.

"If he be a Roman citizen, let him come and make his claim at the tribune to-morrow, in legal form. But I would have you remember, ancient sir, that I shall require you to prove your citizenship, before we proceed to the question of purchase."

"The law does not demand that," quoth Peter.

"Knock that fellow down, apparitor!" Whereat Peter vanished, and an ominous growl rose from the mob of monks.

"What am I to do, most noble sir?" said Philammon.

"Whatever you like, till the third hour to-morrow — if you are fool enough to appear at the tribune. If you will take my advice, you will knock down these fellows right and left, and run for your life." And Orestes drove on.

Philammon saw that it was his only chance, and did so; and in another minute he found himself rushing headlong into the archway of Pelagia's house, with a dozen monks at his heels.

As luck would have it, the outer gates, at which the Goths had just entered, were still open; but the inner ones which led into the court beyond were fast. He tried them, but in vain. There was an open door in the wall on his right: he rushed through it, into a long range of stables, and into the arms of Wulf and Smid, who were unsaddling and feeding, like true warriors, their own horses.

"Souls of my fathers!" shouted Smid, "here's our young monk come back! What brings you here head over heels in this way, young curly-pate?"

"Save me from those wretches!" pointing to the monks, who were peeping into the doorway.

Wulf seemed to understand it all in a moment; for, snatching up a heavy whip, he rushed at the foe, and with a few tremendous strokes cleared the doorway, and shut-to the door.

Philammon was going to explain and thank, but Smid I stopped his mouth.

"Never mind, young one, you are our guest now. Come in, and you shall be as welcome as ever. See what comes of running away from us at first."

"You do not seem to have benefited much by leaving me for the monks," said old Wulf. "Come in by the inner door. Smid! go and turn those monks out of the gateway."

But the mob, after battering the door for a few minutes, had yielded to the agonized entreaties of Peter, who assured them that if those incarnate fiends once broke out upon them, they would not leave a Christian alive in Alexandria. So it was agreed to leave a few to watch for Philammon's coming out; and the rest, balked of their prey, turned the tide of their wrath against the Prefect, and rejoined the mass of their party, who were still hanging round his chariot, ready for mischief.

In vain the hapless shepherd of the people attempted to drive on. The apparitors were frightened, and hung back; and without their help it was impossible to force the horses through the mass of tossing arms and beards in front. The matter was evidently growing serious.

"The bitterest ruffians in all Nitria, your Excellency," whispered one of the guards, with a pale face; "and two hundred of them, at the least. The very same set, I will be sworn, who nearly murdered Dioscuros."

"If you will not allow me to proceed, my holy brethren," said Orestes, trying to look collected, "perhaps it will not be contrary to the canons of the church if I turn back. Leave the horses' heads alone. Why, in God's name, what do you want?"

"Do you fancy we have forgotten Hieracas?" cried a voice from the rear; and at that name, yell upon yell arose, till the mob, gaining courage from its own noise, burst out into open threats. "Revenge for the blessed martyr, Hieracas!" "Revenge for the wrongs of the church!" "Down with the friend of Heathens, Jews, and Barbarians I" "Down with the favourite of Hypatia!" "Tyrant!" "Butcher!"

And the last epithet so smote the delicate fancy of the crowd, that a general cry arose of "Kill the butcher!" and one furious monk attempted to clamber into the chariot. An apparitor tore him down, and was dragged to the ground in his turn. The monks closed in. The guards, finding the enemy number ten to their one, threw down their weapons in a panic, and vanished; and in; another minute the hopes of Hypatia and the gods would have been lost for ever, and Alexandria robbed of the blessing of being ruled by the most finished gentleman-south of the Mediterranean, had it not been for unexpected-succour; of which it will be time enough, considering who and what is in danger, to speak in a future chapter.

CHAPTER XVII
A STRAY GLEAM

THE last blue headland of Sardinia was fading fast on the north-west horizon, and a steady breeze bore before it innumerable ships, the wrecks of Heraclian's armament, plunging and tossing impatiently in their desperate homeward race toward the coast of Africa. Far and wide, under a sky of cloudless blue, the white sails glittered on the glittering sea, as gaily now, above their loads of shame and disappointment, terror and pain, as when, but one short month before, they bore with them only wild hopes and gallant daring. Who can calculate the sum of misery in that hapless flight?.... And yet it was but one, and that one of the least known and most trivial, of the tragedies of that age of woe; one petty death-spasm among the unnumbered throes which were shaking to dissolution the Babylon of the West. Her time had come. Even as Saint John beheld her in his vision, by agony after agony, she was rotting to her well-earned doom. Tyrannizing it luxuriously over all nations, she had sat upon the mystic beast — building her power on the brute animal appetites of her dupes and slaves: but she had duped herself even more than them. She was finding out by bitter lessons that it was "to the beast," and not to her, that her vassal kings of the earth had been giving their power and strength; and the ferocity and lust which she had pampered so cunningly in them, had become her curse and her destruction..... Drunk with the blood of the saints; blinded by her own conceit and jealousy to the fact that she had been crushing and extirpating out of her empire for centuries past all which was noble, purifying, regenerative, divine, she sat impotent and doting, the prey of every fresh adventurer, the slave of her own slaves..... "And the kings of the earth who had sinned with her, hated the harlot, and made her desolate and naked, and devoured her flesh, and burned her with fire. For God had put into their hearts to fulfil his will, and to agree, and to give their kingdom to the beast, until the words of God should be fulfilled.".... Everywhere sensuality, division, hatred, treachery, cruelty, uncertainty, terror; the vials of God's wrath poured out. Where was to be the end of it all? asked every man of his neighbour, generation after generation; and received for answer only, "It is better to die than to live."

And yet, in one ship out of that sad fleet, there was peace; peace amid shame and terror; amid the groans of the wounded, and the sighs of the starving; amid all but blank despair. The great triremes and quinqueremes rushed onward past the lagging transports, careless, in the mad race for safety, that they were leaving the greater number of their comrades defenceless in the rear of the flight; but from one little fishing-craft alone no base entreaties, no bitter execrations greeted the passing flash and roll of their mighty oars. One after another, day by day, they came rushing up out of the northern offing, each like a huge hundred-footed dragon, panting and quivering, as if with terror, at every loud pulse of its oars, hurling the wild water right and left with the mighty share of its beak, while from the bows some gorgon or chimæra, elephant or boar stared out with brazen eyes toward the coast of Africa, as if it, too, like the human beings which it carried, was dead to every care but that of dastard flight. Past they rushed, one after another; and off the poop some shouting voice chilled all hearts for a moment, with the fearful news that the Emperor's Neapolitan fleet was in full chase..... And the soldiers on board that little vessel looked silently and steadfastly into the silent steadfast face of the old Prefect, and Victoria saw him shudder, and turn his eyes away — and stood up among the rough fighting men, like a goddess, and cried aloud that "The Lord would protect his own"; and they believed her, and were still; till many days and many ships were past, and the little fishing-craft, outstripped even by the transports and merchant-men, as it strained and crawled along-before its single square-sail, was left alone upon the sea.

And where was Raphael Aben-Ezra?

He was sitting, with Bran's head between his knees, at the door of a temporary awning in the vessel's stern, which shielded the wounded men from sun and spray; and as he sat he could hear from within the tent the gentle voices of Victoria and her brother, as they tended the sick like ministering angels, or read to them words of divine hope and comfort — in which his home-less heart felt that he had no share.....

"As I live, I would change places now with any one of those poor mangled ruffians, to have that voice speaking such words to me.... and to believe them.".... And he went on perusing the manuscript which he held in his hand.

* * * * * *

"Well!" he sighed to himself after a while, "at least it is the most complimentary, not to say hopeful, view of our destinies with which I have met since I threw away my nurse's belief that the seed of David was fated to conquer the whole earth, and set up a second Roman Empire at Jerusalem, only worse than the present one, in that the devils of superstition and bigotry would be added to those of tyranny and rapine."

A hand was laid on his shoulder, and a voice asked, "And what may this so hopeful view be?"

"Ah! my dear General!" said Raphael, looking up. "I have a poor bill of fare whereon to exercise my culinary powers this morning. Had it not been for that shark who was so luckily deluded last night, I should have been reduced to the necessity of stewing my friend the fat decurion's big boots."

"They would have been savoury enough, I will warrant, after they had passed under your magical hand."

"It is a comfort, certainly, to find that after all one did learn something useful in Alexandria! So I will even go forward at once, and employ my artistic skill."

"Tell me first what it was about which I heard you just now soliloquizing, as so hopeful a view of some matter or other?"

"Honestly — if you will neither betray me to your son and daughter, nor consider me as having in anywise committed myself — it was Paul of Tarsus' notion of the history and destinies of our stiff-necked nation. See what your daughter has persuaded me into reading!" And he held up a manuscript of the Epistle to the Hebrews.

"It is execrable Greek. But it is sound philosophy, I cannot deny. He knows Plato better than all the ladies and gentlemen in Alexandria put together, if my opinion on the point be worth having."

"I am a plain soldier, and no judge on that point, sir. He may or may not know Plato; but I am right sure that he knows God."

"Not too fast," said Raphael, with a smile. "You do not know, perhaps, that I have spent the last ten years of my life among men who professed the same knowledge?"

"Augustine, too, spent the best ten years of his life among such; and yet he is now combating the very errors which he once taught."

"Having found, he fancies, something better?"

"Having found it, most truly. But you must talk to him yourself, and argue the matter over, with one who can argue. To me such questions are an unknown land."

"Well.... Perhaps I may be tempted to do even that. At least, a thoroughly converted philosopher — for poor dear Synesius is half heathen still, I often fancy, and hankers after the wisdom of the Egyptian — will be a curious sight; and to talk with so famous and so learned a man would always be a pleasure; but to argue with him, or any other human being, none whatsoever."

"Why, then?"

"My dear sir, I am sick of syllogisms, and probabilities, and pros and contras. What do I care if, on weighing both sides, the nineteen pounds' weight of questionable arguments against, are overbalanced by the twenty pounds' weight of equally questionable arguments for? Do you not see that my belief of the victorious proposition will be proportioned to the one overbalancing pound only, while the whole other nineteen will go for nothing?"

"I really do not."

"Happy are you, then. I do, from many a sad experience. No, my worthy sir. I want a faith past arguments; one which, whether I can prove it or not to the satisfaction of the lawyers, I believe to my own satisfaction, and act on it as undoubtingly and unreasoningly as I do upon my own newly rediscovered personal identity. I don't want to possess a faith. I want a faith which will possess me. And if I ever arrived at such a one, believe me, it would be by some such practical demonstration as this very tent has given me."

"This tent?"

"Yes, sir, this tent; within which I have seen you and your children lead a life of deeds as new to me the Jew, as they would be to Hypatia the Gentile. I have watched you for many a day, and not in vain. When I saw you, an experienced officer, encumber your flight with wounded men, I was only surprised. But since I have seen you and your daughter, and, strangest of all, your gay young Alcibiades of a son, starving yourselves to feed those poor ruffians — performing for them, day and night, the offices of menial slaves — comforting them, as no man ever comforted me — blaming no one but yourselves, caring for every one but yourselves, sacrificing nothing but yourselves; and all this without hope of fame or reward, or dream of appeasing the wrath of any god or goddess, but simply because you thought it right.... When I saw that, sir, and more which I have seen; and when, reading in this book here, I found most unexpectedly those very grand moral rules which you were practising, seeming to spring unconsciously, as natural results, from the great thoughts, true or false, which had preceded them; then, sir, I began to suspect that the creed which could produce such deeds as I have watched within the last few days, might have on its side not merely a slight preponderance of probabilities, but what we Jews used once to call, when we believed in it — or in anything — the mighty power of God."

And as he spoke, he looked into the Prefect's face with the look of a man wrestling in some deadly struggle; so intense and terrible was the earnestness of his eye, that even the old soldier shrank before it.

"And therefore," he went on, "therefore, sir, beware of your own actions, and of your children's. If, by any folly or baseness, such as I have seen in every human being whom I ever met as yet, upon this accursed stage of fools, you shall crush my new-budding hope that there Is something somewhere which will make me what I know that I ought to be, and can be — If you shall crush that, I say, by any misdoing of yours, you had better have been the murderer of my firstborn; with such a hate — a hate which Jews alone can feel — will I hate you and yours."

"God help us and strengthen us!" said the old warrior in a tone of noble humility.

"And now," said Raphael, glad to change the subject, after this unwonted outburst, "we must once more seriously consider whether it is wise to hold on our present course. If you return to Carthage, or to Hippo ———"

"I shall be beheaded."

"Most assuredly. And how much soever you may consider such an event a gain to yourself, yet for the sake of your son and your daughter ———"

"My dear sir," interrupted the Prefect, "you mean kindly. But do not, do not tempt me. By the Count's side I have fought for thirty years, and by his side I will die, as I deserve."

"Victorius! Victoria!" cried Raphael; "help me! Your father," he went on, as they came out from the tent, "is still decided on losing his own head, and throwing away ours, by going to Carthage."

"For my sake — for our sakes — father!" cried Victoria, clinging to him.

"And for my sake, also, most excellent sir," said Raphael, smiling quietly. "I have no wish to be so uncourteous as to urge any help which I may have seemed to afford you. But I hope that you will recollect that I have a life to lose, and that it is hardly fair of you to imperil it, as you intend to do. If you could help or save Heraclian, I should be dumb at once. But now, for a mere point of honour to destroy fifty good soldiers, who know not their right hands from their left — Shall I ask their opinion?"

"Will you raise a mutiny against me, sir?" asked the old man, sternly.

"Why not mutiny against Philip drunk, in behalf of Philip sober? But really, I will obey you.... only you must obey us..... What is Hesiod's definition of the man who will neither counsel himself nor be counselled by his friends?.... Have you no trusty acquaintances in Cyrenaica, for instance?"

The Prefect was silent.

"Oh, hear us, my father! Why not go to Euodius? He is your old comrade — a well-wisher, too, to this.... this expedition..... And recollect, Augustine must be there now. He was about to sail for Berenice, in order to consult Synesius and the Pentapolitan bishops, when we left Carthage."

And at the name of Augustine the old man paused.

"Augustine will be there; true. And this our friend must meet him. And thus at least I should have his advice. If he thinks it my duty to return to Carthage, I can but do so, after all. But the soldiers?"

"Excellent sir," said Raphael, "Synesius and the Pentapolitan landlords — who can hardly call their lives their own, thanks to the Moors — will be glad enough to feed and pay them, or any other brave fellows with arms in their hands, at this moment. And my friend Victorius, here, will enjoy, I do not doubt, a little wild campaigning against marauding blacka-moors."

The old man bowed silently. The battle was won.

The young tribune, who had been watching his father's face with the most intense anxiety, caught at the gesture, and hurrying forward, announced the change of plan to the soldiery. It was greeted with a shout of joy, and in another five minutes the sails were about, the rudders shifted, and the ship on her way toward the western point of Sicily, before a steady north-west breeze.

"Ah!" cried Victoria, delighted. "And now you will see Augustine! You must promise me to talk to him!"

"This, at least, I will promise, that whatsoever the great sophist shall be pleased to say, shall meet with a patient hearing from a brother sophist. Do not be angry. at the term. Recollect that I am somewhat tired, like my ancestor Solomon, of wisdom and wise men, having found it only too like madness and folly. And you cannot surely expect me to believe in man, while I do not yet believe in God?"

Victoria sighed. "I will not believe you. Why always pre-tend to be worse than you are?"

"That kind souls like you may be spared the pain of find-ing me worse than I seem..... There, let us say no more; except that I heartily wish that you would hate me!"

"Shall I try?"

"That must be my work, I fear, not yours. However, I shall give you good cause enough before long, doubt it not."

Victoria sighed again, and retired into the tent to nurse the sick.

"And now, sir," said the Prefect, turning to Raphael and his son; "do not mistake me. I may have been weak, as worn-out and hopeless men are wont to be; but do not think of me as one who has yielded to adversity in fear for his own safety. As God hears me, I desire nothing better than to die; and I only turn out of my course on the understanding that if Augustine so advise, my children hold me free to return to Carthage and meet my fate. All I pray for is, that my life may be spared until I can place my dear child in the safe shelter of a nunnery."

"A nunnery?"

"Yes, indeed; I have intended ever since her birth, to dedicate her to the service of God. And in such times as these, what better lot for a defenceless girl?"

"Pardon me!" said Raphael; "but I am too dull to comprehend what benefit or pleasure your Deity will derive from the celibacy of your daughter..... Except, indeed, on one supposition, which, as I have some faint remnants of reverence and decency reawakening in me just now, I must leave to be uttered only by the pure lips of sexless priests."

"You forget, sir, that you are speaking to a Christian."

"I assure you, no! I had certainly been forgetting it till the last two minutes, in your very pleasant and rational society. There is no danger henceforth of my making so silly a mistake."

"Sir!" said the Prefect, reddening at the undisguised contempt of Raphael's manner..... "When you know a little more of St. Paul's Epistles, you will cease to insult the opinions and feelings of those who obey them, by sacrificing their most precious treasures to God."

"Oh, it is Paul of Tarsus, then, who gives you the advice? I thank you for informing me of the fact; for it will save me the trouble of any future study of his works. Allow me, therefore, to return by your hands this manuscript of his with many thanks from me to that daughter of yours, by whose perpetual imprisonment you intend to give pleasure to your Deity. Henceforth the less communication which passes between me and any member of your family, the better." And he turned away.

"But, my dear sir!" said the honest soldier, really chagrined, "you must not! — we owe you too much, and love you too well to part thus for the caprice of a moment. If any word of mine has offended you — forget it, and forgive me, I beseech you!" and he caught both Raphael's hands in his own.

"My very dear sir," answered the Jew, quietly; "let me ask the same forgiveness of you; and believe me, for the sake of past pleasant passages, I shall not forget my promise about the mortgage..... But — here we must part. To tell you the truth, I half-an-hour ago was fearfully near becoming neither more nor less than a Christian. I had actually deluded myself into the fancy that the Deity of the Galileans might be, after all, the God of our old Hebrew forefathers — of Adam and Eve, of Abraham and David, and of the rest who believed that children and the fruit of the womb were an heritage and gift which cometh of the Lord —

and that Paul was right — actually right — in his theory that the church was the development and fulfilment of our old national polity..... I must thank you for opening my eyes to a mistake which, had I not been besotted for the moment, every monk and nun would have contradicted by the mere fact of their existence, and reserve my nascent faith for some Deity who takes no delight in seeing his creatures stultify the primary laws of their being. Farewell!"

And while the Prefect stood petrified with astonishment, he retired to the further extremity of the deck, muttering to himself—

"Did I not know all along that this gleam was too sudden and too bright to last? Did I not know that he, too, would prove himself, like all the rest — an ass?.... Fool I to have looked for common sense on such an earth as this!.... Back to chaos again, Raphael Aben-Ezra, and spin ropes of sand to the end of the farce !"

And mixing with the soldiers, he exchanged no word with the Prefect and his children, till they reached the port of Berenice; and then putting the necklace into Victoria's hands, vanished among the crowds upon the quay, no one knew whither.

CHAPTER XVIII
THE PREFECT TESTED

WHEN we lost sight of Philammon, his destiny had hurled him once more among his old friends the Goths, in search of two important elements of human comfort, freedom and a sister. The former he found at once, in a large hall where sundry Goths were lounging and toping, into the nearest corner of which he shrank, and stood, his late terror and rage forgotten altogether in the one new and absorbing thought — His sister might be in that house!.... and yielding to so sweet a dream, he began fancying to himself which of all those gay maidens she might be who had become in one moment more dear, more great to him, than all things else in heaven or earth. That fair-haired, rounded Italian? That fierce, luscious, aquiline-faced Jewess? That delicate, swart, sidelong-eyed Copt? No. She was Athenian, like himself. That tall, lazy Greek girl, then, from beneath whose sleepy lids flashed, once an hour, sudden lightnings, revealing depths of thought and feeing uncultivated, perhaps even unsuspected, by their possessor? Her? Or that, her seeming sister? Or the next?.... Or — Was it Pelagia herself, most beautiful and most sinful of them all? Fearful thought t He blushed scarlet at the bare imagination: yet why, in his secret heart, was that the most pleasant hypothesis of them all? And suddenly flashed across him that observation of one of the girls on board the boat, on his likeness to Pelagia. Strange, that he had never recollected it before! It must be so! And yet on what a slender thread, woven of scattered hints and surmises, did that "must" depend! He would be sane; he would wait; he would have patience. Patience, with a sister yet unfound, perhaps perishing? Impossible!

Suddenly the train of his thoughts was changed perforce:
—

"Come! come and see! There's a fight in the streets," called one of the damsels down the stairs, at the highest pitch of her voice.

"I shan't go," yawned a huge fellow, who was lying on his back on a sofa.

"Oh come up, my hero," said one of the girls. "Such a

charming riot, and the Prefect himself in the middle of it! We have not had such a one in the street this month."

"The princes won't let me knock any of these donkey-riders on the head, and seeing other people do it only makes me envious. Give me the wine-jug — curse the girl! she has run upstairs!"

The shouting and trampling came nearer; and in another minute Wulf came rapidly downstairs, through the hall into the harem-court, and into the presence of the Amal.

"Prince — here is a chance for us. These rascally Greeks are murdering their Prefect under our very windows."

"The lying cur! Serve him right for cheating us. He has plenty of guards. Why can't the fool take care of himself?"

"They have all run away, and I saw some of them hiding among the mob. As I live, the man will be killed in five minutes more."

"Why not?"

"Why should he, when we can save him and win his favour for ever? The men's fingers are itching for a fight; it's a bad plan not to give hounds blood now and then, or they lose the knack of hunting."

"Well, it wouldn't take five minutes."

"And heroes should show that they can forgive when an enemy is in distress."

"Very true! Like an Amal too!" And the Amal sprang up and shouted to his men to follow him.

"Good-by, my pretty one. Why, Wulf," cried he, as he burst out into the court, "here's our monk again! By Odin, you're welcome, my handsome boy! come along and fight too, young fellow; what were those arms given you for?"

"He is my man," said Wulf, laying his hand on Philammon's shoulder, "and blood he shall taste." And out the three hurried, Philammon, in his present reckless mood, ready for anything.

"Bring your whips. Never mind swords. Those rascals are not worth it," shouted the Amal, as he hurried down the passage brandishing his heavy thong, some ten feet In length, threw the gate open, and the next moment recoiled from a dense crush of people who surged in — and surged out again as rapidly, as the Goth, with the combined force of his weight and arm, hewed his way straight through them, felling a wretch at every blow, and followed up by his terrible companions.

They were but just in time. The four white blood-horses were plunging and rolling over each other, and Orestes reeling in his chariot, with a stream of blood running down his face, and the hands of twenty wild monks clutching at him. "Monks again!" thought Philammon; and as he saw among them more than one hateful face, which he recollected in Cyril's court-yard on that fatal night, a flush of fierce revenge ran through him.

"Mercy!" shrieked the miserable Prefect — "I am a Christian! I I swear that I am a Christian! the Bishop Atticus baptized me at Constantinople!"

"Down with the butcher! down with the heathen tyrant, who refuses the adjuration on the Gospels rather than be reconciled to the patriarch! Tear him out of the chariot!" yelled the monks.

"The craven hound!" said the Amal, stopping short, "I won't help him!" But in an instant Wulf rushed forward, and struck right and left; the monks recoiled, and Philammon, burning to prevent so shameful a scandal to the faith to which he still clung convulsively, sprung into the chariot and caught Orestes in his arms.

"You are safe, my lord; don't struggle," whispered he, while the monks flew on him. A stone or two struck him, but they only quickened his determination, and in another moment the whistling of the whips round his head, and the yell and backward rush of the monks, told him that he was safe. He carried his burden safely within the doorway of Pelagia's house, into the crowd of peeping and shrieking damsels, where twenty pair of the prettiest hands in Alexandria seized on Orestes, and drew him into the court.

"Like a second Hylas, carried off by the nymphs!" simpered he, as he vanished into the harem, to reappear in five minutes, his head bound up with silk handkerchiefs, and with as much of his usual impudence as he could muster.

"Your Excellency — heroes all — I am your devoted slave. I owe you life itself; and more, the valour of your succour is only surpassed by the deliciousness of your cure. I would gladly undergo a second wound to enjoy a second time the services of such hands, and to see such feet busying themselves on my behalf."

"You wouldn't have said that five minutes ago," quoth the Amal, looking at him very much as a bear might at a monkey.

"Never mind the hands and feet, old fellow, they are none of yours!" bluntly observed a voice from behind, probably Smid's, and a laugh ensued.

"My saviours, my brothers!" said Orestes, politely ignoring the laughter. "How can I repay you? Is there anything in which my office here enables me — I will not say to reward, for that would be a term beneath your dignity as free barbarians — but to gratify you?"

"Give us three days' pillage of the quarter!" shouted some one.

"Ah, true valour is apt to underrate obstacles; you forget your small numbers."

"I say," quoth the Amal; "I say, take care, Prefect. — If you mean to tell me that we forty couldn't cut all the throats in Alexandria in three days, and yours into the bargain, and keep your soldiers at bay all the time ——— "

"Half of them would join us!" cried some one. "They are half our own flesh and blood after all!"

"Pardon me, my friends, I do not doubt it a moment. I know enough of the world never to have found a sheep-dog yet who would not, on occasion, help to make away with a little of the mutton which he guarded. Eh, my venerable sir?" turning to Wulf, with a knowing bow.

Wulf chuckled grimly, and said something to the Amal in German about being civil to guests.

"You will pardon me, my heroic friends," said Orestes, "but, with your kind permission, I will observe that I am somewhat faint and disturbed by late occurrences. To trespass on your hospitality further would be an impertinence. If, therefore, I might send a slave to find some of my apparitors ——— "

"No, by all the Gods!" roared the Amal; "you're my guest now — my lady's at least. And no one ever went out of my house sober yet if I could help it. Set the cooks to work, my men! The Prefect shall feast with us like an emperor, and we'll send him home to-night as drunk as he can wish. Come along, your Excellency; we're rough fellows, we Goths; but by the Valkyrs, no one can say that we neglect our guests!"

"It is a sweet compulsion," said Orestes, as he went in.

"Stop, by the bye! Didn't one of you men catch a monk?"

"Here he is, prince, with his elbows safe behind him." And a tall, haggard, half-naked monk was dragged forward.

"Capital! bring him in. His Excellency shall judge him while dinner's cooking, and Smid shall have the hanging of him. He hurt nobody in the scuffle; he was thinking of his dinner."

"Some rascal bit a piece out of my leg, and I tumbled down," grumbled Smid.

"Well, pay out this fellow for it, then. Bring a chair, slaves! Here, your Highness, sit there and judge."

"Two chairs'." said some one; "the Amal shan't stand, before the emperor himself."

"By all means, my dear friends. The Amal and I will act as the two Cæsars, with divided empire. I presume we shall have little difference of opinion as to the hanging of this worthy."

"Hanging's too quick for him."

"Just what I was about to remark — there are certain judicial formalities, considered generally to be conducive to the stability, if not necessary to the existence, of the Roman empire——"

"I say, don't talk so much," shouted a Goth. "If you want to have the hanging of him yourself, do. We thought we would save you trouble."

"Ah, my excellent friend, would you rob me of the delicate pleasure of revenge? I intend to spend at least four hours to-morrow in killing this pious martyr. He will have a good time to think, between the beginning and the end of the rack."

"Do you hear that, master monk?" said Smid, chucking him under the chin, while the rest of the party seemed to think the whole business an excellent joke, and divided their ridicule openly enough between the Prefect and his victim.

"The man of blood has said it. I am a martyr," answered the monk, in a dogged voice.

"You will take a good deal of time in becoming one."

"Death may be long, but glory is everlasting."

"True. I forgot that, and will save you the said glory, if I can help it, for a year or two. Who was it struck me with the stone?"

No answer.

"Tell me, and the moment he is in my lictors' hands I pardon you freely."

The monk laughed. "Pardon? Pardon me eternal bliss, and the things unspeakable, which God has prepared for those who love him? Tyrant and butcher! I struck thee, thou second Dioclesian — I hurled the stone — I, Ammonius. Would to heaven it had smitten thee through, thou Sisera, like the nail of Jael the Kenite!"

"Thanks, my friend. Heroes, you have a cellar for monks as well as for wine? I will trouble you with this hero's psalm-singing to-night, and send my apparitors for him in the morning."

"If he begins howling when we are in bed, your men won't find much of him left in the morning," said the Amal. "But here come the slaves, announcing dinner."

"Stay," said Orestes; "there is one more with whom I have an account to settle — that young philosopher there."

"Oh, he is coming in, too. He never was drunk in his life, I'll warrant, poor fellow, and it's high time for him to begin." And the Amal laid a good-natured bear's paw on Philammon's shoulder, who hung back in perplexity, and cast a piteous look towards Wulf.

Wulf answered it by a shake of the head, which gave Philammon courage to stammer out a courteous refusal. The Amal swore an oath at him which made the cloister ring again, and with a quiet shove of his heavy hand, sent him staggering half across the court: but Wulf interposed.

"The boy is mine, prince. He is no drunkard, and I will not let him become one. Would to heaven," added he, under his breath, "that I could say the same to some others. Send us out our supper here, when you are done. Half a sheep or so will do between us; and enough of the strongest to wash it down with. Smid knows my quantity."

"Why in heaven's name are you not coming in?"

"That mob will be trying to burst the gates again before two hours are out; and as some one must stand sentry, it may as well be a man who will not have his ears stopped up by wine and women's kisses. The boy will stay with me."

So the party went in, leaving Wulf and Philammon alone in the outer hall.

There the two sat for some half-hour, casting stealthy glances at each other, and wondering, perhaps, each of them vainly enough, what was going on in the opposite brain. Philammon, though his heart was full of his sister, could not help noticing the air of deep sadness which hung about the scarred and weatherbeaten features of the old warrior. The grimness which he had remarked on their first meeting seemed to be now changed into a settled melancholy. The furrows round his mouth and eyes had become deeper and sharper. Some perpetual indignation seemed smouldering in the knitted brow and protruding upper lip. He sat there silent and motionless for some half-hour, his chin resting on his hands, and they again upon the butt of his axe, apparently in deep thought, and listening with a silent sneer at the clinking of glasses and dishes within.

Philammon felt too much respect both for his. age, and his stately sadness, to break the silence. At last some louder burst of merriment than usual aroused him.

"What do you call that?" said he, speaking in Greek.

"Folly and vanity."

"And what does she there — the Alruna — the prophet-woman, call it?"

"Whom do you mean?"

"Why, the Greek woman whom we went to hear talk this morning?"

"Folly and vanity."

"Why can't she cure that Roman hairdresser there of it, then?"

Philammon was silent — "Why not, indeed!"

"Do you think she could cure any one of it?"

"Of what?"

"Of getting drunk, and wasting their strength and their fame, and their hard-won treasures upon eating and drinking, and fine clothes, and bad women."

"She is most pure herself, and she preaches purity to all who hear her."

"Curse preaching. I have preached for these four months."

"Perhaps she may have some more winning arguments — perhaps ——"

"I know. Such a beautiful bit of flesh and blood as she is might get a hearing, when a grizzled old head-splitter like me was called a dotard. Eh? Well. It's natural."

A long silence.

"She is a grand woman. I never saw such a one, and I have seen many. There was a prophetess once, lived in an island in the Weser-stream — and when a man saw her, even before she spoke a word, one longed to crawl to her feet on all-fours, and say, 'There, tread on me; I am not fit for you to wipe your feet upon.' And many a warrior did it.... Perhaps I may have done it myself, before now..... And this one is strangely like her. She would make a prince's wife, now."

Philammon started. What new feeling was it, which made him so indignant at the notion?

"Beauty? What's body without soul? What's beauty without wisdom? What's beauty without chastity? Beast! fool! wallowing in the mire which every hog has fouled!"

"Like a jewel of gold in a swine's snout, so is a fair woman who is without discretion."

"Who said that?"

"Solomon, the king of Israel."

"I never heard of him. But he was a right Sagaman, whoever said it. And she is a pure maiden, that other one?"

"Spotless as the" — blessed Virgin, Philammon was going to say — but checked himself. There were sad recollections about the words.

Wulf sat silent for a few minutes, while Philammon's thoughts reverted at once to the new purpose for which alone life seemed worth having..... To find his sister! That one thought had in a few hours changed and matured the boy into the man. Hitherto he had been only the leaf before the wind, the puppet of every new impression; but now circumstance, which had been leading him along in such soft fetters for many a month, was become his deadly foe; and all his energy and cunning, all his little knowledge of man and of society, rose up sturdily and shrewdly to fight in this new cause. Wulf was now no longer a phenomenon to be wondered at, but an instrument to be used. The broken hints which he had just given of discontent with Pelagia's presence inspired the boy with sudden hope, and cautiously he began to hint at the existence of persons who would be glad to remove her. Wulf caught at the notion, and replied to it with searching questions, till Philammon, finding plain speaking the better part of cunning, told him openly the whole events of the morning, and the mystery which Arsenius had half revealed; and then shuddered with mingled joy and horror as Wulf, after ruminating over the matter for a weary five minutes, made answer —

"And what if Pelagia herself were your sister?"

Philammon was bursting forth in some passionate answer, when the old man stopped him, and went on slowly, looking him through and through —

"Because, when a penniless young monk claims kin with a woman who is drinking out of the wine-cups of the Cæsars, and filling a place for a share of which kings' daughters have been thankful — and will be again before long — why then, though an old man may be too good-natured to call it all a lie at first sight, he can't help supposing that the young monk has an eye to his own personal profit, eh?"

"My profit?" cried poor Philammon, starting up. "Good God! what object on earth can I have, but to rescue her from this infamy to purity and holiness?"

He had touched the wrong chord.

"Infamy? you accursed Egyptian slave!" cried the Prince, starting up in his turn, red with passion, and clutching at the whip which hung over his head. "Infamy? As if she, and you too, ought not to consider yourselves blest in her being allowed to wash the feet of an Amal!"

"Oh, forgive me!" said Philammon, terrified at the fruits of his own clumsiness. "But you forget — you forget, she is not married to him!"

"Married to him? A freedwoman? No; thank Freya! he has not fallen as low as that, at least; and never shall, if I kill the witch with my own hands. A freedwoman!"

Poor Philammon! And he had been told but that morning that he was a slave. He hid his face in his hands, and burst into an agony of tears.

"Come, come," said the testy warrior, softened at once. "Woman's tears don't matter; but somehow I never could bear to make a man cry. When you are cool, and have learnt common courtesy, we'll talk more about this. So! Hush; enough is enough. Here comes the supper, and I am as hungry as Loke."

And he commenced devouring like his namesake, "the grey beast of the wood," and forcing, in his rough hospitable

way, Philammon to devour also, much against his will and stomach.

"There. I feel happier now!" quoth Wulf, at last. "There is
nothing to be done in this accursed place but to eat. I get no
fighting, no hunting. I hate women as they hate me. I don't know
anything, indeed, that I don't hate, except eating and singing.
And now, what with those girls' vile unmanly harps and flutes,
no one cares to listen to a true rattling war-song. There they are
at it now, with their catterwauling, squealing all together like a
set of starlings on a foggy morning! We'll have a song, too, to
drown the noise." And he burst out with a wild rich melody,
acting, in uncouth gestures and a suppressed tone of voice, the
scene which the words described: —

> An elk looked out of the pine forest;
> He snuffed up east, he snuffed down west,
> > Stealthy and still.
> His mane and his horns were heavy with snow;
> I laid my arrow across my bow,
> > Stealthy and still.

And then, quickening his voice, as his whole face blazed up into
fierce excitement —

> The bow it rattled, the arrow flew,
> It smote his blade-bones through and through,
> > Hurrah!
> I sprang at his throat like a wolf of the wood,
> And I warmed my hands in the smoking blood,
> > Hurrah!

And, with a shout that echoed and rang from wall to wall, and
pealed away above the roofs, he leapt to his feet with a gesture
and look of savage frenzy which made Philammon recoil. But
the passion was gone in an instant, and Wulf sat down again,
chuckling to himself —

"There — that is something like a warrior's song. That
makes the old blood spin along again I But this debauching fur-
nace of a climate! — no man can keep his muscle, or his courage, or his money, or anything else in it. May the gods curse the
day when first I saw it!"

Philammon said nothing, but sat utterly aghast at an out-
break so unlike Wulf's usual caustic reserve, and stately self-
restraint, and shuddering at the thought that it might be an in-

stance of that dæmoniac possession to which these barbarians were supposed by Christians and by Neo-Platonists to be peculiarly subject. But the horror was not yet at its height; for in another minute the doors of the women's court flew open, and, attracted by Wulf's shout, out poured the whole Bacchanalian crew, with Orestes, crowned with flowers, and led by the Amal and Pelagia, reeling in the midst, wine-cup in hand.

"There is my philosopher, my preserver, my patron saint!" hiccuped he. "Bring him to my arms, that I may encircle his lovely neck with pearls of India, and barbaric gold!"

"For God's sake let me escape!" whispered he to Wulf, as the rout rushed upon him. Wulf opened the door in an instant, and he dashed through it. As he went, the old man held out his hand —

"Come and see me again, boy ! Me only. The old warrior will not hurt you!"

There was a kindly tone in the voice, a kindly light in the eye, which made Philammon promise to obey. He glanced one look back through the gateway as he fled, and just saw a wild whirl of Goths and girls, spinning madly round the court in the world-old Teutonic waltz; while, high above their heads, in the uplifted arms of the mighty Amal, was tossing the beautiful figure of Pelagia, tearing the garland from her floating hair to pelt the dancers with its roses. And that might be his sister! He hid his face and fled, and the gate shut out the revellers from his eyes; and it is high time that it should shut them out from ours also.

Some four hours more had passed. The revellers were sleeping off their wine, and the moon shining bright and cold across the court, when Wulf came out, carrying a heavy jar of wine, followed by Smid, a goblet in each hand.

"Here, comrade, out into the middle, to catch a breath of night-air. Are all the fools asleep?"

"Every mother's son of them. Ah! this is refreshing after that room. What a pity it is that all men are not born with heads like ours!"

"Very sad, indeed," said Wulf, filling his goblet.

"What a quantity of pleasure they lose in this life! There they are, snoring like hogs. Now, you and I are good to finish this jar, at least."

"And another after it, if our talk is not over by that time."

"Why, are you going to hold a council of war?"

"That is as you take it. Now, look here, Smid. Whomsoever I cannot trust, I suppose! may trust you, eh?"

"Well!" quoth Smid, surlily, putting down his goblet, "that is a strange question to ask of a man who has marched, and hungered, and plundered, and conquered, and been well beaten by your side for five-and-twenty years, through all lands between the Wesel and Alexandria!"

"I am growing old, I suppose, and so I suspect every one. But hearken to me, for between wine and ill-temper out it must come. You saw that Alruna-woman?"

"Of course."

"Well?"

"Well?"

"Why, did not you think she would make a wife for any man?"

"Well?"

"And why not for our Amal?"

"That's his concern as well as hers, and hers as well as ours."

"She? Ought she not to think herself only too much honoured by marrying a son of Odin? Is she going to be more dainty than Placidia?"

"What was good enough for an emperor's daughter must be good enough for her."

"Good enough? And Adolf only a Bait, while Amalric is a full-blooded Amal — Odin's son by both sides?"

"I don't know whether she would understand that."

"Then we would make her. Why not carry her off, and marry her to the Amal whether she chose or not? She would be well content enough with him in a week, I will warrant."

"But there is Pelagia in the way."

"Put her out of the way, then."

"Impossible."

"It was this morning; a week hence it may not be. I heard a promise made to-night which will do it, if there be the spirit of a Goth left in the poor besotted lad whom we know of."

"Oh, he is all right at heart; never fear him. But what was the promise?"

"I will not tell till it is claimed. I will not be the man to shame my own nation and the blood of the gods. But if that drunken Prefect recollects it — why let him recollect it. And what is more, the monk-boy who was here tonight —— "

"Ah, what a well-grown lad that is wasted!"

"More than suspects — and if his story is true, I more than suspect too — that Pelagia is his sister."

"His sister! But what of that?"

"He wants, of course, to carry her off, and make a nun other."

"You would not let him do such a thing to the poor child?"

"If folks get in my way, Smid, they must go down. So much the worse for them; but old Wulf was never turned back yet by man or beast, and he will not be now."

"After all, it will serve the hussy right. But Amalric?"

"Out of sight, out of mind."

"But they say the Prefect means to marry the girl."

"He? That scented ape? She would not be such a wretch."

"But he does intend; and she intends too. It is the talk of the whole town. We should have to put him out of the way first."

"Why not? Easy enough, and a good riddance for Alexandria. Yet if we made away with him we should be forced to take the city too; and I doubt whether we have hands enough for that."

"The guards might join us. I will go down to the barracks and try them, if you choose, to-morrow. I am boon-companion with a good many of them already. But, after all, Prince Wulf — of course you are always right; we all know that — but what's the use of marrying this Hypatia to the Amal?"

"Use?" said Wulf, smiting down his goblet on the pavement. "Use? you purblind old hamster-rat, who think of nothing but filling your own cheek-pouches! — To give him a wife worthy of a hero, as he is, in spite of all — a wife who will make him sober instead of drunk, wise instead of a fool, daring instead of a sluggard — a wife who can command the rich people for us, and give us a hold here, which if once we get, let us see who will break it! Why, with those two ruling in Alexandria, we might be masters of Africa in three months. We'd send to Spain for the Wendels, to move on Carthage; we'd send up the Adriatic for the Longbeards, to land in Pentapolis; we'd sweep the whole coast without losing a man, now it is drained of troops by that fool Heraclian's Roman expedition; make the Wendels and Longbeards shake hands here in Alexandria; draw lots for their shares of the coast; and then — !"

"And then what?"

"Why, when we had settled Africa, I would call out a crew of picked heroes, and sail away south for Asgard — I'd try that Red Sea this time — and see Odin face to face, or die searching for him."

"Oh!" groaned Smid. "And I suppose you would expect me to come too, instead of letting me stop halfway, and settle there among the dragons and elephants. Well, well, wise men are like moorlands — ride as far as you will on the sound ground, you are sure to come upon a soft place at last. However, I will go down to the guards to-morrow, if my head don't ache."

"And I will see the boy about Pelagia. Drink to our plot!"

And the two old iron-heads drank on, till the stars paled out, and the eastward shadows of the cloister vanished in the blaze of dawn.

CHAPTER XIX
JEWS AGAINST CHRISTIANS

THE little porter, after having carried Arsenius's message to Miriam, had run back in search of Philammon and his foster-father; and not finding them, had spent the evening in such frantic rushings to and fro, as produced great doubts of his sanity among the people of the quarter. At last hunger sent him home to supper; at which meal he tried to find vent for his excited feelings in his favourite employment of beating his wife. Whereon Miriam's two Syrian slave-girls, attracted by her screams, came to the rescue, threw a pail of water over him, and turned him out of doors. He, nothing discomfited, likened himself smilingly to Socrates conquered by Xantippe; and, philosophically yielding to circumstances, hopped about like a tame magpie for a couple of hours at the entrance of the alley, pouring forth a stream of light raillery on the passers-by, which several times endangered his personal safety; till at last Philammon, hurrying breathlessly home, rushed into his arms.

"Hush! Hither with me I Your star still prospers. She calls for you."

"Who?"

"Miriam herself. Be secret as the grave. You she will see and speak with. The message of Arsenius she rejected in language which it is unnecessary for philosophic lips to repeat. Come; but give her good words — as are fit to an enchantress who can stay the stars in their courses, and command the spirits of the third heaven."

Philammon hurried home with Eudæmon. Little cared he now for Hypatia's warning against Miriam..... Was he not in search of a sister?

"So, you wretch, you are back again!" cried one of the girls, as they knocked at the outer door of Miriam's apartments. "What do you mean by bringing young men here at this time of night?"

"Better go down, and beg pardon of that poor wife of yours. She has been weeping and praying for you to her crucifix all the evening, you ungrateful little ape!"

"Female superstitions — but I forgive her..... Peace, barbarian women! I bring this youthful philosopher hither by your mistress's own appointment."

"He must wait, then, in the ante-room. There is a gentleman with my mistress at present."

So Philammon waited in a dark, dingy ante-room, luxuriously furnished with faded tapestry, and divans which lined the walls; and fretted and fidgeted, while the two girls watched him over their embroidery out of the corners of their eyes, and agreed that he was a very stupid person for showing-no inclination to return their languishing glances.

In the meanwhile, Miriam, within, was listening, with a smile of grim delight, to a swarthy and weatherbeaten young Jew.

"I knew, mother in Israel, that all depended on my pace; and night and day I rode from Ostia toward Tarentum: but the messenger of the uncircumcised was better mounted than I; I therefore bribed a certain slave to lame his horse, and passed him by a whole stage on the second day. Nevertheless, by night the Philistine had caught me up again, the evil angels helping him; and my soul was mad within me."

"And what then, Jonadab Bar-Zebudah?"

"I bethought me of Ehud, and of Joab also, when he was pursued by Asahel, and considered much of the lawfulness of the deed, not being a man of blood. Nevertheless, we were together in the darkness, and I smote him."

Miriam clapped her hands.

"Then putting on his clothes, and taking his letters and credentials, as was but reasonable, I passed myself off for the messenger of the emperor, and so rode the rest of that journey at the expense of the heathen; and I hereby return you the balance saved."

"Never mind the balance. Keep it, thou worthy son of Jacob. What next?"

"When I came to Tarentum, I sailed in the galley which I had chartered from certain sea-robbers. Valiant men they were, nevertheless, and kept true faith with me. For when we had come halfway, rowing with all our might, behold another galley coming in our wake and about to pass us by, which I knew for an Alexandrian, as did the captain also, who assured me that she had come from hence to Brundusium with letters from Orestes."

"Well?"

"It seemed to me both base to be passed, and more base to waste all the expense wherewith you and our elders had charged themselves; so I took counsel with the man of blood, offering him over and above our bargain, two. hundred gold pieces of my own, which please to pay to my account with Rabbi Ezekiel, who lives by the watergate in Pelusium. Then the pirates, taking counsel, agreed to run down the enemy; for our galley was a sharp-beaked Liburnian, while theirs was only a messenger tri-reme."

"And you did it?"

"Else had I not been here. They were delivered into our hands, so that we struck them full in mid-length, and they sank like Pharaoh and his host."

"So perish all the enemies of the nation!" cried Miriam. "And now it is impossible, you say, for fresh news to arrive for these ten days?"

"Impossible, the captain assured me, owing to the rising of the wind, and the signs of southerly storm."

"Here, take this letter for the Chief Rabbi, and the blessing of a mother in Israel. Thou hast played the man for thy people; and thou shalt go to the grave full of years and honours, with men-servants and maid-servants, gold and silver, children and children's children, with thy foot on the necks of heathens, and the blessing of Abraham, Isaac, and Jacob, to eat of the goose which is fattening in the desert, and the Leviathan which lieth in the great sea, to be meat for all true Israelites at the last day."

And the Jew turned and went out, perhaps, in his simple fanaticism, the happiest man in Egypt at that moment.

He passed out through the ante-chamber, leering at the slave-girls, and scowling at Philammon; and the youth was ushered into the presence of Miriam.

She sat, coiled up like a snake, on a divan, writing busily in a tablet upon her knees, while on the cushions beside her glittered splendid jewels, which she had been fingering over as a child might its toys. She did not look up for a few minutes; and Philammon could not help, in spite of his impatience, looking round the little room, and contrasting its dirty splendour, and heavy odour of wine, and food, and perfumes, with the sunny grace and cleanliness of Greek houses. Against the walls stood presses and chests fretted with fantastic Oriental carving; illuminated rolls of parchment lay in heaps in a corner; a lamp of strange form hung from the ceiling, and shed a dim and lurid light upon an object which chilled the youth's blood for a moment — a bracket against the wall, on which, in a plate of gold, engraven with mystic signs, stood the mummy of an infant's head; one of those teraphim, from which, as Philammon knew, the sorcerers of the East professed to evoke oracular responses.

At last, she looked up, and spoke in a shrill, harsh voice.

"Well, my fair boy, and what do you want with the poor old proscribed Jewess? Have you coveted yet any of the pretty thing's which she has had the wit to make her slave-demons save from the Christian robbers?"

Philammon's tale was soon told. The old woman listened, watching him intently with her burning eye; and then answered slowly —

"Well, and what if you are a slave?"

"Am I one, then? Am I?"

"Of course you are. Arsenius spoke truth. I saw him buy you at Ravenna, just fifteen years ago. I bought your sister at the same time. She is two-and-twenty now. You were four years younger than her, I should say."

"Oh heavens! and you know my sister still! Is she Pelagia?"

"You were a pretty boy," went on the hag, apparently not hearing him. "If I had thought you were going to grow up as beautiful and as clever as you are, I would have bought you myself. The Goths were just marching, and Arsenius gave only eighteen gold pieces for you — or twenty — I am growing old, and forget everything, I think. But there would have been the expense of your education, and your sister cost me in training — oh what sums! Not that she was not worth the money — no, no, the darling!"

"And you know where she is? Oh tell me — in the name of mercy, tell me!"

"Why, then?"

"Why, then? Have you not the heart of a human being in you? Is she not my sister?"

"Well? You have done very well for fifteen years without

your sister — why can you not do as well now? You don't recollect her — you don't love her."

"Not love her? I would die for her — die for you if you will but help me to see her!"

"You would, would you? And if I brought you to her, what then? What if she were Pelagia herself, what then? She is happy enough now, and rich enough. Could you make her happier or richer?"

"Can you ask? I must — I will — reclaim her from the Infamy in which I am sure she lives."

"Ah ha! sir monk? I expected as much. I know, none knows better, what those fine words mean. The burnt child dreads the fire: but the burnt old woman quenches it, you will find. Now listen. I do not say that you shall not see her — I do not say that Pelagia herself is not the woman whom you seek — but — you are in my power. Don't frown and pout. J can deliver you as a slave to Arsenius when I choose. One word from me to Orestes, and you are in fetters as a fugitive."

"I will escape!" cried he, fiercely.

"Escape me?" — She laughed, pointing to the teraph — "Me, who, if you fled beyond Kaf, or dived to the depths of the ocean, could make these dead lips confess where you were, and command demons to bear you back to me upon their wings! Escape me! Better to obey me, and see your sister."

Philammon shuddered, and submitted. The spell of the woman's eye, the terror of her words, which he half believed, and the agony of longing, conquered him, and he gasped out —

"I will obey you — only — only ——— "

"Only you are not quite a man yet, but half a monk still, eh? I must know that before I help you, my pretty boy. Are you a monk still, or a man?"

"What do you mean?"

"Ah, ha, ha!" laughed she, shrilly. "And these Christian dogs don't know what a man means. Are you a monk, then? leaving the man alone, as above your understanding."

"I? — I am a student of philosophy."

"But no man?"

"I am a man, I suppose."

"I don't; if you had been, you would have been making love like a man to that heathen woman many a month ago."

"I — to her?"

"Yes, I — to her!" said Miriam, coarsely imitating his tone of shocked humility. "I, the poor penniless boy-scholar, to her, the great, rich, wise, worshipped she-philosopher, who holds the sacred keys of the inner shrine of the east wind — and just because I am a man, and the handsomest man in Alexandria, and she a woman, and the vainest woman in Alexandria, and therefore I am stronger than she, and can twist her round my finger, and bring her to her knees at my feet when I like, as soon as I open my eyes, and discover that I am a man. Eh, boy? Did she ever teach you that among her mathematics and metaphysics, and gods and goddesses?"

Philammon stood blushing scarlet. The sweet poison had entered, and every vein glowed with it for the first time in his life. Miriam saw her advantage.

"There, there — don't be frightened at your new lesson. After all, I liked you from the first moment I saw you, and asked the teraph about you, and I got an answer — such an answer! — You shall know it some day. At all events, it set the poor old soft-hearted Jewess on throwing away her money. Did you ever guess from whom your monthly gold-piece came?"

Philammon started, and Miriam burst into loud, shrill laughter.

"From Hypatia, I'll warrant! From the fair Greek woman, of course — vain child that you are — never thinking of the poor old Jewess."

"And did you? did you?" gasped Philammon. "Have I to thank you, then, for that strange generosity?"

"Not to thank me, but to obey me; for mind, I can prove your debt to me, every obol, and claim it if I choose. But don't fear; I wont be hard on you, just because you are in my power. I hate every one who is not so. As soon as I have a hold on them, I begin to love them. Old folks, like children, are fond of their own playthings."

"You are indeed, then?" said Philammon, fiercely.

"You are indeed, my beautiful boy," answered she, looking up with so insinuating a smile that he could not be angry. "After all, I know how to toss my balls gently — and for these forty years I have only lived to make young folks happy; so you need not be afraid of the poor softhearted old woman. Now —

you saved Orestes' life yesterday."

"How did you find out that?"

"I? I know everything. I know what the swallows say when they pass each other on the wing, and what the fishes think of in the summer sea. — You, too, will be able to guess some day, without the teraph's help. But in the mean time you must enter Orestes' service? Why? — What are you hesitating about? Do you not know that you are high in his favour? He will make you secretary — raise you to be chamberlain some day, if you know how to make good use of your fortune."

Philammon stood in astonished silence; and at last —

"Servant to that man? What care I for him or his honours? Why do you tantalize me thus? I have no wish on earth but to see my sister!"

"You will be far more likely to see her if you belong to the court of a great officer — perhaps more than an officer — than if you remain a penniless monk. Not that I believe you. Your only wish on earth, eh? Do you not care, then, ever to see the fair Hypatia again?"

"I? Why should I not see her? Am I not her pupil?"

"She will not have pupils much longer, my child. If you wish to hear her wisdom — and much good may it do you — you must go for it henceforth somewhat nearer to Orestes' palace than the lecture-room is. Ah! you start. Have I found you an argument now? No — ask no questions. I explain nothing to monks. But take these letters; to-morrow morning-at the third hour go to Orestes' palace, and ask for his secretary, Ethan the Chaldee. Say boldly that you bring important news of state; and then follow your star: it is a fairer one than you fancy. Go! obey me, or you see no sister."

Philammon felt himself trapped; but, after all, what might not this strange woman do for him? It seemed, if not his only path, still his nearest path to Pelagia; and in the mean while he was in the hag's power, and he must submit to his fate; so he took the letters and went out.

"And so you think that you are going to have her?" chuckled Miriam to herself, when Philammon went out. "To make a penitent of her, eh? — a nun, or a she-hermit; to set her to appease your God by crawling on all-fours among the mummies for twenty years, with a chain round her neck and a clog at

her ankle, fancying herself all the while the bride of the Nazarene? And you think that old Miriam is going to give her up to
you for that? No, no, sir monk! Better she were dead!.... Follow
your dainty bait! — follow it, as the donkey does the grass which
his driver offers him, always an inch from his nose..... You in my
power! — and Orestes in my power!.... I must negotiate that new
loan to-morrow, I suppose..... I shall never be paid. The dog will
ruin me, after all! How much is it, now? Let me see.".... And she
began fumbling in her escritoire, over bonds and notes of hand.
"I shall never be paid: but power! — to have power! To see
those heathen slaves and Christian hounds plotting and vapour-
ing, and fancying themselves the masters of the world, and never
dreaming that we are pulling the strings, and that they are our
puppets! — we, the children of the promises — we, The Nation
— we, the seed of Abraham! Poor fools! I could almost pity
them, as I think of their faces when Messiah comes, and they
find out who were the true lords of the world, after all!.... He
must be Emperor of the South, though, that Orestes; he must,
though I have to lend him Raphael's jewels to make him so. For
he must marry the Greek woman. He shall. She hates him, of
course..... So much the deeper revenge for me. And she loves
that monk. I saw it in her eyes there in the garden. So much the
better for me, too. He will dangle willingly enough at Orestes'
heels for the sake of being near her — poor fool! We will make
him secretary, or chamberlain. He has wit enough for it, they
say, or for anything. So Orestes and he shall be the two jaws of
my pincers, to squeeze what I want out of that Greek Jezebel.....
And then — then for the black agate!"

Was the end of her speech a bathos? Perhaps not; for as
she spoke the last word, she drew from her bosom, where it hung
round her neck by a chain, a broken talisman, exactly similar to
the one which she coveted so fiercely, and looked at it long and
lovingly — kissed it — wept over it — spoke to it — fondled it
in her arms as a mother would a child — murmured over it
snatches of lullabies; and her grim, withered features grew
softer, purer, grander; and rose ennobled, for a moment, to their
long-lost might-have-been, to that personal ideal which every
soul brings with it into the world, which shines, dim and poten-
tial, in the face of every sleeping babe, before it has been
scarred, and distorted, and encrusted in the long tragedy of life.

Sorceress she was, pander and slave-dealer, steeped to the lips in falsehood, ferocity, and avarice; yet that paltry stone brought home to her some thought, true, spiritual, impalpable, unmarketable, before which all her treasures and all her ambition were as worthless in her own eyes as they were in the eyes of the angels of God.

But little did Miriam think that at the same moment a brawny, clownish monk was standing in Cyril's private chamber, and, indulged with the special honour of a cup of good wine in the patriarch's very presence, was telling to him and Arsenius the following history: —

"So I, finding that the Jews had chartered this pirate-ship, went to the master thereof, and finding favour in his eyes, hired myself to row therein, being sure, from what I had overheard from the Jews, that she was destined to bring the news to Alexandria as quickly as possible. Therefore, fulfilling the work which his Holiness had intrusted to my incapacity, I embarked, and rowed continually among the rest; and being unskilled in such labour, received many curses and stripes in the cause of the Church — the which I trust are laid to my account hereafter. Moreover, Satan entered into me, desiring to slay me, and almost tore me asunder, so that I vomited much, and loathed all manner of meat. Nevertheless, I rowed on valiantly, being such as I am, vomiting continually, till the heathens were moved with wonder, and forbore to beat me, giving me strong liquors in pity; wherefore I rowed all the more valiantly day and night, trusting that by my unworthiness the cause of the Catholic Church might be in some slight wise assisted."

"And so it is," quoth Cyril. "Why do you not sit down, man?"

"Pardon me," quoth the monk, with a piteous gesture; "of sitting, as of all carnal pleasure, cometh satiety at the last."

"And now," said Cyril, "what reward am I to give you for your good service?"

"It is reward enough to know that I have done good service. Nevertheless, if the holy patriarch be so inclined without reason, there is an ancient Christian, my mother according to the flesh — —— "

"Come to me to-morrow, and she shall be well seen to. And mind — look to it, if I make you not a deacon of the city, when I promote Peter."

The monk kissed his superior's hand, and withdrew. Cyril turned to Arsenius, betrayed for once into geniality by his delight, and smiting his thigh —

"We have beaten the heathen for once, eh?" And then, In the usual artificial tone of an ecclesiastic — "And what would my father recommend in furtherance of the advantage so mercifully thrown into our hand?"

Arsenius was silent.

"I," went on Cyril, "should be inclined to announce the news this very night, in my sermon."

Arsenius shook his head.

"Why not? why not?" asked Cyril, impatiently.

"Better to keep it secret till others tell it. Reserved knowledge is always reserved strength; and if the man, as I hope he docs not, intends evil to the Church, let him commit himself before you use your knowledge against him. True, you may have a scruple of conscience as to the lawfulness of allowing a sin which you might prevent. To me it seems that the sin lies in the will rather than in the deed, and that sometimes — I only say sometimes — it may be a means of saving the sinner to allow his root of iniquity to bear fruit, and fill him with his own devices."

"Dangerous doctrine, my father."

"Like all sound doctrine — a savour of life or of death, according as it is received. I have not said it to the multitude, but to a discerning brother. And even politically speaking — let him commit himself, if he be really plotting rebellion, and then speak, and smite his Babel tower."

"You think, then, that he does not know of Heraclian's defeat already?"

"If he does, he will keep it secret from the people; and our chances of turning them suddenly will be nearly the same."

"Good. After all, the existence of the Catholic Church in Alexandria depends on this struggle, and it is well to be wary. Be it so. It is well for me that I have you for an adviser."

And thus Cyril, usually the most impatient and intractable of plotters, gave in, as wise men should, to a wiser man than himself, and made up his mind to keep the secret, and to command the monk to keep it also.

Philammon, after a sleepless night, and a welcome visit to

the public baths, which the Roman tyranny, wiser in its generation than modern liberty, provided so liberally for its victims, set forth to the Prefect's palace, and gave his message; but Orestes, who had been of late astonishing the Alexandrian public by an unwonted display of alacrity, was already in the adjoining Basilica. Thither the youth was conducted by an apparitor, and led up the centre of the enormous hall, gorgeous with frescoes and coloured marbles, and surrounded by aisles and galleries, in which the inferior magistrates were hearing causes, and doing such justice as the complicated technicalities of Roman law chose to mete out. Through a crowd of anxious loungers the youth passed to the apse of the upper end, in which the Prefect's throne stood empty, and then turned into a side chamber, where he found himself alone with the secretary, a portly Chaldee eunuch, with a sleek pale face, small pig's eyes, and an enormous turban. The man of pen and paper took the letter, opened it with solemn deliberation, and then, springing to his feet, darted out of the room in most undignified haste, leaving Philammon to wait and wonder. In half-an-hour he returned, his little eyes growing big with some great idea.

"Youth! your star is in the ascendant; you are the fortunate bearer of fortunate news! His Excellency himself commands your presence." And the two went out.

In another chamber, the door of which was guarded by armed men, Orestes was walking up and down in high excitement, looking somewhat the worse for the events of the past night, and making occasional appeals to a gold goblet which stood on the table.

"Ha! No other than my preserver himself I Boy, I will make your fortune. Miriam says that you wish to enter my service."

Philammon, not knowing what to say, thought the best answer would be to bow as low as he could.

"Ah, ha! Graceful, but not quite according to etiquette. You will soon teach him, eh, Secretary? Now to business. Hand me the notes to sign and seal. To the Prefect of the Stationaries ———"

"Here, your Excellency."

"To the Prefect of the Corn-market — How many wheat-ships have you ordered to be unladen?"

"Two, your Excellency."

"Well, that will be largess enough for the time being. To the Defender of the Plebs — The devil break his neck!"

"He may be trusted, most noble; he is bitterly jealous of Cyril's influence. And, moreover, he owes my insignificance much money."

"Good! Now the notes to the Gaol-masters, about the gladiators."

"Here, your Excellency."

"To Hypatia. No. I will honour my bride elect with my own illustrious presence. As I live, here is a morning's work for a man with a racking headache!"

"Your Excellency has the strength of seven. May you live for ever!"

And really, Orestes' power of getting through business, when he chose, was surprising enough. A cold head and a colder heart make many things easy.

But Philammon's whole soul was fixed on those words. "His bride elect!".... Was it that Miriam's hints of the day before had raised some selfish vision, or was it pity and horror at such a fate for her — for his idol? — But he passed five minutes in a dream, from which he was awakened by the sound of another and still dearer name.

"And now, for Pelagia. We can but try."

"Your Excellency might offend the Goth."

"Curse the Goth! He shall have his choice of all the beauties in Alexandria, and be Count of Pentapolis if he likes. But a spectacle I must have; and no one but Pelagia can dance Venus Anadyomene."

Philammon's blood rushed to his heart, and then back again to his brow, as he reeled with horror and shame.

"The people will be mad with joy to see her on the stage once more. Little they thought, the brutes, how I was plotting for their amusement, even when as drunk as Silenus."

"Your nobility only lives for the good of your slaves."

"Here, boy! So fair a lady requires a fair messenger. You shall enter on my service at once, and carry this letter to Pelagia. Why? — why do you not come and take it?"

"To Pelagia?" gasped the youth. "In the theatre? Publicly? Venus Anadyomene?"

"Yes, fool! Were you, too, drunk last night after all?"

"She is my sister!"

"Well, and what of that? Not that I believe you, you villain! So!" said Orestes, who comprehended the matter in an instant. "Apparitors!"

The door opened, and the guard appeared.

"Here is a good boy who is inclined to make a fool of himself. Keep him out of harm's way for a few days. But don't hurt him; for, after all, he saved my life yesterday, when you scoundrels ran away."

And, without further ado, the hapless youth was collared, and led down a vaulted passage into the guardroom, amid the jeers of the guard, who seemed only to owe him a grudge for his yesterday's prowess, and showed great alacrity in fitting him with a heavy set of irons; which done, he was thrust head foremost into a cell of the prison, locked in, and left to his meditations.

CHAPTER XX
SHE STOOPS TO CONQUER

"BUT, fairest Hypatia, conceive yourself struck in the face by a great stone, several hundred howling wretches leaping up at you like wild beasts — two minutes more, and you are torn limb from limb. What would even you do in such a case?"

"Let them tear me limb from limb, and die as I have lived."

"Ah, but —— When it came to fact, and death was staring you in the face?"

"And why should man fear death?"

"Ahem! No, not death, of course; but the act of dying. That may be, surely, under such circumstances, to say the least, disagreeable. If our ideal, Julian the Great, found a little dissimulation necessary, and was even a better Christian than I have ever pretended to be, till he found himself able to throw off the mask, why should not I? Consider me as a lower being than yourself — one of the herd, if you will; but a penitent member thereof, who comes to make the fullest possible reparation, by doing any desperate deed on which you may choose to put him, and prove myself as able and willing, if once I have the power, as Julian himself."

Such was the conversation which passed between Hypatia and Orestes half-an-hour after Philammon had taken possession of his new abode.

Hypatia looked at the Prefect with calm penetration, not unmixed with scorn and fear.

"And pray what has produced this sudden change in your Excellency's earnestness? For four months your promises have been lying-fallow." She did not confess how glad she would have been at heart to see them lying fallow still.

"Because —— This morning' I have news; which I tell to you the first as a compliment. We will take care that all Alexandria knows it before sundown. Heraclian has conquered."

"Conquered?" cried Hypatia, springing from her seat.

"Conquered, and utterly destroyed the emperor's forces at Ostia. So says a messenger on whom I can depend. And even if the news should prove false, I can prevent the contrary report from spreading, or what is the use of being prefect? You demur? Do you not see that if we can keep the notion alive but a week our cause is won?"

"How so?"

"I have treated already with all the officers of the city, and every one of them has acted like a wise man, and given me a promise of help, conditional of course on Heraclian's success, being as tired as I am of that priest-ridden court at Byzantium. Moreover, the stationaries are mine already. So are the soldiery all the way up the Nile. Ah! you have been fancying me idle for these four months, but — — — You forget that you yourself were the prize of my toil. Could I be a sluggard with that goal in sight?"

Hypatia shuddered, but was silent; and Orestes went on: —

"I have unladen several of the wheat-ships for enormous largesses of bread: though those rascally monks of Tabenne had nearly forestalled my benevolence, and I was forced to bribe a deacon or two, buy up the stock they had sent down, and retail it again as my own. It is really most officious of them to persist in feeding gratuitously half the poor of the city! What possible business have they with Alexandria?"

"The wish for popularity, I presume."

"Just so; and then what hold can the government have on a set of rogues whose stomachs are filled without our help?"

"Julian made the same complaint to the high priest of Galatia, in that priceless letter of his."

"Ah, you will set that all right, you know, shortly. Then again, I do not fear Cyril's power just now. He has injured himself deeply, I am happy to say, in the opinion of the wealthy and educated, by expelling the Jews. And as for his mob, exactly at the right moment, the deities — there are no monks here, so I can attribute my blessings to the right source — have sent us such a boon as may put them into as good a humour as we need."

"And what is that?" asked Hypatia.

"A white elephant."

"A white elephant?"

"Yes," he answered, mistaking or ignoring the tone of her answer. "A real, live, white elephant; a thing which has not been seen in Alexandria for a hundred years! It was passing through, with two tame tigers, as a present to the boy at Byzantium, from some hundred-wived kinglet of the Hyperborean Taprobane, or other no-man's-land in the far East. I took the liberty of laying an embargo on them, and, after a little argumentation and a few hints of torture, elephant and tigers are at our service.''

"And of what service are they to be?"

"My dearest madam ———— Conceive.... How are we to win the mob without a show?.... When were there more than two ways of gaining either the whole or part of the Roman empire — by force of arms, or force of trumpery? Can even you invent a third? The former is unpleasantly exciting, and hardly practicable just now. The latter remains; and, thanks to the white elephant, may be triumphantly successful. I have to exhibit something every week. The people are getting tired of that pantomime; and since the Jews were driven out, the fellow has grown stupid and lazy, having lost the more enthusiastic half of his spectators. As for horse-racing, they are sick of it..... Now, suppose we announce, for the earliest possible day — a spectacle — such a spectacle as never was seen before in this generation. You and I — I as exhibitor, you as representative — for the time being only — of the Vestals of old — sit side by side...... Some worthy friend has his instructions, when the people arc beside themselves with rapture, to cry, 'Long live Orestes Cæsar!'.... Another reminds them of Heraclian's victory — another couples your name with mine.... the people applaud.... some Mark Antony steps forward, salutes me as Imperator, Augustus — what you will — the cry is taken up — I refuse as meekly as Julius Cæsar himself — am compelled, blushing, to accept the honour — I rise, make an oration about the future independence of the southern continent — union of Africa and Egypt — the empire no longer to be divided into Eastern and Western, but Northern and Southern. Shouts of applause, at two drachmas per man, shake the skies. Everybody believes that everybody else approves, and follows the lead.... And the thing is won."

"And pray," asked Hypatia, crushing down her contempt and despair, "how is this to bear on the worship of the gods?"

"Why.... why.... if you thought that people's minds were sufficiently prepared, you might rise in your turn, and make an oration — you can conceive one. Set forth how these spectacles, formerly the glory of the empire, had withered under Galilæan superstition.... How the only path toward the full enjoyment of eye and ear was a frank return to those deities, from whose worship they originally sprung, and connected with which they could alone be enjoyed in their perfection..... But I need not teach you how to do that which you have so often taught me: so now to consider our spectacle, which, next to the largess, is the most important part of our plans. I ought to have exhibited to them the monk who so nearly killed me yesterday. That would indeed have been a triumph of the laws over Christianity. He and the wild beasts might have given the people ten minutes' amusement. But wrath conquered prudence; and the fellow has been crucified these two hours. Suppose, then, we had a little exhibition of gladiators. They are forbidden by law, certainly."

"Thank Heaven, they are!"

"But do you not see that is the very reason why we, to assert our own independence, should employ them?"

"No! they are gone. Let them never reappear to disgrace the earth."

"My dear lady, you must not, in your present character, say that in public; lest Cyril should be impertinent enough to remind you that Christian emperors and bishops put them down."

Hypatia bit her lip, and was silent.

"Well, I do not wish to urge anything unpleasant to you.... If we could but contrive a few martyrdoms — but I really fear we must wait a year or two longer, in the present state of public opinion, before we can attempt that."

"Wait? wait for ever! Did not Julian — and he must be our model — forbid the persecution of the Galilæans, considering them sufficiently punished by their own atheism and self-tormenting superstition?"

"Another small error of that great man. He should have recollected that for three hundred years, nothing, not even the gladiators themselves, had been found to put the mob in such good humour as to see a few Christians, especially young and handsome women, burned alive, of thrown to the lions."

Hypatia bit her lip once more. "I can hcar no more of this, sir. You forget that you are speaking to a woman."

"Most supreme wisdom," answered Orestes, in his blandest tone, "you cannot suppose that I wish to pain your ears. But allow me to observe, as a general theorem, that if one wishes to effect any purpose, it is necessary to use the means; and on the whole, those which have been tested by four hundred years' experience will be the safest. I speak as a plain practical statesman — but surely your philosophy will not dissent?"

Hypatia looked down in painful thought. What could she answer? Was it not too true? and had not Orestes fact and experience on his side?

"Well, if you must — but I cannot have gladiators. Why not a — one of those battles with wild beasts? They are disgusting enough: but still they are less inhuman than the others; and you might surely take precautions to prevent the men being hurt."

"Ah! that would indeed be a scentless rose! If there Is neither danger nor bloodshed, the charm is gone. But really wild beasts are too expensive just now; and if I kill down my present menagerie, I can afford no more. Why not have something which costs no money, like prisoners?"

"What! do you rank human being's below brutes?"

"Heaven forbid! But they are practically less expensive. Remember, that without money, we are powerless; we must husband our resources for the cause of the gods."

Hypatia was silent.

"Now, there are fifty or sixty Libyan prisoners just brought in from the desert. Why not let them fight an equal number of soldiers? They are rebels to the empire, taken in war."

"Ah, then," said Hypatia, catching at any thread of self-justification, "their lives are forfeit in any case."

"Of course. So the Christians could not complain of us for that. Did not the most Christian Emperor Constantine set some three hundred German prisoners to butcher each other in the amphitheatre of Treves?"

"But they refused, and died like heroes, each falling on his own sword."

"Ah — those Germans are always unmanageable. My guards, now, are just as stiffnecked. To tell you the truth, I have asked them already to exhibit their prowess on these Libyans, and what do you suppose they answered?"

"They refused, I hope."

'' They told me in the most insolent tone that they were

men, and not stage-players; and hired to fight, and not to butcher. I expected a Socratic dialogue after such a display of dialectic, and bowed myself out."

"They were right."

"Not a doubt of it, from a philosophic point of view; from a practical one they were great pedants, and I an ill-used master. However, I can find unfortunate and misunderstood heroes enough in the prisons, who, for the chance of their liberty, will acquit themselves valiantly enough; and I know of a few old gladiators still lingering about the wineshops, who will be proud enough to give them a week's training. So that may pass. Now for some lighter species of representation to follow — something more or less dramatic."

"You forget that you speak to one who trusts to be, as soon as she has the power, the high-priestess of Athene, and who in the mean while is bound to obey her tutor Julian's commands to the priests of his day, and imitate the Galilæans as much in their abhorrence for the theatre as she hopes hereafter to do in their care for the widow and the stranger."

"Far be it from me to impugn that great man's wisdom. But allow me to remark, that to judge by the present state of the empire, one has a right to say that he failed."

"The Sun-God whom he loved took him to himself, too early, by a hero's death."

"And the moment he was removed, the wave of Christian barbarism rolled back again into its old channel."

"Ah! had he but lived twenty years longer!"

"The Sun-God, perhaps, was not so solicitous as we are for the success of his high-priest's project."

Hypatia reddened — was Orestes, after all, laughing in his sleeve at her and her hopes?

"Do not blaspheme!" she said, solemnly.

"Heaven forbid! I only offer one possible explanation of a plain fact. The other is, that as Julian was not going quite the right way to work to restore the worship of the Olympians, the Sun-God found it expedient to withdraw him from his post, and now sends in his place Hypatia the philosopher, who will be wise enough to avoid Julian's error, and not copy the Galilæans too closely, by imitating a severity of morals at which they are the only true and natural adepts."

"So Julian's error was that of being too virtuous? If it be so, let me copy him, and fail like him. The fault will then not be mine, but fate's."

"Not in being too virtuous himself, most stainless likeness of Athene, but in trying to make others so. He forgot one half of Juvenal's great dictum about 'Panem and Circenses,' as the absolute and overruling necessities of rulers. He tried to give the people the bread without the games..... And what thanks he received for his enormous munificence, let himself and the good folks of Antioch tell — you just quoted his Misopogon ——— "

"Ay — the lament of a man too pure for his age."

"Exactly so. He should rather have been content to keep his purity to himself, and have gone to Antioch not merely as a philosophic high-priest, with a beard of questionable cleanliness, to offer sacrifices to a god in whom — forgive me — nobody in Antioch had believed for many a year. If he had made his entrance with ten thousand gladiators, and our white elephant, built a theatre of ivory and glass in Daphnæ, and proclaimed games in honour of the Sun, or of any other member of the Pantheon ——— — "

"He would have acted unworthily of a philosopher."

"But instead of that one priest draggling up, poor devil, through the wet grass to the deserted altar with his solitary goose under his arm, he would have had every goose in Antioch — forgive my stealing a pun from Aristophanes — running open-mouthed to worship any god, known or unknown — and to see the sights."

"Well," said Hypatia, yielding perforce to Orestes' cutting arguments. "Let us then restore the ancient glories of the Greek drama. Let us give them a trilogy of Æschylus or Sophocles."

"Too calm, my dear madam. The Eumenides might do certainly, or Philoctetes, if we could but put Philoctetes to real pain, and make the spectators sure that he was yelling in good earnest."

"Disgusting!"

"But necessary, like many disgusting things."

"Why not try the Prometheus?"

"A magnificent field for stage effect, certainly. What with those ocean nymphs in their winged chariot, and Ocean on his griffin..... But I should hardly think it safe to re-introduce Zeus and Hermes to the people under the somewhat ugly light in which Æschylus exhibits them."

"I forgot that," said Hypatia. "The Orestean trilogy will be best, after all."

"Best? perfect — divine! Ah, that it were to be my fate to go down to posterity as the happy man who once more revived Æschylus's masterpieces on a Grecian stage! But — — — Is there not, begging the pardon of the great tragedian, too much reserve in the Agamemnon for our modern taste? If we could have the bath scene represented on the stage, and an Agamemnon who could be really killed — though I would not insist on that, because a good actor might make it a reason for refusing the part — but still the murder ought to take place in public."

"Shocking! an outrage on all the laws of the drama. Does not even the Roman Horace lay down as a rule the — *Ne pueros coram populo Medea trucidet?*"

"Fairest and wisest, I am as willing a pupil of the dear old Epicurean as any man living — even to the furnishing of my chamber; of which fact the Empress of Africa may some day assure herself. But we are not now discussing the art of poetry, but the art of reigning; and, after all, while Horace was sitting in his easy-chair, giving his countrymen good advice, a private man, who knew somewhat better than he what the mass admired, was exhibiting forty thousand gladiators at his mother's funeral."

" But the canon has its foundation in the eternal laws of beauty. It has been accepted and observed."

"Not by the people for whom it was written. The learned Hypatia has surely not forgotten, that within sixty years after the Ars Poetica was written, Annæus Seneca, or whosoever wrote that very bad tragedy called the Medea, found it so necessary that she should, in despite of Horace, kill her children before the people, that he actually made her do it!"

Hypatia was still silent — foiled at every point, while Orestes ran on with provoking glibness.

"And consider, too, even if we dare alter Æschylus a little, we could find no one to act him."

"Ah, true! fallen, fallen days!"

"And really, after all, omitting the questionable compliment to me, as candidate for a certain dignity, of having my namesake kill his mother, and then be hunted over the stage by furies —"

"But Apollo vindicates and purifies him at last. What a noble occasion that last scene would give for winning them back to their old reverence for the god!"

"True, but at present the majority of spectators will believe more strongly in the horrors of matricide and furies than in Apollo's power to dispense therewith. So that I fear must be one of your labours of the future."

"And it shall be," said Hypatia. But she did not speak cheerfully.

"Do you not think, moreover," went on the tempter, "that those old tragedies might give somewhat too gloomy a notion of those deities whom we wish to re-introduce — I beg pardon, to re-honour? The history of the house of Atreus is hardly more cheerful, in spite of its beauty, than one of Cyril's sermons on the day of judgment, and the Tartarus prepared for hapless rich people."

"Well," said Hypatia, more and more listlessly; "it might be more prudent to show them first the fairer and more graceful side of the old Myths. Certainly the great age of Athenian tragedy had its playful reverse in the old comedy."

"And in certain Dionysiac sports and processions which shall be nameless, in order to awaken a proper devotion for the gods in those who might not be able to appreciate Æschylus and Sophocles."

"You would not re-introduce them?"

"Pallas forbid! but give as fair a substitute for them as we can."

"And are we to degrade ourselves because the masses are degraded?"

"Not in the least. For my own part, this whole business, like the catering for the weekly pantomimes, is as great a bore to me as it could have been to Julian himself. But, my dearest madam — 'Panem and Circenses' — they must be put into good humour; and there is but one way — by ' the lust of the flesh, and the lust of the eye, and the pride of life,' as a certain Galilæan correctly defines the time-honoured Roman method."

"Put them into good humour? I wish to lustrate them afresh for the service of the gods. If we must have comic representations, we can only have them conjoined to tragedy, which, as Aristotle defines it, will purify their affections by pity and terror."

Orestes smiled.

"I certainly can have no objection to so good a purpose. But do you not think that the battle between the gladiators and the Libyans will have done that sufficiently beforehand? I can conceive nothing more fit for that end, unless it be Nero's method of sending his guards among the spectators themselves, and throwing them down to the wild beasts in the arena. How thoroughly purified by pity and terror must every worthy shopkeeper have been, when he sat uncertain whether he might not follow his fat wife into the claws of the nearest lion!"

"You are pleased to be witty, sir," said Hypatia, hardly able to conceal her disgust.

"My dearest bride elect, I only meant the most harmless of reductiones ad absurdum of an abstract canon of Aristotle, with which I, who am a Platonist after my mistress's model, do not happen to agree. But do, I beseech you, be ruled, not by me, but by your own wisdom. You cannot bring the people to appreciate your designs at the first sight. You are too wise, too pure, too lofty, too farsighted for them. And therefore you must get power to compel them. Julian, after all, found it necessary to compel — if he had lived seven years more he would have found it necessary to persecute."

"The gods forbid that — that such a necessity should ever arise here."

"The only way to avoid it, believe me, is to allure and to indulge. After all, it is for their good."

"True," sighed Hypatia. "Have your way, sir."

"Believe me, you shall have yours in turn. I ask you to be ruled by me now, only that you may be in a position to rule me and Africa hereafter."

"And such an Africa! Well, if they are born low and earthly, they must, I suppose, be treated as such; and the fault of such a necessity is Nature's, and not ours. — Yet it is most degrading! — But still, if the only method by which the philosophic few can assume their rights, as the divinely-appointed rulers of the world, is by indulging those lower beings whom they govern for their good — why be it so. It is no worse necessity than many another which the servant of the gods must endure in days like these."

"Ah," said Orestes, refusing to hear the sigh, or to see the bitterness of the lip which accompanied the speech—— "now Hypatia is herself again; and my counsellor, and giver of deep and celestial reasons for all things at which poor I can only snatch and guess by vulpine cunning. So now for our lighter entertainment. What shall it be?"

"What you will, provided it be not, as most such are, unfit for the eyes of modest women. I have no skill in catering for folly."

"A pantomime, then? We may make that as grand and as significant as we will, and expend too on it all our treasures in the way of gewgaws and wild beasts."

"As you like."

"Just consider, too, what a scope for mythologic learning a pantomime affords. Why not have a triumph of some deity? Could I commit myself more boldly to the service of the gods? Now — who shall it be?"

"Pallas — unless, as I suppose, she is too modest and too sober for your Alexandrians?"

"Yes — it does not seem to me that she would be appreciated — at all events for the present. Why not try Aphrodite? Christians as well as Pagans will thoroughly understand her; and I know no one who would not degrade the virgin goddess by representing her, except a certain lady, who has already, I hope, consented to sit in that very character, by the side of her too much honoured slave; and one Pallas is enough at a time in any theatre."

Hypatia shuddered. He took it all for granted, then — and claimed her conditional promise to the uttermost. Was there no escape? She longed to spring up and rush away, into the streets, into the desert — anything to break the hideous net which she had wound around herself. And yet — was it not the cause of the gods — the one object of her life? And after all, if he the hateful was to be her emperor, she at least was to be an empress; and do what she would — and half in irony, and half in the attempt to hurl herself perforce into that which she knew that she must go through, and forget misery in activity, she answered as cheerfully as she could.

"Then, my goddess, thou must wait the pleasure of these

base ones! At least the young Apollo will have charms even for them."

"Ay, but who will represent him? This puny generation does not produce such figures as Pylades and Bathyllus — except among those Goths. Besides, Apollo must have golden hair; and our Greek race has intermixed itself so shamefully with these Egyptians, that our stage-troop is as dark as Andromeda, and we should have to apply again to those accursed Goths, who have nearly "(with a bow)" all the beauty, and nearly all the money and the power, and will, I suspect, have the rest of it before I am safe out of this wicked world, because they have not nearly, but quite, all the courage. Now — Shall we ask a Goth to dance Apollo? for we can get no one else."

Hypatia smiled in spite of herself at the notion. "That would be too shameful! I must forego the god of light himself, if I am to see him in the person of a clumsy barbarian."

"Then why not try my despised and rejected Aphrodite? Suppose we had her triumph, finishing with a dance of Venus Anadyomene. Surely that is a graceful myth enough."

"As a myth; but on the stage in reality?"

" Not worse than what this Christian city has been looking at for many a year. We shall not run any danger of corrupting morality, be sure."

Hypatia blushed.

"Then you must not ask for my help."

"Or for your presence at the spectacle? For that be sure is a necessary point. You are too great a person, my dearest madam, in the eyes of these good folks to be allowed to absent yourself on such an occasion. If my little stratagem succeeds, it will be half owing to the fact of the people knowing that in crowning me, they crown Hypatia..... Come now — do you not see that as you must needs be present at their harmless scrap of mythology, taken from the authentic and undoubted histories of those very gods whose worship we intend to restore, you will consult your own comfort most in agreeing to it cheerfully, and in lending me your wisdom towards arranging it? Just conceive now, a triumph of Aphrodite, entering preceded by wild beasts led in chains by Cupids, the white elephant and all — what a field for the plastic art! You must have a thousand groupings, dispersions, regroupings, in as perfect bas-relief style as those of any Sophoclean drama. Allow me only to take this paper and pen — —— "

And he began sketching rapidly group after group.

"Not so ugly, surely?"

"They are very beautiful, I cannot deny," said poor Hypatia.

"Ah, sweetest Empress I you forget sometimes that I, too, world-worn, as I am, am a Greek, with as intense a love of the beautiful as even you yourself have. Do not fancy that every violation of correct taste does not torture me as keenly as it does you. Some day, I hope, you will have learnt to pity and to excuse the wretched compromise between that which ought to be and that which can be, in which we hapless statesmen must struggle on, half-stunted, and wholly misunderstood — Ah, well! Look, now, at these fauns and dryads among the shrubs upon the stage, pausing in startled wonder at the first blast of music which proclaims the exit of the goddess from her temple."

"The temple? Why, where are you going to exhibit?"

"In the Theatre, of course. Where else pantomimes?"

"But will the spectators have time to move all the way from the Amphitheatre after that — those ——?"

"The Amphitheatre? We shall exhibit the Libyans, too, in the Theatre."

"Combats in the Theatre sacred to Dionusos?"

"My dear lady " — penitently — " I know it is an offence against all the laws of the drama."

"Oh, worse than that! Consider what an impiety toward the god, to desecrate his altar with bloodshed?"

"Fairest devotee, recollect that, after all, I may fairly borrow Dionusos' altar in this my extreme need; for I saved its very existence for him, by preventing the magistrates from filling up the whole orchestra with benches for the patricians, after the barbarous Roman fashion. And besides, what possible sort of representation, or misrepresentation, has not been exhibited in every theatre of the empire for the last four hundred years? Have we not had tumblers, conjurers, allegories, martyrdoms, marriages, elephants on the tight rope, learned horses, and learned asses too, if we may trust Apuleius of Madaura; with a good many other spectacles of which we must not speak in the presence of a vestal? It is an age of execrable taste, and we must act accordingly."

"Ah!" answered Hypatia; "the first step in the downward career of the drama began when the successors of Alexander dared to profane theatres which had re-echoed the choruses of Sophocles and Euripides by degrading the altar of Dionusos into a stage for pantomimes!"

"Which your pure mind must, doubtless, consider not so very much better than a little fighting. But, after all, the Ptolemies could not do otherwise. You can only have Sophoclean dramas in a Sophoclean age; and theirs was no more of one than ours is, and so the drama died a natural death; and when that happens to man or thing, you may weep over it if you will, but you must, after all, bury it, and get something else in its place — except, of course, the worship of the gods."

"I am glad that you except that, at least," said Hypatia, somewhat bitterly. "But why not use the amphitheatre for both spectacles?"

"What can I do? I am over head and ears in debt already; and the amphitheatre is half in ruins, thanks to that fanatic edict of the late emperor's against gladiators. There is no time or money for repairing it; and besides, how pitiful a poor hundred of combatants will look in an arena built to hold two thousand! Consider, my dearest lady, in what fallen times we live!"

"I do, indeed!" said Hypatia. "But I will not see the altar polluted by blood. It is the desecration which it has undergone already which has provoked the god to withdraw the poetic inspiration."

"I do not doubt the fact. Some curse from Heaven, certainly, has fallen on our poets, to judge by their exceeding badness. Indeed, I am inclined to attribute the insane vagaries of the water-drinking monks and nuns, like those of the Argive women, to the same celestial anger. But I will see that the sanctity of the altar is preserved, by confining the combat to the stage. And as for the pantomime which will follow, if you would only fall in with my fancy of the triumph of Aphrodite, Dionusos would hardly refuse his altar for the glorification of his own lady-love."

"Ah — that myth is a late, and in my opinion a degraded one."

"Be it so: but recollect, that another myth makes her, and not without reason, the mother of all living beings. Be sure that

Dionusos will have no objection, or any other god either, to allow her to make her children feel her conquering might; for they all know well enough, that if we can once get her well worshipped here, all Olympus will follow in her train."

"That was spoken of the celestial Aphrodite, whose symbol is the tortoise, the emblem of domestic modesty and chastity: not of that baser Pandemic one."

"Then we will take care to make the people aware of whom they are admiring by exhibiting in the triumph whole legions of tortoises; and you yourself shall write the chant, while I will see that the chorus is worthy of what it has to sing. No mere squeaking double flute and a pair of boys: but a whole army of cyclops and graces, with such trebles and such bass-voices! It shall make Cyril's ears tingle in his palace!"

"The chant! A noble office for me, truly! That is the very part of the absurd spectacle to which you used to say the people never dreamed of attending. All which is worth settling you seem to have settled for yourself before you deigned to consult me."

"I said so? Surely you must mistake. But if any hired poetaster's chant do pass unheeded, what has that to do with Hypatia's eloquence and science, glowing with the treble inspiration of Athene, Phœbus, and Dionusos? And as for having arranged beforehand — my adorable mistress, what more delicate compliment could I have paid you?"

"I cannot say that it seems to me to be one."

"How? After saving you every trouble which I could, and racking my overburdened wits for stage-effects and properties, have I not brought hither the darling children of my own brain, and laid them down ruthlessly, for life or death, before the judgment-seat of your lofty and unsparing criticism?"

Hypatia felt herself tricked: but there was no escape now.

"And who, pray, is to disgrace herself, and me, as Venus Anadyomene?"

"Ah! that is the most exquisite article in all my bill of fare! What if the kind gods have enabled me to exact a promise from — whom, think you?"

"What care I? How can I tell?" asked Hypatia, who suspected and dreaded that she could tell.

"Pelagia herself!"

Hypatia rose angrily.

"This, sir, at least, is too much! It was not enough for you, it seems, to claim, or rather to take for granted, so imperiously, so mercilessly, a conditional promise — weakly, weakly made, in the vain hope that you would help forward aspirations of mine which you have let lie fallow for months — in which I do not believe that you sympathize now! — It was not enough for you to declare yourself publicly yesterday a Christian, and to come hither this morning to flatter me into the belief that you will dare, ten days hence, to restore the worship of the gods whom you have abjured! — It was not enough to plan without me all those movements in which you told me I was to be your fellow-counsellor — the very condition which you yourself offered! — It was not enough for you to command me to sit in that theatre, as your bait, your puppet, your victim, blushing and shuddering at sights unfit for the eyes of gods and men: — but, over and above all this, I must assist in the renewed triumph of a woman who has laughed down my teaching, seduced away my scholars, braved me in my very lecture-room — who for four years has done more than even Cyril himself to destroy all the virtue and truth which I have toiled to sow — and toiled in vain! Oh, beloved gods! where will end the tortures through which your martyr must witness for you to a fallen race?"

And, in spite of all her pride, and of Orestes' presence, her eyes filled with scalding tears.

Orestes' eyes had sunk before the vehemence of her just passion: but as she added the last sentence in a softer and sadder tone, he raised them again, with a look of sorrow and entreaty, as his heart whispered —

"Fool! — fanatic! But she is too beautiful'. Win her I must and will !"

"Ah! dearest, noblest Hypatia! what have I done? Unthinking fool that I was! In the wish to save you trouble — in the hope that I could show you, by the aptness of my own plans, that my practical statesmanship was not altogether an unworthy helpmate for your loftier wisdom — wretch that I am, I have offended you; and I have ruined the cause of those very gods for whom, I swear, I am as ready to sacrifice myself as ever you can be!"

The last sentence had the effect which it was meant to

have.

"Ruined the cause of the gods?" asked she, in a startled tone.

"Is it not ruined, without your help? And what am I to understand from your words but that — hapless man that I am! — you leave me and them henceforth to our own unassisted strength?"

"The unassisted strength of the gods is omnipotence."

"Be it so. But — why is Cyril, and not Hypatia, master of the masses of Alexandria this day? Why but because he and his have fought, and suffered, and died too, many a hundred of them, for their god, omnipotent as they believe him to be? Why are the old gods forgotten, my fairest logician? — for forgotten they are."

Hypatia trembled from head to foot, and Orestes went on more blandly than ever.

"I will not ask an answer to that question of mine. All I entreat is forgiveness for — what for I know not: but I have sinned, and that is enough for me. What if I have been too confident — too hasty? Are you not the prize for which I strain? and will not the preciousness of the victor's wreath excuse some impatience in his struggle for it? Hypatia has forgotten who and what the gods have made her — she has not even consulted her own mirror, when she blames one of her innumerable adorers for a forwardness which ought to be rather imputed to him as a virtue."

And Orestes stole meekly such a glance of adoration, that Hypatia blushed, and turned her face away..... After all, she was woman..... And she was a fanatic..... And she was to be an empress..... And Orestes' voice was as melodious, and his manner as graceful, as ever charmed the heart of woman.

"But Pelagia?" she said, at last, recovering herself.

"Would that I had never seen the creature! But, after all, I really fancied that in doing what I have done I should gratify you."

"Me?"

"Surely if revenge be sweet, as they say, it could hardly find a more delicate satisfaction than in the degradation of one who ——— "

"Revenge, sir? Do you dream that I am capable of so base

a passion?"

"I? Pallas forbid!" said Orestes, finding himself on the wrong path again. "But recollect that the allowing this spectacle to take place might rid you for ever of an unpleasant — I will not say rival."

"How, then?"

"Will not her reappearance on the stage, after all her proud professions of contempt for it, do something towards reducing her in the eyes of this scandalous little town to her true and native level? She will hardly dare thenceforth to go about parading herself as the consort of a god-descended hero, or thrusting herself unbidden into Hypatia's presence, as if she were the daughter of a consul."

"But I cannot — I cannot allow it even to her. After all, Orestes, she is a woman. And can I, philosopher as I am, help to degrade her even one step lower than she lies already?"

Hypatia had all but said "a woman even as I am"; but Neo-Platonic philosophy taught her better; and she checked the hasty assertion of anything like a common sex or common humanity between two beings so antipodal.

"Ah," rejoined Orestes, "that unlucky word degrade! Unthinking that I was, to use it, forgetting that she herself will be no more degraded in her own eyes, or any one's else, by hearing again the plaudits of those 'dear Macedonians,' on whose breath she has lived for years, than a peacock when he displays his train. Unbounded vanity and self-conceit are not unpleasant passions, after all, for their victim. After all, she is what she is, and her being so is no fault of yours. Oh, it must be! indeed it must!"

Poor Hypatia! The bait was too delicate, the tempter too wily; and yet she was ashamed to speak aloud the philosophic dogma which flashed a ray of comfort and resignation through her mind, and reminded her that after all there was no harm in allowing lower natures to develop themselves freely in that direction which Nature had appointed for them, and in which only they could fulfil the laws of their being, as necessary varieties in the manifold whole of the universe. So she cut the interview short with —

"If it must be, then.... I will now retire, and write the ode. Only, I refuse to have any communication whatsoever with — I am ashamed of even mentioning her name. I will send the ode to you, and she must adapt her dance to it as best she can. By her taste, or fancy rather, I will not be ruled."

"And I," said Orestes, with a profusion of thanks, "will retire to rack my faculties over the 'dispositions.' On this day week we exhibit — and conquer! Farewell, queen of wisdom! Your philosophy never shows to better advantage than when you thus wisely and gracefully subordinate that which is beautiful in itself to that which is beautiful relatively and practically."

He departed; and Hypatia, half dreading her own thoughts, sat down at once to labour at the ode. Certainly it was a magnificent subject. What etymologies, cosmogonies, allegories, myths, symbolisms between all heaven and earth, might she not introduce — if she could but banish that figure of Pelagia dancing to it all, which would not be banished, but hovered, like a spectre, in the background of all her imaginations. She became quite angry, first with Pelagia, then with herself, for being weak enough to think of her. Was it not positive defilement of her mind to be haunted by the image of so defiled a being? She would purify her thoughts by prayer and meditation. But to whom of all the gods should she address herself? To her chosen favourite, Athene? She who had promised to be present at that spectacle? Oh, how weak she had been to yield! And yet she had been snared into it. Snared — there was no doubt of it — by the very man whom she had fancied that she could guide and mould to her own purposes. He had guided and moulded her now against her self-respect, her compassion, her innate sense of right. Already she was his tool. True, she had submitted to be so for a great purpose. But suppose she had to submit again hereafter — always henceforth? And what made the thought more poignant was, her knowledge that he was right; that he knew what to do, and how to do it. She could not help admiring him for his address, his quickness, his clear practical insight: and yet she despised, mistrusted, all but hated him. But what if his were the very qualities which were destined to succeed? What if her purer and loftier aims, her resolutions — now, alas! broken — never to act but on the deepest and holiest principles and by the most sacred means, were destined never to exert themselves in practice, except conjointly with miserable stratagems and cajoleries such as these? What if statecraft, and not philosophy and religion, were the appointed rulers of mankind? Hideous thought! And yet — she who had all her life tried to be self-dependent, originative, to face and crush the hostile mob of circumstance and custom, and do battle single-handed with Christianity and a fallen age — how was it that in her first important and critical opportunity of action she had been dumb, irresolute, passive, the victim, at last, of the very corruption which she was to exterminate? She did not know yet that those who have no other means for regenerating a corrupted time than dogmatic pedantries concerning the dead and unreturning past, must end, in practice, by borrowing insincerely, and using clumsily, the very weapons of that novel age which they deprecate, and "sewing new cloth into old garments," till the rent become patent and Incurable. But in the mean while, such meditations as these drove from her mind for that day both Athene, and the ode, and philosophy, and all things but — Pelagia the wanton.

In the mean while, Alexandrian politics flowed onward in their usual pure and quiet course. The public buildings were placarded with the news of Heraclian's victory; and groups of loungers expressed, loudly enough, their utter indifference as to who might rule at Rome — or even at Byzantium. Let Heraclian or Honorius be emperor, the capitals must be fed; and while the Alexandrian wheat-trade was uninjured, what matter who received the tribute? Certainly, as some friends of Orestes found means to suggest, it might not be a bad thing for Egypt, if she could keep the tribute in her own treasury, instead of sending it to Rome without any adequate return, save the presence of an expensive army..... Alexandria had been once the metropolis of an independent empire..... Why not again? Then came enormous largesses of corn, proving, more satisfactorily to the mob than to the shipowners, that Egyptian wheat was better employed at home than abroad. Nay, there were even rumours of a general amnesty for all prisoners; and as, of course, every evil-doer had a kind of friend, who considered him an injured martyr, all parties were well content, on their own accounts at least, with such a move.

And so Orestes' bubble swelled, and grew, and glittered every day with fresh prismatic radiance; while Hypatia sat at home, with a heavy heart, writing her ode to Venus Urania, and submitting to Orestes' daily visits.

One cloud, indeed, not without squalls of wind and rain,

disfigured that sky which the Prefect had invested with such serenity by the simple expedient, well known to politicians, of painting it bright-blue, since it would not assume that colour of its own accord. For, a day or two after Ammonius's execution, the Prefect's guards informed him that the corpse of the crucified man, with the cross on which it hung, had vanished. The Nitrian monks had come down in a body, and carried them off before the very eyes of the sentinels. Orestes knew well enough that the fellows must have been bribed to allow the theft; hut he dare not say so to men on whose good humour his very life might depend: so, stomaching the affront as best he could, he vowed fresh vengeance against Cyril, and went on his way. But, behold! — within four-and-twenty hours of the theft, a procession of all the rascality, followed by all the piety, of Alexandria, — monks from Nitria counted by the thousand, — priests, deacons, archdeacons, Cyril himself, in full pontificals, and, borne aloft in the midst, upon a splendid bier, the missing corpse, its nail-pierced hands and feet left uncovered for the pitying gaze Church.

Under the very palace windows, from which Orestes found it expedient to retire for the time being, out upon the quays, and up the steps of the Cæsareum, defiled that new portent; and in another half-hour, a servant entered, breathlessly, to inform the shepherd of people, that his victim was lying in state in the centre of the nave, a martyr duly canonized, — Ammonius now no more, but henceforth Thaumasius the wonderful, on whose heroic virtues and more heroic faithfulness unto the death, Cyril was already descanting from the pulpit, amid thunders of applause at every allusion to Sisera at the brook Kishon, Sennacherib in the house of Nisroch, and the rest of the princes of this world who come to nought.

Here was a storm! To order a cohort to enter the church and bring away the body, was easy enough: to make them do it, in the face of certain death, not so easy. Besides, it was too early yet for so desperate a move as would be involved in the violation of a church..... So Orestes added this fresh item to the long column of accounts which he intended to settle with the patriarch; cursed for half-an-hour in the name of all divinities, saints, and martyrs, Christian and Pagan; and wrote off a lamentable history of his wrongs and sufferings to the very Byzantine court against which he was about to rebel, in the comfortable assurance that

Cyril had sent, by the same post, a counterstatement, contradicting it in every particular.... Never mind..... In case he failed in rebelling, it was as well to be able to prove his allegiance up to the latest possible date; and the more completely the two statements contradicted each other, the longer it would take to sift the truth out of them; and thus so much time was gained, and so much the more chance, meantime, of a new leaf being turned over in that Sibylline oracle of politicians — the Chapter of Accidents. And, for the time being, he would make a pathetic appeal to respectability and moderation in general, of which Alexandria, wherein some hundred thousand tradesmen and merchants had property to lose, possessed a goodly share.

Respectability responded promptly to the appeal; and loyal addresses and deputations of condolence flowed in from every quarter, expressing the extreme sorrow with which the citizens had beheld the late disturbances of civil order, and the contempt which had been so unfortunately evinced for the constituted authorities: but taking, nevertheless, the liberty to remark, that while the extreme danger to property which might ensue from the further exasperation of certain classes, prevented their taking those active steps on the side of tranquillity to which their feelings inclined them, the known piety and wisdom of their esteemed patriarch made it presumptuous in them to offer any opinion on his present conduct, beyond the expression of their firm belief that he had been unfortunately misinformed as to those sentiments of affection and respect which his excellency the Prefect was well known to entertain towards him. They ventured, therefore, to express a humble hope that, by some mutual compromise, to define which would be an unwarrantable intrusion on their part, a happy reconciliation would be effected, and the stability of law, property, and the Catholic Faith, ensured..... All which Orestes heard with blandest smiles, while his heart was black with curses; and Cyril answered by a very violent though a very true and practical harangue on the text, "How hardly shall they that have riches enter into the kingdom of heaven."

So respectability and moderation met with its usual hapless fate, and, soundly cursed by both parties, in the vain attempt to please both, wisely left the upper powers to settle their own affairs, and went home to their desks and counters, and did a very brisk business all that week on the strength of the approaching festival. One hapless innkeeper only tried to carry out in practice the principles which the deputation from his guild had so eloquently advocated; and being convicted of giving away bread in the morning to the Nitrian monks, and wine in the evening to the Prefect's guards, had his tavern gutted, and his head broken, by a joint plebiscitum of both the parties whom he had conciliated, who afterwards fought a little together, and then, luckily for the general peace, mutually ran away from each other.

Cyril in the mean while, though he was doing a foolish thing, was doing it wisely enough. Orestes might curse, and respectability might deplore, those nightly sermons, which shook the mighty arcades of the Cӕsareum, but they could not answer them. Cyril was right, and knew that he was right. Orestes was a scoundrel, hateful to God, and' to the enemies of God. The middle classes were lukewarm covetous cowards; the whole system of government was a swindle and an injustice; all men's hearts were mad with crying, "Lord, how long?" The fierce bishop had only to thunder forth text on text, from every book of scripture, old and new, in order to array on his side not merely the common sense and right feeling, but the bigotry and ferocity of the masses.

In vain did the good Arsenius represent to him not only the scandal but the unrighteousness of his new canonization. "I must have fuel, my good father," was his answer, "wherewith to keep alight the flame of zeal. If I am to be silent as to Heraclian's defeat, I must give them some other irritant, which will put them in a proper temper to act on that defeat, when they are told of it. If they hate Orestes, does he not deserve it? Even if he is not altogether as much in the wrong in this particular case as they fancy he is, are there not a thousand other crimes of his which deserve their abhorrence even more? At all events, he must proclaim the empire, as you yourself say, or we shall have no handle against him. He will not dare to proclaim it, if he knows that we are aware of the truth. And if we are to keep the truth in reserve, we must have something else to serve mean while as a substitute for it."

And poor Arsenius submitted with a sigh, as he saw Cyril making a fresh step in that alluring path of evil-doing that good might come, which led him in after-years into many a fearful sin, and left his name disgraced, perhaps for ever, in the judgment of generations, who know as little of the pandemonium against which he fought, as they do of the intense belief which sustained him in his warfare; and who have therefore neither understanding nor pardon for the occasional outrages and errors of a man no worse, even if no better, than themselves.

CHAPTER XXI
THE SQUIRE-BISHOP

IN a small and ill-furnished upper room of a fortified country-house, sat Synesius, the Bishop of Cyrene.

A goblet of wine stood beside him, on the table, but it was untasted. Slowly and sadly, by the light of a tiny lamp, he went on writing a verse or two, and then burying his face in his hand, while hot tears dropped between his fingers on the paper; till a servant entering, announced Raphael Aben -Ezra.

Synesius rose, with a gesture of surprise, and hurried towards the door. "No, ask him to come hither to me. To pass through those deserted rooms at night is more than I can bear." And he awaited for his guest at the chamber-door, and, as he entered, caught both his hands in his, and tried to speak; but his voice was choked within him.

"Do not speak," said Raphael, gently, leading him to his chair again. "I know all."

"You know all? And are you, then, so unlike the rest of the world, that you alone have come to visit the bereaved and the deserted in his misery?"

"I am like the rest of the world, after all; for I came to you on my own selfish errand, to seek comfort. Would that I could give it instead! But the servants told me all, below."

"And yet you persisted in seeing me, as if I could help you? Alas! I can help no one now. Here I am at last, utterly alone, utterly helpless. As I came from my mother's womb, so shall I return again. My last child — my last and fairest — gone after the rest! — Thank God, that I have had even a day's peace wherein to lay him by his mother and his brothers; though He alone knows how long the beloved graves may remain unrifled. Let it have been shame enough to sit here in my lonely tower, and watch the ashes of my Spartan ancestors, the sons of Hercules himself, my glory and my pride, sinful fool that I was! cast to the winds by barbarian plunderers..... When wilt thou make an end, O Lord, and slay me?"

"And how did the poor boy die?" asked Raphael, in hope of soothing sorrow by enticing it to vent itself in words.

"The pestilence. — What other fate can we expect, who breathe an air tainted with corpses, and sit under a sky darkened with carrion-birds? But I could endure even that, if I could work, if I could help. But to sit here, imprisoned now for months between these hateful towers; night after night to watch the sky, red with burning homesteads; day after day to have my ears ring with the shrieks of the dying and the captives — for they have begun now to murder every male, down to the baby at the breast — and to feel myself utterly fettered, impotent, sitting here like some palsied idiot, waiting for my end! — I long to rush out, and fall fighting, sword in hand: but I am their last, their only hope. The governors care nothing for our supplications. In vain have I memorialized Gennadius and Innocent, with what little eloquence my misery has not stunned in me. But there is no resolution, no unanimity left in the land. The soldiery are scattered in small garrisons, employed entirely in protecting the private property of their officers. The Ausurians defeat them piecemeal, and, armed with their spoils, actually have begun to be-leaguer fortified towns; and now there is nothing left for us, but to pray that, like Ulysses, we may be devoured the last. What am I doing? I am selfishly pouring out my own sorrows, instead of listening to yours."

"Nay, friend, you are talking of the sorrows of your country, not of your own. As for me, I have no sorrow — only a despair: which, being irremediable, may well wait. But you — oh, you must not stay here. Why not escape to Alexandria?"

"I will die at my post, as I have lived, the father of my people. When the last ruin comes, and Cyrene itself is besieged, I shall return thither from my present outpost, and the conquerors shall find the bishop in his place before the altar. There I have offered for years the unbloody sacrifice to Him, who will perhaps require of me a bloody one, that so the sight of an altar, polluted by the murder of His priest, may end the sum of Pentapolitan woe, and arouse Him to avenge His slaughtered sheep! There, we will talk no more of it. This at least I have left in my power, to make you welcome. And after supper you shall tell me what brings you hither."

And the good bishop, calling his servants, set to work to show his guest such hospitality as the invaders had left in his power.

Raphael's usual insight had not deserted him when, in his utter perplexity, he went, almost instinctively, straight to Synesius. The Bishop of Cyrene, to judge from the charming private letters which he has left, was one of those many-sided, volatile, restless men, who taste joy and sorrow, if not deeply or permanently, yet abundantly and passionately. He lived, as Raphael had told Orestes, in a whirlwind of good deeds, meddling and toiling for the mere pleasure of action; and as soon as there was nothing to be done, which, till lately, had happened seldom enough with him, paid the penalty for past excitement in fits of melancholy. A man of magniloquent and flowery style, not without a vein of self-conceit; yet withal of overflowing kindliness, racy humour, and unflinching courage, both physical and moral; with a very clear practical faculty, and a very muddy speculative one — though, of course, like the rest of the world, he was especially proud of his own weakest side, and professed the most passionate affection for philosophic meditation; while his detractors hinted, not without a show of reason, that he was far more of an adept in soldiering and dog-breaking than in the mysteries of the unseen world.

To him Raphael betook himself, he hardly knew why; certainly not for philosophic consolation; perhaps because Synesius was, as Raphael used to say, the only Christian from whom he had ever heard a hearty laugh; perhaps because he had some wayward hope, unconfessed even to himself, that he might meet at Synesius's house the very companions from whom he had just fled. He was fluttering round Victoria's new and strange brilliance, like a moth round the candle, as he confessed, after supper, to his host; and now he was come hither, on the chance of being able to singe his wings once more.

Not that his confession was extracted without much trouble to the good old man, who, seeing at once that Raphael had some weight upon his mind, which he longed to tell, and yet was either too suspicious or too proud to tell, set himself to ferret out the secret, and forgot all his sorrows for the time, as soon as he found a human being to whom he might do good. But Raphael was inexplicably wayward and unlike himself. All his smooth and shallow persiflage, even his shrewd satiric humour, had vanished. He seemed parched by some inward fever; restless, moody, abrupt, even peevish; and Synesius's curiosity rose with his disappointment, as Raphael went on obstinately declining to consult the very physician before whom he had presented himself as patient.

"And what can you do for me, if I did tell you?"

"Then allow me, my very dear friend, to ask this. As you deny having visited me on my own account, on what account did you visit me?"

"Can you ask? To enjoy the society of the most finished gentleman of Pentapolis."

"And was that worth a week's journey, in perpetual danger of death?"

"As for danger of death, that weighs little with a man who is careless of life. And as for the week's journey, I had a dream one night, on my way, which made me question whether I were wise in troubling a Christian bishop with any thoughts or questions which relate merely to poor human beings like myself, who marry and are given in marriage."

"You forget, friend, that you are speaking to one who has married, and loved — and lost."

"I did not. But you see how rude I am growing. I am no fit company for you, or any man. I believe I shall end by turning robber-chief, and heading a party of Ausurians."

"But," said the patient Synesius, "you have forgotten your dream all this while."

"Forgotten! — I did not promise to tell it you — did I?"

"No; but as it seems to have contained some sort of accusation against my capacity, do you not think it but fair to tell the accused what it was?"

Raphael smiled.

"Well then..... Suppose I had dreamt this. That a philosopher, an academic, and a believer in nothing and in no man, had met at Berenice certain rabbis of the Jews, and heard them reading and expounding a certain book of Solomon — the Song of Songs. You, as a learned man, know into what sort of trumpery allegory they would contrive to twist it; how the bride's eyes were to mean the scribes who were full of wisdom, as the pools of Heshbon were of water; and her stature spreading like a palm-tree, the priests who spread out their hands when blessing the people; and the left hand which should be under her head, the Tephilim which these old pedants wore on their left wrists; and the right hand which should hold her, the Mezuzah which they fixed on the right side of their doors to keep off devils; and so forth."

"I have heard such silly Cabbalisms, certainly."

"You have? Then suppose that I went on, and saw in my dream how this same academic and unbeliever, being himself also a Hebrew of the Hebrews, snatched the roll out of the rabbi's hand, and told them that they were a party of fools for trying to set forth what the book might possibly mean, before they had found out what it really did mean; and that they could only find out that by looking honestly at the plain words to see what Solomon meant by it. And then, suppose that this same apostate Jew, this member of the synagogue of Satan, in his carnal and lawless imaginations, had waxed eloquent with the eloquence of devils, and told them, that the book set forth, to those who had eyes to see, how Solomon the great king, with his three-score queens, and fourscore concubines, and virgins without number, forgets all his seraglio and his luxury in pure and noble love for the undefiled, who is but one; and how as his eyes are opened to see that God made the one man for the one woman, and the one woman to the one man, even as it was in the garden of Eden, so all his heart and thoughts become pure, and gentle, and simple; how the song of the birds, and the scent of the grapes, and the spicy southern gales, and all the simple country pleasures of the glens of Lebanon, which he shares with his own vine-dressers and slaves, become more precious in his eyes than all his palaces and artificial pomp; and the man feels that he is in harmony, for the first time in his life, with the universe of God, and with the mystery of the seasons; that within him, as well as without him, the winter is past, and the rain is over and gone; the flowers appear on the earth, and the voice of the turtle is heard in the land..... And suppose I saw in my dream how the rabbis, when they heard those wicked words, stopped their ears with one accord, and ran upon that son of Belial and cast him out, because he blasphemed their sacred books by his carnal interpretations. And suppose — I only say suppose — that I saw in my dream how the poor man said in his heart, 'I will go to the Christians; they acknowledge the sacredness of this same book; and they say that their God taught them that "in the beginning God made man, male and female." Perhaps they will tell me whether this Song of

Songs does not, as it seems to me to do, show the passage up-wards from brutal polygamy to that monogamy which they so solemnly command, and agree with me, that it is because the Song preaches this that it has a right to take its place among the holy writings?' You, as a Christian bishop, should know what answer such a man would receive..... You are silent? Then I will tell you what answer he seemed to receive in my dream. 'O blas-phemous and carnal man, who pervertest Holy Scripture into a cloak for thine own licentious-ness, as if it spoke of man's base and sensual affections, know that this book is to be spiritually interpreted of the marriage between the soul and its Creator, and that it is from this very book that the Catholic Church derives her strongest arguments in favour of holy virginity, and the glories of a celibate life.' "

Synesius was still silent.

"And what do you think I saw in my dream that that man did when he found these Christians enforcing, as a necessary article of practice, as well as of faith, a baseless and bombastic metaphor, borrowed from that very Neo-Platonism out of which he had just fled for his life? He cursed the day he was born, and the hour in which his father was told, 'Thou hast gotten a man-child,' and said, 'Philosophers, Jews, and Christians, farewell for ever and a day! The clearest words of your most sacred books mean anything or nothing, as the case may suit your fancies; and there is neither truth nor reason under the sun. What better is there for a man, than to follow the example of his people, and to turn usurer, and money-getter, and cajoler of fools in his turn, even as his father was before him?' "

Synesius remained a while in deep thought, and at last —

"And yet you came to me?"

"I did, because you have loved and married; because you have stood out manfully against this strange modern insanity, and refused to give up, when you were made a bishop, the wife whom God had given you. You, I thought, could solve the riddle for me, if any man could."

"Alas, friend! I have begun to distrust, of late, my power of solving riddles. After all, why should they be solved? What matters one more mystery in a world of mysteries? 'If thou marry, thou hast not sinned,' are St. Paul's own words; and let them be enough for us. Do not ask me to argue with you, but to help you. Instead of puzzling me with deep questions, and tempting me to set up my private judgment, as I have done too often already, against the opinion of the Church, tell me your story, and test my sympathy rather than my intellect. I shall feel with you and work for you, doubt not, even though I am unable to explain to myself why I do it."

"Then you cannot solve my riddle?"

"Let me help you," said Synesius with a sweet smile, "to solve it for yourself. You need not try to deceive me. You have a love, an undefiled, who is but one. When you possess her, you will be able to judge better whether your interpretation of the Song is the true one; and if you still think that it is, Synesius, at least, will have no quarrel against you. He has always claimed for himself the right of philosophizing in private, and he will allow the same liberty to you, whether the mob do or not."

"Then you agree with me? Of course you do!"

"Is it fair to ask me whether I accept a novel interpretation, which I have only heard five minutes ago, delivered in a somewhat hasty and rhetorical form?"

"You are shirking the question," said Raphael, peevishly.

"And what if I am? Tell me, point-blank, most self-tormenting of men, can I help you in practice, even though I choose to leave you to yourself in speculation?"

"Well, then, if you will have my story, take it, and judge for yourself of Christian common sense."

And hurriedly, as if ashamed of his own confession, and yet compelled, in spite of himself, to unbosom it, he told Synesius all, from his first meeting with Victoria to his escape from her at Berenice.

The good bishop, to Aben-Ezra's surprise, seemed to treat the whole matter as infinitely amusing. He chuckled, smote his hand on his thigh, and nodded approval at every pause — perhaps to give the speaker courage — perhaps because he really thought that Raphael's prospects were considerably less desperate than he fancied.....

"If you laugh at me, Synesius, I am silent. It is quite enough to endure the humiliation of telling you that I am — confound it! — like any boy of sixteen."

"Laugh at you? — with you, you mean. A convent? Pooh, pooh! The old Prefect has enough sense, I will warrant him, not to refuse a good match for his child."

"You forget that I have not the honour of being a Christian."

"Then we'll make you one. You won't let me convert you, I know; you always used to gibe and jeer at my philosophy. But Augustine comes to-morrow."

"Augustine?"

"He does indeed; and we must be off by daybreak, with all the armed men we can muster, to meet and escort him, and to hunt, of course, going and coming; for we have had no food this fortnight but what our own dogs and bows have furnished us. He shall take you in hand, and cure you of all your Judaism in a week; and then just leave the rest to me; I will manage it somehow or other. It is sure to come right. No; do not be bashful. It will be real amusement to a poor wretch who can find nothing else to do — Heigho! And as for lying under an obligation to me, why, we can square that by your lending me three or four thousand gold pieces — Heaven knows I want them! — on the certainty of never seeing them again."

Raphael could not help laughing in his turn.

"Synesius is himself still, I see, and not unworthy of his ancestor Hercules; and though he shrinks from cleansing the Augean stable of my soul, paws like the war-horse in the valley at the hope of undertaking any lesser labours in my behalf. But, my dear generous bishop, this matter is more serious, and I, the subject of it, have become more serious also, than you fancy. Consider: by the uncorrupt honour of your Spartan forefathers, Agis, Brasidas, and the rest of them, don't you think that you are, in your hasty kindness, tempting me to behave in a way which they would have called somewhat rascally?"

"How then, my dear man? You have a very honourable and praiseworthy desire; and I am willing to help you to compass it."

"Do you think that I have not cast about before now for more than one method of compassing it for myself? My good man, I have been tempted a dozen times already to turn Christian: but there has risen up in me the strangest fancy about conscience and honour..... I never was scrupulous before, Heaven knows — I am not over-scrupulous now — except about her. I cannot dissemble before her. I dare not look in her face when I had a lie in my right hand..... She looks through one — into one — like a clear-eyed awful goddess..... I never was ashamed in my life till my eyes met hers.".....

"But if you really became a Christian?"

"I cannot. I should suspect my own motives. Here is another of these absurd soul-anatomizing scruples which have risen up in me. I should suspect that I had changed my creed because I wished to change it — that if I was not deceiving her I was deceiving myself. If I had not loved her it might have been different: but now — just because I do love her, I will not, I dare not, listen to Augustine's arguments, or my own thoughts on the matter."

"Most wayward of men!" cried Synesius, half peevishly; "you seem to take some perverse pleasure in throwing yourself into the waves again, the instant you have climbed a rock of refuge?"

"Pleasure? Is there any pleasure in feeling oneself at death-grips with the devil? I had given up believing in him for many a year..... And behold, the moment that I awaken to anything noble and right, I find the old serpent alive and strong at my throat! No wonder that I suspect him, you, myself — I, who have been tempted every hour in the last week, temptations to become a devil. Ay," he went on, raising his voice, as all the fire of his intense Eastern nature flashed from his black eyes, "to be a devil! From my childhood till now never have I known what it was to desire, and not to possess. It is not often that I have had to trouble any poor Naboth for his vineyard: but when I have taken a fancy to it, Naboth has always found it wiser to give way. And now.... Do you fancy that I have not had a dozen hellish plots flashing across me in the last week? Look here! This is the mortgage of her father's whole estate. I bought it — whether by the instigation of Satan or of God — of a banker in Berenice, the very day I left them; and now they, and every straw which they possess, are in my power. I can ruin them — sell them as slaves — betray them to death as rebels — and last, but not least, cannot I hire a dozen worthy men to carry her off, and cut the Gordian knot most simply and summarily? And yet I dare not! I must be pure to approach the pure; and righteous, to kiss the feet of the righteous. Whence came this new conscience to me I know not, but come it has; and I dare no more do a base thing toward her, than I dare toward a God, if there be one. This very mortgage — I hate it, curse it, now that I possess it — the tempting devil!"

"Burn it," said Synesius, quietly.

"Perhaps I may. At least, used it never shall be. Compel her? I am too proud, or too honourable, or something or other, even to solicit her. She must come to me; tell me with her own lips that she loves me, that she will take me, and make me worthy of her. She must have mercy on me, of her own free will, or — let her pine and die in that accursed prison; and then a scratch with the trusty old dagger for her father, and another for myself, will save him from any more superstitions, and me from any more philosophic doubts, for a few aeons of ages, till we start again in new lives — he, I suppose, as a jackass, and I as a baboon. What matter? but unless I possess her by fair means, God do so to me, and more also, if I attempt base ones!"

"God be with you, my son, in the noble warfare!" said Synesius, his eyes filling with kindly tears.

"It is no noble warfare at all. It is a base coward fear, in one who never before feared man or devil, and is now fallen low enough to be afraid of a helpless girl!"

"Not so," cried Synesius, in his turn; "it is a noble and a holy fear. You fear her goodness. Could you see her goodness, much less fear it, were there not a Divine Light within you which showed you what, and how awful, goodness was? Tell me no more, Raphael Aben-Ezra, that you do not fear God; for he who fears Virtue, fears Him whose likeness Virtue is. Go on — go on..... Be brave, and His strength will be made manifest in your weakness."

* * * * *

It was late that night before Synesius compelled his guest to retire, after having warned him not to disturb himself if he heard the alarm-bell ring, as the house was well garrisoned, and having set the water-clock by which he and his servants measured their respective watches. And then the good bishop, having disposed his sentinels, took his station on the top of his tower, close by the warning-bell; and as he looked out over the broad lands of his forefathers, and prayed that their desolation might come to an end at last, he did not forget to pray for the desolation of the guest who slept below, a happier and more healthy slumber than he had known for many a week. For before Raphael lay down that night, he had torn to shreds Majoricus's mortgage, and felt a lighter and a better man as he saw the cunning temptation consuming scrap by scrap in the lamp-flame. And then, wearied out with fatigue of body and mind, he forgot Synesius, Victoria, and the rest, and seemed to himself to wander all night among the vine-clad glens of Lebanon, amid the gardens of lilies, and the beds of spices; while shepherds' music lured him on and on, and girlish voices, chanting the mystic idyl of his mighty ancestor, rang soft and fitful through his weary brain.

* * * * *

Before sunrise the next morning, Raphael was faring forth gallantly, well armed and mounted, by Synesius's side, followed by four or five brace of tall brush-tailed greyhounds, and by the faithful Bran, whose lop-ears and heavy jaws, unique in that land of prick-ears and fox-noses, formed the absorbing subject of conversation among some twenty smart retainers, who, armed to the teeth for chase and war, rode behind the bishop on half-starved raw-boned horses, inured by desert training and bad times to do the maximum of work upon the minimum of food.

For the first few miles they rode in silence, through ruined villages and desolated farms, from which here and there a single inhabitant peeped forth fearfully, to pour his tale of woe into the ears of the hapless bishop, and then; instead of asking alms from him, to entreat his acceptance of some paltry remnant of grain or poultry, which hac escaped the hands of the marauders; and as they clung to his hands, and blessed him as their only hope and stay poor Synesius heard patiently again and again the same purposeless tale of woe, and mingled his tears with theirs and then spurred his horse on impatiently, as if to escape from the sight of misery which he could not relieve; while a voice in Raphael's heart seemed to ask him — "Why was thy wealth given to thee, but that thou mightest dry, if but for a day, such tears as these?"

And he fell into a meditation which was not without its fruit in due season, but which lasted till they had left the enclosed country, and were climbing-the slopes of the low rolling hills, over which lay the road from the distant sea. But as they left the signs of war behind them, the volatile temper of the good bishop began to rise. He petted his hounds, chatted to his men, discoursed on the most probable quarter for finding game, and exhorted them cheerfully enough to play the man, as their chance of having anything to eat at night depended entirely on their prowess during the day.

"Ah!" said Raphael at last, glad of a pretext for breaking his own chain of painful thought, "there is a vein of your land-salt. I suspect that you were all at the bottom of the sea once, and that the old Earth-shaker Neptune, tired of your bad ways, gave you a lift one morning, and set you up as dry land, in order to be rid of you."

"It may really be so. They say that the Argonauts returned back through this country from the Southern Ocean, which must have been therefore far nearer us than it is now, and that they carried their mystic vessel over these very hills to the Syrtis. However, we have forgotten all about the sea thoroughly enough since that time. I well remember my first astonishment at the sight of a galley in Alexandria, and the roar of laughter with which my fellow-students greeted my not unreasonable remark, that it looked very like a centipede."

"And do you recollect, too, the argument which I had once with your steward about the pickled fish which I brought you from Egypt; and the way in which, when the jar was opened, the servants shrieked and ran right and left, declaring that the fish-bones were the spines of poisonous serpents?"

"The old fellow is as obstinate as ever, I assure you, in his disbelief in salt-water. He torments me continually by asking me to tell him the story of my shipwreck, and does not believe me after all, though he has heard it a dozen times. 'Sir,' he said to me, solemnly, after you were gone, 'will that strange gentleman pretend to persuade me that anything eatable can come out of his great pond there at Alexandria, when every one can see that the best fountain in the country never breeds anything but frogs and leeches?' "

As he spoke they left the last field behind them, and entered upon a vast sheet of breezy down, speckled with shrubs and copse, and split here and there by rocky glens, ending in fertile valleys, once thick with farms and homesteads.

"Here," cried. Synesius, "are our hunting-grounds. And now for one hour's forgetfulness, and the joys of the noble art! What could old Homer have been thinking of when he forgot to number it among the pursuits which are glorious to heroes, and make man illustrious, and yet could laud in those very words the forum?"

"The forum?" said Raphael. "I never saw it yet make men anything but rascals."

"Brazen-faced rascals, my friend. I detest the whole breed of lawyers, and never meet one without turning him into ridicule; effeminate pettifoggers, who shudder at the very sight of roast venison, when they think of the dangers by which it has been procured. But it is a cowardly age, my friend — a cowardly age. Let us forget it, and ourselves."

"And even philosophy and Hypatia?" said Raphael, archly.

"I have done with philosophy. To fight like an Heracleid, and to die like a bishop, is all I have left — except Hypatia, the perfect, the wise! I tell you, friend, it is a comfort to me, even in my deepest misery, to recollect that the corrupt world yet holds one being so divine ———— "

And he was running on in one of his high-flown laudations of his idol, when Raphael checked him.

"I fear our common sympathy on that subject is rather weakened. I have begun to doubt her lately nearly as much as I doubt philosophy."

"Not her virtue?"

"No, friend; nor her beauty, nor her wisdom; simply her power of making me a better man. A selfish criterion, you will say. Be it so..... What a noble horse that is of yours!"

"He has been — he has been; but worn out now, like his master and his master's fortunes.".....

"Not so, certainly, the colt on which you have done me the honour to mount me."

Ah, my poor boy's pet!.... You are the first person who has crossed him since ———— "

"Is he of your own breeding?" asked Raphael, trying to turn the conversation.

"A cross between that white Nisжan which you sent me, and one of my own mares.''

"Not a bad cross; though he keeps a little of the bull head and greyhound flank of your Africans."

"So much the better, friend. Give me bone — bone and endurance for this rough down country. Your delicate Nisæans are all very well for a few minutes over those flat sands of Egypt: but here you need a horse who will go forty miles a day over rough and smooth, and dine thankfully off thistles at night. Aha, poor little man!" — as a jerboa sprang up from a tuft of bushes at his feet — "I fear you must help to fill our soup-kettle in these hard times."

And with a dexterous sweep of his long whip, the worthy bishop entangled the jerboa's long legs, whisked him up to his saddle-bow, and delivered him to the groom and the game-bag.

"Kill him at once. Don't let him squeak, boy! — he cries too like a child."....

"Poor little wretch!" said Raphael. "What more right, now, have we to eat him than he to eat us?"

"Eh? If he can eat us, let him try. How long have you joined the Manichees?"

"Have no fears on that score. But, as I told you, since my wonderful conversion by Bran, the dog, I have begun to hold dumb animals in respect, as probably quite as good as myself."

"Then you need a further conversion, friend Raphael, and to learn what is the dignity of man; and when that arrives, you will learn to believe, with me, that the life of every beast upon the face of the earth would be a cheap price to pay in exchange for the life of the meanest human being."

"Yes, if they be required for food: but really, to kill them for our amusement!"

"Friend, when I was still a heathen, I recollect well how I used to haggle at that story of the cursing of the fig-tree; but when I learnt to know what man was, and that I had been all my life mistaking for a part of nature that race which was originally, and can be again, made in the likeness of God, then I began to see that it were well if every fig-tree upon earth were cursed, if the spirit of one man could be taught thereby a single lesson. And so I speak of these, my darling field-sports, on which I have not been ashamed, as you know, to write a book."

"And a very charming one: yet you were still a pagan, recollect, when you wrote it."

"I was; and then I followed the chase by mere nature and inclination. But now I know I have a right to follow it-, because it gives me endurance, promptness, courage, self-control, as well as health and cheerfulness; and therefore — Ah! a fresh ostrich-track!"

And stopping short, Synesius began pricking slowly up the hill-side.

"Back!" whispered he, at last. "Quietly and silently. Lie down on your horse's neck, as I do, or the long-necked rogues may see you. They must be close to us over the brow. I know that favourite grassy slope of old. Round under yon hill, or they will get wind of us, and then farewell to them!"

And Synesius and his groom cantered on, hanging each to their horses' necks by an arm and a leg, in a way which Raphael endeavoured in vain to imitate.

Two or three minutes more of breathless silence brought them to the edge of the hill, where Synesius halted, peered down a moment, and then turned to Raphael, his face and limbs quivering with delight, as he held up two fingers, to denote the number of the birds.

"Out of arrow-range! Slip the dogs, Syphax!"

And in another minute Raphael found himself galloping headlong down the hill, while two magnificent ostriches, their outspread plumes waving in the bright breeze, their necks stooped almost to the ground, and their long legs flashing out behind them, were sweeping away before the greyhounds at a pace which no mortal horse could have held for ten minutes.

"Baby that I am still!" cried Synesius, tears of excitement glittering in his eyes;.... while Raphael gave himself up to the joy, and forgot even Victoria, in the breathless rush over rock and bush, sandhill and watercourse.

"Take care of that dry torrent-bed! Hold up, old horse! This will not last two minutes more. They cannot hold their pace against this breeze..... Well tried, good dog, though you did miss him! Ah, that my boy were here! There — they double. Spread right and left, my children, and ride at them as they pass!"

And the ostriches, unable, as Synesius said, to keep their pace against the breeze, turned sharp on their pursuers, and beating the air with outspread wings, came down the wind again, at a rate even more wonderful than before.

"Ride at him Raphael — ride at him, and turn him into those bushes!" cried Synesius, fitting an arrow to his bow.

Raphael obeyed, and the bird swerved into the low scrub; the well-trained horse leapt at him like a cat; and Raphael, who dare not trust his skill in archery, struck with his whip at the long-neck as it struggled past him, and felled the noble quarry to the ground. He was in the act of springing down to secure his prize, when a shout from Synesius stopped him.

"Are you mad? He will kick out your heart! Let the dogs hold him!"

"Where is the other?" asked Raphael, panting.

"Where he ought to be. I have not missed a running shot for many a month."

"Really, you rival the Emperor Commodus himself."

"Ah! I tried his fancy of crescent-headed arrows once, and decapitated an ostrich or two tolerably: but they are only fit for the amphitheatre: they will not lie safely in the quiver on horseback, I find. But what is that?" And he pointed to a cloud of white dust, about a mile down the valley. "A herd of antelopes? If so, God is indeed gracious to us! Come down — whatsoever they are, we have no time to lose."

And collecting his scattered forces, Synesius pushed on rapidly towards the object which had attracted his attention.

"Antelopes!" cried one.

"Wild horses!" cried another.

"Tame ones, rather!" cried Synesius, with a gesture of wrath. "I saw the flash of arms!"

"The Ausurians!" And a yell of rage rang from the whole troop.

"Will you follow me, children?"

"To death!" shouted they.

"I know it. Oh that I had seven hundred of you, as Abraham had! We would see then whether these scoundrels did not share, within a week, the fate of Chedorlaomer's."

"Happy man, who can actually trust your own slaves!" said Raphael, as the party galloped on, tightening their girdles and getting ready their weapons.

"Slaves? If the law gives me the power of selling one or two of them who are not yet wise enough to be trusted to take care of themselves, it is a fact which both I and they have long forgotten. Their fathers grew grey at my father's table, and God grant that they may grow grey at mine! We eat together, work together, hunt together, fight together, jest together, and weep together. God help us all! for we have but one common weal.

Now — do you make out the enemy, boys?"

"Ausurians, your Holiness. The same party who tried Myrsinitis last week. I know them by the helmets which they took from the Markmen."

"And with whom are they fighting?"

No one could see. Fighting they certainly were: but their victims were beyond them, and the party galloped on.

"That was a smart business at Myrsinitis. The Ausurians appeared while the people were at morning prayers. The soldiers, of course, ran for their lives, and hid in the caverns, leaving the matter to the priests."

"If they were of your presbytery, I doubt not they proved themselves worthy of their diocesan."

"Ah, if all my priests were but like them! or my people either!" said Synesius, chatting quietly in full gallop, like a true son of the saddle. "They offered up prayers for victory, sallied out at the head of the peasants, and met the Moors in a narrow pass. There their hearts failed them a little. Faustus, the deacon, makes them a speech; charges the leader of the robbers, like young David, with a stone, beats his brains out therewith, strips him in true Homeric fashion, and routs the Ausurians with their leader's sword; returns and erects a trophy in due classic form, and saves the whole valley."

"You should make him archdeacon." "I would send him and his townsfolk round the province, if I could, crowned with laurel, and proclaim before them at every market-place, 'These are men of God.' With whom can those Ausurians be dealing? Peasants would have been all killed long ago, and soldiers would have run away long ago. It is truly a portent in this country to see a fight last ten minutes. Who can they be? I see them now, and hewing away like men too. They are all on foot but two; and we have not a cohort of infantry left for many a mile round."

"I know who they are!" cried Raphael, suddenly striking spurs into his horse. "I will swear to that armour among a thousand. And there is a litter in the midst of them. On! and fight, men, if you ever fought in your lives!"

"Softly!" cried Synesius. "Trust an old soldier, and perhaps — alas! that he should have to say it — the best left in this wretched country. Round by the hollow, and take the barbarians suddenly in flank. They will not see us then till we are within twenty paces of them. Aha! you have a thing or two to learn yet, Aben-Ezra."

And chuckling at the prospect of action, the gallant bishop wheeled his little troop, and in five minutes more dashed out of the copse with a shout and a flight of arrows, and rushed into the thickest of the fight.

One cavalry skirmish must be very like another. A crash of horses, a flashing of sword-blades, five minutes of blind confusion, and then those who have not been knocked out of their saddles by their neighbours' knees, and have not cut off their own horses' heads instead of their enemy's, find themselves, they know not how, either running away or being run away from — not one blow in ten having taken effect on either side. And even so Raphael, having made vain attempts to cut down several Moors, found himself standing on his head in an altogether undignified posture, among-innumerable horses' legs, in all possible frantic motions. To avoid one, was to get in the way of another; so he philosophically sat still, speculating on the sensation of having his brains kicked out, till the cloud of legs vanished, and he found himself kneeling abjectly opposite the nose of a mule, on whose back sat, utterly unmoved, a tall and reverend man, in episcopal costume. The stranger, instead of bursting out laughing, as Raphael did, solemnly lifted his hand, and gave him his blessing. The Jew sprang to his feet, heedless of all such courtesies, and, looking round, saw the Ausurians galloping off up the hill in scattered groups, and Synesius standing close by him, wiping a bloody sword.

"Is the litter safe?" were his first words.

"Safe; and so are all. I gave you up for killed, when I saw you run through with that lance."

"Run through? I am as sound in the hide as a crocodile," said Raphael, laughing.

"Probably the fellow took the butt instead of the point, in his hurry. So goes a cavalry scuffle. I saw you hit three or four fellows running with the flat of your sword."

"Ah, that explains," said Raphael. "Why, I thought myself once the best swordsman on the Armenian frontier.".…

"I suspect that you were thinking of some one besides the Moors," said Synesius, archly, pointing to the litter; and Raphael, for the first time for many a year, blushed like a boy of fifteen, and then turned haughtily away, and remounted his horse, saying, "Clumsy fool that I was!"

"Thank God rather that you have been kept from the shedding of blood," said the stranger bishop, in a soft, deliberate voice, with a peculiarly clear and delicate enunciation. "If God have given us the victory, why grudge His having spared any other of His creatures besides ourselves?"

"Because there are so many the more of them left to ravish, burn, and slay," answered Synesius. "Nevertheless, I am not going to argue with Augustine."

Augustine! Raphael looked intently at the man, a tall, delicate-featured personage, with a lofty and narrow forehead, scarred like his cheeks with the deep furrows of many a doubt and woe. Resolve, gentle but unbending, was expressed in his thin close-set lips and his clear quiet eye; but the calm of his mighty countenance was the calm of a Worn-out volcano, over which centuries must pass before the earthquake-rents be filled with kindly soil, and the cinder-slopes grow gay with grass and flowers. The Jew's thoughts, however, were soon turned into another channel by the hearty embraces of Majoricus and his son.

"We have caught you again, you truant!" said the young Tribune; "you could not escape us, you see, after all."

"Rather," said the father, "we owe him a second debt of gratitude for a second deliverance. We were right hard bested when you rode up."

"Oh, he brings nothing but good with him whenever he appears; and then he pretends to be a bird of ill omen," said the light-hearted Tribune, putting his armour to rights.

Raphael was in his secret heart not sorry to find that his old friends bore him no grudge for his caprice: but all he answered was —

"Pray thank any one but me; I have, as usual, proved myself a fool. But what brings you here, like Gods e Machinâ? It is contrary to all probabilities. One would not admit so astounding an incident, even in the modern drama."

"Contrary to none whatsoever, my friend. We found Augustine at Berenice, in act to set off to Synesius: we — one of us, that is — were certain that you would be found with him; and we decided on acting as Augustine's guard, for none of the dastard garrison dare stir out."

"One of us," thought Raphael, — "which one?" And, conquering his pride, he asked, as carelessly as he could, for Victoria.

"She is there in the litter, poor child!" said tier father, in a serious tone.

"Surely, not ill?"

"Alas! either the overwrought excitement of months of heroism broke down when she found us safe at last, or some stroke from God ————.... Who can tell what I may not have deserved? — But she has been utterly prostrate in body and mind, ever since we parted from you at Berenice."

The blunt soldier little guessed the meaning of his own words. But Raphael, as he heard, felt a pang shoot through his heart, too keen for him to discern whether it sprung from joy or from despair.

"Come," cried the cheerful voice of Synesius, "come, Aben-Ezra; you have knelt for Augustine's blessing already, and now you must enter into the fruition of it. Come, you two philosophers must know each other. Most holy, I entreat you to preach to this friend of mine, at once the wisest and the foolishest of men."

"Only the latter," said Raphael; "but open to any speech of Augustine's, at least when we are safe home, and game enough for Synesius's new guests killed."

And turning away, he rode silent and sullen by the side of his companions, who began at once to consult together as to the plans of Majoricus and his soldiers.

In spite of himself, Raphael soon became interested in Augustine's conversation. He entered into the subject of Cyrenian misrule and ruin as heartily and shrewdly as any man of the world; and when all the rest were at a loss, the prompt practical hint which cleared up the difficulty was certain to come from him. It was by his advice that Majoricus had brought his soldiery hither; it was his proposal that they should be employed for a fixed period in defending these remote southern boundaries of the province; he checked the impetuosity of Synesius, cheered the despair of Majoricus, appealed to the honour and the Christianity of the soldiers, and seemed to have a word — and that the right word — for every man; and after a while, Aben-Ezra quite forgot the stiffness and deliberation of his manner, and the quaint use of Scripture texts in far-fetched illustrations of every opinion which he propounded. It had seemed at first a mere affectation; but the arguments which it was employed to enforce were in themselves so moderate and so rational, that Raphael began to feel, little by little, that his apparent pedantry was only the result of a wish to refer every matter, even the most vulgar, to some deep and divine rule of right and wrong.

" But you forget all this while, my friends," said Majoricus at last, "the danger which you incur by sheltering proclaimed rebels."

"The King of kings has forgiven your rebellion, in that while he has punished you by the loss of your lands and honours, he has given you your life for a prey in this city of refuge. It remains for you to bring forth worthy fruits of penitence; of which I know none better than those which John the Baptist commanded to the soldiery of old, 'Do no violence to any man, and be content with your wages.' "

"As for rebels and rebellion," said Synesius, "they are matters unknown among us; for where there is no king there can be no rebellion. Whosoever will help us against Ausurians is loyal in our eyes. And as for our political creed, it is simple enough — namely, that the emperor never dies, and that his name is Agamemnon, who fought at Troy; which any of my grooms will prove to you syllogistically enough to satisfy Augustine himself. As thus —

"Agamemnon was the greatest and the best of kings.

"The emperor is the greatest and the best of kings.

"Therefore, Agamemnon is the emperor, and conversely.''

"It had been well," said Augustine, with a grave smile, "if some of our friends had held the same doctrine, even at the expense of their logic."

"Or if," answered Synesius, "they believed with us, that the emperor's chamberlain is a clever old man, with a bald head like my own, Ulysses by name, who was rewarded with the prefecture of all lands north of the Mediterranean, for putting out the Cyclop's eye two years ago. However, enough of this. But, you see, you are not in any extreme danger of informers and intriguers..... The real difficulty is, how you will be able to obey Augustine, by being content with your wages. For," lowering his voice, "you will get literally none."

"It will be as much as we deserve," said the young Tribune; "but my fellows have a trick of eating ———— "

"They are welcome, then, to all deer and ostriches which they can catch. But! am not only penniless, but reduced myself to live, like the Læstrygons, on meat and nothing else; all crops and stocks for miles round being either burnt or carried off."

"E nihilo nihil!" said Augustine, having nothing else to say. But here Raphael woke up on a sudden with —

"Did the Pentapolitan wheat-ships go to Rome?"

"No; Orestes stopped them when he stopped the Alexandrian convoy."

"Then the Jews have the wheat, trust them for it; and what they have, I have. There are certain monies of mine lying at interest in the seaports, which will set that matter to rights for a month or two. Do you find an escort tomorrow, and I will find wheat."

"But, most generous of friends, I can neither repay you interest nor principal."

"Be it so. I have spent so much money during the last thirty years in doing nothing but evil, that it is hard if I may not at last spend a little in doing good. — Unless his Holiness of Hippo thinks it wrong for you to accept the good will of an infidel?"

"Which of these three," said Augustine, "was neighbour to him who fell among thieves, but he who had mercy on him? Verily, my friend Raphael Aben-Ezra, thou art not far from the kingdom of God."

"Of which God?" asked Raphael, slily.

"Of the God of thy forefather Abraham, whom thou shalt hear us worship this evening, if He will. Synesius, have you a church wherein I can perform the evening service, and give a word of exhortation to these my children?"

Synesius sighed. "There is a ruin, which was last month a church."

"And is one still. Man did not place there the presence of God, and man cannot expel it."

And so, sending out hunting-parties right and left in chase of everything which had animal life, and picking up before nightfall a tolerably abundant supply of game, they went homewards, where Victoria was intrusted to the care of Synesius's old stewardess, and the soldiery were marched straight into the church; while Synesius's servants, to whom the Latin service would have been unintelligible, busied themselves in cooking the still warm game.

Strangely enough it sounded to Raphael that evening, to hear, among those smoke-grimed pillars and fallen rafters, the grand old Hebrew psalms of his nation ring aloft, to the very chants, too, which were said by the Rabbi to have been used in the Temple-worship of Jerusalem..... They, and the invocations, thanksgivings, blessings, the very outward ceremonial itself, were all Hebraic, redolent of the thoughts, the words of his own ancestors. That lesson from the book of Proverbs, which Augustine's deacon was reading in Latin — the blood of the man who wrote these words was flowing in Aben-Ezra's veins..... Was it a mistake, an hypocrisy? or were they indeed worshipping, as they fancied, the Ancient One who spoke face to face with his forefathers, the Archetype of man, the Friend of Abraham and of Israel?

And now the sermon began; and as Augustine stood for a moment in prayer in front of the ruined altar, every furrow in his worn face lit up by a ray of moonlight which streamed in through the broken roof, Raphael waited impatiently for his speech. What would he, the refined dialectician, the ancient teacher of heathen rhetoric, the courtly and learned student, the ascetic celibate and theosopher, have to say to those coarse war-worn soldiers. Thracians and Markmen, Gauls and Belgians, who sat watching there, with those sad earnest faces? What one thought or feeling in common could there be between Augustine and his congregation?

At last, after signing himself with the cross, he began. The subject was one of the psalms which had just been read — a battle psalm, concerning Moab and Amalek, and the old border wars of Palestine. What would he make of that?

He seemed to start lamely enough, in spite of the exquisite grace of his voice, and manner, and language, and the epigrammatic terseness of every sentence. He spent some minutes over the inscription of the psalm — allegorized it — made it mean something which it never did mean in the writer's mind, and which it, as Raphael well knew, never could mean, for his interpretation was founded on a sheer mis-translation. He punned on the Latin version — derived the meaning of Hebrew words from Latin etymologies..... And as he went on with the psalm itself, the common sense of David seemed to evaporate in mysticism. The most fantastic and far-fetched illustrations, drawn from the commonest objects, alternated with mysterious theosophic dogma. Where was that learning for which he was so famed? Where was that reverence for the old Hebrew Scriptures which he professed? He was treating David as ill as Hypatia used to treat Homer — worse even than old Philo did, when in the home life of the old patriarchs, and in the mighty acts of Moses and Joshua, he could find nothing but spiritual allegories wherewith to pamper the private experiences of the secluded theosophist. And Raphael felt very much inclined to get up and go away, and still more inclined to say, with a smile, in his haste, "All men are liars."....

And yet, what an illustration that last one was! No mere fancy, but a real deep glance into the working of the material universe, as symbolic of the spiritual and unseen one. And not drawn, as Hypatia's were, exclusively from some sublime or portentous phenomenon, but from some dog, or kettle, or fish-wife, with a homely insight worthy of old Socrates himself. How personal he was becoming, too!.... No long bursts of declamation, but dramatic dialogue and interrogation, by-hints, and un-expected hits at one and the other most common-place soldier's failing..... And yet each pithy rebuke was put in a universal, comprehensive form, which made Raphael himself wince — which might, he thought, have made any man, or woman either, wince in like manner. Well, whether or not Augustine knew truths for all men, he at least knew sins for all men, and for him-self as well as his hearers. There was no denying that. He was a real man, right or wrong. What he rebuked in others, he had felt in himself, and fought it to the death-grip, as the flash and quiver of that worn face proclaimed..... But yet, why were the Edomites, by an utterly mistaken pun on their name, to signify one sort of sin, and the Ammonites another, and the Amalekites another? What had that to do with the old psalm? What had it to do with the present auditory? Was not this the wildest and lowest form of that unreal, subtilizing, mystic pedantry, of which he had sick-ened long ago in Hypatia's lecture-room, till he fled to Bran, the dog, for honest practical realities?

No..... Gradually, as Augustine's hints became more practical and pointed, Raphael saw that there was in his mind a most real and organic connexion, true or false, in what seemed at first mere arbitrary allegory. Amalekites, personal sins, Ausurian robbers and ravishers, were to him only so many different forms of one and the same evil. He who helped any of them fought against the righteous God; he who fought against them fought for that God; but he must conquer the Amalekites within, if he expected to conquer the Amalekites without. Could the legionaries permanently put down the lust and greed around them, while their own hearts were enslaved to lust and greed within? Would they not be helping it by example, while they pretended to crush it by sword-strokes? Was it not a mockery, an hypocrisy? Could God's blessing be on it? Could they restore unity and peace to the country while there was neither unity nor peace within them? What had produced the helplessness of the people, the imbecility of the military, but inward helplessness, inward weakness? They were weak against Moors, because they were weak against enemies more deadly than Moors. How could they fight for God outwardly, while they were fighting against Him inwardly? He would not go forth with their hosts. How could He, when He was not among their hosts? He, a spirit, must dwell in their spirits..... And then the shout of a King would be among them, and one of them should chase a thousand..... Or if not — if both people and soldiers required still further chastening-and humbling — what matter, provided that they were chastened and humbled? What matter if their faces were confounded, if they were thereby driven to seek His Name, who alone was the Truth, the Light, and the Life? What if they were slain? Let them have conquered the inward enemies, what matter to them if the outward enemies seemed to prevail for a moment? They should be recompensed at the resurrection of the just, when death was swallowed up in victory. It would be seen then who had really conquered in the eyes of the just God — they, God's ministers, the defenders of peace and justice, or the Ausurians, the enemies thereof..... And then, by some quaintest turn of fancy, he introduced a word of pity and hope, even for the wild Moorish robbers. It might be good for them to have succeeded thus far; they might learn from their Christian captives, purified by affliction, truths which those captives had forgotten in prosperity. And, again, it might be good for them, as well as for Christians, to be confounded and made like chaff before the wind, that so they too might learn His Name..... And so on, through and in spite of all conceits, allegories, overstrained interpretations, Augustine went on evolving from the Psalms, and from the past, and from the future, the assertion of a Living, Present God, the eternal enemy of discord, injustice, and evil, the eternal helper and deliverer of those who were enslaved and crushed thereby in soul or body..... It was all. most strange to Raphael..... Strange in its utter unlikeness to any teaching, Platonist or Hebrew, which he had ever heard before, and stranger still in its agreement with those teachings; in the instinctive ease with which it seemed to unite and justify them all by the talisman of some one idea — and what that might be, his Jewish prejudices could not prevent his seeing, and yet would not allow him to acknowledge. But, howsoever he might redden with Hebrew pride; howsoever he might long to persuade himself that Augustine was building up a sound and right practical structure on the foundation of a sheer lie; he could not help watching, at first with envy, and then with honest pleasure, the faces of the rough soldiers, as they gradually lightened up into fixed attention, into cheerful and solemn resolve.

"What wonder?" said Raphael to himself, "what wonder, after all? He has been speaking to these wild beasts as to sages and saints; he has been telling them that God is as much with them as with prophets and psalmists..... I wonder if Hypatia, with all her beauty, could have touched their hearts as he has done?"

And when Raphael rose at the end of this strange discourse, he felt more like an old Hebrew than he had done since he sat upon his nurse's knee, and heard legends about Solomon and the Queen of Sheba. What if Augustine were right after all? What if the Jehovah of the old Scriptures were not merely the national patron of the children of Abraham, as the Rabbis held; not merely, as Philo held, the Divine Wisdom which inspired a few elect sages, even among the heathen; but the Lord of the whole earth, and of the nations thereof? — And suddenly, for the first time in his life, passages from the psalms and prophets flashed across him, which seemed to assert this. What else did that whole book of Daniel and the history of Nebuchadnezzar mean — if not that? Philosophic latitudinarianism had long ago cured him of the Rabbinical notion of the Babylonian conqueror as an incarnate fiend, devoted to Tophet, like Sennacherib before him. He had long in private admired the man, as a magnificent human character, a fairer one, in his eyes, than either Alexander or Julius Cæsar..... What if Augustine had given him a hint which might justify his admiration?.... But more..... What if Augustine were right in going even further than Philo and Hypatia? What if this same Jehovah, Wisdom, Logos, call him what they might, were actually the God of the spirits, as well as of the bodies of all flesh? What if he was as near — Augustine said that he was — to the hearts of those wild Markmen, Gauls, Thracians, as to Augustine's own heart? What if he were — Augustine said he was — yearning after, enlightening, leading home to himself, the souls of the poorest, the most brutal, the most sinful? — What if he loved man as man, and not merely one favoured race or one favoured class of minds?.... And in the light of that hypothesis, that strange story of the Cross of Calvary seemed not so impossible after all..... But then, celibacy and asceticism, utterly non-human as they were, what had they to do with the theory of a human God?

And filled with many questionings, Raphael was not sorry to have the matter brought to an issue that very evening, in Synesius's sitting-room. Majoricus, in his blunt, soldierlike way, set Raphael and Augustine at each other without circumlocution; and Raphael, after trying to smile and pooh-pooh away the subject, was tempted to make a jest on a seeming fallacious conceit of Augustine's — found it more difficult than he thought to trip up the serious and wary logician, lost his temper a little — a sign, perhaps, of returning health in a sceptic — and soon found himself fighting desperately, with Synesius backing him, apparently for the mere pleasure of seeing a battle, and Majoricus making him more and more cross by the implicit dogmatic faith with which he hewed at one Gordian knot after another, till Augustine had to save himself from his friends by tripping the good Prefect gently up, and leaving him miles behind the disputants, who argued on and on, till broad daylight shone in, and the sight of the desolation below recalled all parties to more material weapons, and a sterner warfare.

But little thought Raphael Aben-Ezra, as he sat there, calling up every resource of his wit and learning, in the hope, half malicious, half honestly cautious, of upsetting the sage of Hippo, and forgetting all heaven and earth in the delight of battle with his peers, that in a neighbouring chamber, her tender limbs outspread upon the floor, her face buried in her dishevelled locks, lay Victoria, wrestling all night long for him in prayer and bitter tears, as the murmur of busy voices reached her eager ears, longing in vain to catch the sense of words, on which hung now her hopes and bliss — how utterly and entirely, she had never yet confessed to herself, though she dare confess it to that Son of Man to whom she prayed, as to One who felt with tenderness and insight beyond that of a brother, a father, even of a mother, for her maiden's blushes and her maiden's woes.

CHAPTER XXII
PANDEMONIUM

BUT where was Philammon all that week?

For the first day or two of his imprisonment he had raved like some wild beast entrapped. His new-found purpose and energy, thus suddenly dammed back and checked, boiled up in frantic rage. He tore at the bars of his prison; he rolled himself, shrieking, on the floor. He called in vain on Hypatia, on Pelagia, on Arsenius — on all but God. Pray he could not, and dare not; for to whom was he to pray? To the stars? — to the Abysses and the Eternities?....

Alas! as Augustine said once, bitterly enough, of his own Manichæan teachers, Hypatia had taken away the living God, and given him instead the four Elements..... And in utter bewilderment and hopeless terror he implored the pity of every guard and gaoler who passed along the corridor, and conjured them, as brothers, fathers, men, to help him. Moved at once by his agony and by his exceeding beauty, the rough Thracians, who knew enough of their employer's character to have little difficulty in believing his victim to be innocent, listened to him and questioned him. But when they offered the very help which he implored, and asked him to tell his story, the poor boy's tongue clave to the roof of his mouth. How could he publish his sister's shame? And yet she was about to publish it herself!.... And instead of words, he met their condolences with fresh agonies, till they gave him up as mad; and, tired by his violence, compelled him, with blows and curses, to remain quiet: and so the week wore out, in dull and stupified despair, which trembled on the very edge of idiocy. Night and day were alike to him. The food which was thrust in through his grate remained untasted; hour after hour, day after day, he sat upon the ground, "is head buried in his hands, half-dozing from mere exhaustion of body and mind. Why should he care to stir, to eat, to live? He had but one purpose in heaven and earth; and that one purpose was impossible.

At last his cell-door grated on its hinges. "Up, my mad youth!" cried a rough voice. "Up, and thank the favour of the gods, and the bounty of our noble — ahem! — Prefect. To-day he gives freedom to all prisoners. And' I suppose a pretty boy like you may go about your business, as well as uglier rascals!"

Philammon looked up in the gaoler's face with a dim, half-comprehension of his meaning.

"Do you hear?" cried the man, with a curse. "You. are free. Jump up, or I shut the door again, and your one chance is over."

"Did she dance Venus Anadyomene?"

"She! Who?"

"My sister! Pelagia!"

"Heaven only knows what she has not danced in her time! But they say she dances to-day once more. Quick! out, or I shall not be ready in time for the sports. They; begin an hour hence. Free admission into the theatre to-day for all — rogues and honest men, Christians and heathens. — Curse the boy! he's as mad as ever."

So indeed Philammon seemed; for springing suddenly to his feet, he rushed out past the gaoler, upsetting him into the corridor, and fled wildly from the prison among the crowd of liberated ruffians, ran from the prison home, from home to the baths, from the baths to the theatre, and was soon pushing his way, regardless of etiquette, towards the lower tiers of benches, in order, he hardly knew why, to place himself as near as possible to the very sight which he dreaded and abhorred.

As fate would have it, the passage by which he had entered opened close to the Prefect's chair of state, where; sat Orestes, gorgeous in his robes of office, and by him — to Philammon's surprise and horror — Hypatia herself.

More beautiful than ever, her forehead sparkling, like Juno's own, with a lofty tiara of jewels, her white Ionic robe half hidden by a crimson shawl, there sat the vestal, the philosopher. What did she there? But the boy's eager eyes, accustomed but too well to note every light and shade of feeling which crossed that face, saw in a moment how wan and haggard was its expression. She wore a look of constraint, of half-terrified self-resolve, as of a martyr: and yet not an undoubting martyr; for as Orestes turned his head at the stir of Philammon's intrusion, and flashing with anger at the sight, motioned him fiercely back, Hypatia turned too, and as her eyes met her pupil's, she blushed crimson, and started, and seemed in act to motion him back also; and then, recollecting herself, whispered something to Orestes which quieted his wrath, and composed herself, or rather sunk into her place again, as one who was determined to abide the worst.

A knot of gay young gentlemen, Philammon's fellow-students, pulled him down among them, with welcome and laughter; and before he could collect his thoughts, the curtain in front of the stage had fallen, and the sport began.

The scene represented a background of desert mountains, and on the stage itself, before a group of temporary huts, stood huddling together the black Libyan prisoners, some fifty men, women and children, bedizened with gaudy feathers and girdles of tasselled leather, brandishing their spears and targets, and glaring out with white eyes on the strange scene before them, in childish awe and wonder.

Along the front of the stage a wattled battlement had been erected, while below, the hyposcenium had been painted to represent rocks, thus completing the rough imitation of a village among the Libyan hills.

Amid breathless silence, a herald advanced, and proclaimed that these were prisoners taken in arms against the Roman senate and people, and therefore worthy of immediate death: but that the Prefect, in his exceeding clemency toward them, and especial anxiety to afford the greatest possible amusement to the obedient and loyal citizens of Alexandria, had determined, instead of giving them at once to the beasts, to allow them to fight for their lives, promising to the survivors a free pardon if they acquitted themselves valiantly.

The poor wretches on the stage, when this proclamation was translated to them, set up a barbaric yell of joy, and brandished their spears and targets more fiercely than ever.

But their joy was short. The trumpets sounded the attack; a body of gladiators, equal in number to the savages, marched out from one of the two great side-passages, made their obeisance to the applauding spectators, and planting their scaling-ladders against the front of the stage, mounted to the attack.

The Libyans fought like tigers; yet from the first Hypatia, and Philammon also, could see that their promised chance of life was a mere mockery. Their light darts and naked limbs were no match for the heavy swords and complete armour of their brutal assailants, who endured carelessly a storm of blows and thrusts on heads and faces protected by visored helmets: yet so fierce was the valour of the Libyans, that even they recoiled twice, and twice the scaling-ladders were hurled down again, while more than one gladiator lay below, rolling in the death-agony.

And then burst forth the sleeping devil in the hearts of that great brutalized multitude. Yell upon yell of savage triumph, and still more savage disappointment, rang from every tier of that vast ring of seats, at each blow and parry, onslaught and repulse; and Philammon saw with horror and surprise that luxury, refinement, philosophic culture itself, were no safeguards against the infection of blood-thirstiness. Gay and delicate ladies, whom he had seen three days before simpering delight at Hypatia's heaven-ward aspirations, and some, too, whom he seemed to recollect in Christian churches, sprang from their seats, waved their hands and handkerchiefs, and clapped and shouted to the gladiators. For, alas! there was no doubt as to which side the favour of the spectators inclined. With taunts, jeers, applause, entreaties, the hired ruffians were urged on to their work of blood. The poor wretches heard no voice raised in their favour; nothing but contempt, hatred, eager lust of blood, glared from those thousands of pitiless eyes; and, brokenhearted, despairing, they flagged and drew back one by one. A shout of triumph greeted the gladiators as they climbed over the battlement, and gained a footing on the stage. The wretched blacks broke up, and fled wildly from corner to corner, looking vainly for an outlet.....

And then began a butchery..... Some fifty men, women, and children were cooped together in that narrow space..... And yet Hypatia's countenance did not falter. Why should it? What were their numbers, beside the thousands who had perished year by year for centuries, by that and far worse deaths, in the amphitheatres of that empire, for that faith which she was vowed to re-establish. It was part of the great system; and she must endure it.

Not that she did not feel; for she, too, was woman; and her heart, raised far above the brutal excitement of the multitude, lay calmly open to the most poignant stings of pity. Again and again she was in the act to entreat mercy for some shrieking woman or struggling child; but before her lips could shape the words, the blow had fallen, or the wretch was whirled away from her sight in the dense undistinguishable mass of slayers and slain. Yes, she had begun, and she must follow to the end..... And, after all, what were the lives of those few semi-brutes, returning thus a few years earlier to the clay from which they sprang, compared with the regeneration of a world?.... And it would be over in a few minutes more, and that black writhing heap be still for ever, and the curtain fall..... And then for Venus Anadyomene, and art, and joy, and peace, and the graceful wisdom and beauty of the old Greek art, calming and civilizing all hearts, and softening them into pure devotion for the immortal myths, the immortal deities, who had inspired their forefathers in the glorious days of old..... But still the black heap writhed; and she looked away, up, down, and round, everywhere, to avoid the sickening sight; and her eye caught Philammon's gazing at her with looks of horror and disgust..... A thrill of shame rushed through her heart, and blushing scarlet, she sank her head, and whispered to Orestes, —

"Have mercy! — spare the rest!"

"Nay, fairest vestal! The mob has tasted blood, and they must have their fill of it, or they will turn on us for aught I know. Nothing so dangerous as to check a brute, whether he be horse, dog, or man, when once his spirit is up. Ha! there is a fugitive! How well the little rascal runs!"

As he spoke, a boy, the only survivor, leaped from the stage, and rushed across the orchestra toward them, followed by a rough cur-dog.

"You shall have this youth, if he reaches us."

Hypatia watched breathless. The boy had just arrived at the altar in the centre of the orchestra, when he saw a gladiator close upon him. The ruffian's arm was raised to strike, when, to the astonishment of the whole theatre, boy and dog turned valiantly to bay, and leaping on the gladiator, dragged him between them to the ground. The triumph was momentary. The uplifted hands, the shout of "Spare him!" came too late. The man, as he lay, buried his sword in the slender body of the child, and then rising, walked coolly back to the side passages, while the poor cur stood over the little corpse, licking its hands and face, and making the whole building ring with his doleful cries. The attendants entered, and striking their hooks into corpse after corpse, dragged them out of sight, marking their path by long red furrows in the sand; while the dog followed, until his inauspicious howling-s died away down distant passages.

Philammon felt sick and giddy, and half rose to escape. But Pelagia!.... No — he must sit it out, and see the worst, if worse than this was possible. He looked round. The people were coolly sipping wine and eating cakes, while they chatted admirably about the beauty of the great curtain, which had fallen and hidden the stage, and represented, on a ground of deep-blue sea, Europa carried by the bull across the Bosphorus, while Nereids and Tritons played around.

A single flute within the curtain began to send forth luscious strains, deadened and distant, as if through far-off glens and woodlands; and from the side passages issued three Graces, led by Peitho, the goddess of persuasion, bearing a herald's staff in her hand. She advanced to the altar in the centre of the orchestra, and informed the spectators that, during the absence of Ares in aid of a certain great military expedition, which was shortly to decide the diadem of Rome, and the liberty, prosperity, and supremacy of Egypt and Alexandria, Aphrodite had returned to her lawful allegiance, and submitted for the time being to the commands of her husband, Hephæstus; that he, as the deity of artificers, felt a peculiar interest in the welfare of the city of Alexandria, the workshop of the world, and had, as a sign of his especial favour, prevailed upon his fair spouse to exhibit, for this once, her beauties to the assembled populace, and, in the unspoken poetry of motion, to represent to them the emotions with which, as she arose new-born from the sea, she first surveyed that fair expanse of heaven and earth of which she now reigned undisputed queen.

A shout of rapturous applause greeted this announcement, and forthwith limped from the opposite slip the lame deity himself, hammer and pincers on shoulder, followed by a train of gigantic Cyclops, who bore on their shoulders various pieces of gilded metal work.

Hephæstus, who was intended to supply the comic element in the vast pantomimic pageant, shambled forward with studied uncouthness, amid roars of laughter; surveyed the altar with ludicrous contempt; raised his mighty hammer, shivered it to pieces with a single blow, and beckoned to his attendants to carry off the fragments, and replace it with something more fitting for his august spouse.

With wonderful quickness the metal open-work was put in its place, and fitted together, forming a frame of coral branches intermingled with dolphins, Nereids, and Tritons. Four gigantic Cyclops then approached, staggering under the weight of a circular slab of green marble, polished to a perfect mirror, which they placed on the framework. The Graces wreathed its circumference with garlands of sea-weed, shells, and corallines, and the mimic sea was complete.

Peitho and the Graces retired a few steps, and grouped themselves with the Cyclops, whose grimed and brawny limbs, and hideous one-eyed masks, threw out in striking contrast the delicate hue and grace of the beautiful maiden figures; while Hephæstus turned toward the curtain, and seemed to await impatiently the forthcoming of the goddess.

Every lip was breathless with expectation as the flutes swelled louder and nearer; horns and cymbals took up the harmony; and, to a triumphant burst of music, the curtain rose, and a simultaneous shout of delight burst from ten thousand voices.

The scene behind represented a magnificent temple, half hidden in an artificial wood of tropic trees and shrubs, which filled the stage. Fauns and Dryads peeped laughing from among their stems, and gorgeous birds, tethered by unseen threads, fluttered and sang among their branches. In the centre, an overarching avenue of palms led from the temple doors to the front of the stage, from which the mimic battlements had disappeared, and had been replaced, in those few moments, by a broad slope of smooth greensward, leading down into the orchestra, and fringed with myrtles, roses, apple-trees, poppies, and crimson hyacinths, stained with the life-blood of Adonis.

The folding doors of the temple opened slowly; the crash of instruments resounded from within; and preceded by the musicians came forth the triumph of Aphrodite, and passed down the slope, and round the outer ring of the orchestra.

A splendid car, drawn by white oxen, bore the rarest and gaudiest of foreign flowers and fruits, which young girls, dressed as Hours and Seasons, strewed in front of the procession and among the spectators.

A long line of beautiful youths and maidens, crowned with garlands, and robed in scarfs of purple gauze, followed by two and two. Each pair carried or led a pair of wild animals, captives of the conquering might of Beauty.

Foremost were borne, on the wrists of the actors, the birds especially sacred to the goddess — doves and sparrows, wry-necks and swallows; and a pair of gigantic Indian tortoises, each ridden by a lovely nymph, showed that Orestes had not forgotten one wish, at least, of his intended bride.

Then followed strange birds from India, parakeets, pea-cocks, pheasants, silver and golden; bustards and ostriches: the latter, bestridden each by a tiny cupid, were led on in golden leashes, followed by antelopes and oryxes, elks from beyond the Danube, four-horned rams from the Isles of the Hyperborean Ocean, and the strange hybrid of the Libyan hills, believed by all spectators to be half-bull, half-horse. And then a murmur of de-lighted awe ran through the theatre, as bears and leopards, lions and tigers, fettered in heavy chains of gold, and made gentle for the occasion by narcotics, paced sedately down the slope, obedi-ent to their beautiful guides; while behind them, the unwieldly bulk of two double-horned rhinoceroses, from the far south, was overtopped by the long slender necks and large soft eyes of a pair of giraffes, such as had not been seen in Alexandria for more than fifty years.

A cry arose of "Orestes! Orestes! Health to the illustrious Prefect! Thanks for his bounty!" And a hired voice or two among the crowd cried, "Hail to Orestes! Hail, Emperor of Af-rica!".... But there was no response.

"The rose is still in the bud," simpered Orestes to Hypatia. He rose, beckoned and bowed the crowd into silence; and then, after a short pantomimic exhibition of rapturous gratitude and humility, pointed triumphantly to the palm avenue, among the shadows of which appeared the wonder of the day — the huge tusks and trunk of the white elephant himself.

There it was at last! Not a doubt of it! A real elephant, and yet as white as snow. Sight never seen before in Alexandria — never to be seen again! "Oh, thrice-blest men of Macedonia!" shouted some worthy on high, "the gods are bountiful to you this day!" And all mouths and eyes confirmed the opinion, as they opened wider and yet wider to drink in the inexhaustible joy and glory.

On he paced solemnly, while the whole theatre resounded to his heavy tread, and the Fauns and Dryads fled in terror. A choir of nymphs swung round him hand in hand, and sang, as they danced along, the conquering might of Beauty, the tamer of beasts and men and deities. Skirmishing parties of little winged cupids spread themselves over the orchestra, from left to right, and pelted the spectators with perfumed comfits, shot among them from their tiny bows arrows of fragrant sandal-wood, or swung smoking censers, which loaded the air with intoxicating odours.

The procession came on down the slope, and the elephant approached the spectators; his tusks were wreathed with roses and myrtles; his ears were pierced with splendid ear-rings, a jewelled frontlet hung between his eyes; Eros himself, a lovely winged boy, sat on his neck, and guided him' with the point of a golden arrow. But what precious thing was it which that shell-formed car upon his back contained? The goddess? Pelagia Aphrodite herself?

Yes; whiter than the snow-white elephant — more rosy than the pink-tipped shell in which she lay, among crimson cushions and silver gauze, there shone the goddess, thrilling all hearts with those delicious smiles, and glances of the bashful playful eyes, and grateful wavings of her tiny hand, as the whole theatre rose with one accord, and ten thousand eyes were concentrated on the unequalled loveliness beneath them.

Twice the procession passed round the whole circumference of the orchestra, and then returning from the foot of the slope toward the central group around Hephæstus, deployed right and left in front of the stage. The lions and tigers were led away into the side passages; the youths and maidens combined themselves with the gentler animals into groups lessening gradually from the centre to the wings, and stood expectant, while the elephant came forward, and knelt behind the platform destined for the goddess.

The valves of the shell closed. The Graces unloosed the fastenings of the car. The elephant turned his trunk over his back, and guided by the hands of the girls, grasped the shell, and lifting it high in air, deposited it on the steps at the back of the platform.

Hephæstus limped forward, and with his most uncouth gestures, signified the delight which he had in bestowing such a sight upon his faithful artisans of Alexandria, and the unspeakable enjoyment which they were to expect from the mystic dance of the goddess; and then retired, leaving the Graces to advance in front of the platform, and with their arms twined round each other, begin Hypatia's song of invocation.

As the first strophe died away, the valves of the shell reopened, and discovered Aphrodite crouching on one knee within. She raised her head, and gazed around the vast circle of seats. A mild surprise was on her countenance, which quickened into delighted wonder, and bashfulness struggling with the sense of new enjoyment and new powers. She glanced downward at herself; and smiled, astonished at her own loveliness; then upward at the sky; and seemed ready, with an awful joy, to spring up into the boundless void. Her whole figure dilated; she seemed to drink in strength from every object which met her in the great universe around; and slowly, from among the shells and sea-weeds, she rose to her full height, the mystic cestus glittering round her waist, in deep festoons of emeralds and pearls, and stepped forward upon the marble sea-floor, wringing the dripping perfume from her locks, as Aphrodite rose of old.

For the first minute the crowd was too breathless with pleasure to think of applause. But the goddess seemed to require due homage; and when she folded her arms across her bosom, and stood motionless for an instant, as if to demand the worship of the universe, every tongue was loosed, and a thunderclap of "Aphrodite!" rung out across the roofs of Alexandria, and startled Cyril in his chamber at the Serapeium, and weary muleteers on distant sand-hills, and dozing mariners far out at sea.

And then began a miracle of art, such as was only possible among a people of the free and exquisite physical training, and the delicate aesthetic perception of those old Greeks, even in their most fallen days. A dance, in which every motion was a word, and rest as eloquent as motion; in which every attitude was a fresh motive for a sculptor of the purest school, and the highest physical activity was manifested, not as in the coarser comic pantomimes, in fantastic bounds and unnatural distortions, but in perpetual delicate modulations of a stately and self-restraining grace. The artist was for the moment transformed into the goddess. The theatre, and Alexandria, and the gorgeous pageant beyond, had vanished from her imagination, and therefore from the imagination of the spectators, under the constraining inspiration of her art, and they and she alike saw nothing but the lonely sea around Cythera, and the goddess hovering above its emerald mirror, raying forth on sea, and air, and shore, beauty, and joy, and love.....

Philammon's eyes were bursting from his head with shame and horror: and yet he could not hate her; not even despise her. He would have done so, had there been the faintest trace of human feeling in her countenance, to prove that some germ of moral sense lingered within: but even the faint blush and the downcast eye with which she had entered the theatre, were gone; and the only expression on her face was that of intense enjoyment of her own activity and skill, and satisfied vanity, as of a petted child..... Was she accountable? A reasonable soul, capable of right or wrong at all? He hoped not..... He would trust not..... And still Pelagia danced on; and for a whole age of agony, he could see nothing in heaven or earth but the bewildering maze of those white feet, as they twinkled over their white image in the marble mirror..... At last it was over. Every limb suddenly collapsed, and she stood drooping in soft self-satisfied fatigue, awaiting the burst of applause which rang through Philammon's ears, proclaiming to heaven and earth, as with a mighty trumpet-blast, his sister's shame.

The elephant rose, and moved forward to the side of the slabs. His back was covered with crimson cushions, on which it seemed Aphrodite was to return without her shell. She folded her arms across her bosom, and stood smiling, as the elephant gently wreathed his trunk around her waist, and lifted her slowly from the slab, in act to place her on his back.....

The little feet, clinging half fearfully together had just risen from the marble — The elephant started, dropped his delicate burden heavily on the slab, looked down, raised his forefoot, and throwing his trunk into the air, gave a shrill scream of terror and disgust.....

The foot was red with blood — the young boy's blood — which was soaking and bubbling up through the fresh sand where the elephant had trodden, in a round, dark, purple spot.....

Philammon could bear no more. Another moment and he had hurled down through the dense mass of spectators, clearing rank after rank of seats by the sheer strength of madness, leaped the balustrade into the orchestra below, and rushed across the space to the foot of the platform.

"Pelagia! Sister! My sister! Have mercy on me! on yourself! I will hide you! save you! and we will flee together out of this infernal place! this world of devils! I am your brother! Come!"

She looked at him one moment with wide, wild eyes —— The truth flashed on her ——

"Brother!"

And she sprang from the platform into his arms..... A vision of a lofty window in Athens, looking out over far olive-yards and gardens, and the bright roofs and basins of the Piraeus, and the broad blue sea, with the purple peaks of Ӕgina beyond all..... And a dark-eyed boy, with his arm around her neck, pointed laughing to the twinkling masts in the far harbour, and called her sister..... The dead soul woke within her; and with a wild cry she recoiled from him in an agony of shame, and covering her face with both her hands, sank down among the blood-stained sand.

A yell, as of all hell broke loose, rang along that vast circle—

"Down with him!" "Away with him!" "Crucify the slave!" "Give the barbarian to the beasts!" "To the beasts with him, noble Prefect!" A crowd of attendants rushed upon him, and many of the spectators sprang from their seats, and were on the point of leaping down into the orchestra.

Philammon turned upon them like a lion at bay; and clear and loud his voice rose through the roar of the multitude.

"Ay! murder me as the Romans murdered Saint Telemachus! Slaves as besotted and accursed as your besotted and accursed tyrants! Lower than the beasts whom you employ as your butchers! Murder and lust go fitly hand in hand, and the throne of my sister's shame is well built on the blood of innocents! Let my death end the devil's sacrifice, and fill up the cup of your iniquity!"

"To the beasts!" "Make the elephant trample him to powder!"

And the huge brute, goaded on by the attendants, rushed on the youth, while Eros leaped from his neck, and fled weeping up the slope.

He caught Philammon in his trunk and raised him high in

air. For an instant the great bellowing ocean of heads spun round and round. He tried to breathe one prayer, and shut his eyes —— Pelagia's voice rang sweet and clear, even in the shrillness of intense agony —

"Spare him! He is my brother! Forgive him, men of Macedonia! For Pelagia's sake — Your Pelagia! One boon — only this one!"

And she stretched her arms imploringly toward the spectators; and then clasping the huge knees of the elephant, called madly to it in terms of passionate entreaty and endearment.

The men wavered. The brute did not. Quietly he lowered his trunk, and set down Philammon on his feet. The monk was saved. Breathless and dizzy, he found himself hurried away by the attendants, dragged through dark passages, and hurled out into the street, with curses, warnings, and congratulations, which fell on an unheeding ear.

But Pelagia kept her face still hidden in her hands, and rising, walked slowly back, crushed by the weight of some tremendous awe, across the orchestra, and up the slope; and vanished among the palms and oleanders, regardless of the applause and entreaties, and jeers, and threats, and curses, of that great multitude of sinful slaves.

For a moment all Orestes' spells seemed broken by this unexpected catastrophe. A cloud, whether of disgust or of disappointment, hung upon every brow. More than one Christian rose hastily to depart, touched with real remorse and shame at the horrors of which they had been the willing witnesses. The common people behind, having glutted their curiosity with all that there was to see, began openly to murmur at the cruelty and heathenry of it. Hypatia, utterly unnerved, hid her face in both her hands. Orestes alone rose with the crisis. Now, or never, was the time for action; and stepping forward, with his most graceful obeisance, waved his hand for silence, and began: his well-studied oration.

"Let me not, O men of Macedonia, suppose that you can be disturbed from that equanimity which befits politicians, by so light an accident as the caprice of a dancer. The spectacle which I have had the honour and delight of exhibiting to you — (Roars and applause from the liberated prisoners and the young gentlemen) — and on which it seemed to me you have deigned to look with not altogether unkindly eyes — (Fresh applause, in which the Christian mob, relenting, began to join) — is but a pleasant prelude to that more serious business for which I have drawn you here together. Other testimonials of my good intentions have not been wanting in the release of suffering innocence, and in the largess of food, the growth and natural property of Egypt, destined by your late tyrants to pamper the luxury of a distant court..... Why should I boast? — yet even now this head is weary, these limbs fail me, worn out in ceaseless efforts for your welfare, and in the perpetual administration of the strictest justice. For a time has come in which the Macedonian race, whose boast is the gorgeous city of Alexander, must rise again to the political pre-eminence which they held of old, and becoming once more the masters of one-third of the universe, be treated by their rulers as freemen, citizens, heroes, who have a right to choose and to employ their rulers — Rulers, did I say? Let us forget the word, and substitute in its place the more philosophic term of ministers. To be your minister — the servant of you all — To sacrifice myself, my leisure, health, life, if need be, to the one great object of securing the independence of Alexandria — This is my work, my hope, my glory — longed for through weary years; now for the first time possible by the fall of the late puppet Emperor of Rome. Men of Macedonia, remember that Honorius reigns no more! An African sits on the throne of the Cæsars! Heraclian, by one decisive victory, has gained, by the favour of — of Heaven, the imperial purple; and a new era opens for the world. Let the conqueror of Rome balance his account with that Byzantine court, so long the incubus of our Trans-Mediterranean wealth and civilization; and let a free, independent, and united Africa rally round the palaces and docks of Alexandria, and find there its natural centre of polity and of prosperity."

A roar of hired applause interrupted him: and not a few, half for the sake of his compliments and fine words, half from a natural wish to be on the right side — namely, the one which happened to be in the ascendant for the time being — joined..... The city authorities were on the point of crying, "Imperator Orestes ": but thought better of it; and waited for some one else to cry first — being respectable. Whereon the Prefect of the Guards, being a man of some presence of mind, and also not in anywise respectable, pricked up the Prefect of the Docks with the point of his dagger, and bade him, with a fearful threat, take care how he played traitor. The worthy burgher roared incontinently — whether with pain or patriotism; and the whole array of respectabilities — having found a Curtius who would leap into the gulf, joined in unanimous chorus, and saluted Orestes as Emperor; while Hypatia, amid the shouts of her aristocratic scholars, rose and knelt before him, writhing inwardly with shame and despair, and entreated him to accept that tutelage of Greek commerce, supremacy, and philosophy which was forced on him by the unanimous voice of an adoring people.....

"It is false!" shouted a voice from the highest tiers, appropriated to the women of the lower classes, which made all turn their heads in bewilderment.

"False! false! You are tricked! He is tricked! Heraclian was utterly routed at Ostia, and is fled to Carthage, with the emperor's fleet in chase."

"She lies! Drag the beast down!" cried Orestes, utterly thrown off his balance by the sudden check.

"She? He! I, a monk, brought the news! Cyril has known it — every Jew in the Delta has known it, for a week past! So perish all the enemies of the Lord, caught 'o their own snare!"

And bursting desperately through the women who surrounded him, the monk vanished.

An awful silence fell on all who heard. For a minute every man looked in his neighbour's face as if he longed to cut his throat, and get rid of one witness, at least, of his treason. And then arose a tumult, which Orestes in vain attempted to subdue. Whether the populace believed the monk's words or not, they were panic-stricken at the mere possibility of their truth. Hoarse with denying, protesting, appealing, the would-be emperor had at last to summon his guards around him and Hypatia, and make his way out of the theatre as best he could; while the multitude melted away like snow before the rain, and poured out into the streets in eddying and roaring streams, to find every church placarded by Cyril with the particulars of Heraclian's ruin.

CHAPTER XXIII
NEMESIS

THAT evening was a hideous one in the palace of Orestes. His agonies of disappointment, rage, and terror were at once so shameful and so fearful, that none of his slaves dare approach him; and it was not till late that his confidential secretary, the Chaldean eunuch, driven by terror of the exasperated Catholics, ventured into the tiger's den, and represented to him the immediate necessity for action.

What could he do? He was committed — Cyril only knew how deeply. What might not the wily archbishop have discovered? What might he not pretend to have, discovered? What accusations might he not send off on the spot to the Byzantine Court?

"Let the gates be guarded, and no one allowed to leave the city," suggested the Chaldee.

"Keep in monks? as well keep in rats! No; we must send off a counter-report, instantly."

"What shall I say, your Excellency?" quoth the ready scribe, pulling out pen and inkhorn from his sash.

"What do I care? Any lie which comes to hand. What in the devil's name are you here for at all, but to invent a lie when I want one?"

"True, most noble," and the worthy sat meekly down to his paper.... but did not proceed rapidly.

"I don't see anything that would suit the emergency, unless I stated, with your august leave, that Cyril, and not you, celebrated the gladiatorial exhibition; which might hardly appear credible?"

Orestes burst out laughing, in spite of himself. The sleek Chaldee smiled and purred in return. The victory was won; and Orestes, somewhat more master of himself, began to turn his vulpine cunning to the one absorbing question of the saving of his worthless neck.

"No, that would be too good. Write, that we had discovered a plot on Cyril's part to incorporate the whole of the African churches (mind and specify Carthage and Hippo) under his own jurisdiction, and to throw off allegiance to the Patriarch of Constantinople, in case of Heraclian's success."

The secretary purred delighted approval, and scribbled away now with right good heart.

"Heraclian's success, your Excellency."

"We of course desired, by every means in our power, to gratify the people of Alexandria, and as was our duty, to excite by every lawful method their loyalty toward the throne of the Cæsars (never mind who sat on it) at so critical a moment."

"So critical a moment."....

"But as faithful Catholics, and abhorring, even in the extremest need, the sin of Uzzah, we dreaded to touch with the unsanctified hands of laymen the consecrated ark of the Church, even though for its preservation."....

"Its preservation, your Excellency...."

"We, therefore, as civil magistrates, felt bound to confine ourselves to those means which were already allowed by law and custom to our jurisdiction; and accordingly made use of those largesses, spectacles, and public execution of rebels, which have unhappily appeared to his holiness the patriarch (too ready, perhaps, to find a cause of complaint against faithful adherents of the Byzantine See) to partake of the nature of those gladiatorial exhibitions, which are equally abhorrent to the spirit of the Catholic Church, and to the charity of the sainted emperors by whose pious edicts they have been long-since abolished."

"Your Excellency is indeed great.... but — pardon your slave's remark — my simplicity is of opinion that it may be asked why you did not inform the Augusta Pulcheria of Cyril's conspiracy?"

"Say that we sent a messenger off three months ago, but that.... Make something happen to him, stupid, and save me the trouble."

"Shall I kill him by Arabs in the neighbourhood of Palmyra, your Excellency?"

"Let me see..... No. They may make inquiries there. Drown him at sea. Nobody can ask questions of the sharks."

"Foundered between Tyre and Crete, from which sad calamity only one man escaped on a raft, and being picked up, after three weeks' exposure to the fury of the elements, by a returning wheat-ship — — — By the bye, most noble, what am I to say about those wheat-ships not having even sailed?"

"Head of Augustus! I forgot them utterly. Say that — say that the plague was making such ravages in the harbour quarter that we feared carrying the infection to the seat of the empire; and let them sail to-morrow."

The secretary's face lengthened.

"My fidelity is compelled to remark, even at the risk of your just indignation, that half of them have been unloaded again for your munificent largesses of the last two days."

Orestes swore a great oath.

"Oh, that the mob had but one throat, that I might give them an emetic! Well, we must buy more corn, that's all."

The secretary's face grew longer still.

"The Jews, most august —— "

"What of them?" yelled the hapless Prefect. "Have they been forestalling?"

"My assiduity has discovered this afternoon that they have been buying up and exporting all the provisions which they could obtain."

"Scoundrels! Then they must have known of Heraclian's failure!"

"Your sagacity has, I fear, divined the truth. They have been betting largely against his success for the last' week, both in Canopus and Pelusium."

"For the last week! Then Miriam betrayed me knowingly!" And Orestes broke forth again into a paroxysm of fury.

"Here — call the tribune of the guard! A hundred gold pieces to the man who brings me the witch alive!"

"She will never be taken alive."

"Dead, then — in any way! Go, you Chaldee hound! what are you hesitating about?"

"Most noble lord," said the secretary, prostrating himself upon the floor, and kissing his master's feet in an agony of fear.... "Remember, that if you touch one Jew you touch all! Remember the bonds! remember the — the — your own most august reputation, in short."

"Get up, brute, and don't grovel there, but tell me what

you mean, like a human being. If old Miriam is once dead, her bonds die with her, don't they?"

"Alas, my lord, you do not know the customs of that accursed folk. They have a damnable practice of treating every member of their nation as a brother, and helping each freely and faithfully without reward; whereby they are enabled to plunder all the rest of the world, and thrive themselves, from the least to the greatest. Don't fancy that your bonds are in Miriam's hands. They have been transferred months ago. Your real creditors may be in Carthage, or Rome, or Byzantium, and they will attack you from thence; while all that you would find if you seized the old witch's property, would be papers, useless to you, belonging to Jews all over the empire, who would rise as one man in defence of their money. I assure you, it is a net without a bound. If you touch one you touch all..... And besides, my diligence, expecting some such command, has already taken the liberty of making inquiries as to Miriam's place of abode; but it appears, I am sorry to say, utterly unknown to any of your Excellency's servants."

"You lie!" said Orestes..... "I would much sooner believe that you have been warning the hag to keep out of the way."

Orestes had spoken, for that once in his life, the exact truth.

The secretary, who had his own private dealings with Miriam, felt every particular atom of his skin shudder at those words; and had he had hair on his head, it would certainly have betrayed him by standing' visibly on end. But as he was, luckily for him, close shaven, his turban remained in its proper place, as he meekly replied, —

"Alas! a faithful servant can feel no keener woe than the causeless suspicion of that sun before whose rays he daily prostrates his —— "

"Confound your periphrases! Do you know where she is?"

"No!" cried the wretched secretary, driven to the lie direct at last; and confirmed the negation with such a string of oaths, that Orestes stopped his volubility with a kick, borrowed of him, under threat of torture, a thousand gold pieces as largess to the soldiery, and ended by concentrating the stationaries round his own palace, for the double purpose of protecting himself in case of a riot, and of increasing the chances of the said riot, by leaving the distant quarters of the city without police.

"If Cyril would but make a fool of himself, now that he is in the full-blown pride of victory — the rascal! — about that Ammonius, or about Hypatia, or anything else, and give me a real handle against him! After all, truth works better than lying now and then. Oh, that I could poison him! But one can't bribe those ecclesiastics; and as for the dagger, one could not hire a man to be torn in pieces by monks. No; I must just sit still, and see what Fortune's dice may turn up. Well; your pedants like Aristides or Epaminondas — thank Heaven, the race of them has died out long ago! — might call this no very creditable piece of provincial legislation; but, after all, it is about as good as any now going, or likely to be going till the world's end; and one can't be expected to strike out a new path. I shall stick to the wisdom of my predecessors, and — oh, that Cyril may make a fool of himself to-night!"

And Cyril did make a fool of himself that night, for the first and last time in his life; and suffers for it, as wise men are wont to do when they err, to this very day and hour: but how much Orestes gained by his foe's false move cannot be decided till the end of this story; perhaps not even then.

CHAPTER XXIV
LOST LAMBS

AND Philammon?!

For a long while he stood in the street outside the theatre, too much maddened to determine on any course of action; and, ere he had recovered his self-possession, the crowd began to pour from every outlet, and filling the street, swept him away in its stream.

Then, as he heard his sister's name, in every tone of pity, contempt, and horror, mingle with their angry exclamations, he awoke from his dream, and, bursting through the mob, made straight for Pelagia's house.

It was fast closed; and his repeated knocks at the gate brought only, after long waiting, a surly negro face to a little wicket.

He asked eagerly and instinctively for Pelagia: of course she had not yet returned. For Wulf: he was not within. And then he took his station close to the gateway, while his heart beat loud with hope and dread.

At last the Goths appeared, forcing their way through the mob in a close column. There were no litters with them. Where, then, were Pelagia and her girls? Where, too, was the hated figure of the Amal? and Wulf, and Smid? The men came on, led by Goderic and Agilmund, with folded arms, knitted brows, downcast eyes; a stern disgust, not unmingled with shame, on every countenance, told Philammon afresh of his sister's infamy.

Goderic passed him close, and Philammon summoned up courage to ask for Wulf.... Pelagia he had not courage to name.

"Out, Greek hound! we have seen enough of your accursed race to-day! What? are you trying to follow us in?" And the young man's sword flashed from its sheath so swiftly, that Philammon had but just time enough to spring back into the street, and wait there, in an agony of disappointment and anxiety, as the gates slid together again, and the house was as silent as before.

For a miserable hour he waited, while the mob thickened instead of flowing away, and the scattered groups of chatterers began to form. themselves into masses, and parade the streets with shouts of "Down with the heathen!" "Down with the idolaters!" "Vengeance on all blaspheming harlots!"

At last the steady tramp of legionaries, and in the midst of the glittering lines of armed men — oh, joy! — a string of litters!

He sprang forward, and called Pelagia's name again and again. Once he fancied he heard an answer: but the soldiers thrust him back.

"She is safe here, young fool, and has seen and been seen quite enough to-day already. Back!"

"Let me speak to her!"

"That is her business. Ours is now to see her home safe."

"Let me go in with you, I beseech!"

"If you want to go in, knock for yourself when we are gone. If you have any business in the house, they will open to you, I suppose. Out, you interfering puppy!"

And a blow of the spear-butt in his chest sent him rolling back into the middle of the street, while the soldiers, having delivered up their charge, returned with the same stolid indifference. In vain Philammon, returning, knocked at the gate. Curses and threats from the negro were all the answer which he received; and at last, wearied into desperation, he wandered away, up one street and down another, struggling in vain to form some plan of action for himself, until the sun was set.

Wearily he went homewards at last. Once the thought of Miriam crossed his mind. It was a disgusting alternative to ask help of her, the very author of his sister's shame: but yet she at least could obtain for him a sight of Pelagia; she had promised as much. But then — the condition which she had appended to her help! To see his sister, and yet to leave her as she was! — Horrible contradiction! But could he not employ Miriam for his own ends? — outwit her? — deceive her? — for it came to that. The temptation was intense: but it lasted only a moment. Could he defile so pure a cause by falsehood? And hurrying past the Jewess's door, hardly daring to look at it, lest the temptation should return, he darted upstairs to his own little chamber, hastily flung open the door, and stopped short in astonishment.

A woman covered from head to foot in a large dark veil, stood in the centre of the chamber.

"Who are you? This is no place for you!" cried he, after a

minute's pause. She replied only by a shudder and a sob..... He caught sight, beneath the folds of the veil, of a too-well-known saffron shawl, and springing upon her like the lion on the lamb, clasped to his bosom his sister.

The veil fell from her beautiful forehead. She gazed into his eyes one moment with a look of terrified inquiry, and saw nothing there but love..... And clinging heart to heart, brother and sister mingled holy kisses, and strained nearer and nearer still, as if to satisfy their last lingering doubts of each other's kin.

Many a minute passed in silent joy..... Philammon dare not speak; he dare not ask her what brought her thither — dare not wake her to recollect the frightful present by questions of the past, of his long-forgotten parents, their home, her history..... And, after all, was it not enough for him that he held her at last? — her, there by her own will — the lost lamb returned to him? — and their tears mingled as their cheeks were pressed together.

At last she spoke.

"I ought to have known you, — I believe I did know you from the first day! When they mentioned your likeness to me, my heart leapt up within me; and a voice whispered.... but I would not hear it! I was ashamed — ashamed to acknowledge my brother, for whom I had sought and longed for years.... ashamed to think that I had a brother..... Ah, God! and ought I not to be ashamed?"

And she broke from him again, and threw herself on the floor.

"Trample upon me; curse me! — anything but part me from him!"

Philammon had not the heart to answer her; but he made an involuntary gesture of sorrowful dissent.

"No! Call me what I am! — what he called me just now! — but do not take me away! Strike me, as he struck me! — anything but parting!"

"Struck you? The curse of God be on him!"

"Ah, do not curse him! — not him! It was not a blow, indeed! — only a push — a touch — and it was my fault — all mine. I angered him — I upbraided him; — I was mad..... Oh, why did he deceive me? Why did he let me dance? — command me to dance?"

"Command you?"

"He said, that we must not break our words. He would not hear me, when I told him that we could deny having-promised. I said that promises made over the wine need never be kept..... Who ever heard of keeping them? And Orestes was drunk, too. But he said that I might teach a Goth to be what I liked, except a liar..... Was not that a strange speech?.... And Wulf bade him be strong, and blest him for it."

"He was right," sobbed Philammon.

"Then I thought he would love me for obeying him, though I loathed it! — Oh, God, how I loathed it!.... But how could I fancy that he did not like my doing it? Who ever heard of any one doing of their own will what they did not like?"

Philammon sobbed again, as the poor civilized savage artlessly opened to him all her moral darkness. What could he say?.... He knew what to say. The disease was so utterly patent, that any of Cyril's school-children could have supplied the remedy. But how to speak it? — how to tell her, before all things, as he longed to do, that there was no hope of her marrying the Amal, and, therefore, no peace for her till she left him?

"Then you did hate the — the ———" said he, at last, catching at some gleam of light.

"Hate it? Do I not belong, body and soul, to him? — him only?.... And yet.... Oh, I must tell you all! When I and the girls began to practise, all the old feelings came back — the love of being admired, and applauded, and cheered; and dancing is so delicious! — so delicious to feel that you are doing anything beautiful perfectly, and better than every one else!.... And he saw that I liked it, and despised me for it..... And, deceitful! — he little guessed how much of the pains which I took were taken to please him, to do my best before him, to win admiration, only that I might take it home and throw it all at his beloved feet, and make the world say once more, 'She has all Alexandria to worship her, and yet she cares for that one Goth more than for ——— ' But he deceived me, true man that he is! He wished to enjoy my smiles to the last moment, and then to cast me off, when I had once given him an excuse..... Too cowardly to upbraid me, he let me ruin myself, to save him the trouble of ruining me. Oh, men, men! all alike! They love us for their own sakes, and we love them for love's sake. We live by love, we die for love, and yet we never find it, but only selfishness dressed up in love's mask..... And then we take up with that, poor, fond, self-blinded creatures that we are! — and in spite of the poisoned hearts around us, persuade ourselves that our latest asp's egg, at least, will hatch into a dove, and that though all men are faithless, our own tyrant can never change, for he is more than man!"

"But he has deceived you! You have found out your mistake. Leave him, then, as he deserves!"

Pelagia looked up, with something of a tender smile. "Poor darling! Little do you know of love!"

Philammon, utterly bewildered by this newest and strangest phase of human passion, could only gasp out —

"But do you not love me, too, my sister?"

"Do I not love you? But not as I love him! Oh, hush, hush! — you cannot understand yet!" And Pelagia hid her face in her hands, while convulsive shudderings ran through every limb.....

"I must do it! I must! I will dare everything, stoop to everything, for love's sake! Go to her! — to the wise woman! — to Hypatia! She loves you! I know that she loves you! She will hear you, though she will not me!"

"Hypatia? Do you know that she was sitting there unmoved at — in the theatre?"

"She was forced! Orestes compelled her! Miriam told me so. And I saw it in her face. As I passed beneath her, I looked up; and she was as pale as ivory, trembling in every limb. There was a dark hollow round her eyes — she had been weeping, I saw. And I sneered in my mad self-conceit, and said, 'She looks as if she was going to be crucified, not married!'.... But now, now! — Oh, go to her! Tell her that I will give her all I have — jewels, money, dresses, house I Tell her that I — I — entreat her pardon, that I will crawl to her feet myself and ask it, if she requires! — Only let her teach me — teach me to be wise and good, and honoured, and respected, as she is! Ask her to tell a poor broken-hearted woman her secret. She can make old Wulf, and him, and Orestes even, and the magistrates, respect her..... Ask her to teach me how to be like her, and to make him respect me again, and I will give her all — all!"

Philammon hesitated. Something within warned him, as the Дæmon used to warn Socrates, that his errand would be bootless. He thought of the theatre, and of that firm, compressed lip: and forgot the hollow eye of misery which accompanied it, in his wrath against his lately-worshipped idol.

"Oh, go! go! I tell you, it was against her will. She felt for me — I saw it — Oh, God! — when I did not feel for myself! And I hated her, because she seemed to despise me in my fool's triumph! She cannot despise me now in my misery..... Go! Go! or you will drive me to the agony of going myself."

There was but one thing to be done.

"You will wait then, here? You will not leave me again?"

"Yes. But you must be quick! If he finds out that I am away, he may fancy.... Ah, heaven! let him kill me, but never let him be jealous of me! Go now! this moment! Take this as an earnest — the cestus which I wore there. Horrid thing! I hate the sight of it! But I brought it with me on purpose, or I would have thrown it into the canal. There; say it is an earnest — only an earnest — of what I will give her!"

In ten minutes more Philammon was in Hypatia's hall. The household seemed full of terror and disturbance; the hall was full of soldiers. At last Hypatia's favourite maid passed, and knew him. Her mistress could not speak with any one. Where was Theon, then? He, too, had shut himself up. Never mind. Philammon must, would speak with him. And he pleaded so passionately and so sweetly, that the soft-hearted damsel, unable to resist so handsome a suppliant, undertook his errand, and led him up to the library, where Theon, pale as death, was pacing to and fro, apparently half beside himself with terror.

Philammon's breathless message fell at first upon unheeding ears.

"A new pupil, sir I Is this a time for pupils; when my house, my daughter's life, is not safe? Wretch that, I am! And have I led her into the snare! I, with my vain ambition and covetousness! Oh, my child! my child! my one treasure! Oh, the double curse which will light upon me, if ——— "

"She asks for but one interview."

"With my daughter, sir? Pelagia! Will you insult me? Do you suppose, even if her own pity should so far tempt her to degrade herself, that I could allow her so to contaminate her purity."

"Your terror, sir, excuses your rudeness."

"Rudeness, sir? the rudeness lies in your intruding on us at such a moment!"

"Then this, perhaps, may, in your eyes at least, excuse me in my turn." And Philammon held out the cestus. "You are a better judge of its value than I. But I am commissioned to say, that it is only an earnest of what she will give willingly and at once, even to the half of her wealth, for the honour of becoming your daughter's pupil." And he laid the jewelled girdle on the table.

The old man halted in his walk. The emeralds and pearls shone like the galaxy. He looked at them; and walked on again more slowly..... What might be their value? What might it not be? At least, they would pay all his debts..... And after hovering to and fro for another minute before the bait, he turned to Philammon. "If you would promise to mention the thing to no one — — "

"I will promise."

"And in case my daughter, as I have a right to expect, shall refuse ——— "

"Let her keep the jewels. Their owner has learnt, thank God, to despise and hate them! Let her keep the jewels — and my curse! For God do so to me, and more also, if I ever see her face again!"

The old man had not heard the latter part of Philammon's speech. He had seized his bait as greedily as a crocodile, and hurried off with it into Hypatia's chamber, while Philammon stood expectant; possessed with a new and fearful doubt. "Degrade herself!" "Contaminate her purity!" If that notion were to be the fruit of all her philosophy? If selfishness, pride, Pharisaism, were all its outcome? Why — had they not been its outcome already? When had he seen her helping, even pitying, the poor, the outcast? When had he heard from her one word of real sympathy for the sorrowing; for the sinful?.... He was still lost in thought when Theon re-entered, bringing a letter.

"From Hypatia to her well-beloved pupil.

"I pity you — how should I not? And more, I thank you for this your request, for it shows me that my unwilling presence at the hideous pageant of to-day, has not alienated from me a soul of which I had cherished the noblest hopes, for which I had sketched out the loftiest destiny. But — how shall I say it? Ask yourself whether a change — apparently impossible — must not take place in her for whom you plead, before she and I can meet?

I am not so inhuman as to blame you for having asked me; I do not even blame her for being what she is. She does but follow her nature; who can be angry with her, if destiny have informed so fair an animal with a too gross and earthly spirit? Why weep over her? Dust she is, and unto dust she will return: while you, to whom a more divine spark was allotted at your birth, must rise, and unrepining, leave below you one only connected with you by the unreal and fleeting bonds of fleshly kin."

Philammon crushed the letter together in his hand, and strode from the house without a word.

The philosopher had no gospel, then, for the harlot! No word for the sinner, the degraded! Destiny forsooth! She was to follow her destiny, and be base, miserable, self-condemned. She was to crush the voice of conscience and reason, as often as it awoke within her, and compel herself to believe that she was bound to be that which she knew herself bound not to be. She was to shut her eyes to that present palpable misery which was preaching to her, with the voice of God himself, that the wages of sin are death. Dust she was, and unto dust she will return! Oh, glorious hope for her, for him, who felt as if an eternity of bliss would be worthless, if it parted him from his new-found treasure! Dust she was, and unto dust she must return!

Hapless Hypatia! If she must needs misapply, after the fashion of her school, a text or two here and there from the Hebrew Scriptures, what suicidal fantasy set her on quoting that one? For now, upon Philammon's memory flashed up in letters of light, old words forgotten for months — and ere he was aware, he found himself repeating aloud and passionately, "I believe in the forgiveness of sins, the resurrection of the body, and the life everlasting,".... and then clear and fair arose before him the vision of the God-man, as He lay at meat in the Pharisee's house; and of her who washed His feet with tears, and wiped them with the hairs of her head..... And from the depths of his agonized heart arose the prayer, "Blessed Magdalene, intercede for her!"

So high he could rise: but not beyond. For the notion of that God-man was receding fast to more and more awful and abysmal heights, in the minds of a generation who were forgetting His love in His power, and practically losing sight of His humanity in their eager doctrinal assertion of His Divinity. And

Philammon's heart re-echoed the spirit of his age, when he felt that for an apostate like himself it were presumptuous to entreat for any light or help from the fountain-head itself. He who had denied his Lord, he who had voluntarily cut himself off from the communion of the Catholic Church — how could he restore himself? How could he appease the wrath of Him who died on the cross, save by years of bitter supplication and self-punishment?....

"Fool! Vain and ambitious fool that I have been! For this I threw away the faith of my childhood! For this I listened to words at which I shuddered; crushed down my own doubts and disgusts; tried to persuade myself that I could reconcile them with Christianity — that I could make a lie fit into the truth! For this I puffed myself up in the vain hope of becoming not as other men are — superior, forsooth, to my kind! It was not enough for me to be a man made in the image of God: but I must needs become a god myself, knowing good and evil. — And here is the end! I call upon my fine philosophy to help me once, in one real practical human struggle, and it folds its arms and sits serene and silent, smiling upon my misery! Oh fool, fool, thou art filled with the fruit of thy own devices! Back to the old faith! Home again, thou wanderer! And yet how home! Are not the gates shut against me? Perhaps against her too.... What if she, like me, were a baptized Christian?"

Terrible and all but hopeless that thought flashed across him, as in the first revulsion of his conscience he plunged utterly and implicitly back again into the faith of his childhood, and all the dark and cruel theories popular in his day rose up before him in all their terrors. In the innocent simplicity of the Laura, he had never felt their force; but he felt them now. If Pelagia were a baptized woman, what was before her but unceasing penance? Before her, as before him, a life of cold and hunger, groans and tears, loneliness and hideous soul-sickening-uncertainty. Life was a dung-eon for them both henceforth. Be it so! There was nothing else to believe in. No other rock of hope in earth or heaven. That at least promised a possibility of forgiveness, of amendment, of virtue, of reward — ay, of everlasting-bliss and glory; and even if she missed of that, better for her the cell in the desert than a life of self-contented impurity! If that latter were her destiny, as Hypatia said, she should at least die fighting-against it, defying it, cursing it! Better virtue with hell, than sin with heaven! And Hypatia had not even promised her a heaven. The resurrection of the flesh was too carnal a notion for her refined and lofty creed. And so, his four months' dream swept away in a moment, he hurried back to his chamber, with one fixed thought before him — the desert; a cell for Pelagia; another for himself. There they would repent, and pray, and mourn out life side by side, if perhaps God would have mercy upon their souls. Yet — perhaps, she might not have been baptized after all. And then she was safe. Like other converts from Paganism, she might become a catechumen, and go on to baptism, where the mystic water would wash away in a moment all the past, and she would begin life afresh, in the spotless robes of innocence. Yet he had been baptized, he knew from Arsenius, before he left Athens; and she was older than he. It was all but impossible: yet he would hope; and breathless with anxiety and excitement, he ran up the narrow stairs and found Miriam standing outside, her hand upon the bolt, apparently inclined to dispute his passage.

"Is she still within?"

"What if she be?"

"Let me pass into my own room."

"Yours? Who has been paying the rent for you, these four months past? You? What can you say to her? What can you do for her? Young pedant, you must be in love yourself before you can help poor creatures who are in love!"

But Philammon pushed past her so fiercely, that the old woman was forced to give way, and with a sinister smile she followed him into the chamber.

Pelagia sprang towards her brother.

"Will she? — will she see me?"

"Let us talk no more of her, my beloved," said Philammon, laying his hands gently on her trembling shoulders, and looking earnestly into her eyes..... Better that we two should work out our deliverance for ourselves, without the help of strangers. You can trust me?"

"You? And can you help me? Will you teach me?"

"Yes, but not here..... We must escape — Nay, hear me, one moment! dearest sister, hear me! Are you so happy here that you can conceive of no better place! And — and, oh, God! that it may not be true after all! — but is there not a hell hereafter?"

Pelagia covered her face with her hands — "The old monk warned me of it!"

"Oh, take his warning.".... And Philammon was bursting forth with some such words about the lake of fire and brimstone as he had been accustomed to hear from Pambo and Arsenius, when Pelagia interrupted him —

"Oh, Miriam! Is it true? Is it possible? What will become of me?" almost shrieked the poor child.

"What if it were true? — Let him tell you how he will save you from it," answered Miriam quietly.

"Will not the Gospel save her from it — unbelieving Jew? Do not contradict me! I can save her."

"If she does what?"

"Can she not repent? Can she not mortify these base affections? Can she not be forgiven? Oh, my Pelagia! forgive me for having dreamed one moment that I could make you a philosopher, when you may be a saint of God, a ——— "

He stopped short suddenly, as the thought about baptism flashed across him, and in a faltering voice asked, "Are you baptized?"

"Baptized?" asked she, hardly understanding the term.

"Yes — by the bishop — in the church."

"Ah," she said, I remember now..... When I was four or five years old..... A tank, and women undressing..... And I was bathed too, and an old man dipped my head under the water three times..... I have forgotten what it all meant — it was so long ago. I wore a white dress, I know, afterwards."

Philammon recoiled with a groan.

"Unhappy child! May God have mercy on you!"

"Will he not forgive me, then? You have forgiven me. He? — he must be more good even than you. — Why not?"

"He forgave you then, freely, when you were baptized;! and there is no second pardon, unless ——— "

"Unless I leave my love!" shrieked Pelagia.

"When the Lord forgave the blessed Magdalene freely, and told her that her faith had saved her — did she live on in sin, or even in the pleasures of this world? No! though God had forgiven her, she could not forgive herself. She fled forth into the desert, and there, naked and barefoot, clothed only with her hair, and feeding on the herb of the field, she stayed fasting and praying till her dying day, never seeing the face of man, but visited and comforted by angels and archangels. And if she, she who never fell again, needed that long penance to work out her own salvation — oh, Pelagia, what will not God require of you, who have broken your baptismal vows, and defiled the white robes, which the tears of penance only can wash clean once more?"

"But I did not know! I did not ask to be baptized! Cruel, cruel parents, to bring me to it! And God! Oh, why did He forgive me so soon? And to go into the deserts! I dare not! I cannot! See me, how delicate and tender I am! I should die of hunger and cold! I should go mad with fear and loneliness! Oh! brother, I brother, is this the Gospel of the Christians? I came to you to be taught how to be wise, and good, and respected, and you tell me that all I can do is to live this horrible life of torture here, on the chance of escaping torture for ever! And how do I know that I shall escape it? How do I know that I shall make myself miserable enough? How do I know that He will forgive me after all? Is this true, I Miriam? Tell me, or I shall go mad!"

"Yes," said Miriam, with a quiet sneer. "This is the gospel and good news of salvation, according to the doctrine of the Nazarenes."

"I will go with you!" cried Philammon. "I will go! I will never leave you! I have my own sins to wash away? — Happy for me if I ever do it! — And I will build you a cell near mine, and kind men will teach us, and we will pray together night and morning, for ourselves and for each other, and weep out our weary lives together ——— "

"Better end them here, at once!" said Pelagia, with a gesture of despair, and dashed herself down on the floor.

Philammon was about to lift her up, when Miriam caught him by the arm, and in a hurried whisper — "Are you mad? Will you ruin your own purpose? Why did you tell her this? Why did you not wait — give her hope — time to collect herself — time to wean herself from her lover, instead of terrifying and disgusting her at the outset, as you have done? Have you a man's heart in you? No word of comfort for that poor creature, nothing but hell, hell, hell — See to your own chance of hell first! It is greater than you fancy!"

"It cannot be greater than I fancy!"

"Then see to it. For her, poor darling! — why, even we Jews, who know that all you Gentiles are doomed to Gehenna alike, have some sort of hope for such a poor untaught creature as that."

"And why is she untaught? Wretch that you are! You have had the training of her! You brought her up to sin and shame! You drove from her recollection the faith in which she was baptized!"

"So much the better for her, if the recollection of it is to make her no happier than it does already. Better to wake unexpectedly in Gehenna when you die, than to endure over and above the dread of it here. And as for leaving her untaught, on your own showing she has been taught too much already. Wiser it would be in you to curse your parents for having had her baptized, than me for giving her ten years' pleasure before she goes to the pit of Tophet. Come, now, don't be angry with me. The old Jewess is your friend, revile her as you will. She shall marry this Goth."

"An Arian heretic!"

"She shall convert him and make a Catholic of him, it you like. At all events, if you wish to win her, you must win her my way. You have had your chance, and spoiled it. Let me have mine. Pelagia, darling! Up, and be a woman! We will find a philtre downstairs to give that ungrateful man, that shall make him more mad about you, before a day is over, than ever you were about him."

"No!" said Pelagia, looking up. "No love-potions! No poisons!"

"Poisons, little fool! Do you doubt the old woman's skill? Do you think I shall make him lose his wits, as Callisphyra did to her lover last year, because she would trust to old Megæra's drugs, instead of coming to me?"

"No! No drugs; no magic! He must love me really, or not at all! He must love me for myself, because I am worth loving, because he honours, worships me — or let me die! I, whose boast was, even when I was basest, that I never needed such mean tricks, but conquered like Aphrodite, a queen in my own right! I have been my own love-charm: when I cease to be that, let me die!"

"One as mad as the other!" cried Miriam, in utter perplexity. "Hist! what is that tramp upon the stairs?"

At this moment heavy footsteps were heard ascending the stairs..... All three stopped aghast: Philammon, because he thought the visitors were monks in search of him; Miriam, because she thought they were Orestes' guards in search of her; and Pelagia, from vague dread of anything and everything....

"Have you an inner room?" asked the Jewess.

"None."

The old woman set her lips firmly, and drew her dagger. Pelagia wrapped her face in her cloak, and stood trembling, bowed down, as if expecting another blow. The door opened, and in walked, neither monks nor guard, but Wulf and Smid.

"Heyday, young monk!" cried the latter worthy, with a loud laugh — "Veils here, too, eh? At your old trade, my worthy portress of hell-gate? Well, walk out now; we have a little business with this young gentleman."

And slipping past the unsuspecting Goths, Pelagia and Miriam hurried downstairs.

"The young one, at least, seems a little ashamed of her errand..... Now, Wulf, speak low; and I will see that no one is listening at the door."

Philammon faced his unexpected visitors with a look of angry inquiry. What right had they, or any man, to intrude at such a moment on his misery and disgrace?.... But he was disarmed the next instant by old Wulf, who advanced to him, and looking him fully in the face with an expression which there was no mistaking, held out his broad brown hand.

Philammon grasped it, and then covering his face with his hands, burst into tears.

"You did right. You are a brave boy. If you had died, no man need have been ashamed to die your death."

"You were there, then?" sobbed Philammon.

"We were."

"And what is more," said Smid, as the poor boy writhed at the admission, "we were mightily minded, some of us, to have leapt down to you and cut you a passage out. One man at least, whom I know of, felt his old blood as hot for the minute as a four-year-old's. The foul curs! And to hoot her, after all! Oh that I may have one good hour's hewing at them before I die!"

"And you shall!" said Wulf. "Boy, you wish to get this

sister of yours into your power?"

"It is hopeless — hopeless! She will never leave her — —
the Amal."

"Are you so sure of that?"

"She told me so with her own lips not ten minutes ago.
That was she who went out as you entered!"

A curse of astonishment and regret burst from Smid.....

"Had I but known her! By the soul of my fathers, she
should have found that it was easier to come here than to go
home again!"

"Hush, Smid! Better as it is. Boy, if I put her into your
power, dare you carry her off!"

Philammon hesitated one moment.

"What I dare you know already. But it would be an unlaw-
ful thing, surely, to use violence."

"Settle your philosopher's doubts for yourself. I have
made my offer. I should have thought that a man in his senses
could give but one answer, much more a mad monk."

"You forget the money matters, prince," said Smid, with a
smile.

"I do not. But I don't think the boy so mean as to hesitate
on that account."

"He may as well know, however, that we promise to send
all her trumpery after her, even to the Amal's presents. As for the
house, we won't trouble her to lend it us longer than we can
help. We intend shortly to move into more extensive premises,
and open business on a grander scale, as the shopkeepers say, —
eh, prince?"

"Her money? — That money? God forgive her!" answered
Philammon. "Do you fancy me base enough to touch it? But I
am resolved. Tell me what to do, and I will do it."

"You know the lane which runs down to the canal, under
the left wall of the house?"

"Yes."

"And a door in the corner tower, close to the landing-
place?"

"I do."

"Be there, with a dozen stout monks, to-morrow, an hour
after sundown, and take what we give you. After that, the concern is yours, not ours."

"Monks?" said Philammon. "I am at open feud with the whole order."

"Make friends with them, then," shortly suggested Smid.

Philammon writhed inwardly. "It makes no difference to you, I presume, whom I bring?"

"No more than it does whether or not you pitch her into the canal, and put a hurdle over her when you have got her," answered Smid; "which is what a Goth would do, if he were in your place."

"Do not vex the poor lad, friend. If he thinks he can mend her instead of punishing her, in Freya's name, let him try. You will be there, then? And mind, I like you I liked you when you faced that great river-hog. I like you better now than ever; for you have spoken to-day lit a Sagaman, and dared like a hero. Therefore mind; if you do not bring a good guard to-morrow night, your life will not be safe. The whole city is out in the streets; and Odin alone knows what will be done, and who will be alive, eight-and-forty hours hence. Mind you! — The mob may do strange things, and they may see still stranger things done. If you once find yourself safe back here, stay where you are, if you value her life or your own. And — if you are wise, let the men whom you bring with you be monks, though it cost your proud stomach ——— "

"That's not fair, prince! You are telling too much!" interrupted Smid, while Philammon gulped down the said proud stomach, and answered, "Be it so!"

"I have won my bet, Smid," said the old man, chuckling, as the two tramped out into the street, to the surprise and fear of all the neighbours, while the children clapped their hands, and the street dogs felt it their duty to bark lustily at the strange figures of their unwonted visitors.

"No play, no pay, Wulf. We shall see to-morrow."

"I knew that he would stand the trial! I knew he was right at heart!"

"At all events, there is no fear of his ill-using the poor thing, if he loves her well enough to go down on his knees to his sworn foes for her."

"I don't know that," answered Wulf, with a shake of the head. "These monks, I hear, fancy that their God likes them the better the more miserable they are: so, perhaps they may fancy that he will like them all the more, the more miserable they make other people. However, it's no concern of ours."

"We have quite enough of our own to see to just now. But mind, no play, no pay."

"Of course not. How the streets are filling! We shall not be able to see the guards to-night, if this mob thickens much more."

"We shall have enough to do to hold our own, perhaps. Do you hear what they are crying there? 'Down with all heathens! Down with barbarians!' That means us, you know."

"Do you fancy no one understands Greek but yourself? Let them come..... It may give us an excuse..... And we can hold the house a week."

"But how can we get speech of the guards?"

"We will slip round by water. And, after all, deeds will win them better than talk. They will be forced to fight on the same side as we, and most probably be glad of our help; for if the mob attacks any one, it will begin with the Prefect."

"And then — Curse their shouting! Let the soldiers once find our Amal at their head, and they will be ready to go with him a mile, where they meant to go a yard."

"The Goths will, and the Markmen, and those Dacians, and Thracians, or whatever the Romans call them. But I hardly trust the Huns."

"The curse of heaven on their pudding faces and pigs eyes! There will be no love lost between us. But there are not twenty of them scattered in different troops; one of us can thrash three of them; and they will be sure to side with the winning party. Besides, plunder, plunder, comrade! When did you know a Hun turn back from that, even if he were only on the scent of a lump of tallow?"

"As for the Gauls and Latins,".... went on Wulf, meditatively, "they belong to any man who can pay them.".....

"Which we can do, like all wise generals, one penny out of our own pocket, and nine out of the enemy's. And the Amal is staunch?"

"Staunch as his own hounds, now there is something to be done on the spot. His heart was in the right place after all. I knew it all along. But he could never in his life see four-and-twenty hours before him. Even now, if that Pelagia gets him under her spell again, he may throw down his sword, and fall as fast asleep as ever.''

"Never fear: we have settled her destiny for her, as far as that is concerned. Look at the mob before the door! We must get in by the postern-gate."

"Get in by the sewer, like a rat! I go my own way. Draw, old hammer and tongs! or run away!"

"Not this time." And sword in hand, the two marched into the heart of the crowd, who gave way before them like a flock of sheep.

"They know their intended shepherds already," said Smid. But at that moment the crowd, seeing them about to enter the house, raised a yell of "Goths! Heathens! Barbarians!" and a rush from behind took place.

"If you will have it, then!" said Wulf. And the two long bright blades flashed round and round their heads, redder and redder every time they swung aloft..... The old men never even checked their steady walk, and knocking at the gate, went in, leaving more than one lifeless corpse at the entrance.

"We have put the coal in the thatch, now, with a vengeance," said Smid, as they wiped their swords inside.

"We have. Get me out a boat and half-a-dozen men, and I and Goderic will go round by the canal to the palace, and settle a thing or two with the guards."

"Why should not the Amal go, and offer our help himself to the Prefect?"

"What? Would you have him after that turn against the hound? For troth and honour's sake he must keep quiet in the matter."

"He will have no objection to keep quiet — trust him for that! But don't forget Sagaman Moneybag, the best of all orators," called Smid laughingly after him, as he went off to man the boat.

CHAPTER XXV
SEEKING AFTER A SIGN

"WHAT answer has he sent back, father?" asked Hypatia, as Theon re-entered her chamber, after delivering that hapless letter to Philammon.

"Insolent that he is! he tore it to fragments, and fled forth without a word."

"Let him go, and desert us like the rest, in our calamity!"

"At least, we have the jewels."

"The jewels? Let them be returned to their owner. Shall we defile ourselves by taking them as wages for anything — above all, for that which is unperformed?"

"But, my child, they were given to us freely. He bade me keep them; and — and, to tell you the truth, I must keep them. After this unfortunate failure, be sure of it, every creditor we have will be clamouring for payment."

"Let them take our house and furniture, and sell us as slaves, then. Let them take all, provided we keep our virtue."

"Sell us as slaves? Are you mad?"

"Not quite mad yet, father," answered she, with a sad smile. "But how should we be worse than we are now, were we slaves? Raphael Aben-Ezra told me that he obeyed my precepts, when he went forth as a houseless beggar; and shall I not have courage to obey them myself, if the need come? The thought of his endurance has shamed my luxury for this many a month. After all, what does the philosopher require but bread and water, and the' clear brook in which to wash away the daily stains of his earthly prison-house? Let what is fated come. Hypatia struggles with the stream no more!"

"My daughter! And have you given up all hope? So soon disheartened! What! is this paltry accident to sweep away the purposes of years? Orestes remains still faithful. His guards have orders to garrison the house for as long as we shall require them."

"Send them away, then. I have done no wrong, and I fear no punishment."

"You do not know the madness of the mob; they are

shouting your name in the streets already, in company with Pelagia's."

Hypatia shuddered. Her name in company with Pelagia's! And to this she had brought herself!

"I have deserved it! I have sold myself to a lie and a disgrace! I have stooped to truckle, to intrigue! I have bound myself to a sordid trickster! Father! never mention his name to me again! I have leagued myself with the impure and the bloodthirsty, and I have my reward!" No more politics for Hypatia from henceforth, my father; no more orations and lectures; no more pearls of Divine wisdom cast before swine. I have sinned in divulging the secrets of the Immortals to the mob. Let them follow their natures! Fool that I was, to fancy that my speech, my plots, could raise them above that which the gods had made them!"

"Then you give up our lectures? Worse and worse!-We shall be ruined utterly!"

"We are ruined utterly already. Orestes? There is no help in him. I know the man too well, my father, not to know that he would give us up to-morrow to the fury of the Christians, were his own base life — even his own baser office — in danger."

"Too true — too true! I fear," said the poor old man, wringing his hands in perplexity. "What will become of us, — of you, rather? What matter what happens to the useless old stargazer? Let him die! To-day or next year is alike to him. But you, — you! Let us escape by' the canal. We may gather up enough, even without these jewels, which you refuse, to pay our voyage to Athens, and' there we shall be safe with Plutarch; he will welcome you — all Athens will welcome you — we will collect a fresh school — and you shall be Queen of Athens, as you have been Queen of Alexandria!"

"No, father. What I know, henceforth I will know for myself only. Hypatia will be from this day alone with the Immortal Gods!"

"You will not leave me?" cried the old man, terrified.

"Never on earth!" answered she, bursting into real human tears, and throwing herself on his bosom. "Never — never! father of my spirit as well as of my flesh! — the parent who has trained me, taught me, educated my soul from the cradle to use her wings! — the only human being who never misunderstood

372

me — never thwarted me — never deceived me!"

"My priceless child! And I have been the cause of your ruin!"

"Not you! — a thousand times not you! I only am to blame! I tampered with worldly politics. I tempted you on to fancy that I could effect what I so rashly undertook. Do not accuse yourself unless you wish to break my heart! We can be happy together yet. — A palm-leaf hut in the desert, dates from the grove, and water from the spring — the monk dares be miserable alone in such a dwelling, and cannot we dare to be happy together in it?"

"Then you will escape?"

"Not to-day. It were base to flee before danger comes. We must hold out at our post to the last moment, even if we dare not die at it like heroes. And to-morrow I go to the lecture-room, — to the beloved Museum, for the last time, to take farewell of my pupils. Unworthy as they are, I owe it to myself and to philosophy, to tell them why I leave them."

"It will be too dangerous, — indeed it will!"

"I could take the guards with me, then. And yet — no..... They shall never have occasion to impute fear to the philosopher. Let them see her go forth as usual on her errand, strong in the courage of innocence, secure in the protection of the gods. So, perhaps, some sacred awe, some suspicion of her divineness, may fall on them at last."

"I must go with you."

"No, I go alone. You might incur danger, where I am safe. After all, I am a woman.... and, fierce as they are, they will not dare to harm me."

The old man shook his head.

"Look now," she said, smilingly, laying her hands on his shoulders, and looking into his face..... "You tell me that I am beautiful, you know; and beauty will tame the lion. Do you not think that this face might disarm even a monk?"

And she laughed and blushed so sweetly, that the old man forgot his fears, as she intended that he should, and kissed her, and went his way for the time being, to command all manner of hospitalities to the soldiers, whom he prudently determined to keep in his house as long as he could make them stay there; in pursuance of which wise purpose, he contrived not to see a great deal of pleasant flirtation between his valiant defenders and Hypatia's maids, who, by no means so prudish as their mistress, welcomed as a rare boon from heaven an afternoon's chat with twenty tall men of war.

So they jested and laughed below, while old Theon, having brought out the very best old wine and actually proposed in person, by way of mending matters, the health of the Emperor of Africa, locked himself into the library, and comforted his troubled soul with a tough problem of astronomy, which had been haunting him the whole day, even in the theatre itself. But Hypatia sat still in her chamber, her face buried in her hands, her heart full of many thoughts, her eyes of tears. She had smiled away her father's fears; she could not smile away her own.

She felt, she hardly knew why, but she felt as clearly as if a god had proclaimed it to her bodily ears, that the crisis of her life was come; that her political and active career was over, and that she must now be content to be for herself and in herself alone, all that she was, or might become. The world might be regenerated: but not in her day; — the gods restored: but not by her. It was a fearful discovery, — and yet hardly a discovery. Her heart had told her for years that she was hoping against hope, — that she was struggling against a stream too mighty for her. And now the moment had come when she must either be swept helpless down the current, or, by one desperate effort, win firm land, and let the tide roll on its own way henceforth..... Its own way?.... Not the way of the gods, at least; for it was sweeping their names from off the earth. What if they did not care to be known? What if they were weary of worship and reverence from mortal men, and, self-sufficing in their own perfect bliss, recked nothing for the weal or woe of earth? Must it not be so? Had she not proof of it in everything which she beheld? What did Isis care for her Alexandria? What did Athene care for her Athens?.... And yet Homer and Hesiod, and those old Orphic singers, were of another mind..... Whence got they that strange fancy of gods counselling, warring, intermarrying with mankind, as with some kindred tribe?

"Zeus, father of gods and men.".... Those were words of hope and comfort..... But were they true? Father of men? Impossible! — not father of Pelagia, surely. Not father of the base, the foul, the ignorant..... Father of heroic souls, only, the poets must have meant..... But where were the heroic souls now? Was she one? If so, why was she deserted by the upper powers in her utter need? Was the heroic race indeed extinct? Was she merely assuming, in her self-conceit, an honour to which she had no claim? Or was it all a dream of these old singers? Had they, as some bold philosophers had said, invented gods in their own likeness, and palmed off on the awe and admiration of men their own fair phantoms?.... Ft must be so. If there were gods, to know them was the highest bliss of man. Then would they not teach men of themselves, unveil their own loveliness to a chosen few, even for the sake of their own honour, if not, as she had dreamed once, from love to those who bore a kindred flame to theirs?.... What if there were no gods? What if the stream of fate, which was sweeping away their names, were the only real power? What if that old Pyrrhonic notion were the true solution of the problem of the Universe? What if there were no centre, no order, no rest, no goal, — but only a perpetual flux, a down-rushing change? And before her dizzying brain and heart arose that awful vision of Lucretius, of the homeless Universe falling, falling, falling, for ever from nowhence toward nowhither through the unending ages, by causeless and unceasing gravitation, while the changes and efforts of all mortal things were but the jostling of the dust-atoms amid the everlasting storm....

It could not be! There was a truth, a virtue, a beauty, a nobleness, which could never change, but which were absolute, the same for ever. The God-given instinct of her woman's heart rebelled against her intellect, and, in the name of God, denied its lie..... Yes, — there was virtue, beauty..... And, yet — might not they, too, be accidents of that enchantment, which man calls mortal life; temporary and mutable accidents of consciousness; brilliant sparks, struck out by the clashing of the dust-atoms. Who could tell?

There were those once who could tell. Did not Plotinus speak of a direct mystic intuition of the Deity, an enthusiasm without passion, a still intoxication of the soul, in which she rose above life, thought, reason, herself, to that which she contemplated, the absolute and first One, and united herself with that One, or, rather, became aware of that union which had existed from the first moment in which she emanated from the One? Six times in a life of sixty years had Plotinus risen to that height of mystic union, and known himself to be a part of God. Once had Porphyry attained the same glory. Hypatia, though often attempting, had never yet succeeded in attaining to any distinct vision of a being external to herself; though practice, a firm will, and a powerful imagination, had long since made her an adept in producing, almost at will, that mysterious trance, which was the preliminary step to super natural vision. But her delight in the brilliant, and, as she held, divine imaginations, in which at such times she revelled, had been always checked and chilled by the know ledge that, in such matters, hundreds inferior to her in intellect and in learning, — ay, saddest of all, Christian monks and nuns, boasted themselves her equals, — indeed if their own account of their visions was to be believed, her superiors — by the same methods which she employed. For by celibacy, rigorous fasts, perfect bodily quiescence, and intense contemplation of one thought, they, too, pretended to be able to rise above the body into the heavenly regions and to behold things unspeakable, which, nevertheless like most other unspeakable things, contrived to be most carefully detailed and noised abroad..... And it was with a half feeling of shame that she prepared herself that afternoon for one more, perhaps one last attempt, to scale the heavens, as she recollected how many an illiterate monk and nun, from Constantinople to the Thebaid, was probably employed at that moment exactly as she was. Still, the attempt must be made. In that terrible abyss of doubt, she must have something palpable, real; something beyond her own thoughts, and hopes, and speculations, whereon to rest her weary faith, her weary heart..... Perhaps this time, at least, in her extremest need, a god might vouchsafe some glimpse of his own beauty..... Athene might pity at last..... Or, if not Athene, some archetype, angel, demon..... And then she shuddered at the thought of those evil and deceiving spirits, whose delight it was to delude and tempt the votaries of the gods, in the forms of angels of light. But even in the face of that danger, she must make the trial once again. Was she not pure and spotless as Athene's self? Would not her innate purity enable her to discern, by an instinctive antipathy, those foul beings beneath the fairest mask? At least, she must make the trial.....

And so, with a look of intense humility, she began to lay aside her jewels and her upper robes. Then, baring her bosom and her feet, and shaking her golden tresses loose, she laid herself down upon the couch, crossed her hands upon her breast, and, with upturned ecstatic eyes, waited for that which might befall.

There she lay, hour after hour, as her eye gradually kindled, her bosom heaved, her breath came fast: but there was no more sign of life in those straight still limbs, and listless feet and hands, than in Pygmalion's ivory bride, before she bloomed into human flesh and blood. The sun sank towards his rest; the roar of the city grew louder and louder without; the soldiers revelled and laughed below; but every sound passed through unconscious ears, and went its way unheeded. Faith, hope, reason itself were staked upon the result of that daring effort to scale the highest heaven. And, by one continuous effort of her practised will, which reached its highest virtue, as mystics hold, in its own suicide, she chained down her senses from every sight and sound, and even her mind from every thought, and lay utterly self-resigned, self-emptied, till consciousness of time and place had vanished, and she seemed to herself alone in the abyss.

She dared not reflect, she dared not hope, she dared not rejoice, lest she should break the spell..... Again and again had she broken it at this very point, by some sudden and tumultuous yielding to her own joy or awe; but now her will held firm..... She did not feel her own limbs, hear her own breath..... A light bright mist, an endless network of glittering films, coming, going, uniting, resolving themselves, was above her and around her...... Was she in the body or out of the body?....

* * * * * *

The network faded into an abyss of still clear light..... A still warm atmosphere was around her, thrilling through and through her..... She breathed the light, and floated in it, as a mote in the midday beam..... And still her will held firm.

* * * * * *

Far away, miles, and aeons, and abysses away, through the interminable depths of glory, a dark and shadowy spot. It neared and grew..... A dark globe, ringed, with rainbows..... What might it be? She dared not hope..... It came nearer, nearer, nearer, touched her..... The centre quivered, flickered, took form — a face..... A god's? No — Pelagia's!

Beautiful, sad, craving, reproachful, indignant, awful.....

Hypatia could bear no more; and sprang to her feet with a shriek, to experience in its full bitterness the fearful revulsion of the mystic, when the human reason and will which he has spurned reassert their God-given rights; and after the intoxication of the imagination, comes its prostration and collapse.

And this, then, was the answer of the gods! The phantom of her whom she had despised, exposed, spurned from her! "No, not their answer — the answer of my own soul! Fool that I have been! I have been exerting my will most while I pretended to resign it most! I have been the slave of every mental desire, while I tried to trample on them! What if that network of light, that blaze, that globe of darkness, have been, like the face of Pelagia, the phantoms of my own imagination — ay, even of my own senses? What if I have mistaken for Deity my own self? What if I have been my own light, my own abyss?.... Am I not my own abyss, my own light — my own darkness?" And she smiled bitterly as she said it, and throwing herself again upon the couch, buried her head in her hands, exhausted equally in body and in mind.

At last she rose, and sat, careless of her dishevelled locks, gazing out into vacancy. "Oh, for a sign, for a token! Oh, for the golden days of which the poets sang, when gods walked among men, fought by their side as friends! And yet.... are those old stories credible, pious, even modest? Does not my heart revolt from them? Who has shared more than I in Plato's contempt for the foul deeds, the degrading transformations, which Homer imputes to the gods of Greece? Must I believe them now? Must I stoop to think that gods, who live in a region above all sense, will deign to make themselves palpable to those senses of ours which are whole aeons of existence below them? — degrade themselves to the base accidents of matter? Yes I That, rather than nothing!.... Be it even so. Better, better, better, to believe that Ares fled shrieking and wounded from a mortal man — better to believe in Zeus's adulteries and Hermes' thefts — than to believe that gods have never spoken face to face with men! Let me think, lest I go mad, that beings from that unseen world for which I hunger have appeared, and held communion with mankind, such as no reason nor sense could doubt — even though those beings were more capricious and baser than ourselves! Is there, after all, an unseen world? Oh, for a sign, a sign!"

Haggard and dizzy, she wandered into her "chamber of the gods "; a collection of antiquities, which she kept there rather as matters of taste than of worship. All around her they looked out into vacancy with their white soulless eyeballs, their dead motionless beauty, those cold dreams of the buried generations. Oh that they could speak, and set her heart at rest! At the lower end of the room stood a Pallas, completely armed with aegis, spear, and helmet; a gem of Athenian sculpture, which she had bought from some merchants after the sack of Athens by the Goths. There it stood, severely fair; but the right hand, alas! was gone; and there the maimed arm remained extended, as if in sad mockery of the faith of which the body remained, while the power was dead and vanished.

She gazed long and passionately on the image of her favourite goddess, the ideal to which she had longed for years to assimilate herself; till — was it a dream? was it a frolic of the dying sunlight? or did those lips really bend themselves into a smile?

Impossible! No, not impossible. Had not, only a few years before, the image of Hecate smiled on a philosopher? Were there not stories of moving images, and winking pictures, and all the material miracles by which a dying faith strives desperately — not to deceive others — but persuade itself of it own sanity? It had been — it might be — it was! —

No! there the lips were, as they had been from the beginning, closed upon each other in that stony self-collected calm, which was only not a sneer. The wonder, if it was one, passed: and now — did her eyes play her false, as were the snakes round that Medusa's head upon the shield all writhing, grinning, glaring at her with stony eyes longing to stiffen her with terror into their own likeness?

No! that, too, passed. Would that even it had stayed for it would have been a sign of life! She looked up the face once more: but in vain — the stone was stone; and ere she was aware, she found herself clasping passionately the knees of the marble.

"Athene! Pallas! Adored! Ever Virgin! Absolute reason, springing unbegotten from the nameless One! Hear me! Athene! Have mercy on me! Speak, if be to curse me! Thou who alone wieldest the lightning of thy father, wield them to strike me dead, if thou will only do something! — something to prove thine own existence — something to make me sure that anything exist beside this gross miserable matter, and my miserable soul I stand alone in the centre of the universe! I fall and sicken down the abyss of ignorance, and doubt, and boundless blank and darkness! Oh, have mercy! I know that thou art not this! Thou art everywhere and in all things. But I know that this is a form which pleases thee, which symbolizes thy nobleness! I know that thou hast deigned to speak to those who — Oh, what do I know? Nothing! nothing! nothing!"

And she clung there, bedewing with scalding tears the cold feet of the image, while there was neither sign, not voice, nor any that answered.

On a sudden she was startled by a rustling near; and looking round, saw close behind her the old Jewess.

"Cry aloud!" hissed the hag, in a tone of bitter scorn "Cry aloud, for she is a goddess. Either she is talking or pursuing, or she is on a journey: or perhaps she had grown old, as we all shall do some day, my pretty lady and is too cross and lazy to stir. What! her naught doll will not speak to her, will it not? or even open its eyes, because the wires are grown rusty? Well, we will find a new doll for her, if she chooses."

"Begone, hag! What do you mean by intruding here?" said Hypatia, springing up; but the old woman went on coolly —

"Why not try the fair young gentleman over there?" pointing to a copy of the Apollo which we call Belvedere — "What is his name? Old maids are always cross and jealous, you know. But he — he could not be cruel to such a sweet face as that. Try the fair young lad! Or, perhaps, if you are bashful, the old Jewess might try him for you?"

These last words were spoken with so marked a significance, that Hypatia, in spite of her disgust, found herself asking the hag what she meant. She made no answer for a few seconds, but remained looking steadily into her eyes with a glance of fire, before which even the proud Hypatia, as she had done once before, quailed utterly, so deep was the understanding, so dogged the purpose, so fearless the power, which burned within those withered and sunken sockets.

"Shall the old witch call him up, the fair young Apollo, with the beauty-bloom upon his chin? He shall come! He shall come! I warrant him he must come, civilly enough, when old

Miriam's finger is once held up."

"To you? Apollo, the god of light, obey a Jewess?"

"A Jewess? And you a Greek?" almost yelled the old Woman. "And who are you who ask? And who are your gods, your heroes, your devils, you children of yesterday, compared with us? You, who were a set of half-naked savages squabbling about the siege of Troy, when our Solomon, amid splendours such as Rome and Constantinople never saw, was controlling demons and ghosts, angels and archangels, principalities and powers, by the ineffable name? What science have you that you have not stolen from the Egyptians and Chaldees? And what had the Egyptians which Moses did not teach them? And what have the Chaldees which Daniel did not teach them? What does the world know but from us, the fathers and the masters of magic — us, the lords of the inner secrets of the universe! Come, you Greek baby — as the priests in Egypt said of your forefathers, always children, craving for a new toy, and throwing it away next day — come to the fountain-head of all your paltry wisdom! Name what you will see, and you shall see it!"

Hypatia was cowed; for of one thing-there was no doubt — that the woman utterly believed in her own words; and that was a state of mind of which she had seen so little, that it was no wonder if it acted on her with that overpowering sympathetic force, with which it generally does, and perhaps ought to, act on the human heart. Besides, her school had always looked to the ancient nations of the East for the primæval founts of inspiration, the mysterious lore of mightier races long gone by. Might she not have found it now?

The Jewess saw her advantage in a moment, and ran on, without giving her time to answer —

"What sort shall it be, then? By glass and water, or by the moonlight on the wall, or by the sieve, or by the meal? By the cymbals, or by the stars? By the table of the twenty-four elements, by which the empire was promised to Theodosius the Great, or by the sacred counters of the Assyrians, or by the sapphire of the Hecatic sphere? Shall I threaten, as the Egyptian priests used to do, to tear Osiris again in pieces, or to divulge the mysteries of Isis? I could do so, if I chose; for I know them all, and more. Or shall I use the ineffable name on Solomon's seal, which we alone, of all the nations of the earth, know! No; it would be a pity to waste that upon a heathen. It shall be by the sacred wafer. Look here! — here they are, the wonder-working atomies! Eat no food this day, except one of these every three hours, and come to me to-night at the house of your porter, Eudжmon, bringing with you the black agate; and then — why then, what you have the heart to see, you shall see!"

Hypatia took the wafers, hesitating —

"But what are they?"

"And you profess to explain Homer? Whom did I hear the other morning lecturing away so glibly on the nepenthe which Helen gave the heroes, to till them with the spirit of joy and love; how it was an allegory of the inward inspiration which flows from spiritual beauty, and all that? — Pretty enough, fair lady; but the question still remains, what was it? and I say it was this. Take it and try; and then confess, that while you can talk about Helen, I can act her; and know a little more about Homer than you do, after all."

"I cannot believe you! Give me some sign of your power, or how can I trust you!"

"A sign? — A sign? — Kneel down then there, with your face toward the north; you are over tall for the poor old cripple!"

"I? I never knelt to human being."

"Then consider that you kneel to the handsome idol there, if you will — but kneel!"

And constrained by that glittering eye, Hypatia knelt before her.

"Have you faith? Have you desire? Will you submit? Will you obey? Self-will and pride see nothing, know nothing. If you do not give up yourself, neither God nor devil will care to approach. Do you submit?"

"I do! I do!" cried poor Hypatia, in an agony of curiosity and self-distrust, while she felt her eye quailing and her limbs loosening more and more every moment under that intolerable fascination.

The old woman drew from her bosom a crystal, and placed the point against Hypatia's breast. A cold shiver ran through her..... The witch waved her hands mysteriously round her head, muttering, from time to time, "Down! down, proud spirit!" and then placed the tips of her skinny fingers on the victim's forehead. Gradually her eyelids became heavy; again and again she tried to raise them, and dropped them again before those fixed glaring eyes.... and in another moment she lost consciousness.....

When she awoke, she was kneeling in a distant part of the room, with dishevelled hair and garments. What was it so cold that she was clasping in her arms? The feet of the Apollo! The hag stood by her, chuckling to herself and clapping her hands.

"How came I here? What have I been doing?"

"Saying such pretty things! — paying the fair youth there such compliments, as he will not be rude enough to forget in his visit to-night. A charming prophetic trance You have had! Ah, ha! you are not the only woman who is wiser asleep than awake! Well, you will make a very Pretty Cassandra — or a Clytia, if you have the sense..... It lies with you, my fair lady. Are you satisfied now? Will you have any more signs? Shall the old Jewess blast those blue eyes blind to show that she knows more than the heathen? "

"Oh, I believe you — I believe," cried the poor exhausted maiden. "I will come; and yet ——— "

"Ah! yes! You had better settle first how he shall appear."

"As he wills! — let him only come! Only let me know that he is a god. Abamnon said that gods appeared in a clear, steady, unbearable light, amid a choir of all the lessen deities, archangels, principalities, and heroes, who derive their life from them."

"Abamnon was an old fool, then. Do you think young Phœbus ran after Daphne with such a mob at his heels? or that Jove, when he swam up to Leda, headed a whole Nile-flock of ducks, and plover, and curlews? No, he shall come alone — to you alone; and then you may choose for yourself between Cassandra and Clytia..... Fare-well. Do not forget your wafers, or the agate either, and talk with no one between now and sunset. And then — my pretty lady!"

And laughing to herself, the old hag glided from the room.

Hypatia sat trembling with shame and dread. She, as a disciple of the more purely spiritualistic school of Porphyry, had always looked with aversion, with all but contempt, on those theurgic arts which were so much lauded and employed by Iamblicus, Abamnon, and those who clung lovingly to the old priestly rites of Egypt and Chaldæa They had seemed to her vulgar toys, tricks of legerdemain, suited only for the wonder of the mob..... She began to think of them with more favour now. How did she know that the vulgar did not require signs and wonders to make them believe?.... How, indeed? for did she not want such herself? And she opened Abamnon's famous letter to Porphyry, and read earnestly over, for the twentieth time, his subtle justification of magic, and felt it to be unanswerable. Magic? What was not magical? The whole universe, from the planets over her head to the meanest pebble at her feet, was utterly mysterious, ineffable, miraculous, influencing and influenced by affinities and repulsions as unexpected, as unfathomable, as those which, as Abamnon said, drew the gods towards those sounds, those objects, which, either in form, or colour, or chemical properties, were symbolic of, or akin to, themselves. What wonder in it, after all? Was not love and hatred, sympathy and antipathy, the law of the universe? Philosophers, when they gave mechanical explanations of natural phenomena, came no nearer to the real solution of them. The mysterious "Why?" remained untouched..... All their analyses could only darken with big words the plain fact that the water hated the oil with which it refused to mix, the lime loved the acid which it eagerly received into itself, and, like a lover, grew warm with the rapture of affection. Why not? What right had we to deny sensation, emotion, to them, any more than to ourselves? Was not the same universal spirit stirring in them as in us? And was it not by virtue of that spirit that we thought, and felt, and loved? — Then why not they, as well as we? If the one spirit permeated all things, if its all-energizing presence linked the flower with the crystal as well as with the demon and the god, must it not link together also the two extremes of the great chain of being? bind even the nameless One itself to the smallest creature which bore its creative impress? What greater miracle in the attraction of a god or an angel, by material Incense, symbols, and spells, than in the attraction of one soul to another by the material sounds of the human voice? Was the affinity between spirit and matter implied in that, more miraculous than the affinity between the soul and the body? — than the retention of that soul within that body by the breathing of material air, the eating of material food? Or even, if the physicists were right, and the soul were but a material product or energy of the nerves, and the sole law of the universe the laws of matter, then was not magic even more probable, more rational? Was it not fair by every analogy to suppose that there might be other, higher beings than ourselves, obedient to those laws, and therefore possible to be attracted, even as human beings were, by the baits of material sights and sounds?.... If spirit pervaded all things, then was magic probable; if nothing but matter had existence, magic was morally certain. All that remained in either case was the test of experience..... And had not that test been applied in every age, and asserted to succeed? What more rational, more philosophic, action than to try herself those methods and ceremonies which she was assured on every hand had never failed but through the ignorance or unfitness of the neophyte?.... Abamnon must be right..... She dared not think him wrong; for if this last hope failed, what was there left but to eat and drink, for to-morrow we die?

CHAPTER XXVI
MIRIAM'S PLOT

HE who has worshipped a woman, even against his will and conscience, knows well how storm may follow storm, and earthquake earthquake, before his idol be utterly overthrown. And so Philammon found that evening, as he sat pondering over the strange chances of the day; for, as he pondered, his old feelings towards Hypatia began, in spite of the struggles of his conscience and reason, to revive within him. Not only pure love of her great loveliness, the righteous instinct which bids us welcome and honour beauty, whether in man or woman, as something of real worth — divine, heavenly, ay, though we know not how, in a most deep sense eternal; which makes our reason give the lie to all merely logical and sentimental maunderings of moralists about "the fleeting hues of this our painted clay"; telling men, as the old Hebrew Scriptures tell them, that physical beauty is the deepest of all spiritual symbols; and that though beauty without discretion be the jewel of gold in the swine's snout, yet the jewel of gold it is still, the sacrament of an inward beauty, which ought to be, perhaps hereafter may be, fulfilled in spirit and in truth. Not only this, which whispered to him — and who shall say that the whisper was of the earth, or of the lower world? — "She is too beautiful to be utterly evil;" but the very defect in her creed which he had just discovered, drew him towards her again. She had no Gospel for the Magdalene, because she was a Pagan..... That, then, was the fault of her Paganism, not of herself. She felt for Pelagia: but even if she had not, was not that, too, the fault of her Paganism? And for that Paganism who was to be blamed? She?.... Was he the man to affirm that? Had he not seen scandals, stupidities, brutalities, enough to shake even his faith, educated a Christian? How much more excuse for her, more delicate, more acute, more lofty than he; the child, too, of a heathen father? Her perfections, were they not her own? — her defects, those of her circumstances?.... And had she not welcomed him, guarded him, taught him, honoured him?.... Could he turn against her? — above all now in her distress — perhaps her danger? Was he not bound to her, if by nothing else, by gratitude? Was not he, of all men, bound to believe that all she required to make her perfect was conversion to the true faith?.... And that first dream of converting her arose almost as bright as ever..... Then he was checked by the thought of his first utter failure..... At least, if he could not convert her, he could love her, pray for her..... No, he could not even do that; for to whom could he pray? He had to repent, to be forgiven, to humble himself by penitence, perhaps for years, ere he could hope to be heard even for himself, much less for another..... And so backwards and forwards swayed his hope and purpose, till he was roused from his meditation by the voice of the little porter, summoning him to his evening meal; and recollecting, for the first time, that he had tasted no food that day, he went down, half-unwillingly, and ate.

But as he, the porter, and his negro wife were sitting silently and sadly enough together, Miriam came in, apparently in high good humour, and lingered a moment on her way to her own apartments upstairs.

"Eh? At supper? And nothing but lentils and watermelons, when the flesh-pots of Egypt have been famous any time these two thousand years. Ah! but times are changed since then!.... You have worn out the old Hebrew hints, you miserable Gentiles you, and got a Cæsar instead of a Joseph! Hist, you hussies!" cried she to the girls upstairs, clapping her hands loudly. "Here! bring us down one of those roast chickens, and a bottle of the wine of wines — the wine with the green seal, you careless daughters of Midian, you, with your wits running on the men, I'll warrant, every minute I've been out of the house! Ah, you'll smart for it some day — you'll smart for it some day, you daughters of Adam's first wife!" Down came, by the hands of one of the Syrian slave-girls, the fowl and the wine.

"There, now; we'll all sup together. Wine, that maketh glad the heart of man! — Youth, you were a monk once, so you have read all about that, eh? and about the best wine which goes down sweetly, causing the lips of them that are asleep to speak. And rare wine it was, I warrant, which the blessed Solomon had in his little country cellar up there in Lebanon. We'll try if this is not a very fair substitute for it, though. Come, my little man-monkey, drink and forget your sorrow! You shall be temple-sweeper to Beelzebub yet, I promise you. Look at it there, creaming and curdling, the darling! purring like a cat at the very thought of touching human lips! As sweet as honey, as strong as fire, as clear as amber! Drink, ye children of Gehenna; and make good use of the little time that is left you between this and the unquenchable fire!"

And tossing a cup of it down her own throat, as if it had been water, she watched her companions with a meaning look, as they drank.

The little porter followed her example gallantly. Philammon looked, and longed, and sipped blushingly and bashfully, and tried to fancy that he did not care for it; and sipped again, being willing enough to forget his sorrow also for. a moment; the negress refused with fear and trembling — "She had a vow on her."

"Satan possess you and your vow! Drink, you coal out of Tophet! Do you think it is poisoned? You, the only creature in the world that I should not enjoy ill-using, because every one else ill-uses you already without my help! Drink, I say, or I'll turn you pea-green from head to foot!"

The negress put the cup to her lips, and contrived, for her own reasons, to spill the contents unobserved.

"A very fine lecture that of the Lady Hypatia's the other morning, on Helen's nepenthe," quoth the little porter, growing philosophic as the wine-fumes rose. "Such a power of extracting the cold water of philosophy out of the bottomless pit of Mythus, I never did hear. Did you ever, my Philammonidion?"

"Aha! she and I were talking about that half-an-hour ago," said Miriam.

"What! have you seen her?" asked Philammon, with a flutter of the heart.

"If you mean, did she mention you, — why, then, yes!"

"How? — how?"

"Talked of a young Phœbus Apollo — without mentioning names, certainly, but in the most sensible, and practical, and hopeful way — the wisest speech that I have heard from her this twelvemonth."

Philammon blushed scarlet.

"And that," thought he, "in spite of what passed this morning! — Why, what is the matter with our host?"

"He has taken Solomon's advice, and forgotten his sorrow."

And so, indeed, he had; for he was sleeping sweetly, with open lacklustre eyes, and a maudlin smile at the ceiling; while the negress, with her head fallen on her chest, seemed equally unconscious of their presence.

"We'll see," quoth Miriam; and taking up the lamp, she held the flame unceremoniously to the arm of each of them; but neither winced nor stirred.

"Surely, your wine is not drugged?" said Philammon, in trepidation.

"Why not? What has made them beasts may make us angels. You seem none the less lively for it! Do I?"

"But drugged wine?"

"Why not? The same who made wine made poppy-juice. Both will make man happy. Why not use both?"

"It is poison!"

"It is the nepenthe, as I told Hypatia, whereof she was twaddling mysticism this morning. Drink, child, drink! I have no mind to put you to sleep to-night! I want to make a man of you, or rather, to see whether you are one!"

And she drained another cup, and then went on, half talking to herself, —

"Ay, it is poison; and music is poison; and woman is poison, according to the new creed, Pagan and Christian; and wine will be poison, and meat will be poison, some day; and we shall have a world full of mad Nebuchadnezzars, eating grass like oxen. It is poisonous, and brutal, and devilish, to be a man, and not a monk, and an eunuch, and a dry branch. You are all in the same lie, Christians and philosophers, Cyril and Hypatia! Don't interrupt me, but drink, young fool! —— Ay, and the only man who keeps his manhood, the only man who is not ashamed to be what God has made him, is your Jew. You will find yourselves in want of him after all, some day, you besotted Gentiles, to bring you back to common sense and common manhood. — In want of him and his grand old books, which you despise while you make idols of them, about Abraham, and Jacob, and Moses, and David, and Solomon, whom you call saints, you miserable hypocrites, though they did what you are too dainty to do, and had their wives and their children, and thanked God for a beautiful woman, as Adam did before them, and their sons do after them — Drink, I say — and believed that God had really made the world, and not the devil, and had given them the lordship over it, as you will find out to your cost some day!"

Philammon heard, and could not answer; and on she rambled.

"And music, too? Our priests were not afraid of sack-but and psaltery, dulcimer and trumpet, in the house of the Lord; for they knew who had given them the cunning to make them. Our prophets were not afraid of calling for music, when they wished to prophesy, and letting it soften and raise their souls, and open and quicken them till they saw into the inner harmony of things, and beheld the future in the present; for they knew who made the melody and harmony, and made them the outward symbols of the inward song which runs through sun and stars, storm and tempest, fulfilling His word — in that these sham philosophers the heathen are wiser than those Christian monks. Try it! — try it! Come with me! Leave these sleepers here, and come to my rooms. You long to be as wise as Solomon. Then get at wisdom as Solomon did, and give your heart first to know folly and madness..... You have read the Book of the Preacher?"

Poor Philammon! He was no longer master of himself. The arguments — the wine — the terrible spell of the old woman's voice and eye, and the strong overpowering will which showed out through them, dragged him along in spite of himself. As if in a dream, he followed her up the stairs.

"There, throw away that stupid, ugly, shapeless, philosopher's cloak. So! You have on the white tunic I gave you? And now you look as a human being should. And you have been to the baths to-day? Well — you have the comfort of feeling now like other people, and having that alabaster skin as white as it was created, instead of being tanned like a brute's hide. Drink, I say! Ay — what was that face, that figure made for? Bring a mirror here, hussy! There, look in that, and judge for yourself! Were those lips rounded for nothing? Why were those eyes set in your head, and made to sparkle bright as jewels, sweet as mountain honey? Why were those curls laid ready for soft fingers to twine themselves among them, and look all the whiter among the glossy black knots? Judge for yourself!"

Alas! poor Philammon!

"And after all," thought he, "is it not true, as well as pleasant?"

"Sing to the poor boy, girls! — sing to him! and teach him for the first time in his little ignorant life, the old road to inspiration!"

One of the slave-girls sat down on the divan, and took up a double flute; while the other rose, and accompanying the plaintive dreamy air with a slow dance, and delicate tinklings of her silver armlets and anklets, and the sistrum which she held aloft, she floated gracefully round and round the floor, and sang—

Why were we born, but for bliss?
Why are we ripe, but to fall?
Dream not that duty can bar thee from beauty,
Like water and sunshine, the heir-loom of all.

Lips were made only to kiss;
  Hands were made only to toy;
Eyes were made only to lure on the lonely,
The longing, the loving, and drown them in joy!

Alas, for poor Philammon! And yet no! The very poison brought with it its own antidote; and, shaking off by one strong effort of will the spell of the music and the wine, he sprang to his feet.....

"Never! If love means no more than that — if it is to be a mere delicate self-indulgence, worse than the brute's, because it requires the prostration of nobler faculties, and a selfishness the more huge in proportion to the greatness of the soul which is crushed inward by it — then I will have none of it! I have had my dream — yes I but it was of one who should be at once my teacher and my pupil, my debtor and my queen — who should lean on me, and yet support me — supply my defects, although with lesser light, as the old moon fills up the circle of the new — labour with me side by side in some great work — rising with me for ever as I rose: — and this is the base substitute! Never!"

Whether or not this was unconsciously forced into words by the vehemence of his passion, or whether the old Jewess heard, or pretended to hear, a footstep coming up the stair, she at all events sprang instantly to her feet.

"Hist! Silence, girls! I hear a visitor. What mad maiden has come to beg a love-charm of the poor old witch at this time of night? Or have the Christian bloodhounds tracked the old lioness of Judah to her den at last? We'll see!"

And she drew a dagger from her girdle, and stepped boldly to the door.

As she went out she turned —

"So! my brave young Apollo! You do not admire simple woman? You must have something more learned: and intellectual, and spiritual, and so forth. I wonder. whether Eve, when she came to Adam in the garden, brought with her a certificate of proficiency in the seven s sciences? Well, well — like must after like. Perhaps we shall be able to suit you after all. Vanish, daughters of Midian!"

The girls vanished accordingly, whispering and laughing; and Philammon found himself alone. Although he was somewhat soothed by the old woman's last speech, yet a sense of terror, of danger, of coming temptation, kept him standing sternly on his feet, looking warily round the chamber, lest a fresh siren should emerge from behind some curtain or heap of pillows.

On one side of the room he perceived a doorway, filled by a curtain of gauze, from behind which came the sound of whispering voices. His fear, growing with the general excitement of his mind, rose into anger as he began to suspect some snare; and he faced round towards the curtain, and stood like a wild beast at bay, ready, with uplifted arm, for all evil spirits, male or female.

"And he will show himself? How shall I accost him?" whispered a well-known voice — could it be Hypatia's? And then the guttural Hebrew accent of the old woman answered —

"As you spoke of him this morning ——— "

"Oh! I will tell him all, and he must — he must have mercy! But he? — so awful, so glorious! ——— "

What the answer was, he could not hear: but the next moment a sweet heavy scent, as of narcotic gums, filled the room — mutterings of incantations — and then a blaze of light, in which the curtain vanished, and disclosed to his astonished eyes, enveloped in a glory of luminous smoke, the hag standing by a tripod, and, kneeling by her, Hypatia herself, robed in pure white, glittering with diamonds and gold, her lips parted, her head thrown back, her arms stretched out in an agony of expectation.

In an instant, before he had time to stir, she had sprung through the blaze, and was kneeling at his feet.

" Phœbus! beautiful, glorious, ever young! Hear me! only

a moment! only this once!"

Her drapery had caught fire from the tripod, but she did not heed it. Philammon instinctively clasped her in his arms, and crushed it out, as she cried —

"Have mercy on me! Tell me the secret! I will obey thee! I have no self — I am thy slave! Kill me, if thou wilt: but speak!"

The blaze sank into a soft, warm, mellow gleam, and beyond it what appeared?

The negro-woman, with one finger upon her lips, as with an imploring, all but despairing, look, she held up to him her little crucifix.

He saw it. What thoughts flashed through him, like the lightning bolt, at that blessed sign of infinite self-sacrifice, I say not; let those who know it judge for themselves. But in another instant he had spurned from him the poor deluded maiden, whose idolatrous ecstasies he saw instantly were not meant for himself, and rushed desperately across the room, looking for an outlet.

He found a door in the darkness — a room — a window — and in another moment he had leapt twenty feet into the street, rolled over, bruised and bleeding, rose again like an Antæus, with new strength, and darted off towards the archbishop's house.

And poor Hypatia lay half senseless on the floor, with the Jewess watching her bitter tears — not merely of disappointment, but of utter shame. For as Philammon fled she had recognised those well-known features; and the veil was lifted from her eyes, and the hope and the self. respect of Theon's daughter were gone for ever.

Her righteous wrath was too deep for upbraidings. Slowly she rose; returned into the inner room; wrapped her cloak deliberately around her; and went silently away, with one look at the Jewess of solemn scorn and defiance.

"Ah! I can afford a few sulky looks to-night!" said the old woman to herself, with a smile, as she picked up from the floor the prize for which she had been plotting so long — Raphael's half of the black agate.

"I wonder whether she will miss it! Perhaps she will have no fancy for its company, any longer, now that she has discovered what over-palpable archangels appear when she rubs it. But if she does try to recover it.... why — let her try her strength with mine: — or, rather, with a Christian mob."

And then, drawing from her bosom the other half of the talisman, she fitted the two pieces together again and again, fingering them over, and poring upon them with tear-brimming eyes, till she had satisfied herself that the fracture still fitted exactly; while she murmured to herself from time to time — "Oh, that he were here! Oh, that he would return now — now! It may be too late tomorrow! Stay — I will go and consult the teraph; it may know where he is."....

And she departed to her incantations; while Hypatia threw herself upon her bed at home, and filled the chamber with a long, low wailing, as of a child in pain, until the dreary dawn broke on her shame and her despair. And then she rose, and rousing herself for one great effort, calmly prepared a last oration, in which she intended to bid farewell for ever to Alexandria and to the schools.

Philammon mean while was striding desperately up the main street which led towards the Serapeium. But he was not destined to arrive there as soon as he had hoped to do. For ere he had gone half-a-mile, behold a crowd advancing towards him blocking up the whole street.

The mass seemed endless. Thousands of torches flared above their heads, and from the heart of the procession rose a solemn chant, in which Philammon soon recognised a well-known Catholic hymn. He was half-minded to turn up some by-street, and escape meeting them. But on attempting to do so, he found every avenue which he tried similarly blocked up by a tributary stream of people; and, almost ere he was aware, was entangled in the vanguard of the great column.

"Let me pass!" cried he, in a voice of entreaty.

"Pass, thou heathen?"

In vain he protested his Christianity.

"Origenist, Donatist, heretic! Whither should a good Catholic be going to-night, save to the Cæsareium?"

"My friends, my friends, I have no business at the Cæsareium!" cried he, in utter despair. "I am on my way to seek a private interview with the patriarch, on matters of importance."

"Oh, liar! who pretends to be known to the patriarch, and yet is ignorant that this night he visits at the Cæsareium the most sacred corpse of the martyr Ammonius!''

"What! Is Cyril with you?"

"He and all his clergy."

"Better so; better in public," said Philammon to himself; and, turning, he joined the crowd.

Onward, with chant and dirge, they swept out through the Sun-gate, upon the harbour esplanade, and wheeled to the right along the quay, while the torchlight bathed in a red glare the great front of the Cæsareium, and the tall obelisks before it, and the masts of the thousand ships which lay in the harbour on their left; and last, but not least, before the huge dim mass of the palace which bounded the esplanade in front, a long line of glittering helmets and cuirasses, behind a barrier of cables which stretched from the shore to the corner of the museum.

There was a sudden halt; a low ominous growl; and then the mob pressed onward from behind, surged up almost to the barrier. The soldiers dropped the points of their lances, and stood firm. Again the mob recoiled; again surged forward. Fierce cries arose; some of the boldest stooped to pick up stones: but, luckily, the pavement was too firm for them..... Another moment, and the whole soldiery of Alexandria would have been fighting for life and death against fifty thousand Christians.....

But Cyril had not forgotten his generalship. Reckless as that night's events proved him to be about arousing the passions of his subjects, he was yet far too wary to risk the odium and the danger of a night attack, which even if successful, would have cost the lives of hundreds. He knew well enough the numbers and the courage of the enemy, and the certainty that, in case of a collision, no quarter would be given or accepted on either side..... Beside, if a battle must take place — and that, of course, must happen sooner or later — it must not happen in his presence and under his sanction. He was in the right now, and Orestes in the wrong; and in the right he would keep — at least till his express to Byzantium should have returned, and Orestes was either proscribed or superseded. So looking forward to some such chance as this, the wary prelate had schooled his aides-de-camp, the deacons of the city, and went on his way up the steps of the Cæsareium, knowing that they could be trusted to keep the peace outside.

And they did their work well. Before a blow had been

struck, or even an insult passed on either side, they had burst through the front rank of the mob, and by stout threats of excommunication, enjoined not only peace, but absolute silence until the sacred ceremony which was about to take place should be completed; and enforced their commands by marching up and down like sentries between the hostile ranks for the next weary two hours, till the very soldiers broke out into expressions of admiration, and the tribune of the cohort, who had no great objection, but also no great wish, to fight, paid them a high-flown compliment on their laudable endeavours to maintain public order, and received the somewhat ambiguous reply, that the "weapons of their warfare were not carnal, that they wrestled not against flesh and blood, but against principalities and powers"…. an answer which the tribune, being now somewhat sleepy, thought it best to leave unexplained.

In the mean while, there had passed up the steps of the Temple a gorgeous line of priests, among whom glittered, more gorgeous than all, the stately figure of the pontiff. They were followed close by thousands of monks, not only from Alexandria and Nitria, but from all the adjoining towns and monasteries. And as Philammon, unable for some half-hour more to force his way into the church, watched their endless stream, he could well believe the boast which he had so often heard in Alexandria, that one half of the population of Egypt was at that moment in "religious orders."

After the monks, the laity began to enter; but even then so vast was the crowd, and so dense the crush upon the steps, that before he could force his way into the church, Cyril's sermon had begun.

* * * * * *

— "What went ye out for to see? A man clothed in soft raiment? Nay, such are in kings' palaces, and in the palaces of prefects who would needs be emperors, and cast away the Lord's bonds from them, — of whom it is written, that He that sitteth in the heavens laugheth them to scorn, and taketh the wicked in their own snare, and maketh the devices of princes of none effect. Ay, in kings' palaces, and in theatres too, where the rich of this world, poor in faith, deny their covenant, and defile their baptismal robes that they may do honour to the devourers of the earth. Woe to them who think that they may partake of the cup of the Lord and the cup of devils. Woe to them who will praise with the same mouth Aphrodite the fiend, and her of whom it is written that He was born of a pure Virgin. Let such be excommunicate from the cup of the Lord, and from the congregation of the Lord, till they have purged away their sins by penance and by almsgiving. But for you, ye poor of this world, rich in faith, you whom the rich despise, hale before the judgment seats, and blaspheme that holy name whereby ye are called — what went ye out into the wilderness to see? A prophet? — Ay, and more than a prophet — a martyr! More than a prophet, more than a king, more than a prefect: whose theatre was the sands of the desert, whose throne was the cross, whose crown was bestowed, not by heathen philosophers and daughters of Satan, deceiving men with the works of their fathers, but by angels and archangels; a crown of glory, the victor's laurel, which grows for ever in the paradise of the highest heaven. Call him no more Ammonius, call him Thaumasius, wonderful! Wonderful in his poverty, wonderful in his zeal, wonderful in his faith, wonderful in his fortitude, wonderful in his death, most wonderful in the manner of that death. Oh, thrice blessed, who has merited the honour of the cross itself! What can follow, but that one so honoured in the flesh should also be honoured in the life which he now lives, and that from the virtue of these thrice-holy limbs the leper should be cleansed, the dumb should speak, the very dead be raised? Yes; it were impiety to doubt it. Consecrated by the cross, this flesh shall not only rest in hope but work in power. Approach, and be healed! Approach, and see the glory of the saints, the glory of the poor. Approach, and learn that that which man despises, God hath highly esteemed; that that which man rejects, God accepts; that that which roan punishes, God rewards. Approach, and see how God hath chosen the foolish things of this world to confound the wise, and the weak things of this world to confound the strong. Man abhors the cross: The Son of God condescended to endure it! Man tramples on the poor: The Son of God hath not where to lay his head. Man passes by the sick as useless: The Son of God chooses them to be partakers of his sufferings, that the glory of God may be made manifest in them. Man curses the publican, while he employs him to fill his coffers with the plunder of the poor: The Son of God calls him from the receipt of custom to be an apostle, higher than the kings of the earth. Man casts away the harlot like a faded flower, when he has tempted her to become the slave of sin for a season: and The Son of God calls her, the defiled, the despised, the forsaken, to Himself, accepts her tears, blesses her offering, and declares that her sins are forgiven, for she hath loved much: while to whom little is forgiven the same loveth little."....

Philammon heard no more. With the passionate and impulsive nature of a Greek fanatic, he burst forward through the crowd, toward the steps which led to the choir, and above which, in front of the altar, stood the corpse of Ammonius, enclosed in a coffin of glass, beneath a gorgeous canopy; and never stopping till he found himself in front of Cyril's pulpit, he threw himself upon his face upon the pavement, spread out his arms in the form of a cross, and lay silent and motionless before the feet of the multitude.

There was a sudden whisper and rustle in the congregation: but Cyril, after a moment's pause, went on —

"Man, in his pride and self-sufficiency, despises humiliation, and penance, and the broken and the contrite heart and tells thee that only as long as thou doest well unto thyself will he speak well of thee: The Son of God says that he that humbleth himself, even as this our penitent brother, he it is who shall be exalted. He it is of whom it is written that his father saw him afar off, and ran to meet him, and bade put the best robe on him, and a ring on his hand, and shoes on his feet, and make merry and be glad with the choir of angels who rejoice over one sinner that repenteth. Arise, my son, whosoever thou art; and go in peace for this night, remembering that he who said 'My belly cleaveth unto the pavement,' hath said also, 'Rejoice not against me, Satan, mine enemy, for when I fall I shall arise!' "

A thunderclap of applause, surely as pardonable as any an Alexandrian church ever heard, followed this dexterous, and yet most righteous, turn of the patriarch's oratory: but Philammon raised himself slowly and fearfully to his knees, and blushing scarlet, endured the gaze of ten thousand eyes.

Suddenly, from beside the pulpit, an old man sprang forward, and clasped him round the neck. It was Arsenius.

"My son! my son!" sobbed he, almost aloud.

"Slave, as well as son, if you will!" whispered Philammon. "One boon from the patriarch; and then home to the Laura for ever!"....

"Oh, twice-blest night," rolled on above the deep rich voice of Cyril, "which beholds at once the coronation of a martyr, and the conversion of a sinner; which increases at the same time the ranks of the church triumphant, and of the church militant; and pierces celestial essences with a twofold rapture of thanksgiving, as they welcome on high a victorious, and on earth a repentant, brother!"

And at a sign from Cyril, Peter the Reader stepped forward, and led away, gently enough, the two weepers, who were welcomed as they passed by the blessings, and prayers, and tears even of those fierce fanatics of Nitria. Nay, Peter himself, as he turned to leave them together in the sacristy, held out his hand to Philammon.

"I ask your forgiveness," said the poor boy, who plunged eagerly and with a sort of delight into any and every self-abasement.

"And I accord it," quoth Peter; and returned to the church, looking, and probably feeling, in a far more pleasant mood than usual.

CHAPTER XXVII
THE PRODIGAL'S RETURN

ABOUT ten o'clock the next morning, as Hypatia, worn out with sleepless sorrow, was trying to arrange her thoughts for the farewell lecture, her favourite maid announced that a messenger from Synesius waited below. A letter from Synesius? A gleam of hope flashed across her mind. From him, surely, might come something of comfort, of advice. Ah! if he only knew how sorely she was bested!

"Let him send up his letter."

"He refuses to deliver it to any one but yourself. And I think," — added the damsel, who had, to tell the truth, at that moment in her purse a substantial reason for so thinking — "I think it might be worth your ladyship's while to see him."

Hypatia shook her head impatiently.

"He seems to know you well, madam, though he refuses to tell his name: but he bade me put you in mind of a black agate — I cannot tell what he meant — of a black agate, and a spirit which was to appear when you rubbed it."

Hypatia turned pale as death. Was it Philammon again? She felt for the talisman — it was gone! She must have lost it last night in Miriam's chamber. Now she saw the true purpose of the old hag's plot — .... deceived, tricked, doubly tricked! And what new plot was this?

"Tell him to leave the letter, and begone.... My father? What? Who is this? Whom are you bringing to me at such a moment?"

And as she spoke, Theon ushered into the chamber no other than Raphael Aben-Ezra, and then retired.

He advanced slowly towards her, and falling on one knee, placed in her hand Synesius's letter.

Hypatia trembled from head to foot at the unexpected apparition..... Well; at least he could know nothing of last night and its disgrace. But not daring to look him in the face, she took the letter, and opened it..... If she had hoped for comfort from it, her hope was not realized.

"Synesius to the Philosopher:

"Even if Fortune cannot take from me all things, yet what she can take she will. And yet of two things, at least, she shall not rob me — to prefer that which is best, and to succour the oppressed. Heaven forbid that she should overpower my judgment, as well as the rest of me! Therefore I do hate injustice; for that I can do; and my will is to stop it; but the power to do so is among the things of which she has bereaved me — before, too, she bereaved me of my children.....

       'Once, in old times, Milesian men were strong.'

And there was a time when I, too, was a comfort to my friends, and when you used to call me a blessing to every one except myself, as I squandered for the benefit of others the favour with which the great regarded me..... My hands they were — then ..... But now I am left desolate of all: unless you have any power. For you and virtue I count among those good things, of which none can deprive me. But you always have power, and will have it, surely, now — using it as nobly as you do.

"As for Nicæus and Philolaus, two noble youths, and kinsmen of my own, let it be the business of all who honour you, both private men and magistrates, to see that they return possessors of their just rights." [5]

"Of all who honour me!" said she, with a bitter sigh: and then looked up quickly at Raphael, as if fearful of having betrayed herself. She turned deadly pale. In his eyes was a look of solemn pity, which told her that he knew — not all? — surely not all?

"Have you seen the — Miriam?" gasped she, rushing desperately at that which she most dreaded.

"Not yet. I arrived but one hour ago; and Hypatia's welfare is still more important to me than my own."

"My welfare? It is gone!"

"So much the better. I never found mine till I lost it."

"What do you mean?"

Raphael lingered, yet without withdrawing his gaze, as if he had something of importance to say, which he longed and yet feared to utter. At last —

"At least, you will confess that I am better drest than when we met last. I have returned, you see, like a certain demoniac of

---

[5] An authentic letter of Synesius to Hypatia.

Gadara, about whom we used to argue, clothed — and perhaps also in my right mind..... God knows!

"Raphael! are you come here to mock me? You know — you cannot have been here an hour without knowing — that but yesterday I dreamed of being" — and she dropped her eyes — " an empress; that to-day I am ruined; to-morrow, perhaps, proscribed. Have you no speech for me but your old sarcasms and ambiguities?"

Raphael stood silent and motionless.

"Why do you not speak? What is the meaning of this sad, earnest look, so different from your former self?.... You have something strange to tell me!"

"I have," said he, speaking very slowly. "What — what would Hypatia answer if, after all, Aben-Ezra said, like the dying Julian, 'The Galilæan has conquered'?"

"Julian never said it! It is a monkish calumny."

"But I say it."

"Impossible!"

"I say it!"

"As your dying speech? The true Raphael Aben-Ezra, then, lives no more!"

"But he may be born again."

"And die to philosophy, that he may be born again into barbaric superstition! Oh worthy metempsychosis I Farewell, sir!" And she rose to go.

"Hear me! — hear me patiently this once, noble, beloved Hypatia! One more sneer of yours, and I may become again the same case-hardened fiend which you knew me of old — to all, at least, but you. Oh, do not think me ungrateful, forgetful! What do I not owe to you, whose pure and lofty words alone kept smouldering in me the dim remembrance that there was a Right, a Truth, an unseen world of spirits, after whose pattern man should aspire to live?"

She paused, and listened in wonder. What faith had she of her own? She would at least hear what he had found.....

"Hypatia, I am older than you — wiser than you, if wisdom be the fruit of the tree of knowledge. You know but one side of the medal, Hypatia, and the fairer; I have seen its reverse as well as its obverse. Through every form of human thought, of human action, of human sin and folly, have I been wandering for years, and found no rest — as little in wisdom as in folly, in spiritual dreams as in sensual brutality. I could not rest in your Platonism — I will tell you why hereafter. I went on to Stoicism, Epicurism, Cynicism, Scepticism, and in that lowest deep I found a lower depth, when I became sceptical of Scepticism itself."

"There is a lower deep still," thought Hypatia to herself, as she recollected last night's magic; but she did not speak.

"Then, in utter abasement, I confessed myself lower than the brutes, who had a law, and obeyed it, while I was my own lawless God, devil, harpy, whirlwind..... I needed even my own dog to awaken in me the brute consciousness of my own existence, or of anything without myself. I took her, the dog, for my teacher, and obeyed her, for she was wiser than I. And she led me back — the poor dumb beast — like a God-sent and God-obeying angel, to human nature, to mercy, to self-sacrifice, to belief, to worship — to pure and wedded love."

Hypatia started..... And in the struggle to hide her own bewilderment, answered almost without knowing it —

"Wedded love?.... Wedded love? Is that, then, the paltry bait by which Raphael Aben-Ezra has been tempted to desert philosophy?"

"Thank Heaven!" said Raphael to himself. "She does not care for me, then! If she had, pride would have kept her from that sneer." "Yes, my dear lady," answered he, aloud, "to desert philosophy, the search after wisdom; because wisdom itself had sought for me, and found me. But, indeed, I had hoped that you would have approved of my following your example for once in my life, and resolving, like you, to enter into the estate of wedlock."

"Do not sneer at me!" cried she, in her turn, looking up at him with shame and horror, which made him repent of uttering the words. "If you do not know — you will soon, too soon! Never mention that hateful dream to me, if you wish to have speech of me more!"

A pang of remorse shot through Raphael's heart. Who but he himself had plotted that evil marriage? But she gave him no opportunity of answering her, and went on hurriedly —

"Speak to me rather about yourself. What is this strange and sudden betrothal? What has it to do with Christianity? I had thought that it was rather by the glories of celibacy — gross and superstitious as their notions of it are — that the Galilæans tempted their converts."

"So had I, my dearest lady," answered he, as, glad return the subject for a moment, and perhaps a little nettle by her contemptuous tone, he resumed something of his old arch and careless manner. "But — there is no accounting for man's agreeable inconsistencies — one morning found myself, to my astonishment, seized by two bishops and betrothed, whether I chose or not, to a young lady who but a few days before had been destined for a nunnery."

"Two bishops?"

"I speak simple truth. The one was Synesius, of course; — that most incoherent and most benevolent of busy bodies chose to betray me behind my back: — but I will not trouble you with that part of my story. The real wonder is, that the other episcopal match-maker was Augustine of Hippo himself!"

"Anything to bribe a convert," said Hypatia, contemptuously.

"I assure you, no. He informed me, and her also openly and uncivilly enough, that he thought us very much to be pitied for so great a fall..... But as we neither of us seemed to have any call for the higher life of celibacy, he could not press it on us..... We should have trouble in the flesh. But if we married we had not sinned. To which I answered that my humility was quite content to sit in the very lowest ranks, with Abraham Isaac, and Jacob..... He replied by an encomium of virginity, in which I seemed to hear again the voice of Hypatia herself."

"And sneered at it inwardly, as you used to sneer at me."

"Really, I was in no sneering mood at that moment and whatsoever I may have felt inclined to reply, he was kind enough to say for me and himself the next minute."

"What do you mean?"

"He went on, to my utter astonishment, by such an eulogium on wedlock as I never heard from Jew or heathen and ended by advice to young married folk so thorough excellent and to the point, that I could not help telling him, when he stopped, what a pity I thought it that he had not himself married, and made some good woman happy by putting his own recipes into practice..... And at that, Hypatia, I saw an expression on his face which made me wish for the moment that I had bitten out this impudent tongue of mine, before I so rashly touched some deep old wound..... That man has wept bitter tears ere now, be sure of it..... But he turned the conversation instantly, like a well-bred gentleman as he is, by saying, with the sweetest smile, that though he had made it a solemn rule never to be a party to making up any marriage, yet in our case Heaven had so plainly pointed us out for each other, &c. &c., that he could not refuse himself the pleasure.... and ended by a blessing as kindly as ever came from the lips of man."

"You seem wonderfully taken with the sophist of Hippo," said Hypatia, impatiently; "and forget, perhaps, that his opinions, especially when, as you confess, they are utterly inconsistent with themselves, are not quite as important to me as they seem to have become to you."

"Whether he be consistent or not about marriage," said Raphael, somewhat proudly, "I care little. I went to him to tell me, not about the relation of the sexes, on which point I am probably as good a judge as he — but about God; and on that subject he told me enough to bring me back to Alexandria, that I might undo, if possible, somewhat of the wrong which I have done to Hypatia."

"What wrong have you done me?.... You are silent? Be sure, at least, that whatsoever it may be, you will not wipe it out by trying to make a proselyte of me!"

"Be not too sure of that. I have found too great a treasure not to wish to share it with Theon's daughter."

"A treasure?" said she, half scornfully.

"Yes, indeed. You recollect my last words, when we Parted there below a few months ago?"

Hypatia was silent. One terrible possibility at which he had hinted flashed across her memory for the first time Since;.... but she spurned proudly from her the heaven-sent warning.

"I told you that, like Diogenes, I went forth to seek a man. Did I not promise you, that when I had found one you should be the first to hear of him? And I have found a man."

Hypatia waved her beautiful hand. "I know whom you would say.... that crucified one. Be it so. I want not a man, but a god."

"What sort of a god, Hypatia? A god made up a our own

intellectual notions, or rather of negations of then — of infinity and eternity, and invisibility, and impassibility — and why not of immortality, too, Hypatia? For I recollect we used to agree that it was a carnal degrading of the Supreme One to predicate of Him so merely human a thin as virtue."

Hypatia was silent.

"Now I have always had a sort of fancy that what we wanted, as the first predicate of our Absolute One, was that He was to be not merely an infinite God — whatever that meant, which I suspect we did not always see quite clearly — or an eternal one — or an omnipotent one — or every merely a one God at all; none of which predicates, I fear did we understand more clearly than the first: but that He must be a righteous God: — or rather, as we used sometimes to say that He was to have no predicate — Righteousness itself. And all along, I could not help remembering that my old sacred Hebrew books told me of such a once and feeling that they might have something to tell me which ———— "

"Which I did not tell you! And this, then, cause your air of reserve, and of sly superiority over the woman whom you mocked by calling her your pupil! I little suspected you of so truly Jewish a jealousy! Why, o, why, did you not tell me this?"

"Because I was a beast, Hypatia; and had all but for gotten what this righteousness was like; and was afraid to find out lest it should condemn me. Because I was devil, Hypatia; and hated righteousness, and neither wished to see you righteous, or God righteous either, because there you would both have been unlike myself. God be merciful to me a sinner!"

She looked up in his face. The man was changed as by miracle — and yet not changed. There was the same gallant consciousness of power, the same subtle and humorous twinkle in those strong ripe Jewish features and those glittering eyes: and yet every line in his face was softened, sweetened; the mask of sneering faineance was gone — imploring tenderness and earnestness beamed from his whole countenance. The chrysalis case had fallen off, and disclosed the butterfly within. She sat looking at him, and past her hand across her eyes, as if to try whether the apparition would not vanish. He, the subtle! — he, the mocker! — he, the Lucian of Alexandria! — he whose depth and power had awed her, even in his most polluted days..... And this was the end of him.....

"It is a freak of cowardly superstition..... Those Christians have been frightening him about his sins and their Tartarus."

She looked again into his bright, clear, fearless face, and was ashamed of her own calumny. And this was the end of him — of Synesius — of Augustine — of learned and unlearned, Goth and Roman..... The great flood would have its way, then..... Could she alone fight against it?

She could! Would she submit? — She? Her will should stand firm, her reason free, to the last — to the death if need be..... And yet last night! — last night!

At last she spoke, without looking up.

"And what if you have found a man in that crucified one? Have you found in him a God also?"

"Does Hypatia recollect Glaucon's definition of the perfectly righteous man?.... How, without being guilty of one unrighteous act, he must labour his life long under the imputation of being utterly unrighteous, in order that his disinterestedness may be thoroughly tested, and by proceeding in such a course, arrive inevitably, as Glaucon says, not only in Athens of old, or in Judæa of old, but, as you yourself will agree, in Christian Alexandria at this moment, at — do you remember, Hypatia? — bonds, and the scourge, and lastly, at the cross itself..... If Plato's idea of the righteous man be a crucified one, why may not mine also? If as we both — and old Bishop Clemens, too — as good a Platonist as we, remember — and Augustine himself, would agree, Plato in speaking those strange words, spoke not of himself, but by The Spirit of God, why should not others have spoken by the same Spirit when they spoke the same words?"

"A crucified man.... Yes. But a crucified God, Raphael! I shudder at the blasphemy."

"So do my poor dear fellow-countrymen. Are they the more righteous in their daily doings, Hypatia, on account of their fancied reverence for the glory of One who probably knows best how to preserve and manifest His own glory? But you assent to the definition? Take care! said he, with one of his arch smiles, "I have been fighting with Augustine, and have become of late a terrible dialectician. Do you assent to it?"

"Of course — it is Plato's."

"But do you assent merely because it is written in the book

called Plato's, or because your reason tells you that it is true?.... You will not tell me. Tell me this, then at least. Is not the perfectly righteous man the highest specimen of men?"

"Surely," said she, half carelessly: but not unwilling like a philosopher and a Greek, as a matter of course, to embark in anything like a word-battle, and to shut out sadder thoughts for a moment.

"Then must not the Autanthropos, the archetypal and ideal man, who is more perfect than any individual specie men, be perfectly righteous also?"

"Yes."

"Suppose, then, for the sake of one of those pleasant old games of ours, an argument, that he wished to manifest his righteousness to the world..... The only method for him, according to Plato, would be Glaucon's, of calumny and persecution, the scourge and the cross?"

"What words are these, Raphael? Material scourge and crosses for an eternal and spiritual idea?"

"Did you ever yet, Hypatia, consider at leisure what the archetype of man might be like?"

Hypatia started, as at a new thought, and confessed — as every Neo-Platonist would have done — that she had never done so.

"And yet our master, Plato, bade us believe that there was a substantial archetype of each thing, from a flowed to a nation, eternal in the heavens. Perhaps we have not been faithful Platonists enough heretofore, my dearest tutor. Perhaps, being philosophers, and somewhat of Pharisees to boot, we began all our lucubrations as we did our prayers, by thanking God that we were not as other men were; and so misread another passage in the Republic which we used in pleasant old days to be fond of quoting."

"What was that?" asked Hypatia, who became more and more interested every moment.

"That philosophers were men."

"Are you mocking me? Plato defines the philosopher as the man who seeks after the objects of knowledge, while others seek after those of opinion."

"And most truly. But what if, in our eagerness to assert that wherein the philosopher differed from other men, we had overlooked that in which he resembled other men; and so forgot that, after all, man was a genus whereof the philosopher was only a species?"

Hypatia sighed.

"Do you not think, then, that as the greater contains the less, and the archetype of the genus that of the species, we should have been wiser if we had speculated a little more on the archetype of man as man, before we meddled with a part of that archetype, — the archetype of the philosopher?.... Certainly it would have been the easier course, for there are more men than philosophers, Hypatia; and every man is a real man, and a fair subject for examination, while every philosopher is not a real philosopher — our friends the Academics, for instance, and even a Neo-Platonist or two whom we know? You seem impatient. Shall I cease?"

"You mistook the cause of my impatience," answered she, looking up at him with her great sad eyes. "Go on."

"Now — for I am going to be terribly scholastic — is it not the very definition of man, that he is, alone of all known things, a spirit temporarily united to an animal body?"

"Enchanted in it, as in a dungeon, rather," said she, sighing.

"Be it so if you will. But — must we not say that the archetype — the very man — that if he is the archetype, he too will be, or must have been, once at least, temporarily enchanted into an animal body?.... You are silent. I will not press you..... Only ask you to consider at your leisure whether Plato may not justify somewhat from the charge of absurdity the fisherman of Galilee, where he said that He in whose image man is made was made flesh, and dwelt with him bodily there by the lake side at Tiberias, and that he beheld his glory, the glory as of the only-begotten of the Father."

"That last question is a very different one. God made flesh! My reason revolts at it."

"Old Homer's reason did not."

Hypatia started, for she recollected her yesterday's cravings after those old, palpable, and human deities. And — "Go on," she cried, eagerly.

"Tell me, then — This archetype of man, if it exists anywhere, it must exist eternally in the mind of God? At least, Plato would have so said?"

"Yes."

"And derive its existence immediately from Him?"

"Yes."

"But a man is one willing person, unlike to all others."

"Yes."

"Then this archetype must be such."

"I suppose so.''

"But possessing the faculties and properties of all men in their highest perfection."

"Of course."

"How sweetly and obediently my late teacher becomes my pupil!"

Hypatia looked at him with her eyes full of tears.

"I never taught you anything, Raphael."

"You taught me most, beloved lady, when you least thought of it. But tell me one thing more. Is it not the property of every man to be a son? For you can conceive of a man as not being a father, but not as not being a son."

"Be it so."

"Then this archetype must be a son also."

"Whose son, Raphael?"

"Why not of 'Zeus, father of gods and men'? For we agreed that it — we will call it he, now, having agreed that it is a person — could owe its existence to none but God himself."

"And what then?" said Hypatia, fixing those glorious eyes full on his face, in an agony of doubt, but yet, as Raphael declared to his dying day, of hope and joy.

"Well, Hypatia, and must not a son be of the same species as his father? 'Eagles,' says the poet, 'do not beget doves.' Is the word son anything but an empty and false metaphor, unless the son be the perfect and equal likeness of his father?"

"Heroes beget sons worse than themselves, says the poet."

"We are not talking now of men as they are, whom Homer's Zeus calls the most wretched of all the beasts of the field; we are talking — are we not? — of a perfect and archetypal Son, and a perfect and archetypal Father, in a perfect and eternal world, wherein is neither growth, decay, nor change; and of a perfect and archetypal generation, of which the only definition can be, that like begets its perfect like?.... You are silent. Be so, Hypatia.... We have gone up too far into the abysses."....

And so they both were silent for a while. And Raphael thought solemn thoughts about Victoria, and about ancient signs of Isaiah's, which were to him none the less prophecies concerning The Man whom he had found, because he prayed and trusted that the same signs might be repeated to himself, and a child given to him also, as a token that, in spite of all his baseness, "God was with him."

But he was a Jew, and a man: Hypatia was a Greek, and a woman — and for that matter, so were the men of her school. To her, the relations and duties of common humanity shone with none of the awful and divine meaning which they did in the eyes of the converted Jew, awakened for the first time in his life to know the meaning of his own scriptures, and become an Israelite indeed. And Raphael's dialectic, too, though it might silence her, could not convince her. Her creed, like those of her fellow-philosophers, was one of the fancy and the religious sentiment, rather than of the reason and the moral sense. All the brilliant cloud-world in which she had revelled for years, — cosmogonies, emanations, affinities, symbolisms, hierarchies, abysses, eternities, and the rest of it — though she could not rest in them, not even believe in them — though they had vanished into thin air at her most utter need, — yet — they were too pretty to be lost sight of for ever; and, struggling against the growing conviction of her reason, she answered at last, —

"And you would have me give up, as you seem to have done, the sublime, the beautiful, the heavenly, for a dry and barren chain of dialectic — in which, for aught I know, — for after all, Raphael, I cannot cope with you — I am a woman — a weak woman!"

And she covered her face with her hands.

"For aught you know, what?" asked Raphael, gently.

"You may have made the worse appear the better reason."

"So said Aristophanes of Socrates. But hear me once more, beloved Hypatia. You refuse to give up the beautiful, the sublime, the heavenly? What if Raphael Aben-Ezra, at least, had never found them till now? Recollect what I said just now — what if our old Beautiful, and Sublime, and Heavenly, had been the sheerest materialism, notions spun by our own brains out of the impressions of pleasant things, and high things, and low

412

things, and awful things, which we had seen with our bodily eyes? What if I had discovered that the spiritual is not the intellectual, but the moral; and that the spiritual world is not, as we used to make it, a world of our own intellectual abstractions, or of our own physical emotions, religious or other, but a world of righteous or unrighteous persons? What if I had discovered that one law of the spiritual world, in which all others were contained, was righteousness; and that disharmony with that law, which we called unspirituality, was not being vulgar, or clumsy, or ill-taught, or unimaginative, or dull, but simply being unrighteous? What if I had discovered that righteousness, and it alone, was the beautiful, righteousness the sublime, the heavenly, the Godlike — ay, God Himself? And, what if it had dawned on me, as by a great sunrise, what that righteousness was like? What if I had seen a human being, a woman, too, a young weak girl, showing forth the glory and the beauty of God? Showing me that the beautiful was to mingle unshrinking, for duty's sake, with all that is most foul and loathsome; that the sublime was to stoop to the most menial offices, the most outwardly-degrading self-denials; that to be heavenly, was to know that the commonest relations, the most vulgar duties, of earth, were God's commands, and only to be performed aright by the help of the same spirit by which He rules the Universe; that righteousness was to love, to help, to suffer for — if need be, to die for — those who, in themselves, seem fitted to arouse no feelings except indignation and disgust? What if, for the first time, I trust not for the last time, in my life, I saw this vision; and at the sight of it my eyes were opened, and I knew it for the likeness and the glory of God? What if I, a Platonist, like John of Galilee, and Paul of Tarsus, yet, like them, a Hebrew of the Hebrews, had confessed to myself — If the creature can love thus, how much more its archetype? If weak woman can endure thus, how much more a Son of God? If for the good of others, man has strength to sacrifice himself in part, God will have strength to sacrifice Himself utterly. If He has not done it, He will do it: or He will be less beautiful, less sublime, less heavenly, less righteous than my poor conception of Him, ay, than this weak playful girl! Why should I not believe those who tell me that He has done it already? What if their evidence be, after all, only probability? I do not want mathematical demonstration to prove to me that when a child was in danger his father saved him — neither do I here. My reason, my heart, every faculty of me, except this stupid sensuous experience, which I find deceiving me every moment, which cannot even prove to me my own existence, accepts that story of Calvary as the most natural, most probable, most necessary of earthly events, assuming only that God is a righteous Person, and not some dream of an all-pervading necessary spirit — nonsense which, in its very terms, confesses its own materialism."

Hypatia answered with a forced smile.

"Raphael Aben-Ezra has deserted the method of the severe dialectician for that of the eloquent lover."

"Not altogether," said he, smiling in return. "For suppose that I had said to myself, We Platonists agree that the sight of God is the highest good."

Hypatia once more shuddered at last night's recollections.

"And if He be righteous, and righteousness be — as I know it to be — identical with love, then He will desire that highest good for men far more than they can desire it for themselves..... Then He will desire to show Himself and His own righteousness to them..... Will you make answer, dearest Hypatia, or shall I?.... or does your silence give consent? At least let me go on to say this, that it God do desire to show His righteousness to men, His only perfect method, according to Plato, will be that of calumny, persecution, the scourge, and the cross, that so He, like Glaucon's righteous man, may remain for ever free from any suspicion of selfish interest, or weakness of endurance..... Am I deserting the dialectic method now, Hypatia?.... You are still silent? You will not hear me, I see..... At some future day, the philosopher may condescend to lend a kinder ear to the words of her greatest debtor..... Or, rather, she may condescend to hear, in her own heart, the voice of that Archetypal Man, who has been loving her, guiding her, heaping her with every perfection of body and of mind, inspiring her with all pure and noble longings, and only asks of her to listen to her own reason, her own philosophy, when they proclaim Him as the giver of them, and to impart them freely and humbly, as He has imparted them to her, to the poor, and the brutish, and the sinful, whom He loves as well as He loves her..... Farewell!"

"Stay!" said she, springing up; "whither are you going?"

"To do a little good before I die, having done much evil.

To farm, plant, and build, and rescue a little corner of Ormuzd's earth, as the Persians would say, out of the dominion of Ahriman. To fight Ausurian robbers, feed Thracian mercenaries, save a few widows from starvation, and a few orphans from slavery..... Perhaps to leave behind me a son of David's line, who will be a better Jew, because a better Christian, than his father..... We shall have trouble in the flesh, Augustine tells us..... But, as I answered him, I really have had so little thereof yet, that my fair share may probably be rather a useful education than otherwise. Farewell!"

"Stay!" said she. "Come again! — again! And her..... Bring her..... I must see her! She must be noble, indeed, to be worthy of you."

"She is many a hundred miles away."

"Ah? Perhaps she might have taught something to me — me, the philosopher! You need not have feared me. ... I have no heart to make converts now..... Oh, Raphael Aben-Ezra, why break the bruised reed? My plans are scattered to the winds, my pupils worthless, my fair name tarnished, my conscience heavy with the thought of my own cruelty..... If you do not know all, you will know it but too soon..... My last hope, Synesius, implores for himself the hope which I need from him..... And, over and above it all..... You!.... Et tu, Brute! Why not fold my mantle round me, like Julius of old, and die!"

Raphael stood looking sadly at her, as her whole face sank into utter prostration.

* * * * * *

"Yes — come..... The Galilæan..... If he conquers strong men, can the weak maid resist him? Come soon..... This afternoon..... My heart is breaking fast."

"At the eighth hour this afternoon?"

"Yes..... At noon I lecture.... take my farewell, rather, for ever of the schools..... Gods! What have I to say?.... And tell me about him of Nazareth. Farewell!"

"Farewell, beloved lady I At the ninth hour, you shall hear of him of Nazareth."

Why did his own words sound to him strangely pregnant, all but ominous? He almost fancied that not he, but some third person had spoken them. He kissed Hypatia's hand. It was as cold as ice; and his heart, too, in spite of all his bliss, felt cold and heavy, as he left the room.

As he went down the steps into the street, a young man sprang from behind one of the pillars, and seized his arm.

"Aha! my young Coryphæus of pious plunderers! What do you want with me?"

Philammon, for it was he, looked at him an instant, and recognised him.

"Save her! for the love of God, save her!"

"Whom?"

"Hypatia!"

"How long has her salvation been important to you, my good friend?"

"For God's sake," said Philammon, "go back and warn her! She will hear you — you are rich — you used to be her friend — I know you — I have heard of you.... Oh, if you ever cared for her — if you ever felt for her a thousandth part of what I feel — go in and warn her not to stir from home!"

"I must hear more of this," said Raphael, who saw that the boy was in earnest. "Come in with me, and speak to her father."

"No! not in that house! Never in that house again! Do not ask me why: but go yourself. She will not hear me. Did you — did you prevent her from listening?"

"What do you mean?"

"I have been here — ages! I sent a note in by her maid, and she returned no answer."

Raphael recollected then, for the first time, a note which he had seen brought to her during the conversation.

"I saw her receive a note. She tossed it away. Tell me your story. If there is reason in it, I will bear your message myself. Of what is she to be warned?"

"Of a plot — I know that there is a plot — against her among the monks and Parabolani. As I lay in bed this morning in Arsenius's room — they thought I was asleep —— "

"Arsenius? Has that venerable fanatic, then, gone the way of all monastic flesh, and turned persecutor?"

"God forbid! I heard him beseeching Peter the Reader to refrain from something, I cannot tell what; but I caught her name.... I heard Peter say, 'She that hindereth will hinder till she be taken out of the way.' And when he went out into the passage I heard him say to another, 'That thou doest, do quickly!' "....

"These are slender grounds, my friend."

"Ah, you do not know of what those men are capable!"

"Do I not? Where did you and I meet last?"

Philammon blushed and burst forth again. "That was enough for me. I know the hatred which they bear her, the crimes which they attribute to her. Her house would have been attacked last night had it not been for Cyril..... And I know Peter's tone. He spoke too gently and softly not to mean something devilish. I watched all the morning for an opportunity of escape, and here I am! — Will you take my message, or see her ———— "

"What?"

"God only knows, and the devil whom they worship instead of God."

Raphael hurried back into the house — "Could he see Hypatia?" She had shut herself up in her private room, strictly commanding that no visitor should be admitted..... "Where was Theon, then?" He had gone out by the canal gate half-an-hour before, with a bundle of mathematical papers under his arm, no one knew whither..... "Imbecile old idiot!" and he hastily wrote on his tablet —

"Do not despise the young monk's warning. I believe him to speak the truth. As you love yourself and your father, Hypatia, stir not out to-day."

He bribed a maid to take the message upstairs; and past his time in the hall in warning the servants. But they would not believe him. It was true the shops were shut in some quarters, and the Museum Gardens empty; people were a little frightened after yesterday. But Cyril, they had heard for certain, had threatened excommunication only last night to any Christian who broke the peace; and there had not been a monk to be seen in the streets the whole morning. And as for any harm happening to their mistress — impossible! "The very wild beasts would not tear her," said the huge negro porter, "if she were thrown into the amphitheatre."

Whereat a maid boxed his ears for talking of such a thing; and then, by way of mending it, declared that she knew for certain that her mistress could turn aside the lightning, and call legions of spirits to fight for her with a nod..... What was to be done with such idolaters? And yet who could help liking them the better for it?

At last the answer came down, in the old graceful, studied, self-conscious handwriting.

"It is a strange way of persuading me to your new faith, to bid me beware, on the very first day of your preaching, of the wickedness of those who believe it. I thank you: but your affection for me makes you timorous. I dread nothing. They will not dare. Did they dare now, they would have dared long ago. As for that youth — to obey or to believe his word, even to seem aware of his existence, were shame to me henceforth. Because he is insolent enough to warn me, therefore I will go. Fear not for me. You would not wish me, for the first time in my life, to fear for myself. I must follow my destiny. I must speak the words which I have to speak. Above all, I must let no Christian say, that the philosopher dared less than the fanatic. If my Gods are Gods, then will they protect me: and if not, let your God prove his rule as seems to him good."

Raphael tore the letter to fragments..... The guards, at least, were not gone mad like the rest of the world. It wanted half-an-hour of the time of her lecture. In the interval he might summon force enough to crush all Alexandria. And turning suddenly, he darted out of the room and out of the house.

"Quem Deus vult perdere ———— !" cried he to Philammon, with a gesture of grief. "Stay here and stop her! — make a last appeal! Drag the horses' heads down, if you can! I will be back in ten minutes." And he ran off for the nearest gate of the Museum gardens.

On the other side of the gardens lay the court-yard of the palace. There were gates in plenty communicating between them. If he could but see Orestes, even alarm the guard in time!....

And he hurried through the walks and alcoves, now deserted by the fearful citizens, to the nearest gate. It was fast, and barricaded firmly on the outside.

Terrified, he ran on to the next; it was barred also. He saw the reason in a moment, and maddened as he saw it. The guards, careless about the Museum, or reasonably fearing no danger from the Alexandrian populace to the glory and wonder of their city, or perhaps wishing wisely enough to concentrate their forces in the narrowest space, had contented themselves with cutting off all communication with the gardens, and so converting the lofty partition-wall into the outer enceinte of their marble citadel. At all events, the doors leading from the Museum itself might be open. He knew them every one, every hall, passage, statue, picture, almost every book in that vast treasure-house of ancient civilization. He found an entrance; hurried through well-known corridors to a postern through which he and Orestes had lounged a hundred times, their lips full of bad words, their hearts of worse thoughts, gathered in those records of the fair wickedness of old..... It was fast. He beat upon it; but no one answered. He rushed on and tried another. No one answered there. Another — still silence and despair!....

He rushed upstairs, hoping that from the windows above he might be able to call to the guard. The prudent soldiers had locked and barricaded the entrances to the upper floors of the whole right wing, lest the palace court should be commanded from thence. Whither now? Back — and whither then? Back, round endless galleries, vaulted halls, staircases, doorways, some fast, some open, up and down, trying this way and that, losing himself at whiles in that enormous silent labyrinth. And his breath failed him, his throat was parched, his face burned as with the simoom wind, his legs were trembling under him. His presence of mind, usually so perfect, failed him utterly. He was baffled, netted; there was a spell upon him. Was it a dream? Was it all one of those hideous nightmares of endless pillars beyond pillars, stairs above stairs, rooms within rooms, changing, shifting, lengthening out for ever and for ever before the dreamer, narrowing, closing in on him, choking him? Was it a dream? Was he doomed to wander for ever and for ever in some palace of the dead, to expiate the sin which he had learnt and done therein? His brain, for the first time in his life, began to reel. He could recollect nothing but that something dreadful was to happen — and that he had to prevent it, and could not..... Where was he now? In a little by-chamber..... He had talked with her there a hundred times, looking out over the Pharos and the blue Mediterranean..... What was that roar below?.... A sea of weltering yelling heads, thousands on thousands, down to the very beach; and from their innumerable throats one mighty war-cry — "God, and the Mother of God!" Cyril's hounds were loose..... He reeled from the window, and darted frantically away again.... whither, he knew not, and never knew until his dying day.

And Philammon?.... Sufficient for the chapter, as for the day, is the evil thereof.

CHAPTER XXVIII
WOMAN'S LOVE

PELAGIA had past that night alone in sleepless sorrow, which was not diminished by her finding herself the next morning palpably a prisoner in her own house. Her girls told her that they had orders — they would not say from whom — to prevent her leaving her own apartments. And though some of them made the announcement with sighs and tears of condolence, yet more than one, she could see, was well inclined to make her feel that her power was over, and that there were others besides herself who might aspire to the honour of reigning favourite.

What matter to her? Whispers, sneers, and saucy answers fell on her ear unheeded. She had one idol, and she had lost it; one power, and it had failed her. In the heaven above, and in the earth beneath, was neither peace, nor help, nor hope; nothing-but black, blank, stupid terror and despair. The little weak infant soul, which had just awakened in her, had been crushed and stunned in its very birth-hour; and instinctively she crept away to the roof of the tower where her apartments were, to sit and weep alone.

There she sat, hour after hour, beneath the shade of the large windsail, which served in all Alexandrian houses the double purpose of a shelter from the sun and a ventilator for the rooms below; and her eye roved carelessly over that endless sea of roofs and towers, and masts, and glittering canals, and gliding boats: but she saw none of them — nothing but one beloved face, lost, lost for ever.

At last a low whistle roused her from her dream. She looked up. Across the narrow lane, from one of the embrasures of the opposite house-parapet, bright eyes were peering at her. She moved angrily to escape them.

The whistle was repeated, and a head rose cautiously above the parapet..... It was Miriam's. Casting a careful look around, Pelagia went forward. What could the old woman want with her?

Miriam made interrogative signs, which Pelagia understood as asking her whether she was alone; and the moment that an answer in the negative was returned, Miriam rose, tossed over to her feet a letter weighted with a pebble, and then vanished again.

"I have watched here all day. They refused me admittance below. Beware of Wulf, of every one. Do not stir from your chamber. There is a plot to carry you off to-night, and give you up to your brother the monk; you are betrayed; be brave!"

Pelagia read it with blanching cheek and staring eyes and took, at least, the last part of Miriam's advice. For walking down the stair, she passed proudly through her own rooms, and commanding back the girls who would have stayed her, with a voice and gesture at which they quailed, went straight down, the letter in her hand, to the apartment where the Amal usually spent his midday hours.

As she approached the door, she heard loud voices within..... His! — yes; but Wulf's also. Her heart fail her, and she stopped a moment to listen..... She heard Hypatia's name; and mad with curiosity, crouched down at the lock, and hearkened to every word.

"She will not accept me, Wulf."

"If she will not, she shall go farther and fare worse. Besides, I tell you, she is hard run. It is her last chance, and she will jump at it. The Christians are mad with her; if a storm blows up, her life is not worth — that!"

"It is pity that we have not brought her hither already."

"It is; but we could not. We must not break with Orestes till the palace is in our hands."

"And will it ever be in our hands, friend?"

"Certain. We were round at every picquet last night, and the very notion of an Amal's leading them made them so eager, that we had to bribe them to be quiet rather than to rise."

"Odin! I wish I were among them now!"

"Wait till the city rises. If the day pass over without a riot, I know nothing. The treasure is all on board, is it not?"

"Yes, and the galleys ready. I have been working like a horse at them all the morning, as you would let me do nothing else. And Goderic will not be back from the palace, you say, till nightfall!"

"If we are attacked first, we are to throw up a fire-signal to him, and he is to come off hither with what Goths he can muster.

If the palace is attacked first, he is to give us the signal, and we are to pack up and row round thither. And in the mean while, he is to make that hound of a Greek prefect as drunk as he can."

"The Greek will see him under the table! He has drugs, I know, as all these Roman rascals have, to sober him when he likes; and then he sets to work and drinks again. Send off old Smid, and let him beat the armourer if he can."

"A very good thought!" said Wulf, and came out instantly for the purpose of putting it in practice.

Pelagia had just time to retreat into an adjoining doorway: but she had heard enough; and as Wulf passed, she sprang to him and caught him by the arm.

"Oh, come in hither! Speak to me one moment; for mercy's sake speak to me!" and she drew him, half against his will, into the chamber, and throwing herself at his feet, broke out into a childlike wail.

Wulf stood silent, utterly discomfited by this unexpected submission, where he had expected petulant and artful resistance. He almost felt guilty and ashamed, as he looked down into that beautiful imploring face, convulsed with simple sorrow, as of a child for a broken toy..... At last she spoke.

"Oh, what have I done — what have I done? Why must you take him from me? What have I done but love him, honour him, worship him? I know you love him; and I love you for it. — I do indeed! But you — what is your love to mine? Oh, I would die for him — be torn in pieces for him — now, this moment!"....

Wulf was silent.

"What have I done but love him? What could I wish but to make him happy? I was rich enough, praised, and petted; .... and then he came, ... glorious as he is, like a god among men — among apes rather — and I worshipped him: was I wrong in that? I gave up all for him: was I wrong in that? I gave him myself: what could I do more? He condescended to like me — he, the hero! Could I help submitting? I loved him: could I help loving him? Did I wrong him in that? Cruel, cruel Wulf?"....

Wulf was forced to be stern, or he would have melted at once.

"And what was your love worth to him? What has it done for him? It has made him a sot, an idler, a laughingstock to these

Greek dogs, when he might have been their conqueror, their king. Foolish woman, who cannot see that your love has been his bane, his ruin! He, who ought by now to have been sitting upon the throne of the Ptolemies, the lord of all south of the Mediterranean — as he shall be still!"

Pelagia looked at him wide-eyed, as if her mind was taking in slowly some vast new thought, under the weight of which it reeled already. Then she rose slowly.

"And he might be Emperor of Africa."

"And he shall be; but not ———— "

"Not with me!" she almost shrieked. "No! not with wretched, ignorant, polluted me! I see — oh, God, I see it all I And this is why you want him to marry her — her ———— "

She could not utter the dreaded name.

Wulf could not trust himself to speak; but he bowed his head in acquiescence.

* * * * * *

"Yes — I will go — up into the desert — with Philammon — and you shall never hear of me again. And I will be a nun, and pray for him, that he may be a great king, and conquer all the world. You will tell him why I went away, will you not? Yes, I will go, — now, at once ———— "

She turned away hurriedly, as if to act upon her promise, and then she sprang again to Wulf with a sudden shudder.

"I cannot, Wulf! — I cannot leave him! I shall go mad if I do! Do not be angry; — I will promise anything — take any oath you like, if you will only let me stay here. Only as a slave — as anything — if I may but look at him sometimes. No — not even that — but to be under the same roof with him, only — Oh, let me be but a slave in the kitchen! I will make over all I have to him — to you — to any one! And you shall tell him that I am gone — dead, if you will. — Only let me stay! And I will wear rags, and grind in the mill. .... Even that will be delicious, to know that he is eating the bread which I have made! And if I ever dare speak to him — even to come near him — let the steward hang me up by the wrists, and whip me, like the slave which I deserve to be!.... And then shall I soon grow old and ugly with grief, and there will be no more danger then, dear Wulf, will there, from this accursed face of mine? Only promise me that, and — — There! he is calling you! Don't let him come in and see me! — I cannot bear it! Go to him, quick, and tell him all. — No, don't tell him yet."....

And she sank down again on the floor, as Wulf went out, murmuring to himself, —

"Poor child! poor child! well for thee this day if thou wert dead, and at the bottom of Hela!"

And Pelagia heard what he said.

Gradually, amid sobs and tears, and stormy confusion of impossible hopes and projects, those words took root in her mind, and spread, till they filled her whole heart and brain.

"Well for me if I were dead?"

And she rose slowly.

"Well for me if I were dead? And why not? Then it would indeed be all settled. There would be no more danger from poor little Pelagia then."....

She went slowly, firmly, proudly, into the well-known chamber..... She threw herself upon the bed, and covered the pillow with kisses. Her eye fell on the Amal's sword, which hung across the bed's-head, after the custom of Gothic warriors. She seized it, and took it down, shuddering.

"Yes!.... Let it be with this, if it must be. And it must be. I cannot bear it! Anything but shame! To have fancied all my life — vain fool that I was! — that every one loved and admired me, and to find that they were despising me, hating me, all along! Those students at the lecture-room door told me I was despised. — The old monk told me so — Fool that I was! I forgot it next day! — For he — he loved me still! — Ah — how could I believe them, till his own lips had said it?.... Intolerable!.... And yet women as bad as I am have been honoured — when they were dead. What was that song-which I used to sing about Epicharis, who hung herself in the litter, and Leaina, who bit out her tongue, lest the torture should drive them to betray their lovers? There used to be a statue of Leaina, they say, at Athens, — a lioness without a tongue..... And whenever I sang the song, the theatre used to rise, and shout, and call them noble and blessed..... I never could tell why then; but I know now! — I know now! Perhaps they may call me noble, after all. At least, they may say 'She was a — a — but she dare die for the man she loved!'.... Ay, but God despises me too, and hates me. He will send me to eternal fire. Philammon said so — though he was my

brother. The old monk said so — though he wept as he said it.....
The flames of hell for ever! Oh, not for ever! Great, dreadful
God! Not for ever! Indeed, I did not know! No one taught me
about right and wrong, and I never knew that I had been baptized
— indeed, I never knew! And it was so pleasant — so pleasant to
be happy, and praised, and loved, and to see happy faces round
me. How could I help it? The birds there who are singing in the
darling, beloved court — they do what they like, and Thou art
not angry with them for being happy? And Thou wilt not be
more cruel to me than to them, great God — for what did I know
more than they? Thou hast made the beautiful sunshine, and the
pleasant, pleasant world, and the flowers and the birds — Thou
wilt not send me to burn for ever and ever? Will not a hundred
years be punishment enough — or a thousand? Oh, God! is not
this punishment enough already, — to have to leave him, just as
— just as I am beginning to long to be good, and to be worthy of
him?.... Oh, have mercy — mercy — mercy — and let me go
after I have been punished enough! Why may I not turn into a
bird, or even a worm, and come back again out of that horrible
place, to see the sun shine, and the flowers grow once more? Oh,
am I not punishing myself already? Will not this help to
atone?.... Yes — I will die! — and perhaps so God may pity
me!"

And with trembling hands she drew the sword from its
sheath and covered the blade with kisses.

"Yes — on this sword — with which he won his battles.
That is right — his to the last! How keen and cold it looks! Will
it be very painful?.... No — I will not try the point, or my heart
might fail me. I will fall on it at once: let it hurt me as it may, it
will be too late to draw back then. And after all it is his sword —
It will not have the heart to torture me much. And yet he struck
me himself this morning!"

And at that thought, a long wild cry of misery broke from
her lips, and rang through the house. Hurriedly she fastened the
sword upright to the foot of the bed, and tore open her tunic.....
"Here — under this widowed bosom, where his head will never
lie again! There are footsteps in the passage! Quick, Pelagia!
Now —— "

And she threw up her arms wildly, in act to fall.....

"It is his step! And he will find me, and never know that it is for him I die!"

The Amal tried the door. It was fast. With a single blow he burst it open, and demanded —

"What was that shriek? What is the meaning of this? Pelagia!"

Pelagia, like a child caught playing with a forbidden toy, hid her face in her hands, and cowered down.

"What is it?" cried he, lifting her.

But she burst from his arms.

"No, no! — never more! I am not worthy of you! Let me die, wretch that I am! I can only drag you down. You must be a king. You must marry her — the wise woman!"

"Hypatia! She is dead!"

"Dead?" shrieked Pelagia.

"Murdered, an hour ago, by those Christian devils."

Pelagia put her hands over her eyes, and burst into tears. Were they of pity or of joy?.... She did not ask herself; and we will not ask her.

"Where is my sword? Soul of Odin! why is it fastened here?"

"I was going to — Do not be angry!.... They told me that I had better die, and —— "

The Amal stood thunderstruck for a moment.

Oh, do not strike me again! Send me to the mill. Kill me now with your own hand! Anything but another blow!"

"A blow? — Noble woman!" cried the Amal, clasping her in his arms.

The storm was past; and Pelagia had been nestling to that beloved heart, cooing like a happy dove, for many a minute before the Amal aroused himself and her.....

"Now! — quick! We have not a moment to lose. Up to the tower, where you will be safe; and then to show these curs what comes of snarling round the wild wolves' den!"

CHAPTER XXIX
NEMESIS

AND was the Amal's news true, then?

Philammon saw Raphael rush across the street into the Museum gardens. His last words had been a command to stay where he was; and the boy obeyed him. The black porter who let Raphael out told him somewhat insolently, that his mistress would see no one, and receive no messages: but he had made up his mind: complained of the sun, quietly ensconced himself behind a buttress, and sat coiled up on the pavement, ready for a desperate spring. The slave stared at him: but he was accustomed to the vagaries of philosophers; and thanking the gods that he was not born in that station of life, retired to his porter's cell, and forgot the whole matter.

There Philammon waited a full half-hour. It seemed to him hours, days, years. And yet Raphael did not return; and yet no guards appeared. Was the strange Jew a traitor? Impossible! — his face had shown a desperate earnestness of terror as intense as Philammon's own..... Yet why did he not return?

Perhaps he had found out that the streets were clear; their mutual fears groundless..... What meant that black knot of men some two hundred yards off, hanging about the mouth of the side street, just opposite the door which led to her lecture-room? He moved to watch them: they had vanished. He lay down again and waited..... There they were again. It was a suspicious post. That street ran along the back of the Cæsareium, a favourite haunt of monks, communicating by innumerable entries and back buildings with the great Church itself..... And yet, why should there not be a knot of monks there? What more common in every street of Alexandria? He tried to laugh away his own fears. And yet they ripened, by the very intensity of thinking on them, into certainty. He knew that something terrible was at hand. More than once he looked out from his hiding-place — the knot of men was still there;.... it seemed to have increased, to draw nearer. If they found him, what would they not suspect? What did he care? He would die for her, if it came to that — not that it could come to that: but still, he must speak to her — he must warn her. Passenger after passenger, carriage after carriage passed along the street; student after student entered the lecture-room: but he never saw them, not though they passed him close. The sun rose higher and higher, and turned his whole blaze upon the corner where Philammon crouched, till the pavement scorched like hot iron, and his eyes were dazzled by the blinding glare: but he never heeded it. His whole heart, and sense, and sight, were riveted upon that well-known door, expecting it to open.....

At last, a curricle, glittering with silver, rattled round the corner and stopped opposite him. She must be coming now. The crowd had vanished. Perhaps it was, after all, a fancy of his own. No; there they were, peeping round the corner, close to the lecture-room — the hellhounds! A slave brought out an embroidered cushion — and then Hypatia herself came forth, looking more glorious than ever; her lips set in a sad firm smile; her eyes up. lifted, inquiring, eager, and yet gentle, dimmed by some great inward awe, as if her soul was far away aloft, and face to face with God.

In a moment he sprang up to her, caught her robe convulsively, threw himself on his knees before her —

"Stop! Stay! You are going to destruction!"

Calmly she looked down upon him.

"Accomplice of witches! Would you make of Theon's daughter a traitor like yourself?"

He sprung up, stepped back, and stood stupified with shame and despair.....

She believed him guilty, then!.... It was the will of God!

The plumes of the horses were waving far down the street before he recovered himself, and rushed after her, shouting he knew not what.

It was too late! A dark wave of men rushed from the ambuscade, surged up round the car.... swept forward.... she had disappeared! and as Philammon followed breathless, the horses galloped past him madly homeward with the empty carriage.

Whither were they dragging her? To the Cæsareium, the Church of God himself? Impossible? Why thither of all places on the earth? Why did the mob, increasing momentarily by hundreds, pour down upon the beach, and return brandishing flints, shells, fragments of pottery?

She was upon the church steps before he caught them up, invisible among the crowd; but he could track her by the fragments of her dress.

Where were her gay pupils now? Alas! they had barricaded themselves shamefully in the Museum, at the first rush which swept her from the door of the lecture-room. Cowards! he would save her!

And he struggled in vain to pierce the dense mass of Parabolani and monks, who, mingled with the fish-wives and dock-workers, leaped and yelled around their victim. But what he could not do, another and a weaker did — even the little porter. Furiously — no one knew how or whence — he burst up as if from the ground in the thickest of the crowd, with knife, teeth, and nails, like a venomous wildcat, tearing his way toward his idol. Alas! he was torn down himself, rolled over the steps, and lay there half dead, in an agony of weeping, as Philammon sprung up past him into the church.

Yes. On into the church itself! Into the cool dim shadow, with its fretted pillars, and lowering domes, and candles, and incense, and blazing altar, and great pictures, looking from the walls athwart the gorgeous gloom. And right in front, above the altar, the colossal Christ watching unmoved from off the wall, his right hand raised to give a blessing — or a curse?

On, up the nave, fresh shreds of her dress strewing the holy pavement — up the chancel steps themselves — up to the altar — right underneath the great still Christ: and there even those hell-hounds paused.....

She shook herself free from her tormentors, and springing back, rose for one moment to her full height, naked, snow-white against the dusky mass around — shame and indignation in those wide clear eyes, but not a stain of fear. With one hand she clasped her golden locks around her; the other long white arm was stretched upward toward the great still Christ appealing — and who dare say, in vain? — from man to God. Her lips were opened to speak; but the words that should have come from them reached God's ear alone; for in an instant Peter struck her down, the dark mass closed over her again..... and then wail on wail, long, wild, ear-piercing, rang along the vaulted roofs, and thrilled like the trumpet of avenging angels through Philammon's ears.

Crushed against a pillar, unable to move in the dense mass, he pressed his hands over his ears. He could not shut out those shrieks! When would they end? What In the name of the God of mercy were they doing? Tearing her piecemeal? Yes, and worse than that. And still the shrieks rang on, and still the great Christ looked down on Philammon with that calm, intolerable eye, and would not turn away. And over his head was written in the rainbow, "I am the same, yesterday, to-day, and for ever"! The same as he was in Judæa of old, Philammon? Then what are these, and in whose temple? And he covered his face with his hands, and longed to die.

It was over. The shrieks had died away into moans; the moans to silence. How long had he been there? An hour, or an eternity? Thank God it was over! For her sake — but for theirs? But they thought not of that as a new cry rose through the dome.

"To the Cinaron! Burn the bones to ashes! Scatter them into the sea!".... And the mob poured past him again.....

He turned to flee: but, once outside the church, he sank exhausted, and lay upon the steps, watching with stupid horror the glaring of the fire, and the mob who leaped and yelled like demons round their Moloch sacrifice.

A hand grasped his arm; he looked up; it was the porter.

"And this, young butcher, is the Catholic and apostolic Church?"

"No! Eudæmon, it is the church of the devils of hell!" And gathering himself up, he sat upon the steps and buried his head within his hands. He would have given life itself for the power of weeping: but his eyes and brain were hot and dry as the desert.

Eudæmon looked at him awhile. The shock had sobered the poor fop for once.

"I did what I could to die with her!" said he.

"I did what I could to save her!" answered Philammon.

"I know it. Forgive the words which I just spoke. Did we not both love her?"

And the little wretch sat down by Philammon's side, and as the blood dripped from his wounds upon the pavement, broke out into a bitter agony of human tears.

There are times when the very intensity of our misery is a boon, and kindly stuns us till we are unable to torture ourselves by thought. And so it was with Philammon then. He sat there, he knew not how long.

"She is with the gods," said Eudæmon at last.

"She is with the God of gods," answered Philammon; and they both were silent again.

Suddenly a commanding voice aroused them. They looked up, and saw before them Raphael Aben-Ezra.

He was pale as death, but calm as death. One look into his face told them that he knew all.

"Young monk," he said, between his closed teeth, "you seem to have loved her?"

Philammon looked up, but could not speak.

"Then arise, and flee for your life into the farthest corner of the desert, ere the doom of Sodom and Gomorrha fall upon this accursed city. Have you father, mother, brother, sister, — ay, cat, dog, or bird for which you care, within its walls?"

Philammon started; for he recollected Pelagia..... That evening, so Cyril had promised, twenty trusty monks were to have gone with him to seize her.

"You have? Then take them with you, and escape, and remember Lot's wife. Eudæmon, come with me. You must lead me to your house, to the lodging of Miriam the Jewess. Do not deny! I know that she is there. For the sake of her who is gone I will hold you harmless, ay, reward you richly, if you prove faithful. Rise!"

Eudæmon, who knew Raphael's face well, rose and led the way trembling; and Philammon was left alone.

They never met again. But Philammon knew that he had been in the presence of a stronger man than himself, and of one who hated even more bitterly than he himself that deed at which the very sun, it seemed, ought to have veiled his face. And his words, "Arise, and flee for thy life," uttered as they were with the stern self-command and writhing lip of compressed agony, rang through his ears like the trump of doom. Yes, he would flee. He had gone forth to see the world, and he had seen it, Arsenius was in the right after all. Home to the desert! But first he would go himself, alone, to Pelagia, and implore her once more to flee with him. Beast, fool, that he had been, to try to win her by force — by the help of such as these! God's kingdom was not a kingdom of fanatics yelling for a doctrine, but of willing, loving, obedient hearts. If he could not win her heart, her will, he would go alone, and die praying for her.

He sprang from the steps of the Cæsareium, and turned up the street of the Museum. Alas! it was one roaring sea of heads! They were sacking Theon's house — the house of so many memories! Perhaps the poor old man too had perished! Still — his sister! He must save her and flee. And he turned up a side street and tried to make his way onward.

Alas again! the whole of the dock-quarter was up and out. Every street poured its tide of furious fanatics into the main river; and ere he could reach Pelagia's house the sun was set, and close behind him, echoed by ten thousand voices, was the cry of "Down with all heathens! Root out all Arian Goths! Down with idolatrous wantons! Down with Pelagia Aphrodite!"

He hurried down the alley, to the tower door, where Wulf had promised to meet him. It was half open, and in the dusk he could see a figure standing in the doorway. He sprang up the steps, and found, not Wulf, but Miriam.

"Let me pass!"

"Wherefore?"

He made no answer, and tried to push past her.

"Fool, fool, fool!" whispered the hag, holding the door against him with all her strength. "Where are your fellow-kidnappers? Where are your band of monks?"

Philammon started back. How had she discovered his plan?

"Ay — where are they? Besotted boy! Have you not seen enough of monkery this afternoon, that you must try still to make that poor girl even such a one as yourselves? Ay, you may root out your own human natures it you will, and make yourselves devils in trying to become angels: but woman she is, and woman she shall live or die!"

"Let me pass!" cried Philammon, furiously.

"Raise your voice — and I raise mine; and then your life is not worth a moment's purchase. Fool, do you think I speak as a Jewess? I speak as a woman — as a nun! I was a nun once, madman — the iron entered into my soul! — God do so to me, and more also, if it ever enter into another soul while I can prevent it! You shall not have her! I will strangle her with my own hand first!" And turning from him, she darted up the winding stair.

He followed: but the intense passion of the old hag hurled her onward with the strength and speed of a young Maenad. Once Philammon was near passing her. But be recollected that he did not know his way, and contented himself with keeping close behind, and making the fugitive his guide.

Stair after stair, he fled upward, till she turned suddenly into a chamber door. Philammon paused. A few feet above him the open sky showed at the stair-head. They were close, then, to the roof! One moment more, and the hag darted out of the room again, and turned to flee upward still. Philammon caught her by the arm, hurled her back into the empty chamber, shut the door upon her; and with a few bounds gained the roof, and met Pelagia face to face.

"Come!" gasped he breathlessly. "Now is the moment! Come, while they are all below!" and he seized her hand.

But Pelagia only recoiled.

"No, no," whispered she in answer, "I cannot, cannot — he has forgiven me all, all! and I am his for ever! And now, just as he is in danger, when he may be wounded — ah, heaven! would you have me do anything so base as to desert him?"

"Pelagia, Pelagia, darling sister!" cried Philammon, in an agonized voice, "think of the doom of sin! Think of the pains of hell!"

"I have thought of them this day: and I do not believe you! No — I do not! God is not so cruel as you say! And if he were: — to lose my love, that is hell! Let me burn hereafter, if I do but keep him now!"

Philammon stood stupified and shuddering. All his own early doubts flashed across him like a thunderbolt, when in the temple-cave he had seen those painted ladies at their revels, and shuddered, and asked himself, were they burning for ever and ever?

"Come!" gasped he once again; and throwing himself on his knees before her, covered her hands with kisses, wildly entreating: but in vain.

"What is this?" thundered a voice; not Miriam's, but the Amal's. He was unarmed: but he rushed straight upon Philammon.

"Do not harm him!" shrieked Pelagia; "he is my brother — my brother of whom I told you!"

"What does he here?" cried the Amal, who instantly divined the truth.

Pelagia was silent.

"I wish to deliver my sister, a Christian, from the sinful embraces of an Arian heretic; and deliver her I will, or die!"

"An Arian?" laughed the Amal. "Say a heathen at once, and tell the truth, young fool! Will you go with him, Pelagia, and turn nun in the sand-heaps?"

Pelagia sprang towards her lover; Philammon caught her by the arm for one last despairing appeal: and in a moment, neither knew how, the Goth and the Greek were locked in deadly struggle, while Pelagia stood in silent horror, knowing that a call for help would bring instant death to her brother.

It was over in a few seconds. The Goth lifted Philammon like a baby in his arms, and bearing him to the parapet, attempted to hurl him into the canal below. But the active Greek had wound himself like a snake around him, and held him by the throat with the strength of despair. Twice they rolled and tottered on the parapet; and twice recoiled. A third fearful lunge — the earthen wall gave way; and down to the dark depths, locked in each other's arms, fell Goth and Greek.

Pelagia rushed to the brink, and gazed downward into the gloom, dumb and dry-eyed with horror. Twice they turned over together in mid-air..... The foot of the tower, as was usual in Egypt, sloped outwards towards the water. They must strike upon that — and then!.... It seemed an eternity ere they touched the masonry..... The Amal was undermost..... She saw his fair floating locks dash against the cruel stone. His grasp suddenly loosened, his limbs collapsed; two distinct plunges broke the dark sullen water; and then all was still but the awakened ripple, lapping angrily against the wall.

Pelagia gazed down one moment more, and then, with a shriek which rang along roof and river, she turned, and fled down the stairs and out into the night.

Five minutes afterwards, Philammon, dripping, bruised, and bleeding, was crawling up the water-steps at the lower end of the lane. A woman rushed from the postern door, and stood on the quay edge, gazing with clasped hands into the canal. The moon fell full on her face. It was Pelagia. She saw him, knew him, and recoiled.

436

"Sister! — my sister! Forgive me!"

"Murderer!" she shrieked, and dashing aside his outspread hands, fled wildly up the passage.

The way was blocked with bales of merchandise: but the dancer bounded over them like a deer; while Philammon, half stunned by his fall, and blinded by his dripping locks, stumbled, fell, and lay, unable to rise. She held on for a few yards towards the torch-lit mob, which was surging and roaring in the main street above, then turned suddenly into a side. alley, and vanished; while Philammon lay groaning upon the pavement, without a purpose or a hope upon earth.

Five minutes more, and Wulf was gazing over the broken parapet, at the head of twenty terrified spectators, male and female, whom Pelagia's shriek had summoned.

He alone suspected that Philammon had been there; and shuddering at the thought of what might have happened, he kept his secret.

But all knew that Pelagia had been on the tower; all had seen the Amal go up thither. Where were they now? And why was the little postern gate found open, and shut only just in time to prevent the entrance of the mob?

Wulf stood, revolving in a brain but too well practised in such cases, all possible contingencies of death and horror. At last—

"A rope and a light, Smid!" he almost whispered.

They were brought, and Wulf, resisting all the entreaties of the younger men to allow them to go on the perilous search, lowered himself through the breach.

He was about two-thirds down, when he shook the rope, and called, in a stifled voice, to those above —

"Haul up. I have seen enough."

Breathless with curiosity and fear, they hauled him up. He stood among them for a few moments, silent, as if stunned by the weight of some enormous woe.

"Is he dead?"

"Odin has taken his son home, wolves of the Goths!" And he held out his right hand to the awe-struck ring, and burst into an agony of weeping..... A clotted tress of long fair hair lay in his palm.

It was snatched; handed from man to man..... One after

another recognised the beloved golden locks. And then, to the utter astonishment of the girls who stood round, the great simple hearts, too brave to be ashamed of tears, broke out, and wailed like children..... Their Amal! Their heavenly man! Odin's own son, their joy and pride, and glory! Their "Kingdom of heaven," as his name declared him, who was all that each wished to be, and more, and yet belonged to them, bone of their bone, flesh of their flesh! Ah, it is bitter to all true human hearts to be robbed of their ideal, even though that ideal be that of a mere wild bull, and soulless gladiator.....

At last Smid spoke: —

"Heroes, this is Odin's doom; and the Allfather is just. Had we listened to Prince Wulf four months ago, this had never been. We have been cowards and sluggards, and Odin is angry with his children. Let us swear to be Prince Wulf's men, and follow him to-morrow where he will!"

Wulf grasped his outstretched hand lovingly —

"No, Smid, son of Troll! These words are not yours to speak. Agilmund son of Cniva, Goderic son of Ermenric, you are Baits, and to you the succession appertains. Draw lots here, which of you shall be our chieftain."

"No! no! Wulf!" cried both the youths at once. "You are the hero! you are the Sagaman! We are not worthy; we have been cowards and sluggards, like the rest. Wolves of the Goths, follow the Wolf, even though he lead you to the land of the giants!"

A roar of applause followed.

"Lift him on the shield," cried Goderic, tearing-off his buckler. "Lift him on the shield! Hail, Wulf king! Wulf, king of Egypt!"

And the rest of the Goths, attracted by the noise, rushed up the tower-stairs in time to join in the mighty shout of "Wulf, king of Egypt!" — as careless of the vast multitude which yelled and surged without, as boys are of the snow against the window-pane.

"No!" said Wulf, solemnly, as he stood on the uplifted shield. "If I be indeed your king, and ye my men, wolves of the Goths, to-morrow we will go forth of this place, hated of Odin, rank with the innocent blood of the Alruna maid. Back to Adolf; back to our own people! Will you go?"

"Back to Adolf!" shouted the men.

"You will not leave us to be murdered?" cried one of the girls. "The mob are breaking the gates already!"

"Silence, silly one! Men — we have one thing to do. The Amal must not go to the Valhalla without fair attendance."

"Not the poor girls?" said Agilmund, who took for granted that Wulf would wish to celebrate the Amal's funeral in true Gothic fashion by a slaughter of slaves.

"No..... One of them I saw behave this very afternoon worthy of a Vala. And they, too — they may make heroes' wives after all, yet..... Women are better than I fancied, even the worst of them. No. Go down, heroes, and throw the gates open; and call in the Greek hounds to the funeral supper of a son of Odin."

"Throw the gates open?"

"Yes. Goderic, take a dozen men, and be ready in the east hall. Agilmund, go with a dozen to the west side of the court — there in the kitchen; and wait till you hear my war-cry. Smid and the rest of you, come with me through the stables close to the gate — as silent as Hela."

And they went down — to meet, full on the stairs below, old Miriam.

Breathless and exhausted by her exertion, she had fallen heavily before Philammon's strong arm; and lying half stunned for a while, recovered just in time to meet her doom.

She knew that it was come, and faced it like herself.

"Take the witch!" said Wulf, slowly — "Take the corrupter of heroes — the cause of all our sorrows!"

Miriam looked at him with a quiet smile.

"The witch is accustomed long ago to hear fools lay on her the consequences of their own lust and laziness."

"Hew her down, Smid, son of Troll, that she may pass the Amal's soul and gladden it on her way to Niflheim."

Smid did it: but so terrible were the eyes which glared upon him from those sunken sockets, that his sight was dazzled. The axe turned aside, and struck her shoulder. She reeled, but did not fall.

"It is enough," she said, quietly.

"The accursed Grendel's daughter numbed my arm!" said

Smid. "Let her go! No man shall say that I struck a woman twice."

"Nidhogg waits for her, soon or late," answered Wulf.

And Miriam, coolly folding her shawl around her, turned and walked steadily down the stair; while all men breathed more freely, as if delivered from some accursed and supernatural spell.

"And now," said Wulf, "to your posts, and vengeance!"

The mob had weltered and howled ineffectually around the house for some half-hour. But the lofty walls, opening on the street only by a few narrow windows in the higher stories, rendered it an impregnable fortress. Suddenly, the iron gates were drawn back, disclosing to the front rank the court, glaring empty and silent and ghastly in the moonlight. For an instant they recoiled, with a vague horror, and dread of treachery: but the mass behind pressed them onward, and in swept the murderers of Hypatia, till the court was full of choking wretches, surging against the walls and pillars in aimless fury. And then, from under the archway on each side, rushed a body of tall armed men, driving back all incomers more; the gates slid together again upon their grooves; and the wild beasts of Alexandria were trapped at last.

And then began a murder grim and great. From three different doors issued a line of Goths, whose helmets and mailshirts made them invulnerable to the clumsy weapons of the mob, and began hewing their way right through the living mass, helpless from their close-packed array. True, they were but as one to ten; but what are ten curs before one lion?.... And the moon rose higher and higher, staring down ghastly and unmoved upon that doomed court of the furies, and still the bills and swords hewed on and on, and the Goths drew the corpses, as they found room, towards a dark pile in the midst, where old Wulf sat upon a heap of slain, singing the praises of the Amal and the glories of Valhalla, while the shrieks of his lute rose shrill above the shrieks of the flying and the wounded, and its wild waltz-time danced and rollicked on swifter and swifter as the old singer maddened, in awful mockery of the terror and agony around.

And so, by men and purposes which recked not of her, as is the wont of Providence, was the blood of Hypatia avenged in part that night.

In part only. For Peter the Reader, and his especial associ-
ates, were safe in sanctuary at the Cæsareium, clinging to the
altar. Terrified at the storm which they had raised, and fearing
the consequences of an attack upon the palace, they had left the
mob to run riot at its will; and escaped the swords of the Goths,
to be reserved for the more awful punishment of impunity.

CHAPTER XXX
EVERY MAN TO HIS OWN PLACE

IT was near midnight. Raphael had been sitting some three hours in Miriam's inner chamber, waiting in vain for her return. To recover, if possible, his ancestral wealth; to convey it, without a day's delay, to Cyrene; and, if possible, to persuade the poor old Jewess to accompany him, and there to soothe, to guide, perhaps to convert her, was his next purpose: — at all events, with or without his wealth, to flee from that accursed city. And he counted impatiently the slow hours and minutes which detained him in an atmosphere which seemed reeking with innocent blood, black with the lowering curse of an avenging God. More than once, unable to bear the thought, he rose to depart, and leave his wealth behind: but he was checked again by the thought of his own past life. How had he added his own sin to the great heap of Alexandrian wickedness! How had he tempted others, pampered others in evil! Good God! how had he not only done evil with all his might, but had pleasure in those who did the same! And now, now he was reaping the fruit of his own devices. For years past, merely to please his lust of power, his misanthropic scorn, he had been making that wicked Orestes wickeder than he was even by his own base will and nature; and his puppet had avenged itself upon him! He, he had prompted him to ask Hypatia's hand..... He had laid, half in sport, half in envy of her excellence, that foul plot against the only human being whom he loved.... and he had destroyed her! He, and not Peter, was the murderer of Hypatia! True, he had never meant her death..... No; but had he not meant for her worse than death? He had never foreseen..... No; but only because he did not choose to foresee. He had chosen to be a god; to kill and to make alive by his own will and law: and behold, he had become a devil by that very act. Who can — and who dare, even if he could — withdraw the sacred veil from those bitter agonies of inward shame and self-reproach, made all the more intense by his clear and undoubting knowledge that he was forgiven? What dread of punishment, what blank despair, could have pierced that great heart so deeply as did the thought that the God whom he had hated and defied had returned him good for evil, and rewarded him not according to his iniquities? That discovery, as Ezekiel of old had warned his forefathers, filled up the cup of his self-loathing..... To have found at last the hated and dreaded name of God: and found that it was Love!.... To possess Victoria, a living, human likeness, however imperfect, of that God; and to possess in her a home, a duty, a purpose, a fresh clear life of righteous labour, perhaps of final victory..... That was his punishment; that was the brand of Cain upon his forehead; and he felt it greater than he could bear.

But at least there was one thing to be done. Where he had sinned, there he must make amends; not as a propitiation, not even as a restitution; but simply as a confession of the truth which he had found. And as his purpose shaped itself, he longed and prayed that Miriam might return, and make it possible.

And Miriam did return. He heard her pass slowly through the outer room, learn from the girls who was within, order them out of the apartments, close the outer door upon them; at last she entered, and said quietly —

"Welcome! I have expected you. You could not surprise old Miriam. The teraph told me, last night, that you would be here.".....

Did she see the smile of incredulity upon Raphael's face, or was it some sudden pang of conscience which made her cry out—

".... No! I did not! I never expected you! I am a liar, a miserable old liar, who cannot speak the truth, even if I try! Only look kind! Smile at me, Raphael! — Raphael come back at last to his poor, miserable, villanous old mother! Smile on me but once, my beautiful, my son! my son!"

And springing to him, she clasped him in her arms.

"Your son?"

"Yes, my son! Safe at last! Mine at last! I can prove it now! The son of my womb, though not the son of my vows!" And she laughed hysterically. "My child, my heir, for whom I have toiled and hoarded for three-and-thirty years! Quick! here are my keys. In that cabinet are all my papers — all I have is yours. Your jewels are safe — buried with mine. The negro-woman, Eudæmon's wife, knows where. I made her swear secrecy upon her little wooden idol, and, Christian as she is, she has been honest. Make her rich for life. She hid your poor old mother, and kept her safe to see her boy come home. But give nothing to her little husband; he is a bad fellow, and beats her. — Go, quick! take your riches, and away!.... No; stay one moment — just one little moment — that the poor old wretch may feast her eyes with the sight of her darling once more before she dies!"

"Before you die? Your son? God of my fathers, what is the meaning of all this, Miriam? This morning I was the son of Ezra the merchant of Antioch!"

"His son and heir, his son and heir I He knew all at last. We told him on his death-bed! I swear that we told him, and he adopted you!"

"We! Who?"

"His wife and I. He craved for a child, the old miser, and we gave him one — a better one than ever came of his family. But he loved you, accepted you, though he did know all. He was afraid of being laughed at after he was dead — afraid of having it known that he was childless, the old dotard! No — he was right — true Jew in that, after all!"

"Who was my father, then?" interrupted Raphael, in utter bewilderment.

The old woman laughed a laugh so long and wild, that Raphael shuddered.

"Sit down at your mother's feet. Sit down.... just to please the poor old thing! Even if you do not believe her, just play at being her child, her darling, for a minute before she dies; and she will tell you all.... perhaps there is time yet!"

And he sat down..... "What if this incarnation of all wickedness were really my mother?.... And yet — why should I shrink thus proudly from the notion? Am I so pure myself as to deserve a purer source?".... And the old woman laid her hand fondly on his head, and her skinny fingers played with his soft locks, as she spoke hurriedly and thick.

"Of the house of Jesse, of the seed of Solomon; not a rabbi from Babylon to Rome dare deny that! A king's daughter I am, and a king's heart I had, and have, like Solomon's own, my son!.... A kingly heart..... It made me dread and scorn to be a slave, a plaything, a soulless doll, such as Jewish women are condemned to be by their tyrants, the men. I craved for wisdom, renown, power — power — power! and my nation refused them to me; because, forsooth, I was a woman! So I left them. I went to the Christian priests..... They gave me what I asked..... They gave me more..... they pampered my woman's vanity, my pride, my self-will, my scorn of wedded bondage, and bade me be a saint, the judge of angels and archangels, the bride of God! Liars! liars! And so — if you laugh, you kill me, Raphael — and so Miriam, the daughter of Jonathan — Miriam, of the house of David — Miriam, the descendant of Ruth and Rachab, of Rachel and Sara, became a Christian nun, and shut herself up to see visions, and dream dreams, and fattened her own mad self-conceit upon the impious fancy that she was the spouse of the Nazarene, Joshua Bar-Joseph, whom she called Jehovah-Ishi — — Silence! If you stop me a moment, it may be too late. I hear them calling me already; and I made them promise not to take me before I had told all to my son — the son of my shame!"

"Who calls you?" asked Raphael; but after one strong shudder she ran on, unheeding, —

"But they lied, lied, lied! I found them out that day..... Do not look up at me, and I will tell you all. There was a riot — a fight between the Christian devils and the Heathen devils — and the convent was sacked, Raphael, my son! — Sacked!.... Then I found out their blasphemy..... Oh, God! I shrieked to him, Raphael! I called on him to rend his heavens and come down — to pour out his thunderbolts upon them — to cleave the earth and devour them — to save the wretched helpless girl who adored him, who had given up father, mother, kinsfolk, wealth, the light of heaven, womanhood itself for him — who worshipped, meditated over him, dreamed of him night and day..... And, Raphael, he did not hear me.... he did not hear me.... did not hear me!.... And then I knew it all for a lie! a lie!"

"And you knew it for what it is!" cried Raphael through his sobs, as he thought of Victoria, and felt every vein burning with righteous wrath.

— "There was no mistaking that test, was there?.... For nine months I was mad. And then your voice, my baby, my joy, my pride — that brought me to myself once more! And I shook off the dust of my feet against those Galilæan priests, and went back to my own nation, where God had set me from the beginning. I made them — the Rabbis, my father, my kin — I made them all receive me. They could not stand before my eye. I can make people do what I will, Raphael! I could — I could make you emperor now, if I had but time left! I went back. I palmed you off on Ezra as his son, I and his wife, and made him believe that you had been born to him while he was in Byzantium..... And then — to live for you! And I did live for you. For you I travelled from India to Britain, seeking wealth. For you I toiled, hoarded, lied, intrigued, won money by every means, no matter how base — for was it not for you? And I have conquered! You are the richest Jew south of the Mediterranean, you, my son! And you deserve your wealth. You have your mother's soul in you, my boy! I watched you, gloried in you — in your cunning, your daring, your learning, your contempt for these Gentile hounds. You felt the royal blood of Solomon within you! You felt that you were a young lion of Judah, and they the jackals who followed to feed upon your leavings! And now, now! Your only danger is past! The cunning woman is gone — the sorceress who tried to take my young lion in her pitfall, and has fallen into the midst of it herself; and he is safe, and returned to take the nations for a prey, and grind their bones to powder, as it is written, 'he couched like a lion, he lay down like a lioness's whelp, and who dare rouse him up?' "

"Stop!" said Raphael, "I must speak! Mother! I must! As you love me, as you expect me to love you, answer! Had you a hand in her death? Speak!"

"Did I not tell you that I was no more a Christian? Had I remained one — who can tell what I might not have done? All I, the Jewess, dare do was — Fool that I am! I have forgotten all this time the proof — the proof —— "

"I need no proof, mother. Your words are enough," said Raphael, as he clasped her hand between his own, and pressed it to his burning forehead. But the old woman hurried on — "See! See the black agate which you gave her in your madness!"

"How did you obtain that?"

"I stole it — stole it, my son; as thieves steal, and are crucified for stealing. What was the chance of the cross to a mother yearning for her child? — to a mother who put round her baby's neck, three-and-thirty black years ago, that broken agate, and kept the other half next her own heart by day and night? See! See how they fit! Look, and believe your poor old sinful mother! Look, I say!" and she thrust the talisman into his hands.

"Now, let me die! I vowed never to tell this secret but to you: never to tell it to you, until the night I died. Farewell, my son! Kiss me but once — once, my child, my joy! Oh, this makes up for all! Makes up even for that day, the last on which I ever dreamed myself the bride of the Nazarene!"

Raphael felt that he must speak, now or never. Though it cost him the loss of all his wealth, and a mother's curse, he must speak. And not daring to look up, he said gently, —

"Men have lied to you about Him, mother: but has He ever lied to you about Himself? He did not lie to me when He sent me out into the world to find a man, and sent me back again to you with the good news that The Man is born into the world."

But to his astonishment, instead of the burst of bigoted indignation which he had expected, Miriam answered in a low, confused, abstracted voice, —

"And did He send you hither? Well — that was more like what I used to fancy Him..... A grand thought it is after all — a Jew the king of heaven and earth!.... Well — I shall know soon.... I loved Him once,.... and perhaps.... perhaps...."

Why did her head drop heavily upon his shoulder? He turned — a dark stream of blood was flowing from her lips I He sprang to his feet. The girls rushed in. They tore open her shawl, and saw the ghastly wound, which she had hidden with such iron resolution to the last. But it was too late. Miriam the daughter of Solomon was gone to her own place.

* * * * * *

Early the next morning, Raphael was standing in Cyril's anteroom, awaiting an audience. There were loud voices within; and after a while a tribune whom he knew well hurried out, muttering curses —

"What brings you here, friend?" said Raphael.

"The scoundrel will not give them up," answered he, in an undertone.

"Give up whom?"

"The murderers. They are in sanctuary now at the Cæsareium. Orestes sent me to demand them: and this fellow defies him openly!" And the tribune hurried out.

Raphael, sickened with disgust, half-turned to follow him: but his better angel conquered, and he obeyed the summons of the deacon who ushered him in.

Cyril was walking up and down, according to his custom, with great strides. When he saw who was his visitor, he stopped short with a look of fierce inquiry. Raphael entered on business at once, with a cold calm voice.

" You know me, doubtless; and you know what I was. I am now a Christian catechumen. I come to make such restitution as I can for certain past ill-deeds done in this city. You will find among these papers the trust-deeds for such a yearly sum of money as will enable you to hire a house of refuge for a hundred fallen women, and give such dowries to thirty of them yearly as will enable them to find suitable husbands. I have set down every detail of my plan. On its exact fulfilment depends the continuance of my gift."

Cyril took the document eagerly, and was breaking out with some commonplace about pious benevolence, when the Jew stopped him.

"Your Holiness's compliments are unnecessary. It is to your office, not to yourself, that this business relates."

Cyril, whose conscience was ill enough at ease that morning, felt abashed before Raphael's dry and quiet manner, which bespoke, as he well knew, reproof more severe than all open upbraidings. So looking down, not without something like a blush, he ran his eye hastily over the paper; and then said, in his blandest tone, —

"My brother will forgive me for remarking, that while I acknowledge his perfect right to dispose of his charities as he will, it is somewhat startling to me, as Metropolitan of Egypt, to find not only the Abbot Isidore of Pelusium, but the secular Defender of the Plebs, a civil officer, implicated, too, in the late conspiracy, associated with me as co-trustees."

"I have taken the advice of more than one Christian bishop on the matter. I acknowledge your authority, by my presence here. If the Scriptures say rightly, the civil magistrates are as much God's ministers as you; and I am therefore bound to acknowledge their authority also. I should have preferred associating the Prefect with you in the trust: but as your dissensions with the present occupant of that post might have crippled my scheme, I have named the Defender of the Plebs, and have already put into his hands a copy of this document. Another copy has been sent to Isidore, who is empowered to receive all moneys from my Jewish bankers in Pelusium."

"You doubt, then, either my ability or my honesty?" said Cyril, who was becoming somewhat nettled.

"If your Holiness dislikes my offer, it is easy to omit your name in the deed. One word more. If you deliver up to justice the murderers of my friend Hypatia, I double my bequest on the spot."

Cyril burst out instantly —

"Thy money perish with thee! Do you presume to bribe me into delivering up my children to the tyrant?"

"I offer to give you the means of showing more mercy, provided that you will first do simple justice."

"Justice?" cried Cyril. "Justice? If it be just that Peter should die, sir, see first whether it was not just that Hypatia should die. Not that I compassed it. As I live, I would have given my own right hand that this had not happened! But now that it is done — let those who talk of justice look first in which scale of the balance it lies! Do you fancy, sir, that the people do not know their enemies from their friends? Do you fancy that they are to sit with folded hands, while a pedant makes common cause with a profligate, to drag them back again into the very black gulf of outer darkness, ignorance, brutal lust, grinding slavery, from which The Son of God died to free them, from which they are painfully and slowly struggling upward to the light of day? You, sir, if you be a Christian catechumen, should know for yourself what would have been the fate of Alexandria had the devil's plot of two days since succeeded. What if the people struck too fiercely? They struck in the right place. What if they have given the rein to passions fit only for heathens? Recollect the centuries of heathendom which bred those passions in them, and blame not my teaching, but the teaching of their forefathers. That very Peter..... What if he have for once given place to the devil, and avenged where he should have forgiven? Has he no memories which may excuse him for fancying, in a just paroxysm of dread, that idolatry and falsehood must be crushed at any risk? — He who counts back for now three hundred years, in persecution after persecution, martyrs, sir! martyrs — if you know what that word implies — of his own blood and kin; who, when he was but a seven years' boy, saw his own father made a sightless cripple to this day, and his elder sister, a consecrated nun, devoured alive by swine in the open streets, at the hands of those who supported the very philosophy, the very gods, which Hypatia attempted yesterday to restore. God shall judge such a man; not I, nor you!"

"Let God judge him, then, by delivering him to God's minister."

"God's minister? That heathen and apostate prefect? When he has expiated his apostacy by penance, and returned publicly to the bosom of the Church, it will be time enough to obey him: till then he is the minister of none but the devil. And no ecclesiastic shall suffer at the tribunal of an infidel. Holy Writ forbids us to go to law before the unjust. Let the world say of me what it will. I defy it and its rulers. I have to establish the kingdom of God in this city, and do it I will, knowing that other foundation can no man lay than that which is laid, which is Christ."

"Wherefore, you proceed to lay it afresh. A curious method of proving that it is laid already."

"What do you mean?" asked Cyril, angrily.

"Simply that God's kingdom, if it exists at all, must be a sort of kingdom, considering Who is The King of it, which would have established itself without your help some time since; probably, indeed, if the Scriptures of my Jewish forefathers are to be believed, before the foundation of the world; and that your business was to believe that God was King of Alexandria, and had put the Roman law there to crucify all murderers, ecclesiastics included, and that crucified they must be accordingly, as high as Haman himself."

"I will hear no more of this, sir! I am responsible to God alone, and not to you: let it be enough that by virtue of the authority committed to me, I shall cut off these men from the Church of God, by solemn excommunication, for three years to come."

"They are not cut off, then, it seems, as yet?"

"I tell you, sir, that I shall cut them off! Do you come here to doubt my word?"

"Not in the least, most august sir. But I should have fancied that, according to my carnal notions of God's Kingdom and The Church, they had cut off themselves most effectually already, from the moment when they cast away the Spirit of God, and took to themselves the spirit of murder and cruelty; and that all which your most just and laudable excommunication could effect, would be to inform the public of that fact. However, farewell! My money shall be forthcoming in due time; and that is the most important matter between us at this moment. As for your client Peter and his fellows, perhaps the most fearful punishment which can befall them, is to go on as they have begun. I only hope that you will not follow in the same direction."

"I?" cried Cyril, trembling with rage.

"Really I wish your Holiness well when I say so. If my notions seem to you somewhat secular, yours — forgive me — seem to me somewhat atheistic; and I advise you honestly to take care lest while you are busy trying to establish God's kingdom, you forget what it is like, by shutting your eyes to those of its laws which are established already. I have no doubt that with your Holiness's great powers you will succeed in establishing something. My only dread is, that when it is established, you should discover to your horror that it is the devil's kingdom and not God's."

And without waiting for an answer, Raphael bowed himself out of the august presence, and sailing for Berenice that very day, with Euджmon and his negro wife, went to his own place; there to labour and to succour, a sad and stern, and yet a loving and a much-loved man, for. many a year to come.

And now we will leave Alexandria also, and taking a forward leap of some twenty years, see how all other persons mentioned in this history went, likewise, each to his own place.

* * * * * *

A little more than twenty years after, the wisest and holiest man in the East was writing of Cyril, just deceased —

"His death made those who survived him joyful; but it grieved most probably the dead; and there is cause to fear, lest, finding his presence too troublesome, they should send him back to us..... May it come to pass, by your prayers, that he may obtain mercy and forgiveness, and that the immeasurable grace of God may prevail over his wickedness!"....

So wrote Theodoret, in days when men had not yet intercalated into Holy Writ that line of an obscure modern hymn, which proclaims to man the good news that "There is no repentance in the grave." Let that be as it may, Cyril has gone to his own place. What that place is in history is but too well known. What it is in the sight of Him unto whom all live for ever, is no concern of ours. May He whose mercy is over all his works, have mercy upon all, whether orthodox or unorthodox, Papist or Protestant, who, like Cyril, begin by lying for the cause of truth; and setting off upon that evil road, arrive surely, with the Scribes and Pharisees of old, sooner or later at their own place!

True, he and his monks had conquered; but Hypatia did not die unavenged. In the hour of that unrighteous victory, the Church of Alexandria received a deadly wound. It had admitted and sanctioned those habits of doing evil that good may come, of pious intrigue, and at last of open persecution, which are certain to creep in wheresoever men attempt to set up a merely religious empire, independent of human relationships and civil laws; — to "establish," in short, a "theocracy," and by that very act confess their secret disbelief that God is ruling already. And the Egyptian Church grew, year by year, more lawless and inhuman. Freed from enemies without, and from the union which fear compels, it turned its ferocity inward, to prey on its own vitals, and to tear itself in pieces, by a voluntary suicide, with mutual anathemas and exclusions, till it ended as' a mere chaos of idolatrous sects, persecuting each other for metaphysical propositions, which, true or false, were equally heretical in their mouths, because they used them only as watchwords of division. Orthodox or unorthodox, they knew not God, for they knew neither righteousness, nor love, nor peace..... They "hated their brethren, and walked on still in darkness, not knowing whither they were going".... till Amrou and his Mahommedans appeared; and whether they discovered the fact or not, they went to their own place.....

Though the mills of God grind slowly, yet they grind exceeding
    small;
Though He stands and waits with patience, with exactness grinds He
    all. —

And so found, in due time, the philosophers as well as the ecclesiastics of Alexandria.

Twenty years after Hypatia's death, philosophy was nickering down to the very socket. Hypatia's murder was its death-blow. In language tremendous and unmistakable, philosophers had been informed that mankind had done with them; that they had been weighed in the balances, and found wanting; that if they had no better Gospel than that to preach, they must make way for those who had. And they did make way. We hear little or nothing of them or their wisdom henceforth, except at Athens, where Proclus, Marinus, Isidore, and others, kept up "the golden chain of the Platonic succession," and descended deeper and deeper, one after the other, into the realms of confusion — confusion of the material with the spiritual, of the subject with the object, the moral with the intellectual; self-consistent in one thing only, — namely, in their exclusive Pharisaism; utterly unable to proclaim any good news for man as man, or even to conceive of the possibility of such, and gradually looking with more and more complacency on all superstitions which did not involve that one idea, which alone they hated, — namely, the Incarnation; craving after signs and wonders, dabbling in magic, astrology, and barbarian fetichisms; bemoaning the fallen age, and barking querulously at every form of human thought except their own; writing pompous biographies, full of bad Greek, worse taste, and still worse miracles.....

> —— That last drear mood
> Of envious sloth, and proud decrepitude;
> No faith, no art, no king, no priest, no God;
> While round the freezing founts of life in snarling ring,
> Crouch'd on the bareworn sod,
> Babbling about the unreturning spring,
> And whining for dead gods, who cannot save,
> The toothless systems shiver to their grave.

The last scene of their tragedy was not without a touch of pathos..... In the year 529, Justinian finally closed, by imperial edict, the schools of Athens. They had nothing-more to tell the world, but what the world had yawned over a thousand times before: why should they break the blessed silence by any more such noises? The philosophers felt so themselves. They had no mind to be martyrs, for they had nothing-for which to testify. They had no message for mankind, and mankind no interest for them. All that was left for them was to take care of their own souls; and fancying that they saw something like Plato's ideal republic in the pure monotheism of the Guebres, their philosophic emperor the Khozroo, and his holy caste of magi, seven of them set off to Persia, to forget the hateful existence of Christianity in that realized ideal. Alas for the facts! The purest monotheism, they discovered, was perfectly compatible with bigotry and ferocity, luxury and tyranny, serails and bowstring's, incestuous marriages and corpses exposed to the beasts of the field and the fowls of the air; and in reasonable fear for their own necks, the last seven Sages of Greece returned home, weary-hearted, into the Christian Empire from which they had fled, fully contented with the permission, which the Khozroo had obtained for them from Justinian, to hold their peace, and die among-decent people. So among decent people they died, leaving behind them, as their last legacy to mankind, Simplicius's Commentaries on Epictetus's Enchiridion, an essay on the art of egotism, by obeying which, whosoever list may become as perfect a Pharisee as ever darkened the earth of God. Peace be to their ashes!.... They are gone to their own place.

* * * * * *

Wulf, too, had gone to his own place, wheresoever that may be. He died in Spain, full of years and honours, at the court of Adolf and Placidia, having resigned his sovereignty into the hands of his lawful chieftain, and having lived long enough to see Goderic and his younger companions in arms settled with their Alexandrian brides up on the sunny slopes from which they had expelled the Vandals and the Suevi, to be the ancestors of "bluest-blooded" Castilian nobles. Wulf died, as he had lived, a heathen. Placidia, who loved him well, as she loved all righteous and noble souls, had succeeded once in persuading him to accept baptism. Adolf himself acted as one of his sponsors; and the old warrior was in the act of stepping into the font, when he turned suddenly to the bishop, and asked where were the souls of his heathen ancestors? "In hell," replied the worthy prelate. Wulf drew back from the font, and threw his bearskin cloak around him..... "He would prefer, if Adolf had no objection, to go to his own people." [6] And so he died unbaptized, and went to his own place.

Victoria was still alive and busy: but Augustine's warning had come true — she had found trouble in the flesh. The day of

---

[6] A fact.

the Lord had come, and Vandal tyrants were now the masters of the fair corn-lands of Africa. Her father and brother were lying by the side of Raphael Aben-Ezra, beneath the ruined walls of Hippo, slain, long years before, in the vain attempt to deliver their country from the invading swarms. But they had died the death of heroes; and Victoria was content. And it was whispered, among the down-trodden Catholics, who clung to her as an angel of mercy, that she, too, had endured strange misery and disgrace; that her delicate limbs bore the scars of fearful tortures; that a room in her house, into which none ever entered but herself, contained a young boy's grave; and that she passed long nights of prayer upon the spot, where lay her only child, martyred by the hands of Arian persecutors. Nay, some of the few who, having dared to face that fearful storm, had survived its fury, asserted that she herself, amid her own shame and agony, had cheered the shrinking boy on to his glorious death. But though she had found trouble in the flesh, her spirit knew none. Clear-eyed and joyful as when she walked by her father's side on the field of Ostia, she went to and fro among the victims of Vandal rapine and persecution, spending upon the maimed, the sick, the ruined, the small remnants of her former wealth, and winning, by her purity and her piety, the reverence and favour even of the barbarian conquerors. She had her work to do, and she did it, and was content; and, in good time, she also went to her own place.

Abbot Pambo, as well as Arsenius, had been dead several years; the abbot's place was filled, by his own dying command, by a hermit from the neighbouring deserts, who had made himself famous for many miles round, by his extraordinary austerities, his ceaseless prayers, his loving wisdom, and, it was rumoured, by various cures which could only be attributed to miraculous powers. While still in the prime of his manhood, he was dragged, against his own entreaties, from a lofty cranny of the cliffs to preside over the Laura of Scetis, and ordained a deacon at the advice of Pambo, by the bishop of the diocese, who, three years afterwards, took on himself to command him to enter the priesthood. The elder monks considered it an indignity to be ruled by so young a man: but the monastery throve and grew rapidly under his government. His sweetness, patience, and humility, and above all, his marvellous understanding of the doubts and temptations of his own generation, soon drew around him all whose sensitiveness or waywardness had made them unmanageable in the neighbouring monasteries. As to David in the mountains, so to him, every one who was discontented, and every one who was oppressed, gathered themselves. The neighbouring abbots were at first inclined to shrink from him, as one who ate and drank with publicans and sinners: but they held their peace, when they saw those whom they had driven out as reprobates labouring peacefully and cheerfully under Philammon. The elder generation of Scetis, too, saw, with some horror, the new influx of sinners: but their abbot had but one answer to their remonstrances — "Those who are whole need not a physician, but those who are sick."

Never was the young abbot heard to speak harshly of any human being. "When thou hast tried in vain for seven years," he used to say, "to convert a sinner, then only wilt thou have a right to suspect him of being a worse man than thyself." That there is a seed of good in all men, a Divine Word and Spirit striving with all men, a gospel and good news which would turn the hearts of all men, if abbots and priests could but preach it aright, was his favourite doctrine, and one which he used to defend, when, at rare intervals, he allowed himself to discuss any subject, from the writings of his favourite theologian, Clement of Alexandria. Above all, he stopped, by stern rebuke, any attempt to revile either heretics or heathens. "On the Catholic Church alone," he used to say, "lies the blame of all heresy and unbelief: for if she were but for one day that which she ought to be, the world would be converted before nightfall." To one class of sins, indeed, he was inexorable — all but ferocious; to the sins, namely, of religious persons. In proportion to any man's reputation for orthodoxy and sanctity, Philammon's judgment of him was stern and pitiless. More than once events proved him to have been unjust: when he saw himself to be so, none could confess his mistake more frankly, or humiliate himself for it more bitterly: but from his rule he never swerved; and the Pharisees of the Nile dreaded and avoided him, as much as the publicans and sinners loved and followed him.

One thing only in his conduct gave some handle for scandal, among the just persons who needed no repentance. It was well known that in his most solemn devotions, on those long nights of unceasing prayer and self-discipline, which won him a reputation for superhuman sanctity, there mingled always with his prayers the names of two women. And, when some worthy elder, taking courage from his years, dared to hint kindly to him that such conduct caused some scandal to the weaker brethren, "It is true," answered he; "tell my brethren that I pray nightly for two women: both of them young; both of them beautiful; both of them beloved by me more than I love my own soul; and tell them, moreover, that one of the two was a harlot, and the other a heathen." The old monk laid his hand on his mouth, and retired.

The remainder of his history it seems better to extract from an unpublished fragment of the Hagiologia Nilotica of Graidio-colosyrtus Tabenniticus, the greater part of which valuable work was destroyed at the taking of Alexandria under Amrou, A. D. 640.

"Now when the said abbot had ruled the monastery of Scetis seven years with uncommon prudence, resplendent in virtue and in miracles, it befell that one morning he was late for the Divine office. Whereon a certain ancient brother, who was also a deacon, being sent to ascertain the cause of so unwonted a defection, found the holy man extended upon the floor of his cell, like Balaam in the flesh, though far differing from him in the spirit, having fallen into a trance, but having his eyes open. Who, not daring to arouse him, sat by him until the hour of noon, judging rightly that something from heaven had befallen him. And at that hour, the saint arising without astonishment, said, 'Brother, make ready for me the divine elements, that I may consecrate them.' And he asking the reason wherefore, the saint replied, 'That I may partake thereof with all my brethren, ere I depart hence. For know assuredly that, within the seventh day, I shall migrate to the celestial mansions. For this night stood by me in a dream, those two women, whom I love, and for whom I pray; the one clothed in a white, the other in a ruby-coloured garment, and holding each other by the hand; who said to me, "That life after death is not such a one as you fancy: come, therefore, and behold with us what it is like." ' Troubled at which words, the deacon went forth: yet on account not only of holy obedience, but also of the sanctity of the blessed abbot, did not hesitate to prepare according to his command the divine elements; which the abbot having consecrated, distributed among his brethren, reserving only a portion of the most holy bread and wine; and then, having bestowed on them all the kiss of peace, he took the paten and chalice in his hands, and went forth from the monastery towards the desert; whom the whole fraternity followed weeping, as knowing that they should see his face no more. But he, having arrived at the foot of a certain mountain, stopped, and blessing them, commanded them that they should follow him no farther, and dismissed them with these words: 'As ye have been loved, so love. As ye have been judged, so judge. As ye have been forgiven, so forgive.' And so ascending, was taken away from their eyes. Now they, returning astonished, watched three days with prayer and fasting: but at last the eldest brother, being ashamed, like Elisha before the entreaties of Elijah's disciples, sent two of the young men to seek their master.

"To whom befell a thing noteworthy and full of miracles. For ascending the same mountain where they had left the abbot, they met with a certain Moorish people, not averse to the Christian verity, who declare that certain days before a priest had passed by them, bearing a paten and chalice, and blessing them in silence, proceeded across the desert in the direction of the cave of the holy Amma.

"And they inquiring who this Amma might be, the Moors answered that some twenty years ago there had arrived in those mountains a woman more beautiful than had ever before been seen in that region, dressed in rich garments; who after a short sojourn among their tribe, having distributed among them the jewels which she wore, had embraced the eremitic life, and sojourned upon the highest peak of a neighbouring mountain; till, her garments failing her, she became invisible to mankind, saving to a few women of the tribe, who went up from time to time to carry her offerings of fruit and meal, and to ask the blessing of her prayers. To whom she rarely appeared, veiled down to her feet in black hair of exceeding length and splendour.

"Hearing these things, the two brethren doubted for a while: but at last, determining to proceed, arrived at sunset upon the summit of the said mountain.

"Where, behold a great miracle. For above an open grave, freshly dug in the sand, a cloud of vultures and obscene birds hovered, whom two lions, fiercely contending, drove away with their talons, as if from some sacred deposit therein enshrined. Towards whom the two brethren, fortifying themselves with the sign of the holy cross, ascended. Whereupon the lions, as having fulfilled the term of their guardianship, retired; and left to the brethren a sight which they beheld with astonishment, and not without tears.

"For in the open grave lay the body of Philammon the abbot; and by his side, wrapt in his cloak, the corpse of a woman of exceeding beauty, such as the Moors had described. Whom embracing straitly, as a brother a sister, and joining his lips to hers, he had rendered up his soul to God; not without bestowing on her, as it seemed, the most holy sacrament; for by the grave-side stood the paten and the chalice emptied of their divine contents.

"Having beheld which things awhile in silence, they considered that the right understanding of such matters pertained to the judgment-seat above, and was unnecessary to be comprehended by men consecrated to God. Whereon, filling in the grave with all haste, they returned weeping to the Laura, and declared to them the strange things which they had beheld, and whereof I the writer, having collected these facts from sacrosanct and most trustworthy mouths, can only say that wisdom is justified of all her children.

"Now, before they returned, one of the brethren searching the cave wherein the holy woman dwelt, found there neither food, furniture, nor other matters; saving one bracelet of gold, of large size and strange workmanship, en-graven with foreign characters, which no one could decipher. The which bracelet, being taken home to the Laura of Scetis, and there dedicated in the chapel to the memory of the holy Amma, proved beyond all doubt the sanctity of its former possessor, by the miracles which its virtue worked; the fame whereof spreading abroad throughout the whole Thebaid, drew innumerable crowds of suppliants to that holy relic. But it came to pass, after the Vandalic persecution wherewith Huneric and Genseric the king devastated Africa, and enriched the Catholic Church with innumerable martyrs, that certain wandering barbarians of the Vandalic race, imbued with the Arian pravity, and made insolent by success, boiled over from the parts of Mauritania into the Thebaid region. Who plundering and burning all monasteries, and insulting the consecrated virgins, at last arrived even at the monastery of Scetis, where they not only, according to their impious custom, defiled the altar, and carried off the sacred vessels. but also bore away that most holy relic, the chief glory of the Laura, — namely, the bracelet of the holy Amma, impiously pretending that it had belonged to a warrior of their tribe, and thus expounding the writing thereon engraven —

For Amalric Amal's Son Smid Troll's Son Made, Me.

Wherein whether they spoke truth or not, yet their sacrilege did not remain unpunished; for attempting to return homeward toward the sea by way of the Nile, they were set upon while weighed down with wine and sleep, by the country people, and to a man miserably destroyed. But the pious folk, restoring the holy gold to its pristine sanctuary, were not unrewarded: for since that day it grows glorious with ever fresh miracles — as of blind restored to sight, paralytics to strength, demoniacs to sanity — to the honour of the orthodox Catholic Church, and of its ever-blessed saints."

* * * * * *

So be it. Pelagia and Philammon, like the rest, went to their own place; to the only place where such in such days could find rest; to the desert and the hermit's cell, and then forward into that fairy land of legend and miracle, wherein all saintly lives were destined to be enveloped for many a century thenceforth.

And now, readers, farewell. I have shown you New Foes under an Old Face — your own likenesses in toga and tunic, instead of coat and bonnet. One word before we part. The same devil who tempted these old Egyptians tempts you. The same God who would have saved these old Egyptians if they had willed, will save you, if you will. Their sins are yours, their errors yours, their doom yours, their deliverance yours. There is nothing new under the sun. The thing which has been, it is that which shall be. Let him that is without sin among you cast the first stone, whether at Hypatia or Pelagia, Miriam or Raphael, Cyril or Philammon.

ANDROMEDA

Over the sea, past Crete, on the Syrian shore to the
    southward,
Dwells in the well-tilled lowland a dark-haired Æthiop
    people,
Skilful with needle and loom, and the arts of the dyer
    and carver,
Skilful, but feeble of heart; for they know not the lords
    of Olympus,
Lovers of men; neither broad-browed Zeus, nor Pallas
    Athené,
Teacher of wisdom to heroes, bestower of might in the
    battle;
Share not the cunning of Hermes, nor list to the songs
    of Apollo.
Fearing the stars of the sky, and the roll of the blue
    salt water,
Fearing all things that have life in the womb of the seas
    and the rivers,
Eating no fish to this day, nor ploughing the main, like
    the Phœnics,
Manful with black-beaked ships, they abide in a
    sorrowful region,
Vexed with the earthquake, and flame, and the
    sea-floods, scourge of Poseidon.
Whelming the dwellings of men, and the toils of the
    slow-footed oxen,
Drowning the barley and flax, and the hard-earned gold
    of the harvest,
Up to the hillside vines, and the pastures skirting the
    woodland,
Inland the floods came yearly; and after the waters a
    monster,
Bred of the slime, like the worms which are bred from
    the muds of the Nile-bank,
Shapeless, a terror to see; and by night it swam out to

the seaward,
Daily returning to feed with the dawn, and devoured of
the fairest,
Cattle, and children, and maids, till the terrified people
fled inland.
Fasting in sackcloth and ashes they came, both the
king and his people,
Came to the mountain of oaks, to the house of the
terrible sea-gods,
Hard by the gulf in the rocks, where of old the world-
wide deluge
Sank to the inner abyss; and the lake where the fish of
the goddess
Holy, undying, abide; whom the priests feed daily with
dainties.
There to the mystical fish, high-throned in her chamber
of cedar,
Burnt they the fat of the flock; till the flame shone far
to the seaward.
Three days fasting they prayed: but the fourth day the
priests of the goddess
Cunning in spells, cast lots, to discover the crime of
the people.
All day long they cast, till the house of the monarch
was taken,
Cepheus, king of the land; and the faces of all gathered
blackness.
Then once more they cast; and Cassiopœia was
taken,
Deep-bosomed wife of the king, whom oft far-seeing
Apollo
Watched well-pleased from the welkin, the fairest of
Æthiop women:
Fairest, save only her daughter; for down to the ankle
her tresses
Rolled, blue-black as the night, ambrosial, joy to be-
holders.
Awful and fair she arose, most like in her coming to
Hebe,
Queen before whom the Immortals arise, as she comes

on Olympus,

Out of the chamber of gold, which her son Hephæstos
has wrought her.

Such in her stature and eyes, and the broad white light
of her forehead

Stately she came from her place, and she spoke in the
midst of the people.

'Pure are my hands from blood: most pure this heart
in my bosom.

Yet one fault I remember this day; one word have I
spoken;

Rashly I spoke on the shore, and I dread lest the sea
should have heard it.

Watching my child at her bath, as she plunged in the
joy of her girlhood,

Fairer I called her in pride than Atergati, queen of the
ocean.

Judge ye if this be my sin, for I know none other.'
She ended;

Wrapping her head in her mantle she stood, and the
people were silent.

Answered the dark-browed priests, 'No word, once
spoken, returneth

Even if uttered unwitting. Shall gods excuse our
rashness?

That which is done, that abides; and the wrath of the
sea is against us;

Hers, and the wrath of her brother, the Sun-god, lord of
the sheepfolds.

Fairer than her hast thou boasted thy daughter? Ah
folly! for hateful,

Hateful are they to the gods, whoso, impious, liken a
mortal,

Fair though he be, to their glory; and hateful is that
which is likened,

Grieving the eyes of their pride, and abominate,
doomed to their anger.

What shall be likened to gods? The unknown, who
deep in the darkness

Ever abide, twyformed, many-handed, terrible,

shapeless.

Woe to the queen; for the land is defiled, and the
   people accursed.

Take thou her therefore by night, thou ill-starred
   Cassiopœia,

Take her with us in the night, when the moon sinks
   low to the westward;

Bind her aloft for a victim, a prey for the gorge of the
   monster,

Far on the sea-girt rock, which is washed by the surges
   for ever;

So may the goddess accept her, and so may the land
   make atonement,

Purged by her blood from its sin: so obey thou the
   doom of the rulers.'

Bitter in soul they went out, Cepheus and Cassiopœia,

Bitter in soul; and their hearts whirled round, as the
   leaves in the eddy.

Weak was the queen, and rebelled: but the king, like a
   shepherd of people,

Willed not the land should waste; so he yielded the
   life of his daughter.

Deep in the wane of the night, as the moon sank low
   to the westward,

They by the shade of the cliffs, with the horror of
   darkness around them,

Stole, as ashamed, to a deed which became not the
   light of the sunshine,

Slowly, the priests, and the queen, and the virgin
   bound in the galley.

Slowly they rowed to the rocks: but Cepheus far in the
   palace

Sate in the midst of the hall, on his throne, like a
   shepherd of people,

Choking his woe, dry-eyed, while the slaves wailed
   loudly around him.

They on the sea-girt rock, which is washed by the
   surges for ever,

Set her in silence, the guiltless, aloft with her face to
   the eastward.

Under a crag of the stone, where a ledge sloped down
     to the water;
There they set Andromeden, most beautiful, shaped
     like a goddess,
Lifting her long white arms wide-spread to the walls of
     the basalt,
Chaining them, ruthless, with brass; and they called on
     the might of the Rulers.
'Mystical fish of the seas, dread Queen whom Æthiops
     honour,
Whelming the land in thy wrath, unavoidable, sharp as
     the sting-ray,
Thou, and thy brother the Sun, brain-smiting, lord of
     the sheepfold,
Scorching the earth all day, and then resting at night in
     thy bosom,
Take ye this one life for many, appeased by the blood
     of a maiden,
Fairest, and born of the fairest, a queen, most priceless
     of victims.'
Thrice they spat as they went by the maid: but her
     mother delaying
Fondled her child to the last, heart-crushed; and the
     warmth of her weeping
Fell on the breast of the maid, as her woe broke forth
     into wailing.
'Daughter! my daughter! forgive me! O curse not
     the murderess! Curse not!
How have I sinned, but in love? Do the gods grudge
     glory to mothers?
Loving I bore thee in vain in the fate-cursed bride-bed
     of Cepheus,
Loving I fed thee and tended, and loving rejoiced in
thy
     beauty,
Blessing thy limbs as I bathed them, and blessing thy
     locks as I combed them;
Decking thee, ripening to woman, I blest thee: yet
     blessing I slew thee!
How have I sinned, but in love? O swear to me, swear

to thy mother,
Never to haunt me with curse, as I go to the grave in
    my sorrow,
Childless and lone: may the gods never send me
    another, to slay it!
See, I embrace thy knees — soft knees, where no babe
    will be fondled —
Swear to me never to curse me, the hapless one, not in
    the death-pang.'
Weeping she clung to the knees of the maid; and the
    maid low answered —
'Curse thee! Not in the death-pang!' The heart of
    the lady was lightened.
Slowly she went by the ledge; and the maid was alone
    in the darkness.
Watching the pulse of the oars die down, as her own
    died with them,
Tearless, dumb with amaze she stood, as a
    storm-stunned nestling
Fallen from bough or from eave lies dumb, which the
    home-going herdsman
Fancies a stone, till he catches the light of its terrified
    eyeball.
So through the long long hours the maid stood helpless
    and hopeless,
Wide-eyed, downward gazing in vain at the black
blank
    darkness.
Feebly at last she began, while wild thoughts bubbled
    within her —
'Guiltless I am: why thus then? Are gods more
    ruthless than mortals?
Have they no mercy for youth? no love for the souls
    who have loved them?
Even as I loved thee, dread sea, as I played by thy
    margin,
Blessing thy wave as it cooled me, thy wind as it
    breathed on my forehead,
Bowing my head to thy tempest, and opening my heart
    to thy children,

Silvery fish, wreathed shell, and the strange lithe things
  of the water,
Tenderly casting them back, as they gasped on the
  beach in the sunshine,
Home to their mother — in vain! for mine sits childless
  in anguish!
Oh dread sea! false sea! I dreamed what I dreamed of
  thy goodness;
Dreamed of a smile in thy gleam, of a laugh in the
  plash of thy ripple:
False and devouring thou art, and the great world dark
  and despiteful.'
Awed by her own rash words she was still: and her
  eyes to the seaward
Looked for an answer of wrath: far off, in the heart of
  the darkness,
Bright white mists rose slowly; beneath them the
  wandering ocean
Glimmered and glowed to the deepest abyss; and the
  knees of the maiden
Trembled and sank in her fear, as afar, like a dawn in
  the midnight,
Rose from their seaweed chamber the choir of the
  mystical sea-maids.
Onward toward her they came, and her heart beat loud
  at their coming,
Watching the bliss of the gods, as they wakened the
  cliffs with their laughter.
Onward they came in their joy, and before them the
  roll
      of the surges
Sank, as the breeze sank dead, into smooth green
  foam-flecked marble,
Awed, and the crags of the cliff, and the pines of the
  mountain were silent.
Onward they came in their joy, and around them the
  lamps of the sea nymphs,
Myriad fiery globes, swam panting and heaving; and
  rainbows
Crimson and azure and emerald, were broken in star-

showers, lighting

Far through the wine-dark depths of the crystal, the
gardens of Nereus,

Coral and sea-fan and tangle, the blooms and the palms
of the ocean.

Onward they came in their joy, more white than the
foam which they scattered,

Laughing and singing, and tossing and twining, while
eager, the Tritons

Blinded with kisses their eyes, unreproved, and above
them in worship

Hovered the terns, and the seagulls swept past them on
silvery pinions

Echoing softly their laughter; around them the
wan-toning dolphins

Sighed as they plunged, full of love; and the great
sea-horses which bore them

Curved up their crests in their pride to the delicate
arms of the maidens,

Pawing the spray into gems, till a fiery rainfall,
unharming,

Sparkled and gleamed on the limbs of the nymphs, and
the coils of the mermen.

Onward they went in their joy, bathed round with the
fiery coolness,

Needing nor sun nor moon, self-lighted, immortal: but
others,

Pitiful, floated in silence apart; in their bosoms the
sea-boys,

Slain by the wrath of the seas, swept down by the anger
of Nereus;

Hapless, whom never again on strand or on quay shall
their mothers

Welcome with garlands and vows to the temple, but
wearily pining

Gaze over island and bay for the sails of the sunken;
they heedless

Sleep in soft bosoms for ever, and dream of the surge
and the sea-maids.

Onward they past in their joy; on their brows neither

sorrow nor anger;
Self-sufficing, as gods, never heeding the woe of the
    maiden.
She would have shrieked for their mercy: but shame
    made her dumb; and their eyeballs
Stared on her careless and still, like the eyes in the
    house of the idols.
Seeing they saw not, and passed, like a dream, on the
    murmuring ripple.
Stunned by the wonder she gazed, wide-eyed, as the
    glory departed.
'Oh fair shapes! far fairer than I! Too fair to be
    ruthless!
Gladden mine eyes once more with your splendour,
    unlike to my fancies;
You, then, smiled in the sea-gleam, and laughed in the
    plash of the ripple.
Awful I deemed you and formless; inhuman, mon-
strous
        as idols;
Lo, when ye came, ye were women, more loving and
    lovelier, only;
Like in all else; and I blest you: why blest ye not me
    for my worship?
Had you no mercy for me, the guiltless? Ye pitied the
    sea-boys,
Why not me, then, more hapless by far? Does your
    sight and your knowledge
End with the marge of the waves? Is the world which
    ye dwell in not our world?'

Over the mountain aloft ran a rush and a roll and a
    roaring;
Downward the breeze came indignant, and leapt with a
    howl to the water,
Roaring in cranny and crag, till the pillars and clefts of
    the basalt
Rang like a god-swept lyre, and her brain grew mad
    with the noises;
Crashing and lapping of waters, and sighing and

tossing of weed-beds,
Gurgle and whisper and hiss of the foam, while
    thundering surges
Boomed in the wave-worn halls, as they champed at
the
    roots of the mountain.
Hour after hour in the darkness the wind rushed fierce
    to the landward,
Drenching the maiden with spray; she shivering, weary
    and drooping,
Stood with her heart full of thoughts, till the
    foam-crests gleamed in the twilight,
Leaping and laughing around, and the east grew red
    with the dawning.
Then on the ridge of the hills rose the broad bright
    sun in his glory,
Hurling his arrows abroad on the glittering crests of the
    surges,
Gilding the soft round bosoms of wood, and the downs
    of the coastland,
Gilding the weeds at her feet, and the foam-laced teeth
    of the ledges,
Showing the maiden her home through the veil of her
    locks, as they floated
Glistening, damp with the spray, in a long black cloud
    to the landward.
High in the far-off glens rose thin blue curls from the
    homesteads;
Softly the low of the herds, and the pipe of the
    out-going herdsman,
Slid to her ear on the water, and melted her heart into
    weeping.
Shuddering, she tried to forget them; and straining her
    eyes to the seaward,
Watched for her doom, as she wailed, but in vain, to
    the terrible Sun-god.
'Dost thou not pity me, Sun, though thy wild dark
    sister be ruthless,
Dost thou not pity me here, as thou seest me desolate,
    weary,

Sickened with shame and despair, like a kid torn young
      from its mother?
What if my beauty insult thee, then blight it: but me —
      Oh spare me!
Spare me yet, ere he be here, fierce, tearing,
      unbearable! See me,
See me, how tender and soft, and thus helpless! See
      how I shudder,
Fancying only my doom. Wilt thou shine thus bright,
      when it takes me?
Are there no deaths save this, great Sun? No fiery
      arrow,
Lightning, or deep-mouthed wave? Why thus? What
      music in shrieking,
Pleasure in warm live limbs torn slowly? And dar'st
      thou behold them!
Oh, thou hast watched worse deeds! All sights are
      alike to thy brightness!
What if thou waken the birds to their song, dost thou
      waken no sorrow;
Waken no sick to their pain; no captive to wrench at
      his fetters?
Smile on the garden and fold, and on maidens who sing
      at the milking;
Flash into tapestried chambers, and peep in the eyelids
      of lovers,
Showing the blissful their bliss — Dost love, then, the
      place where thou smilest?
Lovest thou cities aflame, fierce blows, and the shrieks
      of the widow?
Lovest thou corpse-strewn fields, as thou lightest the
      path of the vulture?
Lovest thou these, that thou gazest so gay on my tears,
      and my mother's,
Laughing alike at the horror of one, and the bliss of
      another?
What dost thou care, in thy sky, for the joys and
      sorrows of mortals?
Colder art thou than the nymphs: in thy broad bright
      eye is no seeing.

Hadst thou a soul — as much soul as the slaves in the
      house of my father,
Wouldst thou not save? Poor thralls! they pitied me,
      clung to me weeping,
Kissing my hands and my feet — What are gods, more
      ruthless than mortals?
Worse than the souls which they rule? Let me die:
      they war not with ashes!'
Sudden she ceased, with a shriek: in the spray, like
      a hovering foam-bow,
Hung, more fair than the foam-bow, a boy in the bloom
      of his manhood,
Golden-haired, ivory-limbed, ambrosial; over his
      shoulder
Hung for a veil of his beauty the gold-fringed folds of
      the goat-skin,
Bearing the brass of his shield, as the sun flashed clear
      on its clearness.
Curved on his thigh lay a falchion; and under the gleam
      of his helmet
Eyes more blue than the main shone awful, around him
      Athené
Shed in her love such grace, such state, and terrible
      daring.
Hovering over the water he came, upon glittering
      pinions,
Living, a wonder, outgrown from the tight-laced gold
      of his sandals;
Bounding from billow to billow, and sweeping the
      crests like a sea-gull;
Leaping the gulfs of the surge, as he laughed in the joy
      of his leaping.
Fair and majestic he sprang to the rock; and the maiden
      in wonder
Gazed for awhile, and then hid in the dark-rolling wave
      of her tresses,
Fearful, the light of her eyes; while the boy (for her
      sorrow had awed him)
Blushed at her blushes, and vanished, like mist on the
      cliffs at the sunrise.

Fearful at length she looked forth: he was gone: she,
    wild with amazement,
Wailed for her mother aloud: but the wail of the wind
    only answered.
Sudden he flashed into sight, by her side; in his pity
    and anger
Moist were his eyes; and his breath like a rose-bed, as
    bolder and bolder,
Hovering under her brows, like a swallow that haunts
    by the house-eaves,
Delicate-handed, he lifted the veil of her hair; while the
    maiden
Motionless, frozen with fear, wept loud; till his lips
    unclosing
Poured from their pearl-strung portal the musical wave
    of his wonder.
'Ah,' well spoke she, the wise one, the grey-eyed
    Pallas Athené, —
'Known to Immortals alone are the prizes which lie for
    the heroes
Ready prepared at their feet; for requiring a little, the
    rulers
Pay back the loan tenfold to the man who, careless of
    pleasure,
Thirsting for honour and toil, fares forth on a perilous
    errand
Led by the guiding of gods, and strong in the strength
    of Immortals.
Thus have they led me to thee: from afar, unknowing,
    I marked thee,
Shining, a snow-white cross on the dark-green walls of
    the sea-cliff;
Carven in marble I deemed thee, a perfect work of the
    craftsman.
Likeness of Amphitrité, or far-famed Queen Cythereia.
Curious I came, till I saw how thy tresses streamed in
    the sea-wind,
Glistening, black as the night, and thy lips moved slow
    in thy wailing.
Speak again now — Oh speak! For my soul is stirred to

avenge thee;
Tell me what barbarous horde, without law,
      unrighteous and heartless,
Hateful to gods and to men, thus have bound thee, a
      shame to the sunlight,
Scorn and prize to the sailor: but my prize now; for a
      coward,
Coward and shameless were he, who so finding a
      glorious jewel
Cast on the wayside by fools, would not win it and
      keep it and wear it,
Even as I will thee; for I swear by the head of my
      father,
Bearing thee over the sea-wave, to wed thee in Argos
      the fruitful,
Beautiful, meed of my toil no less than this head which
      I carry,
Hidden here fearful — Oh speak!'
      But the maid, still dumb with amazement,
Watered her bosom with weeping, and longed for her
      home and her mother.
Beautiful, eager, he wooed her, and kissed off her tears
      as he hovered,
Roving at will, as a bee, on the brows of a rock
      nymph-haunted,
Garlanded over with vine, and acanthus, and
      clambering roses,
Cool in the fierce still noon, where streams glance clear
      in the mossbeds,
Hums on from blossom to blossom, and mingles the
      sweets as he tastes them.
Beautiful, eager, he kissed her, and clasped her yet
      closer and closer,
Praying her still to speak —
                'Not cruel nor rough did my mother
Bear me to broad-browed Zeus in the depths of the
      brass-covered dungeon;
Neither in vain, as I think, have I talked with the
      cunning of Hermes,
Face unto face, as a friend; or from grey-eyed Pallas

Athené
Learnt what is fit, and respecting myself, to respect in
    my dealings
Those whom the gods should love; so fear not; to
    chaste espousals
Only I woo thee, and swear, that a queen, and alone
    without rival
By me thou sittest in Argos of Hellas, throne of my
    fathers,
Worshipped by fair-haired kings: why callest thou still
    on thy mother?
Why did she leave thee thus here? For no foeman has
    bound thee; no foeman
Winning with strokes of the sword such a prize, would
    so leave it behind him.'
Just as at first some colt, wild-eyed, with quivering
    nostril,
Plunges in fear of the curb, and the fluttering robes of
    the rider;
Soon, grown bold by despair, submits to the will of his
    master,
Tamer and tamer each hour, and at last, in the pride of
    obedience,
Answers the heel with a curvet, and arches his neck to
    be fondled,
Cowed by the need that maid grew tame; while the
hero
    indignant
Tore at the fetters which held her; the brass, too
    cunningly tempered,
Held to the rock by the nails, deep wedged; till the boy,
    red with anger,
Drew from his ivory thigh, keen flashing, a falchion of
    diamond —
'Now let the work of the smith try strength with the
    arms of Immortals!'
Dazzling it fell; and the blade, as the vine-hook shears
    off the vine-bough,
Carved through the strength of the brass, till her arms
    fell soft on his shoulder.

Once she essayed to escape: but the ring of the water
    was round her,
Round her the ring of his arms; and despairing she
    sank on his bosom.
Then, like a fawn when startled, she looked with a
    shriek to the seaward.
'Touch me not, wretch that I am! For accursed, a
    shame and a hissing,
Guiltless, accurst no less, I await the revenge of the
    sea-gods.
Yonder it comes! Ah go! Let me perish unseen, if I
    perish!
Spare me the shame of thine eyes, when merciless
    fangs must tear me
Piecemeal! Enough to endure by myself in the light
    of the sunshine
Guiltless, the death of a kid!'
                But the boy still lingered
    around her,
Loth, like a boy, to forego her, and wakened the cliffs
    with his laughter.
'Yon is the foe, then? A beast of the sea? I had
    deemed him immortal
Titan, or Proteus' self, or Nereus, foeman of sailors:
Yet would I fight with them all, but Poseidon, shaker
    of mountains,
Uncle of mine, whom I fear, as is fit; for he haunts on
    Olympus,
Holding the third of the world; and the gods all rise at
    his coming.
Unto none else will I yield, god-helped: how then to a
    monster
Child of the earth and of night, unreasoning, shapeless,
    accursed?'
'Art thou, too, then a god?'
              'No god I,' smiling he answered,
'Mortal as thou, yet divine: but mortal the herds of the
    ocean,
Equal to men in that only, and less in all else; for they
    nourish

Blindly the life of the lips, untaught by the gods,
  without wisdom:
Shame if I fled before such!'
    In her heart new life was enkindled,
Worship and trust, fair parents of love: but she
  answered him sighing.
'Beautiful, why wilt thou die? Is the light of the
  sun, then, so worthless,
Worthless to sport with thy fellows in flowery glades
  of the forest,
Under the broad green oaks, where never again shall I
  wander,
Tossing the ball with my maidens, or wreathing the
  altar in garlands,
Careless, with dances and songs, till the glens rang
  loud to our laughter.
Too full of death the great earth is already; the halls
  full of weepers,
Quarried by tombs all cliffs, and the bones gleam white
  on the sea-floor
Numberless, gnawn by the herds who attend on the
  pitiless sea-gods,
Even as mine will be soon: and yet noble it seems to
  me, dying,
Giving my life for the many, to save to the arms of
  their lovers
Maidens and youths for awhile: thee, fairest of all,
  shall I slay thee?
Add not thy bones to the many, thus angering idly the
  dread ones!
Either the monster will crush, or the sea-queen's self
  overwhelm thee,
Vengeful, in tempest and foam, and the thundering
  walls of the surges.
Why wilt thou follow me down? can we love in the
  black blank darkness?
Love in the realms of the dead, in the land where all is
  forgotten?
Why wilt thou follow me down? is it joy, on the
  desolate oozes,

Meagre to flit, grey ghosts in the depths of the grey salt
    water?
Beautiful! why wilt thou die, and defraud fair girls of
    thy manhood?
Surely one waits for thee longing, afar in the isles of
    the ocean.
Go thy way; I mine; for the gods grudge pleasure to
    mortals.'
Sobbing she ended her moan, as her neck, like a
    storm-bent lily,
Drooped with the weight of her woe, and her limbs
    sank, weary with watching,
Soft on the hard-ledged rock: but the boy, with his eye
    on the monster,
Clasped her, and stood, like a god; and his lips curved
    proud as he answered —
'Great are the pitiless sea-gods: but greater the Lord
    of Olympus;
Greater the Ægis-wielder, and greater is she who
    attends him.
Clear-eyed Justice, her name is, the counsellor, loved
    of Athené;
Helper of heroes, who dare, in the god-given might of
    their manhood
Greatly to do and to suffer, and far in the fens and the
    forests
Smite the devourers of men, Heaven-hated, brood of
    the giants,
Twyformed, strange, without like, who obey not the
    golden-haired Rulers.
Vainly rebelling they rage, till they die by the swords
    of the heroes,
Even as this must die, for I burn with the wrath of my
    father,
Wandering, led by Athené; and dare whatsoever
    betides me.
Led by Athené I won from the grey-haired terrible
    sisters
Secrets hidden from men, when I found them asleep on
    the sand-hills,

Keeping their eye and their tooth, till they showed me
the perilous pathway
Over the waterless ocean, the valley that led to the
Gorgon.
Her too I slew in my craft, Medusa, the beautiful
horror;
Taught by Athené I slew her, and saw not herself, but
her image,
Watching the mirror of brass, in the shield which a
goddess had lent me;
Cleaving her brass-scaled throat, as she lay with her
adders around her,
Fearless I bore off her head, in the folds of the mystical
goat-skin,
Hide of Amaltheié, fair nurse of the Ægis-wielder.
Hither I bear it, a gift to the gods, and a death to my
foemen,
Freezing the seer to stone; so hide thine eyes from
the horror.
Kiss me but once, and I go.'
                          Then lifting her neck, like a
sea-bird
Peering up over the wave, from the foam-white swells
of her bosom,
Blushing she kissed him: afar on the topmost Idalian
summit
Laughed in the joy of her heart, far-seeing, the queen
Aphrodité.
Loosing his arms from her waist he flew upward,
awaiting the sea-beast.
Onward it came from the southward, as bulky and
black as a galley,
Lazily coasting along, as the fish fled leaping before
it;
Lazily breasting the ripple, and watching by sandbar
and headland,
Listening for laughter of maidens at bleaching, or song
of the fisher,
Children at play on the pebbles, or cattle that pawed
on the sandhills.

Rolling and dripping it came, where bedded in
glistening purple
Cold on the cold sea-weeds lay the long white sides of
the maiden,
Trembling, her face in her hands, and her tresses afloat
on the water.
As when an osprey aloft, dark-eyebrowed, royally
crested,
Flags on by creek and by cove, and in scorn of the
anger of Nereus
Ranges, the king of the shore; if he see on a glittering
shallow,
Chasing the bass and the mullet, the fin of a wallowing
dolphin,
Halting, he wheels round slowly, in doubt at the weight
of his quarry,
Whether to clutch it alive, or to fall on the wretch like
a plummet,
Stunning with terrible talon the life of the brain in the
hindhead:
Then rushes up with a scream, and stooping the wrath
of his eyebrows
Falls from the sky like a star, while the wind rattles
hoarse in his pinions.
Over him closes the foam for a moment; then from the
sand-bed
Rolls up the great fish, dead, and his side gleams white
in the sunshine.
Thus fell the boy on the beast, unveiling the face of
the Gorgon;
Thus fell the boy on the beast; thus rolled up the beast
in his horror,
Once, as the dead eyes glared into his; then his sides,
death-sharpened,
Stiffened and stood, brown rock, in the wash of the
wandering water.
Beautiful, eager, triumphant, he leapt back again to
his treasure;
Leapt back again, full blest, towards arms spread wide
to receive him.

Brimful of honour he clasped her, and brimful of love
she caressed him,
Answering lip with lip; while above them the queen
Aphrodité
Poured on their foreheads and limbs, unseen, ambrosial
odours,
Givers of longing, and rapture, and chaste content in
espousals.
Happy whom ere they be wedded anoints she, the
Queen Aphrodité!
Laughing she called to her sister, the chaste Tritonid
Athené,
Seest thou yonder thy pupil, thou maid of the
Ægis-wielder,
How he has turned himself wholly to love, and caresses
a damsel;
Dreaming no longer of honour, or danger, or Pallas
Athené?
Sweeter, it seems, to the young my gifts are; so yield
me the stripling;
Yield him me now, lest he die in his prime, like hapless
Adonis.'
Smiling she answered in turn, that chaste Tritonid
Athené:
'Dear unto me, no less than to thee, is the wedlock of
heroes;
Dear, who can worthily win him a wife not unworthy;
and noble,
Pure with the pure to beget brave children, the like of
their father.
Happy, who thus stands linked to the heroes who were,
and who shall be;
Girdled with holiest awe, not sparing of self; for his
mother
Watches his steps with the eyes of the gods; and his
wife and his children
Move him to plan and to do in the farm and the camp
and the council.
Thence comes weal to a nation: but woe upon woe,
when the people

Mingle in love at their will, like the brutes, not heeding
the future.'
Then from her gold-strung loom, where she wrought
in her chamber of cedar,
Awful and fair she arose; and she went by the glens of
Olympus;
Went by the isles of the sea, and the wind never ruffled
her mantle;
Went by the water of Crete, and the black-beaked fleets
of the Phœnics;
Came to the sea-girt rock which is washed by the
surges for ever,
Bearing the wealth of the gods, for a gift to the bride of
a hero.
There she met Andromeden and Persea, shaped like
Immortals;
Solemn and sweet was her smile, while their hearts
beat cloud at her coming;
Solemn and sweet was her smile, as she spoke to the
pair in her wisdom.
'Three things hold we, the Rulers, who sit by the
founts of Olympus,
Wisdom, and prowess, and beauty; and freely we pour
them on mortals;
Pleased at our image in man, as father at his in his
children.
One thing only we grudge to mankind, when a hero,
unthankful,
Boasts of our gifts as his own, stiffnecked, and
dishonours the givers,
Turning our weapons against us. Him Até follows
avenging;
Slowly she tracks him and sure, as a lyme-hound;
sudden she grips him,
Crushing him, blind in his pride, for a sign and a terror
to folly.
This we avenge, as is fit; in all else never weary of
giving.
Come then, damsel, and know if the gods grudge
pleasure to mortals.'

Loving and gentle she spoke: but the maid stood in
      awe, as the goddess
Plaited with soft swift finger her tresses, and decked
      her in jewels,
Armlet and anklet and earbell; and over her shoulders
      a necklace,
Heavy, enamelled, the flower of the gold and the brass
      of the mountain.
Trembling with joy she gazed, so well Hæphaistos had
      made it,
Deep in the forges of Ætna, while Charis his lady
      beside him,
Mingled her grace in his craft, as he wrought for his
sister Athené.
Then on the brows of the maiden a veil bound Pallas
Athené;
Ample it fell to her feet, deep-fringed, a wonder of
weaving.
Ages and ages agone it was wrought on the heights of
Olympus,
Wrought in the gold-strung loom, by the finger of
      cunning Athené.
In it she wove all creatures that teem in the womb of
      the ocean;
Nereid, siren, and triton, and dolphin, and arrowy
      fishes
Glittering round, many-hued, on the flame-red folds of
the mantle.
In it she wove, too, a town where grey-haired kings sat
in judgment;
Sceptre in hand in the market they sat, doing right by
the people,
Wise: while above watched Justice, and near,
      far-seeing Apollo.
Round it she wove for a fringe all herbs of the earth
      and the water,
Violet, asphodel, ivy, and vine-leaves, roses and lilies,
Coral and sea-fan, and tangle, the blooms and the
      palms of the ocean:
Now from Olympus she bore it, a dower to the bride of

a hero.

Over the limbs of the damsel she wrapt it: the maid still trembled,

Shading her face with her hands; for the eyes of the goddess were awful.

Then, as a pine upon Ida when southwest winds blow landward,

Stately she bent to the damsel, and breathed on her: under her breathing

Taller and fairer she grew; and the goddess spoke in her wisdom.

'Courage I give thee; the heart of a queen, and the mind of Immortals,

Godlike to talk with the gods, and to look on their eyes unshrinking;

Fearing the sun and the stars no more, and the blue salt water;

Fearing us only, the lords of Olympus, friends of the heroes;

Chastely and wisely to govern thyself and thy house and thy people,

Bearing a godlike race to thy spouse, till dying I set thee

High for a star in the heavens, a sign and a hope to the seamen,

Spreading thy long white arms all night in the heights of the æther,

Hard by thy sire and the hero thy spouse, while near thee thy mother

Sits in her ivory chair, as she plaits ambrosial tresses.

All night long thou wilt shine; all day thou wilt feast on Olympus,

Happy, the guest of the gods, by thy husband, the god begotten.'

Blissful, they turned them to go: but the fair-tressed Pallas Athené

Rose, like a pillar of tall white cloud, toward silver Olympus,

Far above ocean and shore, and the peaks of the isles and the mainland;

Where no frost nor storm is, in clear blue windless
        abysses,
High in the home of the summer, the seats of the happy
Immortals,
Shrouded in keen deep blaze, unapproachable; there
        ever youthful
Hebé, Harmonié, and the daughter of Jove,
        Aphrodité,
Whirled in the white-linked dance with the
        gold-crowned Hours and the Graces,
Hand within hand, while clear piped Phœbe, queen of
        the woodlands.
All day long they rejoiced: but Athené still in her
        chamber
Bent herself over her loom, as the stars rang loud to her
        singing,
Chanting of order and right, and of foresight, warden
        of nations;
Chanting of labour and craft, and of wealth in the port
        and the garner,
Chanting of valour and fame, and the man who can fall
        with the foremost,
Fighting for children and wife, and the field which his
        father bequeathed him.
Sweetly and solemnly sang she, and planned new
        lessons for mortals:
Happy, who hearing obey her, the wise unsullied
        Athené.

SONGS, BALLADS

THE TIDE ROCK

How sleeps yon rock, whose half-day's bath is done,
With broad bright side beneath the broad bright sun,
Like sea-nymph tired, on cushioned mosses sleeping.
Yet, nearer drawn, beneath her purple tresses
From drooping brows we find her slowly weeping.
      So many a wife for cruel man's caresses
      Must inly pine and pine, yet outward bear
      A gallant front to this world's gaudy glare.

THE OUBIT

I

It was an hairy oubit, sae proud he crept alang;
A feckless hairy oubit, and merrily he sang —
'My minnie bad me bide at hame until I won my
      wings;
I shew her soon my soul's aboon the works o' creeping
      things.'

II

This feckless hairy oubit cam' hirpling by the linn,
A swirl o' wind cam' doun the glen, and blew that
      oubit in:
O when he took the water, the saumon fry they rose,
And tigg'd him a' to pieces sma', by head and tail and
      toes.

III

Tak' warning then, young poets a', by this poor oubit's
      shame;
Though Pegasus may nicher loud, keep Pegasus at
      hame.

O hand your hands frae inkhorns, though a' the Muses
    woo;
For critics lie, like saumon fry, to mak' their meals o'
    you.

THE STARLINGS

I

Early in spring time, on raw and windy mornings,
Beneath the freezing house-eaves I heard the starlings
    sing —
'Ah dreary March month, is this then a time for
    building wearily?
Sad, sad, to think that the year is but begun.'

II

Late in the autumn, on still and cloudless evenings,
Among the golden reed-beds I heard the starlings
    sing —
'Ah that sweet March month, when we and our mates
    were courting merrily;
Sad, sad, to think that the year is all but done.'

OH, THOU HADST BEEN A WIFE FOR SHAKSPEARE'S SELF

Oh, thou hadst been a wife for Shakspeare's self!
No head, save some world-genius, ought to rest
Above the treasures of that perfect breast;
Or nightly draw fresh light from those keen stars
Through which thy soul awes ours: yet thou art
    bound —
Oh waste of nature! — to a craven hound;
To shameless lust, and childish greed of pelf;
Athené to a Satyr: was that link
Forged by The Father's hand? Man's reason bars
The bans which God allowed. — Ay, so we think:
Forgetting, thou hadst weaker been, full blest,

Than thus made strong by suffering; and more
great
In martyrdom, than throned as Cæsar's mate.

A MARCH

Dreary East winds howling o'er us;
Clay-lands knee-deep spread before us;
Mire and ice and snow and sleet;
Aching backs and frozen feet;
Knees which reel as marches quicken,
Ranks which thin as corpses thicken;
While with carrion birds we eat,
Calling puddle-water sweet,
As we pledge the health of our general, who fares as
rough as we:
What can daunt us, what can turn us, led to death by
such as he?

AIRLY BEACON

I

Airly Beacon, Airly Beacon;
Oh the pleasant sight to see
Shires and towns from Airly Beacon,
While my love climbed up to me!

II

Airly Beacon, Airly Beacon;
Oh the happy hours we lay
Deep in fern on Airly Beacon,
Courting through the summer's day!

III

Airly Beacon, Airly Beacon;
Oh the weary haunt for me,
All alone on Airly Beacon,
With his baby on my knee!

A FAREWELL

I

My fairest child, I have no song to give you;
    No lark could pipe to skies so dull and grey;
Yet, ere we part, one lesson I can leave you
    For every day.

II

Be good, sweet maid, and let who will be clever;
    Do noble things, not dream them, all day long:
And so make life, death, and that vast for-ever
    One grand, sweet song.

ODE TO THE NORTHEAST WIND

Welcome, wild Northeaster!
    Shame it is to see
Odes to every zephyr;
    Ne'er a verse to thee.

Welcome, black Northeaster!
    O'er the German foam;
O'er the Danish moorlands,
    From thy frozen home.

Tired we are of summer,
    Tired of gaudy glare,
Showers soft and steaming,
    Hot and breathless air.

Tired of listless dreaming,
    Through the lazy day:
Jovial wind of winter
    Turn us out to play!

Sweep the golden reed-beds;
    Crisp the lazy dyke;
Hunger into madness
    Every plunging pike.

Fill the lake with wild fowl;
      Fill the marsh with snipe;
While on dreary moorlands
      Lonely curlew pipe.

Through the black fir-forest
      Thunder harsh and dry,
Shattering down the snow flakes
      Off the curdled sky.

Hark! The brave Northeaster!
      Breast-high lies the scent,
On by holt and headland,
      Over heath and bent.

Chime, ye dappled darlings,
      Through the sleet and snow!
Who can over-ride you?
      Let the horses go!

Chime, ye dappled darlings,
      Down the roaring blast;
You shall see a fox die
      Ere an hour be past.

Go! and rest to-morrow,
      Hunting in your dreams,
While our skates are ringing
      O'er the frozen streams.

Let the luscious South-wind
      Breathe in lovers' sighs,
While the lazy gallants
      Bask in ladies' eyes.

What does he but soften
      Heart alike and pen?
'Tis the hard grey weather
      Breeds hard English men.

What's the soft Southwester?
      'Tis the ladies' breeze,
Bringing home their true loves
      Out of all the seas:

But the black Northeaster,
      Through the snow-storm hurled,
Drives our English hearts of oak
      Seaward round the world!

Come! as came our fathers,
      Heralded by thee,
Conquering from the eastward,
      Lords by land and sea.

Come; and strong within us
      Stir the Vikings' blood;
Bracing brain and sinew;
      Blow, thou wind of God!

TO G—

A hasty jest I once let fall —
      As jests are wont to be, untrue —
      As if the sum of joy to you
Were hunt and pic-nic, rout and ball.

Your eyes met mine: I did not blame;
      You saw it: but I touched too near
      Some noble nerve; a silent tear
Spoke soft reproach, and lofty shame.

I do not wish those words unsaid.
      Unspoilt by praise and pleasure, you
      In that one look to woman grew,
While with a child, I thought, I played.

Next to mine own beloved so long!
      I have not spent my heart in vain.
      I watched the blade; I see the grain;
A woman's soul, most soft, yet strong.

SAINT MAURA

A. D. 304.

Thank God! Those gazers' eyes are gone at last!

The guards are crouching underneath the rock;
The lights are fading in the town below,
Around the cottage which this morn was ours.
Kind sun, to set, and leave us here alone;
Alone upon our crosses with our God;
While all the angels watch us from the stars!
Kind moon, to shine so clear and full on him,
And bathe his limbs in glory, for a sign
Of what awaits him! Oh look on him, Lord!
Look, and remember how he saved thy lamb!

      Oh listen to me, teacher, husband, love,
Never till now loved utterly! Oh say,
Say you forgive me? No — you must not speak:
You said it to me hours ago — long hours!
Now you must rest, and when to-morrow comes
Speak to the people, call them home to God,
A deacon on the Cross, as in the Church,
And plead from off the tree with outspread arms,
To show them that the Son of God endured
For them — and me. Hush! I alone will speak,
And wile away the hours till dawn for you.
I know you have forgiven me; as I lay
Beneath your feet, while they were binding me,
I knew I was forgiven then! When I cried
'Here am I, husband! The lost lamb returned,
All re-baptized in blood!' and you said, 'Come!
Come to thy bride-bed, martyr, wife once more!'
From that same moment all my pain was gone;
And ever since those sightless eyes have smiled
Love — love! Alas, those eyes! They made me fall.
I could not bear to see them bleeding, dark,
Never, no never to look into mine;
Never to watch me round the little room
Singing about my work, or flash on me
Looks bright with counsel. — Then they drove me mad
With talk of nameless tortures waiting you —
And I could save you! You would hear your love —
They knew you loved me, cruel men! And then —
Then came a dream, to say one little word,
One easy wicked word, we both might say,

And no one hear us, but the lictors round,
One tiny sprinkle of the incense grains,
And both, both free! And life had just begun —
Only three months — short months — your wedded
      wife!
Only three months within the cottage there —
Hoping I bore your child....
Ah! husband! Saviour! God! think gently of me!
I am forgiven!..
      And then another dream;
A flash — so quick, I could not bear the blaze,
I could not see the smoke among the light —
To wander out through unknown lands, and lead
You by the hand through hamlet, port, and town,
On, on, until we died; and stand each day
To glory in you, as you preached and prayed
From rock and bourne-stone, with that voice, those
      words,
Mingled of fire and honey — you would wake,
Bend, save whole nations! would not that atone
For one short word? — ay, make it right, to save
You, you, to fight the battles of the Lord?
And so — and so — alas! you knew the rest!
You answered me...
Ah cruel words! No! Blessed, godlike words!
You had done nobly had you struck me dead,
Instead of striking me to life! — the temptress!..
'Traitress! apostate! dead to God and me!' —
'The smell of death upon me?' — so it was!
True! true! well spoken, hero! Oh they snapped,
Those words, my madness, like the angel's voice
Thrilling the graves to birth-pangs. All was clear.
There was but one right thing in the world to do;
And I must do it... Lord, have mercy! Christ!
Help through my womanhood: or I shall fail
Yet, as I failed before!.. I could not speak —
I could not speak for shame and misery,
And terror of my sin, and of the things
I knew were coming: but in heaven, in heaven!
There we should meet, perhaps — and by that time

I might be worthy of you once again —
Of you, and of my God... So I went out.

Will you hear more, and so forget the pain?
And yet I dread to tell you what comes next;
Your love will feel it all again for me.
No! it is over; and the woe that's dead
Rises next hour a glorious angel. Love!
Say, shall I tell you? Ah! your lips are dry!
To-morrow, when they come, we must entreat,
And they will give you water. One to-day,
A soldier, gave me water in a sponge
Upon a reed, and said, 'Too fair! too young!
She might have been a gallant soldier's wife!'
And then I cried, 'I am a soldier's wife!
A hero's!' And he smiled, but let me drink.
God bless him for it!
                                So they led me back:
And as I went, a voice was in my ears
Which rang through all the sunlight, and the breath
And blaze of all the garden slopes below,
And through the harvest-voices, and the moan
Of cedar-forests on the cliffs above,
And round the shining rivers, and the peaks
Which hung beyond the cloud-bed of the west,
And round the ancient stones about my feet.
Out of all heaven and earth it rang, and cried
'My hand hath made all these. Am I too weak
To give thee strength to say so?' Then my soul
Spread like a clear blue sky within my breast,
While all the people made a ring around,
And in the midst the judge spoke smilingly —
'Well? hast thou brought him to a better mind?'
'No! He has brought me to a better mind!' —
I cried, and said beside — I know not what —
Words which I learnt from thee — I trust in God
Nought fierce or rude — for was I not a girl
Three months ago beneath my mother's roof?
I thought of that. She might be there! I looked —
She was not there! I hid my face and wept.

And when I looked again, the judge's eye
Was on me, cold and steady, deep in thought —
'She knows what shame is still; so strip her.' 'Ah!'
I shrieked,' Not that, Sir! Any pain! So young
I am — a wife too — I am not my own,
But his — my husband's!' But they took my shawl,
And tore my tunic off, and there I stood
Before them all.... Husband! you love me still?
Indeed I pleaded! Oh, shine out, kind moon,
And let me see him smile! Oh! how I prayed,
While some cried 'Shame!' And some 'She is too
        young!'
And some mocked — ugly words: God shut my ears.
And yet no earthquake came to swallow me.
While all the court around, and walls, and roofs,
And all the earth and air were full of eyes,
Eyes, eyes, which scorched my limbs like burning
        flame,
Until my brain seemed bursting from my brow:
And yet no earthquake came! And then I knew
This body was not yours alone, but God's —
His loan — He needed it: and after that
The worst was come, and any torture more
A change — a lightening; and I did not shriek —
Once only — once, when first I felt the whip —
It coiled so keen around my side, and sent
A fire-flash through my heart which choked me —
then
I shrieked — that once. The foolish echo rang
So far and long — I prayed you might not hear.
And then a mist, which hid the ring of eyes,
Swam by me, and a murmur in my ears
Of humming bees around the limes at home;
And I was all alone with you and God.
And what they did to me I hardly know;
I felt, and did not feel. Now I look back,
It was not after all so very sharp —
So do not pity me. It made me pray;
Forget my shame in pain, and pain in you,
And you in God: and once, when I looked down,

And saw an ugly sight — so many wounds!
'What matter?' thought I. 'His dear eyes are dark;
For them alone I kept this skin so white —
A foolish pride! As God wills now. 'Tis just.'
       But then the judge spoke out in haste, 'She is
       mad,
Or fenced by magic arts! She feels no pain!'
He did not know I was on fire within:
Better he should not; so his sin was less:
Then he cried fiercely, 'Take the slave away,
And crucify her by her husband's side!'
And at those words a film came on my face —
A sickening rush of joy — was that
That my reward? I rose, and tried to go —
But all the eyes had vanished, and the judge;
And all the buildings melted into mist;
So how they brought me here I cannot tell.
Here, here, by you, until the judgment-day,
And after that for ever and for ever!
Ah! If I could but reach that hand! One touch!
One finger tip, to send the thrill through me
I felt but yesterday! — No! I can wait: —
Another body! — Oh, new limbs are ready,
Free, pure, instinct with soul through every nerve,
Kept for us in the treasuries of God.
They will not mar the love they try to speak,
They will not fail my soul, as these have done.'

Will you hear more? Nay — you know all the rest;
Yet those poor eyes — alas! they could not see
My waking, when you hung above me there
With hands outstretched to bless the penitent —
Your penitent — even like The Lord Himself —
I gloried in you! — like The Lord Himself!
Sharing His very sufferings, to the crown
Of thorns which they had put on that dear brow
To make you like Him — show you as you were!
I told them so! I bid them look on you,
And see there what was the highest throne on earth —
The throne of suffering, where the Son of God

Endured and triumphed for them. But they laughed;
All but one soldier, grey, with many scars;
And he stood silent. Then I crawled to you,
And kissed your bleeding feet, and called aloud —
You heard me! You know all! I am at peace.
Peace, peace, as still and bright as is the moon
Upon your limbs, came on me at your smile,
And kept me happy, when they dragged me back
From that last kiss, and spread me on the cross,
And bound my wrists and ancles — Do not sigh:
I prayed, and bore it: and since they raised me up
My eyes have never left your face, my own, my own,
Nor will, till death comes!...
                    Do I feel much pain?
Not much. Not maddening. None I cannot bear.
It has become like part of my own life,
Or part of God's life in me — honour — bliss!
I dreaded madness, and instead comes rest;
Rest deep and smiling, like a summer's night.
I should be easy, now if I could move....
I cannot stir. Ah God! these shoots of fire
Through all my limbs! Hush, selfish girl! He hears
        you!
Who ever found the cross a pleasant bed?
Yes; I can bear it, love. Pain is no evil
Unless it conquers us. These little wrists, now —
You said, one blessed night, they were too slender,
Too soft and slender for a deacon's wife —
Perhaps a martyr's: — You forgot the strength
Which God can give. The cord has cut them through;
And yet my voice has never faltered yet.
Oh! do not groan, or I shall long and pray
That you may die: and you must not die yet.
Not yet — they told us we might live three days...
Two days for you to preach! Two days to speak
Words which may wake the dead!

Hush! is he sleeping?
They say that men have slept upon the cross;
So why not he?... Thanks, Lord! I hear him

breathe:
And he will preach thy word to-morrow! — save
Souls, crowds, for Thee! And they will know his worth
Years hence — poor things, they know not what they
        do! —
And crown him martyr; and his name will ring
Through all the shores of earth, and all the stars
Whose eyes are sparkling through their tears to see
His triumph — Preacher! Martyr! — Ah — and me?
If they must couple my poor name with his,
Let them tell all the truth — say how I loved him,
And tried to damn him by that love! Oh Lord!
Returning good for evil! and was this
The payment I deserved for such a sin?
To hang here on my cross, and look at him
Until we kneel before Thy throne in heaven!

THE WATCHMAN

I

'Watchman, what of the night?'
        'The stars are out in the sky;
And the merry round moon will be rising soon,
        For us to go sailing by.'

II

'Watchman, what of the night?'
        'The tide flows in from the sea;
There's water to float a little cockboat
        Will carry such fishers as we.'

III

'Watchman, what of the night?'
        'The night is a fruitful time;
When to many a pair are born children fair,
        To be christened at morning chime.'

THE WORLD'S AGE

I

Who will say the world is dying?
      Who will say our prime is past?
Sparks from Heaven, within us lying,
      Flash, and will flash till the last.
Fools! who fancy Christ mistaken,
      Man a tool to buy and sell;
Earth a failure, God-forsaken,
      Anteroom of Hell.

II

Still the race of Hero-spirits
      Pass the lamp from hand to hand;
Age from age the Words inherits —
      'Wife, and Child, and Fatherland.'
Still the youthful hunter gathers
      Fiery joy from wold and wood;
He will dare as dared his fathers
      Give him cause as good.

III

While a slave bewails his fetters;
      While an orphan pleads in vain;
While an infant lisps his letters,
      Heir of all the ages' gain;
While a lip grows ripe for kissing;
      While a moan from man is wrung;
Know, by every want and blessing,
      That the world is young.

EARLY POEMS

IN AN ILLUMINATED MISSAL

I would have loved: there are no mates in heaven:
I would be great: there is no pride in heaven;
I would have sung, as doth the nightingale
The summer's night aneath the moonè pale:
But saintès hymnes alone in heaven prevail.
My love, my song, my skill, my high intent,
Have I within this seely book y-pent:
And all that beauty which from every part
I treasured still alway within mine heart,
Whether of form or face angelical,
Or herb or flower, or lofty cáthedral,
Upon these sheets below doth lie y-spred,
In quaint devices deftly blazonèd.
  Lord, in this tome to thee I sanctify
  The sinful fruits of worldly fantasy.

THE WEIRD LADY

I

The swevens came up round Harold the Earl,
  Like motes in the sunnés beam;
And over him stood the Weird Lady,
In her charmèd castle over the sea,
  Sang 'Lie thou still and dream.'

II

'Thy steed is dead in his stall, Earl Harold,
  Since thou hast bid with me;
The rust has eaten thy harness bright,
And the rats have eaten thy greyhound light,
  That was so fair and free.'

III

Mary Mother she stooped from heaven;
She wakened Earl Harold out of his sweven,
    To don his harness on;
And over the land and over the sea
He wended abroad to his own countrie,
    A weary way to gon.

IV

O but his beard was white with eld,
    O but his hair was gray;
He stumbled on by stock and stone,
And as he journeyed he made his moan
    Along that weary way.

V

Earl Harold came to his castle wall;
    The gate was burnt with fire;
Roof and rafter were fallen down,
The folk were strangers all in the town,
    And strangers all in the shire.

VI

Earl Harold came to a house of nuns,
    And he heard the dead-bell toll;
He saw the sexton stand by a grave;
'Now Christ have mercy, who did us save,
    Upon yon fair nun's soul.'

VII

The nuns they came from the convent gate
    By one, by two, by three;
They sang for the soul of a lady bright
Who died for the love of a traitor knight:
    It was his own lady.

VIII

He stayed the corpse beside the grave;
    'A sign, a sign!' quod he.
'Mary Mother who rulest heaven
Send me a sign if I be forgiven
    By the woman who so loved me.'

IX

A white dove out of the coffin flew;
    Earl Harold's mouth it kist;
He fell on his face, wherever he stood;
And the white dove carried his soul to God
    Or ever the bearers wist.

PALINODIA 1841

Ye mountains, on whose torrent-furrowed slopes,
And bare and silent brows uplift to heaven,
I envied oft the soul which fills your wastes
Of pure and stern sublime, and still expanse
Unbroken by the petty incidents
Of noisy life: Oh hear me once again!

Winds, upon whose racked eddies, far aloft,
Above the murmur of the uneasy world,
My thoughts in exultation held their way:
Whose tremulous whispers through the rustling glade
Were once to me unearthly tones of love,
Joy without object, wordless music, stealing
Through all my soul, until my pulse beat fast
With aimless hope, and unexpressed desire —
Thou sea, who wast to me a prophet deep
Through all thy restless waves, and wasting shores,
Of silent labour, and eternal change;
First teacher of the dense immensity
Of ever-stirring life, in thy strange forms
Of fish, and shell, and worm, and oozy weed:
To me alike thy frenzy and thy sleep
Have been a deep and breathless joy: Oh hear!

Mountains, and winds, and waves, take back your
    child!
Upon thy balmy bosom, Mother Nature,
Where my young spirit dreamt its years away,
Give me once more to nestle: I have strayed
Far through another world, which is not thine.
Through sunless cities, and the weary haunts

Of smoke-grimed labour, and foul revelry
My flagging wing has swept. A mateless bird's
My pilgrimage has been; through sin, and doubt,
And darkness, seeking love. Oh hear me, Nature!
Receive me once again: but not alone;
No more alone, Great Mother! I have brought
One who has wandered, yet not sinned, like me.
Upon thy lap, twin children, let us lie;
And in the light of thine immortal eyes
Let our souls mingle, till The Father calls
To some eternal home the charge He gives thee.

A NEW FOREST BALLAD

I

Oh she tripped over Ocknell plain,
     And down by Bradley Water;
And the fairest maid of the forest side
     Was Jane, the keeper's daughter.

II

She went and went through the broad grey lawns
     As down the red sun sank,
And chill as the scent of a new-made grave
     The mist smelt cold and dank.

III

'A token, a token!' that fair maid cried,
     'A token that bodes me sorrow;
For they that smell the grave by night
     Will see the corpse to-morrow.

IV

'My own true love in Burley Walk
     Does hunt to-night, I fear;
And if he meet my father stern,
     His game may cost him dear.

V

'Ah, here's a curse on hare and grouse,
     A curse on hart and hind;

And a health to the squire in all England,
    Leaves never a head behind.'
VI

Her true love shot a mighty hart
    Among the standing rye,
When on him leapt that keeper old
    From the fern where he did lie.
VII

The forest laws were sharp and stern,
    The forest blood was keen;
They lashed together for life and death
    Beneath the hollies green.
VIII

The metal good and the walnut wood
    Did soon in flinders flee;
They tost the orts to south and north,
    And grappled knee to knee.
IX

They wrestled up, they wrestled down,
    They wrestled still and sore;
Beneath their feet the myrtle sweet
    Was stamped to mud and gore.
X

Ah cold pale moon, thou cruel pale moon,
    That starest with never a frown
On all the grim and the ghastly things
    That are wrought in thorpe and town;
XI

And yet cold pale moon, thou cruel pale moon,
    That night hadst never the grace
To lighten two dying Christian men
    To see one another's face.
XII

They wrestled up, they wrestled down,
    They wrestled sore and still:
The fiend who blinds the eyes of men
    That night he had his will.

XIII

Like stags full spent, among the bent
    They dropped awhile to rest;
When the young man drove his saying knife
    Deep in the old man's breast.

XIV

The old man drove his gunstock down
    Upon the young man's head;
And side by side, by the water brown,
    Those yeomen twain lay dead.

XV

They dug three graves in Lyndhurst yard,
    They dug them side by side;
Two yeomen lie there, and a maiden fair,
    A widow and never a bride.

THE RED KING

The King was drinking in Malwood Hall,
There came in a monk before them all;
He thrust by squire, he thrust by knight,
Stood over against the dais aright;
And, 'The word of the Lord, thou cruel Red King,
The word of the Lord to thee I bring.
A grimly sweven I dreamt yestreen;
I saw thee lie under the hollins green,
And thorough thine heart an arrow keen;
And out of thy body a smoke did rise,
Which smirched the sunshine out of the skies;
So if thou God's anointed be
I rede thee unto thy soul thou see.
For mitre and pall thou hast y-sold,
False knight to Christ, for gain and gold;
And for this thy forest were digged down all,
Steading and hamlet and churches tall;
And Christés poor were ousten forth,
To beg their bread from south to north.
So tarry at home, and fast and pray,

Lest fiends hunt thee in the judgment day.'

The monk he vanished where he stood;
King William sterte up wroth and wod;
Quod he, 'Fools' wits will jump together;
The Hampshire ale and the thunder weather
Have turned the brains for us both, I think;
And monks are curst when they fall to drink.
A lothly sweven I dreamt last night,
How there hoved anigh me a griesly knight,
Did smite me down to the pit of hell;
I shrieked and woke, so fast I fell.
There's Tyrrel as sour as I, perdie,
So he of you all shall hunt with me;
A grimly brace for a hart to see.'

The Red King down from Malwode came;
His heart with wine was all a-flame,
His eyne were shotten, red as blood,
He rated and swore, wherever he rode.

They roused a hart, that grimly brace,
A hart of ten, a hart of grease,
Fled over against the kingés place.
The sun it blinded the kingés ee,
A fathom behind his hocks shot he:
        'Shoot thou,' quod he, 'in the fiendés name,
To lose such a quarry were seven years' shame,'
And he hove up his hand to mark the game.
Tyrrel he shot full light, God wot;
For whether the saints they swerved the shot,
Or whether by treason, men knowen not,
But under the arm, in a secret part,
The iron fled through the kingés heart.
The turf it squelched where the Red King fell;
And the fiends they carried his soul to hell,
Quod 'His master's name it hath sped him well.'

Tyrrel he smited full grim that day,
Quod 'Shooting of kings is no bairns play;'
And he smote in the spurs, and fled fast away.
As he pricked along by Fritham plain,

The green tufts flew behind like rain;
The waters were out, and over the sward:
He swam his horse like a stalwart lord;
Men clepen that water Tyrrel's ford.
By Rhinefield and by Osmondsleigh,
Through glade and furze brake fast drove he,
Until he heard the roaring sea;
Quod he, 'Those gay waves they call me.'
By Mary's grace a seely boat
On Christchurch bar did lie afloat;
He gave the shipmen mark and groat,
To ferry him over to Normandie,
And there he fell to sanctuarie;
God send his soul all bliss to see.

And fend our princes every one,
From foul mishap and trahison;
But kings that harrow Christian men,
Shall England never bide again.
                    The End.

Printed in Great Britain
by Amazon.co.uk, Ltd.,
Marston Gate.